JOHN GALSWORTHY

# Collected Works

JOHN GALSWORTHY
1867–1933

# JOHN GALSWORTHY

# A Modern Comedy

## THE WHITE MONKEY
## A SILENT WOOING
## THE SILVER SPOON
## PASSERS BY

*Original illustrations by*
CHRISTOPHER W. BRADBURY

*Distributed by*
HERON BOOKS

*Published by arrangement with*
*William Heinemann Ltd*

TO

## MY WIFE

WITHOUT WHOM I KNOW NOT WHAT

COULD HAVE BEEN WRITTEN,

THIS SECOND TRILOGY OF

THE FORSYTE CHRONICLES

IS

## DEDICATED

# CONTENTS

Preface

## BOOK I

## THE WHITE MONKEY

### PART I

### PART II

## PART III

## BOOK II

## THE SILVER SPOON

### PART I

# PREFACE

IN naming this second part of The Forsyte Chronicles 'A Modern Comedy' the word comedy is stretched, perhaps, as far as the word Saga was stretched to cover the first part. And yet, what but a comedic view can be taken, what but comedic significance gleaned, of so restive a period as that in which we have lived since the war? An Age which knows not what it wants, yet is intensely pre-occupied with getting it, must evoke a smile, if rather a sad one.

To render the forms and colours of an epoch is beyond the powers of any novelist, and very far beyond the powers of this novelist; but to try and express a little of its spirit was undoubtedly at the back of his mind in penning this trilogy. Like the Irishman's chicken, our Present runs about so fast that it cannot be summed up; it can at most be snapshotted while it hurries looking for its Future without notion where, what, or when that Future will be.

The England of 1886, when the Forsyte Saga began, also had no Future, for England then expected its Present to endure, and rode its bicycle in a sort of dream, disturbed only by two bogles—Mr. Gladstone and the Irish Members.

The England of 1926—when the Modern Comedy closes—with one foot in the air and the other in a Morris Oxford, is going round and round like a kitten after its tail, muttering: "If one could only see where one wants to stop!"

Everything being now relative, there is no longer absolute dependence to be placed on God, Free Trade, Marriage, Consols, Coal, or Caste.

Everywhere being now overcrowded, there is no place where anyone can stay for long, except the mere depopulated country-side, admittedly too dull, and certainly too unprofitable to dwell in.

Everyone, having been in an earthquake which lasted four years, has lost the habit of standing still.

And yet, the English character has changed very little, if at all. The General Strike of 1926, with which the last part of this trilogy begins, supplied proof of that. We are still a people that cannot be rushed, distrustful of extremes, saved by the grace of our defensive humour, well-tempered, resentful of interference, improvident and

i

wasteful, but endowed with a certain genius for recovery. If we believe in nothing much else, we still believe in ourselves. That salient characteristic of the English will bear thinking about. Why, for instance, do we continually run ourselves down? Simply because we have not got the inferiority complex and are indifferent to what other people think of us. No people in the world seems openly less sure of itself; no people is secretly more sure. Incidentally, it might be worth the while of those who own certain public mouths inclined to blow the British trumpet to remember, that the blowing of one's own trumpet is the insidious beginning of the inferiority complex. Only those strong enough to keep silent about self are strong enough to be sure of self. The epoch we are passing through is one which favours misjudgment of the English character, and of the position of England. There never was a country where real deterioration of human fibre had less chance than in this island, because there is no other country whose climate is so changeable, so tempering to character, so formative of grit, and so basically healthy. What follows in this preface should be read in the light of that remark.

In the present epoch, no Early Victorianism survives. By Early Victorianism is meant that of the old Forsytes, already on the wane in 1886; what has survived, and potently, is the Victorianism of Soames and his generation, more self-conscious, but not sufficiently self-conscious to be either self-destructive or self-forgetful. It is against the background of this more or less fixed quantity that we can best see the shape and colour of the present intensely self-conscious and all-questioning generation. The old Forsytes—Old Jolyon, Swithin and James, Roger, Nicholas and Timothy—lived their lives without ever asking whether life was worth living. They found it interesting, very absorbing from day to day, and even if they had no very intimate belief in a future life, they had very great faith in the progress of their own positions, and in laying up treasure for their children. Then came Young Jolyon and Soames and their contemporaries, who, although they had imbibed with Darwinism and the 'Varsities, definite doubts about a future life, and sufficient introspection to wonder whether they themselves were progressing, retained their sense of property and their desire to provide for, and to live on in their progeny. The generation which came in when Queen Victoria went out, through new ideas about the treatment of children, because of new modes of loco- motion, and owing to the Great War, has decided that everything requires re-valuation. And, since there is, seemingly, very little

ii

future before property, and less before life, is determined to live now or never, without bothering about the fate of such offspring as it may chance to have. Not that the present generation is less fond of its children than were past generations—human nature does not change on points so elementary—but when everything is keyed to such pitch of uncertainty, to secure the future at the expense of the present no longer seems worth while.

This is really the fundamental difference between the present and the past generations. People will not provide against that which they cannot see ahead.

All this, of course, refers only to that tenth or so of the population whose eyes are above the property line; below that line there are no Forsytes, and therefore no need for this preface to dip. What average Englishman, moreover, with less than three hundred a year ever took thought for the future, even in Early Victorian days?

This Modern Comedy, then, is staged against a background of that more or less fixed quantity, Soames, and his co-father-in-law, light weight and ninth baronet, Sir Lawrence Mont, with such subsidiary neo-Victorians as the self-righteous Mr. Danby, Elderson, Mr. Blythe, Sir James Foskisson, Wilfred Bentworth, and Hilary Charwell. Pooling their idiosyncrasies, qualities, and mental attitudes, one gets a fairly comprehensive and steady past against which to limn the features of the present—Fleur and Michael, Wilfred Desert, Aubrey Greene, Marjorie Ferrar, Norah Curfew, Jon, the Rafaelite, and other minor characters. The multiple types and activities of to-day—even above the Plimsoll line of property— would escape the confines of twenty novels, so that this Modern Comedy is bound to be a gross under-statement of the present generation, but not perhaps a libel on it. Symbolism is boring, so let us hope that a certain resemblance between the case of Fleur and that of her generation chasing the serenity of which it has been defrauded may escape notice. The fact remains that for the moment, at least, youth is balancing, twirling on the tiptoes of uncertainty. What is to come? Will contentment yet be caught? How will it all settle down? Will things ever again settle down— who knows? Are there to come fresh wars, and fresh inventions hot-foot on those not yet mastered and digested? Or will Fate decree another pause, like that of Victorian times, during which re-valuated life will crystallise, and give property and its brood of definite beliefs a further innings?

But, however much or little 'A Modern Comedy' may be

deemed to reflect the spirit of an Age, it continues in the main to relate the tale of life which sprang from the meeting of Soames and Irene in a Bournemouth drawing-room in 1881, a tale which could but end when its spine snapped, and Soames 'took the ferry' forty-five years later.

The chronicler, catechised (as he often is) concerning Soames, knows not precisely what he stands for. Taking him for all in all he was honest, anyway. He lived and moved and had his peculiar being, and, now he sleeps. His creator may be pardoned for thinking there was something fitting about his end, for, however far we have travelled from Greek culture and philosophy, there is still truth in the old Greek proverb: "That which a man most loves shall in the end destroy him."

JOHN GALSWORTHY

# BOOK I

## THE WHITE MONKEY

"No retreat, no retreat
They must conquer or die
Who have no retreat!"

*Mr. Gay.*

TO

MAX  BEERBOHM

# PART I

## Chapter I

### PROMENADE

COMING down the steps of 'Snooks' Club, so nicknamed by George Forsyte in the late 'eighties, on that momentous mid-October afternoon of 1922, Sir Lawrence Mont, ninth baronet, set his fine nose towards the east wind, and moved his thin legs with speed. Political by birth rather than by nature, he reviewed the revolution which had restored his Party to power with a detachment not devoid of humour. Passing the Remove Club, he thought: 'Some sweating into shoes, there! No more confectioned dishes. A woodcock—without trimmings, for a change!'

The captains and the kings had departed from 'Snooks' before he entered it, for he was not of 'that catch-penny crew, now paid off, no sir; fellows who turned their tails on the land the moment the war was over. Pah!' But for an hour he had listened to echoes, and his lively twisting mind, embedded in deposits of the past, sceptical of the present and of all political protestations and pronouncements, had recorded with amusement the confusion of patriotism and personalities left behind by the fateful gathering. Like most landowners, he distrusted doctrine. If he had a political belief, it was a tax on wheat; and so far as he could see, he was now alone in it—but then he was not seeking election; in other words, his principle was not in danger of extinction from the votes of those who had to pay for bread. Principles—he mused—*au fond* were pocket; and he wished the deuce people wouldn't pretend they weren't! Pocket, in the deep sense of that word, of course, self-interest as member of a definite community. And how the devil was this definite community, the English nation, to exist, when all its land was going out of cultivation, and all its ships and docks in danger of destruction by aeroplanes? He had listened that hour past for a single mention of the land. Not one! It was not practical politics! Confound the fellows! They had to wear their breeches out—keeping seats or getting them. No connection between

3

posteriors and posterity! No, by George! Thus reminded of
posterity, it occurred to him rather suddenly that his son's wife
showed no signs as yet. Two years! Time they were thinking about
children. It was dangerous to get into the habit of not having
them, when a title and estate depended. A smile twisted his lips
and eyebrows which resembled spinneys of dark pothooks. A
pretty young creature, most taking; and knew it, too! Whom was
she not getting to know? Lions and tigers, monkeys and cats—her
house was becoming quite a menagerie of more or less celebrities.
There was a certain unreality about that sort of thing! And
opposite a British lion in Trafalgar Square Sir Lawrence thought:
'She'll be getting these to her house next! She's got the collecting
habit. Michael must look out—in a collector's house there's always
a lumber-room for old junk, and husbands are liable to get into it.
That reminds me: I promised her a Chinese Minister. Well, she
must wait now till after the General Election.'

Down Whitehall, under the grey easterly sky, the towers of
Westminster came for a second into view. 'A certain unreality in
that, too,' he thought. 'Michael and his fads! Well, it's the fashion
—Socialistic principles and a rich wife. Sacrifice with safety! Peace
with plenty! Nostrums—ten a penny!'

Passing the newspaper hubbub of Charing Cross, frenzied by the
political crisis, he turned up to the left towards Danby and Winter,
publishers, where his son was junior partner. A new theme for a
book had just begun to bend a mind which had already produced
a 'Life of Montrose, Far Cathay', that work of Eastern travel, and
a fanciful conversation between the shades of Gladstone, and
Disraeli—entitled 'A Duet' With every step taken, from 'Snooks'
eastward, his erect thin figure in Astrakhan-collared coat, his thin
grey-moustached face, and tortoise-shell rimmed monocle under
the lively dark eyebrow, had seemed more rare. It became almost
a phenomenon in this dingy back street, where carts stuck like
winter flies, and persons went by with books under their arms, as
if educated.

He had nearly reached the door of Danby's when he encountered
two young men. One of them was clearly his son, better dressed
since his marriage, and smoking a cigar—thank goodness—instead
of those eternal cigarettes; the other—ah! yes—Michael's sucking
poet and best man, head in air, rather a sleek head under a velour
hat! He said:

"Ha, Michael!"

"*Hallo*, Bart! You know my governor, Wilfrid? Wilfrid Desert.

'Copper Coin'—some poet, Bart, I tell you. You must read him We're going home. Come along!"

Sir Lawrence went along.

"What happened at 'Snooks'?"

"*Le roi est mort.* Labour can start lying, Michael—election next month."

"Bart was brought up, Wilfrid, in days that knew not Demos."

"Well, Mr. Desert, do *you* find reality in politics now?"

"Do you find reality in anything, sir?"

"In income tax, perhaps."

Michael grinned.

"Above knighthood," he said, "there's no such thing as simple faith."

"Suppose your friends came into power, Michael—in some ways not a bad thing, help 'em to grow up—what could they do, eh? Could they raise national taste? Abolish the cinema? Teach English people to cook? Prevent other countries from threatening war? Make us grow our own food? Stop the increase of town life? Would they hang dabblers in poison gas? Could they prevent flying in war-time? Could they weaken the possessive instinct—anywhere? Or do anything, in fact, but alter the incidence of possession a little? All party politics are top dressing. We're ruled by the inventors, and human nature; and we live in Queer Street, Mr. Desert."

"Much my sentiments, sir."

Michael flourished his cigar.

"Bad old men, you two!"

And removing their hats, they passed the Cenotaph.

"Curiously symptomatic—that thing," said Sir Lawrence; "monument to the dread of swank—most characteristic. And the dread of swank——"

"Go on, Bart," said Michael.

"The fine, the large, the florid—all off! No far-sighted views, no big schemes, no great principles, no great religion, or great art—æstheticism in cliques and backwaters, small men in small hats."

"As panteth the heart after Byron, Wilberforce, and the Nelson Monument. My poor old Bart! What about it, Wilfrid?"

"Yes, Mr. Desert—what about it?"

Desert's dark face contracted.

"It's an age of paradox," he said. "We all kick up for freedom, and the only institutions gaining strength are Socialism and the Roman Catholic Church. We're frightfully self-conscious about art

—and the only art development is the cinema. We're nuts on peace—and all we're doing about it is to perfect poison gas."

Sir Lawrence glanced sideways at a young man so bitter.

"And how's publishing, Michael?"

"Well, 'Copper Coin' is selling like hot cakes; and there's quite a movement in 'A Duet'. What about this for a new ad.: 'A Duet, by Sir Lawrence Mont, Bart. The most distinguished Conversation ever held between the Dead.' That ought to get the psychic. Wilfrid suggested 'G.O.M. and Dizzy—broadcasted from Hell.' Which do you like best?"

They had come, however, to a policeman holding up his hand against the nose of a van horse, so that everything marked time. The engines of the cars whirred idly, their drivers' faces set towards the space withheld from them; a girl on a bicycle looked vacantly about her, grasping the back of the van, where a youth sat sideways with his legs stretched out towards her. Sir Lawrence glanced again at young Desert. A thin, pale-dark face, good-looking, but a hitch in it, as if not properly timed; nothing *outré* in dress or manner, and yet socially at large; less vivacious than that lively rascal, his own son, but as anchorless, and more sceptical—might feel things pretty deeply, though! The policeman lowered his arm.

"You were in the war, Mr. Desert?"

"Oh, yes."

"Air service?"

"And line. Bit of both."

"Hard on a poet."

"Not at all. Poetry's only possible when you may be blown up at any moment, or when you live in Putney."

Sir Lawrence's eyebrow rose. "Yes?"

"Tennyson, Browning, Wordsworth, Swinburne—they could turn it out; *ils vivaient, mais si peu.*"

"Is there not a third condition favourable?"

"And that, sir?"

"How shall I express it—a certain cerebral agitation in connection with women?"

Desert's face twitched, and seemed to darken.

Michael put his latchkey into the lock of his front door.

6

# Chapter II

## HOME

THE house in South Square, Westminster, to which the young Monts had come after their Spanish honeymoon two years before, might have been called 'emancipated'. It was the work of an architect whose dream was a new house perfectly old, and an old house perfectly new. It followed therefore, no recognised style or tradition, and was devoid of structural prejudice; but it soaked up the smuts of the metropolis with such special rapidity that its stone already respectably resembled that of Wren. Its windows and doors had gently rounded tops. The high-sloping roof, of a fine sooty pink, was almost Danish, and two 'ducky little windows' looked out of it, giving an impression that very tall servants lived up there. There were rooms on each side of the front door, which was wide and set off by bay trees in black and gold bindings. The house was thick through, and the staircase, of a broad chastity, began at the far end of a hall which had room for quite a number of hats and coats and cards. There were four bathrooms; and not even a cellar underneath. The Forsyte instinct for a house had co-operated in its acquisition. Soames had picked it up for his daughter, undecorated, at that psychological moment when the bubble of in-flation was pricked, and the air escaping from the balloon of the world's trade. Fleur, however, had established immediate contact with the architect—an element which Soames himself had never quite got over—and decided not to have more than three styles in her house: Chinese, Spanish, and her own. The room to the left of the front door, running the breadth of the house, was Chinese, with ivory panels, a copper floor, central heating, and cut-glass lustres. It contained four pictures—all Chinese—the only school in which her father had not yet dabbled. The fireplace, wide and open, had Chinese dogs with Chinese tiles for them to stand on. The silk was chiefly of jade green. There were two wonderful old black tea-chests, picked up with Soames's money at Jobson's—not a bargain. There was no piano, partly because pianos were too uncompromisingly occidental, and partly because it would have taken up much room. Fleur aimed at space—collecting people rather than furniture or *bibelots*. The light, admitted by windows at both ends, was unfortunately not Chinese. She would stand sometimes in the centre of this room, thinking—how to 'bunch' her guests, how to make her room more Chinese without making it uncomfortable; how to seem to know all about literature and politics; how to accept everything her father gave her, without making him aware that his taste had no sense of the future; how to keep hold of Sibley Swan, the new literary star, and to get hold of Gurdon Minho, the old; of how Wilfrid Desert was getting too fond of her; of what was really her style in dress; of why Michael had such funny ears; and sometimes she stood not thinking at all— just aching a little.

When those three came in she was sitting before a red lacquer tea-table, finishing a very good tea. She always had tea brought in rather early, so that she could have a good quiet preliminary 'tuck-in' all by herself, because she was not quite twenty-one, and this was her hour for remembering her youth. By her side Ting-a-ling was standing on his hind feet, his tawny forepaws on a Chinese foot-stool, his snubbed black and tawny muzzle turned up towards the fruits of his philosophy.

"That'll do, Ting. No more, ducky! *No more!*"

The expression of Ting-a-ling answered:

"Well, then, stop, too! Don't subject me to torture!"

A year and three months old, he had been bought by Michael out of a Bond Street shop window on Fleur's twentieth birthday, eleven months ago.

Two years of married life had not lengthened her short dark chestnut hair; had added a little more decision to her quick lips, a little more allurement to her white-lidded, dark-lashed hazel eyes, a little more poise and swing to her carriage, a little more chest and hip measurement; had taken a little from waist and calf measurement, a little colour from cheeks a little less round, and a little sweetness from a voice a little more caressing.

She stood up behind the tray, holding out her white round arms without a word. She avoided unnecessary greetings or farewells. She would have had to say them so often, and their purpose was better served by look, pressure, and slight inclination of head to one side.

With circular movement of her squeezed hand, she said:

"Draw up. Cream, sir? Sugar, Wilfrid? Ting has had too much— don't feed him! Hand things, Michael. I've heard all about the meeting at 'Snooks'. You're not going to canvass for Labour, Michael—canvassing's so silly. If anyone canvassed me, I should vote the other way at once."

"Yes, darling; but you're not the average elector."

Fleur looked at him. Very sweetly put! Conscious of Wilfrid biting his lips, of Sir Lawrence taking that in, of the amount of silk leg she was showing, of her black and cream teacups, she adjusted these matters. A flutter of her white lids—Desert ceased to bite his lips; a movement of her silk legs—Sir Lawrence ceased to look at him. Holding out her cups, she said:

"I suppose I'm not modern enough?"

Desert, moving a bright little spoon round in his magpie cup, said without looking up:

"As much more modern than the moderns, as you are more ancient."

"'Ware poetry!" said Michael.

But when he had taken his father to see the new cartoons by Aubrey Greene, she said:

"Kindly tell me what you meant, Wilfrid."

Desert's voice seemed to leap from restraint.

"What does it matter? I don't want to waste time with that."

"But I want to know. It sounded like a sneer."

"A sneer? From me? Fleur!"

"Then tell me."

"I meant that you have all their restlessness and practical get-thereness; but you have what they haven't, Fleur—power to turn one's head. And mine is turned. You know it."

"How would Michael like that—from *you*, his best man?"

Desert moved quickly to the windows.

Fleur took Ting-a-ling on her lap. Such things had been said to her before; but from Wilfrid it was serious. Nice to think she had his heart, of course! Only, where on earth could she put it, where it wouldn't be seen except by her? He was incalculable—did strange things! She was a little afraid—not of him, but of that quality in him. He came back to the hearth, and said:

"Ugly, isn't it? Put that damn' dog down, Fleur; I can't see your face. If you were really fond of Michael—I swear I wouldn't; but you're not, you know."

Fleur said coldly:

"You know very little; I *am* fond of Michael."

Desert gave his little jerky laugh.

"Oh yes; not the sort that counts."

Fleur looked up.

"It counts quite enough to make one safe."

"A flower that I can't pick."

9

Fleur nodded.

"Quite sure, Fleur? Quite, quite sure?"

Fleur stared; her eyes softened a little, her eyelids, so excessively white, drooped over them; she nodded. Desert said slowly:

"The moment I believe that, I shall go East."

"East?"

"Not so stale as going West, but much the same—you don't come back."

Fleur thought: 'The East? I should love to know the East! Pity one can't manage that, too. Pity!'

"You won't keep me in your Zoo, my dear. I shan't hang around and feed on crumbs. You know what I feel—it means a smash of some sort."

"It hasn't been my fault, has it?"

"Yes; you've collected me, as you collect everybody that comes near you."

"I don't know what you mean."

Desert bent down, and dragged her hand to his lips.

"Don't be riled with me; I'm too unhappy."

Fleur let her hand stay against his hot lips.

"Sorry, Wilfrid."

"All right, dear. I'll go."

"But you're coming to dinner to-morrow?"

Desert said violently:

"*To-morrow?* Good God—no! What d'you think I'm made of?"

He flung her hand away.

"I don't like violence, Wilfrid."

"Well, good-bye; I'd better go."

The words "And you'd better not come again" trembled up to her lips, but were not spoken. Part from Wilfrid—life would lose a little warmth! She waved her hand. He was gone. She heard the door closing. Poor Wilfrid?—nice to think of a flame at which to warm her hands! Nice but rather dreadful! And suddenly, dropping Ting-a-ling, she got up and began to walk about the room. To-morrow! Second anniversary of her wedding-day! Still an ache when she thought of what it had not been. But there was little time to think—and she made less. What good in thinking? Only one life, full of people, of things to do and have, of things wanted— a life only void of—one thing, and that—well, if people had it, they never had it long! On her lids two tears, which had gathered, dried without falling. Sentimentalism! No! The last thing in the world—the unforgivable offence! Whom should she put next

10

to whom to-morrow? And whom should she get in place of Wilfrid, if Wilfrid wouldn't come—silly boy! One day—one night—what difference? Who should sit on her right, and who on her left? Was Aubrey Greene more distinguished, or Sibley Swan? Were they either as distinguished as Walter Nazing or Charles Upshire? Dinner of twelve, exclusively literary and artistic, except for Michael and Alison Charwell. Ah! Could Alison get her Gurdon Minho—just one writer of the old school, one glass of old wine to mellow effervescence? He didn't publish with Danby and Winter; but he fed out of Alison's hand. She went quickly to one of the old tea-chests, and opened it. Inside was a telephone.

"Can I speak to Lady Alison—Mrs. Michael Mont . . . Yes . . . That you, Alison? . . . Fleur speaking. Wilfrid has fallen through to-morrow night . . . Is there any chance of your bringing Gurdon Minho? I don't know him, of course; but he might be interested. You'll try? . . . That'll be ever so delightful. Isn't the 'Snooks' Club meeting rather exciting? Bart says they'll eat each other now they've split . . . About Mr. Minho. Could you let me know to-night? Thanks—thanks awfully! . . . Good-bye!"

Failing Minho, whom? Her mind hovered over the names in her address book. At so late a minute it must be someone who didn't stand on ceremony; but except Alison, none of Michael's relations would be safe from Sibley Swan or Nesta Gorse, and their subversive shafts; as to the Forsytes—out of the question; they had their own sub-acid humour (some of them), but they were not modern, not really modern. Besides, she saw as little of them as she could—they dated, belonged to the dramatic period, had no sense of life without beginning or end. No! If Gurdon Minho was a frost, it would have to be a musician, whose works were hieroglyphical with a dash of surgery; or, better, perhaps, a psychoanalyst. Her fingers turned the pages till she came to those two categories. Hugo Solstis? A possibility; but suppose he wanted to play them something recent? There was only Michael's upright Grand, and that would mean going to his study. Better Gerald Hanks—he and Nesta Gorse would get off together on dreams; still, if they did, there would be no actual loss of life. Yes, failing Gurdon Minho, Gerald Hanks; he would be free—and put him between Alison and Nesta. She closed the book, and, going back to her jade-green settee, sat gazing at Ting-a-ling. The little dog's prominent round eyes gazed back; bright, black, very old. Fleur thought: 'I *don't* want Wilfrid to drop off.' Among all the crowd who came and went, here, there and everywhere, she cared for nobody. Keep up with them, keep up with everything, of course! It was all frightfully amusing, frightfully necessary! Only—only—what?

Voices! Michael and Bart coming back. Bart had noticed Wilfrid, He *was* a noticing old Bart. She was never very comfortable when he was about—lively and twisting, but with something settled and ancestral in him; a little like Ting-a-ling—something judgmatic, ever telling her that she was fluttering and new. He was anchored, could only move to the length of his old-fashioned cord, but he could drop on to things disconcertingly. Still, he admired her, she felt—oh! yes.

Well! What had he thought of the cartoons? Ought Michael to publish them, and with letterpress or without? Didn't he think the cubic called 'Still Life'—of the Government—too frightfully funny, especially the 'old bean' representing the Prime? For answer she was conscious of a twisting, rapid noise; Sir Lawrence was telling her of his father's collection of electioneering cartoons. She did wish Bart would not tell her about his father; he had been so distinguished, and he must have been so dull, paying all his calls on horseback, with trousers strapped under his boots. He and Lord Charles Cariboo and the Marquis of Forfar had been the last three 'callers' of that sort. If only they hadn't, they'd have been clean forgot. She had that dress to try, and fourteen things to see to, and Hugo's concert began at eight-fifteen! Why did people of the last generation always have so much time? And, suddenly, she looked down. Ting-a-ling was licking the copper floor. She took him up: "Not that, darling; nasty!" Ah! the spell was broken! Bart was going, reminiscent to the last. She waited at the foot of the stairs till Michael shut the door on him, then flew. Reaching her room, she turned on all the lights. Here was her own style—a bed which did not look like one, and many mirrors. The couch of Ting-a-ling occupied a corner, whence he could see himself in three. She put him down, and said: "Keep quiet, now!" His attitude to the other dogs in the room had long become indifferent; though of his own breed and precisely his colouring, they had no smell and no licking power in their tongues—nothing to be done with them, imitative creatures, incredibly unresponsive.

Stripping off her dress, Fleur held the new frock under her chin.

"May I kiss you?" said a voice, and there was Michael's image behind her own reflection in the glass.

"My dear boy, there isn't time! Help me with this." She slipped the frock over her head. "Do those three top hooks. How do you

12

like it? Oh! and—Michael! Gurdon Minho may be coming to dinner to-morrow—Wilfrid can't. Have you read his things? Sit down and tell me something about them. All novels, aren't they? What sort?"

"Well, he's always had something to say. And his cats are good. He's a bit romantic, of course."

"Oh! Have I made a gaff?"

"Not a bit; jolly good shot. The vice of our lot is, they say it pretty well, but they've nothing to say. They won't last."

"But that's just why they will last. They won't date."

"Won't they? My gum!"

"Wilfrid will last."

"Ah! Wilfrid has emotions, hates, pities, wants; at least sometimes; when he has, his stuff is jolly good. Otherwise, he just makes a song about nothing—like the rest."

Fleur tucked in the top of her undergarment.

"But, Michael, if that's so, we—I've got the wrong lot."

Michael grinned.

"My dear child! The lot of the hour is always right; only you've got to watch it, and change it quick enough."

"But d'you mean to say that Sibley isn't going to live?"

"Sib? Lord, no!"

"But he's so perfectly sure that almost everybody else is dead or dying. Surely he has critical genius!"

"If I hadn't more judgment than Sib, I'd go out of publishing to-morrow."

"You—more than Sibley Swan?"

"Of course, I've more judgment than Sib. Why! Sib's judgment is just his opinion of Sib—common or garden impatience of anyone else. He doesn't even read them. He'll read one specimen of every author and say : 'Oh! that fellow! He's dull, or he's moral, or he's sentimental, or he dates, or he drivels'—I've heard him dozens of times. That's if they're alive. Of course, if they're dead, it's different. He's always digging up and canonising the dead; that's how he's got his name. There's always a Sib in literature. He's a standing example of how people can get taken at their own valuation. But as to lasting—of course he won't; he's never creative, even by mistake."

Fleur had lost the thread. Yes! It suited her—quite a nice line! Off with it! Must write those three notes before she dressed.

Michael had begun again.

"Take my tip, Fleur. The really big people don't talk—and don't bunch—they paddle their own canoes in what seem backwaters. But it's the backwaters that make the main stream. By Jove, that's a *mot*, or is it a bull; and are bulls *mots* or *mots* bulls?"

"Michael, if you were me, would you tell Frederic Wilmer that he'll be meeting Hubert Marsland at lunch next week? Would it bring him or would it put him off?"

"Marsland's rather an old duck, Wilmer's rather an old goose—I don't know."

"Oh! do be serious, Michael—you never give me any help in arranging—No! Don't maul my shoulders please."

"Well, darling, I *don't* know. I've no genius for such things, like you. Marsland paints windmills, cliffs and things—I doubt if he's heard of the future. He's almost a Mathew Maris for keeping out of the swim. If you think he'd like to meet a Vertiginist——"

"I didn't ask you if he'd like to meet Wilmer; I asked you if Wilmer would like to meet him."

"Wilmer will just say: 'I like little Mrs. Mont, she gives deuced good grub'—and so you do, ducky. A Vertiginist wants nourishing, you know, or it wouldn't go to his head."

Fleur's pen resumed its swift strokes, already become slightly illegible. She murmured:

"I think Wilfrid would help—you won't be there; one—two—three. What women?"

"Four painters—pretty and plump; no intellect."

Fleur said crossly:

"I can't get them plump; they don't go about now." And her pen flowed on:

"DEAR WILFRID,—Wednesday—lunch; Wilmer, Hubert Marsland, two other women. Do help me live it down.

"Yours ever,

"FLEUR."

"Michael, your chin is like a bootbrush."

"Sorry, old thing; your shoulders shouldn't be so smooth. Bart gave Wilfrid a tip as we were coming along."

Fleur stopped writing. "Oh!"

"Reminded him that the state of love was a good stunt for poets."

"*A propos* of what?"

"Wilfrid was complaining that he couldn't turn it out now."

"Nonsense! His last things are his best."

14

"Well, that's what I think. Perhaps he's forestalled the tip. Has he, d'you know?"

Fleur turned her eyes towards the face behind her shoulder. No, it had its native look—frank, irresponsible, slightly faun-like, with its pointed ears, quick lips, and nostrils.

She said slowly,

"If *you* don't know, nobody does."

A snuffle interrupted Michael's answer. Ting-a-ling, long, low, slightly higher at both ends, was standing between them, with black muzzle upturned. "My pedigree is long," he seemed to say: "but my legs are short—what about it?"

## Chapter III

### MUSICAL

ACCORDING to a great and guiding principle, Fleur and Michael Mont attended the Hugo Solstis concert, not because they anticipated pleasure, but because they knew Hugo. They felt, besides, that Solstis, an Englishman of Russo-Dutch extraction, was one of those who were restoring English music, giving to it a wide and spacious freedom from melody and rhythm, while investing it with literary and mathematical charms. And one never could go to a concert given by any of this school without using the word 'interesting' as one was coming away. To sleep to this restored English music, too, was impossible. Fleur, a sound sleeper, had never even tried. Michael had, and complained afterwards that it had been like a nap in Liège railway station. On this occasion they occupied those gangway seats in the front row of the dress circle of which Fleur had a sort of natural monopoly. There Hugo and the rest could see her taking her place in the English restoration movement. It was easy, too, to escape into the corridor and exchange the word 'interesting' with side-whiskered cognoscenti; or, slipping out a cigarette from the little gold case, wedding present of Cousin Imogen Cardigan, get a whiff or two's repose. To speak quite honestly, Fleur had a natural sense of rhythm which caused her discomfort during those long and 'interesting' passages which evidenced, as it were, the composer's rise and fall from his bed of thorns. She secretly loved a tune, and the impossibility of ever confessing this without losing hold of Solstis, Baff, Birdigal, MacLewis, Clorane, and other English restoration composers, sometimes taxed to its limits a nature which had its Spartan side. Even

15

A MODERN COMEDY

tu Michael she would not 'confess'; and it was additionally trying when, with his native disrespect of persons, accentuated by life in the trenches and a publisher's office, he would mutter: "Gad! Get on with it!" or: "Cripes! Ain't he took bad!" especially as she knew that Michael was really putting up with it better than herself, having a more literary disposition, and a less dancing itch in his toes.

The first movement of the new Solstis composition—'Phantasmagoria Piémontesque'—to which they had come especially to listen, began with some drawn-out chords.

"What oh!" said Michael's voice in her ear: "Three pieces of furniture moved simultaneously on a parquet floor!"

In Fleur's involuntary smile was the whole secret of why her marriage had not been intolerable. After all, Michael was a dear! Devotion and mercury—jesting and loyalty—combined, they piqued and touched even a heart given away before it was bestowed on him. 'Touch' without 'pique' would have bored; 'pique' without 'touch' would have irritated. At this moment he was at peculiar advantage! Holding on to his knees, with his ears standing up, eyes glassy from loyalty to Hugo, and tongue in cheek, he was listening to that opening in a way which evoked Fleur's admiration. The piece would be 'interesting'—she fell into the state of outer observation and inner calculation very usual with her nowadays. Over there was L.S.D., the greater dramatist; she didn't know him —yet. He looked rather frightening, his hair stood up so straight. And her eye began picturing him on her copper floor against a Chinese picture. And there—yes! Gurdon Minho! Imagine *his* coming to anything so modern! His profile *was* rather Roman—of the Aurelian period! Passing on from that antique, with the pleased thought that by this time to-morrow she might have collected it, she quartered the assembly face by face—she did not want to miss anyone important.

'The furniture' had come to a sudden standstill.

"Interesting!" said a voice over her shoulder. Aubrey Greene! Illusive, rather moonlit, with his silky fair hair brushed straight back, and his greenish eyes—his smile always made her feel that he was 'getting' at her. But, after all, he was a cartoonist!

"Yes, isn't it?"

He curled away. He might have stayed a little longer—there wouldn't be time for anyone else before those songs of Birdigal's! Here came the singer Charles Powls! How stout and efficient he looked, dragging little Birdigal to the piano.

16

Charming accompaniment—rippling, melodious!

The stout, efficient man began to sing. How different from the accompaniment! The song hit every note just off the solar plexus, it mathematically prevented her from feeling pleasure. Birdigal must have written it in horror of someone calling it 'vocal'. Vocal! Fleur knew how catching the word was; it would run like a measle round the ring, and Birdigal would be no more! Poor Birdigal! But this was 'interesting'. Only, as Michael was saying: "O, my Gawd!"

Three songs! Powls was wonderful—so loyal! Never one note hit so that it rang out like music! Her mind fluttered off to Wilfrid. To him, of all the younger poets, people accorded the right to say something; it gave him such a position—made him seem to come out of life, instead of literature. Besides, he had done things in the war, was a son of Lord Mullyon, would get the Mercer Prize probably for 'Copper Coin'. If Wilfrid abandoned her, a star would fall from the firmament above her copper floor. He had no right to leave her in the lurch. He must learn not to be violent—not to think physically. No! she couldn't let Wilfrid slip away; nor could she have any more sob-stuff in her life, searing passions, *cul de sacs*, aftermaths. She had tasted of that; a dulled ache still warned her.

Birdigal was bowing, Michael saying: "Come out for a whiff! The next thing's a dud!" Oh! ah! Beethoven. Poor old Beethoven! So out of date—one did *rather* enjoy him!

The corridor, and refectory beyond, were swarming with the restoration movement. Young men and women with faces and heads of lively and distorted character, were exchanging the word 'interesting'. Men of more massive type, resembling sedentary matadors, blocked all circulation. Fleur and Michael passed a little way along, stood against the wall, and lighted cigarettes. Fleur smoked hers delicately—a very little one in a tiny amber holder. She had the air of admiring blue smoke rather than of making it; there were spheres to consider beyond this sort of crowd—one never knew who might be about!—the sphere, for instance, in which Alison Charwell moved, politico-literary, catholic in taste, but, as Michael always put it: "Convinced, like a sanitary system, that it's the only sphere in the world; look at the way they all write books of reminiscence about each other!" They might, she always felt, disapprove of women smoking in public halls. Consorting delicately with iconoclasm, Fleur never forgot that her feet were in two worlds at least. Standing there, observant of all to

17

left and right, she noted against the wall one whose face was screened by his programme. 'Wilfrid,' she thought, 'and doesn't mean to see me!' Mortified, as a child from whom a sixpence is filched, she said:

"There's Wilfrid! Fetch him, Michael!"

Michael crossed, and touched his best man's sleeve; Desert's face emerged, frowning. She saw him shrug his shoulders, turn and walk into the throng. Michael came back.

"Wilfrid's got the hump to-night; says he's not fit for human society—queer old son!"

How obtuse men were! Because Wilfrid was his pal, Michael did not see; and that was lucky! So Wilfrid really meant to avoid her! Well, she would see! And she said:

"I'm tired, Michael; let's go home."

His hand slid round her arm.

"Sorry, old thing; come along!"

They stood a moment in a neglected doorway, watching Woomans, the conductor, launched towards his orchestra.

"Look at him," said Michael; "guy hung out of an Italian window, legs and arms all stuffed and flying! And look at the Frapka and her piano—that's a turbulent union!"

There was a strange sound.

"Melody, by George!" said Michael.

An attendant muttered in their ears: "Now, sir, I'm going to shut the door." Fleur had a fleeting view of L.S.D. sitting upright as his hair, with closed eyes. The door was shut—they were outside in the hall.

"Wait here, darling; I'll nick a rickshaw."

Fleur huddled her chin in her fur. It was easterly and cold.

A voice behind her said:

"Well, Fleur, am I going East?"

Wilfrid! His collar up to his ears, a cigarette between his lips, hands in pockets, eyes devouring.

"You're very silly, Wilfrid!"

"Anything you like; am I going East?"

"No; Sunday morning—eleven o'clock at the Tate. We'll talk it out."

"*Convenu!*" And he was gone.

Alone suddenly, like that, Fleur felt the first shock of reality. Was Wilfrid truly going to be unmanageable? A taxi-cab ground up; Michael beckoned; Fleur stepped in.

Passing a passionately lighted oasis of young ladies displaying to the interested Londoner the acme of Parisian undress, she felt Michael incline towards her. If she were going to keep Wilfrid, she must be nice to Michael. Only:

"You needn't kiss me in Piccadilly Circus, Michael!"

"Sorry, duckie! It's a little previous—I meant to get you opposite the Partheneum."

Fleur remembered how he had slept on a Spanish sofa for the first fortnight of their honeymoon; how he always insisted that she must not spend anything on him, but must always let him give her what he liked, though she had three thousand a year and he twelve hundred; how jumpy he was when she had a cold—and how he always came home to tea. Yes, he was a dear! But would she break her heart if he went East or West to-morrow?

Snuggled against him, she was surprised at her own cynicism.

A telephone message written out, in the hall, ran: 'Please tell Mrs. Mont I've got Mr. Gurding Minner. Lady Alisson.'

It was restful. A real antique! She turned on the lights in her room, and stood for a moment admiring it. Truly pretty! A slight snuffle from the corner—Ting-a-ling, tan on a black cushion, lay like a Chinese lion in miniature; pure, remote, fresh from evening communion with the Square railings.

"I see you," said Fleur.

Ting-a-ling did not stir; his round black eyes watched his mistress undress. When she returned from the bathroom he was curled into a ball. Fleur thought: 'Queer! How does he know Michael won't be coming?' And slipping into her well-warmed bed, she too curled herself up and slept.

But in the night, contrary to her custom, she awoke. A cry—long, weird, trailing, from somewhere—the river—the slums at the back—rousing memory—poignant, aching—of her honeymoon—Granada, its roofs below, jet, ivory, gold; the watchman's cry, the lines in Jon's letter:

"Voice in the night crying, down in the old sleeping
    Spanish City darkened under her white stars.
What says the voice—its clear, lingering anguish?
Just the watchman, telling his dateless tale of safety?
Just a road-man, flinging to the moon his song?
    No! 'Tis one deprived, whose lover's heart is weeping,
    Just his cry: 'How long?'"

A cry, or had she dreamed it? Jon, Wilfrid, Michael! No use to have a heart!

19

## Chapter IV

## DINING

LADY ALISON CHARWELL, born Heathfield, daughter of the first Earl of Campden, and wife to Lionel Charwell, K.C., Michael's somewhat young uncle, was a delightful Englishwoman brought up in a set accepted as the soul of society. Full of brains, energy, taste, money, and tinctured in its politico-legal ancestry by blue blood, this set was linked to, but apart from 'Snooks' and the duller haunts of birth and privilege. It was gay, charming, free-and-easy, and, according to Michael, "Snobbish, old thing, æsthetically and intellectually, but they'll never see it. They think they're the top notch—quick, healthy, up-to-date, well-bred, intelligent; they simply can't imagine their equals. But you see their imagination is deficient. Their really creative energy would go into a pint pot. Look at their books—they're always *on* something—philosophy, spiritualism, poetry, fishing, themselves; why, even their sonnets dry up before they're twenty-five. They know everything—except mankind outside their own set. Oh! they work—they run the show—they have to; there's no one else with their brains, and energy, and taste. But they run it round and round in their own blooming circle. It's the world to them—and it might be worse. They've patented their own golden age; but it's a trifle fly-blown since the war."

Alison Charwell—in and of this world, so spryly soulful, debonnaire, free, and cosy—lived within a stone's throw of Fleur, in a house pleasant, architecturally, as any in London. Forty years old, she had three children and considerable beauty, wearing a little fine from mental and bodily activity. Something of an enthusiast, she was fond of Michael, in spite of his strange criticisms, so that his matrimonial venture had piqued her from the start. Fleur was dainty, had quick natural intelligence—this new niece was worth cultivation. But, though adaptable and assimilative, Fleur had remained curiously unassimilated; she continued to whet the curiosity of Lady Alison, accustomed to the close borough of choice spirits, and finding a certain poignancy in contact with the New Age on Fleur's copper floor. She met with an irreverence there, which, not taken too seriously, flipped her mind. On that floor she almost felt a back number. It was stimulating.

Receiving Fleur's telephonic enquiry about Gurdon Minho, she had rung up the novelist. She knew him, if not well. Nobody seemed to know him well; amiable, polite, silent, rather dull and austere; but with a disconcerting smile, sometimes ironical, sometimes friendly. His books were now caustic, now sentimental. On both counts it was rather the fashion to run him down, though he still seemed to exist.

She rang him up. Would he come to a dinner to-morrow at her young nephew, Michael Mont's, and meet the younger generation? His answer came, rather high-pitched:

"Rather! Full fig, or dinner jacket?"

"How awfully nice of you! they'll be ever so pleased. Full fig, I believe. It's the second anniversary of their wedding." She hung up the receiver with the thought: 'He must be writing a book about them!'

Conscious of responsibility, she arrived early.

It was a grand night at her husband's Inn, so that she brought nothing with her but the feeling of adventure, pleasant after a day spent in fluttering over the decision at 'Snooks'. She was received only by Ting-a-ling, who had his back to the fire, and took no notice beyond a stare. Sitting down on the jade green settee, she said:

"Well, you funny little creature, don't you know me after all this time?"

Ting-a-ling's black shiny gaze seemed saying: "You recur here, I know; most things recur. There is nothing new about the future."

Lady Alison fell into a train of thought: The new generation! Did she want her own girls to be of it! 'She would like to talk to Mr. Minho about that—they had had a very nice talk down at Beechgroves before the war. Nine years ago—Sybil only six, Joan only four then! Time went, things changed! A new generation! And what was the difference! "I think we had more tradition!" she said to herself softly.

A slight sound drew her eyes up from contemplation of her feet. Ting-a-ling was moving his tail from side to side on the hearth-rug, as if applauding. Fleur's voice, behind her, said:

"Well, darling, I'm awfully late. It *was* good of you to get me Mr. Minho. I do hope they'll all behave. He'll be between you and me, anyway; I'm sticking him at the top, and Michael at the bottom, between Pauline Upshire and Amabel Nazing. You'll have Sibley on your left, and I'll have Aubrey on my right, then Nesta Gorse and Walter Nazing; opposite them Linda Frewe and Charles

21

Upshire. Twelve. You know them all. Oh! and you mustn't mind if the Nazings and Nesta smoke between the courses. Amabel will do it. She comes from Virginia—it's the reaction. I do hope she'll have some clothes on; Michael always says it's a mistake when she has; but having Mr. Minho makes one a little nervous. Did you see Nesta's skit in 'The Bouquet'? Oh, too frightfully amusing—clearly meant for L.S.D.! Ting, my Ting, are you going to stay and see all these people? Well, then, get up here or you'll be trodden on. Isn't he Chinese? He does so round off the room."

Ting-a-ling laid his nose on his paws, in the centre of a jade green cushion.

"Mr. Gurding Minner!"

The well-known novelist looked pale and composed. Shaking the two extended hands, he gazed at Ting-a-ling, and said:

"How nice! How are *you*, my little man?"

Ting-a-ling did not stir. "You take me for a common English dog, sir!" his silence seemed to say.

"Mr. and Mrs. Walter Nazon, Miss Lenda Frow."

Amabel Nazing came first, clear alabaster from her fair hair down to the six inches of gleaming back above her waist-line, shrouded alabaster from four inches below the knee to the gleaming toes of her shoes; the eminent novelist mechanically ceased to commune with Ting-a-ling.

Walter Nazing, who followed a long way up above his wife, had a tiny line of collar emergent from swathes of black, and a face, cut a hundred years ago, that slightly resembled Shelley's. His literary productions were sometimes felt to be like the poetry of that bard, and sometimes like the prose of Marcel Proust. "What oh!" as Michael said.

Linda Frewe, whom Fleur at once introduced to Gurdon Minho, was one about whose work no two people in her drawing-room ever agreed. Her works 'Trifles' and 'The Furious Don' had quite divided all opinion. Genius according to some, drivel according to others, those books always roused an interesting debate whether a slight madness enhanced or diminished the value of art. She herself paid little attention to criticism—she produced.

"*The* Mr. Minho? How interesting! I've never read anything of yours."

Fleur gave a little gasp.

"What—don't you know Mr. Minho's cats? But they're wonderful. Mr. Minho, I do want Mrs. Walter Nazing to know you. Amabel—Mr. Gurdon Minho."

"Oh! Mr. Minho—how perfectly lovely! I've wanted to know you ever since my cradle."

Fleur heard the novelist say quietly:

"I could wish it had been longer;" and passed on in doubt to greet Nesta Gorse and Sibley Swan, who came in, as if they lived together, quarrelling over L.S.D., Nesta upholding him because of his 'panache', Sibley maintaining that wit had died with the Restoration; this fellow was alive!

Michael followed with the Upshires and Aubrey Greene, whom he had encountered in the hall. The party was complete.

Fleur loved perfection, and that evening was something of a nightmare. Was it a success? Minho was so clearly the least brilliant person there; even Alison talked better. And yet he had such a fine skull. She did hope he would not go away early. Someone would be almost sure to say 'Dug up!' or 'Thick and bald!' before the door closed behind him. He was pathetically agreeable, as if trying to be liked, or, at least, not despised too much. And there must, of course, be more in him than met the sense of hearing. After the crab soufflé he did seem to be talking to Alison, and all about youth. Fleur listened with one ear.

"Youth feels . . . main stream of life . . . not giving it what it wants. Past and future getting haloes . . . Quite! Contemporary life no earthly just now . . . No . . . Only comfort for us—we'll be antiquated, some day, like Congreve, Sterne, Defoe . . . have our chance again . . . *Why?* What *is* driving them out of the main current? Oh! Probably surfeit . . . newspapers . . . photographs. Don't see life itself, only reports . . . reproductions of it; all seems shoddy, lurid, commercial . . . Youth says: 'Away with it, let's have the past or the future!'"

He took some salted almonds, and Fleur saw his eyes stray to the upper part of Amabel Nazing. Down there the conversation was like Association football—no one kept the ball for more than one kick. It shot from head to head. And after every set of passes someone would reach out and take a cigarette, and blow a blue cloud across the unclothed refectory table. Fleur enjoyed the glow of her Spanish room—its tiled floor, richly coloured fruits in porcelain, its tooled leather, copper articles, and Soames's Goya above a Moorish divan. She headed the ball promptly when it came her way, but initiated nothing. Her gift was to be aware of everything at once. "Mrs. Michael Mont presented" the brilliant irrelevances of Linda Frewe, the pricks and stimulations of Nesta Gorse, the moonlit sliding innuendoes of Aubrey Greene, the

23

upturning strokes of Sibley Swan, Amabel Nazing's little cool American audacities, Charles Upshire's curious bits of lore, Walter Nazing's subversive contradictions, the critical intricacies of Pauline Upshire; Michael's happy-go-lucky slings and arrows, even Alison's knowledgeable quickness, and Gurdon Minho's silences—she presented them all, showed them off, keeping her eyes and ears on the ball of talk lest it should touch earth and rest. Brilliant evening; but—a success?

On the jade green settee, when the last of them had gone and Michael was seeing Alison home, she thought of Minho's 'Youth—not getting what it wants.' No! Things didn't fit. "They don't fit, do they, Ting!" But Ting-a-ling was tired, only the tip of one ear quivered. Fleur leaned back and sighed. Ting-a-ling uncurled himself, and putting his forepaws on her thigh, looked up in her face. "Look at me," he seemed to say, "I'm all right. I get what I want, and I want what I get. At present I want to go to bed."

"But I don't," said Fleur, without moving.

"Just take me up!" said Ting-a-ling.

"Well," said Fleur, "I suppose—— It's a nice person, but not the right person, Ting."

Ting-a-ling settled himself on her bare arms.

"It's all right," he seemed to say. "There's a great deal too much sentiment and all that, out of China. Come on!"

## Chapter V

### EVE

THE Honourable Wilfrid Desert's rooms were opposite a picture gallery off Cork Street. The only male member of the aristocracy writing verse that anyone would print, he had chosen them for seclusion rather than for comfort. His 'junk', however, was not devoid of the taste and luxury which overflows from the greater houses of England. Furniture from the Hampshire seat of the Cornish nobleman, Lord Mullyon, had oozed into two vans, when Wilfrid settled in. He was seldom to be found, however, in his nest, and was felt to be a rare bird, owing his rather unique position among the younger writers partly to his migratory reputation. He himself hardly, perhaps, knew where he spent his time, or did his work, having a sort of mental claustrophobia, a dread of being hemmed in by people. When the war broke out he had just left Eton; when the war was over he was twenty-three, as old a young

man as ever turned a stave. His friendship with Michael, begun
in hospital, had languished and renewed itself suddenly, when in
1920 Michael joined Danby and Winter, publishers, of Blake Street,
Covent Garden. The scattery enthusiasm of the sucking publisher
had been roused by Wilfrid's verse. Hob-nobbing lunches over the
poems of one in need of literary anchorage, had been capped by
the firm's surrender to Michael's insistence. The mutual intoxica-
tion of the first book Wilfrid had written and the first book Michael
had sponsored was crowned at Michael's wedding. Best man!
Since then, so far as Desert could be tied to anything, he had been
tied to those two; nor, to do him justice, had he realised till a
month ago that the attraction was not Michael, but Fleur. Desert
never spoke of the war, it was not possible to learn from his own
mouth an effect which he might have summed up thus: "I lived
so long with horror and death; I saw men so in the raw; I put hope
of anything out of my mind so utterly, that I can never more have
the faintest respect for theories, promises, conventions, moralities,
and principles. I have hated too much the men who wallowed in
them while I was wallowing in mud and blood. Illusion is off. No
religion and no philosophy will satisfy me—words, all words. I
have still my senses—no thanks to them; am still capable—I find—
of passion; can still grit my teeth and grin; have still some feeling
of trench loyalty, but whether real or just a complex, I don't yet
know. I am dangerous, but not so dangerous as those who trade
in words, principles, theories, and all manner of fanatical idiocy
to be worked out in the blood and sweat of other men. The war's
done one thing for me—converted life to comedy. Laugh at it—
there's nothing else to do!"

Leaving the concert hall on the Friday night, he had walked
straight home to his rooms. And lying down full length on a
monk's seat of the fifteenth century, restored with down cushions
and silk of the twentieth, he crossed his hands behind his head and
delivered himself to these thoughts: 'I am not going on like this.
She has bewitched me. It doesn't mean anything to her. But it
means hell to me. I'll finish with it on Sunday—Persia's a good
place. Arabia's a good place—plenty of blood and sand! She's incapable of giving anything up. How has she hooked herself into
me? By trick of eyes, and hair, by her walk, by the sound of her
voice—by trick of warmth, scent, colour. Fling her cap over the
windmill—not she! What then? Am I to hang about her Chinese
fireside and her little Chinese dog; and have this ache and this fever
because I can't be kissing her? I'd rather be flying again in the

middle of Boche whiz-bangs! Sunday! How women like to drag out agonies! It'll be just this afternoon all over again. "How unkind of you to go, when your friendship is so precious to me! Stay, and be my tame cat, Wilfrid!" No, my dear, for once you're up against it! And—so am I, by the Lord! . . .'

When in that gallery which extends asylum to British art, those two young people met so accidentally on Sunday morning in front of Eve smelling at the flowers of the Garden of Eden, there were present also six mechanics in various stages of decomposition, a custodian and a couple from the provinces, none of whom seemed capable of observing anything whatever. And, indeed, that meeting was inexpressive. Two young people, of the disillusioned class, exchanging condemnations of the past. Desert with his off-hand speech, his smile, his well-tailored informality, suggested no aching heart. Of the two Fleur was the paler and more interesting. Desert kept saying to himself: "No melodrama—that's all it would be!" And Fleur was thinking: 'If I can keep him ordinary like this, I shan't lose him, because he'll never go away without a proper outburst.'

It was not until they found themselves a second time before the Eve, that he said:

"I don't know why you asked me to come, Fleur. It's playing the goat for no earthly reason. I quite understand your feeling. I'm a bit of 'Ming' that you don't want to lose. But it's not good enough, my dear; and that's all about it."

"How horrible of you, Wilfrid!"

"Well! Here we part! Give us your flipper."

His eyes—rather beautiful—looked dark and tragic above the smile on his lips, and she said stammering:

"Wilfrid—I—I don't know. I want time. I can't bear you to be unhappy. Don't go away! Perhaps I—I shall be unhappy, too; I—I don't know."

Through Desert passed the bitter thought: 'She *can't* let go—she doesn't know how.' But he said quite softly: "Cheer up, my child; you'll be over all that in a fortnight. I'll send you something to make up. Why shouldn't I make it China—one place is as good as another? I'll send you a bit of real 'Ming', of a better period than this."

Fleur said passionately:

"You're insulting! Don't!"

"I beg your pardon. I don't want to leave you angry."

"What is it you want of me?"

26

"Oh! no—come! This is going over it twice. Besides, since Friday I've been thinking. I want nothing, Fleur, except a blessing and your hand. Give it me! Come on!"

Fleur put her hand behind her back. It was too mortifying! He took her for a cold-blooded, collecting little cat—clutching and playing with mice that she didn't want to eat!

"You think I'm made of ice," she said, and her teeth caught her upper lip: "Well, I'm not!"

Desert looked at her; his eyes were very wretched. "I didn't mean to play up your pride," he said. "Let's drop it, Fleur. It isn't any good."

Fleur turned and fixed her eyes on the Eve—rumbustious-looking female, care-free, avid, taking her fill of flower perfume! Why not be care-free, take anything that came along? Not so much love in the world that one could afford to pass, leaving it unsmelled, unplucked. Run away! Go to the East! Of course, she couldn't do anything extravagant like that! But, perhaps—— What did it matter? one man or another, when neither did you really love!

From under her drooped, white, dark-lashed eyelids she saw the expression on his face, and that he was standing stiller than the statues. And suddenly she said: "You will be a fool to go. Wait!" And without another word or look, she walked away, leaving Desert breathless before the avid Eve.

## Chapter VI

### 'OLD FORSYTE' AND 'OLD MONT'

MOVING away, in the confusion of her mood, Fleur almost trod on the toes of a too-familiar figure standing before an Alma Tadema with a sort of grey anxiety, as if lost in the mutability of market values.

"Father! *You* up in town? Come along to lunch, I have to get me quick."

Hooking his arm and keeping between him and Eve, she guided him away, thinking: 'Did he see us? Could he have seen us?'

"Have you got enough on?" muttered Soames.

"Heaps!"

"That's what you women always say. East wind, and your neck like that! Well, I don't know."

"No, dear, but I do."

The grey eyes appraised her from head to foot.

27

"What are you doing here?" he said. And Fleur thought: 'Thank God he didn't see. He'd never have asked if he had.' And she answered:

"I take an interest in art, darling, as well as you."

"Well, I'm staying with your aunt in Green Street. This east wind has touched my liver. How's your—how's Michael?"

"Oh, he's all right—a little cheap. We had a dinner last night."

Anniversary! The realism of a Forsyte stirred in him, and he looked under her eyes. Thrusting his hand into his overcoat pocket, he said:

"I was bringing you this."

Fleur saw a flat substance wrapped in pink tissue paper.

"Darling, what is it?"

Soames put it back into his pocket.

"We'll see later. Anybody to lunch?"

"Only Bart."

"Old Mont! Oh, Lord!"

"Don't you like Bart, dear?"

"Like him? He and I have nothing in common."

"I thought you fraternised rather over the state of things."

"He's a reactionary," said Soames.

"And what are you, ducky?"

"I? What should *I* be?" With these words he affirmed that policy of non-commitment which, the older he grew, the more he perceived to be the only attitude for a sensible man.

"How is Mother?"

"Looks well. I see nothing of her—she's got her own mother down—they go gadding about."

He never alluded to Madame Lamotte as Fleur's grandmother—the less his daughter had to do with her French side, the better.

"Oh!" said Fleur. "There's Ting and a cat!" Ting-a-ling, out for a breath of air, and tethered by a lead in the hands of a maid, was snuffling horribly and trying to climb a railing whereon was perched a black cat, all hunch and eyes.

"Give him to me, Ellen. Come with Mother, darling!"

Ting-a-ling came, indeed, but only because he couldn't go, bristling and snuffling and turning his head back.

"I like to see him natural," said Fleur.

"Waste of money, a dog like that," Soames commented. "You should have had a bull-dog and let him sleep in the hall. No end of burglaries. Your aunt had her knocker stolen."

"I wouldn't part with Ting for a hundred knockers."

"One of these days you'll be having *him* stolen—fashionable breed."

Fleur opened her front door. "Oh!" she said, "Bart's here, already!"

A shiny hat was reposing on a marble coffer, present from Soames, intended to hold coats and discourage moth. Placing his hat alongside the other, Soames looked at them. They were too similar for words, tall, high, shiny, and with the same name inside. He had resumed the 'tall hat' habit after the failure of the general and coal strikes in 1921, his instinct having told him that revolution would be at a discount for some considerable period.

"About this thing," he said, taking out the pink parcel, "I don't know what you'll do with it, but here it is."

It was a curiously carved and coloured bit of opal in a ring of tiny brilliants.

"Oh!" Fleur cried: "What a delicious thing!"

"Venus floating on the waves, or something," murmured Soames. "Uncommon. You want a strong light on it."

"But it's lovely. I shall put it on at once."

Venus! If Dad had known! She put her arms round his neck to disguise her sense of *à propos*. Soames received the rub of her cheek against his own well-shaved face with his usual stillness. Why demonstrate when they were both aware that his affection was double hers?

"Put it on then," he said, "and let's see."

Fleur pinned it at her neck before an old lacquered mirror. "It's a jewel. Thank you, darling! Yes, your tie is straight. I like that white piping. You ought always to wear it with black. Now, come along!" And she drew him into her Chinese room. It was empty.

"Bart must be up with Michael, talking about his new book."

"Writing at his age?" said Soames.

"Well, ducky, he's a year younger than you."

"I don't write. Not such a fool. Got any more new-fangled friends?"

"Just one—Gurdon Minho, the novelist."

"Another of the new school?"

"Oh, no, dear! Surely you've heard of Gurdon Minho; he's older than the hills."

"They're all alike to me," muttered Soames. "Is he well thought of?"

"I should think his income is larger than yours. He's almost a classic—only waiting to die."

29

"I'll get one of his books and read it. What name did you say?"

"Get 'Big and Little Fishes,' by Gurdon Minho. You can remember that, can't you? Oh! here they are! Michael, look at what Father's given me."

Taking his hand, she put it up to the opal at her neck. 'Let them both see,' she thought, 'what good terms we're on.' Though her father had not seen her with Wilfrid in the gallery, her conscience still said: "Strengthen your respectability, you don't quite know how much support you'll need for it in future."

And out of the corner of her eye she watched those two. The meetings between 'Old Mont' and 'Old Forsyte'—as she knew Bart called her father when speaking of him to Michael—always made her want to laugh, but she never quite knew why. Bart knew everything, but his knowledge was beautifully bound, strictly edited by a mind tethered to the 'eighteenth century'. Her father only knew what was of advantage to him, but the knowledge was unbound, and subject to no editorship. If he *was* late Victorian, he was not above profiting if necessary by even later periods. 'Old Mont' had faith in tradition; 'Old Forsyte' none. Fleur's acuteness had long perceived a difference which favoured her father. Yet 'Old Mont's' talk was so much more up-to-date, rapid, glancing, garrulous, redolent of precise information; and 'Old Forsyte's' was constricted, matter-of-fact. Really impossible to tell which of the two was the better museum specimen; and both so well-preserved!

They did not precisely shake hands; but Soames mentioned the weather. And almost at once they all four sought that Sunday food which by a sustained effort of will Fleur had at last deprived of reference to the British character. They partook, in fact, of lobster cocktails, and a mere risotto of chickens' livers, an omelette *au rhum*, and dessert trying to look as Spanish as it could.

"I've been in the Tate," Fleur said; "I do think it's touching."

"Touching?" queried Soames with a sniff.

"Fleur means, sir, that to see so much old English art together is like looking at a baby show."

"I don't follow," said Soames stiffly. "There's some very good work there."

"But not grown-up, sir."

"Ah! You young people mistake all this crazy cleverness for maturity."

"That's not what Michael means, Father. It's quite true that English painting has no wisdom teeth. You can see the difference in a moment, between it and any Continental painting."

30

"And thank God for it!" broke in Sir Lawrence. "The beauty of this country's art is its innocence. We're the oldest country in the world politically, and the youngest æsthetically. What do you say, Forsyte?"

"Turner is old and wise enough for me," said Soames curtly. "Are you coming to the P.P.R.S. Board on Tuesday?"

"Tuesday? We were going to shoot the spinneys, weren't we, Michael?"

Soames grunted. "I should let them wait," he said. "We settle the report."

It was through 'Old Mont's' influence that he had received a seat on the Board of that flourishing concern, the Providential Premium Reassurance Society, and, truth to tell, he was not sitting very easily in it. Though the law of averages was, perhaps, the most reliable thing in the world, there were circumstances which had begun to cause him disquietude. He looked round his nose. Light weight, this narrow-headed, twisting-eyebrowed baronet of a chap —like his son before him! And he added suddenly: "I'm not easy. If I'd realised how that chap Elderson ruled the roost, I doubt if I should have come on to that Board."

One side of 'Old Mont's' face seemed to try to leave the other.

"Elderson!" he said. "His grandfather was my grandfather's parliamentary agent at the time of the Reform Bill; he put him through the most corrupt election ever fought—bought every vote —used to kiss all the farmers' wives. Great days, Forsyte, great days!"

"And over," said Soames. "I don't believe in trusting a man's judgment as far as we trust Elderson's; I don't like this foreign insurance."

"My dear Forsyte—first-rate head, Elderson; I've know him all my life, we were at Winchester together."

Soames uttered a deep sound. In that answer of 'Old Mont's' lay much of the reason for his disquietude. On the Board they had all, as it were, been at Winchester together! It was the very deuce! They were all so honourable that they dared not scrutinise each other, or even their own collective policy. Worse than their dread of mistake or fraud was their dread of seeming to distrust each other. And this was natural, for to distrust each other was an immediate evil. And, as Soames knew, immediate evils are those which one avoids. Indeed, only that tendency, inherited from his father, James, to lie awake between the hours of two and four, when the chrysalis of faint misgiving becomes so readily the butter-

31

fly of panic, had developed his uneasiness. The P.P.R.S. was so imposing a concern, and he had been connected with it so short a time, that it seemed presumptuous to smell a rat; especially as he would have to leave the Board and the thousand a year he earned on it if he raised smell of rat without rat or reason. But what if there were a rat? That was the trouble! And here sat 'Old Mont' talking of his spinneys and his grandfather. The fellow's head was too small! And visited by the cheerless thought: 'There's nobody here, not even my own daughter, capable of taking a thing seriously,' he kept silence. A sound at his elbow roused him. That marmoset of a dog, on a chair between him and his daughter, was sitting up! Did it expect him to give it something? Its eyes would drop out one of these days. And he said: "Well, what do *you* want?" The way the little beast stared with those boot-buttons! "Here," he said, offering it a salted almond. "You don't eat these."

Ting-a-ling did.

"He has a passion for them, Dad. Haven't you, darling?"

Ting-a-ling turned his eyes up at Soames, through whom a queer sensation passed. 'Believe the little brute likes me,' he thought, 'he's always looking at me.' He touched the dog's nose with the tip of his finger. Ting-a-ling gave it a slight lick with his curly blackish tongue.

"Poor fellow!" muttered Soames involuntarily, and turned to 'Old Mont'.

"Don't mention what I said."

"My dear Forsyte, what was that?"

Good Heavens! And he was on a Board with a man like this! What had made him come on, when he didn't want the money, or any more worries—goodness knew. As soon as he had become a director, Winifred and others of his family had begun to acquire shares to neutralise their income tax—seven per cent. preference—nine per cent. ordinary—instead of the steady five they ought to be content with. There it was, he couldn't move without people following him. He had always been so safe, so perfect a guide in the money maze! To be worried at his time of life! His eyes sought comfort from the opal at his daughter's neck—pretty thing, pretty neck! Well! She seemed happy enough—had forgotten her infatuation of two years ago! That was something to be thankful for. What she wanted now was a child to steady her in all this modern scrimmage of twopenny-ha'penny writers and painters and musicians. A loose lot, but she had a good little head on her. If she had a child, he would put another twenty thousand into her settlement. That was one thing about her mother—steady in money matters, good French method. And Fleur—so far as he knew —cut her coat according to her cloth. What was that? The word 'Goya' had caught his ear. New life of him coming out? H'm! That confirmed his slowly growing conviction that Goya had reached top point again.

"Think I shall part with that," he said, pointing to the picture. "There's an Argentine over here."

"Sell your Goya, sir?" It was Michael speaking. "Think of the envy with which you're now regarded!"

"One can't have everything," said Soames.

"That reproduction we've got for 'The New Life' has turned out first-rate. 'Property of Soames Forsyte, Esquire.' Let's get the book out first, sir, anyway."

"Shadow or substance, eh, Forsyte?"

Narrow-headed baronet chap—was he mocking?

"*I've* no family place," he said.

"No, but we have, sir," murmured Michael; "you could leave it to Fleur, you know."

"Well," said Soames, "we shall see if that's worth while." And he looked at his daughter.

Fleur seldom blushed, but she picked up Ting-a-ling and rose from the Spanish table. Michael followed suit. "Coffee in the other room," he said. 'Old Forsyte' and 'Old Mont' stood up, wiping their moustaches.

## Chapter VII

### 'OLD MONT' AND 'OLD FORSYTE'

THE offices of the P.P.R.S. were not far from the College of Arms. Soames, who knew that 'three dexter buckles on a sable ground gules' and a 'pheasant proper' had been obtained there at some expense by his Uncle Swithin in the 'sixties of the last century, had always pooh-poohed the building, until, about a year ago, he had been struck by the name Golding in a book which he had absently taken up at the Connoisseurs' Club. The affair purported to prove that William Shakespeare was really Edward de Vere, Earl of Oxford. The mother of the earl was a Golding—so was the mother of Soames! The coincidence struck him; and he went on reading. The tome left him with judgment suspended over the main issue, but a distinct curiosity as to whether he was not of the same

33

blood as Shakespeare. Even if the earl were not the bard, he felt
that the connection could only be creditable, though, so far as he
could make out, Oxford was a shady fellow. Recently appointed
on the Board of the P.P.R.S., so that he passed the college every
other Tuesday, he had thought: 'Shan't go spending a lot of money
on it, but might look in one day.' Having looked in, it was astonishing how taken he had been by the whole thing. Tracing his mother
had been quite like a criminal investigation, nearly as ramified and
fully as expensive. Having begun, the tenacity of a Forsyte could
hardly bear to leave him short of the mother of Shakespeare de
Vere, even though she would be collateral; unfortunately, he could
not get past a certain William Gouldyng, Ingerer—whatever that
might be, and he was almost afraid to enquire—of the time of
Oliver Cromwell. There were still four generations to be un-
ravelled, and he was losing money and the hope of getting anything for it. This it was which caused him to gaze askance at the
retired building while passing it on his way to the Board on the
Tuesday after the lunch at Fleur's. Two more wakeful early mornings had screwed him to the pitch of bringing his doubts to a head
and knowing where he stood in the matter of the P.P.R.S.; and this
sudden reminder that he was spending money here, there and everywhere, when there was a possibility, however remote, of financial
liability somewhere else, sharpened the edge of a nerve already
stropped by misgivings. Neglecting the lift and walking slowly up
the two flights of stairs, he 'went over' his fellow-directors for the
fifteenth time. Old Lord Fontenoy was there for his name, of
course; seldom attended, and was what they called 'a dud'—h'm!—
nowadays; the chairman, Sir Luke Sharman, seemed always to be
occupied in not being taken for a Jew. His nose was straight, but
his eyelids gave cause for doubt. His surname was impeccable, but
his Christian dubious; his voice was reassuringly roughened, but
his clothes had a suspicious tendency towards gloss. Altogether a
man who, though shrewd, could not be trusted—Soames felt—to
be giving his whole mind to other business. As for 'Old Mont'—
what was the good of a ninth baronet on a Board? Guy Meyricke,
King's Counsel, last of the three who had been 'together', was a
good man in court, no doubt, but with no time for business and no
real sense of it! Remained that converted Quaker, old Cuthbert
Mothergill—whose family name had been a by-word for successful
integrity throughout the last century, so that people still put
Mothergills on to boards almost mechanically—rather deaf, nice
clean old chap, and quite bland, but nothing more. A perfectly

34

honest lot, no doubt, but perfunctory. None of them really giving their minds to the thing! In Elderson's pocket, too, except perhaps Sharman, and he on the wobble. And Elderson himself—clever chap, bit of an artist, perhaps; managing director from the start, with everything at his finger-tips! Yes! That was the mischief! Prestige of superior knowledge, and years of success—they all kow-towed to him, and no wonder! Trouble with a man like that was that if he once admitted to having made a mistake he destroyed the legend of his infallibility. Soames had enough infallibility of his own to realise how powerful was its impetus towards admit-ting nothing. Ten months ago, when he had come on to the Board, everything had seemed in full sail; exchanges had reached bottom, so they all thought—the 'reassurance of foreign contracts' policy, which Elderson had initiated about a year before, had seemed, with rising exchanges, perhaps the brightest feather in the cap of possi-bility. And now, a twelvemonth later, Soames suspected darkly that they did not know where they were—and the general meet-ing only six weeks off! Probably not even Elderson knew; or, if he did, he was keeping knowledge which ought to belong to the whole directorate severely to himself.

He entered the board-room without a smile. All there—even Lord Fontenoy and 'Old Mont'—given up his spinneys, had he! Soames took his seat at the end on the fireside. Staring at Elderson, he saw, with sudden clearness, the strength of the fellow's position; and, with equal clearness, the weakness of the P.P.R.S. With this rising and falling currency, they could never know exactly their liability—they were just gambling. Listening to the minutes and other routine business, with his chin clasped in his hand, he let his eyes move from face to face—old Mothergill, Elderson, Mont opposite; Sharman at the head; Fontenoy, Meyricke, back to him-self—decisive board of the year. He could not, must not, be placed in any dubious position! At his first general meeting on this con-cern, he must not face the shareholders without knowing exactly where he stood. He looked again at Elderson—sweetish face, bald head rather like Julius Cæsar's, nothing to suggest irregularity or excessive optimism—in fact, somewhat resembling that of old Uncle Nicholas Forsyte, whose affairs had been such an example to the last generation but one. The managing director having com-pleted his exposition, Soames directed his gaze at the pink face of dosey old Mothergill, and said:

"I'm not satisfied that these accounts disclose our true position. I want the Board adjourned to this day week, Mr. Chairman, and during the week I want every member of the Board furnished with exact details of the foreign contract commitments which do *not* mature during the present financial year. I notice that those are lumped under a general estimate of liability. I am not satisfied with that. They ought to be separately treated." Shifting his gaze past Elderson to the face of 'Old Mont', he went on: "Unless there's a material change for the better on the Continent, which I don't anticipate (quite the contrary), I fully expect those commitments will put us in Queer Street next year."

The scraping of feet, shifting of legs, clearing of throats which accompany a slight sense of outrage greeted the words 'Queer Street'; and a sort of satisfaction swelled in Soames; he had rattled their complacency, made them feel a touch of the misgiving from which he himself was suffering.

"We have always treated our commitments under one general estimate, Mr. Forsyte."

Plausible chap!

"And to my mind wrongly. This foreign contract business is a new policy. For all I can tell, instead of paying a dividend, we ought to be setting this year's profits against a certain loss next year."

Again that scrape and rustle.

"My dear sir, absurd!"

The bulldog in Soames snuffled.

"So you say!" he said. "Am I to have those details?"

"The Board can have what details it likes, of course. But permit me to remark on the general question that it *can* only be a matter of estimate. A conservative basis has always been adopted."

"That is a matter of opinion," said Soames; "and in my view it should be the Board's opinion after very careful discussion of the actual figures."

'Old Mont' was speaking.

"My dear Forsyte, to go into every contract would take us a week, and then get us no further; we can but average it out."

"What we have not got in these accounts," said Soames, "is the relative proportion of foreign risk to home risk—in the present state of things a vital matter."

The chairman spoke.

"There will be no difficulty about that, I imagine, Elderson! But in any case, Mr. Forsyte, we should hardly be justified in penalising the present year for the sake of eventualities which we hope will not arise."

"I don't know," said Soames. "We are here to decide policy according to our common sense, and we must have the fullest opportunity of exercising it. That is my point. We have not enough information."

That 'plausible chap' was speaking again:

"Mr. Forsyte seems to be indicating a lack of confidence in the management." Taking the bull by the horns—was he?

"Am I to have that information?"

The voice of old Mothergill rose cosy in the silence.

"The Board could be adjourned, perhaps, Mr. Chairman; I could come up myself at a pinch. Possibly we could all attend. The times are very peculiar—we mustn't take any unnecessary risks. The policy of foreign contracts is undoubtedly somewhat new to us. We have no reason so far to complain of the results. And I am sure we have the utmost confidence in the judgment of our managing director. Still, as Mr. Forsyte has asked for this information, I think perhaps we ought to have it. What do you say, my lord?"

"I can't come up next week. I agree with the chairman that on these accounts we couldn't burke this year's dividend. No good getting the wind up before we must. When do the accounts go out, Elderson?"

"Normally at the end of this week."

"These are not normal times," said Soames. "To be quite plain, unless I have that information I must tender my resignation." He saw very well what was passing in their minds. A newcomer making himself a nuisance—they would take his resignation readily—only it would look awkward just before a general meeting unless they could announce "wife's ill-health" or something satisfactory, which he would take very good care they didn't.

The chairman said coldly:

"Well, we will adjourn the Board to this day week; you will be able to get us those figures, Elderson?"

"Certainly."

Into Soames's mind flashed the thought: 'Ought to ask for an independent scrutiny.' But he looked round. Going too far—perhaps—if he intended to remain on the Board—and he had no wish to resign—after all, it was a big thing, and a thousand a year! No! Mustn't overdo it!

Walking away, he savoured his triumph doubtfully, by no means sure that he had done any good. His attitude had only closed the 'all together' attitude round Elderson. The weakness of his position was that he had nothing to go on, save an uneasiness, which when examined was found to be simply a feeling that he hadn't enough control himself. And yet, there couldn't be two managers—you must trust your manager!

A voice behind him tittupped: "Well, Forsyte, you gave us quite a shock with your alternative. First time I remember anything of the sort on that Board."

"Sleepy hollow," said Soames.

"Yes, I generally have a nap. It gets very hot in there. Wish I'd stuck to my spinneys. They come high, even as early as this."

Incurably frivolous, this tittupping baronet!

"By the way, Forsyte, I wanted to say: With all this modern birth control and the rest of it, one gets uneasy. We're not the royal family; but don't you feel with me it's time there was a movement in heirs?"

Soames did, but he was not going to confess to anything so indelicate about his own daughter.

"Plenty of time," he muttered.

"I don't like that dog, Forsyte."

Soames stared.

"Dog!" he said. "What's that to do with it?"

"I like a baby to come before a dog. Dogs and poets distract young women. My grandmother had five babies before she was twenty-seven. She was a Montjoy; wonderful breeders, you remember them—the seven Montjoy sisters—all pretty. Old Montjoy had forty-seven grandchildren. You don't get it nowadays, Forsyte."

"Country's over-populated," said Soames grimly.

"By the wrong sort—less of them, more of ourselves. It's almost a matter for legislation."

"Talk to your son," said Soames.

"Ah! but they think us fogeys, you know. If we could only point to a reason for existence. But it's difficult, Forsyte, it's difficult."

"They've got everything they want," said Soames.

"Not enough, my dear Forsyte, not enough; the condition of the world is on the nerves of the young. England's dished, they say, Europe's dished. Heaven's dished, and so is Hell! No future in anything but the air. You can't breed in the air; at least, I doubt it—the difficulties are considerable."

Soamnes sniffed.

"If only the journalists would hold their confounded pens," he said; for, more and more of late, with the decrescendo of scare in

38

the daily Press, he was regaining the old sound Forsyte feeling of security. "We've only to keep clear of Europe," he added.

"Keep clear and keep the ring! Forsyte, I believe you've hit it. Good friendly terms with Scandinavia, Holland, Spain, Italy, Turkey—all the outlying countries that we can get at by sea. And let the others dree their weirds. It's an idea!" How the chap rattled on!

"I'm no politician," said Soames.

"Keep the ring! The new formula. It's what we've been coming to unconsciously! And as to trade—to say we can't do without trading with this country or with that—bunkum, my dear Forsyte. The world's large—we can."

"I don't know anything about that," said Soames. "I only know we must drop this foreign contract assurance."

"Why not confine it to the ring countries? Instead of 'balance of power', 'keep the ring'! Really, it's an inspiration!"

Thus charged with inspiration, Soames said hastily:

"I leave you here, I'm going to my daughter's."

"Ah! I'm going to my son's. Look at these poor devils!"

Down by the Embankment at Blackfriars a band of unemployed were trailing dismally with money-boxes.

"Revolution in the bud! There's one thing that's always forgotten, Forsyte, it's a great pity."

"What's that?" said Soames, with gloom. The fellow would tittup all the way to Fleur's!

"Wash the working-class, put them in clean, pleasant-coloured jeans, teach 'em to speak like you and me, and there'd be an end of class feeling. It's all a matter of the senses. Wouldn't you rather share a bedroom with a clean, neat-clothed plumber's assistant who spoke and smelled like you than with a profiteer who dropped his aitches and reeked of opoponax? Of course you would."

"Never tried," said Soames, "so don't know."

"Pragmatist! But believe me, Forsyte — if the working-class would concentrate on baths and accent instead of on their political and economic tosh, equality would be here in no time."

"I don't want equality," said Soames, taking his ticket to Westminster.

The 'tittupping' voice pursued him entering the tube lift.

"Æsthetic equality, Forsyte, if we had it, would remove the wish for any other. Did you ever catch an impecunious professor wishing he was the King?"

"No," said Soames, opening his paper.

# Chapter VIII

## BICKET

BENEATH its veneer of cheerful irresponsibility, the character of Michael Mont had deepened during two years of anchorage and continuity. He had been obliged to think of others; and his time was occupied. Conscious, from the fall of the flag, that he was on sufferance with Fleur, admitting as whole the half-truth: '*Il y a toujours un qui baise, et l'autre qui tend la joue,*' he had developed real powers of domestic consideration; and yet he did not seem to redress the balance in his public or publishing existence. He found the human side of his business too strong for the monetary. Danby and Winter, however, were bearing up against him, and showed, so far, no signs of the bankruptcy prophesied for them by Soames on being told of the principles which his son-in-law intended to introduce. No more in publishing than in any other walk of life was Michael finding it possible to work too much on principle. The field of action was so strewn with facts—human, vegetable and mineral.

On this same Tuesday afternoon, having long tussled with the price of those vegetable facts, paper and linen, he was listening with his pointed ears to the plaint of a packer discovered with five copies of 'Copper Coin' in his overcoat pocket, and the too obvious intention of converting them to his own use.

Mr. Danby had 'given him the sack'—he didn't deny that he was going to sell them, but what would Mr. Mont have done? He owed rent—and his wife wanted nourishing after pneumonia—wanted it bad. 'Dash it!' thought Michael, 'I'd snoop an edition to nourish Fleur after pneumonia!'

"And I can't live on my wages with prices what they are. I can't, Mr. Mont, so help me!"

Michael swivelled. "But look here, Bicket, if we let you snoop copies, all the packers will snoop copies; and if they do, where are Danby and Winter? In the cart. And, if they're in the cart, where are all of you? In the street. It's better that one of you should be in the street than that all of you should, isn't it?"

"Yes, sir, I quite see your point—it's reason; but I can't live on reason, the least thing knocks you out, when you're on the bread line. Ask Mr. Danby to give me another chance."

"Mr. Danby always says that a packer's work is particularly confidential, because it's almost impossible to keep a check on it."

"Yes, sir, I should feel that in future; but with all this unemployment and no reference, I'll never get another job. What about my wife?"

To Michael it was as if he had said: "What about Fleur?" He began to pace the room; and the young man Bicket looked at him with large dolorous eyes. Presently he came to a standstill, with his hands deep plunged into his pockets and his shoulders hunched.

"I'll ask him," he said; "but I don't believe he will; he'll say it isn't fair on the others. You had five copies; it's pretty stiff, you know—means you've had 'em before, doesn't it? What?"

"Well, Mr. Mont, anything that'll give me a chance, I don't mind confessin'. I have 'ad a few previous, and it's just about kept my wife alive. You've no idea what that pneumonia's like for poor people."

Michael pushed his fingers through his hair.

"How old's your wife?"

"Only a girl—twenty."

Twenty! Just Fleur's age!

"I'll tell you what I'll do, Bicket; I'll put it up to Mr. Desert; if he speaks for you, perhaps it may move Mr. Danby."

"Well, Mr. Mont, thank you—you're a gentleman, we all sy that."

"Oh! hang it! But look here, Bicket, you were reckoning on those five copies. Take this to make up, and get your wife what's necessary. Only for goodness' sake don't tell Mr. Danby."

"Mr. Mont, I wouldn't deceive you for the world—I won't sy a word, sir. And my wife—well!"

A sniff, a shuffle—Michael was alone, with his hands plunged deeper, his shoulders hunched higher. And suddenly he laughed. Pity! Pity was pop! It was all dam' funny. Here he was rewarding Bicket for snooping 'Copper Coin'! A sudden longing possed him to follow the little packer and see what he did with the two pounds —see whether 'the pneumonia' was real or a figment of the brain behind those dolorous eyes. Impossible, though! Instead he must ring up Wilfrid and ask him to put in a word with old Danby. His own word was no earthly. He had put it in too often! Bicket! Little one knew of anybody, life was deep and dark, and upside down! What was honesty? Pressure of life *versus* power of resistance—the result of that fight, when the latter won, was honesty! But why resist? Love thy neighbour as thyself—but not more! And wasn't it a darned sight harder for Bicket on two pounds a week to

41

love him, than for him on twenty-four pounds a week to love
Bicket? . . .

"Hallo! . . . That you, Wilfrid? . . . Michael speaking. . . .
One of our packers has been sneaking copies of 'Copper Coin'. He's
'got the sack'—poor devil! I wondered if you'd mind putting in a
word for him—old Dan won't listen to me . . . yes, got a wife—
Fleur's age; pneumonia, so he says. Won't do it again with yours
anyway, insurance by common gratitude—what! . . . Thanks, old
man, awfully good of you—will you bob in, then? We can go
round home together . . . Oh! Well! You'll bob in anyway.
Aurev!"

Good chap, old Wilfrid! Real good chap—underneath! Underneath—what?

Replacing the receiver, Michael saw a sudden great cloud of
sights and scents and sounds, so foreign to the principles of his firm
that he was in the habit of rejecting instantaneously every manuscript which dealt with them. The war might be 'off'; but it was
still 'on' within Wilfrid, and himself. Taking up a tube, he spoke:

"Mr. Danby in his room? Right! If he shows any signs of flitting,
let me know at once. . . ."

Between Michael and his senior partner a gulf was fixed, not less
deep than that between two epochs, though partially filled in by
Winter's middle-age and accommodating temperament. Michael
had almost nothing against Mr. Danby except that he was always
right—Philip Norman Danby, of Sky House, Campden Hill, a man
of sixty and some family, with a tall forehead, a preponderance of
body to leg, and an expression both steady and reflective. His eyes
were perhaps rather close together, and his nose rather thin, but he
looked a handsome piece in his well-proportioned room. He glanced
up from the formation of a correct judgment on a matter of
advertisement when Wilfrid Desert came in.

"Well, Mr. Desert, what can I do for you? Sit down!"

Desert did not sit down, but looked at the engravings, at his
fingers, at Mr. Danby, and said:

"Fact is, I want you to let that packer chap off, Mr. Danby."

"Packer chap. Oh! Ah! Bicket. Mont told you, I suppose?"

"Yes; he's got a young wife down with pneumonia."

"They all go to our friend Mont with some tale or other, Mr.
Desert—he has a very soft heart. But I'm afraid I can't keep this
man. It's a most insidious thing. We've been trying to trace a
leak for some time."

Desert leaned against the mantelpiece and stared into the fire.

42

"Well, Mr. Danby," he said, "your generation may like the soft in literature, but you're precious hard in life. Ours won't look at softness in literature, but we're a deuced sight less hard in life."

"I don't think it's hard," said Mr. Danby, "only just."

"Are you a judge of justice?"

"I hope so."

"Try four years' hell, and have another go."

"I really don't see the connection. The experience you've been through, Mr. Desert, was bound to be warping."

Wilfrid turned and started at him.

"Forgive my saying so, but sitting here and being just is much more warping. Life is pretty good purgatory, to all except about thirty per cent. of grown-up people."

Mr. Danby smiled.

"We simply couldn't conduct our business, my dear young man, without scrupulous honesty in everybody. To make no distinction between honesty and dishonesty would be quite unfair. You know that perfectly well."

"I don't know anything perfectly well, Mr. Danby; and I mistrust those who say they do."

"Well, let us put it that there are rules of the game which must be observed, if society is to function at all."

Desert smiled, too: "Oh! hang rules! Do it as a favour to me. I wrote the rotten book."

No trace of struggle showed in Mr. Danby's face; but his deep-set, close-together eyes shone a little.

"I should be only too glad, but it's a matter—well, of conscience, if you like. I'm not prosecuting the man. He must leave—that's all."

Desert shrugged his shoulders.

"Well, good-bye!" and he went out.

On the mat was Michael in two minds.

"Well?"

"No go. The old blighter's too just."

Michael stivered his hair.

"Wait in my room five minutes while I let the poor beggar know, then I'll come along."

"No," said Desert, "I'm going the other way."

Not the fact that Wilfrid was going the other way—he almost always was—but something in the tone of his voice and the look on his face obsessed Michael's imagination while he went downstairs to seek Bicket. Wilfrid was a rum chap—he went 'dark' so suddenly!

In the nether regions he asked:

"Bicket gone?"

"No, sir, there he is."

There he was, in his shabby overcoat, with his pale narrow face, and his disproportionately large eyes, and his sloping shoulders.

"Sorry, Bicket, Mr. Desert has been in, but it's no go."

"No, sir?"

"Keep your pecker up, you'll get something."

"I'm afryde not, sir. Well, I thank you very 'eartily; and I thank Mr. Desert. Good-night, sir; and good-bye!"

Michael watched him down the corridor, saw him waver into the dusky street.

"Jolly!" he said, and laughed. . . .

The natural suspicions of Michael and his senior partner that a tale was being pitched were not in fact justified. Neither the wife nor the pneumonia had been exaggerated; and wavering away in the direction of Blackfriars Bridge, Bicket thought not of his turpitude nor of how just Mr. Danby had been, but of what he should say to her. He should not, of course, tell her that he had been detected in stealing; he must say he had 'got the sack for cheeking the foreman'; but what would she think of him for doing that, when everything as it were depended on his not cheeking the foreman? This was one of those melancholy cases of such affection that he had been coming to his work day after day feeling as if he had 'left half his guts' behind him in the room where she lay, and when at last the doctor said to him:

"She'll get on now, but it's left her very run down—you must feed her up," his anxiety had hardened into a resolution to have no more. In the next three weeks he had 'pinched' eighteen 'Copper Coins', including the five found in his overcoat. He had only 'pitched on' Mr. Desert's book because it was 'easy sold', and he was sorry now that he hadn't pitched on someone else's. Mr. Desert had been very decent. He stopped at the corner of the Strand, and went over his money. With the two pounds given him by Michael and his wages he had seventy-five shillings in the world, and going into the Stores he bought a meat jelly and a tin of Benger's food that could be made with water. With pockets bulging he took a bus, which dropped him at the corner of his little street on the Surrey side. His wife and he occupied the two ground-floor rooms, at eight shillings a week, and he owed for three weeks. 'Py that!' he thought, 'and have a roof until she's well.' It would help him over the news, too, to show her a receipt for the rent and some good food. How lucky they had been careful to have no baby! He sought the basement. His landlady was doing the week's washing. She paused, in sheer surprise at such full and voluntary payment, and inquired after his wife.

"Doing nicely, thank you."

"Well, I'm glad of that, it must be a relief to your mind."

"It is," said Bicket.

The landlady thought: 'He's a thread-paper—reminds me of a shrimp before you bile it, with those eyes.'

"Here's your receipt, and thank you. Sorry to 'ave seemed nervous about it, but times are 'ard."

"They are," said Bicket. "So long!"

With the receipt and the meat jelly in his left hand, he opened the door of his front room.

His wife was sitting before a very little fire. Her bobbed black hair, crinkly towards the ends, had grown during her illness; it shook when she turned her head and smiled. To Bicket—not for the first time—that smile seemed queer, 'pathetic-like', mysterious —as if she saw things that one didn't see oneself. Her name was Victorine, and he said: "Well, Vic? This jelly's a bit of all right, and I've pyde the rent." He sat on the arm of the chair and she put her hand on his knee—her thin arm emerging blue-white from the dark dressing-gown.

"Well, Tony?"

Her face—thin and pale with those large dark eyes and beautifully formed eyebrows—was one that "looked at you from somewhere; and when it looked at you—well! it got you right inside!"

It got him now and he said: "How've you been breathin'?"

"All right—much better. I'll soon be out now."

Bicket twisted himself round and joined his lips to hers. The kiss lasted some time, because all the feelings which he had not been able to express during the past three weeks to her or to anybody, got into it. He sat up again, "sort of exhausted," staring at the fire, and said: "News isn't bright—lost my job, Vic."

"Oh! Tony! Why?"

Bicket swallowed.

"Fact is, things are slack, and they're reducin'."

There had surged into his mind the certainty that sooner than tell her the truth he would put his head under the gas!

"Oh! dear! What shall we do, then?"

Bicket's voice hardened.

"Don't you worry—I'll get something;" and he whistled.

"But you liked that job."

"Did I? I liked some o' the fellers; but as for the job—why, what was it? Wrappin' books up in a bysement all dy long. Let's have something to eat and get to bed early—I feel as if I could sleep for a week, now I'm shut of it."

Getting their supper ready with her help, he carefully did not look at her face for fear it might "get him agyne inside!" They had only been married a year, having made acquaintance on a tram, and Bicket often wondered what had made her take to him, eight years her senior and C3 during the war! And yet she must be fond of him, or she'd never look at him as she did.

"Sit down and try this jelly."

He himself ate bread and margarine and drank cocoa, he seldom had any particular appetite.

"Shall I tell you what I'd like?" he said; "I'd like Central Austrylia. We had a book in there about it; they sy there's quite a movement. I'd like some sun. I believe if we 'ad sun we'd both be twice the size we are. I'd like to see colour in your cheeks, Vic."

"How much does it cost to get out there?"

"A lot more than we can ly hands on, that's the trouble. But I've been thinkin'. England's about done. There's too many like me."

"No," said Victorine: "There aren't enough."

Bicket looked at her face, then quickly at his plate.

"What myde you take a fancy to me?"

"Because you don't think first of yourself, that's why."

"Used to before I knew you. But I'd do anything for you, Vic."

"Have some of this jelly, then, it's awful good."

Bicket shook his head.

"If we could wyke up in Central Austrylia," he said. "But there's only one thing certain, we'll wyke up in this blighted little room. Never mind, I'll get a job and earn the money yet."

"Could we win it on a race?"

"Well, I've only got forty-seven bob all told, and if we lose it, where'll you be? You've got to feed up, you know. No, I must get a job."

"They'll give you a good recommend, won't they?"

Bicket rose and stacked his plate and cup.

"They would, but that job's off—overstocked."

Tell her the truth? Never! So help him!

In their bed, one of those just too wide for one and just not wide enough for two, he lay, with her hair almost in his mouth, thinking what to say to his Union, and how to go to work to get a job. And in his thoughts as the hours drew on he burned his boats. To draw his unemployment money he would have to tell his Union what the trouble was. Blow the Union! He wasn't going to be accountable to them! *He* knew why he'd pinched the books; but it was nobody else's business, nobody else could understand his feelings, watching her so breathless, pale and thin. Strike out for himself! And a million and a half out o' work! Well, he had a fortnight's keep, and something would turn up—and he might risk a bob or two and win some money, you never knew. She turned in her sleep. 'Yes,' he thought, 'I'd do it agyne. . . .'

Next day, after some hours on foot, he stood under the grey easterly sky in the grey street, before a plate-glass window protecting an assortment of fruits and sheaves of corn, lumps of metal, and brilliant blue butterflies, in the carefully golden light of advertised Australia. To Bicket, who had never been out of England, not often out of London, it was like standing outside Paradise. The atmosphere within the office itself was not so golden, and the money required considerable; but it brought Paradise nearer to take away pamphlets which almost burned his hands, they were so warm.

Later, he and she, sitting in the one armchair—advantage of being thin—pored over these alchemised pages and inhaled their glamour.

"D'you think it's true, Tony?"

"If it's thirty per cent. true it's good enough for me. We just must get there somehow. Kiss me."

From around the corner in the main road the rumbling of the trams and carts, and the rattling of their window-pane in the draughty dry easterly wind increased their feeling of escape into a gas-lit·Paradise.

## Chapter IX

## CONFUSION

TWO hours behind Bicket, Michael wavered towards home. Old Danby was right as usual—if you couldn't trust your packers, you might shut up shop! Away from Bicket's eyes, he doubted. Perhaps the chap hadn't a wife at all! Then Wilfrid's manner usurped the place of Bicket's morals. Old Wilfrid had been abrupt and queer the last three times of meeting. Was he boiling-up for verse?

He found Ting-a-ling at the foot of the stairs in a conservative

47

attitude. "I am not going up," he seemed saying, "until someone carries me—at the same time it is later than usual!"

"Where's your mistress, you heraldic little beast?"

Ting-a-ling snuffled. "I could put up with it," he implied, "if *you* carried me—these stairs are laborious!"

Michael took him up. "Let's go and find her."

Squeezed under an arm harder than his mistress', Ting-a-ling stared as if with black-glass eyes; and the plume of his emergent tail quivered.

In the bedroom Michael dropped him so absent-mindedly that he went to his corner plume pendent, and crouched there in dudgeon.

Nearly dinner time and Fleur not in! Michael went over his sketchy recollection of her plans. To-day she had been having Hubert Marsland and that Vertiginist—what was his name?—to lunch. There would have been fumes to clear off. Vertiginists—like milk—made carbonic acid gas in the lungs! Still! Half-past seven! What was happening to-night? Weren't they going to that play of L.S.D.'s? No—that was to-morrow! Was there conceivably nothing? If so, of course she would shorten her unoccupied time as much as possible. He made that reflection humbly. Michael had no illusions, he knew himself to be commonplace, with only a certain redeeming liveliness, and, of course, his affection for her. He even recognised that his affection was a weakness, tempting him to fussy anxieties, which on principle he restrained. To enquire, for instance, of Coaker or Philps—their man and their maid—when she had gone out, would be thoroughly against that principle. The condition of the world was such that Michael constantly wondered if his own affairs were worth paying attention to; but then the condition of the world was also such that sometimes one's own affairs seemed all that were worth paying attention to. And yet his affairs were, practically speaking, Fleur; and if he paid too much attention to them, he was afraid of annoying her.

He went into his dressing-room and undid his waistcoat.

'But no!' he thought; 'if she finds me "dressed" already, it'll put too much point on it.' So he did up his waistcoat and went downstairs again. Coaker was in the hall.

"Mr. Forsyte and Sir Lawrence looked in about six, sir. Mrs. Mont was out. What time shall I serve dinner?"

"Oh! about a quarter-past eight. I don't think we're going out."

He went into the drawing-room and passing down its Chinese emptiness, drew aside the curtain. The square looked cold and dark and draughty; and he thought: 'Bicket—pneumonia—I hope

48

she's got her fur coat.' He took out a cigarette and put it back. If she saw him at the window she would think him fussy; and he went up again to see if she had put on her fur!

Ting-a-ling, still couchant, greeted him plume dansetti arrested as at disappointment. Michael opened a wardrobe. She had! Good! He was taking a sniff round, when Ting-a-ling passed him trottant, and her voice said: "Well, my darling!" Wishing that he was, Michael emerged from behind the wardrobe door. Heaven! She looked pretty, coloured by the wind! He stood rather wistfully silent.

"Hallo, Michael! I'm rather late. Been to the Club and walked home."

Michael had a quite unaccountable feeling that there was suppression in that statement. He also suppressed, and said: "I was just looking to see that you'd got your fur, it's beastly cold. Your dad and Bart have been and went away fasting."

Fleur shed her coat and dropped into a chair. "I'm tired. Your ears are sticking up so nicely to-night, Michael."

Michael went on his knees and joined his hands behind her waist. Her eyes had a strange look, a scrutiny which held him in suspense, a little startled.

"If you got pneumonia," he said, "I should go clean out of curl."

"Why on earth should I?"

"You don't know the connection—never mind, it wouldn't interest you. We're not going out, are we?"

"Of course we are. It's Alison's monthly."

"Oh! Lord! If you're tired we could cut that."

"My dear! Impos.! She's got all sorts of people coming."

Stifling a disparagement, he sighed out: "Right-o! War-paint?"

"Yes, white waistcoat. I like you in white waistcoats."

Cunning little wretch? He squeezed her waist and rose. Fleur laid a light stroke on his hand, and he went into his dressing-room comforted. . . .

But Fleur sat still for at least five minutes—not precisely 'a prey to conflicting emotions,' but the victim of very considerable confusion. Two men within the last hour had done this thing—knelt at her knees and joined their fingers behind her waist. Undoubtedly she had been rash to go to Wilfrid's rooms. The moment she got there she had perceived how entirely unprepared she really was to commit herself to what was physical. True he had done no more than Michael. But—Goodness!—she had seen the fire she was playing with, realised what torment he was in.

49

She had strictly forbidden him to say a word to Michael, but intuitively she knew that in his struggle between loyalties she could rely on nothing. Confused, startled, touched, she could not help a pleasant warmth in being so much loved by two men at once, nor an itch of curiosity about the upshot. And she sighed. She had added to her collection of experiences—but how to add further without breaking up the collection, and even perhaps the collector, she could not see.

After her words to Wilfrid before the Eve: "You will be a fool to go—wait!" she had known he would expect something before long. Often he had asked her to come and pass judgment on his 'junk'. A month, even a week, ago she would have gone without thinking more than twice about it, and discussed his 'junk' with Michael afterwards! But now she thought it over many times, and but for the fumes of lunch, and the feeling, engendered by the society of the 'Vertiginist', of Amabel Nazing, of Linda Frewe, that scruples of any kind were 'stuffy', sensations of all sorts 'the thing'. she would probably still have been thinking it over now. When they departed, she had taken a deep breath and her telephone receiver from the Chinese tea-chest.

If Wilfrid were going to be in at half-past five, she would come and see his 'junk'.

His answer: "My God! Will you?" almost gave her pause. But dismissing hesitation with the thought: 'I will be Parisian—Proust!' she had started for her Club. Three-quarters of an hour, with no more stimulant than three cups of China tea, three back numbers of the 'Glass of Fashion', three back views of country members 'dead in chairs', had sent her forth a careful quarter of an hour behind her time.

On the top floor Wilfrid was standing in his open doorway, pale as a soul in purgatory. He took her hand gently, and drew her in. Fleur thought with a little thrill: 'Is this what it's like? *Du côté de chez Swann!*' Freeing her hand, she began at once to flutter round the 'junk', clinging to it piece by piece.

Old English 'junk' rather manorial, with here and there an Eastern or First Empire bit, collected by some bygone Desert, nomadic, or attached to the French court. She was afraid to sit down, for fear that he might begin to follow the authorities; nor did she want to resume the intense talk of the Tate Gallery. 'Junk' was safe, and she only looked at him in those brief intervals when he was not looking at her. She knew she was not playing the game according to 'La Garçonne' and Amabel Nazing; that, indeed, she

was in danger of going away without having added to her sensations. And she couldn't help being sorry for Wilfrid; his eyes
yearned after her, his lips were bitter to look at. When at last
from sheer exhaustion of 'junk' she sat down, he had flung himself
at her feet Half hypnotised, with her knees against his chest, as
safe as she could hope for, she really felt the tragedy of it—his
horror of himself, his passion for herself. It was painful, deep; it
did not fit in with what she had been led to expect; it was not in
the period, and how—how was she to get away without more pain
to him and to herself? When she *had* got away, with one kiss
received but not answered, she realised that she had passed through
a quarter of an hour of real life, and was not at all sure that she
liked it. . . . But now, safe in her own room, undressing for
Alison's monthly, she felt curious as to what she would have been
feeling if things had gone as far as was proper according to the
authorities. Surely she had not experienced one-tenth of the
thoughts or sensations that would have been assigned to her in any
advanced piece of literature! It had been disillusioning, or else she
was deficient, and Fleur could not bear to feel deficient. And,
lightly powdering her shoulders, she bent her thoughts towards
Alison's monthly.

Though Lady Alison enjoyed an occasional encounter with the
younger generation, the Aubrey Greenes and Linda Frewes of this
life were not conspicuous by their presence at her gatherings. Nesta
Gorse, indeed, had once attended, but one legal and two literary
politicos who had been in contact with her, had complained of it
afterwards. She had, it seemed, rent little spiked holes in the
garments of their self-esteem. Sibley Swan would have been
welcome, for his championship of the past, but he seemed, so far,
to have turned up his nose and looked down it. So it was not the
intelligentsia, but just intellectual society, which was gathered
there when Fleur and Michael entered, and the conversation had
all the sparkle and all the '*savoir faire*' incidental to talk about art
and letters by those who—as Michael put it—"fortunately had not
to *faire*."

"All the same, these are the guys," he muttered in Fleur's ear,
"who make the names of artists and writers. What's the stunt,
to-night?"

It appeared to be the London *début* of a lady who sang Balkan
folk songs. But in a refuge to the right were four tables set out for
bridge. They were already filled. Among those who still stood

listening, were, here and there, a Gurdon Minho, a society painter
and his wife, a sculptor looking for a job. Fleur, wedged between
Lady Feynte, the painter's wife, and Gurdon Minho himself, began
planning an evasion. There—yes, there was Mr. Chalfont! At
Lady Alison's, Fleur, an excellent judge of '*milieu*', never wasted
her time on artists and writers—she could meet *them* anywhere.
Here she intuitively picked out the biggest 'bug', politico-literary,
and waited to pin him. Absorbed in the idea of pinning Mr.
Chalfont, she overlooked a piece of drama passing without.

Michael had clung to the top of the stairway, in no mood for
talk and skirmish; and, leaning against the balustrade, wasp-thin in
his long white waistcoat, with hands deep thrust into his trousers'
pockets, he watched the turns and twists of Fleur's white neck, and
listened to the Balkan songs, with a sort of blankness in his brain.
The word: "Mont!" startled him. Wilfrid was standing just below.
Mont? He had not been that to Wilfrid for two years!

"Come down here."

On that half-landing was a bust of Lionel Charwell, K.C., by
Boris Strumolowski, in the genre he had cynically adopted when
June Forsyte gave up supporting his authentic but unrewarded
genius. It had been almost indistinguishable from any of the other
busts in that year's Academy, and was used by the young Char-
wells to chalk moustaches on.

Beside this object Desert leaned against the wall with his eyes
closed. His face was a study to Michael.

"What's wrong, Wilfrid?"

Desert did not move. "You've got to know—I'm in love with
Fleur."

"What!"

"I'm not going to play the snake. You're up against me. Sorry,
but there it is! You can let fly!" His face was death-pale, and its
muscles twitched. In Michael, it was the mind, the heart that
twitched. What a very horrible, strange, "too beastly" moment!
His best friend—his best man! Instinctively he dived for his
cigarette-case—instinctively handed it to Desert. Instinctively they
both took cigarettes, and lighted each other's. Then Michael said:

"Fleur—knows?"

Desert nodded: "She doesn't know I'm telling you—wouldn't
have let me. You've nothing against her—yet." And, still with
closed eyes, he added: "I couldn't help it."

It was Michael's own subconscious thought! Natural! Natural!
Fool not to see how natural! Then something shut-to within him,

52

and he said: "Decent of you to tell me; but—aren't you going to clear out?"

Desert's shoulders writhed against the wall.

"I thought so; but it seems not."

"Seems? I don't understand."

"If I knew for certain I'd no chance—but I don't," and he suddenly looked at Michael: "Look here, it's no good keeping gloves on. I'm desperate, and I'll take her from you if I can."

"Good God!" said Michael. "It's the limit!"

"Yes! Rub it in! But, I tell you, when I think of you going home with her, and of myself," he gave a dreadful little laugh, "I advise you *not* to rub it in."

"Well," said Michael, "as this isn't a Dostoievsky novel, I suppose there's no more to be said."

Desert moved from the wall and laid his hand on the bust of Lionel Charwell.

"You realise, at least, that I've gone out of my way—perhaps dished myself—by telling you. I've not bombed without declaring war."

"No," said Michael dully.

"You can chuck my books over to some other publisher." Michael shrugged.

"Good-night, then," said Desert. "Sorry for being so primitive."

Michael looked straight into his 'best man's' face. There was no mistaking its expression of bitter despair. He made a half-movement with his hand, uttered half the word "Wilfrid," and, as Desert went down, he went upstairs.

Back in his place against the balustrade, he tried to realise that life was a laughing matter, and couldn't. His position required a serpent's cunning, a lion's courage, a dove's gentleness: he was not conscious of possessing such proverbial qualities. If Fleur had loved him as he loved her, he would have had for Wilfrid a real compassion. It was so natural to fall in love with Fleur! But she didn't—oh! no, she didn't! Michael had one virtue—if virtue it be—a moderate opinion of himself, a disposition to think highly of his friends. He had thought highly of Desert; and—odd!—he still did not think lowly of him. Here was his friend trying to do him mortal injury, to alienate the affection—more honestly, the toleration—of his wife; and yet he did not think him a cad. Such leniency, he knew, was hopeless; but the doctrines of free-will, and free contract, were not to him mere literary conceptions, they were part of his nature. To apply duress, however desirable, would not

53

be on his cards. And something like despair ravaged the heart of him, watching Fleur's ingratiating little tricks with the great Gerald Chalfont. If she left him for Wilfrid! But surely—no—her father, her house, her dog, her friends, her—her collection of—of—she would not—could not give *them* up? But suppose she kept everything, Wilfrid included! No, no! She wouldn't! Only for a second did that possibility blur the natural loyalty of his mind.

Well, what to do? Tell her—talk the thing out? Or wait and watch? For what? Without deliberate spying, he could not watch. Desert would come to their house no more. No! Either complete frankness; or complete ignoring—and that meant living with the sword of Damocles above his head! No! Complete frankness! And not do anything that seemed like laying a trap! He passed his hand across a forehead that was wet. If only they were at home, away from that squalling and these cultivated jackanapes! Could he go in and hook her out? Impossible without some reason! Only his brain-storm for a reason! He must just bite on it. The singing ceased. Fleur was looking round. Now she would beckon! On the contrary, she came towards him. He could not help the cynical thought: 'She's hooked old Chalfont!' He loved her, but he knew her little weaknesses. She came up and took hold of his sleeve.

"I've had enough, Michael, let's slip off; d'you mind?"

"Quick!" he said, "before they spot us!"

In the cold air outside he thought: 'Now? Or in her room?'

"I think," said Fleur, "that Mr. Chalfont is overrated—he's nothing but a mental yawn. He's coming to lunch to-morrow week."

Not now—in her room!

"Whom do you think to meet him, besides Alison?"

"Nothing jazzy."

"Of course not; but it must be somebody intriguing, Michael. Bother! sometimes I think it isn't worth it."

Michael's heart stood still. Was that a portent—sign of 'the primitive' rising within his adored practitioner of social arts? An hour ago he would have said:

"You're right, my child; it jolly well isn't!" But now—any sign of change was ominous! He slipped his arm in hers.

"Don't worry, we'll snare the just-right cuckoos, somehow."

"A Chinese Minister would be perfect," mused Fleur, "with Minho and Bart—four men—two women—cosy. I'll talk to Bart."

Michael had opened their front door. She passed him; he lingered to see the stars, the plane trees, a man's figure motionless, collared

54

to the eyes, hatted down to them. 'Wilfrid!' he thought: 'Spain! Why Spain? And all poor devils who are in distress—the heart— oh! darn the heart!' He closed the door.

But soon he had another to open, and never with less enthusiasm. Fleur was sitting on the arm of a chair, in the dim lavender pyjamas she sometimes wore just to keep in with things, staring at the fire. Michael stood, looking at her and at his own reflection beyond in one of the five mirrors—white and black, the pierrot pyjamas she had bought him. 'Figures in a play,' he thought, 'figures in a play! Is it real?' He moved forward and sat on the chair's other arm.

"Hang it!" he muttered. "Wish I were Antinous!" And he slipped from the arm into the chair, to be behind her face, if she wanted to hide it from him.

"Wilfrid's been telling me," he said quietly.

Off his chest! What now? He saw the blood come flushing into her neck and cheek.

"Oh! What business—how do you mean 'telling you'?"

"Just that he's in love with you—nothing more—there's nothing more to tell, is there?" And drawing his feet up on to the chair, he clasped his hands hard round his knees. Already—already he had asked a question! Bite on it! Bite on it! And he shut his eyes.

"Of course," said Fleur, very slowly, "there's nothing more. If Wilfrid chooses to be so silly."

Chooses! The word seemed unjust to one whose own 'silliness' was so recent—so enduring! And—curious! his heart wouldn't bound. Surely it ought to have bounded at her words!

"Is that the end of Wilfrid, then?"

"The end? I don't know."

Ah! Who knew anything—when passion was about?

"Well," he said, holding himself hard together, "don't forget I love you awfully!"

He saw her eyelids flicker, her shoulders shrugging.

"Am I likely to?"

Bitter, cordial, simple—which? Suddenly her hands came round and took him by the ears. Holding them fast she looked down at him, and laughed. And again his heart *would* not bound. If she did not lead him by the nose, she——! But he clutched her to him in the chair. Lavender and white and black confused—she returned his kiss. But from the heart? Who knew? Not Michael.

## Chapter X

## PASSING OF A SPORTSMAN

SOAMES, disappointed of his daughter, said: "I'll wait," and took his seat in the centre of the jade green settee, oblivious of Ting-a-ling before the fire, sleeping off the attentions of Amabel Nazing, who had found him 'just too cunning'. Grey and composed, with one knee over the other, and a line between his eyes, he thought of Elderson and the condition of the world, and of how there was always something. And the more he thought, the more he wondered why he had ever been such a flat as to go on to a Board which had anything to do with foreign contracts. All the old wisdom that in the nineteenth century had consolidated British wealth, all the Forsyte philosophy of attending to one's own business, and taking no risks, the close-fibred national individualism which refused to commit the country to chasing this wild goose or that, held within him silent demonstration. Britain was on the wrong tack politically to try and influence the Continent, and the P.P.R.S. on the wrong tack monetarily to insure business outside Britain. The special instinct of his breed yearned for resumption of the straight and private path. Never meddle with what you couldn't control! 'Old Mont' had said: "Keep the ring!" Nothing of the sort: Mind one's own business! That was the real 'formula'. He became conscious of his calf—Ting-a-ling was sniffing at his trousers.

"Oh!" said Soames. "It's you!"

Placing his forepaws against the settee, Ting-a-ling licked the air.

"Pick you up?" said Soames. "You're too long." And again he felt that faint warmth of being liked.

'There's something about me that appeals to him,' he thought, taking him by the scruff and lifting him on to a cushion. "You and I," the little dog seemed saying with his stare—Chinese little object! The Chinese knew what they were about, they had minded their own business for five thousand years!

'I shall resign,' thought Soames. But what about Winifred, and Imogen, and some of the Rogers and Nicholases who had been putting money into this thing because he was a director? He wished they wouldn't follow him like a lot of sheep! He rose from the settee. It was no good waiting, he would walk on to Green Street

56

and talk to Winifred at once. She would have to sell again, though the shares had dropped a bit. And without taking leave of Ting-a-ling, he went out.

All this last year he had almost enjoyed life. Having somewhere to come and sit and receive a certain sympathy once at least a week, as in old days at Timothy's, was of incalculable advantage to his spirit. In going from home Fleur had taken most of his heart with her; but Soames had found it almost an advantage to visit his heart once a week rather than to have it always about. There were other reasons conducing to light-heartedness. That diabolical foreign chap, Prosper Profond, had long been gone he didn't know where, and his wife had been decidedly less restive and sarcastic ever since. She had taken up a thing they called Coué, and grown stouter. She used the car a great deal. Altogether she was more domestic. Then, too, he had become reconciled to Gauguin—a little slump in that painter had convinced him that he was still worth attention, and he had bought three more. Gauguin would rise again! Soames almost regretted his intuition of that second coming, for he had quite taken to the chap. His colour, once you got used to it, was very attractive. One picture, especially, which meant nothing so far as he could see, had a way of making you keep your eyes on it. He even felt uneasy when he thought of having to part with the thing at an enhanced price. But, most of all, he had been feeling so well, enjoying a recrudescence of youth in regard to Annette, taking more pleasure in what he ate, while his mind dwelt almost complacently on the state of money. The pound going up in value; Labour quiet! And now they had got rid of that Jack-o'-lantern, they might look for some years of solid Conservative administration. And to think, as he did, stepping across St. James's Park towards Green Street, that he had gone and put his foot into a concern which he could not control, made him feel—well, as if the devil had been in it!

In Piccadilly he moused along on the Park side, taking his customary look up at the 'Iseeum' Club. The curtains were drawn, and chinks of light glowed, long and cosy. And that reminded him —someone had said George Forsyte was ill. Certainly he had not seen him in the bay window for months past. Well, George had always eaten and drunk too much. He crossed over and passed beneath the Club; and a sudden feeling—he didn't know what—a longing for his own past, a sort of nostalgia—made him stop and mount the steps.

"Mr. George Forsyte in the Club?"

The janitor stared, a grey-haired, long-faced chap, whom he had known from away back in the 'eighties.

"Mr. Forsyte, sir," he said, "is very ill indeed. They say he won't recover, sir."

"What?" said Soames. "Nobody told me that."

"He's very bad—*very* bad indeed. It's the heart."

"The heart! Where is he?"

"At his rooms, sir; just round the corner. They say the doctors have given him up. He *will* be missed here. Forty years I've known him. One of the old school, and a wonderful judge of wine and horses. We none of us last for ever, they say, but I never thought to see him out. Bit too full-blooded, sir, and that's a fact."

With a slight shock Soames realised that he had never known where George lived, so utterly anchored had he seemed to that bay window above.

"Just give me the number of his rooms," he said.

"Belville Row—No. 11, sir; I'm sure I hope you'll find him better. I shall miss his jokes—I shall, indeed."

Turning the corner into Belville Row, Soames made a rapid calculation. George was sixty-six, only one year younger than himself! If George was really *in extremis* it would be quite unnatural! 'Comes of not leading a careful life,' he thought; 'always rackety—George! When was it I made his will?' So far as he remembered, George had left his money to his brothers and sisters —no one else to leave it to. The feeling of kinship stirred in Soames, the instinct of family adjustment. George and he had never got on—opposite poles of temperament—still he would have to be buried, and who would see to it if not Soames, who had seen to so many Forsyte burials in his time? He recalled the nickname George had once given him, 'the undertaker'! H'm! Here was poetical justice! Belville Row! Ah! No. 11—regular bachelor-looking place! And putting his hand up to the bell, he thought: 'Women!' What had George done about women all his life?

His ring was answered by a man in a black cut-away coat with a certain speechless reticence.

"My cousin, Mr. George Forsyte? How is he?"

The man compressed his lips.

"Not expected to last the night, sir."

Soames felt a little clutch beneath his Jaeger vest.

"Conscious?"

"Yes, sir."

"Could you show him my card? He might possibly like to see me."

"Will you wait in here, sir?" Soames passed into a low room panelled up to the level of a man's chest, and above that line decorated with prints. George—a collector! Soames had never supposed he had it in him! On those walls, wherever the eye roved, were prints coloured and uncoloured, old and new, depicting the sports of racing and prize-fighting! Hardly an inch of the red wall space visible! About to examine them for marks of value, Soames saw that he was not alone. A woman—age uncertain in the shaded light—was sitting in a very high-backed chair before the fire with her elbow on the arm of it, and a handkerchief held to her face. Soames looked at her, and his nostrils moved in a stealthy sniff. 'Not a lady,' he thought. 'Ten to one but there'll be complications.' The muffled voice of the cut-away man said:

"I'm to take you in, sir." Soames passed his hand over his face and followed.

The bedroom he now entered was in curious contrast. The whole of one wall was occupied by an immense piece of furniture, all cupboards and drawers. Otherwise there was nothing in the room but a dressing-table with silver accoutrements, an electric radiator alight in the fireplace, and a bed opposite. Over the fireplace was a single picture, at which Soames glanced mechanically. What! Chinese! A large whitish sidelong monkey, holding the rind of a squeezed fruit in its outstretched paw. Its whiskered face looked back at him with brown, almost human eyes. What on earth had made his inartistic cousin buy a thing like that and put it up to face his bed? He turned and looked at the bed's occupant. "The only sportsman of the lot," as Montague Dartie in his prime had called him, lay with his swollen form outlined beneath a thin quilt. It gave Soames quite a turn to see that familiar beef-coloured face pale and puffy as a moon, with dark corrugated circles round eyes which still had their japing stare. A voice, hoarse and subdued, but with the old Forsyte timbre, said:

"Hallo, Soames! Come to measure me for my coffin?"

Soames put the suggestion away with a movement of his hand; he felt queer looking at that travesty of George. They had never got on, but——!

And in his flat, unemotional voice he said:

"Well, George! You'll pick up yet. You're no age. Is there anything I can do for you?"

A grin twitched George's pallid lips.

"Make me a codicil. You'll find paper in the dressing-table drawer."

Soames took out a sheet of 'Iseeum' Club notepaper. Standing at the table, he inscribed the opening words of a codicil with his stylographic pen, and looked round at George. The words came with a hoarse relish.

"My three screws to young Val Dartie, because he's the only Forsyte that knows a horse from a donkey." A throaty chuckle sounded ghastly in the ears of Soames. "What have you said?"

Soames read: "I hereby leave my three racehorses to my kinsman, Valerius Dartie, of Wansdon, Sussex, because he has special knowledge of horses."

Again the throaty chuckle. "You're a dry file, Soames. Go on. To Milly Moyle, of 12, Claremont Grove, twelve thousand pounds, free of legacy duty."

Soames paused on the verge of a whistle.

The woman in the next room!

The japing in George's eyes had turned to brooding gloom.

"It's a lot of money," Soames could not help saying.

George made a faint choleric sound.

"Write it down, or I'll leave her the lot."

Soames wrote. "Is that all?"

"Yes. Read it!"

Soames read. Again he heard that throaty chuckle.

"That's a pill. You won't let *that* into the papers. Get that chap in, and you and he can witness."

Before Soames reached the door, it was opened and the man himself came in.

"The—er—vicar, sir," he said in a deprecating voice, "has called. He wants to know if you would like to see him."

George turned his face, his fleshy grey eyes rolled.

"Give him my compliments," he said, "and say I'll see him at the funeral."

With a bow the man went out, and there was silence.

"Now," said George, "get him in again. I don't know when the flag'll fall."

Soames beckoned the man in. When the codicil was signed and the man gone, George spoke:

"Take it, and see she gets it. I can trust you, that's one thing about you, Soames."

Soames pocketed the codicil with a very queer sensation.

"Would you like to see her again?" he said.

George stared up at him a long time before he answered.

"No. What's the good? Give me a cigar from that drawer."

Soames opened the drawer.

"Ought you?" he said.

George grinned. "Never in my life done what I ought; not going to begin now. Cut it for me."

Soames nipped the end of the cigar. 'Shan't give him a match, he thought. 'Can't take the responsibility.' But George did not ask for a match. He lay quite still, the unlighted cigar between his pale lips, the curved lids down over his eyes.

"Good-bye," he said, "I'm going to have a snooze."

"Good-bye," said Soames. "I—I hope—you—you'll soon——"

George reopened his eyes—fixed, sad, jesting, they seemed to quench the shams of hope and consolation. Soames turned hastily and went out. He felt bad, and almost unconsciously turned again into the sitting-room. The woman was still in the same attitude; the same florid scent was in the air. Soames took up the umbrella he had left there, and went out.

"This is my telephone number," he said to the servant waiting in the corridor; "let me know."

The man bowed.

Soames turned out of Belville Row. Never had he left George's presence without the sense of being laughed at. Had he been laughed at now? Was that codicil George's last joke? If he had not gone in this afternoon, would George ever have made it, leaving a third of his property away from his family to that florid woman in the high-backed chair? Soames was beset by a sense of mystery. How could a man joke at death's door? It was, in a way, heroic. Where would he be buried? Somebody would know— Francie or Eustace. And what would they think when they came to know about that woman in the chair—twelve thousand pounds! 'If I can get hold of that white monkey, I will,' he thought suddenly. 'It's a good thing.' The monkey's eyes, the squeezed-out fruit—was life all a bitter jest and George deeper than himself? He rang the Green Street bell.

Mrs. Dartie was very sorry, but Mrs. Cardigan had called for her to dine and make a fourth at the play.

Soames went in to dinner alone. At the polished board below which Montague Dartie had now and again slipped, if not quite slept, he dined and brooded. "I can trust you, that's one thing about you, Soames." The words flattered and yet stung him. The depths of that sardonic joke! To give him a family shock and trust him to carry the shock out! George had never cared twelve thousand pounds for a woman who smelled of patchouli. No! It was a final gibe at his family, the Forsytes, at Soames himself! Well! one by one those who had injured or gibed at him—Irene, Bosinney, old and young Jolyon, and now George, had met their fates. Dead, dying, or in British Columbia! He saw again his cousin's eyes above that unlighted cigar, fixed, sad, jesting—poor devil! He got up from the table, and nervously drew aside the curtains. The night was fine and cold. What happened to one— after? George used to say that he had been Charles the Second's cook in a former existence! But reincarnation was all nonsense, weak-minded theorising! Still, one would be glad to hold on if one could, after one was gone. Hold on, and be near Fleur! What noise was that? Gramophone going in the kitchen! When the cat was away, the mice——! People were all alike—take what they could get, and give as little as they could for it. Well! he would smoke a cigarette. Lighting it at a candle—Winifrid dined by candle-light, it was the 'mode' again—he thought: 'Has he still got that cigar between his teeth?' A funny fellow, George—all his days a funny fellow! He watched a ring of smoke he had made without intending to—very blue, he never inhaled! Yes! George had lived too fast, or he would not have been dying twenty years before his time—too fast! Well, there it was, and he wished he had a cat to talk to! He took a little monster off the mantelboard. Picked up by his nephew Benedict in an Eastern bazaar the year after the War, it had green eyes—'Not emeralds,' thought Soames, 'some cheap stone!'

"The telephone for you, sir."

He went into the hall and took up the receiver.

"Yes?"

"Mr. Forsyte has passed away, sir—in his sleep, the doctor says."

"Oh!" said Soames: "Had he a cig——? Many thanks." He hung up the receiver.

Passed away! And, with a nervous movement, he felt for the codicil in his breast pocket.

## Chapter XI

### VENTURE

FOR a week Bicket had seen 'the job', slippery as an eel, evasive as a swallow, for ever passing out of reach. A pound for keep, and three shillings invested on a horse, and he was down to twenty-four bob. The weather had turned sou'-westerly and Victorine had gone out for the first time. That was something off his mind, but the cramp of the unemployed sensation, that fearful craving for the means of mere existence, a protesting, agonising anxiety, was biting into the very flesh of his spirit. If he didn't get a job within a week or two, there would be nothing for it but the work-house, or the gas. 'The gas,' thought Bicket, 'if she will, I will. I'm fed up. After all, what is it? In her arms I wouldn't mind.' Instinct, however, that it was not so easy as all that to put one's head under the gas, gave him a brain-wave that Monday night. Balloons—that chap in Oxford Street to-day! Why not? He still had the capital for a flutter in them, and no hawker's licence needed. His brain, working like a squirrel in the small hours, grasped the great, the incalculable advantage of coloured balloons over all other forms of commerce. You couldn't miss the man who sold them—there he was for every eye to see, with his many radiant circumferences dangling in front of him! Not much profit in them, he had gathered—a penny on a sixpenny globe of coloured air, a penny on every three small twopenny globes; still their salesman was alive, and probably had pitched him a poor tale for fear of making his profession seem too attractive. Over the Bridge, just where the traffic—no, up by St. Paul's! He knew a passage where he could stand back a yard or two, like that chap in Oxford Street! But to the girl sleeping beside him he said nothing. No word to her till he had thrown the die. It meant gambling with his last penny. For a bare living he would have to sell—why, three dozen big and four dozen small balloons a day would only be twenty-six shillings a week profit, unless that chap was kidding. Not much towards Austrylia' out of that! And not a career—Victorine would have a shock! But it was neck or nothing now—he must try it, and in off hours go on looking for a job.

Our thin capitalist, then, with four dozen big and seven dozen small on a tray, two shillings in his pocket, and little in his stomach, took his stand off St. Paul's at two o'clock next day. Slowly he blew up and tied the necks of two large and three small, magenta, green and blue, till they dangled before him. Then with the smell of rubber in his nostrils, and protruding eyes, he stood back on the kerb and watched the stream go by. It gratified him to see that most people turned to look at him. But the first person to address him was a policeman, with:

"I'm not sure you can stand there."

Bicket did not answer, his throat felt too dry. He had heard of the police. Had he gone the wrong way to work? Suddenly he gulped, and said: "Give us a chance, constable; I'm right on my bones. If I'm in the way, I'll stand anywhere you like. This is new to me, and two bob's all I've got left in the world besides a wife."

The constable, a big man, looked him up and down. "Well, we'll see. I shan't make trouble for you if no one objects."

Bicket's gaze deepened thankfully.

"I'm much obliged," he said; "tyke one for your little girl—to please me."

"I'll buy one," said the policeman, "and give you a start. I go off duty in an hour, you 'ave it ready—a big one, magenta."

He moved away. Bicket could see him watching. Edging into the gutter, he stood quite still; his large eyes clung to every face that passed; and, now and then, his thin fingers nervously touched his wares. If Victorine could see him! All the spirit within him mounted. By Golly! he would get out of this somehow into the sun, into a life that was a life!

He had been standing there nearly two hours, shifting from foot to unaccustomed foot, and had sold four big and five small—six-penny worth of profit—when Soames, who had changed his route to spite those fellows who couldn't get past William Gouldyng, Ingerer, came by on his way to the P.P.R.S. board. Startled by a timid murmur: "Balloon, sir, best quality," he looked round from that contemplation of St. Paul's which had been his lifelong habit, and stopped in sheer surprise.

"Balloon!" he said. "What should I want with a balloon?"

Bicket smiled. Between those green and blue and orange globes and Soames's grey self-containment there was incongruity which even he could appreciate.

"Children like 'em—no weight, sir, waistcoat pocket."

"I dare say," said Soames, "but I've no children."

"Grandchildren, sir."

"Nor any grandchildren."

"Thank you, sir."

Soames gave him one of those rapid glances with which he was accustomed to gauge the character of the impecunious. 'A poor, harmless little rat!' he thought. "Here, give me two—how much?"

"A shilling, sir, and much obliged."

"You can keep the change," said Soames hurriedly, and passed on, astonished. Why on earth he had bought the things, and for more than double their price, he could not conceive. He did not

recollect such a thing having happened to him before. Extremely peculiar! And suddenly he realised why. The fellow had been humble, mild—to be encouraged, in these days of Communistic bravura. After all, the little chap was—was on the side of Capital, had invested in those balloons! Trade! And, raising his eyes towards St. Paul's again, he stuffed the nasty-feeling things down into his overcoat pocket. Somebody would be taking them out, and wondering what was the matter with him! Well, he had other things to think of! . . .

Bicket, however, stared after him, elated. Two hundred and fifty odd per cent. profit on those two—that was something like. The feeling, that not enough women were passing him here, became less poignant—after all, women knew the value of money, no extra shillings out of them! If only some more of these shiny-hatted old millionaires would come along!

At six o'clock, with a profit of three and eightpence, to which Soames had contributed just half, he began to add the sighs of deflating balloons to his own; untying them with passionate care he watched his coloured hopes one by one collapse, and stored them in the drawer of his tray. Taking it under his arm, he moved his tired legs in the direction of the Bridge. In a full day he might make four to five shillings—— Well, it would just keep them alive, and something might turn up! He was his own master, anyway, accountable neither to employer nor to union. That knowledge gave him a curious lightness inside, together with the fact that he had eaten nothing since breakfast.

'Wonder if he was an alderman,' he thought; 'they say those aldermen live on turtle soup.' Nearing home, he considered nervously what to do with the tray? How prevent Victorine from knowing that he had joined the ranks of Capital, and spent his day in the gutter? Ill luck! She was at the window! He must put a good face on it. And he went in whistling.

"What's that, Tony?" she said, pointing to the tray.

"Ah! ha! Great stunt—this! Look 'ere!"

Taking a balloon out from the tray, he blew. He blew with a desperation he had not yet put into the process. They said the things would swell to five feet in circumference. He felt somehow that if he could get it to attain those proportions, it would soften everything. Under his breath the thing blotted out Victorine, and the room, till there was just the globe of coloured air. Nipping its neck between thumb and finger, he held it up, and said:

"There you are; not bad value for sixpence, old girl!" and he

65

peered round it. Lord, she was crying! He let the 'blymed' thing go; it floated down, the air slowly evaporating till a little crinkled wreck rested on the dingy carpet. Clasping her heaving shoulders, he said desperately:

"Cheerio, my dear, don't quarrel with bread and butter. I shall get a job, this is just to tide us over. I'd do a lot worse than that for you. Come on, and get my tea, I'm hungry, blowin' up those things."

She stopped crying, looked up, said nothing—mysterious with those big eyes! You'd say she had thoughts! But what they were Bicket could not tell. Under the stimulus of tea, he achieved a certain bravado about his new profession. To be your own master! Go out when you liked, come home when you liked—lie in bed with Vic if he jolly well pleased. A lot in that! And there rose in Bicket something truly national, something free and happy-go-lucky, resenting regular work, enjoying a spurt, and a laze-off, craving independence—something that accounted for the national life, the crowds of little shops, of middlemen, casual workers, tramps, owning their own souls in their own good time, and damning the consequences—something inherent in the land, the race, before the Saxons and their conscience and their industry came in—something that believed in swelling and collapsing coloured air, demanded pickles and high flavours without nourishment—yes, all that something exulted above Bicket's kipper and his tea, good and strong. He would rather sell balloons than be a packer any day, and don't let Vic forget it! And when she was able to take a job, they would get on fine, and not be long before they'd saved enough to get out of it to where those blue butterflies came from. And he spoke of Soames. A few more aldermen without chlidren—say two a day, fifteen bob a week outside legitimate trade. Why, in under a year they'd have the money! And once away, Vic would blow out like one of those balloons: she'd be twice the size, and a colour in her cheeks to lay over that orange and magenta. Bicket became full of air. And the girl, his wife, watched with her large eyes and spoke little; but she did not cry again, or, indeed, throw any water, warm or cold, on him who sold balloons.

## Chapter XII

# FIGURES AND FACTS

WITH the exception of old Fontenoy—in absence as in presence ornamental—the Board was again full; Soames, conscious of special ingratiation in the manner of 'that chap' Elderson, prepared himself for the worst. The figures were before them; a somewhat colourless show, appearing to disclose a state of things which would pass muster, if within the next six months there were no further violent disturbances of currency exchange. The proportion of foreign business to home business was duly expressed in terms of two to seven; German business, which constituted the bulk of the foreign, had been lumped—Soames noted—in the middle section, of countries only half bankrupt, and taken at what might be called a conservative estimate.

During the silence which reigned while each member of the Board digested the figures, Soames perceived more clearly than ever the quandary he was in. Certainly, these figures would hardly justify the foregoing of the dividend earned on the past year's business. But suppose there were another Continental crash and they became liable on the great bulk of their foreign business, it might swamp all profits on home business next year, and more besides. And then his uneasiness about Elderson himself—founded he could not tell on what, intuitive, perhaps silly.

"Well, Mr. Forsyte," the chairman was speaking; "there are the figures. Are you satisfied?"

Soames looked up; he had taken a resolution.

"I will agree to this year's dividend on condition that we drop this foreign business in future, lock, stock and barrel." The manager's eyes hard and bright, met his, then turned towards the chairman.

"That appears to savour of the panicky," he said; "the foreign business is responsible for a good third of our profit this year."

The chairman seemed to garner the expressions of his fellow-directors, before he said:

"There is nothing in the foreign situation at the moment, Mr. Forsyte, which gives particular cause for alarm. I admit that we should watch it closely——"

"You can't," interjected Soames. "Here we are four years from the Armistice, and we know no more where we stand than we did then. If I'd realised our commitment to this policy, I should never have come on the Board. We must drop it."

"Rather an extreme view. And hardly a matter we can decide in a moment."

The murmur of assent, the expression, faintly ironical, of 'that chap's' lips, jolted the tenacity in Soames.

"Very well! Unless you're prepared to tell the shareholders in the report that we are dropping foreign business, you drop me. I must be free to raise the question myself at the general meeting." He did not miss the shift and blink in the manager's eyes. That shot had gone home!

The Chairman said:

"You put a pistol to our heads."

"I am responsible to the shareholders," said Soames, "and I shall do my duty by them."

"So we all are, Mr. Forsyte; and I hope we shall all do our duty."

"Why not confine the foreign business to the small countries—their currency is safe enough?"

'Old Mont', and his precious 'ring'!

"No," said Soames, "we must go back to safety."

"Splendid isolation, Forsyte?"

"Meddling was all very well in the war, but in peace—politics or business—this half-and-half interference is no good. We can't control the foreign situation."

He looked around him, and was instantly conscious that with those words he had struck a chord. 'I'm going through with this!' he thought.

"I should be glad, Mr. Chairman"—the manager was speaking—"if I might say a word. The policy was of my initiation, and I think I may claim that it has been of substantial benefit to the Society so far. When, however, a member of the Board takes so strong a view against its continuance, I certainly don't press the Board to continue it. The times *are* uncertain, and a risk, of course, is involved, however conservative our estimates."

'Now why?' thought Soames: 'What's he ratting for?'

"That's very handsome of you, Elderson; Mr. Chairman, I think we may say that is very handsome of our manager."

Old Dosey Cosey! Handsome! The old woman!

The chairman's rather harsh voice broke a silence.

"This is a very serious point of policy. I should have been glad to have Lord Fontenoy present."

"If I am to endorse the report," said Soames shortly, "it must be

68

decided to-day. I have made up my mind. But please yourselves."

He threw in those last three words from a sort of fellow feeling—it was unpleasant to be dragooned! A moment's silence, and then discussion assumed that random volubility which softens a decision already forced on one. A quarter of an hour thus passed before the chairman said:

"We are agreed then, gentlemen, that the report shall contain the announcement that, in view of Continental uncertainty, we are abandoning foreign risks for the present."

Soames had won. Relieved and puzzled, he walked away alone.

He had shown character; their respect for him had gone up, he could see; their liking for him down, if they'd ever had any—he didn't know! But why had Elderson veered round? He recalled the shift and blink of the fellow's steely eyes at the idea of the question being raised at the general meeting.

That had done it! But why? Were the figures faked? Surely not! That would be too difficult, in the face of the accountants. If Soames had faith, it was in chartered accountants. Sandis and Jevon were tip-top people. It couldn't be that! He glanced up from the pavement. The dome of St. Paul's was dim already in the evening sky—nothing to be had out of it! He felt badly in need of someone to talk to; but there was nobody; and he quickened his pace among the hurrying crowd. His hand, driven deep into his overcoat pocket, came into sudden contact with some foreign sticky substance. 'Gracious!' he thought: 'those things!' Should he drop them in the gutter? If only there were a child he could take them home to! He must get Annette to speak to Fleur. He knew what came of bad habits from his own experience of long ago. Why shouldn't he speak to her himself? He was staying the night there! But there came on him a helpless sense of ignorance. These young people! What did they really think and feel? Was old Mont right? Had they given up interest in everything except the moment, abandoned all belief in continuity, and progress? True enough that Europe was in Queer Street. But look at the state of things after the Napoleonic Wars. He couldn't remember his grandfather 'Superior Dosset', the old chap had died five years before he was born, but he perfectly remembered how Aunt Ann, born in 1799, used to talk about "that dreadful Bonaparte—we used to call him Boney, my dear;" of how her father could get eight or ten per cent. for his money; and of what an impression 'those Chartists' had made on Aunts Juley and Hester, and that was long afterwards. Yet, in spite of all that, look at the Victorian

era—a golden age, things worth collecting, children worth having!
Why not again! Consols had risen almost continuously since
Timothy died. Even if Heaven and Hell had gone, they couldn't
be the reason; none of his uncles had believed in either, and yet
had all made fortunes, and all had families, except Timothy and
Swithin. No! It couldn't be the want of Heaven and Hell! What,
then, was the reason of the change—if change there really were?
And suddenly it was revealed to Soames. They talked too much—
too much and too fast! They got to the end of interest in this and
that and the other. They ate life and threw away the rind, and—
and——. By the way, he must buy that picture of George's! . . .
Had these young folk more mind than his own generation? And
if so—why? Was it diet? That lobster cocktail Fleur had given
him the Sunday before last. He had eaten the thing—very nasty!
But it hadn't made him want to talk. No! He didn't think it could
be diet. Besides—Mind! Where were the minds now that equalled
the Victorians—Darwin, Huxley, Dickens, Disraeli, even old Gladstone? Why, he remembered judges and advocates who seemed
giants compared with those of the present day, just as he remembered that the judges of James his father's youth had seemed giants
to James compared with those of Soames's prime. According to
that, mind was steadily declining. It must be something else.
There was a thing they called psycho-analysis, which so far as he
could understand attributed people's action not to what they ate
at breakfast, or the leg they got out of bed with, as in the good old
days, but to some shock they had received in the remote past and
entirely forgotten. The subconscious mind! Fads! Fads and
microbes! The fact was this generation had no digestion. His
father and his uncles had all complained of liver, but they had
never had anything the matter with them—no need of any of
these vitamins, false teeth, mental healing, newspapers, psycho-
analysis, spiritualism, birth control, osteopathy, broadcasting, and
what not. 'Machines!' thought Soames. 'That's it—I shouldn't
wonder!' How could you believe in anything when everything
was going round so fast? When you couldn't count your chickens
—they ran about so? But Fleur had got a good little head on
her! 'Yes,' he mused, 'and French teeth, she can digest anything.
Two years! I'll speak to her before she gets the habit confirmed.
Her mother was quick enough about it!' And perceiving the
Connoisseurs' Club in front of him, he went in.

The hall porter came out of his box. A gentleman was waiting.

"What gentleman?" said Soames, sidelong.

"I think he's your nephew, sir, Mr. Dartie."

"Val Dartie! H'm! Where?"

"In the little room, sir."

The little room—all the accommodation considered worthy of such as were not Connoisseurs—was at the end of a passage, and in no taste at all, as if the Club were saying: "See what it is not to be one of us!" Soames entered it, and saw Val Dartie smoking a cigarette and gazing with absorption at the only object of interest, his own reflection in the glass above the fire

He never saw his nephew without wondering when he would say: "Look here, Uncle Soames, I'm up a stump." Breeding race-horses! There could only be one end to that!"

"Well?" he said, "how are *you*?"

The face in the glass turned round, and became the back of a clipped sandyish head.

"Oh! bobbish, thanks! *You* look all right, Uncle Soames. I just wanted to ask you: Must I take these screws of old George Forsyte's? They're dashed bad."

"Gift horse in the mouth?" said Soames.

"Well," said Val, "but they're *so* dashed bad; by the time I've paid legacy duty, boxed them to a sale, and sold them, there won't be a sixpence. One of them falls down when you look at it. And the other two are broken-winded. The poor old boy kept them, because he couldn't get rid of them. They're about five hundred years old."

"Thought you were fond of horses," said Soames. "Can't you turn them out?"

"Yes," said Val, drily; "but I've got my living to make. I haven't told my wife, for fear she should suggest that. I'm afraid I might see them in my dreams if I sold them. They're only fit for the kennels. Can I write to the executors and say I'm not rich enough to take them?"

"You can," said Soames, and the words: "How's your wife?" died unspoken on his lips. She was the daughter of his enemy, young Jolyon. That fellow was dead, but the fact remained.

"I will, then," said Val. "How did his funeral go off?"

"Very simple affair—I had nothing to do with it." The days of funerals were over. No flowers, no horses, no plumes—a motor hearse, a couple of cars or so, was all the attention paid nowadays to the dead. Another sign of the times!

"I'm staying the night at Green Street," said Val. "I suppose you're not there, are you?"

"No," said Soames, and did not miss the relief in his nephew's countenance.

"Oh! by the way, Uncle Soames—do you advise me to buy P.P.R.S shares?"

"On the contrary. I'm going to advise your mother to sell. Tell her I'm coming in to-morrow."

"Why? I thought——"

"Never mind my reasons!" said Soames shortly.

"So long, then!"

Exchanging a chilly hand-shake, he watched his nephew withdraw.

So long! An expression, old as the Boer war, that he had never got used to—meant nothing so far as he could see! He entered the reading-room. A number of Connoisseurs were sitting and standing about, and Soames, least clubbable of men, sought the solitude of an embrasured window. He sat there polishing the nail of one forefinger against the back of the other, and chewing the cud of life. After all, what was the point of anything? There was George! He had had an easy life—never done any work! And here was himself, who had done a lot of work! And sooner or later they would bury him too, with a motor hearse probably! And there was his son-in-law, young Mont, full of talk about goodness knew what—and that thin-cheeked chap who had sold him the balloons this afternoon. And old Fontenoy, and that waiter over there; and the out-of-works and the in-works; and those chaps in Parliament, and the parsons in their pulpits—what were they all for? There was the old gardener down at Mapledurham pushing his roller over and over the lawn, week after week, and if he didn't, what would the lawn be like? That was life—gardener rolling lawn! Put it that there was another life—he didn't believe it, but for the sake of argument—that life must be just the same. Rolling lawn—to keep it lawn! What point in lawn? Conscious of pessimism, he rose. He had better be getting back to Fleur's—they dressed for dinner! He supposed there was something in dressing for dinner, but it was like lawn—you came unrolled—undressed again, and so it went on! Over and over and over to keep up to a pitch, that was—ah! what *was* the pitch for?

Turning into South Square, he cannoned into a young man, whose head was craned back as if looking after someone he had parted from. Uncertain whether to apologise or to wait for an apology, Soames stood still.

The young man said abruptly: "Sorry, sir," and moved on; dark, neat-looking chap with a hungry look obviously unconnected with his stomach. Murmuring : "Not at all!" Soames moved forward and rang his daughter's bell. She opened to him herself. She was in hat and furs—just in. The young man recurred to Soames. Had he left her there? What a pretty face it was! He should certainly speak to her. If she once took to gadding about!

He put it off, however, till he was about to say "Good-night"— Michael having gone to the political meeting of a Labour candidate, as if he couldn't find something better to do!

"Now you've been married two years, my child, I suppose you'll be looking towards the future. There's a great deal of nonsense talked about children. The whole thing's much simpler. I hope you feel that."

Fleur was leaning back among the cushions of the settee, swinging her foot. Her eyes became a little restless, but her colour did not change.

"Of course!" she said; "only there's no hurry, Dad."

"Well, I don't know," Soames murmured. "The French and the royal family have a very sound habit of getting it over early. There's many a slip and it keeps them out of mischief. You're very attractive, my child—I don't want to see you take too much to gad-about ways. You've got all sorts of friends."

"Yes," said Fleur.

"You get on well with Michael, don't you?"

"Oh! yes."

"Well, then, why not? You must remember that your son will be a what-you-call-it."

In those words he compromised with his instinctive dislike of titles and flummery of that nature.

"It mightn't be a son," said Fleur.

"At your age that's easily remedied."

"Oh, I don't want a lot, Dad. One, perhaps, or two."

"Well," said Soames, "I should almost prefer a daughter, something like—well, something like you."

Her softened eyes flew, restive, from his face to her foot, to the dog, all over the room.

"I don't know, it's a tie—like digging your own grave in a way."

"I shouldn't put it as high as that," murmured Soames, persuasively.

"No man would, Dad."

"Your mother wouldn't have got on at all without you," and recollection of how near her mother had been to not getting on at

73

all with her—of how, but for him, she would have made a mess of it, reduced him to silent contemplation of the restive foot.

"Well," he said, at last, "I thought I'd mention it. I—I've got your happiness at heart."

Fleur rose and kissed his forehead.

"I know, Dad," she said, "I'm a selfish pig. I'll think about it. In fact, I—I have thought about it."

"That's right," said Soames; "that's right! You've a good head on you—it's a great consolation to me. Good-night, my dear!"

And he went up to his bed. If there was point in anything, it was in perpetuation of oneself, though, of course, that begged the question. 'Wonder,' he thought, 'if I ought to have asked her whether that young man——!' But young people were best left alone. The fact was, he didn't understand them. His eye lighted on the paper bag containing those—those things he had bought. He had brought them up from his overcoat to get rid of them—but how? Put into the fire, they would make a smell. He stood at his dressing-table, took one up and looked at it. Good Lord! And, suddenly, rubbing the mouthpiece with his handkerchief, he began to blow the thing up. He blew until his cheeks were tired, and then, nipping the aperture, took a bit of the dental cotton he used on his teeth every night and tied it up. There the thing was! With a pettish gesture he batted the balloon. Off it flew—purple and extravagant, alighting on his bed. H'm! He took up the other, and did the same to it. Purple and green! The deuce! If anyone came in and saw! He threw up the window, batted them, balloon after balloon, into the night, and shut the window down. There they'd be in the dark, floating about. His lips contracted in a nervous grin. People would see them in the morning. Well! What else could you do with things like that?

## Chapter XIII

## TENTERHOOKS

MICHAEL had gone to the Labour candidate's meeting partly because he wanted to, and partly out of fellow feeling for 'old Forsyte', whom he was always conscious of having robbed. His father-in-law had been very decent about Fleur, and he liked the 'old man' to have her to himself when he could.

In a constituency which had much casual and no trades-union labour to speak of, the meeting would be one of those which

74

enabled the intellectuals of the Party to get it 'off their chests'. Sentiment being 'slop', and championship mere condescension, one might look for sound economic speeches which left out discredited factors, such as human nature. Michael was accustomed to hearing people disparaged for deprecating change because human nature was constant; he was accustomed to hearing people despised for feeling compassion; he knew that one ought to be purely economic. And anyway that kind of speech was preferable to the tub-thumpings of the North or of the Park, which provoked a nasty under-lying class spirit in himself.

The meeting was in full swing when he arrived, the candidate pitilessly exposing the fallacies of a capitalism which, in his view, had brought on the war. For fear that it should bring on another, it must be changed for a system which would ensure that nations should not want anything too much. The individual—said the candidate—was in every respect superior to the nation of which he formed a part; and the problem before them was to secure an economic condition which would enable the individual to function freely in his native superiority. In that way alone, he said, would they lose those mass movements and emotions which imperilled the sanity of the world. He spoke well. Michael listened, purring almost audibly, till he found that he was thinking of himself, Wilfrid and Fleur. Would he ever function so freely in a native superiority that he did not want Fleur too much? And did he wish to? He did not. That seemed to introduce human nature into the speaker's argument. Didn't everybody want something too much? Wasn't it natural? And if so, wouldn't there always be a collective wanting too much—pooling of primary desire, such as the desire of keeping your own head above water? The candidate's argument seemed to him suddenly to leave out heat, to omit friction, to be that of a man in an armchair after a poor lunch. He looked attentively at the speaker's shrewd, dry, doubting face. 'No juice!' he thought. And when 'the chap' sat down, he got up and left the hall.

This Wilfrid business had upset him horribly. Try as he had to put it out of his mind, try as he would to laugh it off, it continued to eat into his sense of security and happiness. Wife and best friend! A hundred times a day he assured himself that he trusted Fleur. Only, Wilfred was so much more attractive than himself. and Fleur deserved the best of everything. Besides, Wilfrid was going through torture, and it was not a pleasant thought! How end the thing, restore peace of mind to himself, to him, to her? She had told him nothing; and it simply was impossible to ask. No way even of showing his anxiety! The whole thing was just 'dark', and, so far as he could see, would have to stay so; nothing to be done but screw the lid on tighter, be as nice as he could to her, try not to feel bitter about him. Hades!

He turned down Chelsea Embankment. Here the sky was dark and wide and streaming with stars. The river wide, dark and gleaming with oily rays from the Embankment lamps. The width of it all gave him relief. Dash the dumps! A jolly, queer, muddled, sweet and bitter world; an immensely intriguing game of chance, no matter how the cards were falling at the moment! In the trenches he had thought: 'Get out of this, and I'll never mind anything again!' How seldom now he remembered thinking that! The human body renewed itself—they said—in seven years. In three years' time his body would not be the body of the trenches, but a whole-time peace body with a fading complex. If only Fleur would tell him quite openly what she felt, what she was doing about Wilfrid, for she must be doing something! And Wilfrid's verse? Would his confounded passion—as Bart suggested—flow in poetry? And if so, who would publish it? A miserable business! Well the night was beautiful, and the great thing not to be a pig. Beauty and not being a pig! Nothing much else to it—except laughter— the comic side! Keep one's sense of humour, anyway! And Michael searched, while he strode beneath plane trees half-stripped of leaves and plume-like in the dark, for the fun in his position. He failed to find it. There seemed absolutely nothing funny about love. Possibly he might fall out of love again some day, but not so long as she kept him on her tenterhooks. Did she do it on purpose? Never! Fleur simply could not be like those women who kept their husbands hungry and fed them when they wanted dresses, furs, jewels. Revolting!

He came in sight of Westminster. Only half-past ten! Suppose he took a cab to Wilfrid's rooms, and tried to have it out with him. It would be like trying to make the hands of a clock move backwards to its ticking. What use in saying: "You love Fleur—well, don't!" or in Wilfrid saying it to him. 'After all, I was first with Fleur,' he thought. Pure chance, perhaps, but fact! Ah! And wasn't that just the danger? He was no longer a novelty to her— nothing unexpected about him now! And he and she had agreed times without number that novelty was the salt of life, the essence of interest and drama. Novelty now lay with Wilfrid! Lord! Lord! Possession appeared far from being nine points of the law! He rounded-in from the Embankment towards home—jolly part of

London, jolly Square; everything jolly except just this infernal complication. Something, soft as a large leaf, tapped twice against his ear. He turned, astonished; he was in empty space, no tree near. Floating in the darkness, a round thing—he grabbed, it bobbed. What? A child's balloon! He secured it between his hands, took it beneath a lamp-post—green, he judged. Queer! He looked up. Two windows lighted, one of them Fleur's! Was this the bubble of his own happiness expelled? Morbid! Silly ass! Some gust of wind —a child's plaything lodged and loosened! He held the balloon gingerly. He would take it in and show it to her. He put his latch-key in the door. Dark in the hall—gone up! He mounted, swinging the balloon on his finger. Fleur was standing before a mirror.

"What on earth's that?" she said.

The blood returned to Michael's heart. Curious how he had dreaded its having anything to do with her!

"Don't know, darling; fell on my hat—must belong to heaven." And he batted it.

The balloon floated, dropped, bounded twice, wobbled and came to rest.

"You *are* a baby, Michael. I believe you bought it."

Michael came closer, and stood quite still.

"My hat! What a misfortune to be in love!"

"You think so!"

"*Il y a toujours un qui baise, et l'autre qui ne tend pas la joue.*"

"But I do."

"Fleur!"

Fleur smiled.

"*Baise* away."

Embracing her, Michael thought: 'She holds me—does with me what she likes; I know nothing of her!'

And there arose a small sound—from Ting-a-ling smelling the balloon.

# PART II

## Chapter I

### THE MARK FALLS

THE state of the world had been getting more and more on Soames's nerves ever since the general meeting of the P.P.R.S. It had gone off with that fatuity long associated by him with such gatherings— a watertight rigmorale from the chairman; butter from two reliable shareholders; vinegar from shareholders not so reliable; and the usual 'gup' over the dividend. He had gone there glum, come away glummer. From a notion once taken into his head Soames parted more slowly than a cheese parts from its mites. Two-sevenths of foreign business, nearly all German! And the mark falling! It had begun to fall from the moment that he decided to support the dividend. And why? What was in the wind? Contrary to his custom, he had taken to sniffing closely the political columns of his paper. The French—he had always mistrusted them, especially since his second marriage—the French were going to play old Harry, if he was not greatly mistaken! Their papers, he noticed, never lost a chance of having a dab at English policy; seemed to think they could always call the tune for England to pipe to! And the mark and the franc, and every other sort of money, falling. And, though in Soames was that which rejoiced in the thought that one of his country's bits of paper could buy a great quantity of other countries' bits of paper, there was also that which felt the whole thing silly and unreal, with an ever-growing consciousness that the P.P.R.S. would pay no dividend next year. The P.P.R.S. was a big concern; no dividend would be a sign, no small one, of bad management. Assurance was one of the few things on God's earth which could and should be conducted without real risk. But for that he would never have gone on the Board. And to find assurance had not been so conducted and that by himself, was— well! He had caused Winifred to sell, anyway, though the shares had already fallen slightly. "I thought it was such a good thing,

Soames," she had said plaintively: "it's rather a bore, losin' money on these shares." He had answered without mercy: "If you don't sell, you'll lose more." And she had done it. If the Rogers and Nicholases who had followed him into it hadn't sold too—well, it was their look out! He had made Winifred warn them. As for himself, he had nothing but his qualifying shares, and the missing of a dividend or two would not hurt one whose director's fees more than compensated. It was not, therefore, private uneasiness so much as resentment at a state of things connected with foreigners and the slur on his infallibility.

Christmas had gone off quietly at Mapledurham. He abominated Christmas, and only observed it because his wife was French, and her national festival New Year's Day. One could not go so far as to observe that, encouraging a foreign notion. But Christmas with no child about—he still remembered the holly and snapdragons of Park Lane in his own childhood—the family parties; and how disgusted he had been if he got anything symbolic—the thimble, or the ring—instead of the shilling. They had never gone in for Santa Claus at Park Lane, partly because they could see through the old gentleman, and partly because he was not at all a late thing. Emily, his mother, had seen to that. Yes; and, by the way, that William Gouldyng, Ingerer, had so stumped those fellows at the Heralds' College, that Soames had dropped the enquiry—it was just encouraging them to spend his money for a sentimental satisfaction which did not materialise. That narrow-headed chap, 'Old Mont', peacocked about his ancestry; all the more reason for having no ancestry to peacock about. The Forsytes and the Goldings were good English country stock—that was what mattered. And if Fleur and her child, if one came, had French blood in them—well, he couldn't help it now.

In regard to the coming of a grandchild, Soames knew no more than in October. Fleur had spent Christmas with the Monts; she was promised to him, however, before long, and her mother must ask her a question or two!

The weather was extremely mild; Soames had even been out in a punt fishing. In a heavy coat he trailed a line for perch and dace, and caught now and then a roach—precious little good, the servants wouldn't eat them, nowadays! His grey eyes would brood over the grey water under the grey sky; and in his mind the mark would fall. It fell with a bump on that eleventh of January when the French went and occupied the Ruhr. He said to Annette at breakfast: "Your country's cracked! Look at the mark now!"

"What do I care about the mark?" she had answered over her coffee. "I care that they shall not come again into my country. I hope they will suffer a little what we have suffered."

"You," said Soames; "you never suffered anything."

Annette put her hand where Soames sometimes doubted the existence of a heart.

"I have suffered here," she said.

"I didn't notice it. You never went without butter. What do you suppose Europe's going to be like now for the next thirty years! How about British trade?"

"We French see before our noses," said Annette with warmth. "We see that the beaten must be kept the beaten, or he will take revenge. You English are so sloppy."

"Sloppy, are we?" said Soames. "You're talking like a child. Could a sloppy people ever have reached our position in the world?"

"That is your selfishness. You are cold and selfish."

"Cold, selfish and sloppy—they don't go together. Try again."

"Your slop is in your thought and your talk; it is your instinct that gives you your success, and your English instinct is cold and selfish, Soames. You are a mixture, all of you, of hypocrisy, stupidity and egoism."

Soames took some marmalade.

"Well," he said, "and what are the French?—cynical, avaricious and revengeful. And the Germans are sentimental, heady and brutal. We can all abuse each other. There's nothing for it but to keep clear. And that's what you French won't do."

Annette's handsome person stiffened.

"When you are tied to a person, as I am tied to you, Soames, or as we French are tied to the Germans, it is necessary to be top dog, or to be bottom dog."

Soames stayed his toast.

"Do you suppose yourself top dog in this house?"

"Yes, Soames."

"Oh! Then you can go back to France to-morrow."

Annette's eyebrows rose quizzically.

"I would wait a little longer, my friend; you are still too young."

But Soames had already regretted his remark; he did not wish any disturbance at his time of life, and he said more calmly:

"Compromise is the essence of any reasonable existence between individuals or nations. We can't have the fat thrown into the fire every few years."

"That is so English," murmured Annette. "We others never know what you English will do. You always wait to see which way the cat jumps."

However deeply sympathetic with such a reasonable characteristic, Soames would have denied it at any ordinary moment—to confess to temporising was not, as it were, done. But, with the mark falling like a cartload of bricks, he was heated to the point of standing by his nature.

"And why shouldn't we? Rushing into things that you'll have to rush out of! I don't want to argue. French and English never did get on, and never will."

Annette rose. "You speak the truth, my friend. *Entente, mais pas cordiale*. What are you doing to-day?"

"Going up to town," said Soames glumly. "Your precious Government has put business into Queer Street with a vengeance."

"Do you stay the night?"

"I don't know."

"*Adieu*, then, *jusqu'au revoir!*" And she got up.

Soames remained brooding above his marmalade—with the mark falling in his mind—glad to see the last of her handsome figure, having no patience at the moment for French tantrums. An irritable longing to say to somebody "I told you so" possessed him. He would have to wait, however, till he found somebody to say it to.

A beautiful day, quite warm; and, taking his umbrella as an assurance against change, he set out for the station.

In the carriage going up they were talking about the Ruhr. Averse from discussion in public, Soames listened from behind his paper. The general sentiment was surprisingly like his own. In so far as it was unpleasant for the Huns—all right; in so far as it was unpleasant for British trade—all wrong; in so far as love of British trade was active and hate of Huns now passive—more wrong than right. A Francophil remark that the French were justified in making themselves safe at all cost, was coldly received. At Maidenhead a man got in whom Soames connected automatically with disturbance. He had much grey hair, a sanguine face, lively eyes, twisting eyebrows, and within five minutes had asked in a breezy voice whether anyone had heard of the League of Nations. Confirmed in his estimate, Soames looked round the corner of his paper. Yes, that chap would get off on some hobby-horse or other! And there he went! The question—said the newcomer—was not whether the Germans should get one in the eye, the British one in

81

the pocket, or the French one in the heart, but whether the world should get peace and goodwill. Soames lowered his paper. If—this fellow said—they wanted peace, they must sink their individual interests, and think in terms of collective interest. The good of all was the good of one! Soames saw the flaw at once; that might be, but the good of one was not the good of all. He felt that if he did not take care he would be pointing this out. The man was a perfect stranger to him, and no good ever came of argument. Unfortunately his silence amid the general opinion that the League of Nations was 'no earthly', seemed to cause the newcomer to regard him as a sympathiser; the fellow kept on throwing his eyebrows at him! To put up his paper again seemed too pointed, and his position was getting more and more false when the train ran in at Padding-ton. He hastened to a cab. A voice behind him said:

"Hopeless lot, sir, eh! Glad to see *you* saw my point."

"Quite!" said Soames. "Taxi!"

"Unless the League of Nations functions, we're all for Gehenna."

Soames turned the handle of the cab door.

"Quite!" he said again. "Poultry!" and got in. He was not going to be drawn. The fellow was clearly a firebrand!

In the cab the measure of his disturbance was revealed. He had said 'Poultry', an address that 'Forsyte, Bustard and Forsyte' had abandoned two-and-twenty years ago when, merged with 'Cuthcott, Holliday and Kingson,' they became 'Cuthcott, Kingson and Forsyte'. Rectifying the error, he sat forward, brooding. Fall of the mark! The country was sound about it, yes—but when they failed to pay the next dividend, could they rely on resentment against the French instead of against the directors? Doubtful! The directors ought to have seen it coming! That might be said of the other directors, but not of himself—here was a policy that he personally never would have touched. If only he could discuss the whole thing with someone—but old Gradman would be out of his depth in a matter of this sort. And, on arrival at his office, he gazed with a certain impatience at that changeless old fellow, sitting in his swivel chair.

"Ah! Mr. Soames, I was hopin' you might come in this morning. There's a young man been round to see you from the P.P.R.S. Wouldn't give his business, said he wanted to see you privately. Left his number on the phone."

"Oh!" said Soames.

"Quite a young feller—in the office."

"What did he look like?"

"Nice, clean young man. I was quite favourably impressed— name of Butterfield."

"Well, ring him up, and let him know I'm here." And going over to the window, he stood looking out on to a perfectly blank wall.

Suited to a sleeping partner, his room was at the back, free from disturbance. Young man! The call was somewhat singular! And he said over his shoulder: "Don't go when he comes, Gradman, I know nothing of him."

The world changed, people died off, the mark fell, but Gradman was there—embodiment, faithful and grey, of service and integrity —an anchor.

Gradman's voice, grating, ingratiating, rose.

"This French news—it's not nice, Mr. Soames. They're a hasty lot. I remember your father, Mr. James, coming into the office the morning the Franco-Prussian war was declared—quite in his prime then, hardly more than sixty, I should say. Why, I recall his very words: 'There,' he said, 'I told them so.' And here they are—at it still. The fact is, they're cat and dog."

Soames, who had half turned, resumed his contemplation of a void. Poor old Gradman dated! What would he say when he heard that they had been insuring foreign business? Stimulated by the old-time quality of Gradman's presence, his mind ranged with sudden freedom. He himself had another twenty years, perhaps. What would he see in that time? Where would old England be at the end of it? 'In spite of the papers, we're not such fools as we look,' he thought. 'If only we can steer clear of flibberty-gibberting, and pay our way!'

"Mr. Butterfield, sir." H'm! The young man had been very spry. Covered by Gradman's bluff and greasy greeting, he "took a lunar," as his Uncle Roger used to call it. The young fellow, in a neat suit, a turndown collar, with his hat in his hand, was a medium modest-looking chap. Soames nodded.

"You want to see me?"

"Alone, if I might, sir."

"Mr. Gradman here is my right-hand man."

Gradman's voice purred gratingly: "You can state your business. Nothing goes outside these walls, young man."

"I'm in the office of the P.P.R.S., sir. The fact is, accident has just put some information in my hands, and I'm not easy in my mind. Knowing you to be a solicitor, sir, I preferred to come to you, rather than go to the chairman. As a lawyer, would you tell me: Is my first duty to the Society, being in their employ?"

"Certainly," said Soames.

"I don't like this job, sir, and I hope you'll understand that I'm not here for any personal motive—it's just because I feel I ought to."

Soames regarded him steadily. Though large and rather swimming, the young man's eyes impressed him by their resemblance to a dog's. "What's it all about?" he said.

The young man moistened his lips.

"The insurance of our German business, sir."

Soames pricked his ears, already slightly pointed by Nature.

"It's a very serious matter," the young man went on, "and I don't know how it'll affect me, but the fact is, this morning I overheard a private conversation."

"Oh!" said Soames.

"Yes, sir. I quite understand your tone, but the very first words did it. I simply couldn't make myself known after hearing them. I think you'll agree, sir."

"Who were the speakers?"

"The manager, and a man called Smith—I fancy by his accent his name's a bit more foreign—who's done most of the agenting for the German business."

"What were the words?" said Soames.

"Well, sir, the manager was speaking, and then this Smith said: 'Quite so, Mr. Elderson, but we haven't paid you a commission on all this business for nothing; if the mark goes absolutely phut, you will have to see that your Society makes it good for us!'"

The intense longing, which at that moment came on Soames to emit a whistle, was checked by sight of Gradman's face. The old fellow's mouth had opened in the nest of his grizzly short beard; his eyes stared puglike, he uttered a prolonged: "A-ow!"

"Yes," said the young man, "it was a knock-out!"

"Where were you?" asked Soames, sharply.

"In the lobby between the manager's room and the board-room. I'd just come from sorting some papers in the board-room, and the manager's door was open an inch or so. Of course I know the voices well."

"What after?"

"I heard Mr. Elderson say: 'H'ssh! Don't talk like that!' and I slipped back into the board-room. I'd had more than enough, sir, I assure you."

Suspicion and surmise clogged Soames's thinking apparatus. Was this young fellow speaking the truth? A man like Elderson—the risk was monstrous! And, if true, what was the directors' responsibility? But proof—proof? He stared at the young man, who looked upset and pale enough, but whose eyes did not waver. Shake him if he could! And he said sharply:

"Now mind what you're saying! This is most serious!"

"I know that, sir. If I'd consulted my own interest, I'd never have come here. I'm not a sneak."

The words rang true, but Soames did not drop his caution.

"Ever had any trouble in the office?"

"No, sir, you can make enquiry. I've nothing against Mr. Elderson, and he's nothing against me."

Soames thought suddenly: 'Good heavens! He's shifted it on to me, and in the presence of a witness. And I supplied the witness!'

"Have you any reason to suppose," he said, "that they became aware of your being there?"

"They couldn't have, I think."

The implications of this news seemed every second more alarming. It was as if Fate, kept at bay all his life by clever wrist-work, had suddenly slipped a thrust under his guard. No good to get rattled, however—must think it out at leisure!

"Are you prepared, if necessary, to repeat this to the Board?"

The young man pressed his hands together.

"Well, sir, I'd much rather have held my tongue; but if you decide it's got to be taken up, I suppose I must go through with it now. I'm sure I hope you'll decide to leave it alone; perhaps it isn't true—only why didn't Mr. Elderson say: 'You ruddy liar!' ?"

Exactly! Why didn't he? Soames gave a grunt of intense discomfort.

"Anything more?" he said.

"No, sir."

"Very well. You've not told anyone?"

"No, sir."

"Then don't, and leave it to me."

"I'll be only too happy to, sir. Good-morning!"

"Good-morning!"

No—very bad morning! No satisfaction whatever in this sudden fulfilment of his prophetic feeling about Elderson. None!

"What d'you think of that young fellow, Gradman? Is he lying?"

Thus summoned, as it were, from stupor, Gradman thoughtfully rubbed a nose both thick and shining.

A MODERN COMEDY

"It's one word against another, Mr. Soames, unless you get more evidence. But I can't see what the young man has to gain by it."

"Nor I; but you never know. The trouble will be to get more evidence. Can I act without it?"

"It's delicate," said Gradman. And Soames knew that he was thrown back on himself. When Gradman said a thing was delicate, it meant that it was the sort of matter on which he was accustomed to wait for orders—presumptuous even to hold opinion! But had he got one? Well, one would never know! The old chap would sit and rub his nose over it till Kingdom Come.

"I shan't act in a hurry," he said, almost angrily: "I can't see to the end of this."

Every hour confirmed that statement. At lunch the tape of his city club showed the mark still falling—to unheard-of depths! How they could talk of golf, with this business on his mind, he could not imagine!

"I must go and see that fellow," he said to himself. "I shall be guarded. He may throw some light." He waited until three o'clock and repaired to the P.P.R.S.

Reaching the office, he sought the board-room. The chairman was there in conference with the manager. Soames sat down quietly to listen; and while he listened he watched that fellow's face. It told him nothing. What nonsense people talked when they said you could tell character from faces! Only a perfect idiot's face could be read like that. And here was a man of experience and culture, one who knew every rope of business life and polite society. The hairless, neat features exhibited no more concern than the natural mortification of one whose policy had met with such a nasty knock. The drop of the mark had already wiped out any possible profit on the next half-year. Unless the wretched thing recovered, they would be carrying a practically dead load of German insurance. Really it was criminal that no limit of liability had been fixed! How on earth could he ever have overlooked that when he came on the Board? But he had only known of it afterwards. And who could have foreseen anything so mad as this Ruhr business, or realised the slack confidence of his colleagues in this confounded fellow? The words 'gross negligence' appeared 'close up' before his eyes. What if an action lay against the Board! Gross negligence! At his age and with his reputation! Why! The thing was plain as a pikestaff; for omitting a limit of liability this chap had got his commission! Ten per cent. probably, on all that business—he must have netted thousands! A man must be in Queer

Street indeed to take a risk like that! But conscious that his fancy was running on, Soames rose, and turned his back. The action suggested another. Simulate anger, draw some sign from that fellow's self-control! He turned again, and said pettishly: "What on earth were you about, Mr. Manager, when you allowed these contracts to go through without limit of liability? A man of your experience! What was your motive?"

A slight narrowing of the eyes, a slight compression of the lips. He had relied on the word 'motive', but the fellow passed it by.

"For such high premiums as we have been getting, Mr. Forsyte, a limited liability was not possible. This is a most outrageous development, and I'm afraid it must be considered just bad luck."

"Unfortunately," said Soames, "there's no such thing as luck in properly regulated assurance, as we shall find, or I'm much mistaken. I shouldn't be surprised if an action lay against the Board for gross negligence!"

That had got the chairman's goat!—Got his goat? What expressions they used nowadays! Or did it mean the opposite? One never knew! But as for Elderson—he seemed to Soames to be merely counterfeiting a certain flusteration. Futile to attempt to spring anything out of a chap like that. If the thing were true, the fellow must be entirely desperate, prepared for anything and everything. And since from Soames the desperate side of life—the real holes, the impossible positions which demand a gambler's throw—had always been carefully barred by the habits of a prudent nature, he found it now impossible to imagine Elderson's state of mind, or his line of conduct if he were guilty. For all he could tell, the chap might be carrying poison about with him; might be sitting on a revolver like a fellow on the film. The whole thing was too unpleasant, too worrying for words. And without saying any more he went away, taking nothing with him but the knowledge that their total liability on this German business, with the mark valueless, was over two hundred thousand pounds. He hastily reviewed the fortunes of his co-directors. Old Fontenoy was always in low water; the chairman a dark horse; Mont was in land, land right down in value, and mortgaged at that; old Cosey Mothergill had nothing but his name and his director's fees; Meyricke must have a large income, but light come, light go, like most of those big counsel with irons in many fires and the certainty of a judgeship. Not a really substantial man among the lot, except himself!

He ploughed his way along, head down. Public companies! Preposterous system! You had to trust somebody, and there you were! It was appalling!

"Balloons, sir—beautiful colours, five feet circumference. Take one, gentleman!"

"Good gad!" said Soames. As if the pricked bubble of German business were not enough!

## Chapter II

## VICTORINE

ALL through December balloons had been slack—hardly any movement about them, even in Christmas week, and from the Bickets Central Australia was as far ever. The girl Victorine, restored to comparative health, had not regained her position in the blouse department of Messrs. Boney Blayds & Co. They had given her some odd sewing, but not of late, and she had spent much time trying to get work less uncertain. Her trouble was—had always been—her face. It was unusual. People did not know what to make of a girl who looked like that. Why employ one who without qualification of wealth, rank, fashion, or ability (so far as they knew) made them feel ordinary? For—however essential to such as Fleur and Michael—dramatic interest was not primary in the manufacture or sale of blouses, in the fitting-on of shoes, the addressing of envelopes, making-up of funeral wreaths, or the other ambitions of Victorine. Behind those large dark eyes and silent lips, what went on? It worried Boney Blayds & Co., and the more wholesale firms of commerce. The lurid professions—film-super, or mannequin—did not occur to one, of self-deprecating nature, born in Putney.

When Bicket had gone out of a morning with his tray and his balloons not yet blown up, she would stand biting her finger, as though to gnaw her way to some escape from this hand-to-mouth existence which kept her husband thin as a rail, tired as a rook, shabby as a tailless sparrow, and, at the expense of all caste feeling, brought them in no more than just enough to keep them living under a roof. It had long been clear to them both that there was no future in balloons, just a cadging present. And there smouldered in the silent, passive Victorine a fierce resentment. She wanted better things for herself, for him, chiefly for him.

On the morning when the mark was bumping down, she was

88

putting on her velveteen jacket and toque (best remaining items of her wardrobe), having taken a resolve. Bicket never mentioned his old job, and his wife had subtly divined some cause beyond the ordinary for his loss of it. Why not see if she could get him taken back? He had often said: "Mr. Mont's a gent and a sort o' Socialist; been through the war, too; no high-and-mighty about *him*." If she could 'get at' this phenomenon! With the flush of hope and daring in her sallow cheeks, she took stock of her appearance from the window-glasses of the Strand. Her velveteen of jade-green always pleased one who had an eye for colour, but her black skirt—well, perhaps the wear and tear of it wouldn't show if she kept behind the counter. Had she brass enough to say that she came about a manuscript? And she rehearsed with silent lips, pinching her accent: "Would you ask Mr. Mont, please, if I could see him; it's about a manuscript." Yes! and then would come the question: "What name, please?" "Mrs. Bicket?" Never! "Miss Victorine Collins?" All authoresses had maiden names. Victorine—yes! But Collins! It didn't sound like. And no one would know what her maiden name had been. Why not choose one? They often chose. And she searched. Something Italian, like—like—— Hadn't their landlady said to them when they came in: "Is your wife Eyetalian?" Ah! Manuelli! That was certainly Italian—the ice-cream man in Little Ditch Street had it! She walked on practising beneath her breath. If only she could get to see this Mr. Mont!

She entered, trembling. All went exactly as foreseen, even to the pinching of her accent, till she stood waiting for them to bring an answer from the speaking-tube, concealing her hands in their very old gloves. Had Miss Manuelli an appointment? There was no manuscript.

"No," said Victorine, "I haven't sent it yet. I wanted to see him first." The young man at the counter was looking at her hard. He went again to the tube, then spoke.

"Will you wait a minute, please—Mr. Mont's lady secretary is coming down."

Victorine inclined her head towards her sinking heart. A lady secretary! She would never get there now! And there came on her the sudden dread of false pretences. But the thought of Tony standing at his corner, ballooned up to the eyes, as she had spied out more than once, fortified her desperation.

A girl's voice said: "Miss Manuelli? Mr. Mont's secretary, perhaps you could give me a message."

A fresh-faced young woman's eyes were travelling up and down her. Pinching her accent hard, she said: "Oh! I'm afraid I couldn't do that."

The travelling gaze stopped at her face. "If you'll come with me, I'll see if he can see you."

Alone in a small waiting-room, Victorine sat without movement, till she saw a young man's face poked through the doorway, and heard the words:

"Will you come in?"

She took a deep breath, and went. Once in the presence, she looked from Michael to his secretary and back again, subtly daring his youth, his chivalry, his sportsmanship, to refuse her a private interview. Through Michael passed at once the thought: 'Money, I suppose. But what an interesting face!' The secretary drew down the corners of her mouth and left the room.

"Well, Miss—er—Manuelli?"

"Not Manuelli, please—Mrs. Bicket; my husband used to be here."

"What!" The chap that had snooped 'Copper Coin'! Phew! Bicket's yarn—his wife—pneumonia! She looked as if she might have had it.

"He often spoke of you, sir. And, please, he hasn't any work. Couldn't you find room for him again, sir?"

Michael stood silent. Did this terribly interesting-looking girl know about the snooping?

"He just sells balloons in the street now; I can't bear to see him. Over by St. Paul's he stands, and there's no money in it; and we do so want to get out to Australia. I know he's very nervy, and gets wrong with people. But if you *could* take him back here. . . ."

No! she did not know!

"Very sorry, Mrs. Bicket. I remember your husband well, but we haven't a place for him. Are *you* all right again?"

"Oh! yes. Except that I can't get work again either."

What a face for wrappers! Sort of Mona Lisa-ish! Storbert's novel! Ha!

"Well, I'll have a talk with your husband. I suppose you wouldn't like to sit to an artist for a book-wrapper? It might lead to work in that line if you want it. You're just the type for a friend of mine. Do you know Aubrey Greene's work?"

"No, sir."

"It's pretty good—in fact, very good in a decadent way. You wouldn't mind sitting?"

90

"I wouldn't mind anything to save some money. But I'd rather you didn't tell my husband I'd been to see you. He might take it amiss."

"All right! I'll see him by accident. Near St. Paul's, you said? But there's no chance here, Mrs. Bicket. Besides, he couldn't make two ends meet on this job, he told me."

"When I was ill, sir."

"Of course, that makes a difference."

"Yes, sir."

"Well, let me write you a note to Mr. Greene. Will you sit down a minute?"

He stole a look at her while she sat waiting. Really, her sallow, large-eyed face, with its dead-black, bobbed, frizzy-ended hair, was extraordinarily interesting—a little too refined and anæmic for the public; but, dash it all! the public couldn't always have its Reckitt's blue eyes, corn-coloured hair, and poppy cheeks. "She's not a peach," he wrote, "on the main tree of taste; but so striking in her way that she really might become a type, like Beardsley's or Dana's."

When she had taken the note and gone, he rang for his secretary.

"No, Miss Perren, she didn't take anything off me. But some type, eh?"

"I thought you'd like to see her. She wasn't an authoress, was she?"

"Far from it."

"Well, I hope she got what she wanted."

Michael grinned. "Partly, Miss Perren—partly. You think I'm an awful fool, don't you?"

"I'm sure I don't; but I think you're too soft-hearted."

Michael ran his fingers through his hair.

"Would it surprise you to hear that I've done a stroke of business?"

"Yes, Mr. Mont."

"Then I won't tell you what it is. When you've done pouting, go on with that letter to my father about 'Duet': 'We are sorry to say that in the present state of the trade we should not be justified in reprinting the dialogue between those two old blighters; we have already lost money by it!' You must translate, of course. Now can we say something to cheer the old boy up? How about this? 'When the French have recovered their wits, and the birds begin to sing—in short, when spring comes—we hope to reconsider the matter in the light of—of—'—er—what, Miss Perren?"

91

A MODERN COMEDY

" 'The experience we shall have gained.' Shall I leave out about the French and the birds?"

"Excellent! 'Yours faithfully, Danby and Winter.' Don't you think it was a scandalous piece of nepotism bringing the book here at all, Miss Perren?"

"What is 'nepotism'?"

"Taking advantage of your son. He's never made a sixpence by any of his books."

"He's a very distinguished writer, Mr. Mont."

"And we pay for the distinction. Well, he's a good old Bart. That's all before lunch, and mind you have a good one. That girl's figure wasn't usual either, was it? She's thin, but she stands up straight. There's a question I always want to ask, Miss Perren: Why do modern girls walk in a curve with their heads poked forward? They can't all be built like that."

The secretary's cheeks brightened.

"There *is* a reason, Mr. Mont."

"Good! What is it?"

The secretary's cheeks continued to brighten. "I don't really know whether I can——"

"Oh! sorry. I'll ask my wife. Only she's quite straight herself."

"Well, Mr. Mont, it's this, you see: They aren't supposed to have anything be—behind, and, of course, they have, and they can't get the proper effect unless they curve their chests in and poke their heads forward. It's the fashion-plates and mannequins that do it."

"I see," said Michael; "thank you, Miss Perren; awfully good of you. It's the limit, isn't it?"

"Yes, I don't hold with it, myself."

"No, quite!"

The secretary lowered her eyelids and withdrew.

Michael sat down and drew a face on his blotting-paper. It was not Victorine's. . . .

Armed with the note to Aubrey Greene, Victorine had her usual lunch, a cup of coffee and a bit of heavy cake, and took the tube towards Chelsea. She had not succeeded, but the gentleman had been friendly and she felt cheered.

At the studio door was a young man inserting a key—very elegant in smoke-grey Harris tweeds, a sliding young man with no hat, beautifully brushed-back bright hair, and a soft voice.

"Model?" he said.

"Yes, sir, please. I have a note for you from Mr. Mont."

"Michael? Come in."

Victorine followed him in. It was 'not half' sea-green in there; a high room with rafters and a top light, and lots of pictures and drawings on the walls, and as if they had slipped off on to the floor. A picture on an easel of two ladies with their clothes sliding down troubled Victorine. She became conscious of the gentleman's eyes, sea-green like the walls, sliding up and down her.

"Will you sit for anything?" he asked.

Victorine answered mechanically: "Yes, sir."

"Do you mind taking your hat off?"

Victorine took off the toque, and shook out her hair.

"Ah!" said the gentleman. "I wonder."

Victorine wondered what.

"Just sit down on the daïs, will you?"

Victorine looked about her, uncertain. A smile seemed to fly up his forehead and over his slippery bright hair.

"This is your first shot, then?"

"Yes, sir."

"All the better." And he pointed to a small platform.

Victorine sat down on it in a black oak chair.

"You look cold."

"Yes, sir."

He went to a cupboard and returned with two small glasses of a brown fluid.

"Have a Grand Marnier?"

She noticed that he tossed his off in one gulp, and did the same. It was sweet, strong, very nice, and made her gasp.

"Take a cigarete."

Victorine took one from a case he handed, and put it between her lips. He lit it. And again a smile slid up away over the top of his head.

"You draw it in," he said. "Where were you born?"

"In Putney, sir."

"That's very interesting. Just sit still a minute. It's not as bad as having a tooth out, but it takes longer. The great thing is to keep awake."

"Yes, sir."

He took a large piece of paper and a bit of dark stuff, and began to draw.

"Tell me," he said, "Miss——"

"Collins, sir—Victorine Collins." Some instinct made her give her maiden name. It seemed somehow more professional.

"Are you at large?" He paused, and again the smile slid up over his bright hair: "Or have you any other occupation?"

"Not at present, sir. I'm married, but nothing else."

For some time after that the gentleman was silent. It was interesting to see him, taking a look, making a stroke on the paper, taking another look. Hundreds of looks, hundreds of strokes. At last he said: "All right! Now we'll have a rest. Heaven sent you here, Miss Collins. Come and get warm."

Victorine approached the fire.

"Do you know anything about expressionism?"

"No, sir."

"Well, it means not troubling about the outside except in so far as it expresses the inside. Does that convey anything to you?"

"No, sir."

"Quite! I think you said you'd sit for the—er—altogether?"

Victorine regarded the bright and sliding gentleman. She did not know what he meant, but she felt that he meant something out of the ordinary.

"Altogether what, sir?"

"Nude."

"Oh!" She cast her eyes down, then raised them to the sliding clothes of the two ladies. "Like that?"

"No, I shouldn't be treating you cubistically."

A slow flush was burning out the sallow in her cheeks. She said slowly:

"Does it mean more money?"

"Yes, half as much again—more perhaps. I don't want you to if you'd rather not. You can think it over and let me know next time."

She raised her eyes again, and said: "Thank you, sir."

"Righto! Only please don't 'sir' me."

Victorine smiled. It was the first time she had achieved this functional disturbance, and it seemed to have a strange effect. He said hurriedly: "By George! When you smile, Miss Collins, I see you *im*pressionistically. If you've rested, sit up there again."

Victorine went back.

The gentleman took a fresh piece of paper.

"Can you think of anything that will keep you smiling?"

She shook her head. That was a fact.

"Nothing comic at all? I suppose you're not in love with your husband, for instance?"

94

"Oh! yes."

"Well, try that."

Victorine tried that, but she could only see Tony selling his balloons.

"That won't do," said the gentleman. "Don't think of him! Did you ever see 'L'après-midi d'un Faune'?"

"No, sir."

"Well, I've got an idea. 'L'après-midi d'une Dryade.' About the nude you really needn't mind. It's quite impersonal. Think of art, and fifteen bob a day. Shades of Nijinsky, I see the whole thing!"

All the time that he was talking his eyes were sliding off and on to her, and his pencil off and on to the paper. A sort of infection began to ferment within Victorine. Fifteen shillings a day! Blue butterflies!

There was a profound silence. His eyes and hand slid off and on. A faint smile had come on Victorine's face—she was adding up the money she might earn.

At last his eyes and hand ceased moving, and he stood looking at the paper.

"That's all for to-day, Miss Collins. I've got to think it out. Will you give me your address?"

Victorine thought rapidly.

"Please, sir, will you write to me at the post office. I don't want my husband to know that I'm—I'm——"

"Affiliated to art? Well! Name of post office?"

Victorine gave it and resumed her hat.

"An hour and a half, five shillings, thank you. And to-morrow, at half-past two, Miss Collins—not 'sir'."

"Yes, s—, thank you."

Waiting for her bus in the cold January air, the altogether appeared to Victorine improbable. To sit in front of a strange gentleman in her skin! If Tony knew! The slow flush again burned up the sallow in her cheeks. She climbed into the bus. But fifteen shillings! Six days a week—why, it would be four pound ten! In four months she could earn their passage out. Judging by the pictures in there, lots must be doing it. Tony must know nothing, not even that she was sitting for her face. He was all nerves, and that fond of her! He would imagine things; she had heard him say those artists were just like cats. But that gentleman had been very nice, though he did seem as if he were laughing at everything. She wished he had shown her the drawing. Perhaps she would see herself in an exhibition some day. But without—oh! And suddenly she thought: 'If I ate a bit more, I'd look nice like that, too!' And as if to escape from the daring of that thought, she stared up into the face opposite. It had two chins, was calm and smooth and pink, with light eyes staring back at her. People had thoughts, but you couldn't tell what they were! And the smile which Aubrey Greene desired crept out on his model's face.

## Chapter III

## MICHAEL WALKS AND TALKS

THE face Michael drew began by being Victorine's, and ended by being Fleur's. If physically Fleur stood up straight, was she morally as erect? This was the speculation for which he continually called himself a cad. He saw no change in her movements, and loyally refrained from enquiring into the movements he could not see. But his aroused attention made him more and more aware of a certain cynicism, as if she were continually registering the belief that all values were equal and none of much value.

Wilfrid, though still in London, was neither visible nor spoken of. "Out of sight and hearing, out of mind," seemed to be the motto. It did not work with Michael—Wilfrid was constantly in his mind. If Wilfrid were not seeing Fleur, how could he bear to stay within such tantalising reach of her? If Fleur did not want Wilfrid to stay, why had she not sent him away? He was finding it difficult, too, to conceal from others the fact that Desert and he were no longer pals. Often the impetus to go and have it out with him surged up and was beaten back. Either there was nothing beyond what he already knew, or there was something—and Wilfrid would say there wasn't. Michael accepted that without cavil; one did not give a woman away! But he wanted to hear no lies from a war comrade. Between Fleur and himself no word had passed; for words, he felt, would add no knowledge, merely imperil a hold weak enough already. Christmas at the ancestral manor of the Monts had been passed in covert-shooting. Fleur had come and stood with him at the last drive on the second day, holding Ting-a-ling on a lead. The Chinese dog had been exraordinarily excited, climbing the air every time a bird fell, and quite unaffected by the noise of guns. Michael, waiting to miss his birds—he was a poor shot—had watched her eager face emerging from grey fur, her

96

form braced back against Ting-a-ling. Shooting was new to her; and under the stimulus of novelty she was always at her best. He had loved even her "Oh, Michaels!" when he missed. She had been the success of the gathering, which meant seeing almost nothing of her except a sleepy head on a pillow; but, at least, down there he had not suffered from lurking uneasiness.

Putting a last touch to the bobbed hair on the blotting-paper, he got up. St. Paul's, that girl had said. He might stroll up and have a squint at Bicket. Something might occur to him. Tightening the belt of his blue overcoat round his waist, he sallied forth, thin and sprightly, with a little ache in his heart.

Walking east, on that bright, cheerful day, nothing struck him so much as the fact that he was alive, well, and in work. So very many were dead, ill, or out of a job. He entered Covent Garden Amazing place! A human nature which, decade after decade, could put up with Covent Garden was not in danger of extinction from its many ills. A comforting place—one needn't take anything too seriously after walking through it. On this square island were the vegetables of the earth and the fruits of the world, bounded on the west by publishing, on the east by opera, on the north and south by rivers of mankind. Among discharging carts and litter of paper, straw and men out of drawing, Michael walked and sniffed. Smell of its own, Covent Garden, earthy and just not rotten! He had never seen—even in the war—any place that so utterly lacked form. Extraordinarily English! Nobody looked as if they had anything to do with the soil—drivers, hangers-on, packers, and the salesmen inside the covered markets, seemed equally devoid of acquaintanceship with sun, wind, water, earth or air—town types all! And—Golly!—how their faces jutted, sloped, sagged and swelled, in every kind of featural disharmony. What was the English type amongst all this infinite variety of disproportion? There just wasn't one! He came on the fruits, glowing piles, still and bright—foreigners from the land of the sun—globes all the same size and colour. They made Michael's mouth water. 'Something in the sun,' he thought; 'there really is.' Look at Italy, at the Arabs, at Australia—the Australians came from England, and see the type now! Nevertheless—a Cockney for good temper! The more regular a person's form and features, the more selfish they were! Those grape-fruit looked horribly self-satisfied, compared with the potatoes!

He emerged still thinking about the English. Well! They were now one of the plainest and most distorted races of the world; and yet was there any race to compare with them for good temper and for 'guts'? And they needed those in their smoky towns, and their climate—remarkable instance of adaptation to environment, the modern English character! 'I could pick out an Englishman any-where,' he thought, 'and yet, physically, there's no general type now!' Astounding people! So ugly in the mass, yet growing such flowers of beauty, and such strange sprigs—like that little Mrs Bicket; so unimaginative in bulk, yet with such a blooming lot of poets! How would old Danby like it, by the way, when Wilfrid took his next volume to some other firm; or rather what should he—Wilfrid's particular friend!—say to old Danby? Aha! He knew what he should say:

"Yes, sir, but you should have let that poor blighter off who snooped the 'Copper Coins'. Desert hasn't forgotten your refusal." One for old Danby and his eternal in-the-rightness! 'Copper Coin' had done uncommonly well. Its successor would probably do un-commonly better. The book was a proof of what he—Michael— was always saying: The 'cockyolly-bird period' was passing. People wanted life again. Sibley, Walter Nazing, Linda—all those who had nothing to say except that they were superior to such as had—were already measured for their coffins. Not that they would know when they were in them; not blooming likely! They would continue to wave their noses and look down them!

'I'm fed-up with them,' thought Michael. 'If only Fleur would see that looking down your nose is a sure sign of inferiority!' And, suddenly, it came to him that she probably did. Wilfrid was the only one of the whole lot she had ever been thick with; the others were there because—well, because she was Fleur, and had the latest things about her. When, very soon, they were no longer the latest things, she would drop them. But Wilfrid she would not drop. No, he felt sure that she had not dropped, and would not drop Wilfrid.

He looked up. Ludgate Hill! "Near St. Paul's—sells balloons?" And there—sure enough—the poor beggar was!

Bicket was deflating with a view to going off his stand for a cup of cocoa. Remembering that he had come on him by accident, Michael stood for a moment preparing the tones of surprise. Pity the poor chap couldn't blow himself into one of those coloured shapes and float over St. Paul's to Peter. Mournful little cuss he looked, squeezing out the air! Memory tapped sharply on his mind. Balloon—in the square—November the first—joyful night! Special! Fleur! Perhaps they brought luck. He moved and said

98

in an astounded voice: "*You*, Bicket? Is this your stunt now?"

The large eyes of Bicket regarded him over a puce-coloured six-pennyworth.

"Mr. Mont! Often thought I'd like to see you again, sir."

"Same. here, Bicket. If you're not doing anything, come and have some lunch."

Bicket completed the globe's collapse, and, closing his tray-lid. said: "Reelly, sir?"

"Rather! I was just going into a fish place."

Bicket detached his tray.

"I'll leave this with the crossing-sweeper." He did so, and followed at Michael's side.

"Any money in it, Bicket?"

"Bare livin', sir."

"How about this place? We'll have oysters."

A little saliva at the corner of Bicket's mouth was removed by a pale tongue.

At a small table decorated with white oilcloth and a cruet stand, Michael sat down.

"Two dozen oysters, and all that; then two good soles, and a bottle of Chablis. Hurry up, please."

When the white-aproned fellow had gone about it, Bicket said simply:

"My Gawd!"

"Yes, it's a funny world, Bicket."

"It *is*, and that's a fact. This lunch'll cost you a pound, I shouldn't wonder. If I take twenty-five bob a week, it's all I do"

"You touch it there, Bicket. I eat my conscience every day."

Bicket shook his head.

"No, sir, if you've got money, spend it. I would. Be 'appy if you can—there yn't too many that are."

The white-aproned fellow began blessing them with oysters. He brought them fresh-opened, three at a time. Michael bearded them; Bicket swallowed them whole. Presently above twelve empty shells, he said:

"That's where the Socialists myke their mistyke, sir. Nothing keeps me going but the sight of other people spendin' money. It's what we might all come to with a bit of luck. Reduce the world to a level of a pound a dy—and it won't even run to that, they sy! It's not good enough, sir. I'd rather 'ave less with the 'ope of more. Take awy the gamble, and life's a frost. Here's luck!"

"Almost thou persuadest me to be a capitalist, Bicket."

A glow had come up in the thin and large-eyed face behind the greenish Chablis glass.

"I wish to Gawd I had my wife here, sir. I told you about her and the pneumonia. She's all right agyne now, only thin. She's the prize I drew. I don't want a world where you can't draw prizes. If it were all bloomin' conscientious an' accordin' to merit, I'd never have got her. See?"

'Me, too,' thought Michael, mentally drawing that face again.

"We've all got our dreams; mine's blue butterflies—Central Austrylia. The Socialists won't 'elp me to get there. Their ideas of 'eaven don't run beyond Europe."

"Cripes!" said Michael. "Melted butter, Bicket?"

"Thank you, sir."

Silence was not broken for some time, but the soles were.

"What made you think of balloons, Bicket?"

"You don't 'ave to advertise, they do it for you."

"Saw too much of advertising with us, eh?"

"Well, sir, I did use to read the wrappers. Astonished me, I will sy—the number of gryte books."

Michael ran his hands through his hair.

"Wrappers! The same young woman being kissed by the same young man with the same clean-cut jaw. But what can you do, Bicket? They *will have it.* I tried to make a break only this morning—I shall see what comes of it." 'And I hope *you* won't!' he thought: 'Fancy coming on Fleur outside a novel!'

"I did notice a tendency just before I left," said Bicket, "to 'ave cliffs or landskips and two sort of dolls sittin' on the sand or in the grass lookin' as if they didn't know what to do with each other."

"Yes," murmured Michael, "we tried that. It was supposed not to be vulgar. But we soon exhausted the public's capacity. What'll you have now—cheese?"

"Thank you, sir; I've had too much already, but I won't say 'No'."

"Two Stiltons," said Michael.

"How's Mr. Desert, sir?"

Michael reddened.

"Oh! He's all right."

Bicket had reddened also.

"I wish—I wish you'd let him know that it was quite a—an accident my pitchin' on his book. I've always regretted it."

"It's usually an accident, I think," said Michael slowly, "when we snoop other people's goods. We never *want* to."

# THE WHITE MONKEY

Bicket looked up.

"No, sir, I don't agree. 'Alf mankind's predytory—only, I'm not that sort, meself."

In Michael loyalty tried to stammer "Nor is he." He handed his cigarette-case to Bicket.

"Thank you, sir, I'm sure."

His eyes were swimming, and Michael thought: 'Dash it! This is sentimental. Kiss me good-bye and go!' He beckoned up the white-aproned fellow.

"Give us your address, Bicket. If integuments are any good to you, I might have some spare slops."

Bicket backed the bill with his address and said, hesitating: "I suppose, sir, Mrs. Mont wouldn't 'ave anything to spare. My wife's about my height."

"I expect she would. We'll send them along." He saw the 'little snipe's' lips quivering, and reached for his overcoat. "If anything blows in, I'll remember you. Good-bye, Bicket, and good luck."

Going east, because Bicket was going west, he repeated to himself the maxim: "Pity is tripe—pity is tripe!" Then getting on a bus, he was borne back past St. Paul's. Cautiously "taking a lunar" —as old Forsyte put it—he saw Bicket inflating a balloon; little was visible of his face or figure behind that rosy circumference. Nearing Blake Street, he developed an invincible repugnance to work, and was carried on to Trafalgar Square. Bicket had stirred him up. The world was sometimes almost unbearably jolly. Bicket, Wilfrid, and the Ruhr! "Feeling is tosh! Pity is tripe!" He descended from his bus, and passed the lions towards Pall Mall. Should he go into 'Snooks' and ask for Bart? No use—he would not find Fleur there. That was what he really wanted—to see Fleur in the daytime. But —where? She was everywhere to be found, and that was nowhere.

She was restless. Was that his fault? If he had been Wilfrid— would she be restless? 'Yes,' he thought stoutly, 'Wilfrid's restless, too.' They were all restless—all the people he knew. At least all the young ones—in life and in letters. Look at their novels! Hardly one in twenty had any repose, any of that quality which made one turn back to a book as a corner of refuge. They dashed and sputtered and skidded and rushed by like motor-cycles—violent, oh! and clever. How tired he was of cleverness! Sometimes he would take a manuscript home to Fleur for her opinion. He remembered her saying once: "This is exactly like life, Michael, it just rushes—it doesn't dwell on anything long enough to mean anything anywhere. Of course the author didn't mean it for satire,

101

but if you publish it, I advise you to put: 'This awful satire on modern life' outside the cover." And they had. At least, they had put: "This wonderful satire on modern life." Fleur *was* like that! She could see the hurry, but, like the author of the wonderful satire, she didn't know that she herself veered and hurried, or—did she know? Was she conscious of kicking at life, like a flame at air?

He had reached Piccadilly, and suddenly he remembered that he had not called on her aunt for ages. That was a possible draw. He bent his steps towards Green Street.

"Mrs. Dartie at home?"

"Yes, sir."

Michael moved his nostrils. Fleur used—but he could catch no scent, except incense. Winifred burnt joss-sticks when she remembered what a distinguished atmosphere they produced.

"What name?"

"Mr. Mont. My wife's not here, I suppose?"

"No, sir. Only Mrs. Val Dartie."

Mrs. Val Dartie! Yes, he remembered, nice woman—but not a substitute for Fleur! Committed, however, he followed the maid.

In the drawing-room Michael found three people, one of them his father-in-law, who had a grey and brooding aspect, and, from an Empire chair, was staring at blue Australian butterflies' wings under a glass on a round scarlet table. Winifred had jazzed the Empire foundations of her room with a superstructure more suitable to the age. She greeted Michael with fashionable warmth. It was good of him to come when he was so busy with all these young poets. "I thought 'Copper Coin'," she said—"what a *nice* title!—such an intriguing little book. I do think Mr. Desert is clever! What is he doing now?"

Michael said: "I don't know," and dropped on to a settee beside Mrs. Val. Ignorant of the Forsyte family feud, he was unable to appreciate the relief he had brought in with him. Soames said something about the French, got up, and went to the window; Winifred joined him—their voices sounded confidential.

"How is Fleur?" said Michael's neighbour.

"Thanks, awfully well."

"Do you like your house?"

"Oh, fearfully. Won't you come and see it?"

"I don't know whether Fleur would——?"

"Why not?"

"Oh! Well!"

"She's frightfully accessible."

She seemed to be looking at him with more interest than he deserved, to be trying to make something out from his face, and he added:

"You're a relation—by blood as well as marriage, aren't you?"

"Yes."

"Then what's the skeleton?"

"Oh! nothing. I'll certainly come. Only—she has so many friends."

Michael thought: 'I like this woman!' "As a matter of fact," he said, "I came here this afternoon thinking I might find Fleur. I should like her to know you. With all the jazz there is about, she'd appreciate somebody restful.'

"Thank you."

"You've never lived in London?"

"Not since I was six."

"I wish she could get a rest—pity there isn't a d-desert handy." He had stuttered; the word was not pronounced the same—still! He glanced, disconcerted, at the butterflies. "I've just been talking to a little Cockney whose S.O.S. is 'Central Austrylia'. But what do you say—Have we got souls to save?"

"I used to think so, but now I'm not so sure—something's struck me lately."

"What was that?"

"Well, I notice that anyone at all out of proportion, or whose nose is on one side, or whose eyes jut out, or even have a special shining look, always believes in the soul; people who are in proportion, and have no prominent physical features, don't seem to be really interested."

Michael's ears moved.

"By Jove!" he said; "some thought! Fleur's beautifully proportioned—*she* doesn't seem to worry. I'm not—and I certainly do. The people in Covent Garden must have lots of soul. You think 'the soul's' the result of loose-gearing in the organism—sort of special consciousness from not working in one piece."

"Yes, rather like that—what's called psychic power is, I'm almost sure."

"I say, is your life safe? According to your theory, though, we're in a mighty soulful era. I must think over my family. How about yours?"

"The Forsytes! Oh, they're quite too well-proportioned."

"I agree, they haven't any special juts so far as I've seen. The French, too, are awfully close-knit. It really is an idea, only, of course, most people see it the other way. They'd say the soul produces the disproportion, makes the eyes shine, bends the nose, and all that; where the soul is small, it's not trying to get out of the body, whence the barber's block. I'll think about it. Thanks for the tip. Well, do come and see us. Good-bye! I don't think I'll disturb them in the window. Would you mind saying I had to scoot?" Squeezing a slim, gloved hand, receiving and returning a smiling look, he slid out, thinking: 'Dash the soul, where's her body?'

### Chapter IV

### FLEUR'S BODY

FLEUR'S body, indeed, was at the moment in one of those difficult positions which continually threaten the spirit of compromise. It was in fact in Wilfrid's arms; sufficiently, at least, to make her say:

"No, Wilfrid—you promised to be good."

It was a really remarkable tribute to her powers of skating on thin ice that the word 'good' should still have significance. For eleven weeks exactly this young man had danced on the edge of fulfilment, and was even now divided from her by two clenched hands pressed firmly against his chest, and the word 'good'; and this after not having seen her for a fortnight.

When she said it, he let her go, with a sort of violence, and sat down on a piece of junk. Only the sense of damnable iteration prevented him from saying: "It can't go on, Fleur." She knew that! And yet it did! This was what perpetually amazed him. How a poor brute could hang on week after week saying to her and to himself: "Now or never!" when it wasn't either? Subconsciousness, that, until the word 'now' had been reached, Fleur would not know her own mind, alone had kept him dancing. His own feelings were so intense that he almost hated her for indecision. And he was unjust. It was not exactly indecision. Fleur wanted the added richness and excitement which Wilfrid's affection gave to life, but without danger and without loss. How natural! His frightful passionateness was making all the trouble. Neither by her wish, nor through her fault, was he passionate! And yet—it was both nice and proper to inspire passion; and, of course, she had the lurking sense that she was not 'in the mode' to cavil at a lover, especially since life owed her one.

Released, she smoothed herself and said: "Talk of something sensible; what have you been writing?"

"This."

Fleur read. Flushing and biting her lips, she said:

"It's frightfully bitter."

"It's frightfully true. Does *he* ever ask you now whether you see me?"

"Never."

"Why?"

"I don't know."

"What would you answer if he did?"

Fleur shrugged her shoulders.

Desert said quietly: "Yes, that's your attitude. It can't last, Fleur." He was standing by the window. She put the sheets down on his desk and moved towards him. Poor Wilfrid! Now that he was quiet she was sorry.

He said suddenly: "Stop! Don't move! *He's* down there in the street."

Recoiling, she gasped: "Michael! Oh! But how—how could he have known?"

Desert said grimly: "Do you only know him as little as that? Do you suppose he'd be there if he knew you were here?"

Fleur winced.

"Why *is* he there, then?"

"He probably wants to see me. He looks as if he couldn't make up his mind. Don't get the wind up, he won't be let in."

Fleur sat down; she felt weak in the legs. The ice seemed suddenly of an appalling thinness—the water appallingly cold.

"Has he seen you?" she said.

"No."

The thought flashed through him: 'If I were a blackguard, I could force her hand, by moving one step and crooking my finger.' Pity one wasn't a blackguard—at all events, not to that point—things would be so much simpler!

"Where is he now?" asked Fleur.

"Going away."

In profound relief, she sighed out:

"But it's queer, isn't it, Wilfrid?"

"You don't suppose he's easy in his mind, do you?"

Fleur bit her lips. He was jeering, because she didn't or couldn't really love either of them. It was unjust. She *could* have loved— she *had* loved! Wilfrid and Michael—they might go to the deuce!

105

"I wish I had never come here," she said suddenly: "and I'll never come again!"

He went to the door, and held it open.

"You are right."

Fleur stood quite still, her chin on the collar of her fur, her clear-glancing eyes fixed on his face, her lips set and mutinous.

"You think I'm a heartless beast," she said slowly. "So I am—now. Good-bye!"

He neither took her hand nor spoke, he only bowed. His eyes were very tragic. Trembling with mortification, Fleur went out. She heard the door closed, while she was going down the stairs. At the bottom she stood uncertain. Suppose Michael had come back! Almost opposite was that gallery where she had first met him and —Jon. Slip across in there! If he were still hovering round the entrance of the little street, she could tell him with a good con-science where she had been. She peeped. Not in sight! Swiftly she slid across into the doorway opposite. They would be closing in a minute—just on four o'clock! She put down a shilling and slipped in. She must see—in case! She stood revolving—one-man show, the man—Claud Brains! She put down another shilling for a cata-logue, and read as she went out. "No. 7. Woman getting the wind up." It told her everything; and with a lighter heart she skimmed along, and took a taxi. Get home before Michael! She felt relieved, almost exhilarated. So much for skating on thin ice! It wasn't good enough. Wilfrid must go. Poor Wilfrid! Well, he shouldn't have sneered—what did he know of her? Nobody knew anything of her! She was alone in the world. She slipped her latchkey into the hall door. No Michael. She sat down in the drawing-room before the fire, and took up Walter Nazing's last. She read a page three times. It meant no more with every reading—it meant less; he was the kind of author who must be read at a gallop, and given away lest a first impression of wind in the hair be lost in a sensation of wind lower down; but Wilfrid's eyes came between her and the words. Pity! Nobody pitied her; why, then, should she pity them? Besides, pity was 'pop', as Amabel would say. The situation demanded cast-iron sense. But Wilfrid's eyes! Well—she wouldn't be seeing them again! Beautiful eyes when they smiled or when—so much more often—they looked at her with longing, as now between her and the sentence: "Solemnly and with a delicious egoism he more than awfully desired her who snug and rosy in the pink shell of her involuted and so petulant social periphrasis——" Poor Wilfrid! Pity was 'pop', but there was pride! Did she choose that he should go away thinking that she had 'played him up' just out of vanity, as Walter Nazing said American women did? Did she? Would it not be more in the mode, really dramatic—if one 'went over the deep end', as they said, just once? Would that not be something they could both look back on—he in the East he was always talking of, she in this West? The proposition had a momentary popularity in that organism called Fleur. too finely proportioned for a soul according to the theory which Michael was thinking over. Like all popularities, it did not last. First: Would she like it? She did not think she would; one man, without love. was quite enough. Then there was the danger of passing into Wilfrid's power. He was a gentleman, but he was passionate; the cup once sippèd, would he consent to put it down? But more than all was a physical doubt of the last two or three weeks which awaited verification, and which made her feel solemn. She stood up and passed her hands all over her, with a definite recoil from the thought of Wilfrid's hands doing the same. No! To have his friendship, his admiration, but not at that price. She viewed him suddenly, as a bomb set on her copper floor; and in fancy ran and seized and flung him out into the Square —poor Wilfrid! Pity was 'pop'! But one might be sorry for *oneself*. losing him; losing too that ideal of modern womanhood expounded to her one evening by Marjorie Ferrar, pet of the 'panjoys', whose red-gold hair excited so much admiration: "My ambition—old thing—is to be the perfect wife of one man, the perfect mistress of another, and the perfect mother of a third, all at once. It's perfectly possible—they do it in France."

But was it really so perfectly possible—even if pity *was* posh? How be perfect to Michael, when the slightest slip might reveal to him that she was being perfect to Wilfrid; how be perfect to Wilfrid, when every time she was perfect to Michael would be a dagger in Wilfrid's heart? And if—if her physical doubt should mature into certainty, how be perfect mother to the certainty. when she was either torturing two men, or lying to them like a trooperess? Not so perfectly possible as all that! 'If only I were all French!' thought Fleur. . . .

The clicking door startled her—the reason that she was not all French was coming in. He looked very grey, as if he had been thinking too much. He kissed her, and sat down moodily before the fire.

"Have you come for the night, Dad?"

"If I may," murmured Soames. "Business."

"Anything unpleasant. ducky?"

107

Soames looked up as if startled.

"Unpleasant? Why should it be unpleasant?"

"I only thought from your face."

Soames grunted. "This Ruhr!" he said. "I've brought you a picture. Chinese!"

"Oh, Dad! How jolly!"

"It isn't," said Soames; "it's a monkey eating fruit."

"But that's perfect! Where is it—in the hall?"

Soames nodded.

Stripping the coverings off the picture, Fleur brought it in, and setting it up on the jade-green settee, stood away and looked at it. The large white monkey with its brown haunting eyes, as if she had suddenly wrested its interest from the orange-like fruit in its crisped paw, the grey background, the empty rinds all round— bright splashes in a general ghostliness of colour, impressed her at once.

"But, Dad, it's a masterpiece—I'm sure it's of a frightfully good period."

"I don't know," said Soames. "I must look up the Chinese."

"But you oughtn't to give it to me, it must be worth any amount. You ought to have it in your collection."

"They didn't know its value," said Soames, and a faint smile illumined his features. "I gave three hundred for it. It'll be safer here."

"Of course it'll be safe. Only why safer?"

Soames turned towards the picture.

"I can't tell. Anything may come of this."

"Of what, dear?"

"Is 'old Mont' coming in to-night?"

"No, he's at Lippinghall still."

"Well, it doesn't matter—he's no good."

Fleur took his hand and gave it a squeeze.

"Tell me!"

Soames's tickled heart quivered. Fancy her wanting to know what was troubling him! But his sense of the becoming, and his fear of giving away his own alarm, forbade response.

"Nothing you'd understand," he said. "Where are you going to hang it?"

"There, I think; but we must wait for Michael."

Soames grumbled out:

"I saw him just now at your aunt's. Is that the way he attends to business?"

## THE WHITE MONKEY

'Perhaps,' thought Fleur, 'he was only on his way back to the office. Cork Street *is* more or less between! If he passed the end of it, he would think of Wilfrid, he might have been wanting to see him about books.'

"Oh, here's Ting! Well, darling!"

The Chinese dog, let in, as it were, by Providence, seeing Soames, sat down suddenly with snub upturned eyes brilliant. "The expression of your face," he seemed to say, "pleases me. We belong to the past and could sing hymns together, old man."

"Funny little chap," said Soames: "he always knows me."

Fleur lifted him. "Come and see the new monkey, ducky."

"Don't let him lick it."

Held rather firmly by his jade-green collar and confronted by an inexplicable piece of silk smelling of the past, Ting-a-ling raised his head higher and higher to correspond with the action of his nostrils, and his little tongue appeared, tentatively savouring the emanation of his country.

"It's a nice monkey, isn't it, darling?"

"No," said Ting-a-ling, rather clearly. "Put me down!"

Restored to the floor, he sought a patch where the copper came through between two rugs, and licked it quietly.

"Mr. Aubrey Greene, ma'am!"

"H'm!" said Soames.

The painter came gliding and glowing in; his bright hair slipping back, his green eyes sliding off.

"Ah!" he said, pointing to the floor. "That's what I've come about."

Fleur followed his finger in amazement.

"Ting!" she said severely, "stop it! He will lick the copper, Aubrey."

"But how perfectly Chinese! They do everything we don't."

"Dad—Aubrey Greene. My father's just brought me this picture, Aubrey—isn't it a gem?"

The painter stood quite still, his eyes ceased sliding off, his hair ceased slipping back.

"Phew!" he said.

Soames rose. He had waited for the flippant; but he recognised in the tone something reverential, if not aghast.

"By George," said Aubrey Greene, "those eyes! Where did you pick it up, sir?"

"It belonged to a cousin of mine—a racing man. It was his only picture."

109

"Good for him! He must have had taste."

Soames stared. The idea that George should have had taste almost appalled him.

"No," he said, with a flash of inspiration: "What he liked about it was that it makes you feel uncomfortable."

"Same thing! I don't know where I've seen a more pungent satire on human life."

"I don't follow," said Soames dryly.

"Why, it's a perfect allegory, sir! Eat the fruits of life, scatter the rinds, and get copped doing it. When they're still, a monkey's eyes are the human tragedy incarnate. Look at them! He thinks there's something beyond, and he's sad or angry because he can't get at it. That picture ought to be in the British Museum, sir, with the label: 'Civilisation, caught out.'"

"Well, it won't be," said Fleur. "It'll be here, labelled 'The White Monkey.'"

"Same thing."

"Cynicism," said Soames abruptly, "gets you nowhere. If you'd said 'Modernity caught out'——"

"I do, sir; but why be narrow? You don't seriously suppose this age is worse than any other?"

"Don't I?" said Soames. "In my belief the world reached its highest point in the 'eighties, and will never reach it again."

The painter stared.

"That's frightfully interesting. I wasn't born, and I suppose you were about my age then, sir. You believed in God and drove in diligences."

Diligences! The word awakened in Soames a memory which somehow seemed appropriate.

"Yes," he said, "and I can tell you a story of those days that you can't match in these. When I was a youngster in Switzerland with my people, two of my sisters had some black cherries. When they'd eaten about half a dozen they discovered that they all had little maggots in them. An English climber there saw how upset they were, and ate the whole of the rest of the cherries—about two pounds—maggots, stones and all, just to show them. That was the sort of men they were then."

"Oh! Father!"

"Gee! He must have been gone on them."

"No," said Soames, "not particularly. His name was Powley; he wore side whiskers."

"Talking of God and diligences: I saw a hansom yesterday."

110

'More to the point if you'd seen God, thought Soames, but he did not say so; indeed, the thought surprised him, it was not the sort of thing he had ever seen himself.

"You mayn't know it, sir, but there's more belief now than there was before the war—they've discovered that we're not all body."

"Oh!" said Fleur. "That reminds me, Aubrey. Do you know any mediums? Could I get one to come here? On our floor, with Michael outside the door, one would know there couldn't be any hanky. Do the dark *séance* people ever go out?—they're much more thrilling they say."

"Spiritualism!" said Soames. "H'mph!" He could not in half an hour have expressed himself more clearly.

Aubrey Greene's eyes slid off to Ting-a-ling. "I'll see what I can do, if you'll lend me your Peke for an hour or so to-morrow after-noon. I'd bring him back on a lead, and give him every luxury.'

"What do you want him for?"

"Michael sent me a most topping little model to-day. But, you see, she can't smile."

"Michael?"

"Yes. Something quite new; and I've got a scheme. Her smile's like sunlight going off an Italian valley; but when you tell her to, she can't. I thought your Peke could make her, perhaps."

"May I come and see?" said Fleur.

"Yes, bring him to-morrow; but, if I can persuade her, it'll be in the 'altogether'."

"Oh! Will you get me a *séance*, if I lend you Ting?"

"I will."

"H'mph!" said Soames again. *Séances*, Italian sunlight, the 'altogether'! It was time he got back to Elderson, and what was to be done now, and left this fiddling while Rome burned.

"Good-bye, Mr. Greene," he said; "I've got no time."

"Quite, sir," said Aubrey Greene.

"Quite!" mimicked Soames to himself, going out.

Aubrey Greene took his departure a few minutes later, crossing a lady in the hall who was delivering her name to the manservant.

Alone with her body, Fleur again passed her hands all over it. The 'altogether'—was a reminder of the dangers of dramatic conduct.

## Chapter V

## FLEUR'S SOUL

"MRS. VAL DARTIE, ma'am."

A name which could not be distorted even by Coaker affected her like a finger applied suddenly to the head of the sciatic nerve. Holly! Not seen since the day when she did not marry Jon. Holly! A flood of remembrance—Wansdon, the Downs, the gravel pit, the apple orchard, the river, the copse at Robin Hill! No! it was not a pleasant sensation—to see Holly, and she said: "How awfully nice of you to come!"

"I met your husband this afternoon at Green Street; he asked me. What a lovely room!"

"Ting! Come and be introduced! This is Ting-a-ling; isn't he perfect? He's a little upset because of the new monkey. How's Val, and dear Wansdon? It was too wonderfully peaceful."

"It's a nice backwater. I don't get tired of it."

"And——" said Fleur, with a little laugh, "Jon?"

"He's growing peaches in North Carolina. British Columbia didn't do."

"Oh! Is he married?"

"No."

"I suppose he'll marry an American."

"He isn't twenty-two, you know."

"Good Lord!" said Fleur: "Am I only twenty-one? I feel forty-eight."

"That's living in the middle of things and seeing so many people——"

"And getting to know none."

"But don't you?"

"No, it isn't done. I mean we all call each other by our Christian names; but *après*——"

"I like your husband very much."

"Oh! yes, Michael's a dear. How's June?"

"I saw her yesterday—she's got a new painter, of course—Claud Brains. I believe he's what they call a Vertiginist."

Fleur bit her lip.

"Yes, they're quite common. I suppose June thinks he's the only one."

"Well, she thinks he's a genius."

"She's wonderful."

"Yes," said Holly, "the most loyal creature in the world while it lasts. It's like poultry farming—once they're hatched. You never saw Boris Strumolowski?"

"No."

"Well, don't."

"I know his bust of Michael's uncle. It's rather sane."

"Yes. June thought it a pot-boiler, and he never forgave her. Of course it was. As soon as her swan makes money, she looks round for another. She's a darling."

"Yes," murmured Fleur; "I liked June."

Another flood of remembrance—from a tea-shop, from the river, from June's little dining-room, from where in Green Street she had changed her wedding dress under the upward gaze of June's blue eyes. She seized the monkey and held it up.

"Isn't it a picture of 'life'?" Would she have said that if Aubrey Greene hadn't? Still it seemed very true at the moment.

"Poor monkey!" said Holly. "I'm always frightfully sorry for monkeys. But it's marvellous, I think."

"Yes. I'm going to hang it here. If I can get one more I shall have done in this room; only people have so got on to Chinese things. This was luck—somebody died—George Forsyte, you know, the racing one."

"Oh!" said Holly softly. She saw again her old kinsman's japing eyes in the church when Fleur was being married, heard his throaty whisper: "Will she stay the course?" And was she staying it, this pretty filly? "Wish she could get a rest. If only there were a desert handy!" Well, one couldn't ask a question so personal, and Holly took refuge in a general remark.

"What do all you smart young people feel about life, nowadays, Fleur? When one's not of it and has lived twenty years in South Africa, one still feels out of it."

"Life! Oh! well, we know it's supposed to be a riddle, but we've given it up. We just want to have a good time because we don't believe anything can last. But I don't think we know how to have it. We just fly on, and hope for it. Of course, there's art, but most of us aren't artists; besides, expressionism—Michael says it's got no inside. We gas about it, but I suppose it hasn't. I see a frightful lot of writers and painters, you know; they're supposed to be amusing."

Holly listened, amazed. Who would have thought that this girl *saw*? She might be seeing wrong, but anyway she saw!

113

"Surely," she said, "you enjoy yourselves?"

"Well, I like getting hold of nice things, and interesting people; I like seeing everything that's new and worth while, or seems so at the moment. But that's just how it is—nothing lasts. You see, I'm not of the 'Pan-joys', nor of the 'new-faithfuls'."

"The new-faithfuls?"

"Oh! don't you know—it's a sort of faith-healing done on oneself, not exactly the old 'God-good, good-God!' sort; but a kind of mixture of will-power, psycho-analysis, and belief that everything will be all right on the night if you say it will. You must have come across them. They're frightfully in earnest."

"I know," said Holly; "their eyes shine."

"I dare say. I don't believe in them—I don't believe in anyone; or anything—much. How can one?"

"How about simple people, and hard work?"

Fleur sighed. "I dare say. I will say for Michael—*he's* not spoiled. Let's have tea? Tea, Ting?" and, turning up the lights, she rang the bell.

When her unexpected visitor had gone, she sat very still before the fire. To-day, when she had been so very nearly Wilfrid's! So Jon was not married! Not that it made any odds! Things did not come round as they were expected to in books. And anyway sentiment was swosh! Cut it out! She tossed back her hair; and, getting hammer and nail, proceeded to hang the white monkey. Between the two tea-chests with their coloured pearl-shell figures, he would look his best. Since she couldn't have Jon, what did it matter—Wilfrid or Michael, or both, or neither? Eat the orange in her hand, and throw away the rind! And suddenly she became aware that Michael was in the room. He had come in very quietly and was standing before the fire behind her. She gave him a quick look and said:

"I've had Aubrey Greene here about a model you sent him, and Holly—Mrs. Val Dartie—she said she's seen you. Oh! and father's brought us this. Isn't it perfect?"

Michael did not speak.

"Anything the matter, Michael?"

"No, nothing." He went up to the monkey. From behind him now Fleur searched his profile. Instinct told her of a change. Had he, after all, seen her going to Wilfrid's—coming away?

"Some monkey!" he said. "By the way, have you any spare clothes you could give the wife of a poor snipe—nothing too swell?"

114

She answered mechanically: "Yes, of course!" while her brain vorked furiously.

"Would you put them out, then? I'm going to make up a bunch or him myself—they could go together."

Yes! He was quite unlike himself, as if the spring in him had un down. A sort of *malaise* overcame her. Michael not cheerful! t was like the fire going out on a cold day. And, perhaps for the rst time, she was conscious that his cheerfulness was of real importance to her. She watched him pick up Ting-a-ling and sit down. And going up behind him, she bent over till her hair was against his cheek. Instead of rubbing his cheek on hers, he sat quite still, and her heart misgave her.

"What is it?" she said, coaxing.

"Nothing!"

She took hold of his ears.

"But there is. I suppose you know somehow that I went to see Wilfrid."

He said stonily: "Why not?"

She let go, and stood up straight.

"It was only to tell him that I couldn't see him again."

That half-truth seemed to her the whole.

He suddenly looked up, a quiver went over his face; he took her hand.

"It's all right, Fleur. You must do what you like, you know. That's only fair. I had too much lunch."

Fleur withdrew to the middle of the room.

"You're rather an angel," she said slowly, and went out.

Upstairs she looked out garments, confused in her soul.

## Chapter VI

### MICHAEL GETS 'WHAT-FOR'

AFTER his Green Street quest Michael had wavered back down Piccadilly, and, obeying one of those impulses which make people hang around the centres of disturbance, on to Cork Street. He stood for a minute at the mouth of Wilfrid's backwater.

'No,' he thought at last, 'ten to one he isn't in; and if he is, twenty to one that I get any change except bad change!'

He was moving slowly on to Bond Street, when a little light lady, coming from the backwater, and reading as she went, ran into him from behind.

"Why don't you look where you're going! Oh! You? Aren't you the young man who married Fleur Forsyte? I'm her cousin, June. I thought I saw her just now." She waved a hand which held a catalogue with a gesture like the flirt of a bird's wing. "Opposite my gallery. She went into a house, or I should have spoken to her—I'd like to have seen her again."

Into a house! Michael dived for his cigarette-case. Hard-grasping it, he looked up. The little lady's blue eyes were sweeping from side to side of his face with a searching candour.

"Are you happy together?" she said.

A cold sweat broke out on his forehead. A sense of general derangement afflicted him—hers, and his own.

"I beg your pardon?" he gasped.

"I hope you are. She ought to have married my little brother—but I hope you are. She's a pretty child."

In the midst of a dull sense of stunning blows, it staggered him that she seemed quite unconscious of inflicting them. He heard his teeth gritting, and said dully: "Your little brother, who was he?"

"What! Jon—didn't you know Jon? He was too young, of course, and so was she. But they were head over—the family feud stopped that. Well! it's all past. I was at your wedding. I hope you're happy. Have you seen the Claud Brains show at my gallery? He's a genius. I was going to have a bun in here; will you join me? You ought to know his work."

She had paused at the door of a confectioner's. Michael put his hand on his chest.

"Thank you," he said, "I have just had a bun—two, in fact. Excuse me!"

The little lady grasped his other hand.

"Well, good-bye, young man! Glad to have met you. You're not a beauty, but I like your face. Remember me to that child. You should go and see Claud Brains. He's a real genius."

Stock-still before the door, he watched her turn and enter, with a scattered motion, as of flying, and a disturbance among those seated in the pastry-cook's. Then he moved on, the cigarette unlighted in his mouth, dazed, as a boxer from a blow which knocks him sideways, and another which knocks him straight again.

Fleur visiting Wilfrid—at this moment in his rooms up there—in his arms, perhaps! He groaned. A well-fed young man in a new hat skipped at the sound. Never! He could never stick that! He would have to clear out! He had believed Fleur honest! A double life! The night before last she had smiled on him. Oh! God! He dashed across into Green Park. Why hadn't he stood still and let something go over him? And that lunatic's little brother—John— family feud? Himself—a *pis aller*, then—taken without love at all—a makeshift! He remembered now her saying one night at Mapledurham: "Come again when I know I can't get my wish." So that was the wish she couldn't get! A makeshift! 'Jolly,' he thought: 'Oh! jolly!' No wonder, then! What could she care? One man or another! Poor little devil! She had never let him know—never breathed a word! Was that decent of her—or was it treachery? 'No,' he thought, 'if she *had* told me, it wouldn't have made any difference—I'd have taken her at any price. It was decent of her not to tell me.' But how was it he hadn't heard from someone? Family feud? The Forsytes! Except 'Old Forsyte', he never saw them; and 'Old Forsyte' was closer than a fish. Well! he had got what-for! And again he groaned, in the twilight spaces of the Park. Buckingham Palace loomed up unlighted, huge and dreary. Conscious of his cigarette at last, he stopped to strike a match, and drew the smoke deep into his lungs with the first faint sense of comfort.

"You couldn't spare us a cigarette, Mister?"

A shadowy figure with a decent sad face stood beside the statue of Australia, so depressingly abundant!

"Of course!" said Michael; "take the lot." He emptied the case into the man's hand. "Take the case too—'present from West- minster'—you'll get thirty bob for it. Good luck!" He hurried on. A faint: "Hi, Mister!" pursued him unavailingly. Pity was pulp! Sentiment was bilge! Was he going home to wait till Fleur had—finished and come back? Not he! He turned towards Chelsea, batting along as hard as he could stride. Lighted shops, gloomy great Eaton Square, Chester Square, Sloane Square, the King's Road—along, along! Worse than the trenches—far worse— this whipped and scorpioned sexual jealousy! Yes, and he would have felt even worse, but for that second blow. It made it less painful to know that Fleur had been in love with that cousin, and Wilfrid, too, perhaps, nothing to her. Poor little wretch! Well, what's the game now?' he thought. The game of life—in bad weather, in stress? What was it? In the war—what had a fellow done? Somehow managed to feel himself not so dashed important; reached a condition of acquiescence, fatalism, "Who dies if England live" sort of sob-stuff state. The game of life? Was it different? "Bloody but unbowed" might be tripe; still—get up when you were knocked down! The whole was big, oneself was

117

little! Passion, jealousy, ought they properly to destroy one's sportsmanship, as Nazing and Sibley and Linda Frewe would have it? Was the word 'gentleman' a dud? Was it? Did one keep one's form, or get down to squealing and kicking in the stomach?

'I don't know,' he thought, 'I don't know what I shall do when I see her—I simply don't know.' Steel-blue of the fallen evening, bare plane trees, wide river, frosty air! He turned towards home. He opened his front door, trembling, and trembling, went into the drawing-room. . . .

When Fleur had gone upstairs and left him with Ting-a-ling he didn't know whether he believed her or not. If she had kept that other thing from him all this time, she could keep anything! Had she understood his words: "You must do as you like, that's only fair?" He had said them almost mechanically, but they were reasonable. If she had never loved him, even a little, he had never had any right to expect anything; he had been all the time in the position of one to whom she was giving alms. Nothing compelled a person to go on giving alms. And nothing compelled one to go on taking them—except—the ache of want, the ache, the ache!

"You little Djinn! You lucky little toad! Give me some of your complacency—you Chinese atom!" Ting-a-ling turned up his boot-buttons. "When you have been civilised as long as I," they seemed to say: "In the meantime, scratch my chest."

And scrattling in that yellow fur Michael thought: 'Pull yourself together! Man at the South Pole with the first blizzard doesn't sing: "Want to go home! Want to go home!"—he sticks it. Come, get going!' He placed Ting-a-ling on the floor, and made for his study. Here were manuscripts, of which the readers to Danby and Winter had already said: "No money in this, but a genuine piece of work meriting consideration." It was Michael's business to give the consideration; Danby's to turn the affair down with the words: "Write him (or her) a civil letter, say we were greatly interested, regret we do not see our way—hope to have the privilege of considering next effort, and so forth. What!"

He turned up his reading-lamp and pulled out a manuscript he had already begun.

> "No retreat, no retreat; they must conquer or die who have
>     no retreat;
>   No retreat, no retreat; they must conquer or die who have
>     no retreat!"

The black footmen's refrain from 'Polly' was all that happened in his mind. Dash it! He must read the thing! Somehow he finished the chapter. He remembered now. The manuscript was all about a man who, when he was a boy, had been so greatly impressed by the sight of a maidservant changing her clothes in a room over the way, that his married life was a continual struggle not to be unfaithful with his wife's maids. They had just discovered his complex, and he was going to have it out. The rest of the manuscript no doubt would show how that was done. It went most conscientiously into all those precise bodily details which it was now so timorous and Victorian to leave out. Genuine piece of work, and waste of time to go on with it! Old Danby—Freud bored him stiff; and for once Michael did not mind old Danby being in the right. He put the thing back into the drawer. Seven o'clock! Tell Fleur what he had been told about that cousin? Why? Nothing could mend *that!* If only she were speaking the truth about Wilfrid! He went to the window—stars above, and stripes below, stripes of courtyard and back garden. "No retreat, no retreat; they must conquer or die who have no retreat!"

A voice said:

"When will your father be up?"

Old Forsyte! Lord! Lord!

"To-morrow, I believe, sir. Come in! You don't know my den. I think."

"No," said Soames. "Snug! Caricatures. You go in for them— poor stuff!"

"But not modern, sir—a revived art."

"Queering your neighbours—I never cared for them. They only flourish when the world's in a mess and people have given up looking straight before them."

"By Jove!" said Michael; "that's good. Won't you sit down, sir?"

Soames sat down, crossing his knees in his accustomed manner. Slim, grey, close—a sealed book, neatly bound! What was *his* complex? Whatever it was, he had never had it out. One could not even imagine the operation.

"I shan't take away my Goya," he said very unexpectedly; "consider it Fleur's. In fact, if I only knew you were interested in the future, I should make more provision. In my opinion death duties will be prohibitive in a few years' time."

Michael frowned. "I'd like you to know, sir, once for all, that what you do for Fleur, you do for Fleur. I can be Epicurus whenever I like—bread, and on feast days a little bit of cheese."

119

Soames looked up with shrewdness in his glance. "I know that," he said, "I always knew it."

Michael bowed.

"With this land depression your father's hard hit, I should think."

"Well, he talks of being on the look-out for soap or cars; but I shouldn't be surprised if he mortgages again and lingers on."

"A title without a place," said Soames, "is not natural. He'd better wait for me to go, if I leave anything, that is. But listen to me: I've been thinking. Aren't you happy together, you two, that you don't have children?"

Michael hesitated.

"I don't think," he said slowly, "that we have ever had a scrap, or anything like it. I have been—I am—terribly fond of her, but you have known better than I that I only picked up the pieces."

"Who told you that?"

"To-day—Miss June Forsyte."

"*That* woman!" said Soames. "She can't keep her foot out of anything. A boy and girl affair—over months before you married."

"But deep, sir," said Michael gently.

"Deep—who knows at that age? Deep?" Soames paused: "You're a good fellow—I always knew. Be patient—take a long view."

"Yes, sir," said Michael, very still in his chair, "if I can."

"She's everything to me," muttered Soames abruptly.

"And to me—which doesn't make it easier."

The line between Soames's brows deepened.

"Perhaps not. But hold on! As gently as you like, but hold on! She's young. She'll flutter about; there's nothing in it."

'Does he know about the other thing?' thought Michael.

"I have my own worries," went on Soames, "but they're nothing to what I should feel if anything went wrong with her."

Michael felt a twinge of sympathy, unusual towards that self-contained grey figure.

"I shall try my best," he said quietly; "but I'm not naturally Solomon at six stone seven."

"I'm not so sure," said Soames, "I'm not so sure. Anyway, a child—well, a child would be—a—sort of insur——" He baulked, the word was not precisely——!

Michael froze.

"As to that, I can't say anything."

Soames got up.

120

THE WHITE MONKEY

"No," he said wistfully, "I suppose not. It's time to dress."

To dress—to dine, and if to dine, to sleep—to sleep, to dream! And then what dreams might come!

On the way to his dressing-room Michael encountered Coaker; the man's face was long.

"What's up, Coaker?"

"The little dog, sir, has been sick in the drawing-room."

"The deuce he has!"

"Yes, sir; it appears that someone left him there alone. He makes himself felt, sir. I always say: He's an important little dog. . . ."

During dinner, as if visited by remorse for having given them advice and two pictures worth some thousands of pounds, Soames pitched a tale like those of James in his palmy days. He spoke of the French—the fall of the mark—the rise in Consols—the obstinacy of Dumetrius, the picture-dealer, over a Constable skyscape which Soames wanted and Dumetrius did not, but to which the fellow held on just for the sake of a price which Soames did not mean to pay. He spoke of the trouble which he foresaw with the United States over their precious Prohibition. They were a headstrong lot. They took up a thing and ran their heads against a stone wall. He himself had never drunk anything to speak of, but he liked to feel that he could. The Americans liked to feel that he couldn't, that was tyranny. They were overbearing. He shouldn't be surprised if everybody took to drinking over there. As to the League of Nations, a man that morning had palavered it up. That cock wouldn't fight—spend money, and arrange things which would have arranged themselves, but as for anything important, such as abolishing Bolshevism, or poison gas, they never would, and to pretend it was all-me-eye-and-Betty-Martin. It was almost a record for one habitually taciturn, and deeply useful to two young people only anxious that he should continue to talk, so that they might think of other things. The conduct of Ting-a-ling was the sole other subject of consideration. Fleur thought it due to the copper floor. Soames that he must have picked up something in the Square— dogs were always picking things up. Michael suggested that it was just Chinese—a protest against there being nobody to watch his self-sufficiency. In China there were four hundred million people to watch each other being self-sufficient. What would one expect of a Chinaman suddenly placed in the Gobi Desert? He would certainly be sick.

"No retreat, no retreat; they must conquer or die who have no retreat!"

121

When Fleur left them, both felt that they could not so soon again bear each other's company, and Soames said:

"I've got some figures to attend to—I'll go to my room."

Michael stood up. "Wouldn't you like my den, sir?"

"No," said Soames, "I must concentrate. Say good-night to Fleur for me."

Michael remained smoking above the porcelain effigies of Spanish fruits. That white monkey couldn't eat those and throw away the rinds! Would the fruits of his life be porcelain in future? Live in the same house with Fleur, estranged? Live with Fleur as now, feeling a stranger, even an unwelcome stranger? Clear out, and join the Air Force, or the 'Save the Children' corps? Which of the three courses was least to be deplored? The ash of his cigar grew long, dropped incontinent, and grew again; the porcelain fruits mocked him with their sheen and glow; Coaker put his head in and took it away again. (The Governor had got the hump—good sort, the Governor!) Decision waited for him, somewhere, somewhen—Fleur's, not his own. His mind was too miserable and disconcerted to be known; but she would know hers. She had the information which alone made decision possible about Wilfrid, that cousin, her own actions and feelings. Yes, decision would come, and would it matter in a world where pity was punk and only a Chinese philosophy of any use?

But not be sick in the drawing-room, try and keep one's end up, even if there were no one to see one being important! . . .

He had been asleep and it was dark, or all but, in his bed-dressing-room. Something white by his bed. A fragrant faint warmth close to him; a voice saying low: "It's only me. Let me come in your bed, Michael." Like a child—like a child! Michael reached out his arms. The whiteness and the warmth came into them. Curls smothered his mouth, the voice in his ear: "I wouldn't have come, would I, if there'd—if there'd been anything?" Michael's heart, wild, confused, beat against hers.

## Chapter VII

### 'THE ALTOGETHER'

TONY BICKET, replete, was in vein that fine afternoon; his balloons left him freely, and he started for home in the mood of a conqueror.

Victorine, too, had colour in her cheeks. She requited the story of his afternoon with the story of hers. A false tale for a true—no word of Danby and Winter, the gentleman with the sliding smile, of the Grand Marnier, or 'the altogether'. She had no compunction. It was her secret, her surprise; if, by sitting in or out of 'the altogether', not yet decided, she could make their passage money— well, she should tell him she had won it on a horse. That night she asked:

"Am I so very thin, Tony?" more than once. "I do so want to get fat."

Bicket, still troubled that she had not shared that lunch, patted her tenderly, and said he would soon have her as fat as butter—he did not explain how.

They dreamed together of blue butterflies, and awoke to chilly gaslight and a breakfast of cocoa and bread-and-butter. Fog! Bicket was swallowed up before the eyes of Victorine ten yards from the door. She returned to the bedroom with anger in her heart. Who would buy balloons in a fog? She would do anything rather than let Tony go on standing out there all the choking days! Undressing again, she washed herself intensively, in case——! She had not long finished when her landlady announced the presence of a messenger boy. He bore an enormous parcel entitled "Mr. Bicket."

There was a note inside. She read:

"DEAR BICKET,—Here are the togs. Hope they'll be useful.— Yours, MICHAEL MONT."

In a voice that trembled she said to the boy:
"Thank you, it's O.K. Here's twopence."

When his rich whistle was heard writhing into the fog, she flung herself down before the 'togs' in ecstasy. The sexes were divided by tissue paper. A blue suit, a velour hat, some brown shoes, three pairs of socks with two holes in them, four shirts only a little frayed at the cuffs, two black-and-white ties, six collars, not too new, some handkerchiefs, two vests beautifully thick, two pairs of pants, and a brown overcoat with a belt and just two or three nice little stains. She held the blue suit up against her arms and legs, the trousers and sleeves would only need taking-in about two inches. She piled them in a pyramid, and turned with awe to the spoil beneath the tissue paper. A brown knitted frock with little clear yellow buttons—unsoiled, uncreased. How could anybody spare a thing like that! A brown velvet toque with a little tuft of goldeny-brown feathers. She put it on. A pair of pink stays ever so little faded, with only three inches of bone above the waist, and five inches of bone below, pink silk ribbons, and suspenders—a perfect dream. She could not resist putting them on also. Two pairs of brown stockings; brown shoes; two combinations, a knitted camisole. A white silk jumper with a hole in one sleeve, a skirt of lilac linen that had gone a little in the wash; a pair of pallid pink silk pants; and underneath them all an almost black-brown coat, long and warm and cosy, with great jet buttons, and in the pocket six small handkerchiefs. She took a deep breath of sweetness—geranium!

Her mind leaped forward. Clothed, trousseaued, fitted out—blue butterflies—the sun! Only the money for the tickets wanting. And suddenly she saw herself with nothing on standing before the gentleman with sliding eyes. Who cared! The money!

For the rest of the morning she worked feverishly, shortening Tony, mending the holes in his socks, turning the fray of his cuffs. She ate a biscuit, drank another cup of cocoa—it was fattening, and went for the hole in the white silk jumper. One o'clock. In panic she stripped once more, put on a new combination, pair of stockings, and the stays, then paused in superstition. No! Her own dress and hat—like yesterday! Keep the rest until——! She hastened to her bus, overcome alternately by heat and cold. Perhaps he would give her another glass of that lovely stuff. If only she could go swimmy and not care for anything!

She reached the studio as two o'clock was striking, and knocked. It was lovely and warm in there, much warmer than yesterday, and the significance of this struck her suddenly. In front of the fire was a lady with a little dog.

"Miss Collins—Mrs. Michael Mont; she's lending us her Peke, Miss Collins."

The lady—only her own age, and ever so pretty—held out her hand. Geranium! This, then, was she whose clothes——!

She took the hand, but could not speak. If this lady was going to stay, if would be utterly impossible. Before her—so pretty, so beautifully covered—oh! no!

"Now, Ting, be good, and as amusing as you can. Good-bye, Aubrey! Good luck to the picture! Good-bye, Miss Collins; it ought to be wonderful."

Gone! The scent of geranium fading; the little dog snuffling at the door. The sliding gentleman had two glasses in his hands.

'Ah!' thought Victorine, and drank hers at a gulp.

"Now, Miss Collins, you don't mind, do you! You'll find everything in there. It's really nothing. I shall want you lying on your face just here with your elbows on the ground and your head up a little turned this way; your hair as loose as it can be, and your eyes looking at this bone. You must imagine that it's a faun or some other bit of all right. The dog'll help you when he settles down to it. F-a-u-n, you know, not f-a-w-n."

"Yes," said Victorine faintly.

"Have another little tot?"

"Oh! please."

He brought it.

"I quite understand; but you know, really, it's absurd. You wouldn't mind with a doctor. That's right. Look here, I'll put this little cow-bell on the ground. When you're in position, give it a tinkle, and I'll come out. That'll help you."

Victorine murmured:

"You *are* kind.'

"Not at all—it's natural. Now will you start in? The light won't last for ever. Fifteen bob a day, we said."

Victorine saw him slide away behind a screen, and looked at the little cow-bell. Fifteen bob! And fifteen bob! And fifteen bob! Many, many, fifteen bobs before——! But not more times of sitting than of Tony's standing from foot to foot, offering balloons. And as if wound up by that thought, she moved like clockwork off the dais, into the model's room. Cosy in there, too; warm, a green silk garment thrown on a chair. She took off her dress. The beauty of the pink stays struck her afresh. Perhaps the gentleman would like—no, that would be even worse——! A noise reached her—from Ting-a-ling complaining of solitude. If she delayed, she never would——! Stripping hastily, she stood looking at herself in a glass. If only that slim, ivory-white image could move out on to the dais and she could stay here! Oh! It was awful—awful! She couldn't—no! she couldn't. She caught up her final garment again. Fifteen bob! But fifteen bob! Before her eyes, wild and mournful, came a vision: Of a huge dome, and a tiny Tony, with little, little balloons in a hand held out! Something cold and steely formed over her heart as icicles form on a window. If that was all they would do for him, she would do better! She dropped the garment; and, confused, numb, stepped forth in 'the altogether'. Ting-a-ling growled at her above his bone. She reached the cow-bell and lay down on her face as she had been told, with feet in the air, crossed.

Resting her chin on one hand, she wagged the bell. It made a sound like no bell she had ever heard; and the little dog barked—he did look funny!

"Perfect, Miss Collins! Hold that!"

Fifteen bob! and fifteen bob!

"Just point those left toes a bit more. That's right! The flesh tone's perfect! My God, why must one walk before one runs! Drawing's a bore, Miss Collins; one ought to draw with a brush only; a sculptor draws with a chisel, at least when he's a Michelangelo. How old are you?"

"Twenty-one," came from lips that seemed to Victorine quite far away.

"I'm thirty-two. They say our generation was born so old that it can never get any older. Without illusions. Well! I never had any beliefs that I can remember. Had you?"

Victorine's wits and senses were astray, but it did not matter, for he was rattling on:

"We don't even believe in our ancestors. All the same, we're beginning to copy them again. D'you know a book called 'The Sobbing Turtle' that's made such a fuss?—sheer Sterne, very well done; but sheer Sterne, and the author's tongue in his cheek. That's it in a nutshell, Miss Collins—our tongues are in our cheeks—bad sign. Never mind; I'm going to out-Piero Cosimo with this. Your head an inch higher, and that curl out of your eye, please. Thanks! Hold that! By the way, have you Italian blood? What was your mother's name, for instance?"

"Brown."

"Ah! You can never tell with Browns. It may have been Brune —or Bruno—but very likely she was Iberian. Probably all the inhabitants of Britain left alive by the Saxons were called Brown. As a fact, that's all tosh, though. Going back to Edward the Confessor, Miss Collins—a mere thirty generations—we each of us have one thousand and seventy-four million, five hundred and seventy-three thousand, nine hundred and eighty-four ancestors, and the population of this island was then well under a million. We're as inbred as race-horses, but not so nice to look at, are we? I assure you, Miss Collins, you're something to be grateful for. So is Mrs. Mont. Isn't she pretty? Look at that dog!"

Ting-a-ling, indeed, with forelegs braced, and wrinkled nose, was glaring, as if under the impression that Victorine was another bone.

"He's funny," she said, and again her voice sounded far away.

126

Would Mrs. Mont lie here if he'd asked her? *She* would look pretty! But *she* didn't need the fifteen bob!

"Comfortable in that position?"

In alarm, she murmured:

"Oh! yes, thank you!"

"Warm enough?"

"Oh! yes, thank you!"

"That's good. Just a little higher with the head."

Slowly in Victorine the sense of the dreadfully unusual faded. Tony should never know. If he never knew, he couldn't care. She could lie like this all day—fifteen bob, and fifteen bob! It was easy. She watched the quick, slim fingers moving, the blue smoke from the cigarette. She watched the little dog.

"Like a rest? You left your gown; I'll get it for you."

In that green silk gown, beautifully padded, she sat up, with her feet on the floor over the dais edge.

"Cigarette? I'm going to make some Turkish coffee. You'd better walk about."

Victorine obeyed.

"You're out of a dream, Miss Collins. I shall have to do a Mathew Maris of you in that gown."

The coffee, like none she had ever tasted, gave her a sense of well-being. She said:

"It's not like coffee."

Aubrey Greene threw up his hands

"You have said it. The British are a great race—nothing will ever do them in. If they could be destroyed, they must long ago have perished of their coffee. Have some more?"

"Please," said Victorine. There was such a little in the cup.

"Ready, again?"

She lay down, and let the gown drop off.

"That's right! Leave it there—you're lying in long grass, and the green helps me. Pity it's winter; I'd have hired a glade."

Lying in long grass—flowers, too, perhaps. She did love flowers. As a little girl she used to lie in the grass, and make daisy-chains, in the field at the back of her grandmother's lodge at Norbiton. Her grandmother kept the lodge. Every year, for a fortnight, she had gone down there—she had liked the country ever so. Only she had always had something on. It would be nicer with nothing. Were there flowers in Central Australia? With butterflies there must be! In the sun—she and Tony—like the Garden of Eden! . . .

"Thank you, that's all for to-day. Half a day—ten bob. To-

127

morrow morning at eleven. You're a first-rate sitter, Miss Collins."

Putting on the pink stays, Victorine had a feeling of elation. She had done it! Tony should never know! The thought that he never would gave her pleasure. And once more divested of 'the altogether', she came forth.

Aubrey Greene was standing before his handiwork.

"Not yet, Miss Collins," he said; "I don't want to depress you. That hip-bone's too high. We'll put it right to-morrow. Forgive my hand, it's all chalk. *Au revoir!* Eleven o'clock. And we shan't need this chap. No, you don't!"

For Ting-a-ling was showing signs of accompanying the larger bone. Victorine passed out smiling.

## Chapter VIII

### SOAMES TAKES THE MATTER UP

SOAMES had concentrated, sitting before the fire in his bedroom till Big Ben struck twelve. His reflections sum-totalled in a decision to talk it over with 'old Mont' after all. Though light-brained, the fellow was a gentleman, and the matter delicate. He got into bed and slept, but awoke at half-past two. There it was! '*I won't* think of it,' he thought; and instantly began to. In a long life of dealings with money, he had never had such an experience. Perfectly straightforward conformity with the law—itself so often far from perfectly straightforward—had been the *sine qua non* of his career. Honesty, they said, was the best policy. But was it anything else? A normally honest man couldn't keep out of a perfect penitentiary for a week. But then a perfect penitentiary had no relation to prison, or the Bankruptcy Court. The business of working honesty was to keep out of those two institutions. And so far he had never had any difficulty. What, besides the drawing of fees and the drinking of tea, were the duties of a director? That was the point. And how far, if he failed in them, was he liable? It was a director's duty to be perfectly straightforward. But if a director were perfectly straightforward, he couldn't be a director. That was clear. In the first place, he would have to tell his shareholders that he didn't anything like earn his fees. For what did he do on his Boards? Well, he sat and signed his name and talked a little, and passed that which the general trend of business decided must be passed. Did he initiate? Once in a blue moon. Did he calculate?

No, he read calculations. Did he check payments out and in? No, the auditors did that. There was policy! A comforting word, but—to be perfectly straightforward—a director's chief business was to let the existing policy alone. Take his own case! If he had done his duty, he would have stopped this foreign insurance business—which he had instinctively distrusted the moment he heard of it—within a month of sitting on the Board, or, having failed in doing so, resigned his seat. But he had not. Things had been looking better! It was not the moment, and so forth! If he had done his duty as a perfectly straightforward director, indeed, he would never have become a director of the P.P.R.S., because he would have looked into the policy of the Society much more closely than he had before accepting a position on the Board. But what with the names, and the prestige, and not looking a gift horse too closely in the mouth—there it had been! To be perfectly straightforward, he ought now to be circularising the shareholders, saying: "My *laissez-faire* has cost you two hundred odd thousand pounds. I have lodged this amount in the hands of trustees for your benefit, and am suing the rest of the directors for their quotas of the amount." But he was not proposing to do so, because—well—because it wasn't done, and the other directors wouldn't like it. In sum: You waited till the shareholders found out the mess, and you hoped they wouldn't. In fact, just like a Government, you confused the issues, and made the best case you could for yourselves. With a sense of comfort Soames thought of Ireland: The late Government had let the country in for all that mess in Ireland, and at the end taken credit for putting an end to what need never have been! The Peace, too, and the Air Force, and Agriculture, and Egypt—the five most important issues they'd had to deal with—they had put the chestnuts into the fire in every case! But had they confessed to it? Not they. One didn't confess. One said: "The question of policy made it imperative at the time." Or, better still, one said nothing; and trusted to the British character. With his chin resting on the sheet, Soames felt a momentary relief. The late Government weren't sweating into *their* sheets—not they—he was convinced of it! Fixing his eyes on the dying embers in the grate, he reflected on the inequalities and injustices of existence. Look at the chaps in politics and business, whose whole lives were passed in skating on thin ice, and getting knighted for it. They never turned a hair. And look at himself, for the first time in forty years on thin ice, and suffering confoundedly. There was a perfect cult of hoodwinking the public, a perfect cult of avoiding the consequences of administrative acts; and here was he, a man of the world, a man of the law, ignorant of those cults, and—and glad of it. From engrained caution and a certain pride, which had in it a touch of the fine, Soames shrank from that coarse-grained standard of honesty which conducted the affairs of the British public. In anything that touched money he was, he always had been, stiff-necked, stiff-kneed. Money was money, a pound a pound, and there was no way of pretending it wasn't and keeping your self-respect. He got up, drank some water, took a number of deep breaths, and stamped his feet. Who was it said the other day that nothing had ever lost him five minutes' sleep? The fellow must have the circulation of an ox, or the gift of Baron Munchausen. He took up a book. But his mind would only turn over and over the realisable value of his resources. Apart from his pictures, he decided that he could not be worth less than two hundred and fifty thousand pounds, and there was only Fleur—and she already provided for more or less. His wife had her settlement, and could live on it perfectly well in France. As for himself—what did he care? A room at his club near Fleur—he would be just as happy, perhaps happier! And suddenly he found that he had reached a way out of his disturbance and anxiety. By imagining the far-fetched, by facing the loss of his wealth, he had exorcised the demon. The book, 'The Sobbing Turtle', of which he had not read one word, dropped from his hand; he slept. . . .

His meeting with 'Old Mont' took place at 'Snooks' directly after lunch. The tape in the hall, at which he glanced on going in, recorded a further heavy drop in the mark. Just as he thought: The thing was getting valueless!

Sitting there, sipping coffee, the baronet looked to Soames almost offensively spry. Two to one he had realised nothing! 'Well!' thought Soames, 'as old Uncle Jolyon used to say, I shall astonish his weak nerves!'

And without preamble he began.

"How are you, Mont? This mark's valueless. You realise we've lost the P.P.R.S. about a quarter of a million by that precious foreign policy of Elderson's. I'm not sure an action won't lie against us for taking unjustifiable risk. But what I've come to see you about is this." He retailed the interview with the clerk, Butterfield, watching the eyebrows of his listener, and finished with the words: "What do you say?"

Sir Lawrence, whose foot was jerking his whole body, fixed his monocle.

"Hallucination, my dear Forsyte! I've known Elderson all my life. We were at Winchester together."

Again! Again! Oh! Lord! Soames said slowly:

"You can't tell from that. A man who was at Marlborough with me ran away with his mess fund and his colonel's wife, and made a fortune in Chili out of canned tomatoes. The point is this: If the young man's story's true, we're in the hands of a bad hat. It won't do, Mont. Will you tackle him, and see what he says to it? You wouldn't like a story of that sort about yourself. Shall we both go?"

"Yes," said Sir Lawrence, suddenly. "You're right. We'll both go, Forsyte. I don't like it, but we'll both go. He ought to hear it."

"Now?"

"Now."

With solemnity they assumed top hats, and issued.

"I think, Forsyte, we'll take a taxi."

"Yes," said Soames.

The cab ground its way slowly past the lions, then dashed on down to the Embankment. Side by side its occupants held their noses steadily before them.

"He was shooting with me a month ago," said Sir Lawrence. "Do you know the hymn 'O God, our help in ages past'? It's very fine, Forsyte."

Soames did not answer. The fellow was beginning to tittup!

"We had it that Sunday," went on Sir Lawrence. "Elderson used to have a fine voice—sang solos. It's a foghorn now, but a good delivery still." He gave his little whinnying laugh.

'Is it possible,' thought Soames, 'for this chap to be serious?' and he said:

"If we find this is true of Elderson, and conceal it, we could all be put in the dock."

Sir Lawrence refixed his monocle. "The deuce!" he said.

"Will you do the talking," said Soames, "or shall I?"

"I think you had better, Forsyte; ought we to have the young man in?"

"Wait and see," said Soames.

They ascended to the offices of the P.P.R.S. and entered the board-room. There was no fire, the long table was ungarnished; an old clerk, creeping about like a fly on a pane, was filling inkstands out of a magnum.

Soames addressed him:

131

"Ask the manager to be so kind as to come and see Sir Lawrence Mont and Mr. Forsyte."

The old clerk blinked, put down the magnum, and went out.

"Now," said Soames in a low voice, "we must keep our heads. He'll deny it, of course."

"I should hope so, Forsyte; I should hope so. Elderson's a gentleman."

"No liar like a gentleman," muttered Soames, below his breath.

After that they stood in their overcoats before the empty grate, staring at their top hats placed side by side on the table.

"One minute!" said Soames, suddenly, and crossing the room, he opened a door opposite. There, as the young clerk had said, was a sort of lobby between board-room and Manager's Room, with a door at the end into the main corridor. He stepped back, closed the door, and, rejoining Sir Lawrence, resumed his contemplation of the hats.

"Geography correct," he said with gloom.

The entrance of the manager was marked by Sir Lawrence's monocle dropping on to his coat-button with a tinkle. In cutaway black coat, clean-shaven, with grey eyes rather baggy underneath, a pink colour, every hair in place on a rather bald egg-shaped head, and lips alternately pouting, compressed, or smiling, the manager reminded Soames ridiculously of old Uncle Nicholas in his middle period. Uncle Nick was a clever fellow—"cleverest man in London," someone had called him—but none had ever impugned his honesty. A pang of doubt and disinclination went through Soames. This seemed a monstrous thing to have to put to a man of his own age and breeding. But young Butterfield's eyes—so honest and dog-like! Invent a thing like that—was it possible? He said abruptly:

"Is that door shut?"

"Yes; do you feel a draught?" said the manager. "Would you like a fire?"

"No, thank you," said Soames. "The fact is, Mr. Elderson, a young man in this office came to me yesterday with a very queer story. Mont and I think you should hear it."

Accustomed to watching people's eyes, Soames had the impression of a film (such as passes over the eyes of parrots) passing over the eyes of the manager. It was gone at once, if, indeed, it had ever been.

"By all means."

Steadily, with that power he had over his nerves when it came to a point, and almost word for word, Soames repeated a story which he had committed to heart in the watches of the night. He concluded with:

"You'd like him in, no doubt. His name is Butterfield."

During the recital Sir Lawrence had done nothing but scrutinise his finger nails; he now said:

"You had to be told, Elderson."

"Naturally."

The manager was crossing to the bell. The pink in his cheeks looked harder; his teeth showed, they had a pouted look.

"Ask Mr. Butterfield to come here."

There followed a minute of elaborate inattention to each other. Then the young man came in, neat, commonplace, with his eyes on the manager's face. Soames had a moment of compunction. This young fellow held his life in his hands, as it were—one of the great army who made their living out of self-suppression and respectability, with a hundred ready to step into his shoes at his first slip. What was that old tag of the provincial actor's declamation—at which old Uncle Jolyon used to cackle so? "Like a pale martyr with his shirt on fire."

"So, Mr. Butterfield, you have been good enough to exercise your imagination in my regard."

"No, sir."

"You stick to this fantastic story of eavesdropping?"

"Yes, sir."

"We have no further use for your services then. Good-morning!"

The young man's eyes, dog-like, sought the face of Soames; a string twitched in his throat, his lips moved without a sound. He turned and went out.

"So much for that," said the manager's voice; "*he'll* never get another job."

The venom in those words affected Soames like the smell of Russian fat. At the same moment he had the feeling: This wants thinking out. Only if innocent, or guilty and utterly resolved, would Elderson have been so drastic. Which was he?

The manager went on:

"I thank you for drawing my attention to the matter, gentlemen. I have had my eye on that young man for some time. A bad hat all round."

Soames said glumly:

"What do you make out he had to gain?"

"Foresaw dismissal, and thought he would get in first."

"I see," said Soames. But he did not. His mind was back in his own office with Gradman rubbing his nose, shaking his grey head, and Butterfield's: "No, sir, I've nothing again⸓t Mr. Elderson, and he's nothing against me."

'I shall require to know more about that young man,' he thought. The manager's voice again cut through.

"I've been thinking over what you said yesterday, Mr. Forsyte, about an action lying against the Board for negligence. There's nothing in that; our policy has been fully disclosed to the shareholders at two general meetings, and has passed without comment. The shareholders are just as responsible as the Board."

"H'm!" said Soames, and took up his hat. "Are you coming, Mont?"

As if summoned from a long distance, Sir Lawrence galvanitically refixed his monocle.

"It's been very distasteful," he said; "you must forgive us, Elderson. You had to be told. I don't think that young man can be quite all there—he had a peculiar look; but we can't have this sort of thing, of course. Good-bye, Elderson."

Placing their hats on their heads simultaneously the two walked out. They walked some way without speaking. Then Sir Lawrence said:

"Butterfield? My brother-in-law has a head gardener called Butterfield—quite a good fellow. Ought we to look into that young man, Forsyte?"

"Yes," said Soames, "leave him to me."

"I shall be very glad to. The fact is, when one has been at school with a man, one has a feeling, don't you know."

Soames gave vent to a sudden outburst.

"You can't trust anyone nowadays, it seems to me," he said. "It comes of—well, I don't know what it comes of. But I've not done with this matter yet."

## Chapter IX

### SLEUTH

THE Hotch-potch Club went back to the eighteen-sixties. Founded by a posse of young sparks, social and political, as a convenient place in which to smoulder, while qualifying for the hearth of 'Snooks', The Remove, The Wayfarers, Burton's, Ostrich Feather, and other more permanent resorts, the club had, chiefly owing to a remarkable chef in its early days, acquired a stability and distinction of its own. It still, however, retained a certain resemblance to its name, and this was its attraction to Michael—all sorts of people belonged. From Walter Nazing, and young semi-writers and patrons of the stage, who went to Venice, and talked of being amorous in gondolas, or of how so-and-so ought to be made love to; from such to bottle-brushed demi-generals, who had sat on courts-martial and shot men out of hand for the momentary weaknesses of human nature; from Wilfrid Desert (who never came there now) to Maurice Elderson, in the card-room, he could meet them all, and take the temperature of modernity. He was doing this in the Hotch-potch smoking-room, the late afternoon but one after Fleur had come into his bed, when he was informed:

"A Mr. Forsyte, sir, in the hall for you. Not the member we had here many years before he died; his cousin, I think."

Conscious that his associates at the moment would not be his father-in-law's 'dream', nor he theirs, Michael went out, and found Soames on the weighing machine.

"I don't vary," he said, looking up. "How's Fleur?"

"Very well, thank you, sir."

"I'm at Green Street. I stayed up about a young man. Have you any vacancy in your office for a clerk—used to figures. I want a job for him."

"Come in here, sir," said Michael, entering a small room.

Soames followed and looked round him.

"What do you call this?" he said.

"Well, we call it 'the grave'; it's nice and quiet. Will you have a sherry?"

"Sherry!" repeated Soames. "You young people think you've invented sherry; when I was a boy no one dreamed of dining without a glass of dry sherry with his soup, and a glass of fine old sherry with his sweet. Sherry!"

"I quite believe you, sir. There really is nothing new. Venice, for instance—wasn't that the fashion, too; and knitting, and royalties? It's all cyclic. Has your young man got the sack?"

Soames stared. "Yes," he said, "he has. His name is Butterfield; he wants a job."

"That's frightfully rife; we get applications every day. I don't want to be swanky, but ours is a rather specialised business. It has to do with books."

"He strikes me as capable, orderly, and civil; I don't see what

135

more you want in a clerk. He writes a good hand, and, so far as I can see, he tells the truth."

"That's important, of course," said Michael; "but is he a good liar as well? I mean, there's more likely to be something in the travelling line; selling special editions, and that kind of thing Could you open up about him a bit? Anything human is to the good—I don't say old Danby would appreciate that, but he needn't know."

"H'm! Well—he—er—did his duty—quite against his interest—in fact, it's ruination for him. He seems to be married and to have two children."

"Ho, ho! Jolly! If I got him a place, would he—would he be doing his duty again, do you think?"

"I am serious," said Soames; "the young man is on my mind."

"Yes," said Michael, ruminative, "the first thing in such a case is to get him on to someone else's, sharp. Could I see him?"

"I told him to step round and see you to-night after dinner. I thought you'd prefer to look him over in private before considering him for your office."

"Very thoughtful of you, sir! There's just one thing. Don't you think I ought to know the duty he did—in confidence? I don't see how I can avoid putting my foot into my mouth without, do you?"

Soames stared at his son-in-law's face, where the mouth was wide; for the *n*th time it inspired in him a certain liking and confidence; it looked so honest.

"Well," he said, going to the door and ascertaining that it was opaque, "this is matter for a criminal slander action, so for your own sake as well as mine you will keep it strictly to yourself;" and in a low voice he retailed the facts.

"As I expected," he ended, "the young man came to me again this morning. He is naturally upset. I want to keep my hand on him. Without knowing more, I can't make up my mind whether to go further or not. Besides——" Soames hesitated; to claim a good motive was repulsive to him : "I—it seems hard on him. He's been getting three hundred and fifty."

"Dashed hard!" said Michael. "I say, Elderson's a member here."

Soames looked with renewed suspicion at the door—it still seemed opaque, and he said : "The deuce he is! Do you know him?"

"I've played bridge with him," said Michael; "he's taken some of the best off me—snorting good player."

"Ah!" said Soames—he never played cards himself. "I can't take this young man into my own firm for obvious reasons; but I can trust you."

Michael touched his forelock.

"Frightfully bucked, sir. Protection of the poor—some sleuth, too. I'll see him to-night, and let you know what I can wangle."

Soames nodded. 'Good Gad!' he thought; 'what jargon! . . .'

The interview served Michael the good turn of taking his thoughts off himself. Temperamentally he sided already with the young man Butterfield; and, lighting a cigarette, he went into the card-room. Sitting on the high fender, he was impressed—the room was square, and within it were three square card-tables, set askew to the walls, with three triangles of card players.

'If only,' thought Michael, 'the fourth player sat under the table, the pattern would be complete. It's having the odd player loose that spoils the cubes.' And with something of a thrill he saw that Elderson was a fourth player! Sharp and impassive, he was engaged in applying a knife to the end of a cigar. Gosh! what sealed books faces were! Each with pages and pages of private thoughts, interests, schemes, fancies, passions, hopes and fears; and down came death—splosh!—and a creature wiped out, like a fly on a wall, and nobody any more could see its little close mechanism working away for its own ends, in its own privacy and its own importance; nobody any more could speculate on whether it was a clean or a dirty little bit of work. Hard to tell! They ran in all shapes! Elderson, for instance—was he a nasty mess, or just a lamb of God who didn't look it? 'Somehow,' thought Michael, 'I feel he's a womaniser. Now why?' He spread his hands out behind him to the fire, rubbing them together like a fly that has been in treacle. If one couldn't tell what was passing in the mind of one's own wife in one's own house, how on earth could one tell anything from the face of a stranger, and he one of the closest bits of mechanism in the world—an English gentleman of business! If only life were like 'The Idiot' or 'The Brothers Karamazov', and everybody went about turning out their inmost hearts at the tops of their voices! If only club card-rooms had a dash of epilepsy in their composition! But—nothing! Nothing! The world was full of wonderful secrets which everybody kept to themselves without captions or close-ups to give them away!

A footman came in, looked at the fire, stood a moment expressionless as a stork, waiting for an order to ping out, staccato, through the hum, turned and went away.

Mechanism! Everywhere—mechanism! Devices for getting away from life so complete that there seemed no life to get away from.

'It's all,' he thought, 'awfully like a man sending a registered letter to himself. And perhaps it's just as well. Is "life" a good thing—is it? Do I want to see "life" raw again?'

Elderson was seated now, and Michael had a perfect view of the back of his head. It disclosed nothing.

'I'm no sleuth,' he thought; 'there ought to be something in the way he doesn't part his hair behind.' And, getting off the fender, he went home.

At dinner he caught one of his own looks at Fleur and didn't like it. Sleuth! And yet how not try to know what were the real thoughts and feelings of one who held his heart, like an accordion, and made it squeak and groan at pleasure!

"I saw the model you sent Aubrey yesterday," she said. "She didn't say anything about the clothes, but she looked ever so! What a face, Michael! Where did you come across her?"

Through Michael sped the thought: 'Could I make her jealous?' And he was shocked at it. A low-down thought—mean and ornery! "She blew in," he said. "Wife of a little packer we had who took to snooping—er—books. He sells balloons now; they want money badly."

"I see. Did you know that Aubrey's going to paint her in the nude?"

"Phew! No! I thought she'd look good on a wrapper. I say! Ought I to stop that?"

Fleur smiled. "It's more money and her look-out. It doesn't matter to you, does it?"

Again that thought; again the recoil from it!

"Only," he said, "that her husband is a decent little snipe for a snooper, and I don't want to be more sorry for him."

"She won't tell him, of course."

She said it so naturally, so simply, that the words disclosed a whole attitude of mind. One didn't tell one's mate what would tease the poor brute! He saw by the flutter of her white eyelids that she also realised the give-away. Should he follow it up, tell her what June Forsyte had told him—have it all out—all out? But with what purpose—to what end? Would it change things, make her love him? Would it do anything but harass her a little more; and give him the sense that he had lost his wicket trying to drive her to the pavilion? No! Better adopt the principle of secrecy she had unwittingly declared her own, bite on it, and grin. He muttered:

"I'm afraid he'll find her rather thin."

Her eyes were bright and steady; and again he was worried by that low-down thought: 'Could he make her——?'

"I've only seen her once," he added, "and then she was dressed."

"I'm not jealous, Michael."

'No,' he thought, 'I wish to heaven you were!'

The words: "A young man called Butterfill to see you, sir," were like the turning of a key in a cell door.

In the hall the young man 'called Butterfill' was engaged in staring at Ting-a-ling.

'Judging by his eyes,' thought Michael, 'he's more of a dog than that little Djinn!'

"Come up to my study," he said, "it's cold down here. My father-in-law tells me you want a job."

"Yes, sir," said the young man, following up the stairs.

"Take a pew," said Michael; "and a cigarette. Now then! I know all about the turmoil. From your moustache, you were in the war, I suppose, like me! As between fellow-sufferers: Is your story O.K.?"

"God's truth, sir; I only wish it wasn't. I'd nothing to gain and everything to lose. I'd have done better to hold my tongue. It's his word against mine, and here I am in the street. That was my first job since the war, so I can whistle for a reference."

"Wife and two children, I think?"

"Yes, and I've put them in the cart for the sake of my conscience! It's the last time I'll do that, I know. What did it matter to me. whether the Society was cheated? My wife's quite right, I was a fool, sir."

"Probably," said Michael. "Do you know anything about books?"

"Yes, sir; I'm a good book-keeper."

"Holy Moses! *Our* job is getting rid of them. My firm are publishers. We were thinking of putting on an extra traveller. Is your tongue persuasive?"

The young man smiled wanly.

"I don't know, sir."

"Well, look here," said Michael, carried away by the look in his eyes, "it's all a question of a certain patter. But, of course, that's got to be learned. I gather that you're not a reader."

"Well, sir, not a great reader."

139

"That, perhaps, is fortunate. What you would have to do is to impress on the poor brutes who sell books that every one of the books on your list—say about thirty-five—is necessary in large numbers to his business. It's lucky you've just chucked your conscience, because, as a matter of fact, most of them won't be. I'm afraid there's nowhere you could go to to get lessons in persuasion, but you can imagine the sort of thing, and if you like to come here for an hour or two this week, I'll put you wise about our authors, and ready you up to go before Peter."

"Before Peter, sir?"

"The Johnny with the keys; luckily it's Mr. Winter, not Mr. Danby; I believe I could get him to let you in for a month's trial."

"Sir, I'll try my very best. My wife knows about books, she could help me a lot. I can't tell you what I think of your kindness. The fact is, being out of a job has put the wind up me properly. I've not been able to save with two children; it's like the end of the world."

"Right-o, then! Come here to-morrow evening at nine, and I'll stuff you. I believe you've got the face for the job, if you can get the patter. Only one book in twenty is a necessity really, the rest are luxuries. Your stunt will be to make them believe the nineteen are necessaries, and the twentieth a luxury that they need. It's like food or clothes, or anything else in civilisation."

"Yes, sir, I quite understand."

"All right, then. Good-night, and good luck!"

Michael stood up and held out his hand. The young man took it with a queer reverential little bow. A minute later he was out in the street; and Michael in the hall was thinking: 'Pity is tripe! Clean forgot I was a sleuth!'

## Chapter X

### FACE

WHEN Michael rose from the refectory table, Fleur had risen, too. Two days and more since she left Wilfrid's rooms, and she had not recovered zest. The rifling of the oyster Life, the garlanding of London's rarer flowers which kept colour in her cheeks, seemed stale, unprofitable. Those three hours, when from shock off Cork Street she came straight to shocks in her own drawing-room, had dislocated her so that she had settled to nothing since. The wound re-opened by Holly had nearly healed again. Dead lion beside live donkey cuts but dim figure. But she could not get hold again of—what? That was the trouble: What? For two whole days she had been trying. Michael was still strange, Wilfrid still lost, Jon still buried alive, and nothing seemed novel under the sun. The only object that gave her satisfaction during those two dreary, dis-illusioned days was the new white monkey. The more she looked at it, the more Chinese it seemed. It summed up the satirical truth of which she was perhaps subconscious, that all her little modern veerings and flutterings and rushings after the future showed that she believed in nothing but the past. The age had overdone it and must go back to ancestry for faith. Like a little bright fish out of a warm bay, making a splash in chill, strange waters, Fleur felt a subtle nostalgia.

In her Spanish room, alone with her own feelings, she stared at the porcelain fruits. They glowed, cold, uneatable! She took one up. Meant for a passion fruit? Alas! Poor passion! She dropped it with a dull clink on to the pyramid, and shuddered a little. Had she blinded Michael with her kisses? Blinded him to—what? To her incapacity for passion?

'But I'm not incapable,' she thought; 'I'm not. Some day I'll show him; I'll show them all.' She looked up at 'the Goya' hanging opposite. What gripping determination in the painting—what intensity of life in the black eyes of a rather raddled dame! *She* would know what she wanted, and get it, too! No compromise and uncertainty there—no capering round life, wondering what it meant, and whether it was worth while, nothing but hard living for the sake of living!

Fleur put her hands where her flesh ended, and her dress began. Wasn't she as warm and firm—yes, and ten times as pretty, as that fine and evil-looking Spanish dame, with the black eyes and the wonderful lace? And, turning her back on the picture, she went into the hall. Michael's voice and another's! They were coming down! She slipped across into the drawing-room and took up the manuscript of a book of poems, on which she was to give Michael her opinion. She sat, not reading, wondering if he were coming in. She heard the front door close. No! He had gone out! A relief, yet chilling! Michael not warm and cheerful in the house — if it were to go on, it would be wearing. She curled herself up and tried to read. Dreary poems—free verse, blank, introspective, all about the author's inside! No lift, no lilt! Duds! She seemed to have read them a dozen times before. She lay quite still—listening to the click and flutter of the burning logs! If the light were out she might go to sleep. She turned it off, and came back to the settee. She could see herself sitting there, a picture in the firelight; see how lonely she looked, pretty, pathetic, with everything she wished for, and—nothing! Her lip curled. She could even see her own spoiled-child ingratitude. And what was worse, she could see herself seeing it—a triple-distilled modern, so subtly arranged in life-tight compartments that she could not be submerged. If only something would blow in out of the unkempt cold, out of the waste and wilderness of a London whose flowers she plucked. The firelight—soft, uncertain—searched out spots and corners of her Chinese room, as on a stage in one of those scenes, seductive and mysterious, where one waited, to the sound of tambourines, for the next moment of the plot. She reached out and took a cigarette. She could see herself lighting it, blowing out the smoke —her own half-curled fingers, her parted lips, her white rounded arm. She was decorative! Well, and wasn't that all that mattered? To be decorative, and make little decorations; to be pretty in a world that wasn't pretty! In 'Copper Coin' there was a poem of a flicker-lit room, and a spoiled Columbine before the fire, and a Harlequin hovering without, like 'the spectre of the rose'. And suddenly, without warning, Fleur's heart ached. It ached definitely, rather horribly, and, slipping down on to the floor before the fire, she snuggled her face against Ting-a-ling. The Chinese dog raised his head—his black eyes lurid in the glow.

He licked her cheek, and turned his nose away. Huf! Powder! But Fleur lay like the dead. And she saw herself lying—the curve of her hip, the chestnut glow in her short hair; she heard the steady beat of her heart. Get up! Go out! Do something! But what— what was worth doing? What had any meaning in it? She saw herself doing—extravagant things; nursing sick women; tending pale babies; making a speech in Parliament; riding a steeplechase; hoeing turnips in knickerbockers—decorative. And she lay perfectly still, bound by the filaments of her self-vision. So long as she saw herself she would do nothing—she knew it—for nothing would be worth doing! And it seemed to her, lying there so still, that not to see herself would be worse than anything. And she felt that to feel this was to acknowledge herself caged for ever.

Ting-a-ling growled, turning his nose towards the windows. "In here," he seemed to say, "we are cosy; we think of the past. We have no use for anything outside. Kindly go away—whoever it is out there!" And again he growled—a low, continuous sound.

"What is it, Ting?"

Ting-a-ling rose on his fore-legs, with muzzle pointed at the window.

"Do you want your walk?"

"No," said the growl.

Fleur picked him up. "Don't be so silly!" And she went to the window. The curtains were closely drawn; rich, Chinese lined, they excluded the night. Fleur made a chink with one hand, and started back. Against the pane was a face, the forehead pressed against the glass, the eyes closed, as if it had been there a long time. In the dark it seemed featureless, vaguely pale. She felt the dog's body stiffen under her arm—she felt his silence. Her heart pumped. It was ghastly—face without body.

Suddenly the forehead was withdrawn, the eyes opened. She saw—the face of Wilfrid. Could he see in—see her peering out from the darkened room? Quivering all over, she let the curtains fall to. Beckon? Let him in? Go out to him? Wave him away? Her heart beat furiously. How long had he been out there—like a ghost? What did he want of her? She dropped Ting-a-ling with a flump, and pressed her hands to her forehead, trying to clear confusion from her brain. And suddenly she stepped forward and flung the curtains apart. No face! Nothing! He was gone! The dark, draughty square—not a soul in it! Had he ever been—or was the face her fancy? But Ting-a-ling! Dogs had no fancies. He had gone back to the fire and settled down again.

'It's not my fault,' she thought passionately. 'It's not! I didn't want him to love me. I only wanted his—his——!' Again she sank down before the fire. "Oh! Ting, have a feeling heart!" But the Chinese dog, mindful of the flump, made no response. . . .

## Chapter XI

### COCKED HAT

AFTER missing his vocation with the young man Butterfield, Michael had hesitated in the hall. At last he had not gone upstairs again, but quietly out. He walked past the Houses of Parliament and up Whitehall. In Trafalgar Square, it occurred to him that he had a father. Bart might be at 'Snooks', The Coffee House, The Aeroplane; and, with the thought, 'He'd be restful,' he sought the most modern of the three.

143

"Yes, Sir Lawrence Mont is in the lounge, sir."

He was sitting with knees crossed, and a cigar between his finger-tips, waiting for someone to talk to.

"Ah! Michael! Can you tell me why I come here?"

"To wait for the end of the world, sir?"

Sir Lawrence sniggered. "An idea," he said. "When the skies are wrecking civilisation, this will be the best-informed tape in London. The wish to be in at the death is perhaps the strongest of our passions, Michael. I should very much dislike being blown up, especially after dinner; but I should still more dislike missing the next show if it's to be a really good one. The air-raids were great fun, after all."

Michael sighed.

"Yes," he said, "the war got us used to thinking of the millennium, and then it went and stopped, and left the millennium hanging over us. Now we shall never be happy till we get it. Can I take one of your cigars, sir?"

"My dear fellow! I've been reading Frazer again. Extraordinary how remote all superstition seems, now that we've reached the ultimate truth: That enlightenment never can prevail."

Michael stopped the lighting of his cigar.

"Do you really think that, sir?"

"What else can one think? Who can have any reasonable doubt now that with the aid of mechanics the head-strong part of man must do him in? It's an unavoidable conclusion from all recent facts. 'Per ardua ad astra,' 'Through hard knocks we shall see stars.' "

"But it's always been like that, sir, and here we are alive?"

"They say so, but I doubt it. I fancy we're really dead, Michael. I fancy we're only living in the past. I don't think—no, I don't think we can be said to expect a future. We talk of it, but I hardly think we hope for one. Underneath our protestations we sub-consciously deduce. From the mess we've made of it these last ten years, we can feel the far greater mess we shall make of it in the next thirty. Human nature can argue the hind legs off a donkey, but the donkey will be four-legged at the end of the discussion."

Michael sat down suddenly and said:

"You're a bad, bold Bart."

Sir Lawrence smiled.

"I should be glad to think that men really believed in humanity, and all that, but you know they don't—they believe in novelty

144

and getting their own way. With rare exceptions they're still monkeys, especially the scientific variety; and when you put gun-powder and a lighted match into the paws of monkeys, they blow themselves up to see the fun. Monkeys are only safe when deprived of means to be otherwise."

"Lively, that!" said Michael.

"Not livelier than the occasion warrants, my dear boy. I've been thinking. We've got a member here who knows a trick worth twenty of any played in the war—an extraordinarily valuable fellow. The Government have got their eye on him. He'll help the other valuable fellows in France and Germany and America and Russia to make history. Between them, they'll do something really proud—something that'll knock all the other achievements of man into a cocked hat. By the way, Michael, new device of 'Homo sapiens'—the cocked hat."

"Well," said Michael, "what are you going to do about it?"

Sir Lawrence's eyebrow sought his hair.

"Do, my dear fellow? What should I do? Can I go out and grab him and the Government by the slack of their breeches: yes, and all the valuable fellows and Governments of the other countries? No! All I can do is to smoke my cigar and say: 'God rest you, merry gentlemen, let nothing you dismay!' By hook or crook, they will come into their own, Michael; but in the normal course of things I shall be dead before they do."

"I shan't," said Michael.

"No, my dear; but think of the explosions, the sights, the smells. By Jove, you've got something to live for, yet. Sometimes I wish I were your age. And sometimes," Sir Lawrence relighted his cigar, "I don't. Sometimes I think I've had enough of our pretences, and that there's nothing left but to die like gentlemen."

"Some Jeremiad, Dad!"

"Well," said Sir Lawrence, with a twirl of his little grizzled moustache, "I hope I'm wrong. But we're driving fast to a condi-tion of things when millions can be killed by the pressing of a few buttons. What reason is there to suppose that our bumps of benevolence will increase in time to stop our using these great new toys of destruction, Michael!"

" 'Where you know little, place terrors.' "

"Very nice; where did you get that?"

"Out of a life of Christopher Columbus."

"Old C.C.! I could bring myself to wish sometimes that he hadn't been so deucedly inquisitive. We were snugger in the dark ages. There were something to be said for not discovering the Yanks."

"Well," said Michael, "I think we shall pedal through, yet. By the way, about this Elderson stunt: I've just seen the clerk—he doesn't look to me the sort that would have made that up."

"Ah! That! But if Elderson could do such a thing, well—really, anything might happen. It's a complete stumper. He was such a pretty bat, always went in first wicket down. He and I put on fifty-four against Eton. I suppose old Forsyte told you?"

"Yes, he wanted me to find the chap a job."

"Butterfield. Ask him if he's related to old Butterfield the gardener! It would be something to go on. D'you find old Forsyte rather trying?"

Loyal to Fleur, Michael concealed his lips. "No, I get on very well with him."

"He's straight, I admit that."

"Yes," said Michael, "very straight."

"But somewhat reticent."

"Yes," said Michael.

On this conclusion they were silent, as though terrors had been placed beyond it. And soon Michael rose.

"Past ten, I'd better go home."

Returning the way he came, he could think of nothing but Wilfrid. What wouldn't he give to hear him say: "It's all right, old man; I've got over it!"—to wring him by the hand again. Why should one catch this fatal disease called love? Why should one be driven half crazy by it? They said love was Nature's provision against Bart's terrors, against the valuable fellows. An insistent urge—lest the race die out. Prosaic, if true! Not that he cared whether Fleur had children. Queer how Nature camouflaged her schemes—leery old bird! But over-reaching herself a bit, wasn't she? Children might yet go clean out of fashion if Bart was right. A very little more would do it; who would have children for the mere pleasure of seeing them blown up, poisoned, starved to death? A few fanatics would hold on, the rest of the world go barren. The cocked hat! Instinctively Michael straightened his own, ready for crossing under Big Ben. He had reached the centre of Parliament Square, when a figure coming towards him swerved suddenly to its left and made in the direction of Victoria. Tall, with a swing in its walk. Wilfrid! Michael stood still. Coming from—South Square! And suddenly he gave chase. He did not run, but he walked his hardest. The blood beat in his temples, and

146

he felt confused to a pitch past bearing. Wilfrid must have seen him, or he wouldn't have swerved, wouldn't be legging it away like a demon. Black!—black! He was not gaining, Wilfrid had the legs of him—to overtake him, he must run! But there rose in Michael a sort of exaltation. His best friend—his wife! There was a limit. One might be too proud to fight that. Let him go his ways! He stood still, watched the swift figure disappear, and slowly, head down under the now cocked hat, turned towards home. He walked quite quietly, and with a sense of finality. No use making a song about it! No fuss, but no retreat! In the few hundred yards before he reached his Square he was chiefly conscious of the tallness of houses, the shortness of men. Such midgets to have made this monstrous pile, lighted it so that it shone in an enormous glittering heap whose glow blurred the colour of the sky! What a vast business this midget activity! Absurd to think that his love for another midget mattered! He turned his key in the lock, took off his cocked hat and went into the drawing-room. Unlighted—empty? No. She and Ting-a-ling were on the floor before the fire! He sat down on the settee, and was abruptly conscious that he was trembling and sweating as if he had smoked a too strong cigar. Fleur had raised herself, cross-legged, and was staring up at him. He waited to get the better of his trembling. Why didn't she speak? Why was she sitting there, in the dark? 'She knows,' he thought: 'we both know this is the end. O God, let me at least be a sport!' He took a cushion, put it behind him, crossed his legs, and leaned back. His voice surprised him suddenly:

"May I ask you something, Fleur? And will you please answer me quite truly?"

"Yes."

"It's this: I know you didn't love me when you married me. I don't think you love me now. Do you want me to clear out?"

A long time seemed to pass.

"No."

"Do you mean that?"

"Yes."

"Why?"

"Because I don't."

Michael got up.

"Will you answer one thing more?"

"Yes."

"Was Wilfrid here to-night?"

147

"Yes—no. That is——"

His hands clutched each other; he saw her eyes fix on them, and kept them still.

"Fleur, don't!"

"I'm not. He came to the window there. I saw his face—that's all. His face—it—Oh! Michael, don't be unkind to-night!"

Unkind! Unkind! Michael's heart swelled at that strange word.

"It's all right," he stammered. "So long as you tell me what it is you want."

Fleur said, without moving:

"I want to be comforted."

Ah! She knew exactly what to say, how to say it! And going on his knees, he began to comfort her.

## Chapter XII

## GOING EAST

HE had not been on his knees many minutes before they suffered from reaction. To kneel there comforting Fleur brought him a growing discomfort. He believed her to-night, as he had not believed her for months past. But what was Wilfrid doing? Where wandering? The face at the window—face without voice, without attempt to reach her! Michael ached in that illegitimate organ the heart. Withdrawing his arms, he stood up.

"Would you like me to have a look for him? If it's all over—he might—I might——"

Fleur, too, stood up. She was calm enough now.

"Yes, I'll go to bed." With Ting-a-ling in her arms, she went to the door; her face, between the dog's chestnut fur and her own, was very pale, very still.

"By the way," she said, "this is my second no go, Michael; I suppose it means——"

Michael gasped. Currents of emotion, welling, ebbing, swirling, rendered him incapable of speech.

"The night of the balloon," she said: "Do you mind?"

"Mind? Good God! Mind!"

"That's all right, then. _I_ don't. Good-night!"

She was gone. Without reason, Michael thought: 'In the beginning was the Word, and the Word was with God, and the Word was God.' And he stood, as if congealed, overcome by an uncontrollable sense of solidity. A child coming! It was as though the

148

barque of his being, tossed and drifted, suddenly rode tethered—anchor down. He turned and tore at the curtains. Night of stars! Wonderful world! Jolly—jolly! And—Wilfrid! He flattened his face against the glass. Outside there Wilfrid's had been flattened. He could see it if he shut his eyes. Not fair! Dog lost—man lost! S.O.S. He went into the hall, and from the mothless marble coffer rived his thickest coat. He took the first taxi that came by.

"Cork Street! Get along!" Needle in bundle of hay! Quarter-past eleven by Big Ben! The intense relief of his whole being in that jolting cab seemed to him brutal. Salvation! It *was*—he had a strange certainty of that as though he saw Fleur suddenly 'close-up' in a very strong light, concrete beneath her graceful veerings. Family! Continuation! He had been unable to anchor her, for he was not of her! But her child could and would! And, perhaps, he would yet come in with the milk. Why did he love her so—it was not done! Wilfrid and he were donkeys—out of touch, out of tune with the times!

"Here you are, sir—what number?"

"All right! Cool your heels and wait for me! Have a cigarette!"

With one between his own lips which felt so dry, he went down the backwater.

A light in Wilfrid's rooms! He rang the bell. The door was opened, the face of Wilfrid's man looked forth.

"Yes, sir?"

"Mr. Desert in?"

"No, sir. Mr. Desert has just started for the East. His ship sails to-morrow."

"Oh!" said Michael blankly. "Where from?"

"Plymouth, sir. His train leaves Paddington at midnight. You might catch him yet."

"It's very sudden," said Michael, "he never——"

"No, sir. Mr. Desert is a sudden gentleman."

"Well, thanks; I'll try and catch him."

Back in the cab with the words: "Paddington—flick her along!" he thought: 'A sudden gentleman!' Perfect! He remembered the utter suddenness of that little interview beside the bust of Lionel Charwell. Sudden their friendship, sudden its end—sudden even Wilfrid's poems—offspring of a sudden soul! Staring from window to window in that jolting, rattling cab, Michael suffered from St. Vitus's dance. Was he a fool? Could he not let well alone? Pity was posh! And yet! With Wilfrid would go a bit of his heart,

149

and in spite of all he would like him to know that. Upper Brook Street, Park Lane! Emptying streets, cold night, stark plane trees painted-up by the lamps against a bluish dark. And Michael thought: 'We wander! What's the end—the goal? To do one's bit, and not worry! But what is my bit? What's Wilfrid's? Where will he end up, now?'

The cab rattled down the station slope and drew up under cover. Ten minutes to twelve, and a long heavy train on platform one!

'What shall I do?' thought Michael: 'It's so darned crude! Must I go down—carriage by carriage? "Couldn't let you go, old man, without"—blurb!'

Bluejackets! If not drunk—as near as made no matter. Eight minutes still! He began slowly walking along the train. He had not passed four windows before he saw his quarry. Desert was sitting back to the engine in the near corner of an empty first. An unlighted cigarette was in his mouth, his fur collar turned up to his eyes, and his eyes fixed on an unopened paper on his lap. He sat without movement; Michael stood looking at him. His heart beat fast. He struck a match, took two steps, and said:

"Light, old boy?"

Desert stared up at him.

"Thanks," he said, and took the match. By its flare his face was dark, thin, drawn; his eyes dark, deep, tired. Michael leaned in the window. Neither spoke.

"Take your seat, if you're going, sir."

"I'm not," said Michael. His whole inside seemed turning over.

"Where are you going, old man?" he said suddenly.

"Jericho."

"God, Wilfrid, I'm sorry!"

Desert smiled.

"Cut it out!"

"Yes, I know! Shake hands?"

Desert held out his hand.

Michael squeezed it hard.

A whistle sounded.

Desert rose suddenly and turned to the rack above him. He took a parcel from a bag. "Here," he said, "these wretched things! Publish them if you like."

Something clicked in Michael's throat.

"Thanks, old man! That's great! Good-bye!"

A sort of beauty came into Desert's face.

"So long!" he said.

The train moved. Michael withdrew his elbows; quite still, he stared at the motionless figure slowly borne along, away. Carriage after carriage went by him, full of bluejackets leaning out, clamouring, singing, waving handkerchiefs and bottles. Guard's van now—the tail light—all spread—a crimson blur—setting East—going—going—gone!

And that was all—was it? He thrust the parcel into his coat pocket. Back to Fleur, now! Way of the world—one man's meat, another's poison! He passed his hand over his eyes. The dashed things were full of—blurb!

## PART III

### Chapter I

### BANK HOLIDAY

WHITSUNTIDE Bank Holiday was producing its seasonal invasion of Hampstead Heath, and among the ascending swarm were two who meant to make money in the morning and spend it in the afternoon.

Tony Bicket, with balloons and wife, embarked early on the Hampstead Tube.

"You'll see," he said, "I'll sell the bloomin' lot by twelve o'clock, and we'll go on the bust."

Squeezing his arm, Victorine fingered, through her dress, a slight swelling just above her right knee. It was caused by fifty-four pounds fastened in the top of her stocking. She had little feeling now, against balloons. They afforded temporary nourishment, till she had the few more pounds needful for their passage-money. Tony still believed he was going to screw salvation out of his blessed balloons: he was 'that hopeful—Tony', though their heads were only just above water on his takings. And she smiled. With her secret she could afford to be indifferent now to the stigma of gutter hawking. She had her story pat. From the evening paper, and from communion on buses with those interested in the national pastime, she had acquired the necessary information about racing. She even talked of it with Tony, who had street-corner knowledge. Already she had prepared chapter and verse of two imaginary coups; a sovereign made out of stitching imaginary blouses, invested on the winner of the Two Thousand Guineas, and the result on the dead-heater for the Jubilee at nice odds; this with a third winner, still to be selected, would bring her imaginary winnings up to the needed sixty pounds odd she would so soon have saved now out of 'the altogether'. This tale she would pitch to Tony in a week or two, reeling off by heart the wonderful luck she had kept from him until she had the whole of the money. She would slip her forehead against his eyes if he looked at her too hard, and kiss his lips till his head was no longer clear. And in the morning they would wake up and take their passages. Such was the plan of Victorine, with five ten-pound and four one-pound notes in her stocking, attached to the pink silk stays.

'Afternoon of a Dryad' had long been finished, and was on exhibition at the Dumetrius Gallery, with other works of Aubrey Greene. Victorine had paid a shilling to see it; had stood some furtive minutes gazing at that white body glimmering from among grass and spikey flowers, at the face, turned as if saying: "I know a secret!"

"Bit of a genius, Aubrey Greene—that face is jolly good!" Scared, and hiding the face, Victorine had slipped away.

From the very day when she had stood shivering outside the studio of Aubrey Greene she had been in full work. He had painted her three times—always nice, always polite, quite the gentleman! And he had given her introductions. Some had painted her in clothes, some half-draped, some in that 'altogether', which no longer troubled her, with the money swelling her stocking and Tony without suspicion. Not everyone had been 'nice'; advances had been made to her, but she had nipped them in the bud. It would have meant the money quicker, but—Tony! In a fortnight now she could snap her fingers at it all. And often on the way home she stood by that plate-glass window, before the fruits, and the corn, and the blue butterflies. . . .

In the packed railway carriage they sat side by side, Bicket with tray on knee, debating where he had best stand.

"I favour the mokes," he said at last, "up by the pond. People'll have more money than when they get down among the swings and coconuts; and you can go and sit in a chair by the pond, like the seaside—I don't want you with me not till I've sold out."

Victorine pressed his arm.

Along the top and over on to the heath to north and south the holiday swarms surged, in perfect humour, carrying paper bags. Round the pond children, with thin, grey-white, spindly legs, were paddling and shrilly chattering, too content to smile. Elderly couples crawled slowly by, with jutting stomachs, and faces discoloured by the unaccustomed climb. Girls and young men were few, for they were dispersed already on the heath, in search of a madder merriment. On benches, in chairs of green canvas or painted wood, hundreds were sitting, contemplating their feet, as if imagining the waves of the sea. Now and again three donkeys would start, urged from behind, and slowly tittup their burdens along the pond's margin. Hawkers cried goods. Fat dark women told fortunes. Policemen stood cynically near them. A man talked and talked and took his hat round.

Tony Bicket unslung his tray. His cockney voice, wheedling and a little husky, offered his coloured airs without intermission. This was something like! It was brisk! And now and again he gazed through the throng away across the pond, to where Victorine would be seated in a canvas chair, looking different from everyone—he knew.

"Fine balloons—fine balloons! Six for a bob! Big one, Madam? Only sixpence. See the size! Buy, buy! Tyke one for the little boy!"

No 'aldermen' up here, but plenty in the mood to spend their money on a bit of brightness!

At five minutes before noon he snapped his tray to—not a bally balloon left! With six Bank Holidays a week he would make his fortune! Tray under arm, he began to tour the pond. The kiddies were all right, but—good Lord—how thin and pale! If he and Vic had a kid—but not they—not till they got out there! A fat brown kid, chysin' blue butterflies, and the sun oozin' out of him! Rounding the end of the pond, he walked slowly along the chairs. Lying back, elegant, with legs crossed, in brown stockings showing to the knees, and neat brown shoes with the flaps over—My! she looked a treat—in a world of her own, like that! Something caught Bicket by the throat. Gosh! He wanted things for her!

"Well, Vic! Penny!"

"I was thinkin' of Australia."

"Ah! It's a gaudy long wait. Never mind—I've sold the bally lot. Which shall we do, go down among the trees, or get to the swings, at once?"

"The swings," said Victorine.

The Vale of Health was in rhapsodic mood. The crowd flowed here in a slow, speechless stream, to the cries of the booth-keepers, and the owners of swings and coconuts. "Roll—bowl—or pitch! Now for the milky ones! Penny a shy! . . . Who's for the swings? . . . Ices . . . Ices . . . Fine bananas!"

On the giant merry-go-round under its vast umbrella the thirty chain-hung seats were filled with girls and men. Round to the music—slowly—faster—whirling out to the full extent of the chain, bodies bent back, legs stuck forward, laughter and speech dying, faces solemn, a little lost, hands gripping the chains hard.

154

Faster, faster; slowing, slowing to a standstill, and the music silent.

"My word!" murmured Victorine. "Come on, Tony!"

They entered the enclosure and took their seats. Victorine, on the outside, locked her feet, instinctively, one over the other, and tightening her clasp on the chains, curved her body to the motion. Her lips parted:

"Lor, Tony!"

Faster, faster—every nerve and sense given to that motion! O-o-h! It *was* a feeling—flying round like that above the world! Faster—faster! Slower—slow, and the descent to earth.

"Tony—it's 'eaven!"

"Queer feelin' in yer inside, when you're swung right out!"

"I'd like it level with the top. Let's go once more!"

"Right-o!"

Twice more they went—half his profit on balloons! But who cared? He liked to see her face. After that, six shies at the milky ones without a hit, an ice apiece: then arm-in-arm to find a place to eat their lunch. That was the time Bicket enjoyed most, after the ginger-beer and sandwiches; smoking his fag, with his head on her lap, and the sky blue. A long time like that; till at last she stirred.

"Let's go and see the dancin'!"

In the grass enclosure ringed by the running path, some two dozen couples were jigging to a band.

Victorine pulled at his arm. "I *would* love a turn!"

"Well, let's 'ave a go," said Bicket. "This one-legged bloke'll 'old my tray."

They entered the ring.

"Hold me tighter, Tony!"

Bicket obeyed. Nothing he liked better; and slowly their feet moved—to this side and that. They made little way, revolving, keeping time, oblivious of appearances.

"You dance all right, Tony."

"*You* dance a treat!" gasped Bicket.

In the intervals, panting, they watched over the one-legged man; then to it again, till the band ceased for good.

"My word!" said Victorine. "They dance on board ship, Tony!"

Bicket squeezed her waist.

"I'll do the trick yet, if I 'ave to rob the Bank. There's nothin' I wouldn't do for you, Vic."

But Victorine smiled. She had done the trick already.

The crowd with parti-coloured faces, tired, good-humoured,

frowsily scented, strolled over a battlefield thick-strewn with paper bags, banana peel, and newspapers.

"Let's 'ave tea, and one more swing," said Bicket; "then we'll get over on the other side among the trees."

Away over on the far side were many couples. The sun went very slowly down. Those two sat under a bush and watched it go. A faint breeze swung and rustled the birch leaves. There was little human sound out here. All seemed to have come for silence, to be waiting for darkness in the hush. Now and then some stealthy spy would pass and scrutinise.

"Foxes!" said Bicket. "Gawd! I'd like to rub their noses in it!"

Victorine sighed, pressing closer to him.

Someone was playing on a banjo now; a voice singing. It grew dusk, but a moon was somewhere rising, for little shadows stole out along the ground.

They spoke in whispers. It seemed wrong to raise the voice, as though the grove were under a spell. Even their whisperings were scarce. Dew fell, but they paid no heed to it. With hands locked, and cheeks together, they sat very still. Bicket had a thought. This was poetry—this was! Darkness now, with a sort of faint and silvery glow, a sound of drunken singing on the Spaniard's Road, the whirr of belated cars returning from the north—and suddenly an owl hooted.

"My!" murmured Victorine, shivering. "An owl! Fancy! I used to hear one at Norbiton. I 'ope it's not bad luck!"

Bicket rose and stretched himself.

"Come on!" he said: "we've 'ad a dy. Don't you go catchin' cold!"

Arm-in-arm, slowly, through the darkness of the birch-grove, they made their way upwards—glad of the lamps, and the street, and the crowded station, as though they had taken an overdose of solitude.

Huddled in their carriage on the Tube, Bicket idly turned the pages of a derelict paper. But Victorine sat thinking of so much, that it was as if she thought of nothing. The swings and the grove in the darkness, and the money in her stocking. She wondered Tony hadn't noticed when it crackled—there wasn't a safe place to keep it in! What was he looking at, with his eyes so fixed? She peered, and read: " 'Afternoon of a Dryad.' The striking picture by Aubrey Greene, on exhibition at the Dumetrius Gallery."

Her heart stopped beating.

"Cripes!" said Bicket. "Ain't that like you?"

"Like me? No!"

Bicket held the paper closer. "It *is*. It's like you all over. I'll cut that out. I'd like to see that picture."

The colour came up in her cheeks, released from a heart beating too fast now.

" 'Tisn't decent," she said.

"Dunno about that; but it's awful like you. It's even got your smile."

Folding the paper, he began to tear the sheet. Victorine's little finger pressed the notes beneath her stocking.

"Funny," she said slowly, "to think there's people in the world so like each other."

"I never thought there could be one like you. Charin' Cross; we gotta change."

Hurrying along the rat-runs of the Tube, she slipped her hand into his pocket, and soon some scraps of torn paper fluttered down behind her following him in the crush. If only he didn't remember where the picture was!

Awake in the night, she thought:

'I don't care; I'm going to get the rest of the money—that's all about it.'

But her heart moved queerly within her, like that of one whose feet have trodden suddenly the quaking edge of a bog.

## Chapter II

### OFFICE WORK

MICHAEL sat correcting the proofs of *Counterfeits*—the book left by Wilfrid behind him.

"Can you see Butterfield, sir?"

"I can."

In Michael the word Butterfield excited an uneasy pride. The young man fulfilled with increasing success the function for which he had been engaged, on trial, four months ago. The head traveller had even called him 'a find'. Next to 'Copper Coin' he was the finest feather in Michael's cap. The Trade were not buying, yet Butterfield was selling books, or so it was reported; he appeared to have a natural gift of inspiring confidence where it was not justified. Danby and Winter had even entrusted to him the private marketing of the vellum-bound 'Limited' of 'A Duet', by which they were hoping to recoup their losses on the ordinary edition. He was now engaged in working through a list of names considered likely to patronise the little masterpiece. This method of private approach had been suggested by himself.

"You see, sir," he had said to Michael: "I know a bit about Coué. Well, you can't work that on the Trade—they've got no capacity for faith. What can you expect? Every day they buy all sorts of stuff, always basing themselves on past sales. You can't find one in twenty that'll back the future. But with private gentlemen, and especially private ladies, you can leave a thought with them like Coué does—put it into them again and again that day by day in every way the author's gettin' better and better; and ten to one when you go round next, it's got into their subconscious, especially if you take 'em just after lunch or dinner, when they're a bit drowsy. Let me take my own time, sir, and I'll put that edition over for you."

"Well," Michael had answered, "if you can inspire confidence in the future of my governor, Butterfield, you'll deserve more than your ten per cent."

"I can do it, sir; it's just a question of faith."

"But you haven't any, have you?"

"Well, not, so to speak, in the author—but I've got faith that I can give *them* faith in him; that's the real point."

"I see—the three-card stunt; inspire the faith you haven't got, that the card is there, and they'll take it. Well, the disillusion is not immediate—you'll probably always get out of the room in time. Go ahead, then!"

The young man Butterfield had smiled. . . .

The uneasy part of the pride inspired in Michael now by the name was due to old Forsyte's continually saying to him that he didn't know—he couldn't tell—there was that young man and his story about Elderson, and they got no further. . . .

"Good morning, sir. Can you spare me five minutes?"

"Come in, Butterfield. Bunkered with 'Duet'?"

"No, sir. I've placed forty already. It's another matter." Glancing at the shut door, the young man came closer.

"I'm working my list alphabetically. Yesterday I was in the E's." His voice dropped. "Mr. Elderson."

"Phew!" said Michael. "You can give *him* the go-by."

"As a fact, sir, I haven't."

"What! Been over the top?"

"Yes, sir. Last night."

158

THE WHITE MONKEY

"Good for you, Butterfield! What happened?"

"I didn't send my name in, sir—just the firm's card."

Michael was conscious of a very human malice in the young man's voice and face.

"Well?"

"Mr. Elderson, sir, was at his wine. I'd thought it out, and I began as if I'd never seen him before. What struck me was—he took my cue!"

"Didn't kick you out?"

"Far from it, sir. He said at once: 'Put my name down for two copies.'"

Michael grinned. "You both had a nerve."

"No, sir; that's just it. Mr. Elderson got it between wind and water. He didn't like it a little bit."

"I don't twig," said Michael.

"My being in this firm's employ, sir. He knows you're a partner here, and Mr. Forsyte's son-in-law, doesn't he?"

"He does."

"Well, sir, you see the connection—two directors believing me—not him. That's why I didn't miss him out. I fancied it'd shake him up. I happened to see his face in the sideboard glass as I went out. He's got the wind up all right."

Michael bit his forefinger, conscious of a twinge of sympathy with Elderson, as for a fly with the first strand of cobweb round his hind leg.

"Thank you, Butterfield," he said.

When the young man was gone, he sat stabbing his blotting-paper with a paper-knife. What curious 'class' sensation was this? Or was it merely fellow-feeling with the hunted, a tremor at the way things found one out? For, surely, this was real evidence, and he would have to pass it on to his father, and 'Old Forsyte'. Elderson's nerve must have gone phut, or he'd have said: "You impudent young scoundrel—get out of here!" That, clearly, was the only right greeting from an innocent, and the only advisable greeting from a guilty man. Well! Nerve did fail sometimes—even the best. Witness the very proof-sheet he had just corrected:

THE COURT MARTIAL
"'See 'ere! I'm myde o' nerves and blood
The syme as you, not meant to be
Froze stiff up to me ribs in mud.
You try it, like I 'ave, an' see!

159

" 'Aye, you snug beauty brass hats, when
    You stick what I stuck out that d'y,
An' keep yer ruddy 'earts up—then
    You'll learn, maybe, the right to s'y:

" 'Take aht an' shoot 'im in the snow,
    Shoot 'im for cowardice! 'E who serves
His King and Country's got to know
    There's no such bloody thing as nerves.' "

Good old Wilfrid!

"Yes, Miss Perren?"

"The letter to Sir James Foggart, Mr. Mont; you told me to remind you. And will you see Miss Manuelli?"

"Miss Manu—— Oh! Ah! Yes."

Bicket's girl wife, whose face they had used on Storbert's novel, the model for Aubrey Greene's—— Michael rose, for the girl was in the room already.

'I remember that dress!' he thought: 'Fleur never liked it.'

"What can I do for you, Mrs. Bicket? How's Bicket, by the way?"

"Fairly, sir, thank you."

"Still in balloons?"

"Yes."

"Well, we all are, Mrs. Bicket."

"Beg pardon?"

"In the air—don't you think? But you didn't come to tell me that?"

"No, sir."

A slight flush in those sallow cheeks, fingers concerned with the tips of the worn gloves, lips uncertain; but the eyes steady—really an uncommon girl!

"You remember givin' me a note to Mr. Greene, sir?"

"I do; and I've seen the result; it's topping, Mrs. Bicket."

"Yes. But it's got into the papers—my husband saw it there last night; and of course, he doesn't know about me."

Phew! For what had he let this girl in?

"I've made a lot of money at it, sir—almost enough for our passage to Australia; but now I'm frightened. 'Isn't it like you?' he said to me. I tore the paper up, but suppose he remembers the name of the Gallery and goes to see the picture! That's even much more like me! He might go on to Mr. Greene. So would you mind, sir, speaking to Mr. Greene, and beggin' him to say it was someone else, in case Tony did go?"

"Not a bit," said Michael. "But do you think Bicket would mind so very much, considering what it's done for you? It can be quite a respectable profession."

Victorine's hands moved up to her breast.

"Yes," she said, simply. "I have been quite respectable. And I only did it because we do so want to get away, and I couldn't bear seein' him standin' in the gutter there sellin' those balloons in the fogs. But I'm ever so scared, sir, now."

Michael stared.

"My God!" he said; "money's an evil thing!"

Victorine smiled faintly. "The want of it is, I know."

"How much more do you need, Mrs. Bicket?"

"Only another ten pound, about, sir."

"I can let you have that."

"Oh! thank you; but it's not that—I can easy earn it—I've got used to it; a few more days don't matter."

"But how are you going to account for having the money?"

"Say I won it bettin'."

"*Thin!*" said Michael. "Look here! Say you came to me and I advanced it. If Bicket repays it from Australia, I can always put it to your credit again at a bank out there. I've got you into a hole, in a way, and I'd like to get you out of it."

"Oh! no, sir; you did me a service. I don't want to put you about, telling falsehoods for me."

"It won't worry me a bit, Mrs. Bicket. I can lie to the umteenth when there's no harm in it. The great thing for you is to get away sharp. Are there many other pictures of you?"

"Oh! yes, a lot—not that you'd recognise them, I think, they're so square and funny."

"Ah! well—Aubrey Greene has got you to the life!"

"Yes; it's like me all over, Tony says."

"Quite. Well, I'll speak to Aubrey, I shall be seeing him at lunch. Here's the ten pounds! That's agreed, then? You came to me to-day—see? Say you had a brain-wave. I quite understand the whole thing. You'd do a lot for him; and he'd do a lot for you. It's all right—don't cry!"

Victorine swallowed violently. Her hand in the worn glove returned his squeeze.

"I'd tell him to-night, if I were you," said Michael, "and I'll get ready."

When she had gone he thought: 'Hope Bicket won't think I received value for that sixty pounds!' And, pressing his bell, he resumed the stabbing of his blotting-paper.

161

"Yes, Mr. Mont?"

"Now let's get on with it, Miss Perren."

" 'DEAR SIR JAMES FOGGART,—We have given the utmost consideration to your very interesting—er—production. While we are
of opinion that the views so well expressed on the present condition of Britain in relation to the rest of the world are of great
value to all—er—thinking persons, we do not feel that there are
enough—er—thinking persons to make it possible to publish the
book, except at a loss. The—er—thesis that Britain should now
look for salvation through adjustment of markets, population,
supply and demand, within the Empire, put with such exceedingly
plain speech, will, we are afraid, get the goat of all the political
parties; nor do we feel that your plan of emigrating boys and girls
in large quantities before they are spoiled by British town life, can
do otherwise than irritate a working-class which knows nothing
of conditions outside its own country, and is notably averse to
giving its children a chance in any other.' "

"Am I to put that, Mr. Mont?"

"Yes; but tone it in a bit. Er——"

" 'Finally, your view that the land should be used to grow food
is so very unusual in these days, that we feel your book would
have a hostile Press except from the Old Guard and the Die-hard,
and a few folk with vision.' "

"Yes, Mr. Mont?"

" 'In a period of veering—er—transitions'—keep that, Miss
Perren—'and the airy unreality of hopes that have gone up the
spout'—almost keep that—'any scheme that looks forward and
defers harvest for twenty years, must be extraordinarily unpopular.
For all these reasons you will see how necessary it is for you to—
er—seek another publisher. In short, we are not taking any.

" 'With—er—' what you like—'dear Sir James Foggart,

" 'We are your obedient servants,

" 'DANBY and WINTER.' "

"When you've translated that, Miss Perren, bring it in, and I'll
sign it."

"Yes. Only, Mr. Mont—I thought you were a Socialist. This
almost seems—forgive my asking?"

"Miss Perren, it's struck me lately that labels are 'off'. How can
a man be anything at a time when everything's in the air? Look at
the Liberals. They can't see the situation whole because of Free
Trade; nor can the Labour Party because of their Capital levy; nor
can the Tories because of Protection; they're all hag-ridden by

catch-words! Old Sir James Foggart's jolly well right, but nobody's going to listen to him. His book will be waste paper if anybody ever publishes it. The world's unreal just now, Miss Perren; and of all countries we're the most unreal."

"Why, Mr. Mont?"

"Why? Because with the most stickfast of all the national temperaments, we're holding on to what's gone more bust for us than for any other country. Anyway, Mr. Danby shouldn't have left the letter to me, if he didn't mean me to enjoy myself. Oh! and while we're about it—I've got to refuse Harold Master's new book. It's a mistake, but they won't have it."

"Why not, Mr. Mont? 'The Sobbing Turtle' was such a success!"

"Well, in this new thing Master's got hold of an idea which absolutely forces him to say something. Winter says those who hailed 'The Sobbing Turtle' as such a work of art, are certain to be down on this for that; and Mr. Danby calls the book an outrage on human nature. So there's nothing for it. Let's have a shot:

" 'MY DEAR MASTER,—In the exhilaration of your subject it has obviously not occurred to you that you've bust up the show. In 'The Sobbing Turtle' you were absolutely in tune with half the orchestra, and that—er—the noisiest half. You were charmingly archaic, and securely cold-blooded. But now, what have you gone and done? Taken the last Marquesan islander for your hero and put him down in London town! This thing's a searching satire, a real criticism of life. I'm sure you didn't mean to be contemporary, or want to burrow into reality; but your subject has run off with you Cold acid and cold blood are very different things, you know, to say nothing of your having had to drop the archaic. Personally, of course, I think this new thing miles better than 'The Sobbing Turtle', which was a nice little affair, but nothing to make a song about. But I'm not the public, and I'm not the critics. The young and thin will be aggrieved by your lack of modernity, they'll say you're moralising; the old and fat will call you bitter and destructive; and the ordinary public will take your Marquesan seriously, and resent your making him superior to themselves. The prospects, you see, are not gaudy. How d'you think we're going to 'get away' with such a book? Well, we're not! Such is the fiat of the firm. I don't agree with it. I'd publish it to-morrow; but needs must when Danby and Winter drive. So, with every personal regret, I return what is really a masterpiece.

" 'Always yours,
" 'MICHAEL MONT.' "

"D'you know, Miss Perren, I don't think you need translate that?"

"I'm afraid it would be difficult."

"Right-o, then; but do the other, please. I'm going to take my wife out to see a picture; back by four. Oh! and if a little chap called Bicket, that we used to have here, calls any time and asks to see me, he's to come up; but I want warning first. Will you let them know downstairs?"

"Yes, Mr. Mont. Oh! didn't—wasn't that Miss Manuelli the model for the wrapper on Mr. Storbert's novel?"

"She was, Miss Perren; alone I found her."

"She's very interesting-looking, isn't she?"

"She's unique, I'm afraid."

"She needn't mind that, I should think."

"That depends," said Michael; and stabbed his blotting-paper.

## Chapter III

### 'AFTERNOON OF A DRYAD'

FLEUR was still gracefully concealing most of what Michael called 'the eleventh baronet', now due in about two months' time. She seemed to be adapting herself, in mind and body, to the quiet and persistent collection of the heir. Michael knew that, from the first, following the instructions of her mother, she had been influencing his sex, repeating to herself, every evening before falling asleep, and every morning on waking the words: "Day by day, in every way, he is getting more and more male," to infect the subconscious which, everybody now said, controlled the course of events; and that she was abstaining from the words: "I *will* have a boy," for this, setting up a reaction, everybody said, was liable to produce a girl. Michael noted that she turned more and more to her mother, as if the French, or more naturalistic, side of her, had taken charge of a process which had to do with the body. She was frequently at Mapledurham, going down in Soames's car, and her mother was frequently in South Square. Annette's handsome presence, with its tendency to black lace was always pleasing to Michael, who had never forgotten her espousal of his suit in days when it was a forlorn hope. Though he still felt only on the threshold of Fleur's heart, and was preparing to play second fiddle to 'the eleventh baronet', he was infinitely easier in mind since Wilfrid had been gone. And he watched, with a sort of amused adoration, the way

164

in which she focussed her collecting powers on an object that had
no epoch, a process that did not date.

Personally conducted by Aubrey Greene, the expedition to view
his show at the Dumetrius Gallery left South Square after an early
lunch.

"Your Dryad came to me this morning, Aubrey," said Michael
in the cab. "She wanted me to ask you to put up a barrage if by
any chance her husband blows round to accuse you of painting his
wife. It seems he's seen a reproduction of the picture."

"Umm!" murmured the painter: "Shall I, Fleur?"

"Of course you must, Aubrey!"

Aubrey Greene's smile slid from her to Michael.

"Well, what's his name?"

"Bicket."

Aubrey Greene fixed his eyes on space, and murmured slowly:

> "An angry young husband called Bicket
> Said: 'Turn yourself round and I'll kick it;
> You have painted my wife
> In the nude to the life.
> Do you think, Mr. Greene, it was cricket?'"

"Oh! Aubrey!"

"Chuck it!" said Michael, "I'm serious. She's a most plucky
little creature. She's made the money they wanted, and remained
respectable."

"So far as I'm concerned, certainly."

"Well, I should think so."

"Why, Fleur?"

"You're not a vamp, Aubrey!"

"As a matter of fact, she excited my æsthetic sense."

"Much that'd save her from some æsthetes!" muttered Michael.

"Also, she comes from Putney."

"There you have a real reason. Then, you will put up a barrage
if Bicket blows in?"

Aubrey Greene laid his hand on his heart. "And there we are!"

For the convenience of the eleventh baronet Michael had chosen
the hour when the proper patrons of Aubrey Greene would still be
lunching. A shock-headed young man and three pale-green girls
alone wandered among the pictures. The painter led the way at
once to his masterpiece; and for some minutes they stood before it
in a suitable paralysis. To speak too soon in praise would never do;

165

to speak too late would be equally tactless; to speak too fulsomely would jar; to mutter coldly: "Very nice—very nice indeed!" would blight. To say bluntly: "Well, old man, to tell you the truth, I don't like it a little bit!" would get his goat.

At last Michael pinched Fleur gently, and she said:

"It really is charming, Aubrey; and awfully like—at least——"

"So far as one can tell. But really, old man, you've done it in once. I'm afraid Bicket will think so, anyway."

"Dash that!" muttered the painter. "How do you find the colour values?"

"Jolly fine; especially the flesh; don't you think so, Fleur?"

"Yes; only I should have liked that shadow down the side a little deeper."

"Yes?" murmured the painter: "Perhaps!"

"You've caught the spirit," said Michael. "But I tell you what, old man, you're for it—the thing's got meaning. I don't know what the critics will do to you."

Aubrey Greene smiled. "That was the worst of her. She led me on. To get an idea's fatal."

"Personally, I don't agree to that; do you, Fleur?"

"Of course not; only one doesn't say so."

"Time we did, instead of kow-towing to the Café C'rillon. I say, the hair's all right, and so are the toes—they curl as you look at 'em."

"And it is a relief not to get legs painted in streaky cubes. The asphodels rather reminds one of the flowers in Leonardo's 'Virgin of the Rocks', Aubrey."

"The whole thing's just a bit Leonardoish, old man. You'll have to live that down."

"Oh! Aubrey, my father's seen it. I believe he's biting. Something you said impressed him—about our white monkey, d'you remember?"

Aubrey Greene threw up his hands. "Ah! That white monkey—to have painted that! Eat the fruit and chuck the rinds around, and ask with your eyes what it's all about."

"A moral!" said Michael: "Take care, old man! Well! Our taxi's running up. Come along, Fleur; we'll leave Aubrey to his conscience."

Once more in the cab, he took her arm.

"That poor little snipe, Bicket! Suppose I'd come on you as he'll come on his wife!"

"I shouldn't have looked so nice."

"Oh! yes; much nicer; though she looks nice enough, I must say."

"Then why should Bicket mind, in these days of emancipation?"

"Why? Good Lord, ducky! you don't suppose Bicket——! I mean, we emancipated people have got into the habit of thinking we're the world—well! we aren't; we're an excrescence, small, and noisy. We talk as if all the old values and prejudices had gone; but they've no more gone, really, you know, than the rows of villas and little grey houses."

"Why this outburst, Michael?"

"Well, darling, I'm a bit fed-up with the attitude of our crowd. If emancipation were true, one could stick it; but it's not. There isn't ten per cent. difference between now and thirty years ago."

"How do you know? You weren't alive."

"No; but I read the papers, and talk to the man in the street, and look at people's faces. Our lot think they're the tablecloth, but they're only the fringe. D'you know, only one hundred and fifty thousand people in this country have ever heard a Beethoven Symphony? How many, do you suppose, think old B. a back number? Five thousand, perhaps, out of forty-two millions. How's that for emancipation?"

He stopped, observing that her eyelids had drooped.

"I was thinking, Michael, that I should like to change my bed-room curtains to blue. I saw the exact colour yesterday at Harton's. They say blue has an effect on the mind—the present curtains really are too jazzy."

The eleventh baronet!

"Anything you like, darling. Have a blue ceiling if it helps."

"Oh, no! But I think I'll change the carpet, too; there's a lovely powder blue at Harton's."

"Then get it. Would you like to go there now? I can take the Tube back to the office."

"Yes, I think I'd better. I might miss it."

Michael put his head out of the window. "Harton's, please!" And, replacing his hat, he looked at her. Emancipated! Phew!

## Chapter IV

### AFTERNOON OF A BICKET

JUST about that moment Bicket re-entered his sitting-room and deposited his tray. All the morning under the shadow of St. Paul's he had re-lived Bank Holiday. Exceptionally tired in feet and legs, he was also itching mentally. He had promised himself a refreshing look from time to time at what was almost like a photo of Vic herself. And he had lost the picture! Yet he had taken nothing out of his pockets—just hung his coat up. Had it jogged out in the crush at the station, or had he missed his pocket opening and dropped it in the carriage? And he had wanted to see the original, too. He remembered that the Gallery began with a 'D', and at lunch-time squandered a penny-halfpenny to look up the names. Foreign, he was sure—the picture being naked. 'Dumetrius?' Ah!

Back at his post, he had a bit of luck. 'That alderman', whom he had not seen for months, came by. Intuition made him say at once: "Hope I see you well sir. Never forgotten your kindness."

The 'alderman', who had been staring up as if he saw a magpie on the dome of St. Paul's, stopped as though attacked by cramp.

"Kindness?" he said; "what kindness? Oh! balloons! They were no good to me!"

"No, sir, I'm sure," said Bicket humbly.

"Well, here you are!" muttered the 'alderman'; "don't expect it again."

Half a crown! A whole half-crown! Bicket's eyes pursued the hastening form. "Good luck!" he said softly to himself, and began putting up his tray. "I'll go home and rest my feet, and tyke Vic to see that picture. It'll be funny lookin' at it together."

But she was not in. He sat down and smoked a fag. He felt aggrieved that she was out, this the first afternoon he had taken off. Of course she couldn't stay in all day! Still——! He waited twenty minutes, then put on Michael's suit and shoes.

'I'll go and see it alone,' he thought. 'It'll cost half as much. They charge you sixpence, I expect.'

They charged him a shilling—a shilling! One fourth of his day's earnings, to see a picture! He entered bashfully. There were ladies who smelled of scent and had drawling voices but not a patch on Vic for looks. One of them, behind him, said:

"See! There's Aubrey Greene himself! And that's the picture they're talking of—'Afternoon of a Dryad'."

They passed him and moved on. Bicket followed. At the end of the room, between their draperies and catalogues, he glimpsed the picture. A slight sweat broke out on his forehead. Almost life-size, among the flowers and spiky grasses, the face smiled round at him —very image of Vic! Could someone in the world be as like her as all that? The thought offended him, as a collector is offended finding the duplicate of a unique possession.

"It's a wonderful picture, Mr. Greene. What a type!"

A young man without hat, and fair hair sliding back, answered:
"A find, wasn't she?"

"Oh! perfect! the very spirit of a wood-nymph; so mysterious!"

The word that belonged to Vic! It was unholy. There she lay for all to look at, just because some beastly woman was made like her! A kind of rage invaded Bicket's throat, caused his cheeks to burn; and with it came a queer physical jealousy. That painter! What business had he to paint a woman so like Vic as that—a woman that didn't mind lyin' like that! They and their talk about cahryscuro and paganism, and a bloke called Leneardo! Blast their drawling and their tricks! He tried to move away, and could not, fascinated by that effigy, so uncannily resembling what he had thought belonged to himself alone. Silly to feel so bad over a 'coincidence', but he felt like smashing the glass and cutting the body up into little bits. The ladies and the painter passed on, leaving him alone before the picture. Alone, he did not mind so much. The face was mournful-like, and lonely, and—and teasing, with its smile. It sort of haunted you—it did! 'Well!' thought Bicket, 'I'll get home to Vic. Glad I didn't bring her, after all, to see herself-like. If I was an alderman, I'd buy the blinkin' thing, and burn it!'

And there, in the entrance-lobby, talking to a 'dago', stood—his very own 'alderman'! Bicket paused in sheer amazement.

"It's a rithing name, Mr. Forthyte," he heard the Dago say: "hith prithes are going up."

"That's all very well, Dumetrius, but it's not everybody's money in these days—too highly-finished, altogether!"

"Well, Mr. Forthyte, to *you* I take off ten per thent."

"Take off twenty and I'll buy it.'

That Dago's shoulders mounted above his hairy ears—they did; and what a smile!

"Mithter Forthyte ! Fifteen, thir!"

"Well, you're doing me; but send it round to my daughter's in South Square—you know the number. When do you close?"

"Day after to-morrow, thir."

So! The counterfeit of Vic had gone to that 'alderman', had it? Bicket uttered a savage little sound, and slunk out.

He walked with a queer feeling. Had he got unnecessary wind up? After all, it wasn't her. But to know that another woman could smile that way, have frizzy-ended short black hair, and be all curved the same! And at every woman's passing face he looked —so different, so utterly unlike Vic's!

When he reached home she was standing in the middle of the room, with her lips to a balloon. All around her, on the floor, chairs, table, mantelpiece, were the blown-out shapes of his stock; one by one they had floated from her lips and selected their own resting-places: puce, green, orange, purple, blue, enlivening with their colour the dingy little space. All his balloons blown up! And there, in her best clothes, she stood, smiling, queer, excited.

"What in thunder!" said Bicket.

Raising her dress, she took some crackling notes from the top of her stocking, and held them out to him.

"See! Sixty-four pounds, Tony! I've got it all. We can go."

"*What!*"

"I had a brain-wave—went to that Mr. Mont who gave us the clothes, and he's advanced it. We can pay it back, some day. Isn't it a marvel?"

Bicket's eyes, startled like a rabbit's, took in her smile, her excited flush, and a strange feeling shot through all his body, as if *they* were taking *him* in! She wasn't like Vic! No! Suddenly he felt her arms round him, felt her moist lips on his. She clung so tight, he could not move. His head went round.

"At last! At last! Isn't it fine? Kiss me, Tony!"

Bicket kissed; his vertigo was real, but behind it, for the moment stifled, what sense of unreality! . . .

Was it before night, or in the night, that the doubt first came—ghostly, tapping, fluttering, haunting—then, in the dawn, jabbing through his soul, turning him rigid. The money—the picture—the lost paper—that sense of unreality! This story she had told him! Were such things possible? Why should Mr. Mont advance that money? She had seen him—that was certain; the room, the secretary—you couldn't mistake her description of that Miss Perren. Why, then, feel this jabbing doubt? The money—such a lot of money! Not with Mr. Mont—never—he was a gent! Oh! Swine that he was, to have a thought like that—of Vic! He turned his back to her and tried to sleep. But once you got a thought like that—sleep? No! Her face among the balloons, the way she had smothered his eyes and turned his head—so that he couldn't think, couldn't go into it and ask her questions! A prey to dim doubts, achings, uncertainty, thrills of hope, and visions of 'Austrylia'. Bicket arose haggard.

"Well," he said, over their cocoa and margarined bread: "I must see Mr. Mont, that's certain." And suddenly he added: "Vic?" looking straight into her face.

She answered his look—straight, yes, straight. Oh! he was a proper swine! . . .

When he had left the house Victorine stood quite still, with hands pressed against her chest. She had slept less than he. Still as a mouse, she had turned and turned the thought: 'Did I take him in? Did I?' And if not—what? She took out the notes which had bought—or sold?—their happiness, and counted them once more. And the sense of injustice burned within her. Had she wanted to stand like that before men? Hadn't she been properly through it about that? Why, she could have had the sixty pounds three months ago from that sculptor, who was wild about her; or—so he said! But she had stuck it; yes, she had. Tony had nothing against her really—even if he knew it all. She had done it for him —Well! mostly—for him selling those balloons day after day in all weathers! But for her, they would still be stuck, and another winter coming, and unemployment—so they said in the paper— to be worse and worse! Stuck in the fogs and the cold, again! Ugh! Her chest was still funny sometimes; and he always hoarse. And this poky little room, and the bed so small that she couldn't stir without waking him. Why should Tony doubt her? For he did— she had felt it, heard it in his "Vic?" Would Mr. Mont convince him? Tony was sharp! Her head drooped. The unfairness of it all! Some had everything to their hand, like that pretty wife of Mr. Mont's! And if one tried to find a way and get out to a new chance—then—then—this! She flung her hair back. Tony *must* believe—he should! If he wouldn't, let him look out. She had done nothing to be ashamed of! No, indeed! And with the longing to go in front and lead her happiness along, she got out her old tin trunk, and began with careful method to put things into it.

## Chapter V

### MICHAEL GIVES ADVICE

MICHAEL still sat, correcting the proofs of 'Counterfeits'. Save 'Jericho', there had been no address to send them to. The East was wide, and Wilfrid had made no sign. Did Fleur ever think of Wilfrid—well, probably he was forgetting her already. Even passion required a little sustenance.

"A Mr. Forsyte to see you, sir."

Apparition in bookland!

"Ah! Show him in."

Soames entered with an air of suspicion.

"This your place?" he said. "I've looked in to tell you that I've bought that picture of young Greene's. Have you anywhere to hang it?"

"I should think we had," said Michael. "Jolly good, sir, isn't it?"

"Well," muttered Soames, "for these days, yes. He'll make a name."

"He's an intense admirer of that White Monkey you gave us."

"Ah! I've been looking into the Chinese. If I go on buying——" Soames paused.

"They *are* a bit of an antidote, aren't they, sir? That 'Earthly Paradise'! And those geese—they don't seem to mind your counting their feathers, do they?"

Soames made no reply; he was evidently thinking: 'How on earth I missed those things when they first came on the market!' Then, raising his umbrella, and pointing it as if at the book trade, he asked:

"Young Butterfield—how's he doing?"

"Ah! I was going to let you know, sir. He came in yesterday and told me that he saw Elderson two days ago. He went to sell him a copy of my father's 'Limited'; Elderson said nothing and bought two."

"The deuce he did!"

"Butterfield got the impression that his visit put the wind up him. Elderson knows, of course, that I'm in this firm, and your son-in-law."

Soames frowned. "I'm not sure," he said, "that sleeping dogs——! Well, I'm on my way there now."

"Mention the book, sir, and see how Elderson takes it. Would you like one yourself? You're on the list. E, F—Butterfield should be reaching you to-day. It'll save you a refusal. Here it is—nice get-up. One guinea."

" 'A Duet'," read Soames. "What's it about? Musical?"

"Not precisely. A sort of cat-calling between the ghosts of the G.O.M. and Dizzy!"

"I'm not a reader," said Soames. He pulled out a note. "Why didn't you make it a pound? Here's the shilling."

"Thanks awfully, sir; I'm sure my father'll be frightfully bucked to think you've got one."

"Will he?" said Soames, with a faint smile. "D'you ever do any *work* here?"

"Well, we try to turn a doubtful penny."

"What d'you make at it?"

"Personally, about five hundred a year."

"That all?"

"Yes, but I doubt if I'm worth more than three."

"H'm! I thought you'd got over your Socialism."

"I fancy I have, sir. It didn't seem to go with my position."

"No," said Soames. "Fleur seems well."

"Yes, she's splendid. She does the Coué stunt, you know."

Soames stared. "That's her mother," he said; "I can't tell. Good-bye! Oh! I want to know; what's the meaning of that expression 'got his goat'?"

" 'Got his goat'? Oh, raised his dander, if you know what that means, it was before my time."

"I see," said Soames; "I had it right, then. Well!" He turned. His back was very neat and real. It vanished through the doorway, and with it seemed to go the sense of definition.

Michael took up the proofs, and read two poems. Bitter as quinine! The unrest in them—the yearning behind the words! Nothing Chinese there! After all, the ancients—like Old Forsyte, and his father in a very different way—had an anchor down. 'What is it?' thought Michael. 'What's wrong with us? We're quick, and clever, cocksure, and dissatisfied. If only something would enthuse us, or get *our* goats! We've chucked religion, tradition, property, pity; and in their place we put—what? Beauty? Gosh! See Walter Nazing, and the Café C'rillon! and yet —we must be after something! Better world? Doesn't look like it. Future life? Suppose I ought to "look into" spiritualism, as Old Forsyte would say. But—half in this world, half in that—deuced odd if spirits are less restive than we are!'

To what—to what, then, was it all moving?

'Dash it!' thought Michael, getting up, 'I'll try dictating an advertisement!'

"Will you come in, please, Miss Perren? For the new Desert volume—Trade Journals: 'Danby and Winter will shortly issue 'Counterfeits', by the author of 'Copper Coin', the outstanding success of the last publishing season.' I wonder how many publishers have claimed that, Miss Perren, for how many books this year? 'These poems show all the brilliancy of mood, and more than the technical accomplishment of the young author's first volume.' How's that?"

"Brilliancy of mood, Mr. Mont? Do you think?"

"No. But what am I to say? 'All the pangs and pessimism'?"

173

"Oh, no! But possibly: 'All the brilliancy of diction. The strangeness and variety of mood.'"

"Good. But it'll cost more. Say: 'All the brilliant strangeness'; that'll ring their bells in once. We're nuts on 'the strange', but we're not getting it—the *outré*, yes, but not the strange."

"Surely Mr. Desert gets——"

"Yes, sometimes; but hardly anyone else. To be strange, you've got to have guts, if you'll excuse the phrase, Miss Perren."

"Certainly, Mr. Mont. That young man Bicket is waiting to see you."

"He is, is he?" said Michael, taking out a cigarette. "Give me time to tighten my belt, Miss Perren, and ask him up."

'The lie benevolent,' he thought; 'now for it!'

The entrance of Bicket into a room where his last appearance had been so painful, was accomplished with a certain stolidity. Michael stood, back to the hearth, smoking; Bicket, back to a pile of modern novels, with the words 'This great new novel' on it. Michael nodded.

"Hallo, Bicket!"

Bicket nodded.

"Hope you're keeping well, sir?"

"Frightfully well, thank you." And there was silence.

"Well," said Michael at last, "I suppose you've come about that little advance to your wife. It's quite all right; no hurry whatever."

While saying this he had become conscious that the 'little snipe' was dreadfully disturbed. His eyes had a most peculiar look, those large, shrimp-like eyes which seemed, as it were, in advance of the rest of him. He hastened on:

"I believe in Australia myself. I think you're perfectly right, Bicket, and the sooner you go, the better. She doesn't look too strong."

Bicket swallowed.

"Sir," he said, "you've been a gent to me, and it's hard to say things."

"Then don't."

Bicket's cheeks became suffused with blood: queer effect in that pale, haggard face.

"It isn't what you think," he said: "I've come to ask you to tell me the truth." Suddenly he whipped from his pocket what Michael perceived to be a crumpled novel-wrapper.

"I took this from a book on the counter as I came by, downstairs. There! Is that my wife?" He stretched it out.

174

Michael beheld with consternation the wrapper of Storbert's novel. One thing to tell the lie benevolent already determined on—quite another to deny this!

Bicket gave him little time.

"I see it is, from your face," he said. "What's it all mean? I want the truth—I must 'ave it! I'm gettin' wild over all this. If that's 'er fyce there, then that's 'er body in the Gallery—Aubrey Greene; it's the syme nyme. What's it all mean?" His face had become almost formidable; his cockney accent very broad. "What gyme 'as she been plyin'? You gotta tell me before I go aht of 'ere."

Michael's heels came together. He said quietly:

"Steady, Bicket."

"Steady! You'd be steady if *your* wife——! All that money! *You* never advanced it—you never give it 'er—never! Don't tell me you did!"

Michael had taken his line. No lies!

"I lent her ten pounds to make a round sum of it—that's all; the rest she earned—honourably; and you ought to be proud of her."

Bicket's mouth fell open.

"Proud? And how's she earned it? Proud! My Gawd!"

Michael said coldly:

"As a model. I myself gave her the introduction to my friend, Mr. Greene, the day you had lunch with me. You've heard of models, I suppose?"

Bicket's hands tore the wrapper, and the pieces fell to the floor. "Models!" he said: "Pynters—yes, I've 'eard of 'em—Swines!"

"No more swine than you are, Bicket. Be kind enough not to insult my friend. Pull yourself together, man, and take a cigarette."

Bicket dashed the proffered case aside.

"I—I—was stuck on her," he said passionately, "and she's put this up on me!" A sort of sob came out of his lungs.

"You were stuck on her," said Michael; his voice had sting in it. "And when she does her best for you, you turn her down—is that it? Do you suppose she liked it?"

Bicket covered his face suddenly.

"What should I know?" he muttered from behind his hands.

A wave of pity flooded up in Michael. Pity! Blurb!

He said dryly: "When you've quite done, Bicket. D'you happen to remember what *you* did for *her*?"

Bicket uncovered his face and stared wildly. "You've never told her that?"

175

"No; but I jolly well will if you don't pull yourself together."

"What do I care if you do, now—lyin' like that, for all the men in the world! Sixty pounds! Honourably! D'you think I believe that?" His voice had desolation in it.

"Ah!" said Michael. "You don't believe simply because you're ignorant, as ignorant as the swine you talk of. A girl can do what she did and be perfectly honest, as I haven't the faintest doubt she is. You've only to look at her, and hear the way she speaks of it. She did it because she couldn't bear to see you selling those balloons. She did it to get you out of the gutter, and give you both a chance. And now you've got the chance, you kick up like this. Dash it all, Bicket, be a sport! Suppose I tell her what you did for her—d'you think she's going to squirm and squeal? Not she! It was damned human of you, and it was damned human of her; and don't you forget it!"

Bicket swallowed violently again.

"It's all very well," he said sullenly; "it 'asn't 'appened to you."

Michael was afflicted at once. No! It hadn't happened to him! And all his doubts of Fleur in the days of Wilfrid came hitting him.

"Look here, Bicket," he said, "do you doubt your wife's affection? The whole thing is there. I've only seen her twice, but I don't see how you can. If she weren't fond of you, why should she want to go to Australia, when she knows she can make good money here, and enjoy herself if she wants? I can vouch for my friend Greene. He's dashed decent, and I *know* he's played cricket."

But, searching Bicket's face, he wondered: Were all the others she had sat to as dashed decent?

"Look here, Bicket! We all get up against it sometimes; and that's the test of us. You've just *got* to believe in her; there's nothing else to it."

"To myke a show of herself for all the world to see!" The words seemed to struggle from the skinny throat. "I saw that picture bought yesterday by a ruddy alderman."

Michael could not conceal a grin at this description of 'Old Forsyte'.

"As a matter of fact," he said, "it was bought by my own father-in-law as a present to us, to hang in our house. And, mind you, Bicket, it's a fine thing."

"Ah!" cried Bicket, "it *is* a fine thing! Money! It's money bought her. Money'll buy anything. It'll buy the 'eart out of your chest."

And Michael thought: 'I can't get away with it a bit! What

176

price emancipation? He's never heard of the Greeks! And if he had, they'd seem to him a lot of loose-living foreigners. I must quit.' And, suddenly, he saw tears come out of those shrimp's eyes, and trickle down the hollowed cheeks.

Very disturbed, he said hastily:

"When you get out there, you'll never think of it again. Hang it all, Bicket, be a man! She did it for the best. If I were you, I'd never let on to her that I knew. That's what she'd do if I told her how you snooped those 'Copper Coins'."

Bicket clenched his fists—the action went curiousiy with the tears; then, without a word, he turned and shuffled out.

'Well,' thought Michael, 'giving advice is clearly not my stunt! Poor little snipe!'

## Chapter VI

### QUITTANCE

BICKET stumbled, half-blind, along the Strand. Naturally good-tempered, such a nerve-storm made him feel ill, and bruised in the brain. Sunlight and motion slowly restored some power of thought. He had got the truth. But was it the whole and nothing but the truth? Could she have made all that money without——? If he could believe that, then, perhaps—out of this country where people could see her naked for a shilling—he might forget. But—all that money! And even if all earned 'honourable', as Mr. Mont had put it, in how many days, exposed to the eyes of how many men? He groaned aloud in the street. The thought of going home to her—of a scene, of what he might learn if there *were* a scene, was just about unbearable. And yet—must do it, he supposed. He could have borne it better under St. Paul's, standing in the gutter, offering his balloons. A man of leisure for the first time in his life, a blooming 'alderman' with nothing to do but step in and take a ticket to the ruddy butterflies! And he owed that leisure to what a man with nothing to take his thoughts off simply could not bear! He would rather have snaffled the money out of a shop till. Better that on his soul, than the jab of this dark fiendish sexual jealousy. "Be a man!" Easy said! "Pull yourself together! She did it for you!" He would a hundred times rather she had not. Blackfriars Bridge! A dive, and an end in the mud down there? But you had to rise three times; they would fish you out alive, and run you in for it—and nothing gained—not even the pleasure of thinking that

Vic would see what she had done, when she came to identify the body. Dead was dead, anyway, and he would never know what she felt post-mortem! He trudged across the bridge, keeping his eyes before him. Little Ditch Street—how he used to scuttle down it, back to her, when she had pneumonia! Would he never feel like that again? He strode past the window, and went in.

Victorine was still bending over the brown tin trunk. She straightened herself, and on her face came a cold, tired look.

"Well," she said, "I see you know."

Bicket had but two steps to take in that small room. He took them, and put his hands on her shoulders. His face was close, his eyes, so large and strained, searched hers.

"I know you've myde a show of yourself for all London to see; what I want to know is—the rest!"

Victorine stared back at him.

"The rest!" she said—it was not a question, just a repetition, in a voice that seemed to mean nothing.

"Ah!" said Bicket hoarsely; "the rest—Well?"

"If you think there's a 'rest', that's enough."

Bicket jerked his hands away.

"Aoh! for the land's sake, daon't be mysterious. I'm 'alf orf me nut!"

"I see that," said Victorine; "and I see this: You aren't what I thought you. D'you think I liked doing it?" She raised her dress and took out the notes. "There you are! You can go to Australia without me."

Bicket cried hoarsely: "And leave you to the blasted pynters?"

"And leave me to meself. Take them!"

But Bicket recoiled against the door, staring at the notes with horror. "Not me!"

"Well, I can't keep 'em. I earned them to get you out of this."

There was a long silence, while the notes lay between them on the table, still crisp if a little greasy—the long-desired, the dreamed-of means of release, of happiness together in the sunshine. There they lay; neither would take them! What then?

"Vic," said Bicket at last, in a hoarse whisper, "swear you never let 'em touch you!"

"Yes, I can swear that."

And she could smile, too, saying it—that smile of hers! How believe her—living all these months, keeping it from him, telling him a lie about it in the end! He sank into a chair by the table and laid his head on his arms.

Victorine turned and began pulling an old cord round the trunk. He raised his head at the tiny sound. Then she really meant to go away! He saw his life devastated, empty as a coconut on Hampstead Heath; and all defence ran melted out of his cockney spirit. Tears rolled from his eyes.

"When you were ill," he said, "I stole for you. I got the sack for it."

She spun round. "Tony—you never told me! What did you steal?"

"Books. All your extra feedin' was books."

For a long minute she stood looking at him, then stretched out her hands without a word. Bicket seized them.

"I don't care about anything," he gasped, "so 'elp me, so long as you're fond of me, Vic!"

"And I don't neither. Oh! let's get out of this, Tony! this awful little room, this awful country. Let's get out of it all!"

"Yes," said Bicket; and put her hands to his eyes.

## Chapter VII

## LOOKING INTO ELDERSON

SOAMES had left Danby and Winter divided in thought between Elderson and the White Monkey. As Fleur surmised, he had never forgotten Aubrey Greene's words concerning that bit of salvage from the wreck of George Forsyte. "Eat the fruits of life, scatter the rinds, and get copped doing it." His application of them tended towards the field of business.

The country was still living on its capital. With the collapse of the carrying trade and European markets, they were importing food they couldn't afford to pay for. In his opinion they would get copped doing it, and that before long. British credit was all very well, the wonder of the world and that, but you couldn't live indefinitely on wonder. With shipping idle, concerns making a loss all over the place, and the unemployed in swarms, it was a pretty pair of shoes! Even insurance must suffer before long. Perhaps that chap Elderson had foreseen this already, and was simply feathering his nest in time. If one was to be copped in any case, why bother to be honest? This was cynicism so patent, that all the Forsyte in Soames rejected it; and yet it would keep coming back. In a general bankruptcy, why trouble with thrift, far-sightedness, integrity? Even the Conservatives were refusing to call them-

179

selves Conservatives again, as if there were something ridiculous
about the word, and they knew there was really nothing left to
conserve. "Eat the fruit, scatter the rinds, and get copped doing
it." That young painter had said a clever thing—yes, and his
picture was clever, though Dumetrius had done one over the price
—as usual! Where would Fleur hang it? In the hall, he shouldn't
be surprised—good light there; and the sort of people they knew
wouldn't jib at the nude. Curious—where all the nudes went to!
You never saw a nude—no more than you saw the proverbial dead
donkey! Soames had a momentary vision of dying donkeys laden
with pictures of the nude, stepping off the edge of the world.
Refusing its extravagance, he raised his eyes, just in time to see St.
Paul's, as large as life. That little beggar with his balloons wasn't
there to-day! Well—he'd nothing for him! At a tangent his
thoughts turned towards the object of his pilgrimage—the P.P.R.S.
and its half-year's accounts. At his suggestion, they were writing
off that German business wholesale—a dead loss of two hundred
and thirty thousand pounds. There would be no interim dividend,
and even then they would be carrying forward a debit towards the
next half-year. Well! better have a rotten tooth out at once and
done with; the shareholders would have six months to get used to
the gap before the general meeting. He himself had got used to it
already, and so would they in time. Shareholders were seldom
nasty unless startled—a long-suffering lot!

In the board-room the old clerk was still filling his ink-pots from
the magnum.

"Manager in?"

"Yes, sir."

"Say I'm here, will you?"

The old clerk withdrew. Soames looked at the clock. Twelve!
A little shaft of sunlight slanted down the wainscotting and floor.
There was nothing else alive in the room save a bluebottle and the
tick of the clock; not even a daily paper. Soames watched the bluebottle. He remembered how, as a boy, he had preferred bluebottles
and greenbottles to the ordinary fly, because of their bright colour.
It was a lesson. The showy things, the brilliant people, were the
dangerous. Witness the Kaiser, and that precious Italian poet—
what was his name! And this Jack-o'-lantern of their own! He
shouldn't be surprised if Elderson were brilliant in private life.
Why didn't the chap come? Was that encounter with young
Butterfield giving him pause? The bluebottle crawled up the pane,
buzzed down, crawled up again; the sunlight stole inward along

the floor. All was vacuous in the board-room, as though embodying the principle of insurance: "Keep things as they are."

'Can't kick my heels here for ever,' thought Soames, and moved to the window. In that wide street leading to the river, sunshine illumined a few pedestrians and a brewer's dray, but along the main artery at the end the traffic streamed and rattled. London! A monstrous place! And all insured! 'What'll it be like thirty years hence?' he thought. To think that there would be London, without himself to see it! He felt sorry for the place, sorry for himself. Even old Gradman would be gone. He supposed the insurance societies would look after it, but he didn't know. And suddenly he became aware of Elderson. The fellow looked quite jaunty, in a suit of dittoes and a carnation.

"Contemplating the future, Mr. Forsyte?"

"No," said Soames. How had the fellow guessed his thoughts?

"I'm glad you've come in. It gives me a chance to say how grateful I am for the interest you take in the concern. It's rare. A manager has a lonely job."

Was he mocking? He seemed altogether very spry and uppish. Light-heartedness always made Soames suspicious—there was generally some reason for it.

"If every director were as conscientious as you, one would sleep in one's bed. I don't mind telling you that the amount of help I got from the Board before you came on it was—well—negligible."

Flattery! The fellow must be leading up to something!

Elderson went on:

"I can say to you what I couldn't say to any of the others: I'm not at all happy about business, Mr. Forsyte. England is just about to discover the state she's really in."

Faced with this startling confirmation of his own thoughts, Soames reacted.

"No good crying out before we're hurt," he said; "the pound's still high. We're good stayers."

"In the soup, I'm afraid. If something drastic isn't done—we *shall* stay there. And anything drastic, as you know, means disorganisation and lean years before you reap reward."

How could the fellow talk like this, and look as bright and pink as a new penny? It confirmed the theory that he didn't care what happened. And, suddenly, Soames resolved to try a shot.

"Talking of lean years—I came in to say that I think we must call a meeting of the shareholders over this dead loss of the German business." He said it to the floor, and looked quickly up. The result was disappointing. The manager's light-grey eyes met his without a blink.

"I've been expecting that from you," he said.

'The deuce you have!' thought Soames, for it had but that moment come into his mind.

"By all means call one," went on the manager; "but I'm afraid the Board won't like it."

Soames refrained from saying: 'Nor do I.'

"Nor the shareholders, Mr. Forsyte. In a long experience I've found that the less you rub their noses in anything unpleasant, the better for everyone."

"That may be," said Soames, stiffening in contrariety; "but it's all a part of the vice of not facing things."

"I don't think, Mr. Forsyte, that you will accuse *me* of not facing things, in the time to come."

Time to come! Now, what on earth did the fellow mean by that?

"Well, I shall moot it at the next Board," he said.

"Quite!" said the manager. "Nothing like bringing things to a head, is there?"

Again that indefinable mockery, as if he had something up his sleeve. Soames looked mechanically at the fellow's cuffs—beautifully laundered, with a blue stripe; at his holland waistcoat, and his bird's-eye tie—a regular dandy. He would give him a second barrel!

"By the way," he said, "Mont's written a book. I've taken a copy."

Not a blink! A little more show of teeth, perhaps—false, no doubt!

"I've taken two—poor, dear Mont!"

Soames had a sense of defeat. This chap was armoured like a crab, varnished like a Spanish table.

"Well," he said, "I must go."

The manager held out his hand.

"Good-bye, Mr. Forsyte. I'm so grateful to you."

The fellow was actually squeezing his hand. Soames went out confused. To have his hand squeezed was so rare! It undermined him. And yet, it might be the crown of a consummate bit of acting. He couldn't tell. He had, however, less intention even than before of moving for a meeting of the shareholders. No, no! That had just been a shot to get a rise; and it had failed. But the Butterfield shot had gone home, surely! If innocent, Elderson must certainly have alluded to the impudence of the young man's call. And yet such a cool card was capable of failing to rise, just to tease you! No! nothing doing—as they said nowadays. He was as far as ever from a proof of guilt; and to speak truth, glad of it. Such a scandal could serve no purpose save that of blackening the whole concern, directors and all. People were so careless, they never stopped to think, or apportion blame where it was due. Keep a sharp eye open, and go on as they were! No good stirring hornets' nests! He had got so far in thought and progress, when a voice said:

"Well met, Forsyte! Are you going my way?"

'Old Mont', coming down the steps of 'Snooks'!

"I don't know," said Soames.

"I'm off to the Aeroplane for lunch."

"That new-fangled place?"

"Rising, you know, Forsyte—rising."

"I've just been seeing Elderson. He's bought two copies of your book."

"Dear me! Poor fellow!"

Soames smiled faintly. "That's what he said of you! And who d'you think sold them to him? Young Butterfield."

"Is he still alive?"

"He was this morning."

Sir Lawrence's face took on a twist:

"I've been thinking, Forsyte. They tell me Elderson keeps two women."

Soames stared. The idea was attractive; would account for everything.

"My wife says it's one too many, Forsyte. What do you say?"

"I?" said Soames. "I only know the chap's as cool as a cucumber. I'm going in here. Good-bye!"

One could get no help from that baronet fellow; he couldn't take anything seriously. Two women! At Elderson's age! What a life! There were always men like that, not content with one thing at a time—living dangerously. It was mysterious to him. You might look and look into chaps like that, and see nothing. And yet, there they were! He crossed the hall, and went into the room where connoisseurs were lunching. Taking down the menu at the service table, he ordered himself a dozen oysters; but, suddenly remembering that the month contained no 'r', changed them to a fried sole.

# Chapter VIII

## LEVANTED

"NO, dear heart, Nature's 'off'!"

"How d'you mean, Michael?"

"Well, look at the Nature novels we get. Sedulous stuff pitched on Cornish cliffs or Yorkshire moors—ever been on a Yorkshire moor?—it comes off on you; and the Dartmoor brand. Gosh! Dartmoor, where the passions come from—ever been on Dartmoor? Well, they don't, you know. And the South Sea bunch! Oh, la, la! And the poets, the splash-and-splutter school don't get within miles of Nature. The village idiot school is a bit better, certainly. After all, old Wordsworth made Nature, and she's a bromide. Of course, there's raw nature with the small 'n'; but if you come up against that, it takes you all your time to keep alive— the Nature we gas about is licensed, nicely blended and bottled. She's not modern enough for contemporary style."

"Oh! well, let's go on the river, anyway, Michael. We can have tea at 'The Shelter'."

They were just reaching what Michael always called 'this desirable residence', when Fleur leaned forward, and, touching his knee, said:

"I'm not half as nice to you as you deserve, Michael."

"Good Lord, darling! I thought you were."

"I know I'm selfish; especially just now."

"It's only the eleventh baronet."

"Yes; it's a great responsibility. I only hope he'll be like you."

Michael slid in to the landing-stage, shipped his sculls, and sat down beside her.

"If he's like me, I shall disown him. But sons take after their mothers."

"I meant in character. I want him frightfully to be cheerful and not restless, and have the feeling that life's worth while."

Michael stared at her lips—they were quivering; at her cheek, slightly browned by the afternoon's sunning; and, bending sideways, he put his own against it.

"He'll be a sunny little cuss, I'm certain."

Fleur shook her head.

"I don't want him greedy and self-centred; it's in my blood, you

184

know. I can see it's ugly, but I can't help it. How do you manage not to be?"

Michael ruffled his hair with his free hand.

"The sun isn't too hot for you, is it, ducky?"

"No. Seriously, Michael—how?"

"But I *am*. Look at the way I want you. Nothing will cure me of that."

A slight pressure of her cheek on his own was heartening, and he said:

"Do you remember coming down the garden one night, and finding me in a boat just here? When you'd gone, I stood on my head, to cool it. I was on my uppers; I didn't think I'd got an earthly——" He stopped. No! He would not remind her, but that was the night when she said: "Come again when I know I can't get my wish!" The unknown cousin!

Fleur said quietly:

"I was a pig to you, Michael, but I was awfully unhappy. That's gone. It's gone at last; there's nothing wrong now, except my own nature."

Conscious that his feelings betrayed the period, Michael said:

"Oh! if that's all! What price tea?"

They went up the lawn arm-in-arm. Nobody was at home—Soames in London, Annette at a garden party.

"We'll have tea on the verandah, please," said Fleur.

Sitting there, happier than he ever remembered being, Michael conceded a certain value to Nature, to the sunshine stealing down, the scent of pinks and roses, the sighing in the aspens. Annette's pet doves were cooing; and, beyond the quietly-flowing river, the spires of poplar trees rose along the further bank. But, after all, he was only enjoying them because of the girl beside him, whom he loved to touch and look at, and because, for the first time, he felt as if she did not want to get up and flutter off to someone or something else. Curious that there could be, outside oneself, a being who completely robbed the world of its importance, 'snooped', as it were, the whole 'bag of tricks'—and she one's own wife! Very curious, considering what one was! He heard her say:

"Of course, mother's a Catholic; only, living with father down here, she left off practising. She didn't even bother me much. I've been thinking, Michael—what shall we do about *him*?"

"Let him rip."

"I don't know. He must be taught something, because of going

185

to school. The Catholics, you know, really do get things out of
their religion."

"Yes; they go it blind; it's the only logical way now."

"I think having no religion makes one feel that nothing matters."

Michael suppressed the words: "We could bring him up as a sun-
worshipper," and said, instead:

"It seems to me that whatever he's taught will only last till he
can think for himself; then he'll settle down to what suits him."

"But what do *you* think about things, Michael? You're as good
as anyone I know."

"Gosh!" murmured Michael, strangely flattered: "Is that so?"

"What *do* you think? Be serious!"

"Well, darling, doctrinally nothing—which means, of course,
that I haven't got religion. I believe one has to play the game—
but that's ethics."

"But surely it's a handicap not to be able to rely on anything
but oneself? If there's something to be had out of any form of
belief, one might as well have it."

Michael smiled, but not on the surface.

"You're going to do just as you like about the eleventh baronet,
and I'm going to abet you. But considering his breeding—I fancy
he'll be a bit of a sceptic."

"But I don't *want* him to be. I'd rather he were snug, and convinced and all that. Scepticism only makes one restless."

"No white monkey in him? Ah! I wonder! It's in the air, I
guess. The only thing will be to teach him a sense of other people,
as young as possible, with a slipper, if necessary."

Fleur gave him a clear look, and laughed.

"Yes," she said: "Mother used to try, but Father wouldn't let
her."

They did not reach home till past eight o'clock.

"Either your father's here, or mine," said Michael, in the hall;
"there's a prehistoric hat."

"It's Dad's. His is grey inside. Bart's is buff."

In the Chinese room Soames indeed was discovered, with an
opened letter, and Ting-a-ling at his feet. He held the letter out to
Michael, without a word.

There was no date, and no address; Michael read:

"DEAR MR. FORSYTE.—Perhaps you will be good enough to tell
the Board at the meeting on Tuesday that I am on my way to
immunity from the consequences of any peccadillo I may have

been guilty of. By the time you receive this, I shall be there. I have always held that the secret of life, no less than that of business, is to know when not to stop. It will be no use to proceed against me, for my person will not be attachable, as I believe you call it in the law, and I have left no property behind. If your object was to corner me, I cannot congratulate you on your tactics. If, on the other hand, you inspired that young man's visit as a warning that you were still pursuing the matter, I should like to add new thanks to those which I expressed when I saw you a few days ago.

"Believe me, dear Mr. Forsyte,

"Faithfully yours,

"ROBERT ELDERSON."

Michael said cheerfully:

"Happy release! Now you'll feel safer, sir."

Soames passed his hand over his face, evidently wiping off its expression. "We'll discuss it later," he said. "This dog's been keeping me company."

Michael admired him at that moment. He was obviously swallowing his 'grief', to save Fleur.

"Fleur's a bit tired," he said. "We've been on the river, and had tea at 'The Shelter'; Madame wasn't in. Let's have dinner at once, Fleur."

Fleur had picked up Ting-a-ling, and was holding her face out of reach of his avid tongue.

"Sorry you've had to wait, Dad," she murmured, behind the yellow fur; "I'm just going to wash; shan't change."

When she had gone, Soames reached for the letter.

"A pretty kettle of fish!" he muttered. "Where it'll end, I can't tell!"

"But isn't this the end, sir?"

Soames stared. These young people! Here he was, faced with a public scandal, which might lead to he didn't know what—the loss of his name in the city, the loss of his fortune, perhaps; and they took it as if——! They had no sense of responsibility—none! All his father's power of seeing the worst, all James' nervous pessimism, had come to the fore in him during the hour since, at the Connoisseurs' Club, he had been handed that letter. Only the extra 'form' of the generation that succeeded James saved him, now that Fleur was out of the room, from making an exhibition of his fears.

"Your father in town?"

"I believe so, sir."

"Good!" Not that he felt relief. That baronet chap was just as irresponsible—getting him to go on that Board! It all came of mixing with people brought up in a sort of incurable levity, with no real feeling for money.

"Now that Elderson's levanted," he said, "the whole thing must come out. Here's his confession in my hand——"

"Why not tear it up, sir, and say Elderson has developed consumption?"

The impossibility of getting anything serious from this young man afflicted Soames like the eating of heavy pudding.

"You think that would be honourable?" he said grimly.

"Sorry, sir!" said Michael, sobered. "Can I help at all?"

"Yes; by dropping your levity, and taking care to keep wind of this matter away from Fleur."

"I will," said Michael earnestly: "I promise you. I'll Dutch-oyster the whole thing. What's your line going to be?"

"We shall have to call the shareholders together and explain this dicky-dealing. They'll very likely take it in bad part."

"I can't see why they should. How could you have helped it?"

Soames sniffed.

"There's no connection in life between reward and your deserts. If the war hasn't taught you that, nothing will."

"Well," said Michael, "Fleur will be down directly. If you'll excuse me a minute; we'll continue it in our next."

Their next did not occur till Fleur had gone to bed.

"Now, sir," said Michael, "I expect my governor's at the Aeroplane. He goes there and meditates on the end of the world. Would you like me to ring him up, if your Board meeting's to-morrow?"

Soames nodded. He himself would not sleep a wink—why should 'Old Mont'?

Michael went to the Chinese tea-chest.

"Bart? This is Michael. Old For—— my father-in-law is here; he's had a pill. . . . No; Elderson. Could you blow in by any chance and hear? . . . He's coming, sir. Shall we stay down, or go up to my study?"

"Down," muttered Soames, whose eyes were fixed on the white monkey. "I don't know what we're all coming to," he added, suddenly.

"If we did, sir, we should die of boredom."

188

"Speak for yourself. All this unreliability! I can't tell where it's leading."

"Perhaps there's somewhere, sir, that's neither heaven nor hell."

"A man of *his* age!"

"Same age as my dad; it was a bad vintage, I expect. If you'd been in the war, sir, it would have cheered you up no end."

"Indeed!" said Soames.

"It took the linch-pins out of the cart—admitted; but, my Lord! it did give you an idea of the grit there is about, when it comes to being up against it."

Soames stared. Was this young fellow reading him a lesson against pessimism?

"Look at young Butterfield, the other day," Michael went on, "going over the top, to Elderson! Look at the girl who sat for 'the altogether' in that picture you bought us! She's the wife of a packer we had, who got hoofed for snooping books. She made quite a lot of money by standing for the nude, and never lost her wicket. They're going to Australia on it. Yes, and look at that little snooper himself; he snooped to keep her alive after pneumonia, and came down to selling balloons."

"I don't know what you're talking about," said Soames.

"Only grit, sir. You said you didn't know what we were coming to. Well, look at the unemployed! Is there a country in the world where they stick it as they do here? I get awfully bucked at being English every now and then. Don't you?"

The words stirred something deep in Soames; but far from giving it away, he continued to gaze at the white monkey. The restless, inhuman, and yet so human, angry sadness of the creature's eyes! 'No whites to them!' thought Soames: 'that's what does it, I expect!' And George had liked that picture to hang opposite his bed! Well, George had grit—joked with his last breath: very English, George! Very English, all the Forsytes! Old Uncle Jolyon, and his way with shareholders; Swithin, upright, puffy, huge in a too little armchair at Timothy's: 'All these small fry!' he seemed to hear the words again; and Uncle Nicholas, whom that chap Elderson reproduced as it were unworthily, spry and all-there, and pretty sensual, but quite above suspicion of dishonesty. And old Roger, with his crankiness, and German mutton! And his own father, James—how he had hung on, long and frail as a reed, hung on and on! And Timothy, preserved in Consols, dying at a hundred! Grit and body in those old English boys, in spite of their funny ways. And there stirred in Soames a sort of atavistic will-power.

He would see, and they would see—and tha was all about it!

The grinding of a taxi's wheels brought him back from reverie. Here came 'Old Mont', tittuppy, and light in the head as ever, no doubt. And, instead of his hand, Soames held out Elderson's letter.

"Your precious schoolfellow's levanted," he said.

Sir Lawrence read it through, and whistled.

"What do you think, Forsyte—Constantinople?"

"More likely Monte Carlo," said Soames gloomily. "Secret commission—it's not an extraditable offence."

The odd contortions of that baronet's face were giving him some pleasure—the fellow seemed to be feeling it, after all.

"I should think he's really gone to escape his women, Forsyte."

The chap was incorrigible! Soames shrugged his shoulders almost violently.

"You'd better realise," he said, "that the fat is in the fire."

"But surely, my dear Forsyte, it's been there ever since the French occupied the Ruhr. Elderson has cut his lucky; we appoint someone else. What more is there to it?"

Soames had the peculiar feeling of having overdone his own honesty. If an honourable man, a ninth baronet, couldn't see the implications of Elderson's confession, were they really there? Was any fuss and scandal necessary? Goodness knew, *he* didn't want it! He said heavily:

"We now have conclusive evidence of a fraud; we *know* Elderson was illegally paid for putting through business by which the shareholders have suffered a dead loss. How can we keep this knowledge from them?"

"But the mischief's done, Forsyte. How will the knowledge help them?"

Soames frowned.

"We're in a fiduciary position. I'm not prepared to run the risks of concealment. If we conceal, we're accessory after the fact. The thing might come out at any time." If that was caution, not honesty, he couldn't help it.

"I should be glad to spare Elderson's name. We were at——"

"I'm aware of that," said Soames, drily.

"But what risk is there of its coming out, Forsyte? Elderson won't mention it; nor young Butterfield, if you tell him not to. Those who paid the commission certainly won't. And beyond us three here, no one else knows. It's not as if we profited in any way."

Soames was silent. The argument was specious. Entirely unjust, of course, that he should be penalised for what Elderson had done!

"No," he said, suddenly, "it won't do. Depart from the law, and you can't tell where it'll end. The shareholders have suffered this loss and they have the right to all the facts within the directors' knowledge. There might be some means of restitution they could avail themselves of. We can't judge. It may be they've a remedy against ourselves."

"If that's so, Forsyte, I'm with you."

Soames felt disgust. Mont had no business to put it with a sort of gallantry that didn't count the cost; when the cost, if cost there were, would fall, not on Mont, whose land was heavily mortgaged, but on himself, whose property was singularly realisable.

"Well," he said, coldly, "remember that to-morrow. I'm going to bed."

At his open window upstairs he felt no sense of virtue, but he enjoyed a sort of peace. He had taken his line, and there it was!

## Chapter IX

### SOAMES DOESN'T GIVE A DAMN

DURING the month following the receipt of Elderson's letter, Soames aged more than thirty days. He had forced his policy of disclosure on a doubting Board, the special meeting had been called, and, just as, twenty-three years ago, pursuing divorce from Irene, he had to face the public eye, so now he suffered day and night in dread of that undiscriminating optic. The French had a proverb: *"Les absents ont toujours tort!"* but Soames had grave doubts about it. Elderson would be absent from that meeting of the shareholders, but—unless he was much mistaken—he himself, who would be present, would come in for the blame. The French were not to be relied on. What with his anxiety about Fleur, and his misgiving about the public eye, he was sleeping badly, eating little, and feeling below par. Annette had recommended him to see a doctor. That was probably why he did not. Soames had faith in doctors for other people; but they had never—he would say—done anything for *him*, possibly because, so far, there had not been anything to do.

Failing in her suggestion, and finding him every day less sociable, Annette had given him a book on Coué. After running it through, he had meant to leave it in the train, but the theory, however extravagant, had somehow clung to him. After all, Fleur was doing

191

it; and the thing cost you nothing: there might be something in it! There was. After telling himself that night twenty-five times that he was getting better and better, he slept so soundly that Annette, in the next room, hardly slept at all.

"Do you know, my friend," she said at breakfast, "you were snoring last night so that I could not hear the cock crow."

"Why should you want to?" said Soames.

"Well, never mind—if you had a good night. Was it my little Coué who gave you that nice dream?"

Partly from fear of encouraging Coué, and partly from fear of encouraging her, Soames avoided a reply; but he had a curious sense of power, as if he did not care what people said of him.

'I'll do it again to-night,' he thought.

"You know," Annette went on, "you are just the temperament for Coué, Soames. When you cure yourself of worrying, you will get quite fat."

"Fat!" said Soames, looking at her curves. "I'd as soon grow a beard."

Fatness and beards were associated with the French. He would have to keep an eye on himself if he went on with this—er—what was one to call it? Tomfoolery was hardly the word to conciliate the process, even if it did require you to tie twenty-five knots in a bit of string: very French, that, like telling your beads! He himself had merely counted on his fingers. The sense of power lasted all the way up to London; he had the conviction that he could sit in a draught if he wanted to, that Fleur would have her boy all right; and as to the P.P.R.S.—ten to one he wouldn't be mentioned by name in any report of the proceedings.

After an early lunch and twenty-five more assurances over his coffee, he set out for the city.

This Board, held just a week before the special meeting of the shareholders, was in the nature of a dress rehearsal. The details of confrontation had to be arranged, and Soames was chiefly concerned with seeing that a certain impersonality should be preserved. He was entirely against disclosure of the fact that young Butterfield's story and Elderson's letter had been confided to himself. The phrase to be used should be a "member of the Board." He saw no need for anything further. As for explanations, they would fall, of course, to the chairman and the senior director, Lord Fontenoy. He found, however, that the Board thought he himself was the right person to bring the matter forward. No one else— they said—could supply the personal touch, the necessary conviction; the chairman should introduce the matter briefly, then call on Soames to give the evidence within his knowledge. Lord Fontenoy was emphatic.

"It's up to you, Mr. Forsyte. If it hadn't been for you, Elderson would be sitting there to-day. From beginning to end you put the wind up him; and I wish the deuce you hadn't. The whole thing's a confounded nuisance. He was a very clever fellow, and we shall miss him. Our new man isn't a patch on him. If he did take a few thou. under the rose, he took 'em off the Huns."

Old guinea-pig! Soames replied, acidly:

"And the quarter of a million he's lost the shareholders, for the sake of those few thou.? Bagatelle, I suppose?"

"Well, it might have turned out a winner; for the first year it did We all back losers sometimes."

Soames looked from face to face. They did not support this blatant attitude, but in them all, except perhaps 'Old Mont's', he felt a grudge against himself. Their expressions seemed to say: 'Nothing of this sort ever happened till you came on the Board.' He had disturbed their comfort, and they disliked him for it. They were an unjust lot! He said doggedly:

"You leave it to me, do you? Very well!"

What he meant to convey—or whether he meant to convey anything, he did not know; but even that 'old guinea-pig' was more civil afterwards. He came away from the Board, however, without any sense of power at all. There he would be on Tuesday next, bang in the public eye.

After calling to enquire after Fleur, who was lying down rather poorly, he returned home with a feeling of having been betrayed. It seemed that he could not rely, after all, on this fellow with his twenty-five knots. However much better he might become, his daughter, his reputation, and possibly his fortune, were not apparently at the disposition of his subconscious self. He was silent at dinner, and went up afterwards to his picture gallery, to think things over. For half an hour he stood at the open window, alone with the summer evening; and the longer he stood there, the more clearly he perceived that the three were really one. Except for his daughter's sake, what did he care for his reputation or his fortune? His reputation! Lot of fools—if they couldn't see that he was careful and honest so far as had lain within his reach—so much the worse for them! His fortune—well, he had better make another settlement on Fleur and her child at once, in case of accidents; another fifty thousand. Ah! if she were only through her trouble! It was time Annette went up to her for good; and there was a thing they called twilight sleep. To have her suffering was not to be thought of!

The evening lingered out; the sun went down behind familiar trees; Soames's hands, grasping the window-ledge, felt damp with dew; sweetness of grass and river stole up into his nostrils. The sky had paled, and now began to darken; a scatter of stars came out. He had lived here a long time, through all Fleur's childhood— best years of his life; still, it wouldn't break his heart to sell. His heart was up in London. Sell? That was to run before the hounds with a vengeance. No—no!—it wouldn't come to *that*! He left the window and, turning up the lights, began the thousand and first tour of his pictures. He had made some good purchases since Fleur's marriage, and without wasting his money on fashionable favourites. He had made some good sales, too. The pictures in this gallery, if he didn't mistake, were worth from seventy to a hundred thousand pounds; and, with the profits on his sales from time to time, they stood him in at no more than five-and-twenty thousand —not a bad result from a life's hobby, to say nothing of the pleasure! Of course, he might have taken up something—butter-flies, photography, archæology, or first editions; some other sport in which you backed your judgment against the field, and collected the results; but he had never regretted choosing pictures. Not he! More to show for your money, more kudos, more profit, and more risk! The thought startled him a little; had he really taken to pictures because of the risk? A risk had never appealed to him; at least, he hadn't realised it, so far. Had his 'subconscious' some part in the matter? He suddenly sat down and closed his eyes. Try the thing once more; very pleasant feeling, that morning, of not "giving a damn"; he never remembered having it before! He had always felt it necessary to worry—kind of insurance against the worst; but worry was wearing, no doubt about it, wearing. Turn out the light! They said in that book, you had to relax. In the now dim and shadowy room, with the starlight, through many windows, dusted over its reality, Soames, in his easy chair, sat very still. A faint drone rose on the words: "fatter and fatter" through his moving lips. 'No, no,' he thought: 'that's wrong!' And he began the drone again. The tips of his fingers ticked it off; on and on—he would give it a good chance. If only one needn't worry! On and on—"better and better!" If only——! His lips stopped moving; his grey head fell forward into the subconscious. And the stealing starlight dusted over him, too, a little unreality.

## Chapter X

### BUT TAKES NO CHANCES

MICHAEL knew nothing of the City; and, in the spirit of the old cartographers: "Where you know nothing, place terrors," made his way through the purlieus of the Poultry, towards that holy of holies, the offices of Cuthcott, Kingson and Forsyte. His mood was attuned to meditation, for he had been lunching with Sibley Swan at the Café C'rillon. He had known all the guests—seven chaps even more modern than old Sib—save only a Russian so modern that he knew no French and nobody could talk to him. Michael had watched them demolish everything, and the Russian closing his eyes, like a sick baby, at mention of any living name. . . . 'Carry on!' he thought, several of his favourites having gone down in the *mêlée*. 'Stab and bludge! Importance awaits you at the end of the alley.' But he had restrained his irreverence till the moment of departure.

"Sib," he said, rising, "all these chaps here are dead—ought they to be about in this hot weather?"

"What's that?" ejaculated Sibley Swan, amidst the almost painful silence of the chaps.

"I mean—they're alive—so they *must* be damned!" And avoiding a thrown chocolate which hit the Russian, he sought the door.

Outside, he mused: 'Good chaps, really! Not half so darned superior as they think they are. Quite a human touch—getting that Russian on the boko. Phew! It's hot!'

On that first day of the Eton and Harrow match all the forfeited heat of a chilly summer had gathered and shimmered over Michael, on the top of his Bank bus; shimmered over straw hats, and pale, perspiring faces, over endless other buses, business men, policemen, shopmen at their doors, sellers of newspapers, laces, jumping toys, endless carts and cabs, letterings and wires, all the confusion of the greatest conglomeration in the world—adjusted almost to a hair's-breadth, by an unseen instinct. Michael stared and doubted. Was it possible that, with everyone pursuing his own business, absorbed in his own job, the thing could work out? An ant-heap was not busier, or more seemingly confused. Live wires crossed and crossed and crossed—inextricable entanglement, you'd say; and yet, life, the order needful to life, somehow surviving! 'No slouch of a miracle!' he thought, 'modern town life!' And suddenly it seemed to cease, as if demolished by the ruthless dispensation of some super Sibley Swan; for he was staring down a *cul-de-sac*. On both sides, flat houses, recently re-buffed, extraordinarily alike; at the end, a flat buff house, even more alike, and down to it, grey virgin pavement, unstained by horses or petrol; no cars, cats, carts, policemen, hawkers, flies, or bees. No sign of human life, except the names of legal firms to right and left of each open doorway.

" 'Cuthcott, Kingson and Forsyte, Commissioners for Oaths: First Floor.' "

'Rule Britannia!' thought Michael, ascending wide stone steps.

Entering the room to which he had been ushered, he saw an old and pug-faced fellow with a round grizzled beard, a black alpaca coat, and a roomy holland waistcoat round his roomy middle, who rose from a swivel chair.

"Aoh!" he said, "Mr. Michael Mont, I think. I've been expecting you. We shan't be long about it, after Mr. Forsyte comes. He's just stepped round the corner. Mrs. Michael well, I hope?"

"Thanks; as well as——"

"Ye-es; it makes you anxious. Take a seat. Perhaps you'd like to read the draft?"

Thus prescribed for, Michael took some foolscap from a pudgy hand, and sat down opposite. With one eye on the old fellow, and the other on the foolscap, he read steadily.

"It seems to mean something," he said at last.

He saw a gape, as a frog at a fly, settle in the beard; and hastened to repair his error.

"Calculating what's going to happen if something else doesn't, must be rather like being a bookmaker."

He felt at once that he had not succeeded. There was a grumpy mutter:

"We don't waste our time 'ere. Excuse me, I'm busy."

Michael sat, compunctious, watching him tick down a long page of entries. He was like one of those old dogs which lie outside front doors, keeping people off the premises, and notifying their fleas. After less than five minutes of that perfect silence Soames came in.

"You're here, then?" he said.

"Yes, sir; I thought it best to come at the time you mentioned. What a nice cool room!"

"Have you read this?" asked Soames, pointing to the draft.

Michael nodded.

"Did you understand it?"

"Up to a point, I think."

"The interest on *this* fifty thousand," said Soames, "is Fleur's until her eldest child, if it's a boy, attains the age of twenty-one, when the capital becomes his absolutely. If it's a girl, Fleur retains half the income for life, the rest of the income becomes payable to the girl when she attains the age of twenty-one or marries, and the capital of that half goes to her child or children lawfully begotten, at majority or marriage, in equal shares. The other half of the capital falls into Fleur's estate, and is disposable by her will, or follows the laws of intestacy."

"You make it wonderfully clear," said Michael.

"Wait!" said Soames. "If Fleur has no children——"

Michael started.

"Anything is possible," said Soames gravely, "and my experience is that the contingencies not provided for are those which happen. In such a case the income of the whole is hers for life, and the capital hers at death to do as she likes with. Failing that, it goes to the next of kin. There are provisions against anticipation and so forth."

"Ought she to make a fresh will?" asked Michael, conscious of sweat on his forehead.

"Not unless she likes. Her present will covers it."

"Have I to do anything?"

"No. I wanted you to understand the purport before I sign; that's all. Give me the deed, Gradman, and get Wickson in, will you?"

Michael saw the old chap produce from a drawer a fine piece of parchment covered with copper-plate writing and seals, look at it lovingly, and place it before Soames. When he had left the room, Soames said in a low voice:

"This meeting on Tuesday—I can't tell! But, whatever happens, so far as I can see, this ought to stand."

"It's awfully good of you, sir."

Soames nodded, testing a pen.

"I'm afraid I've got wrong with your old clerk," said Michael; "I like the look of him frightfully, but I accidentally compared him to a bookmaker."

Soames smiled. "Gradman," he said, "is a 'character'. There aren't many, nowadays."

Michael was wondering: Could one be a 'character' under the age of sixty?—when the 'character' returned, with a pale man in dark clothes.

Lifting his nose sideways, Soames said at once:

"This is a post-nuptial settlement on my daughter. I deliver this as my act and deed."

He wrote his name, and got up.

The pale person and Gradman wrote theirs, and the former left the room. There was a silence as of repletion.

"Do you want me any more?" asked Michael.

"Yes. I want you to see me deposit it at the bank with the marriage settlement. Shan't come back, Gradman!"

"Good-bye, Mr. Gradman."

Michael heard the old fellow mutter through his beard half buried in a drawer to which he was returning the draft, and followed Soames out.

"Here's where I used to be," said Soames as they went along the Poultry; "and my father before me."

"More genial, perhaps," said Michael.

"The trustees are meeting us at the bank; you remember them?"

"Cousins of Fleur's, weren't they, sir?"

"Second cousins; young Roger's eldest, and young Nicholas'. I chose them youngish. Very young Roger was wounded in the war —he does nothing. Very young Nicholas is at the Bar."

Michael's ears stood up. "What about the next lot, sir? Very, very young Roger would be almost insulting, wouldn't it?"

"There won't be one," said Soames, "with taxation where it is. He can't afford it; he's a steady chap. What are you going to call your boy, if it *is* one?"

"We think Christopher, because of St. Paul's and Columbus. Fleur wants him solid, and I want him enquiring."

"H'm And if it's a girl?"

"Oh!—if it's a girl—Anne."

"Yes," said Soames: "very neat. Here they are!"

They had reached the bank, and in the entrance Michael saw two Forsytes between thirty and forty, whose chinny faces he dimly remembered. Escorted by a man with bright buttons down his front, they all went to a room, where a man without buttons produced a japanned box. One of the Forsytes opened it with a key; Soames muttered an incantation, and deposited the deed. When he and the chinnier Forsyte had exchanged a few remarks with the manager on the question of the bank rate, they all went back to the lobby and parted with the words: "Well, good-bye."

"Now," said Soames, in the din and hustle of the street, "he's provided for, so far as I can see. When exactly do you expect it?"

"It should be just a fortnight."

"Do you believe in this—this twilight sleep?"

"I should like to," said Michael, conscious again of sweat on his forehead. "Fleur's wonderfully calm; she does Coué night and morning."

"That!" said Soames. He did not mention that he himself was doing it, thus giving away the state of his nerves. "If you're going home, I'll come, too."

"Good!"

He found Fleur lying down with Ting-a-ling on the foot of the sofa.

"Your father's here, darling. He's been anointing the future with another fifty thou. I expect he'd like to tell you all about it."

Fleur moved restlessly.

"Presently. If it's going on as hot as this, it'll be rather a bore, Michael."

"Oh! but it won't, ducky. Three days and a thunder-storm."

Taking Ting-a-ling by the chin, he turned his face up.

"And how on earth is your nose going to be put out of joint, old man? There's no joint to put."

"He knows there's something up."

"He's a wise little brute, aren't you, old son?"

Ting-a-ling sniffed.

"Michael!"

"Yes, darling?"

"I don't seem to care about anything now—it's a funny feeling."

"That's the heat."

"No. I think it's because the whole business is too long. Everything's ready, and now it all seems rather stupid. One more person in the world or one more out of it—what does it matter?"

"Don't! It matters frightfully!"

"One more gnat to dance, one more ant to run about!"

Anguished, Michael said again:

"Don't, Fleur! That's just a mood."

"Is Wilfrid's book out?"

"It comes out to-morrow."

"I'm sorry I gave you such a bad time, there. I only didn't want to lose him."

Michael took her hand.

"Nor did I—goodness knows!" he said.

"He's never written, I suppose?"

"No."

"Well, I expect he's all right by now. Nothing lasts."

Michael put her hand to his cheek.

"*I* do, I'm afraid," he said.

The hand slipped round over his lips.

"Give Dad my love, and tell him I'll be down to tea. Oh! I'm so hot!"

Michael hovered a moment, and went out. Damn the heat, upsetting her like this!

He found Soames standing in front of the white monkey.

"I should take this down, if I were you," he muttered, "until it's over."

"Why, sir?" asked Michael, in surprise.

Soames frowned.

"Those eyes!"

Michael went up to the picture. Yes! He was a haunting kind of brute!

"But it's such top-hole work, sir."

Soames nodded.

"Artistically, yes. But at such times you can't be too careful what she sees."

"I believe you're right. Let's have him down."

"I'll hold him," said Soames, taking hold of the bottom of the picture.

"Got him tight? Right-o. Now!"

"You can say I wanted an opinion on his period," said Soames, when the picture had been lowered to the floor.

"There can hardly be a doubt of that, sir—the present!"

Soames stared. "What? Oh! You mean——? Ah! H'm! Don't let her know he's in the house."

"No. I'll lock him up." Michael lifted the picture. "D'you mind opening the door, sir?"

"I'll come back at tea-time," said Soames. "That'll look as if I'd taken him off. You can hang him again, later."

"Yes. Poor brute!" said Michael, bearing the monkey off to limbo.

## Chapter XI

### WITH A SMALL 'n'

ON the night of the Monday following, after Fleur had gone to bed, Michael and Soames sat listening to the mutter of London coming through the windows of the Chinese room opened to the brooding heat.

"They say the war killed sentiment," said Soames suddenly: "Is that true?"

"In a way, yes, sir. We had so much reality that we don't want any more."

"I don't follow you."

"I meant that only reality really makes you feel. So if you pretend there *is* no reality, you don't have to feel. It answers awfully well, up to a point."

"Ah!" said Soames. "Her mother comes up to-morrow morning, to stay. This P.P.R.S. meeting of mine is at half-past two. Good-night!"

Michael, at the window, watched the heat gathered black over the Square. A few tepid drops fell on his outstretched hand. A cat stole by under a lamp-post, and vanished into shadow so thick that it seemed uncivilised.

Queer question of 'Old Forsyte's' about sentiment; odd that he should ask it! 'Up to a point! But don't we all get past that point?' he thought. Look at Wilfrid, and himself—after the war they had deemed it blasphemous to admit that anything mattered except eating and drinking, for to-morrow they died; even fellows like Nazing, and Master, who were never in the war, had felt like that ever since. Well, Wilfrid had got it in the neck; and he himself had got it in the wind; and he would bet that—barring one here and there whose blood was made of ink—they would all get it in the neck or wind soon or late. Why, he would cheerfully bear Fleur's pain and risk, instead of her! But if nothing mattered, why should he feel like that?

Turning from the window, he leaned against the lacquered back of the jade-green settee, and stared at the wall space between the Chinese tea-chests. Jolly thoughtful of the 'old man' to have that white monkey down! The brute was potent—symbolic of the world's mood: beliefs cancelled, faiths withdrawn! And, dash it! not only the young—but the old—were in that temper! 'Old Forsyte', or he would never have been scared by that monkey's eyes; yes, and his own governor, and Elderson, and all the rest. Young and old—no real belief in anything! And yet—revolt sprang up in Michael, with a whirr, like a covey of partridges. It *did* matter that some person or some principle outside oneself should be more precious than oneself—it dashed well did! Sentiment, then, wasn't dead—nor faith, nor belief, which were the same things. They were only shedding shells, working through chrysalis, into—butterflies, perhaps. Faith, sentiment, belief, had gone under-

201

ground, possibly, but they were there, even in 'Old Forsyte' and himself. He had a good mind to put the monkey up again. No use exaggerating his importance! . . . By George! Some flare! A jagged streak of vivid light had stripped darkness off the night. Michael crossed, to close the windows. A shattering peal of thunder blundered overhead; and down came the rain, slashing and sluicing. He saw a man running, black, like a shadow across a dark-blue screen; saw him by the light of another flash, suddenly made lurid and full of small meaning, with face of cheerful anxiety, as if he were saying: "Hang it, I'm getting wet!" Another frantic crash!

'Fleur!' thought Michael; and clanging the last window down, he ran upstairs.

She was sitting up in bed, with a face all round, and young, and startled.

'Brutes!' he thought—guns and the heavens confounded in his mind: 'They've waked her up!'

"It's all right, darling! Just another little summer kick-up! Were you asleep?"

"I was dreaming!" He felt her hand clutching within his own, saw a sudden pinched look on her face, with a sort of rage. What infernal luck!

"Where's Ting?"

No dog was in the corner.

"Under the bed—you bet! Would you like him up?"

"No. Let him stay; he hates it."

She put her head against his arm, and Michael curled his hand round her other ear.

"I never liked thunder much!" said Fleur, "and now it—it hurts!"

High above her hair Michael's face underwent the contortions of an overwhelming tenderness. One of those crashes which seem just overhead sent her face burrowing against his chest, and, sitting on the bed, he gathered her in, close.

"I wish it were over," came, smothered, from her lips.

"It will be directly, darling; it came on so suddenly!" But he knew she didn't mean the storm.

"If I come through, I'm going to be quite different to you, Michael."

Anxiety was the natural accompaniment of such events, but the words: "If I come through" turned Michael's heart right over. Incredible that one so young and pretty should be in even the remotest danger of extinction; incredibly painful that she should be in fear of it! He hadn't realised. She had been so calm, so matter-of-fact about it all.

"Don't!" he mumbled; "of course you'll come through."

"I'm afraid."

The sound was small and smothered, but the words hurt horribly. Nature, with the small 'n', forcing fear into this girl he loved so awfully! Nature kicking up this godless din above her poor little head!

"Ducky, you'll have twilight sleep and know nothing about it; and be as right as rain in no time."

Fleur freed her hand.

"Not if it's not good for him. Is it?"

"I expect so, sweetheart; I'll find out. What makes you think——?"

"Only that it's not natural. I want to do it properly. Hold my hand hard, Michael. I—I'm not going to be a fool. Oh! Someone's knocking—go and see."

Michael opened the door a crack. Soames was there—unnatural —in a blue dressing-gown and scarlet slippers!

"Is she all right?" he whispered.

"Yes, yes."

"In this bobbery she oughtn't to be left."

"No, sir, of course not. I shall sleep on the sofa."

"Call me, if anything's wanted."

"I will."

Soames's eyes slid past, peering into the room. A string worked in his throat, as if he had things to say which did not emerge. He shook his head, and turned. His slim figure, longer than usual, in its gown, receded down the corridor, past the Japanese prints which he had given them. Closing the door again, Michael stood looking at the bed. Fleur had settled down; her eyes were closed, her lips moving. He stole back on tiptoe. The thunder, travelling away south blundered and growled as if regretfully. Michael saw her eyelids quiver, her lips stop, then move again. 'Coué!' he thought.

He lay down on the sofa at the foot of the bed, whence, without sound, he could raise himself and see her. Many times he raised himself. She had dropped off, was breathing quietly. The thunder was faint now, the flashes imperceptible. Michael closed his eyes.

A faint last mutter roused him to look at her once more, high on her pillows by the carefully shaded light. Young—young! Colourless, like a flower in wax! No scheme in her brain, no dread —peaceful! If only she could stay like that and wake up with it all over! He looked away. And there she was at the far end, dim, reflected in a glass; and there to the right, again. She lay, as it were, all round him in the pretty room, the inhabiting spirit—of his heart.

It was quite still now. Through a chink in those powder-blue curtains he could see some stars. Big Ben chimed one.

He had slept, perhaps, dozed at least, dreamed a little. A small sound woke him. A very little dog, tail down, yellow, low and unimportant, was passing down the room, trailing across it to the far corner. 'Ah!' thought Michael, closing his eyes again: 'You!'

## Chapter XII

### ORDEAL BY SHAREHOLDER

REPAIRING, next day, to the Aeroplane Club, where, notably spruce, Sir Lawrence was waiting in the lounge, Michael thought: 'Good old Bart! he's got himself up for the guillotine all right!'

"That white piping will show the blood!" he said. "Old Forsyte's neat this morning, but not so gaudy."

"Ah! How is 'Old Forsyte'? In good heart?"

"One doesn't ask him, sir. How do you feel yourself?"

"Exactly as I used to before the Eton and Winchester match. I think I shall have shandy-gaff at lunch."

When they had taken their seats, Sir Lawrence went on:

"I remember seeing a man tried for murder in Colombo; the poor fellow was positively blue. I think my favourite moment in the past, Michael, is Walter Raleigh asking for a second shirt. By the way, it's never been properly settled yet whether the courtiers of that day were lousy. What are you going to have, my dear fellow?"

"Cold beef, pickled walnuts, and gooseberry-tart."

"Excellent for the character. I shall have curry; they give you a very good Bombay duck here. I rather fancy we shall be fired, Michael. 'Nous sommes trahis!' used to be the prerogative of the French, but I'm afraid we're getting the attitude, too. The Yellow Press has made a difference."

Michael shook his head.

"We say it, but we don't act on it; the climate's too uncertain."

"That sounds deep. This looks very good curry—will you change your mind? Old Fontenoy sometimes comes in here; he has no inside. It'll be serious for him if we're shown the door."

"Deuced rum," said Michael suddenly, "how titles still go down. There can't be any belief in their business capacity."

"Character, my dear fellow—the good old English gentleman. After all, there's something in it."

"I fancy, sir, it's more a case of complex in the shareholders. Their parents show them a lord when they're young."

"Shareholders," said Sir Lawrence; "the world is comprehensive. Who are they, what are they, when are they?"

"This afternoon," said Michael, "and I shall have a good look at them."

"They won't let you in, my dear."

"No?"

"Certainly not."

Michael frowned.

"What paper," he said, "is sure not to be represented?"

Sir Lawrence gave his whinnying laugh.

"*The Field*," he said; "*The Horse and Hound; The Gardener's Weekly*."

"I'll slide in on them."

"You'll see us die game, I hope," said Sir Lawrence, with sudden gravity.

They took a cab together to the meeting, but separated before reaching the door of the hotel.

Michael had thought better of the Press, and took up a position in the passage, whence he could watch for a chance. Stout men, in dark suits, with a palpable look of having lunched off turbot, joints, and cheese, kept passing him. He noticed that each handed the janitor a paper. 'I'll hand him a paper, too,' he thought, 'and scoot in.' Watching for some even stouter men, he took cover between two of them, and approached the door, with an announcement of 'Counterfeits' in his left hand. Handing it across a neighbouring importance, he was quickly into a seat. He saw the janitor's face poked round the door. 'No, my friend,' thought Michael, 'if you could tell duds from shareholders, you wouldn't be in that job!'

He found a report before him, and holding it up, looked at other things. The room seemed to him to have been got by a concert-hall out of a station waiting-room. It had a platform with a long table, behind which were seven empty chairs, and seven inkpots, with seven quill pens upright in them. 'Quills!' thought Michael; 'symbolic, I suppose—they'll all use fountain-pens!'

Back-centre of the platform was a door, and in front, below it, a table,· where four men were sitting, fiddling with notebooks. 'Orchestra,' thought Michael. He turned his attention to the eight or ten rows of shareholders. They looked what they were, but he could not tell why. Their faces were cast in an infinity of moulds, but all had the air of waiting for something they knew they would not get. What sort of lives did they lead, or did their lives lead them? Nearly all wore moustaches. His neighbours to right and left were the same stout shareholders between whom he had slipped in; they both had thick lobes to their ears, and necks even broader than the straight broad backs of their heads. He was a good deal impressed. Dotted here and there he noticed a woman, or a parson. There was practically no conversation, from which he surmised that no one knew his neighbour. He had a feeling that a dog somewhere would have humanised the occasion. He was musing on the colour scheme of green picked out with chocolate and chased with gold, when the door behind the platform was thrown open, and seven men in black coats filed in, and with little bows took their seats behind the quills. They reminded him of people getting up on horses, or about to play the piano—full of small adjustments. That—on the Chairman's right— would be old Fontenoy, with a face entirely composed of features. Michael had an odd conceit: a little thing in a white top-hat sat inside the brain, driving the features eight-in-hand. Then came a face straight from a picture of Her Majesty's Government in 1850, round and pink, with a high nose, a small mouth, and little white whiskers; while at the end on the right was a countenance whose jaw and eyes seemed boring into a conundrum beyond the wall at Michael's back. 'Legal!' he thought. His scrutiny passed back to the Chairman. Chosen? Was he—or was he not? A bearded man, a little behind on the Chairman's left, was already reading from a book, in a rapid monotonous voice. That must be the secretary letting off his minute guns. And in front of him was clearly the new manager, on whose left Michael observed his own father. The dark pothooks over Sir Lawrence's right eye were slightly raised, and his mouth was puckered under the cut line of his small moustache. He looked almost Oriental, quick but still. His left hand held his tortoise-shell-rimmed monocle between thumb and finger. 'Not quite in the scene!' thought Michael; 'poor old Bart!' He had come now to the last of the row. 'Old Forsyte' was sitting precisely as if alone in the world; with one corner of his mouth just drawn down, and one nostril just drawn up, he seemed to Michael quite fascinatingly detached; and yet, not out of the picture. Within that still neat figure, whereof only one patent-leather boot seemed with a slight movement to be living, was intense concentration, entire respect for the proceedings, and yet, a queer contempt for them; he was like a statue of reality, by one who had seen that there was precious little reality in it. 'He chills my soup,' thought Michael, 'but—dash it!—I can't help half admiring him!'

The Chairman had now risen. 'He *is*'—thought Michael; 'no, he isn't—yes—no—I can't tell!' He could hardly attend to what the Chairman said, for wondering whether he was chosen or not, though well aware that it did not matter at all. The Chairman kept steadily on. Distracted, Michael caught words and words: "European situation—misguided policy—French—totally unexpected—position disclosed—manager—unfortunate circumstances shortly to be explained to you—future of this great concern—no reason to doubt——"

'Oil,' thought Michael, 'he is—and yet——!'

"I will now ask one of your directors, Mr. Forsyte, to give you at first hand an account of this painful matter."

Michael saw Soames, pale and deliberate, take a piece of paper from his breast-pocket, and rise. Was it to the occasion?

"I will give you the facts shortly," he said in a voice which reminded Michael of a dry, made-up wine. "On the eleventh of January last I was visited by a clerk in the employ of the Society——"

Familiar with these details, Michael paid them little attention, watching the shareholders for signs of reaction. He saw none, and it was suddenly borne in on him why they wore moustaches: They could not trust their mouths! Character was in the mouth. Moustaches had come in when people no longer went about, like the old Duke, saying: "Think what you damned well like of my character!" Mouths had tried to come in again, of course, before the war; but what with majors, shareholders, and the working-classes, they now had little or no chance! He heard Soames say: "In these circumstances we came to the conclusion that there was nothing for it but to wait and see." Michael saw a sudden quiver pass over the moustaches, as might wind over grass.

'Wrong phrase,' he thought; 'we all do it, but we can't bear being reminded of it.'

207

"Six weeks ago, however," he heard Soames intone, "an accidental incident seems to have warned your late manager that Sir Lawrence and I still entertained suspicions, for I received a letter from him practically admitting that he had taken this secret commission on the German business, and asking me to inform the Board that he had gone abroad and left no property behind him. This statement we have been at pains to verify. In these circumstances we had no alternative but to call you together, and lay the facts before you."

The voice, which had not varied an iota, ceased its recital; and Michael saw his father-in-law return to his detachment—stork on one leg, about to apply beak to parasite, could have inspired no greater sense of loneliness. 'Too like the first account of the battle of Jutland!' he thought: 'He mentioned all the losses, and never once struck the human note.'

A pause ensued, such as occurs before an awkward fence, till somebody has found a gate. Michael rapidly reviewed the faces of the Board. Only one showed any animation. It was concealed in a handkerchief. The sound of the blown nose broke the spell. Two shareholders rose to their feet at once—one of them Michael's neighbour on the right.

"Mr. Sawdry," said the Chairman, and the other shareholder sat down.

With a sonorous clearing of the throat, Michael's neighbour turned his blunt red face towards Soames.

"I wish to ask you, sir, why you didn't inform the Board when you first 'eard of this?"

Soames rose slightly.

"You are aware, I presume, that such an accusation, unless it can be fully substantiated, is a matter for criminal proceedings?"

"No; it would ha' been privileged."

"As between members of the Board, perhaps; but any leakage would have rendered us liable. It was a mere case of word against word."

"Perhaps Sir Lawrence Mont will give us 'is view of that?"

Michael's heart began to beat. There was an air of sprightliness about his father's standing figure.

"You must remember, sir," he said, "that Mr. Elderson had enjoyed our complete confidence for many years; he was a gentleman, and, speaking for myself, an old school-fellow of his, I preferred, in common loyalty, to give his word preference, while—er—keeping the matter in mind."

208

"Oh!" said Michael's neighbour: "What's the Chairman got to say about bein' kept in the dark?"

"We are all perfectly satisfied, sir, with the attitude of our co-directors, in a very delicate situation. You will kindly note that the mischief was already done over this unfortunate assurance, so that there was no need for undue haste."

Michael saw his neighbour's neck grow redder.

"I don't agree," he said. " 'Wait and see'—We might have 'ad that commission out of him, if he'd been tackled promptly." And he sat down.

He had not reached mahogany before the thwarted shareholder had started up.

"Mr. Botterill," said the Chairman.

Michael saw a lean and narrow head, with two hollows in a hairy neck, above a back slightly bent forward, as of a doctor listening to a chest.

"I take it from you, then, sir," he said, "that these two directors represent the general attitude of the Board, and that the Board were content to allow a suspected person to remain manager. The gentleman on your extreme left—Mr. Forsyte, I think—spoke of an accidental incident. But for that, apparently, we should still be in the hands of an unscrupulous individual. The symptoms in this case are very disquieting. There appears to have been gross over-confidence; a recent instance of the sort must be in all our minds. The policy of assuring foreign business was evidently initiated by the manager for his own ends. We have made a severe loss by it. And the question for us shareholders would seem to be whether a Board who placed confidence in such a person, and continued it after their suspicions were aroused, are the right people to direct this important concern."

Throughout this speech Michael had grown very hot. ' "Old Forsyte" was right,' he thought; 'they're on their uppers after all.'

There was a sudden creak from his neighbour on the left.

"Mr. Tolby," said the Chairman.

"It's a serious matter, this, gentlemen. I propose that the Board withdraw, an' leave us to discuss it."

"I second that," said Michael's neighbour on the right.

Searching the vista of the Board, Michael saw recognition gleam for a second in the lonely face at the end, and grinned a greeting.

The Chairman was speaking.

"If that is your wish, gentlemen, we shall be happy to comply with it. Will those who favour the motion hold up their hands?"

All hands were held up, with the exception of Michael's, of two women whose eager colloquy had not permitted them to hear the request, and of one shareholder, just in front of Michael, so motionless that he seemed to be dead.

"Carried," said the Chairman, and rose from his seat.

Michael saw his father smiling, and speaking to 'Old Forsyte' as they both stood up. They all filed out, and the door was closed.

'Whatever happens,' Michael thought, 'I've got to keep my head shut, or I shall be dropping a brick.'

"Perhaps the Press will kindly withdraw, too," he heard someone say.

With a general chinny movement, as if enquiring their rights of no one in particular, the four Pressmen could be seen to clasp their notebooks. When their pale reluctance had vanished, there was a stir among the shareholders, like that of ducks when a dog comes up behind. Michael saw why at once. They had their backs to each other. A shareholder said:

"Perhaps Mr. Tolby, who proposed the withdrawal, will act as Chairman."

Michael's left-hand neighbour began breathing heavily.

"Right-o!" he said. "Anyone who wants to speak, kindly ketch my eye."

Everyone now began talking to his neighbour, as though to get at once a quiet sense of proportion, before speaking. Mr. Tolby was breathing so heavily that Michael felt a positive draught.

"'Ere, gentlemen," he said suddenly, "this won't do! We don't want to be too formal, but we must preserve some order. I'll open the discussion myself. Now, I didn't want to 'urt the feelin's of the Board by plain speakin' in their presence. But, as Mr. What's-'is-name there, said: The public 'as got to protect itself against sharpers, and against slackness. We all know what 'appened the other day, and what'll 'appen again in other concerns, unless we shareholders look after ourselves. In the first place, then, what I say is: They ought never to 'ave touched anything to do with the 'Uns. In the second place, I say they showed bad judgment. And in the third place I say they were too thick together. In my opinion, we should propose a vote of no confidence."

Cries of: "Hear, hear!" mixed with indeterminate sounds, were broken sharply by a loud: "No!" from the shareholder who had seemed dead. Michael's heart went out to him, the more so as he still seemed dead. The negative was followed by the rising of a thin, polished-looking shareholder, with a small grey moustache.

210

"If you'll forgive my saying so, sir," he began, "your proposal seems to me very rough-and-ready justice. I should be interested to know how you would have handled such a situation if you had been on the Board. It is extremely easy to condemn other people!"

"Hear, hear!" said Michael, astonished at his own voice.

"It is all very well," the polished shareholder went on, "when anything of this sort happens, to blame a directorate, but, speaking as a director myself, I should be glad to know whom one is to trust, if not one's manager. As to the policy of foreign insurance, it has been before us at two general meetings; and we have pocketed the profit from it for nearly two years. Have we raised a voice against it?"

The dead shareholder uttered a "No!" so loud that Michael almost patted his head.

The shareholder, whose neck and back were like a doctor's, rose to answer.

"I differ from the last speaker in his diagnosis of the case. Let us admit all he says, and look at the thing more widely. The proof of pudding is in the eating. When a Government makes a bad mistake of judgment, the electorate turns against it as soon as it feels the effects. This is a very sound check on administration; it may be rough and ready, but it is the less of two evils. A Board backs its judgment; when it loses, it should pay. I think, perhaps, Mr. Tolby, being our informal Chairman, was out of order in proposing a vote of no confidence; if that be so, I should be happy to do so, myself."

The dead shareholder's "No!" was so resounding this time that there was a pause for him to speak; he remained, however, without motion. Both of Michael's neighbours were on their feet. They bobbed at each other over Michael's head, and Mr. Tolby sat down.

"Mr. Sawdry," he said.

"Look 'ere, gentlemen," said Mr. Sawdry, "and ladies, this seems to me a case for compromise. The Directors that knew about the manager ought to go; but we might stop at that. The gentleman in front of me keeps on saying 'No.' Let 'im give us 'is views."

"No," said the dead shareholder, but less loudly.

"If a man can't give 'is views," went on Mr. Sawdry, nearly sitting down on Michael, "'e shouldn't interrupt, in my opinion."

A shareholder in the front row now turned completely round so that he faced the meeting.

"I think," he said, "that to prolong this discussion is to waste time; we are evidently in two, if not three, minds. The whole of the business of this country is now conducted on a system of delegated trust; it may be good, it may be bad—but there it is. You've got to trust somebody. Now, as to this particular case, we've had no reason to distrust the Board, so far; and, as I take it, the Board had no previous reason to distrust the late manager. I think it's going too far, at present, to propose anything definite like a vote of no confidence; it seems to me that we should call the Board in and hear what assurances they have to give us against a repetition of anything of the sort in the future."

The sounds which greeted this moderate speech were so inextricable that Michael could not get the sense of them. Not so with the speech which followed. It came from a shareholder on the right, with reddish hair, light eyelashes, a clipped moustache, and a scraped colour.

"I have no objection whatever to having the Board in," he said in a rather jeering voice, "and passing a vote of no confidence in their presence. There is a question, which no one has touched on, of how far, if we turn them out, we could make them liable for this loss. The matter is not clear, but there is a good sporting chance, if we like to take it. Whereas, if we don't turn them out, it's obvious we can't take it, even if we wish."

The impression made by this speech was of quite a different order from any of the others. It was followed by a hush, as though something important had been said at last. Michael stared at Mr. Tolby. The stout man's round, light, rather prominent eye was extraordinarily reflective. 'Trout must look like that,' thought Michael, 'when they see a mayfly.' Mr. Tolby suddenly stood up.

"All right," he said, " 'ave 'em in!"

"Yes," said the dead shareholder. There was no dissent. Michael saw someone rise and ascend the platform.

"Let the Press know!" said Mr. Tolby.


## Chapter XIII

### SOAMES AT BAY

WHEN the door had closed behind the departing directors, Soames sought a window as far as possible from the lunch eaten before the meeting.

"Funeral baked meats, eh, Forsyte?" said a voice in his ear. "Our number's up, I think. Poor old Mothergill's looking very blue. I think he ought to ask for a second shirt!"

Soames's tenacity began wriggling within him.

"The thing wants tackling," he grumbled; "the Chairman's not the man for the job!" Shades of old Uncle Jolyon! He would have made short work of this! It wanted a masterful hand.

"Warning to us all, Forsyte, against loyalty! It's not in the period. Ah! Fontenoy!"

Soames became conscious of features rather above the level of his own.

"Well, Mr. Forsyte, hope you're satisfied? A pretty damned mess! If I'd been the Chairman, I'd never have withdrawn. Always keep hounds under your eye, Mont. Take it off, and they'll go for you! Wish I could get among 'em with a whip; I'd give it those two heavy pug-faced chaps—they mean business! Unless you've got something up your sleeve, Mr. Forsyte, we're dished."

"What should I have up my sleeve?" said Soames coldly.

"Damn it, sir, you put the chestnuts in the fire, it's up to you to pull 'em out. I can't afford to lose these fees!"

Soames heard Sir Lawrence murmur: "Crude, my dear Fontenoy!" and said with malice:

"You may lose more than your fees!"

"Can't! They may have Eaglescourt to-morrow, and take a loss off my hands." A gleam of feeling burned up suddenly in the old eyes: "The country drives you to the wall, skins you to the bone, and expects you to give 'em public service gratis. Can't be done, Mont—can't be done!"

Soames turned away; he had an utter disinclination for talk, like one standing before an open grave, watching a coffin slowly lowered. Here was his infallibility going—going! He had no illusions. It would all be in the papers, and his reputation for sound judgment gone for ever! Bitter! No more would the Forsytes say: "Soames says——" No more would old Gradman follow him with eyes like an old dog's, grudging sometimes, but ever submitting to infallibility. It would be a nasty jar for the old fellow. His business acquaintances—after all, they were not many, now!—would no longer stare with envious respect. He wondered if the reverberations would reach Dumetrius, and the picture market! The sole comfort was: Fleur needn't know. Fleur! Ah! If only her business were safely over! For a moment his mind became empty of all else. Then with a rush the present filled it up again. Why were they all talking as if there were a corpse in the room? Well! There was—the corpse of his infallibility! As for monetary loss—that seemed secondary, remote, incredible—like a

213

future life. Mont had said something about loyalty. He didn't know what loyalty had to do with it! But if they thought he was going to show any white feather, they were extremely mistaken. Acid courage welled up into his brain. Shareholders, directors—they might howl and shake their fists; he was not going to be dictated to. He heard a voice say:

"Will you come in, please, gentlemen?"

Taking his seat again before his unused quill, he noticed the silence—shareholders waiting for directors, directors for shareholders. "Wish I could get among 'em with a whip!" Extravagant words of that 'old guinea-pig's,' but expressive, somehow!

At last the Chairman, whose voice always reminded Soames of a raw salad with oil poured over it, said ironically:

"Well, gentlemen, we await your pleasure."

That stout, red-faced fellow, next to Michael, stood up, opening his pug's mouth.

"To put it shortly, Mr. Chairman, we're not at all satisfied; but before we take any resolution, we want to 'ear what you've got to say."

Just below Soames, someone jumped up and added:

"We'd like to know, sir, what assurances you can offer us against anything of this sort in the future."

Soames saw the Chairman smile—no real backbone in that fellow!

"In the nature of things, sir," he said, "none whatever! You can hardly suppose that if we had known our manager was not worthy of our confidence, we should have continued him in the post for a moment!"

Soames thought: 'That won't do—he's gone back on himself!' Yes, and that other pug-faced chap had seen it!

"That's just the point, sir," he was saying: "Two of you *did* know, and yet, there the fellow was for months afterwards, playin' 'is own 'and, cheatin' the Society for all he was worth, I shouldn't wonder."

One after another, they were yelping now:

"What about your own words?"

"You admitted collective responsibility."

"You said you were perfectly satisfied with the attitude of your co-directors in the matter." Regular pack!

Soames saw the Chairman incline his head as if he wanted to shake it; old Fontenoy muttering, old Mothergill blowing his nose, Meyricke shrugged his sharp shoulders. Suddenly he was cut off

214

from view of them—Sir Lawrence was standing up between.

"Allow me a word! Speaking for myself, I find it impossible to accept the generous attempt of the Chairman to shoulder a responsibility which clearly rests on me. If I made a mistake of judgment in not disclosing our suspicions, I must pay the penalty; and I think it will clear the—er—situation if I tender my resignation to the meeting."

Soames saw him give a little bow, place his monocle in his eye, and sit down.

A murmur greeted the words—approval, surprise, deprecation, admiration? It had been gallantly done. Soames distrusted gallantry—there was always a dash of the peacock about it. He felt curiously savage.

"I, apparently," he said, rising, "am the other incriminated director. Very good! I am not conscious of having done anything but my duty from beginning to end of this affair. I am confident that I made no mistake of judgment. And I consider it entirely unjust that I should be penalised. I have had worry and anxiety enough, without being made a scapegoat by shareholders who accepted this policy without a murmur, before ever I came on the Board, and are now angry because they have lost by it. You owe it to me that the policy has been dropped: you owe it to me that you have no longer a fraudulent person for a manager. And you owe it to me that you were called together to-day to pass judgment on the matter. I have no intention whatever of singing small. But there is another aspect to this affair. I am not prepared to go on giving my services to people who don't value them. I have no patience with the attitude displayed this afternoon. If anyone here thinks he has a grievance against me, let him bring an action. I shall be happy to carry it to the House of Lords, if necessary. I have been familiar with the City all my life, and I have not been in the habit of meeting with suspicions and ingratitude. If this is an instance of present manners, I have been familiar with the City long enough. I do not tender my resignation to the meeting; I resign."

Bowing to the Chairman, and pushing back his chair, he walked doggedly to the door, opened it and passed through.

He sought his hat. He had not the slightest doubt but that he had astonished their weak nerves! Those pug-faced fellows had their mouths open! He would have liked to see what he had left behind, but it was hardly consistent with dignity to open the door again. He took a sandwich instead, and began to eat it with his back to the door and his hat on. He felt better than he had for months. A voice said:

" 'And the subsequent proceedings interested him no more!' I'd no idea, Forsyte, you were such an orator! You gave it 'em between the eyes! Never saw a meeting so knocked out! Well, you've saved the Board by focussing their resentment entirely on yourself. It was very gallant, Forsyte!"

Soames growled through his sandwich:

"Nothing of the sort! Are you out, too?"

"Yes. I pressed my resignation. That red-faced fellow was proposing a vote of confidence in the Board when I left—and they'll pass it, Forsyte—they'll pass it! Something was said about financial liability, by the way!"

"Was there?" said Soames, with a grim smile: "That cock won't fight. Their only chance was to claim against the Board for initiating foreign assurance *ultra vires*; if they're re-affirming the Board, after the question's been raised in open meeting, they're dished. Nothing'll lie against you and me, for not disclosing our suspicions —that's certain."

"A relief, I confess," said Sir Lawrence, with a sigh. "It was the speech of your life, Forsyte!"

Perfectly well aware of that, Soames shook his head. Apart from the horror of seeing himself in print, he was beginning to feel that he had been extravagant. It was always a mistake to lose your temper! A bitter little smile came on his lips. Nobody, not even Mont, would see how unjustly he had been treated.

"Well," he said, "I shall go."

"I think I shall wait, Forsyte, and hear the upshot."

"Upshot? They'll appoint two other fools, and slaver over each other. Shareholders! Good-bye!" He moved to the door.

Passing the Bank of England, he had a feeling of walking away from his own life. His acumen, his judgment, his manner of dealing with affairs—aspersed! They didn't like it; well—he would leave it! Catch him meddling, in future! It was all of a piece with the modern state of things. Hand to mouth, and the steady men pushed to the wall! The men to whom a pound was a pound, and not a mess of chance and paper. The men who knew that the good of the country was the strict, straight conduct of their own affairs. They were not wanted. One by one, they would get the go-by—as he had got it—in favour of Jack-o'-lanterns, revolutionaries, restless chaps, or clever, unscrupulous fellows, like Elderson. It was in the air. No amount of eating your cake and wanting to have it could take the place of common honesty.

He turned into the Poultry before he knew why he had come there. Well, he might as well tell Gradman at once that he must exercise his own judgment in the future. At the mouth of the backwater he paused for a second, as if to print its buffness on his brain. He would resign his trusts, private and all! He had no notion of being sneered at in the family. But a sudden wave of remembrance almost washed his heart into his boots. What a tale of trust deeds executed, leases renewed, houses sold, investments decided on—in that back room up there; what a mint of quiet satisfaction in estates well managed! Ah! well! He would continue to manage his own. As for the others, they must look out for themselves, now. And a precious time they'd have of it, in face of the spirit there was about!

He mounted the stone steps slowly.

In the repository of Forsyte affairs, he was faced by the unusual —not Gradman, but, on the large ripe table, a large ripe melon alongside a straw bag. Soames sniffed. The thing smelled delicious. He held it to the light. Its greeny yellow tinge, its network of threads—quite Chinese! Was old Gradman going to throw its rind about, like that white monkey?

He was still holding it when a voice said:

"Aoh! I wasn't expecting you to-day, Mr. Soames. I was going early; my wife's got a little party."

"So I see!" said Soames, restoring the melon to the table. "There's nothing for you to do at the moment, but I came in to tell you to draw my resignation from the Forsyte trusts."

The old chap's face was such a study that he could not help a smile.

"You can keep me in Timothy's; but the rest must go. Young Roger can attend to them. He's got nothing to do."

A gruff and deprecating: "Dear me! They won't like it!" irritated Soames.

"Then they must lump it! I want a rest."

He did not mean to enter into the reason—Gradman could read it for himself in the *Financial News*, or whatever he took in.

"Then I shan't be seeing you so often, Mr. Soames; there's never anything in Mr. Timothy's. Dear me! I'm quite upset. Won't you keep your sister's?"

Soames looked at the old fellow, and compunction stirred within him—as ever, at any sign that he was appreciated.

"Well," he said, "keep me in hers; I shall be in about my own

A MODERN COMEDY

affairs, of course. Good afternoon, Gradman. That's a fine melon."

He waited for no more words. The old chap! *He* couldn't last much longer, anyway, sturdy as he looked! Well, they would find it hard to match him!

On reaching the Poultry, he decided to go to Green Street and see Winifred—queerly and suddenly home-sick for the proximity of Park Lane, for the old secure days, the efflorescent privacy of his youth under the wings of James and Emily. Winifred alone represented for him now, the past; her solid nature never varied, however much she kept up with the fashions.

He found her, a little youthful in costume, drinking China tea, which she did not like—but what could one do, other teas were 'common'! She had taken to a parrot. Parrots were coming in again. The bird made a dreadful noise. Whether under its influence or that of the China tea—which, made in the English way, of a brand the Chinese grew for foreign stomachs, always upset him— he was soon telling her the whole story.

When he had finished, Winifred said comfortably:

"Well, Soames, I think you did splendidly; it serves them right!"

Conscious that his narrative must have presented the truth as it would not appear to the public, Soames muttered:

"That's all very well; you'll find a very different version in the financial papers."

"Oh! but nobody reads them. I shouldn't worry. Do you do Coué? Such a comfortable little man, Soames; I went to hear him. It's rather a bore sometimes, but it's quite the latest thing."

Soames became inaudible—he never confessed a weakness.

"And how," asked Winifred, "is Fleur's little affair?"

" 'Little affair!' " echoed a voice above his head. That bird! It was clinging to the brocade curtains, moving its neck up and down.

"Polly!" said Winifred: "don't be naughty!"

"Soames!" said the bird.

"I've taught him that. Isn't he rather sweet?"

"No," said Soames. "I should shut him up; he'll spoil your curtains."

The vexation of the afternoon had revived within him suddenly. What was life, but parrotry? What did people see of the real truth? They just repeated each other, like a lot of shareholders, or got their precious sentiments out of *The Daily Liar*. For one person who took a line, a hundred followed on, like sheep!

"You'll stay and dine, dear boy!" said Winifred.

Yes! he would dine. Had she a melon, by any chance? He'd no

218

inclination to go and sit opposite his wife at South Square. Ten to one Fleur would not be down. And as to young Michael—the fellow had been there that afternoon and witnessed the whole thing; he'd no wish to go over it again.

He was washing his hands for dinner, when a maid, outside said: "You're wanted on the phone, sir."

Michael's voice came over the wire, strained and husky:

"That you, sir?"

"Yes. What is it?"

"Fleur. It began this afternoon at three. I've been trying to reach you."

"What?" cried Soames. "How? Quick!"

"They say it's all normal. But it's so awful. They say quite soon, now." The voice broke off.

"My God!" said Soames. "My hat!"

By the front door the maid was asking: "Shall you be back to dinner, sir?"

"Dinner!" muttered Soames, and was gone.

He hurried along, almost running, his eyes searching for a cab. None to be had, of course! None to be had! Opposite the 'Iseeum' Club he got one, open in the fine weather after last night's storm. That storm! He might have known. Ten days before her time. Why on earth hadn't he gone straight back, or at least telephoned where he would be? All that he had been through that afternoon was gone like smoke. Poor child! Poor little thing! And what about twilight sleep? Why hadn't he been there? He might have— nature! Damn it! Nature—as if it couldn't leave even her alone!

"Get on!" he said, leaning out: "Double fare!"

Past the Connoisseurs', and the Palace, and Whitehall; past all preserves whence nature was excluded, deep in the waters of primitive emotion Soames sat, grey, breathless. Past Big Ben— eight o'clock! Five hours! Five hours of it!

"Let it be over!" he muttered aloud: "Let it be over, God!"

## Chapter XIV

### ON THE RACK

WHEN his father-in-law bowed to the Chairman and withdrew, Michael had restrained a strong desire to shout: "Bravo!" Who'd have thought the 'old man' could let fly like that? He had 'got their goats' with a vengeance. Quite an interval of fine mixed vociferation followed, before his neighbour, Mr. Sawdry, made himself heard at last.

"Now that the director implicated has resigned, I shall 'ave pleasure in proposing a vote of confidence in the rest of the Board."

Michael saw his father rise, a little finicky and smiling, and bow to the Chairman. "I take my resignation as accepted also; if you permit me, I will join Mr. Forsyte in retirement."

Someone was saying:

"I shall be glad to second that vote of confidence."

And brushing past the knees of Mr. Sawdry, Michael sought the door. From there he could see that nearly every hand was raised in favour of the vote of confidence; and with the thought: 'Thrown to the shareholders!' he made his way out of the hotel. Delicacy prevented him from seeking out those two. They had saved their dignity; but the dogs had had the rest.

Hurrying west, he reflected on the rough ways of justice. The shareholders had a grievance, of course; and someone had to get it in the neck to satisfy their sense of equity. They had pitched on 'Old Forsyte', who, of all, was least to blame; for if Bart had only held his tongue, they would certainly have lumped him into the vote of confidence. All very natural and illogical; and four o'clock already!

'Counterfeits'! The old feeling for Wilfrid was strong in him this day of publication. One must do everything one could for his book—poor old son! There simply must not be a frost.

After calling in at two big booksellers, he made for his club, and closeted himself in the telephone booth. In old days they 'took cabs and went about'. Ringing-up was quicker—was it? With endless vexations, he tracked down Sibley, Nazing, Upshire, Master, and half a dozen others of the elect. He struck a considered note likely to move them. The book—he said—was bound to 'get the goat of the old guard and the duds generally'; it would want a bit of drum-beating from the cognoscenti. To each of them he appealed as the only one whose praise really mattered. "If you haven't reviewed the book, old chap, will you? It's you who count, of course." And to each he added: "I don't care two straws whether it sells, but I do want old Wilfrid to get his due." And he meant it. The publisher in Michael was dead during that hour in the telephone booth, the friend alive and kicking hard. He came out with sweat running down his forehead, quite exhausted; and it was half-past five.

'Cup of tea—and home!' he thought. He reached his door at six.

THE WHITE MONKEY

Ting-a-ling, absolutely unimportant, was cowering in the far corner of the hall.

"What's the matter, old man?"

A sound from above, which made his blood run cold, answered— a long, low moaning.

"Oh, God!" he gasped, and ran upstairs.

Annette met him at the door. He was conscious of her speaking in French, of being called "*mon cher*," of the words "*vers trois heures*. . . . The doctor says one must not worry—all goes for the best." Again that moan, and the door shut in his face; she was gone. Michael remained standing on the rug with perfectly cold sweat oozing from him, and his nails dug deep into his palms.

'This is how one becomes a father!' he thought: 'This is how I became a son!' That moaning! He could not bear to stay there, and he could not bear to go away. It might be hours, yet! He kept repeating to himself: "One must not worry—must not worry!" How easily said! How meaningless! His brain, his heart, ranging for relief, lighted on the strangest relief which could possibly have come to him. Suppose this child being born, had not been his— had been—been Wilfrid's; how would he have been feeling, here. outside this door? It might—it might so easily have been—since nothing was sacred, now! Nothing except—yes, just that which was dearer than oneself—just that which was in there, moaning. He could not bear it on the rug, and went downstairs. Across and across the copper floor, a cigar in his mouth, he strode in vague, rebellious agony. Why should birth be like this? And the answer was: It isn't—not in China! To have the creed that nothing mattered—and then run into it like this! Something born at such a cost, must matter, should matter. One must see to that! Specula- tion ceased in Michael's brain; he stood, listening terribly. Nothing! He could not bear it down there, and went up again. No sound at first, and then another moan! This time he fled into his study, and ranged round the room, looking at the cartoons of Aubrey Greene. He did not see a single one, and suddenly bethought him of 'Old Forsyte'. He ought to be told! He rang up the 'Connoisseurs', the 'Remove', and his own father's clubs, in case they might have gone there together after the meeting. He draw blank everywhere. It was half-past seven. How much longer was this going on? He went back to the bedroom door; could hear nothing. Then down again to the hall. Ting-a-ling was lying by the front door, now. 'Fed-up!' thought Michael, stroking his back, and mechanically clearing the letter-box. Just one letter—Wilfrid's writing! He took it to the foot of the stairs and read it with half his brain, the other half wondering—wandering up there.

"DEAR MONT,—I start to-morrow to try and cross Arabia. I thought you might like a line in case Arabia crosses me. I have recovered my senses. The air here is too clear for sentiment of any kind; and passion in exile soon becomes sickly. I am sorry I made you so much disturbance. It was a mistake for me to go back to England after the war, and hang about writing drivel for smart young women and inky folk to read. Poor old England—she's in for a bad time. Give her my love; the same to yourselves.

"Yours ever,
"WILFRID DESERT.

"P.S.—If you've published the things I left behind, send any royalties to me care of my governor.—W.D."

Half Michael's brain thought: 'Well, that's that! And the book coming out to-day!' Queer! Was Wilfrid right—was it all a blooming gaff—the inky stream? Was one just helping on England's sickness? Ought they all to get on camels and ride the sun down? And yet, in books were comfort and diversion; and they were wanted! England had to go on—go on! 'No retreat, no retreat, they must conquer or die who have no retreat!' . . . God! There it was again! Back he flew upstairs, with his ears covered and his eyes wild. The sounds ceased; Annette came out to him.

"Her father, *mon cher*; try to find her father!"

"I have—I can't" gasped Michael.

"Try Green Street—Mrs. Dartie. *Courage!* All is normal—it will be quite soon, now."

When he had rung up Green Street and been answered at last, he sat with the door of his study open, waiting for 'Old Forsyte' to come. Half his sight remarked a round hole burnt in his trouser leg—he hadn't even noticed the smell; hadn't even realised that he had been smoking. He must pull himself together for the 'old man' He heard the bell ring, and ran down to open.

"Well?" said Soames.

"Not yet, sir. Come up to my study. It's nearer."

They went up side by side. That trim grey head, with the deep furrow between the eyes, and those eyes staring as if at pain behind them, steadied Michael. Poor old chap! He was 'for it', too! They were both on 'their uppers'!

222

"Have a peg, sir? I've got brandy here."

"Yes," said Soames. "Anything."

With the brandies in their hands, half-raised, they listened—jerked their hands up, drank. They were automatic, like two doll figures worked by the same string.

"Cigarette, sir?" said Michael.

Soames nodded.

With the lighted cigarettes just not in their mouths, they listened, put them in, took them out, puffed smoke. Michael had his right arm across his chest. Soames his left. They formed a pattern, thus, side by side.

"Bad to stick, sir. Sorry!"

Soames nodded. His teeth were clenched. Suddenly his hand relaxed.

"Listen!" he said. Sounds—different—confused!

Michael's hand seized something, gripped it hard; it was cold, thin—the hand of Soames. They sat thus, hand in hand, staring at the doorway, for how long neither knew.

Suddenly that doorway darkened; a figure in grey stood there—Annette!

"It is all r-right! A son!"


Chapter XV

CALM

ON waking from deep sleep next morning, Michael's first thought was: 'Fleur is back!' He then remembered.

To his : "O.K.?" whispered at her door, he received an emphatic nod from the nurse.

In the midst of excited expectation he retained enough modernity to think: 'No more blurb! Go and eat your breakfast quietly!'

In the dining-room Soames was despising the broken egg before him. He looked up as Michael entered, and buried his face in his cup. Michael understood perfectly; they had sat hand in hand! He saw, too, that the journal opened by his plate was of a financial nature.

"Anything about the meeting, sir? Your speech must read like one o'clock!"

With a queer little sound Soames held out the paper. The headlines ran: "Stormy meeting—resignation of two directors—a vote of confidence." Michael skimmed down till he came to:

"Mr. Forsyte, the director involved, in a speech of some length, said he had no intention of singing small. He deprecated the behaviour of the shareholders; he had not been accustomed to meet with suspicions. He tendered his resignation."

Michael dropped the sheet.

"By Jove!" he said—" 'Involved—suspicions'. They've given it a turn, as though——!"

"The papers!" said Soames, and resumed his egg.

Michael sat down, and stripped the skin off a banana. ' "Nothing became him like his death",' he thought: 'Poor old boy!'

"Well, sir," he said, "I was there, and all I can say is: You and my father were the only two people who excited my respect."

"That!" said Soames, putting down his spoon.

Michael perceived that he wished to be alone, and swallowing the banana, went to his study. Waiting for his summons, he rang up his father.

"None the worse for yesterday, sir?"

Sir Lawrence's voice came clear and thin, rather high.

"Poorer and wiser. What's the bulletin?"

"Top-hole."

"Our love to both. Your mother wants to know if he has any hair?"

"Haven't seen him yet. I'm just going."

Annette, indeed, was beckoning from the doorway.

"She wants you to bring the little dog, *mon cher.*"

With Ting-a-ling under his arm, and treading on tiptoe, Michael entered. The eleventh baronet! He did not seem to amount to much, beneath her head bent over him. And surely her hair was darker! He walked up to the bed, and touched it reverently.

Fleur raised her head, and revealed the baby sucking vigorously at her little finger. "Isn't he a monkey?" said her faint voice.

Michael nodded. A monkey clearly—but whether white—that was the question!

"And you, sweetheart?"

"All right now, but it was——" She drew her breath in, and her eyes darkened: "Ting, look!"

The Chinese dog, with nostrils delicately moving, drew backward under Michael's arm. His whole demeanour displayed a knowing criticism. "Puppies," he seemed to say, "we do it in China. Judgment reserved!"

224

"What eyes!" said Michael: "We needn't tell *him* that this was brought from Chelsea by the doctor."

Fleur gave the tiniest laugh.

"Put him down, Michael."

Michael put him down, and he went to his corner.

"I mustn't talk," said Fleur, "but I want to, frightfully; as if I'd been dumb for months."

'Just as I felt,' thought Michael, 'she's been away, away somewhere, utterly away.'

"It was like being held down, Michael. Months of not being yourself."

Michael said softly: "Yes! the process *is* behind the times! Has he got any hair? My mother wants to know."

Fleur revealed the head of the eleventh baronet, covered with dark down.

"Like my grandmother's; but it'll get lighter. His eyes are going to be grey. Oh! and, Michael, about godparents? Alison, of course —but men?"

Michael dwelled a little before answering:

"I had a letter from Wilfrid yesterday. Would you like him? He's still out there, but I could hold the sponge for him in church."

"Is he all right again?"

"He says so."

He could not read the expression of her eyes, but her lips were pouted slightly.

"Yes," she said: "and I think one's enough, don't you? Mine never gave me anything."

"One of mine gave me a Bible, and the other gave me a wigging. Wilfrid, then." And he bent over her.

Her eyes seemed to make him a little ironic apology. He kissed her hair, and moved hurriedly away.

By the door Soames was standing, awaiting his turn.

"Just a minute only, sir," the nurse was saying.

Soames walked up to the bedside, and stood looking at his daughter.

"Dad, dear!" Michael heard her say.

Soames just touched her hand, nodded, as if implying approval of the baby, and came walking back, but, in a mirror, Michael saw his lips quivering.

On the ground floor once more, he had the most intense desire to sing. It would not do; and, entering the Chinese room, he stood staring out into the sunlit square. Gosh! It was good to be alive!

Say what you liked, you couldn't beat it! They might turn their noses up at life, and look down them at it; they might bolster up the future and the past, but—give him the present!

'I'll have that white monkey up again!' he thought. 'I'll see the brute further before he shall depress me!'

He went out to a closet under the stairs, and, from beneath four pairs of curtains done up in moth-preserver and brown paper, took out the picture. He held it away from him in the dim light. The creature's eyes! It was all in those eyes!

"Never mind, old son!" he said: "Up you go!" And he carried it into the Chinese room.

Soames was there.

"I'm going to put him up again, sir."

Soames nodded.

"Would you hold him, while I hook the wire?"

Soames held the picture.

Returning to the copper floor, Michael said:

"All right, sir!" and stood back.

Soames joined him. Side by side they contemplated the white monkey.

"He won't be happy till he gets it," said Michael at last: "The only thing is, you see, he doesn't know what it is."

INTERLUDE

A SILENT WOOING

# A SILENT WOOING

IN February 1924, Jon Forsyte, convalescing from the 'flu, was sitting in the lounge of an hotel at Camden, South Carolina, with his bright hair slowly rising on his scalp. He was reading about a lynching.

A voice behind him said:

"Will you join our picnic over at those old-time mounds to-day?"

Looking up, he saw a young acquaintance called Francis Wilmot, who came from further south.

"Very glad to. Who's going?"

"Why, just Mr. and Mrs. Pulmore Hurrison, and that English novelist, Gurdon Minho, and the Blair girls and their friends, and my sister Anne and I. You could ride over horseback, if you want exercise."

"All right; they've got some new horses in this morning from Columbia."

"Why, that's fine! My sister and I'll ride horseback too, and some of the Blair girls. The Hurrisons can take the others."

"I say," said Jon, "this is a pretty bad case of lynching."

The young man to whom he spoke leaned in the window. Jon admired his face, as of ivory, with dark hair and eyes, and narrow nose and lips, and his lissom free attitude.

"All you Britishers go off the deep-end when you read of a lynching. You haven't got the negro problem up where you are at Southern Pines. They don't have it any to speak of in North Carolina."

"No, and I don't profess to understand it. But I can't see why negroes shouldn't be tried the same as white men. There may be cases where you've got to shoot at sight; but I don't see how you can defend mob law. Once you catch a man, he ought to be tried properly."

"We're not taking any chances with that particular kind of trouble."

"But if a man isn't tried, how can you tell he's guilty?"

"Well, we'd sooner do without an innocent darkie now and again than risk our women."

"I should have thought killing a man for a thing he hadn't done was worse than anything."

"Maybe, in Europe. But not here. Things are in the large, still."

"What do they think about lynching in the north?"

"They squeal a bit, but they've no call to. If we've got negroes, they've got the reds, and they surely have a wholesale way with them."

Jon Forsyte tilted back his rocking-chair, with a puzzled frown.

"I reckon there's too much space in this country still," said Francis Wilmot; "a man has all the chances to get off. So where we feel strong about a thing, we take the law into our own hands."

"Well, every country to its own fashions. What are these mounds we're going to?"

"Old Indian remains that go way back thousands of years, they say. You haven't met my sister? She only came last night."

"No. What time do we start?"

"Noon; it's about an hour's ride by the woods."

At noon then, in riding kit, Jon came out to the five horses, for more than one of the Blair girls had elected to ride. He started between them, Francis Wilmot going ahead with his sister.

The Blair girls were young and pretty with a medium-coloured, short-faced, well-complexioned, American prettiness, of a type to which he had become accustomed during the two and a half years he had spent in the United States. They were at first extremely silent, and then extremely vocal. They rode astride, and very well. Jon learned that they, as well as the givers of the picnic, Mr. and Mrs. Pulmore Hurrison, inhabited Long Island. They asked him many questions about England, to which Jon, who had left at the age of nineteen, invented many answers. He began to look longingly between his horse's ears at Francis Wilmot and his sister, cantering ahead in a silence that, from a distance, seemed extremely restful. Their way led through pine woods—of trees spindly and sparse, and over a rather sandy soil; the sunlight was clear and warm, the air still crisp. Jon rode a single-footing bay horse, and felt as one feels on the first day of recovered health.

The Blair girls wished to know what he thought of the English novelist—they were dying to see a real highbrow. Jon had only

read one of his books, and of the characters therein could only
remember a cat. The Blair girls had read none; but they had heard
that his cats were 'just too cunning'.

Francis Wilmot, reining up in front, pointed at a large mound
which certainly seemed to be unnaturally formed. They all reined
up, looked at it for two minutes in silence, judged it was 'very
interesting', and rode on. In a hollow the occupants of two cars
were disembarking food. Jon led the horses away to tether them
alongside the horses of Wilmot and his sister.

"My sister," said Francis Wilmot.

"Mr. Forsyte," said the sister.

She looked at Jon, and Jon looked at her. She was slim but
distinctly firm, in a long dark-brown coat and breeches and boots;
her hair was bobbed and dark under a soft brown felt hat. Her
face was pale, rather browned, and had a sort of restrained eager-
ness—the brow broad and clear, the nose straight and slightly
sudden, the mouth unreddened, rather wide and pretty. But what
struck Jon were her eyes, which were exactly his idea of a water
nymph's. They slanted a little, and were steady and brown and
enticing; whether there was ever such a slight squint in them he
could not tell, but if there were it was an improvement. He felt
shy. Neither of them spoke.

Francis Wilmot remarked: "I reckon I'm hungry," and they
walked side by side towards the eatables.

Jon said suddenly to the sister:

"You've just come then, Miss Wilmot?"

"Yes, Mr. Forsyte."

"Where from?"

"From Naseby. It's way down between Charleston and
Savannah."

"Oh, Charleston! I liked Charleston."

"Anne likes Savannah best," said Francis Wilmot.

Anne nodded. She was not talkative, it seemed, though her
voice had sounded pleasant in small quantities.

"It's kind of lonesome where we live," said Francis. "Mostly
darkies. Anne's never seen an Englishman to speak to."

Anne smiled. Jon also smiled. Neither pursued the subject. They
arrived at the eatables, spread in a manner calculated to give the
maximum of muscular and digestive exertion. Mrs. Pulmore Hurrison, a lady of forty or so, and of defined features, was seated with
her feet turned up; next to her, Gurdon Minho, the English novelist,
had his legs in a more reserved position; and then came quantities

231

of seated girls, all with pretty unreserved legs; Mr. Pulmore Hurrison, somewhat apart, was pursing a small mouth over the cork of a large bottle. Jon and the Wilmots also sat down. The picnic had begun.

Jon soon realised that everybody was expecting Gurdon Minho to say something beyond "Yes," "Really!", "Ah!", "Quite!" This did not occur. The celebrated novelist was at first almost painfully attentive to what everybody else said, and then seemed to go into a coma. Jon felt a patriotic disappointment, for he himself was, if anything, even more silent. He could see that, among the three Blair girls and their two girl friends, a sort of conspiracy was brewing, to quiz the silent English in the privacy of the future. Francis Wilmot's speechless sister was a comfort to him; he felt that she would neither be entitled nor inclined to join that conspiracy. He took refuge in handing victuals and was glad when the period of eating on constricted stomachs was over. Picnics were like Christmas Day, better in the future and the past than in the present. After the normal period of separation into genders, the baskets were repacked, and all restored into their vehicles. The two cars departed for another mound said to be two miles off. Francis Wilmot and the two Blair girls judged they would get back and watch the polo. Jon asked Anne Wilmot which she wished to do. She elected to see the other mound.

They mounted and pursued a track through the woods in silence, till Jon said:

"Do you like picnics?"

"I certainly do not."

"Nor do I. But riding?"

"I just adore it more than anything in the world."

"More than dancing?"

"Surely. Riding and swimming!"

"Ah! I *thought*——" And he was silent.

"What did you think?"

"Well, I thought somehow you were a good swimmer."

"Why?"

Jon said with embarrassment:

"By your eyes——"

"What! Are they fishy?"

Jon laughed.

"Not exactly. They're like water nymph's."

"I don't just know if that's a compliment."

"Of course it is."

"I thought nymphs weren't respectable."

"Oh! *Water* nymphs—very! Shy, of course."

"Do you have many in England?"

"No. As a matter of fact I've never seen one before."

"Then how do you know?"

"Just a general sense of what's fitting."

"I suppose you had a classical education. Don't you all have that in England?"

"Far from it."

"And how do you like America, Mr. Forsyte?"

"Very much. I get homesick sometimes."

"I'd love to travel."

"You never have?"

She shook her head. "I just stay at home and look after things. But I reckon we'll have to sell the old home—cotton doesn't pay any more."

"I grow peaches near Southern Pines, you know, up in North Carolina; that's paying at present."

"Do you live there alone?"

"No; with my mother."

"Is she Engilsh?"

"Yes."

"Have you a father?"

"He died four years ago."

"Francis and I have been orphans ten years."

"I wish you'd both come and stay with us some day; my mother would be awfully glad."

"Is she like you?"

Jon laughed.

"No. She's beautiful."

The eyes regarded him gravely, the lips smiled faintly.

"I'd just love to come, but Francis and I can't ever be away together."

"But," said Jon, "you're both here."

"We go back to-morrow; I wanted to see Camden." The eyes resumed their steady consideration of Jon's face, "Won't you come back with us instead, and see our home—it's old? Francis would like to have you come."

"Do you always know what your brother would like?"

"Surely."

"That must be jolly. But do you really mean you want me?"

"I certainly do."

233

# A MODERN COMEDY

"I'd enjoy it awfully; I hate hotels. I mean—well, you know——" But as *he* didn't he was not so sure that she did.

She touched her horse, and the single-footing animal broke into a canter.

Along the alleys of the eternal pinewood the sun was in their eyes; a warmed scent rose from pine needles, gum and herbs; the going was sandy and soft; the horses in good mood. Jon felt happy. This girl had strange eyes, enticing; and she rode better even than the Blair girls.

"I suppose all the English ride well?" she said.

"Most do, when they ride at all; but we don't ride much nowadays."

"I'd love to see England; our folk came from England in 1700—Worcestershire. Where is that?"

"It's our middle west," said Jon. "But as unlike as ever you can imagine. It's fruit-growing country—very pretty; white timbered houses, pastures, orchards, woods, green hills. I went there walking one holiday with a school friend."

"It sounds just lovely. Our ancestors were Roman Catholics. They had a place called Naseby; that's why we call ours Naseby. But my grandmother was French Creole, from Louisiana. Is it true that in England they think Creoles have negro blood in them?"

"We're very ignorant," said Jon. "*I* know the Creoles are the old French and Spanish families. You both look as if you had French blood."

"Francis does. Do you think we've passed that mound? We've come all of four miles, and I thought it was only two."

"Does it matter? The other mound was rather overrated."

The lips smiled; she didn't ever quite laugh, it seemed.

"What Indians hereabouts?" asked Jon.

"I'm not too sure; Seminoles, if any, I think. But Francis says these mounds would be from way back before the present tribes. What made you come to America, Mr. Forsyte?"

Jon bit his lip. To give the reason—family feud—broken love affair—was not exactly possible.

"I went first to British Columbia; but I didn't get on too well. Then I heard of peaches in North Carolina."

"But why did you leave England?"

"I suppose I just wanted to see the world."

"Yes," she said. It was a quiet but comprehending sound; Jon was the more gratified, because she had not comprehended. The image of his first love did not often haunt him now—had not for a

234

year or more. He had been so busy with his peaches. Besides,
Holly had written that Fleur had a boy. He said suddenly: "I
think we ought to turn. Look at the sun!" The sun, indeed, was
well down behind the trees.

"My—yes!"

Jon turned his steed. "Let's gallop, it'll be down in half an hour;
and there's no moon till late."

They galloped back along the track. The sun went down even
faster than he had thought, the air grew cold, the light grey. Jon
reined up suddenly.

"I'm awfully sorry; I don't believe we're on the track we came
by from the picnic. I feel we've gone off to the right. The tracks
are all alike and these horses only came in from Columbia yesterday; they don't know the country any more than we do."

The girl laughed.

"We'll be lost."

"M'm! That'll be no joke in these woods. Don't they ever
end?"

"I reckon not, in these parts. It's an adventure."

"Yes; but you'll catch cold. It's jolly cold at night."

"And you've had 'flu!"

"Oh! That's all right. Here's a track to the left. Shall we go on,
or shall we take it?"

"Take it."

They cantered on. It was too dark now for galloping and soon
too dark for cantering. And the track· wound on and on.

"This is a pretty business," said Jon. "I *am* sorry." He peered
towards her riding beside him, and could just see her smile.

"Why! It's lots of fun."

He was glad she thought so, but he could not see it.

"I *have* been an ass. Your brother'll be pretty sick with me."

"He'll know I'm with you."

"If we only had a compass. We may be out all night at this rate.
Here's another fork! Gosh, it *is* going to be dark."

And, almost as he spoke, the last of the light failed; he could
barely see her five yards away. He came up close alongside, and
she touched his sleeve.

"Don't worry," she said; "because that spoils it."

Shifting his reins, he gave her hand a squeeze.

"You're splendid, Miss Wilmot."

"Oh! do call me Anne. Surnames seem kind of chilly when
you're lost."

"Thank you very much. My name's Jon. Without an h, you know—short for Jolyon."

"Jolyon—Jon; I like it."

"Anne's always been my favourite name. Shall we stop till the moon rises, or ride on?"

"When will the moon rise?"

"About ten, I think, judging from last night. And it'll be nearly full. But it's hardly six yet."

"Let's ride on and leave it to the horses."

"Right! Only if they make for anywhere I'm pretty sure it'll be towards Columbia, which must be miles and miles."

They pursued the narrow track at a foot's pace. It was really dark now. Jon said: "Are you cold? You'd be warmer walking. I'll go ahead; stick close enough to see me."

He went ahead, and soon dismounted, feeling cold himself; there was utter silence among the unending trees, and no light.

"I'm cold now," said the voice of Anne. "I'll get off too."

They had trailed on perhaps half an hour like this, leading their horses, and almost feeling their way, when Jon said: "Look! There's some sort of a clearing here! And what's that blackness on the left?"

"It's a mound."

"Which mound, I wonder? The one we saw, or the other, or neither?"

"I reckon we'd better stop here till the moon rises, then maybe we'll see which it is, and know our way."

"You're right. There'll be swamps, I expect. I'll tether the horses to leeward, and we'll try to find a nook. It *is* cold."

He tethered the horses out of the wind, and, turning back, found her beside him.

"It's creepy here," she said.

"We'll find a snug place, and sit down."

He put his hand through her arm, and they moved round the foot of the mound.

"Here," said Jon suddenly; "they've been digging. This'll be sheltered." He felt the ground—dry enough. "Let's squat here and talk."

Side by side, with their backs to the wall of the excavated hollow, they lighted cigarettes, and sat listening to the silence. But for a snuffle or soft stamp now and then from the horses, there wasn't a sound. Trees and wind, both, were too sparse for melody, and nothing but their two selves and their horses seemed alive. A sprinkle of stars in a very dark sky and the deeper blackness of the pine stems was all they could see. Ah! and the glowing tips of their cigarettes, and each other's faces vaguely illumined, now and then, thereby.

"I don't expect you'll ever forgive me for this," said Jon gloomily.

"Why! I'm just loving it."

"Very sweet of you to say so; but you must be awfully cold. Look here—have my coat!"

He had begun to take it off when she said: "If you do that I'll run out into the woods and get really lost."

Jon resumed his coat.

"It might have been one of those Blair girls," he said.

"Would you rather?"

"For your sake, of course. Not for my own—no, indeed!"

They were looking round at each other so that the tips of their cigarettes were almost touching. Just able to see her eyes, he had a very distinct impulse to put his arm round her. It seemed the natural and proper thing to do, but of course it was not 'done !

"Have some chocolate," she said.

Jon ate a very little. The chocolate should be reserved for her!

"This is a real adventure. It *is* black. I'd have been scared alone —seems kind of spooky here."

"Spirits of the old Indians," muttered Jon. "Only I don't believe in spirits."

"You would if you'd had a coloured nanny."

"Did you have one?"

"Surely, with a voice as soft as mush melon. We have one old darkie still, who was a slave as a boy. He's the best of all the negroes round—nearly eighty, with quite white hair."

"Your father couldn't have been in the Civil War, could he?"

"No; my two grandfathers."

"And how old are you, Anne?"

"Nineteen."

"I'm twenty-three."

"Tell me about your home in England."

"I haven't one now." He began an expurgated edition of his youth, and it seemed to him that she listened beautifully. He asked for her story in return; and, while she was telling it, wondered whether he liked her voice or not. It dwelled and slurred, but was soft and had great flavour. When she had finished her simple tale, for she had hardly been away from home, there was silence, till Jon said:

"It's half-past seven only. I'll go and see that the horses are all right; then perhaps you could get a snooze."

He moved round the foot of the mound till he came to the horses and stayed a little talking to them and stroking their noses. A feeling, warm and protective, stirred within him. This was a nice child, and a brave one. A face to remember, with lots behind it. Suddenly he heard her voice, low and as if pretending not to call: "Jon, oh, Jon!" He felt his way back through the darkness. Her hands were stretched out.

"It *is* so spooky! That funny rustling! I've got creeps down my back!"

"The wind's got up a bit. Let's sit back to back—it'll keep you warm. Or, look here, I'll sit against the wall; if you lean up against me you could go to sleep. It's only two hours now—we can ride on by moonlight."

They took up the suggested postures, her back against his side, and her head in the hollow of his arm and shoulder.

"Comfy?"

"Surely. It stops the creeps. Am I too heavy?"

"Not a bit," said Jon.

They smoked and talked a little more. The stars were brighter now, and their eyes more accustomed to the darkness. And they were grateful for each other's warmth. Jon enjoyed the scent, as of hay, that rose from her hair not far below his nose. Then came a long silence, while the warm protective feeling grew and grew within him. He would have liked to slip his arms round and hold her closer. But of course he did not. It was, however, as much as he could do to remain a piece of warmth impersonal enough for her to recline against. This was the very first time since he left England that he had felt an inclination to put his arms round anyone, so badly burnt had he been in that old affair. The wind rose, talked in the trees, died away again; the stillness was greater than ever. He was very wide awake, and it seemed curious to him that she should sleep, for, surely, she was asleep—so still. The stars twinkled, and he gazed up at them. His limbs began to ache and twitch, and suddenly he realised that she was no more asleep than he. She slowly turned her head till he could see her eyes, grave, enticing.

"I'm too heavy," she said, and raised herself; but his arm restored her.

"Not a bit; so long as you're warm and comfy."

Her head settled in again; and the vigil was resumed. They talked a little now of nothing important, and he thought: 'It's queer—one could live months knowing people and not know them half so well as we shall know each other now."

Again a long silence fell; but this time his arm was round her, it was more comfortable so, for both of them. And Jon began to have the feeling that it would be inadvisable for the moon to rise. Had she that feeling too? He wondered. But if she had, the moon in its courses paid no attention. For suddenly he became conscious that it was there, behind the trees somewhere lurking, a curious kind of stilly glimmer creeping about the air, along the ground, in and out of the tree-stems.

"The moon!" he said. She did not stir, and his heart beat rather fast. So! She did not want the moon to rise any more than he! And slowly the creeping glimmer became light, and, between the tree-trunks, stole, invading their bodies till they were visible. And still they sat, unstirring, as if afraid to break a spell. The moon gained power and a cold glory, and rose above the trees; the world was alive once more. Jon thought: 'Could I kiss her?' and at once recoiled. As if she would want! But, as though she divined his thought, she turned her head, and her eyes looked into his. He said:

"I'm in charge of you!"

Her answer was a little sigh, and she got up. They stood, stretching, gazing into the whitened mysterious wood.

"Look, Anne! It *is* the mound. There's the path down to the hollow where we had the picnic. Now we can find the way all right."

"Yes"—a sound he could not interpret. But they went towards the horses, untethered them, and mounted. Between them, they would remember the way now; and they set forth. They rode side by side.

Jon said: "Well, that'll be something to remember."

"Yes, I shall always remember it."

They said no more, except to consult about the way, but this was soon clear, and they cantered. They came out on the polo-ground close to the hotel.

"You go in and relieve your brother's mind. I'll take the horses round, and then come on."

When he entered the hotel lounge Francis Wilmot, still in riding clothes, was alone. His expression was peculiar, not exactly hostile, but certainly not friendly.

239

"Anne's gone up," he said. "I reckon you haven't much bump of locality. You surely had me scared."

"I'm awfully sorry," said Jon humbly, "I forgot the horses were new to the country."

"Well!" said Francis Wilmot, and shrugged his shoulders. Jon looked at the young man steadily.

"You don't think that I got bushed on purpose? Because you look as if you do."

Again Francis Wilmot shrugged his shoulders.

"Forgive me," said Jon, "but aren't you forgetting that your sister's a lady, and that one doesn't behave like a cad with a lady?"

Francis Wilmot did not answer; he went to a window and stood looking out. Jon felt very angry. He sat down on the arm of a long chair, suddenly extremely tired. He sat there looking at the ground, and frowning heavily. Damn the fellow! Had he been bullying Anne? If he had——! A voice behind him said: "I reckon I didn't mean it. I certainly am sorry. It was just the scare. Shake hands!"

Jon stretched out his own impulsively, and they shook hands, looking straight into each other's eyes.

"You must be about through," said Francis Wilmot. "Come on to my room; I've got a flask. I've given Anne a dram already."

They went up. Jon sat in the only chair, Francis Wilmot on the bed.

"Anne tells me she's asked you to come home with us to-morrow. I surely hope you will."

"I should simply love to."

"That's fine!"

They drank, talked a little, smoked.

"Good night," said Jon suddenly, "or I shall go to sleep here."

They shook hands again, and Jon staggered to his room. He fell asleep at once.

They travelled next day, all three, through Columbia and Charleston, to the Wilmot's place. It stood in the bend of a red river, with cotton-fields around, and swampy ground where live oaks grew, melancholy, festooned with Florida moss. The old slave quarters, disused except as kennels, were still standing; the two-storeyed house had flights of wooden steps running up on each side, on to the wide wistaria-covered porch, and needed a coat of paint; and, within, rooms ran one into the other, hung with old portraits of dead Wilmots and de Frevilles; and darkies wandered around and talked their soft drawled speech.

# A SILENT WOOING

Jon was happier than he had been since he landed in the New World three and a half years ago. In the mornings he sauntered with the dogs in the sunlight or tried to write poetry—for the two young Wilmots were busy. After the midday meal he rode with them or with Anne alone. In the evening he learned from her to play the ukulele before a wood fire lighted at sundown, or heard about cotton culture from Francis, with whom, since that moment of animosity, he was on the best of terms.

Between Anne and himself there was little talk; they had, as it were, resumed the silence which had fallen when they sat in the dark under the old Indian mound. But he watched her; indeed, he was always trying to catch the grave enticing look in her dark eyes. More and more she seemed to him unlike any girl he had ever known; quicker, more silent, and with more 'sand'. The days went on, in warm sun, and the nightly scent of wood smoke; and his holiday drew to an end. He could play the ukulele now, and they sang to it—negro spirituals, songs from comic operas, and other immortal works. The last day came, and dismay descended on Jon. To-morrow, early, he was going back to his peaches at Southern Pines! That afternoon, riding with her for the last time, the silence was almost unnatural, and she did not even look at him. Jon went up to change, with panic in his heart. He knew now that he wanted to take her back with him, and he thought he knew that she did not want to come. How he would miss watching for those eyes to be fixed on him. He was thirsty with the wish to kiss her. He went down moodily, and sat in a long chair before the wood fire, pulling a spaniel's ears and watching the room darken. Perhaps she wouldn't even come for a last sing-song. Perhaps there would be nothing more but dinner and an evening à trois; not even a chance to say he loved her and be told that she didn't love him. And he thought miserably: 'It's my fault—I'm a silent fool; I've missed all my chance.' The room darkened till there was nothing but firelight, and the spaniel went to sleep. Jon, too, closed his eyes. It was as if he could wait better, thus—for the worst. When he opened them she was standing in front of him with the ukuleles in her hands.

"Do you want to play, Jon?"

"Yes," said Jon, "let's play. It's the last time;" and he took his ukulele.

She sat down on the rug before the fire, and began to tune hers. Jon slipped down beside the spaniel and began to tune his. The spaniel got up and went away.

A MODERN COMEDY

"What shall we sing?"

"I don't want to sing, Anne. You sing; I'll just accompany."

She didn't look at him! She would not look at him! It was all up! What a fool he'd been!

Anne sang. She sang a crooning phrase—a call over the mountains of Spain. Jon plucked his strings, and the tune plucked his heart. She sang it through. She sang it again, and her eyes slid round. God? She *was* looking at him. She mustn't see that he knew she was! It was too good—that long dark look over the ukulele. Between him and her were her ukulele and his own. He dropped the beastly thing. And, suddenly shifting along the floor, he put his arm round her. Without a word she drooped her head against his shoulder, as when they sat under the Indian mound. He bent his cheek down to her hair. It smelled, as it had then, of hay. And, just as she had screwed her face round in the moonlight, she turned it to him now. But this time Jon kissed her lips.

242

# BOOK II

## THE SILVER SPOON

"But O, the thorns we stand upon!"
                              *Winter's Tale.*

PART I

Chapter I

A STRANGER

THE young man who, at the end of September, 1924, dismounted
from a taxicab in South Square, Westminster, was so unobtrusively
American that his driver had some hesitation in asking for double
his fare. The young man had no hesitation in refusing it.

"Are you unable to read?" he said softly. "Here's four shillings."

With that he turned his back and looked at the house before
which he had descended. This, the first private English house he
had ever proposed to enter, inspired him with a certain uneasiness,
as of a man who expects to part with a family ghost. Comparing
a letter with the number chased in pale brass on the door, he
murmured: "It surely is," and rang the bell.

While waiting for the door to be opened, he was conscious of
extreme quietude, broken by a clock chiming four as if with the
voice of Time itself. When the last boom died, the door yawned
inwards, and a man, almost hairless, said:

"Yes, sir?"

The young man removed a soft hat from a dark head.

"This is Mrs. Michael Mont's house?"

"Correct, sir."

"Will you give her my card, and this letter?"

" 'Mr. Francis Wilmot, Naseby, S.C.' Will you wait in here,
sir?"

Ushered through the doorway of a room on the right, Francis
Wilmot was conscious of a commotion close to the ground, and
some teeth grazing the calf of his leg.

"Dandie!" said the voice of the hairless man, "you little devil!
That dog is a proper little brute with strangers, sir. Stand still!
I've known him bite clean through a lady's stockings."

Francis Wilmot saw with interest a silver-grey dog nine inches
high and nearly as broad, looking up at him with lustrous eyes
above teeth of extreme beauty.

245

"It's the baby, sir," said the hairless man, pointing to a sort of nest on the floor before the fireless hearth; "he *will* go for people when he's with the baby. But once he gets to smelling your trousers, he's all right. Better not touch the baby, though. Mrs. Mont was here a minute ago; I'll take your card up to her."

Francis Wilmot sat down on a settee in the middle of the room; and the dog lay between him and the baby.

And while the young man sat he gazed around him. The room was painted in panels of a sub-golden hue, with a silver-coloured ceiling. A clavichord, little golden ghost of a piano, stood at one end. Glass lustres, pictures of flowers and of a silvery-necked lady swinging a skirt and her golden slippers, adorned the walls. The curtains were of gold and silver. The silver-coloured carpet felt wonderfully soft beneath his feet, the furniture was of a golden wood.

The young man felt suddenly quite home-sick. He was back in the living-room of an old 'Colonial' house in the bend of a lonely South Carolina river, reddish in hue. He was staring at the effigy of his high-collared, red-coated great-grandfather, Francis Wilmot, Royalist major in the War of Independence. They always said it was like the effigy he saw when shaving every morning; the smooth dark hair drooping across his right temple, the narrow nose and lips, the narrow dark hand on the sword-hilt or the razor, the slits of dark eyes gazing steadily out. Young Francis was seeing the darkies working in the cotton-fields under a sun that he did not seem to have seen since he came over here; he was walking with his setter along the swamp edge, where Florida moss festooned the tall dolorous trees; he was thinking of the Wilmot inheritance, ruined in the Civil War, still decayed yet precious, and whether to struggle on with it, or to sell it to the Yank who wanted a week-end run-to from his Charleston dock job, and would improve it out of recognition. It would be lonely there, now that Anne had married that young Britisher, Jon Forsyte, and gone away north, to Southern Pines. And he thought of his sister, thus lost to him, dark, pale, vivid, 'full of sand'. Yes! this room made him home-sick, with its perfection, such as he had never beheld, where the only object out of keeping was that dog, lying on its side now, and so thick through that all its little legs were in the air. Softly he said:

"It's the prettiest room I ever was in."

"What a perfectly charming thing to overhear!"

A young woman, with crinkly chestnut hair above a creamy

face, with smiling lips, a short straight nose, and very white dark-lashed eyelids active over dark hazel eyes, stood near the door. She came towards him, and held out her hand.

Francis Wilmot bowed over it, and said gravely:

"Mrs. Michael Mont?"

"So Jon's married your sister. Is she pretty?"

"She is."

"Very?"

"Yes, indeed."

"I hope baby has been entertaining you."

"He's just great."

"He is, rather. I hear Dandie bit you?"

"I reckon he didn't break the cuticle."

"Haven't you looked? But he's quite healthy. Sit down, and tell me all about your sister and Jon. Is it a marriage of true minds?"

Francis Wilmot sat down.

"It certainly is. Young Jon is a pretty white man, and Anne——"

He heard a sigh.

"I'm very glad. He says in his letter that he's awfully happy. You must come and stay here. You can be as free as you like. Look on us as an hotel."

The young man's dark eyes smiled.

"That's too good of you! I've never been on this side before. They got through the war too soon."

Fleur took the baby out of its nest.

"*This* creature doesn't bite. Look—two teeth, but they don't antagonise—isn't that how you put it?"

"What is its name?"

"Kit—for Christopher. We agreed about its name luckily. Michael—my husband—will be in directly. He's in Parliament, you know. They're not sitting till Monday—Ireland, of course. We only came back for it from Italy yesterday. Italy's so wonder-ful—you must see it."

"Pardon me, but is that the Parliament clock that chimes so loud?"

"Big Ben—yes. He marks time for them. Michael says Parlia-ment is the best drag on Progress ever invented. With our first Labour Government, it's been specially interesting this year. Don't you think it's rather touching the way this dog watches my baby? He's got the most terrific jaw!"

"What kind of dog is he?"

247

"A Dandie Dinmont. We did have a Peke. It was a terrible tragedy. He *would* go after cats; and one day he struck a fighting Tom, and got clawed over both eyes—quite blinded—and so——"

The young man saw her eyes suddenly too bright. He made a soft noise, and said gently: "That was too bad."

"I had to change this room completely. It used to be Chinese. It reminded me too much."

"This little fellow would chaw any cat."

"Luckily he was brought up with kittens. We got him for his legs—they're so bowed in front that he can hardly run, so he just suits the pram. Dan, show your legs!"

The Dandie looked up with a negative sound.

"He's a terrible little 'character'. Do tell me, what's Jon like now? Is he still English?"

The young man was conscious that she had uttered at last something really in her mind.

"He is; but he's a dandy fellow."

"And his mother? She used to be beautiful."

"And is to this day."

"She would be. Grey, I suppose, by now?"

"Yes. You don't like her?"

"Well, I hope she won't be jealous of your sister!"

"I think, perhaps, you're unjust."

"I think, perhaps, I am."

She sat very still, her face hard above the baby's. And the young man, aware of thoughts beyond his reach, got up.

"When you write to Jon," she said suddenly, "tell him that I'm awfully glad, and that I wish him luck. I shan't write to him myself. May I call you Francis?"

Francis Wilmot bowed. "I shall be proud, ma'am."

"Yes; but you must call me Fleur. We're sort of related, you know."

The young man smiled, and touched the name with his lips.

"Fleur! It's a beautiful name!"

"Your room will be ready when you come back. You'll have a bathroom to yourself, of course."

He put his lips to the hand held out.

"It's wonderful," he said. "I was feeling kind of homesick; I miss the sun over here."

In going out, he looked back. Fleur had put her baby back in its nest, and was staring straight before her.

## Chapter II

## CHANGE

BUT more than the death of a dog had caused the regarnishing of Fleur's Chinese room. On the evening of her twenty-second birthday Michael had come home saying:

"Well, my child, I've chucked publishing. With old Danby always in the right—it isn't a career."

"Oh! Michael, you'll be bored to death."

"I'll go into Parliament. It's quite usual, and about the same screw."

He had spoken in jest. Six days later it became apparent that she had listened in earnest.

"You were absolutely right, Michael. It's the very thing for you. You've got ideas."

"Other people's."

"And the gift of the gab. We're frightfully handy for the House, here."

"It costs money, Fleur."

"Yes, I've spoken to Father. It was rather funny—there's never been a Forsyte, you know, anywhere near Parliament. But he thinks it'll be good for me; and that it's all baronets are fit for."

"One has to have a Seat, unfortunately."

"Well, I've sounded your father, too. He'll speak to people. They want young men."

"Ah! And what are my politics?"

"My dear boy, you must know—at thirty."

"I'm not a Liberal. But am I Labour or Tory?"

"You can think it out before the next election!"

Next day, while he was shaving, and she was in her bath, he cut himself slightly and said:

"The land and this unemployment is what I really care about. I'm a Foggartist."

"What?"

"Old Sir James Foggart's book. You read it."

"No."

"Well, you said so."

"So did others."

"Never mind—his eyes are fixed on 1944, and his policy's according. Safety in the Air, the Land, and Child Emigration;

adjustment of Supply and Demand within the Empire; cut our losses in Europe; and endure a worse Present for the sake of a better Future. Everything, in fact, that's unpopular, and said to be impossible."

"Well, you could keep all that to yourself till you get in. You'll have to stand as a Tory."

"How lovely you look!"

"If you get in, you can disagree with everybody. That'll give you a position from the start."

"Some scheme!" murmured Michael.

"You can initiate this—this Foggartism. He isn't mad, is he?"

"No, only too sane, which is much the same thing, of course. You see we've got a higher wage-scale than any other country except America and the Dominions; and it isn't coming down again; we really group in with the new countries. He's for growing as much of our food as we can, and pumping British town children, before they're spoiled, into the Colonies, till Colonial demand for goods equals our supply. It's no earthly, of course, without wholehearted co-operation between the Governments within the Empire."

"It sounds very sensible."

"We published him, you know, but at his own expense. It's a 'faith and the mountain' stunt. He's got the faith all right, but the mountain shows no signs of moving."

Fleur stood up. "Well," she said, "that's settled. Your father says he can get you a nomination as a Tory, and you can keep your own views to yourself. You'll get in on the human touch, Michael."

"Thank you, ducky. Can I help dry you?" . . .

Before redecorating her Chinese room, however, Fleur had waited till after Michael was comfortably seated for a division which professed to be interested in agriculture. She chose a blend between Adam and Louis Quinze. Michael called it the 'bimetallic parlour'; and carried off 'The White Monkey' to his study. The creature's pessimism was not, he felt, suited to political life.

Fleur had initiated her 'salon' with a gathering in February. The soul of society had passed away since the Liberal *débâcle* and Lady Alison's politico-legal coterie no longer counted. Plainer people were in the ascendant. Her Wednesday evenings were youthful, with age represented by her father-in-law, two minor ambassadors, and Pevensey Blythe, editor of *The Outpost*. So unlike his literary style that he was usually mistaken for a Colonial Prime

250

Minister, Blythe was a tall man with a beard, and grey bloodshot eyes, who expressed knowledge in paragraphs that few could really understand. "What Blythe thinks to-day, the Conservative Party will not think to-morrow," was said of him. He spoke in a small voice, and constantly used the impersonal pronoun.

"One is walking in one's sleep," he would say of the political situation, "and will wake up without any clothes on."

A warm supporter of Sir James Foggart's book, characterising it as "the masterpiece of a blind archangel," he had a passion for listening to the clavichord, and was invaluable in Fleur's 'salon'.

Freed from poetry and modern music, from Sibley Swan, Walter Nazing and Hugo Solstis, Fleur was finding time for her son—the eleventh baronet. He represented for her the reality of things. Michael might have posthumous theories, and Labour predatory hopes, but for her the year 1944 would see the eleventh baronet come of age. That Kit should inherit an England worth living in was of more intrinsic importance than anything they proposed in the Commons and were unable to perform. All those houses they were going to build, for instance—very proper, but a little unnecessary if Kit still had Lippinghall Manor and South Square, Westminster, to dwell in. Not that Fleur voiced such cynical convictions, or admitted them even to herself. She did orthodox lip-service to the great god Progress.

The Peace of the World, Hygiene, Trade, and the End of Unemployment, preoccupied all, irrespective of Party, and Fleur was in the fashion; but instinct, rather than Michael and Sir James Foggart, told her that the time-honoured motto: 'Eat your cake and have it', which underlay the platforms of all Parties, was not 'too frightfully' sound. So long as Kit had cake, it was no good bothering too deeply about the rest; though, of course, one must seem to. Fluttering about her 'salon'—this to that person, and that to the other, and to all so pretty, she charmed by her grace, her common sense, her pliancy. Not infrequently she attended at the House, and sat, not listening too much to the speeches, yet picking up, as it were, by a sort of seventh sense (if women in Society all had six, surely Fleur had seven) what was necessary to the conduct of that 'salon'—the rise and fall of the Governmental barometer, the catchwords and clichés of policy; and, more valuable, impressions of personality, of the residuary man within the Member. She watched Michael's career, with the fostering eye of a godmother who has given her godchild a blue morocco prayer-book, in the hope that some day he may remember its existence. Although a sedulous attendant at the House all through the spring and summer, Michael had not yet opened his mouth, and so far she had approved of his silence, while nurturing his desire to know his own mind by listening to his wanderings in Foggartism. If it were indeed the only permanent cure for Unemployment, as he said, she too was a Foggartist; common sense assuring her that the only real danger to Kit's future lay in that national malady. Eliminate Unemployment, and nobody would have time to make a fuss. But her criticisms were often pertinent:

"My dear boy, does a country ever sacrifice the present for the sake of the future?" or: "Do you really think country life is better than town life?" or: "Can you imagine sending Kit out of England at fourteen to some God-forsaken end of the world?" or: "Do you suppose the towns will have it?" And they roused Michael to such persistence and fluency that she felt he would really catch on in time—like old Sir Giles Snoreham, whom they would soon be making a peer, because he had always worn low-crowned hats and advocated a return to hansom cabs. Hats, buttonholes, an eye-glass—she turned over in her mind all such little realities as help a political career.

"Plain glass doesn't harm the sight; and it really has a focusing value, Michael."

"My child, it's never done my Dad a bit of good; I doubt if it's sold three copies of any of his books. No! If I get on, it'll be by talking."

But still she encouraged him to keep his mouth shut.

"It's no good starting wrong, Michael. These Labour people aren't going to last out the year."

"Why not?"

"Their heads are swelling, and their tempers going. They're only on sufferance; people on sufferance have got to be pleasant or they won't be suffered. When they go out, the Tories will get in again and probably last. You'll have several years to be eccentric in, and by the time they're out again, you'll have your licence. Just go on working the human touch in your constituency; I'm sure it's a mistake to forget you've got constituents."

Michael spent most week-ends that summer working the human touch in mid-Bucks; and Fleur spent most week-ends with the eleventh baronet at her father's house near Mapledurham.

Since wiping the dust of the city off his feet, after that affair of Elderson and the P.P.R.S., Soames had become almost too countri-fied for a Forsyte. He had bought the meadows on the far side of the river and several Jersey cows. Not that he was going in for farming or nonsense of that sort, but it gave him an interest to punt himself over and see them milked. He had put up a good deal of glass, too, and was laying down melons. The English melon was superior to any other, and every year's connection with a French wife made him more and more inclined to eat what he grew himself. After Michael was returned for Parliament, Fleur had sent him Sir James Foggart's book, 'The Parlous State of England'. When it came, he said to Annette:

"I don't know what she thinks I want with this great thing!"

"To read it, Soames, I suppose."

Soames sniffed, turning the pages.

"I can't tell what it's all about."

"I will sell it at my bazaar, Soames. It will do for some good man who can read English."

From that moment Soames began almost unconsciously to read the book. He found it a peculiar affair, which gave most people some good hard knocks. He began to enjoy them, especially the chapter deprecating the workman's dislike of parting with his children at a reasonable age. Having never been outside Europe, he had a somewhat sketchy idea of places like South Africa, Australia, Canada, and New Zealand; but this old fellow Foggart, it appeared, had been there, and knew what he was talking about. What he said about their development seemed quite sensible. Children who went out there put on weight at once, and became owners of property at an age when in England they were still delivering parcels, popping in and out of jobs, hanging about street corners, and qualifying for unemployment and Communism. Get them out of England! There was a startling attraction in the idea for one who was English to a degree. He was in favour, too, of what was said about growing food and making England safe in the air. And then, slowly, he turned against it. The fellow was too much of a Jeremiah altogether. He complained to Fleur that the book dealt with nothing but birds in the bush; it was unpractical. What did 'Old Mont' say?'

"He won't read it; he says he knows old Foggart."

"H'm!" said Soames, "I shouldn't be surprised if there were something in it, then." That little-headed baronet was old-fashioned! "Anyway, it shows that Michael's given up those Labour fellows."

"Michael says Foggartism will be Labour's policy when they understand all it means."

"How's that?"

"He thinks it's going to do them much more good than anybody else. He says one or two of their leaders are beginning to smell it out, and that the rest of the leaders are bound to follow in time."

"In that case," said Soames, "it'll never go down with their rank and file." And for two minutes he sat in a sort of trance. Had he said something profound, or had he not?

Fleur's presence at week-ends with the eleventh baronet was extremely agreeable to him. Though at first he had felt a sort of disappointment that his grandchild was not a girl—an eleventh baronet belonged too definitely to the Monts—he began, as the months wore on, to find him 'an engaging little chap', and, in any case, to have him down at Mapledurham kept him away from Lippinghall. It tried him at times, of course, to see how the women hung about the baby—there was something very excessive about motherhood. He had noticed it with Annette; he noticed it now with Fleur. French—perhaps! He had not remembered his own mother making such a fuss; indeed, he could not remember anything that happened when he was one. A week-end, when Madame Lamotte, Annette and Fleur were all hanging over his grandson, three generations of maternity concentrated on that pudgy morsel, reduced him to a punt, fishing for what he felt sure nobody would eat.

By the time he had finished Sir James Foggart's book, the disagreeable summer of 1924 was over, and a more disagreeable September had set in. The mellow golden days that glow up out of a haze which stars with dewdrops every cobweb on a gate, simply did not come. It rained, and the river was so unnaturally full, that the newspapers were at first unnaturally empty—there was literally no news of drought; they filled up again slowly with reports of the wettest summer 'for thirty years'. Calm, greenish with weed and tree shadow, the river flowed unendingly between Soames's damp lawn and his damp meadows. There were no mushrooms. Blackberries tasted of rain. Soames made a point of eating one every year, and, by the flavour, could tell what sort of year it had been. There was a good deal of 'old-man's-beard'. In spite of all this, however, he was more cheerful than he had been for ages. Labour had been 'in', if not in real power, for months, and the heavens had only lowered. Forced by Labour-in-office to take some notice of politics, he would utter prophecies at the breakfast-table. They varied somewhat, according to the news; and, since he always forgot those which did not come true, he was constantly able to

tell Annette that he had told her so. She took no interest, however, occupied, 'like a woman, with her bazaars and jam-making,
running about in the car, shopping in London, attending garden-
parties'; and, in spite of her tendency to put on flesh, still remark-
ably handsome. Jack Cardigan, his niece Imogen's husband, had
made him a sixty-ninth-birthday present of a set of golf-clubs.
This was more puzzling to Soames than anything that had ever
happened to him. What on earth was he to do with them?
Annette, with that French quickness which so often annoyed him,
suggested that he should use them. She was uncomfortable! At
his age——! And then, one week-end in May the fellow himself
had come down with Imogen and, teeing a ball up on half a mole-
hill, had driven it across the river.

"I'll bet you a box of cigars, Uncle Soames, that you don't do
that before we leave on Monday."

"I never bet," said Soames, "and I don't smoke."

"Time you began both. Look here, we'll spend to-morrow learn-
ing to knock the ball!"

"Absurd!" said Soames.

But in his room that night he had stood in his pyjamas swinging
his arms in imitation of Jack Cardigan. The next day he sent the
women out in the car with their lunch; he was not going to have
them grinning at him. He had seldom spent more annoying hours
than those which followed. They culminated in a moment when
at last he hit the ball, and it fell into the river three yards from
the near bank. He was so stiff next morning in arms and ribs, that
Annette had to rub him till he said:

"Look out! you're taking the skin off!"

He had, however, become infected. After destroying some
further portions of his lawn, he joined the nearest golf club, and
began to go round by himself during the luncheon-hour, accompanied by a little boy. He kept at it with characteristic tenacity,
till by July he had attained a certain proficiency; and he began to
say to Annette that it would do her all the good in the world to
take it up, and keep her weight down.

"Merci, Soames," she would reply; "I have no wish to be the
figure of your English Misses, flat as a board before and behind."
She was reactionary, 'like her nation'; and Soames, who at heart
had a certain sympathy with curves, did not seriously press the
point. He found that the exercise jogged both his liver and his
temper. He began to have colour in his cheeks. The day after his
first nine-hole round with Jack Cardigan, who had given him three

255

strokes a hole and beaten him by nine holes, he received a package which, to his dismay, contained a box of cigars. What the fellow was about, he could not imagine! He only discovered when, one evening a few days later, sitting at the window of his picture gallery, he found that he had one in his mouth. Curiously enough, it did not make him sick. It produced rather something of the feeling he used to enjoy after 'doing Coué'—now comparatively out of fashion, since an American, so his sister Winifred said, had found a shorter cut. A suspicion, however, that the family had set Jack Cardigan on, prevented him from indulging his new sensation anywhere but in his picture gallery; so that cigars gathered the halo of a secret vice. He renewed his store stealthily. Only when he found that Annette, Fleur, and others had known for weeks, did he relax his rule, and say openly that the vice of the present day was cigarettes.

"My dear boy," said Winifred, when she next saw him, "everybody's saying you're a different man!"

Soames raised his eyebrows. He was not conscious of any change.

"That chap Cardigan," he said, "is a funny fellow! . . . I'm going to dine and sleep at Fleur's; they're just back from Italy. The House sits on Monday."

"Yes," said Winifred; "very fussy of them—sitting in the Long Vacation."

"Ireland!" said Soames deeply. "A pretty pair of shoes again!" Always had been; always would be!

## Chapter III

### MICHAEL TAKES 'A LUNAR'

MICHAEL had returned from Italy with the longing to 'get on with it', which results from Southern holidays. Countryman by upbringing, still deeply absorbed by the unemployment problem and committed to Foggartism, as its remedy, he had taken up no other hobby in the House, and was eating the country's bread, if somewhat unbuttered, and doing nothing for it. He desired, therefore, to know where he stood, and how long he was going to stand there.

Bent on 'taking this lunar'—as 'Old Forsyte' would call it—at his own position, he walked away from the House that same day, after dealing with an accumulated correspondence. He walked towards Pevensey Blythe, in the office of that self-sufficing weekly:

# THE SILVER SPOON

*The Outpost.* Sunburnt from his Italian holiday and thinned by Italian cookery, he moved briskly, and thought of many things. Passing down on to the Embankment, where a number of unemployed birds on a number of trees were also wondering, it seemed, where they stood and how long they were going to stand there, he took a letter from his pocket to read a second time.

> "12 Sapper's Row,
> "Camden Town.

"HONOURABLE SIR,

"Being young in 'Who's Who', you will not be hard, I think, to those in suffering. I am an Austrian woman who married a German eleven years ago. He was an actor on the English stage, for his father and mother, who are no more living, brought him to England quite young. Interned he was, and his health broken up. He has the neurasthenie very bad so he cannot be trusted for any work. Before the war he was always in a part, and we had some good money; but this went partly when I was left with my child alone, and the rest was taken by the P.T., and we got very little back, neither of us being English. What we did get has all been to the doctor, and for our debts, and for burying our little child, which died happily, for though I loved it much this life which we have is not fit for a child to live. We live on my needle, and that is not earning much, a pound a week and sometimes nothing. The managers will not look at my husband all these years, because he shakes suddenly, so they think he drinks, but, Sir, he has not the money to buy it. We do not know where to turn, or what to do. So I thought, dear Sir, whether you could do anything for us with the P.T.; they have been quite sympatical; but they say they administrate an order and cannot do more. Or if you could get my husband some work where he will be in open air—the doctor say that is what he want. We have nowhere to go in Germany or in Austria, our well-beloved families being no more alive. I think we are like many, but I cannot help asking you, Sir, because we want to keep living if we can, and now we are hardly having any food. Please to forgive me my writing, and to believe your very anxious and humble

> "ANNA BERGFELD."

'God help them!' thought Michael, under a plane tree close to Cleopatra's Needle, but without conviction. For in his view God was not so much interested in the fate of individual aliens as the Governor of the Bank of England in the fate of a pound of sugar bought with the fraction of a Bradbury; He would not arbitrarily interfere with a ripple of the tides set loose by His arrangement of the Spheres. God, to Michael, was a monarch strictly limited by His own Constitution. He restored the letter to his pocket. Poor creatures! But really, with 1,200,000 and more English unemployed, mostly due to that confounded Kaiser and his Navy stunt——! If that fellow and his gang had not started their naval rivalry in 1899, England would have been out of the whole mess, or, perhaps, there never would have been a mess!

He turned up from the Temple station towards the offices of *The Outpost*. He had 'taken' that weekly for some years now. It knew everything, and managed to convey a slight impression that nobody else knew anything; so that it seemed more weighty than any other weekly. Having no particular Party to patronise, it could patronise the lot. Without Imperial bias, it professed a special knowledge of the Empire. Not literary, it made a point of reducing the heads of literary men—Michael, in his publishing days, had enjoyed every opportunity of noticing that. Professing respect for Church and the Law, it was an adept at giving them 'what-for'. It fancied itself on Drama, striking a somewhat Irish attitude towards it. But, perhaps above all, it excelled in neat detraction from political reputations, keeping them in their place, and that place a little lower than *The Outpost's*. Moreover, from its editorials emanated that 'holy ghost' of inspired knowledge in periods just a little beyond average comprehension, without which no such periodical had real importance.

Michael went up the stairs two at a time, and entered a large square room, where Mr. Blythe, back to the door, was pointing with a ruler to a circle drawn on a map.

"This is a bee map," said Mr. Blythe to himself. "Quite the bee-est map I ever saw."

Michael could not contain a gurgle, and the eyes of Mr. Blythe came round, prominent, epileptic, richly encircled by pouches.

"Hallo!" he said defiantly. "You? The Colonial Office prepared this map specially to show the best spots for Settlement schemes. And they've left out Baggersfontein—the very hub."

Michael seated himself on the table.

"I've come in to ask what you think of the situation? My wife says Labour will be out in no time."

"Our charming little lady!" said Mr. Blythe; "Labour will survive Ireland; they will survive Russia; they will linger on in their precarious way. One hesitates to predict their decease. Fear of their Budget may bring them down in February. After the smell of Russian fat has died away—say in November, Mont—one may make a start."

"This first speech," said Michael, "is a nightmare to me. How, exactly, am I to start Foggartism?"

"One will have achieved the impression of a body of opinion before then."

"But will there be one?"

"No," said Mr. Blythe.

"Oh!" said Michael. "And, by the way, what about Free Trade?"

"One will profess Free Trade, and put on duties."

"God and Mammon."

"Necessary in England, before any new departure, Mont. Witness Liberal-Unionism, Tory-Socialism, and——"

"Other ramps," said Michael gently.

"One will glide, deprecate Protection till there is more Protection than Free Trade, then deprecate Free Trade. Foggartism is an end, not a means; Free Trade and Protection are means, not the ends politicians have made them."

Roused by the word 'politician', Michael got off the table; he was coming to have a certain sympathy with those poor devils. They were supposed to have no feeling for the country, and to be wise only after the event. But, really, who could tell what was good for the country, among the mists of talk? Not even old Foggart, Michael sometimes thought.

"You know, Blythe," he said, "that we politicians don't think ahead, simply because we know it's no earthly. Every elector thinks his own immediate good is the good of the country. Only their own shoes pinching will change electors' views. If Foggartism means adding to the price of living now, and taking wage-earning children away from workmen's families for the sake of benefit— ten or twenty years hence—who's going to stand for it?"

"My dear young man," said Mr. Blythe, "conversion is our job. At present our trade-unionists despise the outside world. They've never seen it. Their philosophy is bounded by their smoky little streets. But five million pounds spent on the organised travel of a hundred thousand working men would do the trick in five years. It would infect the working-class with a feverish desire for a place in the sun. The world is their children's for the taking. But who can blame them, when they know nothing of it?"

"Some thought!" said Michael. "Only—what Government will think it? Can I take those maps? . . . By the way," he said at the

A MODERN COMEDY

door, "there are Societies, you know, for sending out children."

Mr. Blythe grunted. "Yes. Excellent little affairs! A few hundred children doing well—concrete example of what might be. Multiply it a hundredfold, and you've got a beginning. You can't fill pails with a teaspoon. Good-bye!"

Out on the Embankment Michael wondered if one could love one's country with a passion for getting people to leave it. But this over-bloated town condition, with its blight and smoky ugliness; the children without a chance from birth; these swarms of poor devils without work, who dragged about and hadn't an earthly, and never would, on present lines; this unbalanced, hand-to-mouth, dependent state of things—surely that wasn't to be for ever the state of the country one loved! He stared at the towers of Westminster, with the setting sun behind them. And there started up before him the thousand familiars of his past—trees, fields and streams, towers, churches, bridges; the English breeds of beasts, the singing birds, the owls, the jays and rooks at Lipping-hall, the little differences from foreign sorts in shrub, flower, lichen, and winged life; the English scents, the English haze, the English grass; the eggs and bacon; the slow good humour, the moderation and the pluck; the smell of rain; the apple-blossom, the heather, and the sea. His country, and his breed—unspoilable at heart! He passed the Clock Tower. The House looked lacey and imposing, more beautiful than fashion granted. Did they spin the web of England's future in that House? Or were they painting camouflage—a screen over old England?

A familiar voice said: "This is a monstrous great thing!"

And Michael saw his father-in-law staring up at the Lincoln statue. "What did they want to put it here for?" said Soames. "It's not English." He walked along at Michael's side. "Fleur well?"

"Splendid. Italy suited her like everything."

Soames sniffed. "They're a theatrical lot," he said. "Did you see Milan cathedral?"

"Yes, sir. It's about the only thing we didn't take to."

"H'm! Their cooking gave me the collywobbles in '82. I dare say it's better now. How's the boy?"

"A1, sir."

Soames made a sound of gratification, and they turned the corner into South Square.

"What's this?" said Soames.

Outside the front door were two battered-looking trunks, a

young man, grasping a bag, and ringing the bell, and a taxi-cab turning away.

"I can't tell you, sir," murmured Michael. "Unless it's the angel Gabriel."

"He's got the wrong house," said Soames, moving forward.

But just then the young man disappeared within.

Soames walked up to the trunks. "Francis Wilmot," he read out. "'S.S. Amphibian.' There's some mistake!"

## Chapter IV

### MERE CONVERSATION

WHEN they came in, Fleur was returning downstairs from showing the young man to his room. Already fully dressed for the evening, she had but little on, and her hair was shingled. . . .

"My dear girl," Michael had said, when shingling came in, "to please me, don't! Your *nuque* will be too bristly for kisses."

"My dear boy," she had answered, "as if one could help it! You're always the same with any new fashion!"

She had been one of the first twelve to shingle, and was just feeling that without care she would miss being one of the first twelve to grow some hair again. Marjorie Ferrar, 'the Pet of the Panjoys', as Michael called her, already had more than an inch. Somehow, one hated being distanced by Marjorie Ferrar. . . .

Advancing to her father, she said:

"I've asked a young American to stay, Dad; Jon Forsyte has married his sister, out there. You're quite brown, darling. How's mother?"

Soames only gazed at her.

And Fleur passed through one of those shamed moments, when the dumb quality of his love for her seemed accusing the glib quality of her love for him. It was not fair—she felt—that he should look at her like that; as if she had not suffered in that old business with Jon more than he; if she could take it lightly now, surely he could! As for Michael—not a word!—not even a joke! She bit her lips, shook her shingled head, and passed into the 'bimetallic parlour'.

Dinner began with soup and Soames deprecating his own cows for not being Herefords. He supposed that in America they had plenty of Herefords?

Francis Wilmot believed that they were going in for Holsteins now.

"Holsteins!" repeated Soames. "They're new since my young days. What's their colour?"

"Parti-coloured," said Francis Wilmot. "The English grass is just wonderful."

"Too damp, with us," said Soames. "We're on the river."

"The river Thames? What size will that be, where it hasn't a tide?"

"Just there—not more than a hundred yards."

"Will it have fish?"

"Plenty."

"And it'll run clear—not red; our Southern rivers have a red colour. And your trees will be willows, and poplars, and elms."

Soames was a good deal puzzled. He had never been in America. The inhabitants were human, of course, but peculiar and all alike, with more face than feature, heads fastened upright on their backs, and shoulders too square to be real. Their voices clanged in their mouths; they pronounced the words 'very' and 'America' in a way that he had tried to imitate without success; their dollar was too high, and they all had motor-cars; they despised Europe, came over in great quantities, and took back all they could; they talked all the time, and were not allowed to drink. This young man cut across all these preconceptions. He drank sherry and only spoke when he was spoken to. His shoulders looked natural; he had more feature than face; and his voice was soft. Perhaps, at least, he despised Europe.

"I suppose," he said, "you find England very small."

"No, sir. I find London very large; and you certainly have the loveliest kind of a countryside."

Soames looked down one side of his nose. "Pretty enough!" he said.

Then came turbot and a silence, broken, low down, behind his chair.

"That dog!" said Soames, impaling a morsel of fish he had set aside as uneatable.

"No, no, Dad! He just wants to know you've seen him!"

Soames stretched down a finger, and the Dandie fell on his side.

"He never eats," said Fleur; "but he has to be noticed."

A small covey of partridges came in, cooked.

"Is there any particular thing you want to see over here, Mr. Wilmot?" said Michael. "There's nothing very un-American left. You're just too late for Regent Street."

"I want to see the Beefeaters; and Cruft's Dog Show; and your blood horses; and the Derby."

"Darby!" Soames corrected. "You can't stay for that—it's not till next June."

"My cousin Val will show you race-horses," said Fleur. "He married Jon's sister, you know."

A 'bombe' appeared. "You have more of this in America, I believe," said Soames.

"We don't have much ice-cream in the South, sir, but we have special cooking—very tasty."

"I've heard of terrapin."

"Well, I don't get frills like that. I live away back, and have to work pretty hard. My place is kind of homey; but I've got some mighty nice darkies that can cook fine—old folk that knew my grannies. The old-time darky is getting scarce, but he's the real thing."

A Southerner!

Soames had been told that the Southerner was a gentleman. He remembered the 'Alabama', too; and his father, James, saying: "I told you so" when the Government ate humble pie over that business.

In the savoury silence that accompanied soft roes on toast, the patter of the Dandie's feet on the parquet floor could be plainly heard.

"This is the only thing he likes," said Fleur. "Dan! go to your master. Give him a little bit, Michael." And she stole a look at Michael, but he did not answer it.

On their Italian holiday, with Fleur in the throes of novelty, sun and wine warmed, disposed to junketing, amenable to his caresses, he had been having his real honeymoon, enjoying, for the first time since his marriage, a sense of being the chosen companion of his adored. And now had come this stranger, bringing reminder that one played but second fiddle to that young second cousin and first lover; and he couldn't help feeling the cup withdrawn again from his lips. She had invited this young man because he came from that past of hers whose tune one could not play. And, without looking up, he fed the Dandie with tid-bits of his favourite edible.

Soames broke the silence.

"Take some nutmeg, Mr. Wilmot. Melon without nutmeg——"

When Fleur rose, Soames followed her to the drawing-room; while Michael led the young American to his study.

"You knew Jon?" said Francis Wilmot.

"No; I never met him."

"He's a great little fellow; and some poet. He's growing dandy peaches."

"Is he going on with that, now he's married?"

"Surely."

"Not coming to England?"

"Not this year. They have a nice home—horses and dogs. They have some hunting there, too. Perhaps he'll bring my sister over for a trip, next fall."

"Oh!" said Michael. "And are you staying long, yourself?"

"Why! I'll go back for Christmas. I'd like to see Rome and Seville; and I want to visit the old home of my people, down in Worcestershire."

"When did they go over?"

"William and Mary. Catholics—they were. Is it a nice part, Worcestershire?"

"Very; especially in the spring. It grows a lot of fruit."

"Oh! You still grow things in this country?"

"Not many."

"I thought that was so, coming on the cars, from Liverpool. I saw a lot of grass and one or two sheep, but I didn't see anybody working. The people all live in the towns, then?"

"Except a few unconsidered trifles. You must come down to my father's; they still grow a turnip or two thereabouts."

"It's sad," said Francis Wilmot.

"It is. We began to grow wheat again in the war; but they've let it all slip back—and worse."

"Why was that?"

Michael shrugged his shoulders: "No accounting for statesmanship. It lets the Land go to blazes when in office; and beats the drum of it when in opposition. At the end of the war we had the best air force in the world, and agriculture was well on its way to recovery. And what did they do? Dropped them both like hot potatoes. It was tragic. What do you grow in Carolina?"

"Just cotton, on my place. But it's mighty hard to make cotton pay nowadays. Labour's high."

"High with you, too?"

"Yes, sir. Do they let strangers into your Parliament?"

"Rather. Would you like to hear the Irish debate? I can get you a seat in the Distinguished Strangers' gallery."

"I thought the English were stiff; but it's wonderful the way you

264

make me feel at home. Is that your father-in-law—the old gentleman?"

"Yes."

"He seems kind of rarefied. Is he a banker?"

"No. But now you mention it—he ought to be."

Francis Wilmot's eyes roved round the room and came to rest on 'The White Monkey'.

"Well, now," he said, softly, "that, surely, is a wonderful picture. Could I get a picture painted by that man, for Jon and my sister?"

"I'm afraid not," said Michael. "You see, he was a Chink—not quite of the best period; but he must have gone West five hundred years ago at least."

"Ah! Well, he had a great sense of animals."

"We think he had a great sense of human beings."

Francis Wilmot stared.

There was something, Michael decided, in this young man unresponsive to satire.

"So you want to see Cruft's Dog Show?" he said. "You're keen on dogs, then?"

"I'll be taking a bloodhound back for Jon, and two for myself. I want to raise bloodhounds."

Michael leaned back, and blew out smoke. To Francis Wilmot, he felt, the world was young, and life running on good tyres to some desirable destination. In England——!

"What is it you Americans want out of life?" he said abruptly.

"Well, I suppose you might say we want success—in the North at all events."

"*We* wanted that in 1824," said Michael.

"Oh! And nowadays?"

"We've had success, and now we're wondering whether it hasn't cooked our goose."

"Well," said Francis Wilmot, "we're sort of thinly populated, compared with you."

"That's it," said Michael. "Every seat here is booked in advance; and a good many sit on their own knees. Will you have another cigar, or shall we join the lady?"

## Chapter V

## SIDE-SLIPS

IF Providence was completely satisfied with Sapper's Row, Camden Town, Michael was not. What could justify those twin dismal rows of three-storeyed houses, so begrimed that they might have been collars washed in Italy? What possible attention to business could make these little ground-floor shops do anything but lose money? From the thronged and tram-lined thoroughfare so pregnantly scented with fried fish, petrol, and old clothes, who would turn into this small backwater for sweetness or for profit? Even the children, made with heroic constancy on its second and third floors, sought the sweets of life outside its precincts; for in Sapper's Row they could neither be run over nor stare at the outside of cinemas. Hand-carts, bicycles, light vans which had lost their nerve and taxicabs which had lost their way, provided all the traffic; potted geraniums and spotted cats supplied all the beauty. Sapper's Row drooped and dithered.

Michael entered from its west end, and against his principles. Here was overcrowded England at its most dismal, and here was he, who advocated a reduction of its population, about to visit some broken-down aliens with the view of keeping them alive. He looked into three of the little shops. Not a soul! Which was worst! Such little shops frequented, or—deserted? He came to No. 12, and looking up, saw a face looking down. It was wax white, movingly listless, above a pair of hands sewing at a garment. 'That,' he thought, 'is my "obedient humble" and her needle.' He entered the shop below, a hairdresser's, containing a dirty basin below a dusty mirror, suspicious towels, bottles, and two dingy chairs. In his shirt-sleeves, astride one of them, reading *The Daily Mail*, sat a shadowy fellow with pale hollow cheeks, twisted moustache, lank hair, and the eyes, at once knowing and tragic, of a philosopher.

"Hair-cut, sir?"

Michael shook his head.

"Do Mr. and Mrs. Bergfeld live here?"

"Upstairs, top floor."

"How do I get up?"

"Through there."

Passing through a curtained aperture, Michael found a stairway,

THE SILVER SPOON

and at its top, stood, hesitating. His conscience was echoing Fleur's comment on Anna Bergfeld's letter: "Yes, I dare say; but what's the good?" when the door was opened, and it seemed to him almost as if a corpse were standing there, with a face as though someone had come knocking on its grave, so eager and so white.

"Mrs. Bergfeld? My name's Mont  You wrote to me."

The woman trembled so, that Michael thought she was going to faint.

"Will you excuse me, sir, that I sit down?" And she dropped on to the end of the bed. The room was spotless, but, besides the bed, held only a small deal washstand, a pot of geranium, a tin trunk with a pair of trousers folded on it, a woman's hat on a peg, and a chair in the window covered with her sewing.

The woman stood up again. She seemed not more than thirty, thin but prettily formed; and her oval face, without colour except in her dark eyes, suggested Rafael rather than Sapper's Row.

"It is like seeing an angel," she said. "Excuse me, sir."

"Queer angel, Mrs. Bergfeld. Your husband not in?"

"No, sir. Fritz has gone to walk."

"Tell me, Mrs. Bergfeld. If I pay your passages to Germany, will you go?"

"We cannot get a passport now; Fritz has been here twenty years, and never back; he has lost his German nationality, sir; they do not want people like us, you know."

Michael stivered up his hair.

"Where are you from yourself?"

"From Salzburg."

"What about going back there?"

"I would like to, but what would we do? In Austria everyone is poor now, and I have no relative left. Here at least we have my sewing."

"How much is that a week?"

"Sometimes a pound; sometimes fifteen shillings. It is bread and the rent."

"Don't you get the dole?"

"No, sir. We are not registered.'

Michael took out a five-pound note and laid it with his card on the washstand. "I've got to think this over, Mrs. Bergfeld. Perhaps your husband will come and see me." He went out quickly, for the ghostly woman had flushed pink.

Repassing through the curtained aperture, he caught the hairdresser wiping out the basin.

"Find 'em, sir?"

"The lady."

"Ah! Seen better days, I should say. The 'usband's a queer customer; 'alf off his nut. Wanted to come in here with me, but I've got to give this job up."

"Oh! How's that?"

"I've got to have fresh air—only got one lung, and that's not very gaudy. I'll have to find something else."

"That's bad, in these days."

The hairdresser shrugged his bony shoulders. "Ah!" he said. "I've been a hairdresser from a boy, except for the war. Funny place this, to fetch up in after where I've been. The war knocked me out." He twisted his little thin moustache.

"No pension?" said Michael.

"Not a bob. What I want to keep me alive is something in the open."

Michael took him in from head to foot. Shadowy, narrow-headed, with one lung.

"But do you know anything about country life?"

"Not a blessed thing. Still, I've got to find something, or peg out."

His tragic and knowing eyes searched Michael's face.

"I'm awfully sorry," said Michael. "Good-bye!"

The hairdresser made a queer jerky little movement.

Emerging from Sapper's Row into the crowded, roaring thoroughfare, Michael thought of a speech in a play he had seen a year or two before. 'The condition of the people leaves much to be desired. I shall make a point of taking up the cudgels in the House. I shall move——!' The condition of the people! What a remote thing! The sportive nightmare of a few dreaming nights, the skeleton in a well-locked cupboard, the discomforting rare howl of a hungry dog! And probably no folk in England less disturbed by it than the gallant six hundred odd who sat with him in 'that House'. For to improve the condition of the people was their job, and that relieved them of a sense of nightmare. Since Oliver Cromwell some sixteen thousand, perhaps, had sat there before them, to the same end. And was the trick done—not precisely! Still *they* were really working for it, and other people were only looking on and telling them how to do it!

Thus was he thinking when a voice said:

"Not got a job about you, sir?"

Michael quickened his steps, then stood still. He saw that the

268

man who had spoken, having cast his eyes down again, had missed this sign of weakness; and he went back to him. They were black eyes in a face round and pasty like a mince-pie. Decent and shabby, quiet and forlorn, he wore an ex-Serviceman's badge.

"You spoke to me?" said Michael.

"I'm sure I don't know why, sir; it just hopped out of me."

"No work?"

"No; and pretty low.

"Married?"

"Widower, sir; two children.

"Dole?"

"Yes; and fair sick of it."

"In the war, I see?"

"Yes, Mespot."

"What sort of a job do you want?"

"Any mortal thing."

"Give me your name and address."

"Henry Boddick, 4 Waltham Buildings, Gunnersbury."

Michael took it down.

"Can't promise anything," he said.

"No, sir."

"Good luck, anyway. Have a cigar?"

"Thank you, and good luck to *you*, sir."

Michael saluted, and resumed his progress; once out of sight of Henry Boddick, he took a taxi. A little more of this, and he would lose the sweet reasonableness without which one could not sit in 'that House'!

'For Sale or to Let' recorded recurrently in Portland Place, somewhat restored his sense of balance.

That same afternoon he took Francis Wilmot with him to the House, and leaving him at the foot of the Distinguished Strangers' stairway, made his way on to the floor.

He had never been in Ireland, so that the debate had for him little relation to reality. It seemed to illustrate, however, the obstacles in the way of agreement on any mortal subject. Almost every speech emphasised the paramount need for a settlement, but declared the impossibility of 'going back' on this, that, or the other factor which precluded such settlement. Still, for a debate on Ireland it seemed good-tempered; and presently they would all go out and record the votes they had determined on before it all began. He remembered the thrill with which he had listened to the first debates after his election; the impression each speech had

given him that somebody must certainly be converted to something and the reluctance with which he had discovered that nobody
ever was. Some force was at work far stronger than any eloquence,
however striking or sincere. The clothes were washed elsewhere;
in here they were but aired before being put on. Still, until people
put thoughts into words, they didn't know what they thought, and
sometimes they didn't know afterwards. And for the hundredth
time Michael was seized by a weak feeling in his legs. In a few
weeks he himself must rise on them. Would the House accord
him its 'customary indulgence'! or would it say: 'Young fellow—
teaching your grandmother to suck eggs—shut up!'

He looked around him.

His fellow members were sitting in all shapes. Chosen of the
people, they confirmed the doctrine that human nature did not
change, or so slowly that one could not see the process—he had
seen their prototypes in Roman statues, in mediæval pictures. . . .
'Plain but pleasant,' he thought, unconsciously reproducing George
Forsyte's description of himself in his palmy days. But did they
take themselves seriously, as under Burke, as under Gladstone
even?

The words 'customary indulgence' roused him from reverie; for
they meant a maiden speech. Ha! yes! the member for Cornmarket. He composed himself to listen. Delivering himself with
restraint and clarity, the speaker seemed suggesting that the
doctrine 'Do unto others as you would they should do unto you'
need not be entirely neglected, even in Ireland; but it was long—
too long—Michael watched the House grow restive. 'Alas! poor
brother!' he thought, as the speaker somewhat hastily sat down.
A very handsome man rose in his place. He congratulated his
honourable friend on his able and well-delivered effort, he only
regretted that it had nothing to do with the business in hand.
Exactly! Michael slipped out. Recovering his 'distinguished
stranger', he walked away with him to South Square.

Francis Wilmot was in a state of some enthusiasm.

"That was fine," he said. "Who was the gentleman under the
curtains?"

"The Speaker?"

"No; I mean the one who didn't speak."

"Exactly; he's the dignity of the House."

"They ought to feed him oxygen; it must be sleepy under there.
I liked the delegate who spoke last. He would 'go' in America; he
had big ideas."

"The idealism which keeps you out of the League of Nations, eh?" said Michael with a grin.

Francis Wilmot turned his head rather sharply.

"Well," he said, "we're like any other people when it comes to bed-rock."

"Quite so," said Michael, "idealism is just a by-product of geography—it's the haze that lies in the middle distance. The farther you are from bed-rock, the less quick you need to be to see it. We're twenty sea-miles more idealistic about the European situation than the French are. And you're three thousand sea-miles more idealistic than we are. But when it's a matter of niggers, we're three thousand sea-miles more idealistic than you; isn't that so?"

Francis Wilmot narrowed his dark eyes.

"It is," he said. "The farther North we go in the States, the more idealistic we get about the negro. Anne and I've lived all our life with darkies, and never had trouble; we love them, and they love us; but I wouldn't trust myself not to join in lynching one that laid his hands on her. I've talked that over many times with Jon. He doesn't see it that way; he says a darky should be tried like a white man; but he doesn't know the real South. His mind is still three thousand sea-miles away."

Michael was silent. Something within him always closed up at mention of a name which he still spelt mentally with an 'h'.

Francis Wilmot added ruminatively: "There are a few saints in every country proof against your theory; but the rest of us, I reckon, aren't above human nature."

"Talking of human nature," said Michael, "here's my father-in-law!"

## Chapter VI

### SOAMES KEEPS HIS EYES OPEN

SOAMES, having prolonged his week-end visit, had been spending the afternoon at the Zoological Gardens, removing his great-nephews, the little Cardigans, from the too close proximity of monkeys and cats. After standing them once more in Imogen's hall, he had roosted at his Club till, idly turning his evening paper, he had come on this paragraph, in the 'Chiff-chaff' column:

"A surprise for the coming Session is being confectioned at the Wednesday gatherings of a young hostess not a hundred yards from Westminster. Her husband, a prospective baronet lately connected with literature, is to be entrusted with the launching in Parliament of a policy which enjoys the peculiar label of Foggartism, derived from Sir James Foggart's book called *The Parlous State of England*. This amusing alarum is attributed to the somewhat fantastic brain which guides a well-known weekly. We shall see what comes of it. In the meantime the enterprising little lady in question is losing no chance of building up her 'salon' on the curiosity which ever surrounds any buccaneering in politics."

Soames rubbed his eyes; then read it again with rising anger. 'Enterprising little lady is losing no chance of building up her "salon".' Who had written that? He put the paper in his pocket— almost the first theft he had ever committed—and all the way across St. James's Park in the gathering twilight he brooded on that anonymous paragraph. The allusion seemed to him unmistakable, and malicious into the bargain. 'Lion-hunter' would not have been plainer. Unfortunately, in a primary sense 'lion-hunter' was a compliment, and Soames doubted whether its secondary sense had ever been 'laid down' as libellous. He was still brooding deeply, when the young men ranged alongside.

"Well, sir?"

"Ah!" said Soames. "I want to speak to you. You've got a traitor in the camp." And without meaning to at all, he looked angrily at Francis Wilmot.

"Now, sir?" said Michael, when they were in his study.

Soames held out the folded paper.

Michael read the paragraph and made a face.

"Whoever wrote that comes to your evenings," said Soames; "that's clear. Who is he?"

"Very likely a she."

"D'you mean to say they print such things by women?"

Michael did not answer. Old Forsyte was behind the times.

"Will they tell me who it is, if I go down to them?" asked Soames.

"No, fortunately."

"How d'you mean 'fortunately'?"

"Well, sir, the Press is a sensitive plant. I'm afraid you might make it curl up. Besides, it's always saying nice things that aren't deserved."

"But this——" began Soames; he stopped in time, and substituted: "Do you mean that we've got to sit down under it?"

"To lie down, I'm afraid."

"Fleur has an evening to-morrow."

# THE SILVER SPOON

"Yes."

"I shall stay up for it, and keep my eyes open."

Michael had a vision of his father-in-law, like a plain clothes man in the neighbourhood of wedding-presents.

But in spite of assumed levity, Michael had been hit. The knowledge that his adored one had the collector's habit, and flitted, alluring, among the profitable, had, so far, caused him only indulgent wonder. But now it seemed more than an amusing foible. The swiftness with which she turned her smile off and on as though controlled by a switch under her shingled hair; the quick turns of her neck, so charming and exposed; the clever roving, disguised so well but not quite well enough, of the pretty eyes; the droop and flutter of their white lids; the expressive hands grasping, if one could so call such slim and dainty apprehensions, her career—all this suddenly caused Michael pain. Still she was doing it for him and Kit! French women, they said, co-operated with their husbands in the family career. It was the French blood in her. Or perhaps just idealism, the desire to have and be the best of whatever bunch there was about! Thus Michael, loyally. But his uneasy eyes roved from face to face of the Wednesday gathering, trying to detect signs of quizzicality.

Soames followed another method. His mind, indeed, was uncomplicated by the currents awash in that of one who goes to bed with the object of his criticism. For him there was no reason why Fleur should not know as many aristocrats, Labour members, painters, ambassadors, young fools, even writing fellows, as might flutter her fancy. The higher up they were, the less likely, he thought with a certain naïveté, they would be to borrow money or get her into a mess. His daughter was as good or better than any of them, and his deep pride was stung to the quick by the notion that people should think she had to claw and scrape to get them round her. It was not she who was after them, but they who were after her! Standing under the Fragonard which he had given her, grizzled, neatly moustached, close-faced, chinny, with a gaze concentrated on nothing in particular, as of one who has looked over much and found little in it, he might have been one of her ambassadors.

A young woman, with red-gold hair, about an inch long on her de-shingled neck, came and stood with her back to him, beside a soft man, who kept washing his hands. Soames could hear every word of their talk.

"Isn't the little Mont amusing? Look at her now, with 'Don

273

Fernando'—you'd think he was her only joy. Ah! There's young Bashly! Off she goes. She's a born little snob. But that doesn't make this a 'salon', as she thinks. To found a 'salon' you want personality, and wit, and the 'don't care a damn' spirit. She hasn't got a scrap. Besides, who is she?"

"Money?" said the soft man.

"Not so very much. Michael's such dead nuts on her that he's getting dull; though it's partly Parliament, of course. Have you heard them talk this Foggartism? All food, children, and the future—the very dregs of dullness."

"Novelty," purred the soft man, "is the vice of our age."

"One resents a nobody like her climbing in on piffle like this Foggartism. Did you read the book?"

"Hardly. Did you?"

"No jolly fear! I'm sorry for Michael. He's being exploited by that little snob."

Penned without an outlet, Soames had begun breathing hard. Feeling a draught, perhaps, the young woman turned to encounter a pair of eyes so grey, so cold, in a face so concentrated, that she moved away. "Who was that old buffer?" she asked of the soft man; "he gave me 'the jim-jams'."

The soft man thought it might be a poor relation—he didn't seem to know anybody.

But Soames had already gone across to Michael.

"Who's the young woman with the red hair?"

"Marjorie Ferrar."

"She's the traitress—turn her out!"

Michael stared.

"But we know her quite well—she's a daughter of Lord Charles Ferrar, and——"

"Turn her out!" said Soames again.

"How do you know that she's the traitress, sir?"

"I've just heard her use the very words of that paragraph, and worse."

"But she's our guest."

"Pretty guest!" growled Soames through his teeth.

"One can't turn a guest out. Besides, she the granddaughter of a marquess and the pet of the Panjoys—it would make the deuce of a scandal."

"Make it, then!"

"We won't ask her again; but really, that's all one can do."

"Is it?" said Soames; and walking past his son-in-law, he went towards the object of his denunciation. Michael followed, much perturbed. He had never yet seen his father-in-law with his teeth bared. He arrived in time to hear him say in a low but quite audible voice:

"You were good enough, madam, to call my daughter a snob in her own house."

Michael saw the de-shingled neck turn and rear, the hard blue eyes stare with a sort of outraged impudence; he heard her laugh, then Soames saying:

"You are a traitress; be so kind as to withdraw."

Of the half-dozen people round, not a soul was missing it! Oh, hell! And he the master of the house! Stepping forward, he put his arm through that of Soames:

"That'll do, sir," he said, quietly; "this is not a Peace Conference."

There was a horrid hush; and in all the group only the soft man's white hands, washing each other, moved.

Marjorie Ferrar took a step towards the door.

"I don't know who this person is," she said; "but he's a liar."

"I reckon not."

At the edge of the little group was a dark young man. His eyes were fixed on Marjorie Ferrar's, whose eyes in turn were fixed on his.

And suddenly, Michael saw Fleur, very pale, standing just behind him. She must have heard it all! She smiled, waved her hand, and said:

"Madame Carelli's going to play."

Marjorie Ferrar walked on towards the door, and the soft man followed her, still washing those hands, as if trying to rid them of the incident. Soames, like a slow dog making sure, walked after them; Michael walked after him. The words "How amusing!" floated back, and a soft echoing snigger. Slam! Both outer door and incident were closed.

Michael wiped his forehead. One half of the brain behind admired his father-in-law; the other thought: 'Well, the old man *has* gone and done it!' He went back into the drawing-room. Fleur was standing near the clavichord, as if nothing had happened. But Michael could see her fingers crisping at her dress; and his heart felt sore. He waited, quivering, for the last chord.

Soames had gone upstairs. Before 'The White Monkey' in Michael's study, he reviewed his own conduct. He regretted nothing. Red-headed cat! 'Born snob!' 'Money? Not very much.'

275

Ha! 'A nobody like her!' Granddaughter of a marquess, was she? Well, he had shown the insolent baggage the door. All that was sturdy in his fibre, all that was acrid in his blood, all that resented patronage and privilege, the inherited spirit of his forefathers, moved within him. Who were the aristocracy, to give themselves airs? Jackanapes! Half of 'em descendants of those who had got what they had by robbery or jobbery! That one should call his daughter, *his* daughter, a snob! He wouldn't lift a finger, wouldn't cross a road, to meet the Duke of Seven Dials himself! If Fleur like to amuse herself by having people round her, why shouldn't she? His blood ran suddenly a little cold. Would she say that he had spoiled her 'salon'? Well! He couldn't help it if she did; better to have had the thing out, and got rid of that cat, and know where they all were. 'I shan't wait up for her,' he thought. 'Storm in a tea-cup!'

The thin strumming of the clavichord came up to him out on the landing, waiting to climb to his room. He wondered if these evenings woke the baby. A gruff sound at his feet made him jump. That dog lying outside the baby's door! He wished the little beggar had been downstairs just now—he would have known how to put his teeth through that red-haired cat's nude stockings. He passed on up, looking at Francis Wilmot's door, which was opposite his own.

That young American chap must have overheard something too; but he shouldn't allude to the matter with him; not dignified. And, shutting his door on the strumming of the clavichord, Soames closed his eyes again as best he could.

## Chapter VII

### SOUNDS IN THE NIGHT

MICHAEL had never heard Fleur cry, and to see her, flung down across the bed, smothering her sobs in the quilt, gave him a feeling akin to panic. She stopped at his touch on her hair, and lay still.

"Buck up, darling!" he said gently. "If you aren't one, what does it matter?"

She struggled up, and sat cross-legged, her flushed face smudged with tears, her hair disordered.

"Who cares what one is? It's what one's labelled."

"Well, we've labelled her 'Traitress'."

276

"As if that made it better! We all talk behind people's backs. Who minds that? But how can I go on when everybody is sniggering and thinking me a lion-hunting snob? She'll cry it all over London in revenge. How can I have any more evenings?"

Was it for her career, or his, that she was sorrowing? Michael went round to the other side of the bed and put his arms about her from behind.

"Never mind what people think, my child. Sooner or later one's got to face that, anyway."

"It's you who aren't facing it. If I'm not thought nice, I can't *be* nice."

"Only the people who really know one matter."

"Nobody knows one," said Fleur sullenly. "The fonder they are, the less they know, and the less it matters what they think."

Michael withdrew his arms.

She sat silent for so long that he went back to the other side of the bed to see if he could tell anything from her face resting moodily on her hands. The grace of her body thus cramped was such that his senses ached. And since caresses would only worry her, he ached the more.

"I hate her," she said at last; "and if I can hurt her, I will."

He would have liked to hurt the 'pet of the Panjoys' himself, but it did not console him to hear Fleur utter that sentiment; it meant more from her than from himself, who, when it came to the point, was a poor hand at hurting people.

"Well, darling," he said, "shall we sleep on it?"

"I said I wouldn't have any more evenings; but I shall."

"Good!" said Michael; "that's the spirit."

She laughed. It was a funny hard little sound in the night. And with it Michael had to remain discontented.

All through the house it was a wakeful night. Soames had the three o'clock tremors, which cigars and the fresh air wherein he was obliged to play his golf had subdued for some time past. He was disturbed, too, by that confounded great clock from hour to hour, and by a stealthy noise between three and four, as of someone at large in the house.

This was, in fact, Francis Wilmot. Ever since his impulsive denial that Soames was a liar, the young man had been in a peculiar state of mind. As Soames surmised, he too had overheard Marjorie Ferrar slandering her hostess; but in the very moment of his refutation, like Saul setting forth to attack the Christians, he had been smitten by blindness. Those blue eyes, pouring into his the light

277

of defiance, had finished with a gleam which seemed to say:
"Young man, you please me!" And it haunted him. That lissome
nymph—with her white skin and red-gold hair, her blue eyes full
of insolence, her red lips full of joy, her white neck fragrant as a
pinewood in sunshine—the vision was abiding. He had been watching her all through the evening; but it was uncanny the way she
had left her image on his senses in that one long moment, so that
now he got no sleep. Though he had not been introduced, he knew
her name to be Marjorie Ferrar, and he thought it 'fine'. Countryman that he was and with little knowledge of women—she was
unlike any woman he had known. And he had given her the lie
direct! This made him so restless that he drank the contents of
his water-bottle, put on his clothes, and stole downstairs. Passing
the Dandie, who stirred as though muttering: "Unusual! But I
know those legs!" he reached the hall, where a milky glimmer
came in through the fanlight. Lighting a cigarette, he sat down on
the marble coat-sarcophagus. It cooled his anatomy, so that he got
off it, turned up the light, saw a telephone directory resting beside
him, and mechanically sought the letter 'F'. There she was!
"Ferrar, Marjorie, 3, River Studios, Wren Street." Switching off
the light, he slipped back the door-chain and stole out. He knew
his way to the river, and went towards it.

It was the hour when sound, exhausted, has laid its head on the
pillow, and one can hear a moth pass. London, in clear air, with
no smoke going up, slept beneath the moon. Bridges, towers,
water, all silvered, had a look as if withdrawn from man. Even
the houses and the trees enjoyed their moony hour apart, and
seemed to breathe out with Francis Wilmot a stanza from 'The
Ancient Mariner':

> 'O Sleep, it is a gentle thing,
> Beloved from pole to pole!
> To Mary Queen the praise be given,
> She sent the gentle sleep from heaven
> That slid into my soul!'

He turned at random to the right along the river. Never in his
life had he walked through a great city at the dead hour. Not a
passion alive, nor a thought of gain; haste asleep, and terrors
dreaming; here and there, no doubt, one turning on his bed; perhaps a soul passing. Down on the water lighters and barges lay
shadowy and abandoned, with red lights burning; the lamps along

278

the Embankment shone without purpose, as if they had been freed. Man was away. In the whole town only himself up and doing—what? Natively shrewd and resourceful in all active situations, the young Southerner had little power of diagnosis, and certainly did not consider himself ridiculous wandering about like this at night, not even when he suddenly felt that if he could 'locate' her windows, he could go home and sleep. He passed the Tate Gallery and saw a human being with moonlit buttons.

"Pardon me, officer," he said, "but where is Wren Street?"

"Straight on and fifth to the right."

Francis Wilmot resumed his march. The 'moving' moon was heeling down, the stars were gaining light, the trees had begun to shiver. He found the fifth turning, walked down 'the block', and was no wiser; it was too dark to read names or numbers. He passed another buttoned human effigy and said:

"Pardon me, officer, but where are River Studios?"

"Comin' away from them; last house on the right."

Francis Wilmot retraced his steps. There it was, then—by itself, back from the street. He stood before it and gazed at dark windows. She might be behind any one of them! Well! He had 'located' her, and, in the rising wind, he turned and walked home. He went upstairs stealthily as he had come down, past the Dandie, who again raised his head, muttered: "Still more unusual, but the same legs!" entered his room, lay down, and fell asleep like a baby.

## Chapter VIII

### ROUND AND ABOUT

GENERAL reticence at breakfast concerning the incident of the night before, made little impression on Soames, because the young American was present, before whom, naturally, one would not discuss it; but he noted that Fleur was pale. In his early-morning vigil legal misgivings had assailed him. Could one call even a red-haired baggage 'traitress' in the hearing of some half-dozen persons with impunity? He went off to his sister Winifred's after breakfast, and told her the whole story.

"Quite right, my dear boy," was her comment. "They tell me that young woman is as fast as they're made. Her father, you know, owned the horse that didn't beat the French horse—I never can remember its name—in that race, the Something Stakes, at— dear me! what was the meeting?"

"I know nothing about racing," said Soames.

But that afternoon at the Connoisseurs' Club a card was brought to him:

> ### LORD CHARLES FERRAR
>
> High Marshes,
>
> Nr. Newmarket.     Burton's Club.

For a moment his knees felt a little weak; but the word 'snob' coming to his assistance, he said dryly: "Show him into the strangers' room." He was not going to hurry himself for this fellow, and finished his tea before repairing to that forlorn corner.

A tallish man was standing in the middle of the little room, thin and upright, with a moustache brushed arrogantly off his lips, and a single eye-glass which seemed to have grown over the right eye, so unaided was it. There were corrugations in his thin weathered cheeks, and in his thick hair flecked at the sides with grey. Soames had no difficulty in disliking him at sight.

"Mr. Forsyte, I believe?"

Soames inclined his head.

"You made use of an insulting word to my daughter last night in the presence of several people."

"Yes; it was richly deserved."

"You were not drunk, then?"

"Not at all," said Soames.

His dry precision seemed to disconcert the visitor, who twisted his moustache, frowned his eyeglass closer to his eye, and said:

"I have the names of those who overheard it. You will be good enough to write to each of them separately, withdrawing your expression unreservedly."

"I shall do nothing of the kind."

A moment's silence ensued.

"You are an attorney, I believe?"

"A solicitor."

"Then you know the consequences of refusal."

"If your daughter likes to go into Court, I shall be happy to meet her there."

"You refuse to withdraw?"

"Absolutely."

"Good-evening, then!"

"Good-evening!"

For two pins he would have walked round the fellow, the bristles rising on his back, but, instead, he stood a little to one side to let him out. Insolent brute! He could so easily hear again the voice of old Uncle Jolyon, characterising some person of the 'eighties as 'a pettifogging little attorney'. And he felt that, somehow or other, he must relieve his mind. 'Old Mont' would know about this fellow—he would go across and ask him.

At 'The Aeroplane' he found not only Sir Lawrence Mont, looking almost grave, but Michael, who had evidently been detailing to his father last evening's incident. This was a relief to Soames, who felt the insults to his daughter too bitterly to talk of them. Describing the visit he had just received, he ended with the words:

"This fellow—Ferrar—what's his standing?"

"Charlie Ferrar? He owes money everywhere, has some useful horses, and is a very good shot."

"He didn't strike me as a gentleman," said Soames.

Sir Lawrence cocked his eyebrow, as if debating whether he ought to answer this remark about one who had ancestors, from one who had none.

"And his daughter," said Soames, "isn't a lady."

Sir Lawrence wagged his head.

"Single-minded, Forsyte, single-minded; but you're right; there's a queer streak in that blood. Old Shropshire's a dear old man; it skipped his generation, but it's there—it's there. His aunt——"

"He called me an attorney," said Soames with a grim smile, "and she called me a liar. I don't know which is worse."

Sir Lawrence got up and looked into St. James's Street. Soames had the feeling that the narrow head perched up on that straight thin back counted for more than his own, in this affair. One was dealing here with people who said and did what they liked and damned the consequences; this baronet chap had been brought up in that way himself, no doubt, he ought to know how their minds worked.

Sir Lawrence turned.

"She may bring an action, Forsyte; it was very public. What evidence have you?"

"My own ears."

Sir Lawrence looked at the ears, as if to gauge their length.

"M'm! Anything else?"

"That paragraph."

"She'll get at the paper. Yes?"

"The man she was talking to."

Michael ejaculated: "Philip Quinsey—put not your trust in Gath!"

"What more?"

"Well," said Soames, "there's what that young American over-heard, whatever it was."

"Ah!" said Sir Lawrence: "Take care she doesn't get at *him*. Is that all?"

Soames nodded. It didn't seem much, now he came to think of it!

"You say she called you a liar. How would it be to take the offensive?"

There was a silence; then Soames said: "Women? No!"

"Quite right, Forsyte! They have their privileges still. There's nothing for it but to wait and see how the cat jumps. Traitress! I suppose you know how much the word costs?"

"The cost," said Soames, "is nothing; it's the publicity!"

His imagination was playing streets ahead of him. He saw him-self already in 'the box', retailing the spiteful purring of that cat, casting forth to the public and the papers the word 'snob', of his own daughter; for if he didn't, he would have no defence. Too painful!

"What does Fleur say?" he asked, suddenly, of Michael.

"War to the knife."

Soames jumped in his chair.

"Ah!" he said: "That's a woman all over—no imagination!"

"That's what I thought at first, sir, but I'm not so sure. She says if Marjorie Ferrar is not taken by the short hairs, she'll put it across everybody—and that the more public the thing is, the less harm she can do."

"I think," said Sir Lawrence, coming back to his chair, "I'll go and see old Shropshire. My father and his shot woodcock together in Albania in 'fifty-four."

Soames could not see the connection, but did not snub the pro-posal. A marquess was a sort of gone-off duke; even in this demo-cratic age, he would have some influence, one supposed.

"He's eighty," went on Sir Lawrence, "and gets gout in the stomach, but he's as brisk as a bee."

Soames could not be sure whether it was a comfort.

"The grass shall not grow, Forsyte. I'll go there now."

They parted in the street, Sir Lawrence moving north—towards Mayfair.

The Marquess of Shropshire was dictating to his secretary a letter to his County Council, urging on them an item of his lifelong programme for the electrification of everything. One of the very first to take up electricity, he had remained faithful to it all his brisk and optimistic days. A short, bird-like old man, in shaggy Lovat tweeds, with a blue tie of knitted silk passed through a ring, bright cheeks and well-trimmed white beard and moustache, he was standing in his favourite attitude, with one foot on a chair, his elbow on his knee, and his chin on his hand.

"Ah! young Mont!" he said: "Sit down."

Sir Lawrence took a chair, crossed his knees, and threaded his finger-tips. He found it pleasing to be called 'young Mont', at sixty-six or so.

"Have you brought me another of your excellent books?"

"No, Marquess; I've come for your advice."

"Ah! Go on, Mr. Mersey: 'In this way, gentlemen, you will save at least three thousand a year to your ratepayers; confer a blessing on the countryside by abolishing the smoke of four filthy chimneys; and make me your obliged servant,

'SHROPSHIRE.'

Thank you, Mr. Mersey. Now, my dear young Mont?"

Having watched the back of the secretary till it vanished, and noted the old peer pivotting his bright eyes, with their expression of one who means to see more every day, on his visitor, Sir Lawrence took his eyeglass between thumb and finger, and said:

"Your granddaughter, sir, and my daughter-in-law want to fight like billy-o."

"Marjorie?" said the old man, and his head fell to one side like a bird's. "I draw the line—a charming young woman to look at, but I draw the line. What has she done now?"

"Called my daughter-in-law a snob and a lion-hunter; and my daughter-in-law's father has called your granddaughter a traitress to her face."

"Bold man," said the Marquess; "bold man! Who is he?"

"His name is Forsyte."

"Forsyte?" repeated the old peer; "Forsyte? The name's familiar —now where would that be? Ah! Forsyte and Treffry—the big tea men. My father had his tea from them direct—real caravan; no such tea now. Is that the——?"

"Some relation, perhaps. This man is a solicitor—retired; chiefly

283

renowned for his pictures. A man of some substance, and probity."

"Indeed! And *is* his daughter a—a lion-hunter?"

Sir Lawrence smiled.

"She's a charmer. Likes to have people about her. Very pretty. Excellent little mother; some French blood."

"Ah!" said the Marquess: "the French! Better built round the middle than our people. What do you want me to do?"

"Speak to your son Charles."

The old man took his foot off the chair, and stood nearly upright. His head moved sideways with a slight continuous motion.

"I never speak to Charlie," he said gravely. "We haven't spoken for six years."

"I beg your pardon, sir. Didn't know. Sorry to have bothered you."

"No, no; pleasure to see you. If I run across Marjorie, I'll see— I'll see. But, my dear Mont, what shall we do with these young women—no sense of service; no continuity; no hair; no figures? By the way, do you know this Power Scheme on the Severn?" He held up a pamphlet: "I've been at them to do it for years. My Colliery among others could be made to pay with electricity; but they won't move. We want some Americans over here."

Sir Lawrence had risen; the old man's sense of service had so clearly taken the bit between its teeth again. He held out his hand.

"Good-bye, Marquess; delighted to see you looking so well."

"Good-bye, my dear young Mont; command me at any time, and let me have another of your nice books."

They shook hands; and from the Lovat clothes was disengaged a strong whiff of peat. Sir Lawrence, looking back, saw the old man back in his favourite attitude, foot on chair and chin on hand, already reading the pamphlet. 'Some boy!' he thought; 'as Michael would say. But what has Charlie Ferrar done not be spoken to for six years? Old Forsyte ought to know. . . .'

In the meantime 'Old Forsyte' and Michael were walking homewards across St. James's Park.

"That young American," said Soames; "what do you suppose made him put his oar in?"

"I don't know, sir; and I don't like to ask."

"Exactly," said Soames, glumly. There was, indeed, something repulsive to him in treating with an American over a matter of personal dignity.

"Do they use the word 'snob' over there?"

"I'm not sure; but, in the States to hunt lions is a form of idealism. They want to associate with what they think better than themselves. It's rather fine."

Soames did not agree; but found difficulty in explaining why. Not to recognise anyone as better than himself or his daughter had been a sort of guiding principle, and guiding principles were not talked about. In fact, it was so deep in him that he hadn't known of it.

"I shan't mention it," he said, "unless he does. What more can this young woman do? She's in a set, I suppose?"

"The Panjoys——'

"Panjoys!"

"Yes, sir; out for a good time at any cost—they don't really count, of course. But Marjorie Ferrar is frightfully in the limelight. She paints a bit; she's got some standing with the Press; she dances; she hunts; she's something of an actress; she goes everywhere week-ending. It's the week-ends that matter, where people have nothing to do but talk. Were you ever at a week-end party, sir?"

"I?" said Soames: "Good Lord—no!"

Michael smiled—incongruity, indeed, could go no farther.

"We must get one up for you at Lippinghall."

"No, thank you."

"You're right, sir; nothing more boring. But they're the *coulisses* of politics. Fleur thinks they're good for me. And Marjorie Ferrar knows all the people we know, and lots more. It *is* awkward."

"I should go on as if nothing had happened," said Soames. "But about that paper? They ought to be warned that this woman is venomous."

Michael regarded his father-in-law quizzically.

On entering, they found the manservant in the hall.

"There's a man to see you, sir, by the name of Bugfill."

"Oh! Ah! Where have you put him, Coaker?"

"Well, I didn't know what to make of him, sir, he shakes all over. I've stood him in the dining-room."

"Excuse me, sir," said Michael.

Soames passed into the 'parlour', where he found his daughter and Francis Wilmot.

"Mr. Wilmot is leaving us, Father. You're just in time to say good-bye."

If there were moments when Soames felt cordial, they were such as these. He had nothing against the young man; indeed, he rather liked the look of him; but to see the last of almost anybody was in a sense a relief; besides, there was this question of what he had

285

overheard, and to have him about the place without knowing would be a continual temptation to compromise with one's dignity and ask him what it was.

"Good-bye, Mr. Wilmot," he said; "if you're interested in pictures—" he paused, and, holding out his hand, added, "you should look in at the British Museum."

Francis Wilmot shook the hand deferentially.

"I will. It's been a privilege to know you, sir."

Soames was wondering why, when the young man turned to Fleur.

"I'll be writing to Jon from Paris, and I'll surely send your love. You've been perfectly wonderful to me. I'll be glad to have you and Michael visit me at any time you come across to the States; and if you bring the little dog, why—I'll just be honoured to let him bite me again."

He bowed over Fleur's hand, and was gone, leaving Soames staring at the back of his daughter's neck.

"That's rather sudden," he said, when the door was closed; "anything upset him?"

She turned on him, and said coldly:

"Why did you make that fuss last night, Father?"

The injustice of her attack was so palpable, that Soames bit his moustache in silence. As if he could help himself, when she was insulted in his hearing!

"What good do you think you've done?"

Soames, who had no notion, made no attempt to enlighten her. He only felt sore inside.

"You've made me feel as if I couldn't look anybody in the face. But I'm going to, all the same. If I'm a lion-hunter and a snob, I'll do it thoroughly. Only I do wish you wouldn't go on thinking I'm a child and can't defend myself."

And still Soames was silent, sore to the soles of his boots.

Fleur flashed a look at him, and said:

"I'm sorry, but I can't help it; everything's queered;" and she too went out of the room.

Soames moved blindly to the window and stood looking out He saw a cab with luggage drive away; saw some pigeons alight, peck at the pavement, and fly off again; he saw a man kissing a woman in the dusk; a policeman light his pipe and go off duty. He saw many human and interesting things; he heard Big Ben chime. Nothing in it all! He was staring at a silver spoon. He himself had put it in her mouth at birth.

## Chapter IX

### POULTRY AND CATS

HE who had been stood in the dining-room, under the name of Bugfill, was still upright. Rather older than Michael, with an inclination to side-whisker, darkish hair, and a pale face stamped with that look of schooled quickness common to so many actors but unfamiliar to Michael, he was grasping the edge of the dining-table with one hand, and a wide-brimmed black hat with the other. The expression of his large, dark-circled eyes was such that Michael smiled and said:

"It's all right, Mr. Bergfeld, I'm not a manager. Do sit down, and smoke."

The visitor silently took the proffered chair and cigarette with an attempt at a fixed smile. Michael sat on the table.

"I gather from Mrs. Bergfeld that you're on the rocks."

"Fast," said the shaking lips.

"Your health, and your name, I suppose?"

"Yes."

"You want an open-air job, I believe? I haven't been able to think of anything very gaudy, but an idea did strike me last night in the stilly watches. How about raising poultry—everybody's doing it."

"If I had my savings."

"Yes, Mrs. Bergfeld told me about them. I can inquire but I'm afraid——"

"It's robbery." The chattered sound let Michael at once into the confidence of the many managers who had refused to employ him who uttered it.

"I know," he said, soothingly, "robbing Peter to pay Paul. That clause in the Treaty was a bit of rank barbarism, of course, camouflage it as they like. Still, it's no good to let it prey on your mind, is it?"

But his visitor had risen. "To take from civilian to pay civilian! Then why not take civilian life for civilian life? What is the difference? And England does it—the leading nation to respect the individual. It is abominable."

Michael began to feel that he was overdoing it.

"You forget," he said, "that the war made us all into barbarians,

287

for the time being; we haven't quite got over it yet. And *your* country dropped the spark into the powder magazine, you know. But what about this poultry stunt?"

Bergfeld seemed to make a violent effort to control himself.

"For my wife's sake," he said, "I will do anything; but unless I get my savings back, how can I start?"

"I can't promise; but perhaps I could start you. That hairdresser below you wants an open-air job, too. What's his name, by the way?"

"Swain."

"How do you get on with him?"

"He is an opinionated man, but we are good friends enough."

Michael got off the table. "Well, leave it to me to think it out. We shall be able to do something, I hope;" and he held out his hand.

Bergfeld took it silently, and his eyes resumed the expression with which they had first looked at Michael.

'That man,' thought Michael, 'will be committing suicide some day, if he doesn't look out.' And he showed him to the door. He stood there some minutes gazing after the German actor's vanishing form, with a feeling as if the dusk were formed out of the dark stories of such as he and the hairdresser and the man who had whispered to him to stand and deliver a job. Well, Bart must lend him that bit of land beyond the coppice at Lippinghall. He would buy a war hut if there were any left and some poultry stock, and start a colony—the Bergfelds, the hairdresser, and Henry Boddick. They could cut the timber in the coppice, and put up the fowl-houses for themselves. It would be growing food—a practical experiment in Foggartism! Fleur would laugh at him. But was there anything one could do nowadays that somebody couldn't laugh at? He turned back into the house Fleur was in the hall.

"Francis Wilmot has gone," she said.

"Why?"

"He's off to Paris."

"What was it he overheard last night?"

"Do you suppose I asked?"

"Well, no," said Michael, humbly. "Let's go up and look at Kit, it's about his bath time."

The eleventh baronet, indeed, was already in his bath.

"All right, nurse," said Fleur, "I'll finish him."

"He's been in three minutes, ma'am."

288

# THE SILVER SPOON

"Lightly boiled," said Michael.

For one aged only fourteen months this naked infant had incredible vigour—from lips to feet he was all sound and motion. He seemed to lend a meaning to life. His vitality was absolute, not relative. His kicks and crows and splashings had the joy of a gnat's dance, or a jackdaw's gambols in the air. He gave thanks not for what he was about to receive, but for what he was receiving. White as a turtle-dove, with pink toes, darker in eyes and hair than he would be presently, he grabbed at the soap, at his mother, at the bath-towelling—he seemed only to need a tail. Michael watched him, musing. This manikin, born with all that he could possibly wish for within his reach—how were they to bring him up? Were they fit to bring him up, they who had been born—like all their generation in the richer classes—emancipated, to parents properly broken-in to worship the fetich—Liberty? Born to everything they wanted, so that they were at wits' end to invent something they could not get; driven to restive searching by having their own way? The war had deprived one of one's own way, but the war had overdone it, and left one grasping at licence. And for those, like Fleur, born a little late for the war, the tale of it had only lowered what respect they could have for anything. With veneration killed, and self-denial 'off', with atavism buried, sentiment derided, and the future in the air, hardly a wonder that modernity should be a dance of gnats, taking itself damned seriously! Such were the reflections of Michael, sitting there above the steam, and frowning at his progeny. Without faith was one fit to be a parent? Well, people were looking for faith again. Only they were bound to hatch the egg of it so hard that it would be addled long before it was a chicken. 'Too self-conscious!' he thought. 'That's our trouble!'

Fleur had finished drying the eleventh baronet, and was dabbing powder over him; her eyes seemed penetrating his skin, as if to gauge the state of health behind it. He watched her take the feet and hands one by one and examine each nail, lost in her scrutiny, unselfconscious in her momentary devotion! And oppressed by the difficulty, as a Member of Parliament, of being devoted, Michael snapped his fingers at the baby and left the nursery. He went to his study and took down a volume of the Encyclopædia Britannica containing the word Poultry. He read about Leghorns, Orpingtons, White Sussex, Bramaputras, and was little the wiser. He remembered that if you drew a chalk-line to the beak of a hen, the hen thought it was tied up. He wished somebody would draw a chalk-line to his beak. Was Foggartism a chalk-line? A voice said:

"Tell Fleur I'm going to her aunt's."

"Leaving us, sir?"

"Yes, I'm not wanted."

What had happened?

"You'll see her before you go, sir?"

"No," said Soames.

Had somebody rubbed out the chalk-line to Old Forsyte's nose?

"Is there any money in poultry-farming, sir?"

"There's no money in anything nowadays."

"And yet the Income Tax returns continue to rise."

"Yes," said Soames; "there's something wrong there."

"You don't think people make their incomes out more than they are?"

Soames blinked. Pessimistic though he felt at the moment, he could not take quite that low view of human nature.

"You'd better see that Fleur doesn't go about abusing that red-haired baggage," he said. "She was born with a silver spoon in her mouth; she thinks she can do what she likes." And he shut Michael in again.

Silver spoon in her mouth. How à propos! . . .

After putting her baby into its cot Fleur had gone to the marqueterie bureau in the little sanctuary that would have been called a boudoir in old days. She sat there brooding. How could her father have made it all glaringly public! Couldn't he have seen that it was nothing so long as it was not public, but everything the moment it was? She longed to pour out her heart, and tell people her opinion of Marjorie Ferrar.

She wrote three letters—one to Lady Alison, and two to women in the group who had overheard it all last night. She concluded her third letter with the words: "A woman like that, who pretends to be a friend and sneaks into one's house to sting one behind one's back, is a snake of the first water. How Society can stick her, I can't think; she hasn't a moral about her nor a decent impulse. As for her charm—Good Lord!" Yes! And there was Francis Wilmot! She had not said all she wanted to say to him.

"My Dear Francis," she wrote:

"I am so sorry you have to run away like this. I wanted to thank you for standing up for me last night. Marjorie Ferrar is

just about the limit. But in London society one doesn't pay attention to backbiting. It has been so jolly to know you. Don't forget
us; and do come and see me again when you come back from Paris.
"Your very good friend,
"FLEUR MONT."

In future she would have nothing but men at her evenings! But
would they come if there were no women? And men like Philip
Quinsey were just as snake-like. Besides, it would look as if she
were really hurt. No! She would have to go on as before, just
dropping people who were 'catty'. But who wasn't? Except Alison,
and heavyweights like Mr. Blythe, the minor Ambassadors, and
three or four earnest politicians, she couldn't be sure about any of
them. It was the thing to be 'catty'. They all scratched other
people's backs, and their faces too when they weren't looking.
Who in Society was exempt from scratches and who didn't
scrtach? Not to scratch a little was so dreadfully dull. She could
not imagine a scratchless life except perhaps in Italy. Those Fra
Angelico frescoes in the San Marco monastery! There was a man
who did not scratch. St. Francis talking to his birds, among his
little flowers, with the sun and the moon and the stars for near
relations. St. Claire! St. Fleur— little sister of St. Francis! To be
unworldly and quite good! To be one who lived to make other
people happy! How new! How exciting, even—for about a week;
and how dull afterwards! She drew aside the curtains and looked
out into the Square. Two cats were standing in the light of a lamp
—narrow, marvellously graceful, with their heads turned towards
each other. Suddenly they began uttering horrible noises, and
became all claws. Fleur dropped the curtain.

## Chapter X

### FRANCIS WILMOT REVERSES

ABOUT that moment Francis Wilmot sat down in the lounge of
the Cosmopolis Hotel, and as suddenly sat up. In the middle of the
parquet floor, sliding and lunging, backing and filling. twisting and
turning in the arms of a man with a face like a mask, was she, to
avoid whom, out of loyalty to Fleur and Michael, he had decided
to go to Paris. Fate! For he could hardly know that she came there
most afternoons during the dancing hours. She and her partner
were easily the show couple; and, fond of dancing, Francis Wilmot

knew he was looking at something special. When they stopped, quite close to him, he said in his soft drawl:

"That was beautiful."

"How do you do, Mr. Wilmot?"

Why! She knew his name! This was the moment to exhibit loyalty! But she had sunk into a chair next his.

"And so you thought me a traitress last night?"

"I did."

"Why?"

"Because I heard you call your hostess a snob."

Marjorie Ferrar uttered an amused sound.

"My dear young man, if one never called one's friends anything worse than that—! I didn't mean you to hear, or that poptious old person in the chin!"

"He was her father," said Francis Wilmot, gravely. "It hurt him."

"Well! I'm sorry!"

A hand without a glove, warm but dry, was put into his. When it was withdrawn the whole of his hand and arm were tingling.

"Do you dance?"

"Yes, indeed, but I wouldn't presume to dance with you."

"Oh! but you must."

Francis Wilmot's head went round, and his body began going round too.

"You dance better than an Englishman, unless he's professional," said her lips six inches from his own.

"I'm proud to hear you say so, ma'am."

"Don't you know my name? or do you always call women ma'am? It's ever so pretty."

"Certainly I know your name and where you live. I wasn't six yards from you this morning at four o'clock."

"What were you doing there?"

"I just thought I'd like to be near you."

Marjorie Ferrar said, as if to herself:

"The prettiest speech I ever heard. Come and have tea with me there to-morrow."

Reversing, side-stepping, doing all he knew, Francis Wilmot said, slowly:

"I have to be in Paris."

"Don't be afraid, I won't hurt you."

"I'm not afraid, but——"

"Well, I shall expect you." And transferring herself again to her mask-faced partner, she looked back at him over her shoulder.

Francis Wilmot wiped his brow. An astonishing experience, another blow to his preconception of a stiff and formal race! If he had not known she was the daughter of a lord, he would have thought her an American. Would she ask him to dance with her again? But she left the lounge without another glance.

An up-to-date young man, a typical young man, would have felt the more jaunty. But he was neither. Six months' training for the Air Service in 1918, one visit to New York, and a few trips to Charleston and Savannah, had left him still a countryman, with a tradition of good manners, work, and simple living. Women, of whom he had known few, were to him worthy of considerable respect. He judged them by his sister, or by the friends of his dead mother, in Savannah, who were all of a certain age. A Northern lady on the boat had told him that Southern girls measured life by the number of men they could attract; she had given him an amusing take-off of a Southern girl. It had been a surprise to this young Southerner. Anne was not like that; she had never had the chance to be, anyway, having married at nineteen the first young man who had asked her!

By the morning's post he received Fleur's little letter. 'Limit!' Limit of what? He felt indignant. He did not go to Paris, and at four o'clock he was at Wren Street.

In her studio Marjorie Ferrar, clad in a flax-blue overall, was scraping at a picture with a little knife. An hour later he was her slave. Cruft's Dog Show, the Beefeaters, the Derby—he could not even remember his desire to see them; he only desired to see one English thing—Marjorie Ferrar. He hardly remembered which way the river flowed, and by mere accident walked East instead of West. Her hair, her eyes, her voice—he 'had fallen for her'! He knew himself for a fool, and did not mind; farther man cannot go. She passed him in a little open car, driving it herself, on her way to a rehearsal. She waved her hand. Blood rushed to his heart and rushed away; he trembled and went pale. And, as the car vanished, he felt lost, as if in a world of shadow, grey and dreary! Ah! There was Parliament! And, near-by, the one spot in London where he could go and talk of Marjorie Ferrar, and that was where she had misbehaved herself! He itched to defend her from the charge of being 'the limit'. He could perceive the inappropriateness of going back there to talk to Fleur of her enemy, but anything was better than not talking of her. So, turning into South Square, he rang the bell.

293

Fleur was in her 'parlour', if not precisely eating bread and honey, at least having tea.

"Not in Paris? How nice! Tea?"

"I've had it," said Francis Wilmot, colouring. "I had it with *her*."

Fleur stared.

"Oh!" she said, with a laugh. "How interesting! Where did she pick you up?"

Without taking in the implication of the words, Francis Wilmot was conscious of something deadly in them.

"She was at the *thé dansant* at my hotel yesterday. She's a wonderful dancer. I think she's a wonderful person altogether; I'd like to have you tell me what you mean by calling her 'the limit'?"

"I'd like to have you tell me why this *volte face* since Wednesday night?"

Francis Wilmot smiled: "You people have been ever so kind to me, and I want you to be friends with her again. I'm sure she didn't mean what she said that night."

"Indeed! Did she tell you that?"

"Why—not exactly! She said she didn't mean us to hear them."

"No?"

He looked at her smiling face, conscious perhaps of deep waters, but youthfully, Americanly, unconscious of serious obstacle to his desire to smooth things out.

"I just hate to think you two are out after each other. Won't you come and meet her at my hotel, and shake hands?"

Fleur's eyes moved slowly over him from head to toe.

"You look as if you might have some French blood in you. Have you?"

"Yes. My grandmother was of French stock."

"Well, I have more. The French, you know, don't forgive easily. And they don't persuade themselves into believing what they want to."

Francis Wilmot rose, and spoke with a kind of masterfulness.

"You're going to tell me what you meant in your letter."

"Am I? My dear young man, the limit of perfection, of course. Aren't you a living proof?"

Aware that he was being mocked, and mixed in his feelings, Francis Wilmot made for the door.

"Good-bye!" he said. "I suppose you'll have no use for me in future."

"Good-bye!" said Fleur.

He went out rueful, puzzled, lonelier even than when he went in. He was guideless, with no one to 'put him wise'! No direct-ness and simplicity in this town. People did not say what they meant; and his goddess—as enigmatic and twisting as the rest! More so—more so—for what did the rest matter?

## Chapter XI

### SOAMES VISITS THE PRESS

SOAMES had gone off to his sister's in Green Street thoroughly up-set. That Fleur should have a declared enemy, powerful in Society, filled him with uneasiness; that she should hold him accountable for it, seemed the more unjust, because, in fact, he was.

An evening spent under the calming influence of Winifred Dartie's common sense, and Turkish coffee, which, though 'liverish stuff', he always drank with relish, restored in him something of the feeling that it was a storm in a tea-cup.

"But that paper paragraph," he said, "sticks in my gizzard."

"Very tiresome, Soames, the whole thing; but I shouldn't bother. People skim those 'chiff-chaff' little notes and forget them the next moment. They're just put in for fun."

"Pretty sort of fun! That paper says it has a million readers."

"There's no name mentioned."

"These political people and whipper-snappers in Society all know each other," said Soames.

"Yes, my dear boy," said Winifred in her comfortable voice, so cosy, and above disturbance, "but nobody takes anything seriously nowadays."

She was sensible. He went up to bed in more cheerful mood.

But retirement from affairs had effected in Soames a deeper change that he was at all aware of. Lacking professional issues to anchor the faculty for worrying he had inherited from James Forsyte, he was inclined to pet any trouble that came along. The more he thought of that paragraph, the more he felt inclined for a friendly talk with the editor. If he could go to Fleur and say: "I've made it all right with those fellows, anyway. There'll be no more of that sort of thing," he would wipe out her vexation. If you couldn't make people in private think well of your daughter, you could surely check public expression of the opposite opinion.

Except that he did not like to get into them, Soames took on the whole a favourable view of 'the papers'. He read *The Times;* his father had read it before him, and he had been brought up on its crackle. It had news—more news for his money than he could get through. He respected its leading articles; and if its great supplements had at times appeared to him too much of a good thing, still it was a gentleman's paper. Annette and Winifred took the *Morning Post*. That also was a gentleman's paper, but it had bees in its bonnet. Bees in bonnets were respectable things, but personally Soames did not care for them. He knew little of the other papers except that those he saw about had bigger headlines and seemed cut into little bits. Of the Press as a whole he took the English view: It was an institution. It had its virtues and its vices —anyway, you had to put up with it.

About eleven o'clock he was walking towards Fleet Street.

At the office of the *Evening Sun* he handed in his card and asked to see the editor. After a moment's inspection of his top-hat, he was taken down a corridor and deposited in a small room. It seemed a 'wandering great place'. Someone would see him, they said.

"Someone?" said Soames. "I want the editor."

'The editor was very busy; could he come again when the rush was over?"

"No," said Soames.

Would he state his business? Soames wouldn't.

The attendant again looked at his top-hat and went away.

Soames waited a quarter of an hour, and was then taken to an even smaller room, where a cheery-looking man in eye-glasses was turning over a book of filed cuttings. He glanced up as Soames entered, took his card from the table, and read from it:

"Mr. Soames Forsyte? Yes?"

"Are you the editor?" asked Soames.

"One of them. Take a seat. What can I do for you?"

Impressed by a certain speed in the air, and desirous of making a good impression, Soames did not sit down, but took from his pocket-book the paragraph.

"I've come about this in your issue of last Thursday."

The cheery man put it up to his eyes, seemed to chew the sense of it a little with his mouth, and said: "Yes?"

"Would you kindly tell me who wrote it"

"We never disclose the names of correspondents, sir."

"Well, as a matter of fact, I know."

The cheery man's mouth opened, as if to emit the words: "Then why did you ask?" but closed in a smile instead.

296

"You'll forgive me," said Soames; "it quite clearly refers to my daughter, Mrs. Michael Mont, and her husband."

"Indeed! You have the advantage of me; but what's the matter with it? Seems rather a harmless piece of gossip."

Soames looked at him. He was too cheery!

"You think so?" he said dryly. "May I ask if you would like to have your daughter alluded to as an enterprising little lady?"

"Why not? It's quite a pleasant word. Besides, there's no name mentioned."

"Do you put things in," asked Soames shrewdly, "in order that they may be Greek to all your readers?"

The cheery man laughed: "Well," he said, "hardly. But really, sir, aren't you rather thin-skinned?"

This was an aspect of the affair that Soames had not foreseen. Before he could ask this editor chap not to repeat his offence, he had apparently to convince him that it *was* an offence; but to do that he must expose the real meaning of the paragraph.

"Well," he said, "if you can't see that the tone of the thing's unpleasant, I can't make you. But I beg you won't let any more such paragraphs appear. I happen to know that your correspondent is actuated by malevolence."

The cheery man again ran his eye over the cutting.

"I shouldn't have judged that. People in politics are taking and giving knocks all the time—they're not mealy-mouthed. This seems perfectly innocuous as gossip goes."

Thus back-handed by the words 'thin-skinned' and 'mealy-mouthed', Soames said testily:

"The whole thing's extremely petty."

"Well, sir, you know, I rather agree. Good-morning!" and the cheery man blandly returned to his file.

The fellow was like an india-rubber ball! Soames clenched his top-hat. Now or never he must make him bound.

"If your correspondent thinks she can vent her spleen in print with impunity, she will find herself very much mistaken." He waited for the effect. There was absolutely none. "Good-morning!" he said, and turned on his heel.

Somehow it had not been so friendly as he had expected. Michael's words "The Press is a sensitive plant" came into his mind He shouldn't mention his visit.

Two days later, picking up the *Evening Sun* at the Connoisseurs', he saw the word 'Foggartism'. H'm! A leader!

"Of the panaceas rife among the young hopefuls in politics, perhaps the most absurd is one which goes by the name of Foggartism. We are in a position to explain the nature of this patent remedy for what is supposed to be the national ill-health before it has been put on the market. Based on Sir James Foggart's book, *The Parlous State of England*, the main article of faith in this crazy creed would appear to be the depletion of British man-power. According to its prophets, we are to despatch to the ends of the Empire hundreds of thousands of our boys and girls as soon as they leave school. Quite apart from the rank impossibility of absorbing them into the life of the slowly developing Dominions, we are to lose this vital stream of labour and defensive material, in order that twenty years hence the demand from our Dominions may equal the supplying power of Great Britain. A crazier proposition was never conceived in woolly brains. Well does the word Foggartism characterise such a proposition. Alongside this emigration 'stunt'—for there is no other term which suits its sensational character—rises a feeble back-to-the-land propaganda. The keystone of the whole professes to be the doctrine that the standard of British wages and living now preclude us from any attempt to rival German production, or to recover our trade with Europe. Such a turning of the tail on our industrial supremacy has probably never before been mooted in this country. The sooner these cheap-jack gerrymanders of British policy realise that the British voter will have nothing to do with so crack-brained a scheme, the sooner it will come to the still birth which is its inevitable fate."

Whatever attention Soames had given to *The Parlous State of England*, he could not be accused of anything so rash as a faith in Foggartism. If Foggartism were killed to-morrow, he, with his inherent distrust of theories and ideas, his truly English pragmatism, could not help feeling that Michael would be well rid of a white elephant. What disquieted him, however, was the suspicion that he himself had inspired this article. Was this that too-cheery fellow's retort?

Decidedly, he should not mention his visit when he dined in South Square that evening.

The presence of a strange hat on the sarcophagus warned him of a fourth party. Mr. Blythe, in fact, with a cocktail in his hand and an olive in his mouth, was talking to Fleur, who was curled up on a cushion by the fire.

"You know Mr. Blythe, Dad?"

Another editor! Soames extended his hand with caution.

Mr. Blythe swallowed the olive. "It's of no importance," he said.

"Well," said Fleur. "*I* think you ought to put it all off, and let them feel they've made fools of themselves."

"Does Michael think that, Mrs. Mont?"

"No; Michael's got his shirt out!" And they all looked round at Michael, who was coming in.

He certainly had a somewhat headstrong air.

According to Michael, they must take it by the short hairs and give as good as they got, or they might as well put up the shutters. They were sent to Parliament to hold their own opinions, not those stuck into them by Fleet Street. If they genuinely believed the Foggart policy to be the only way to cure unemployment, and stem the steady drain into the towns, they must say so, and not be stampeded by every little newspaper attack that came along. Common sense was on their side, and common sense, if you aired it enough, won through in the end. The opposition to Foggartism was really based on an intention to force lower wages and longer hours on Labour, only they daren't say so in so many words. Let the papers jump through their hoops as much as they liked. He would bet that when Foggartism had been six months before the public, they would be eating half their words with an air of eating someone else's! And suddenly he turned to Soames:

"I suppose, sir, you didn't go down about that paragraph?"

Soames, privately, and as a business man, had always so conducted himself that, if cornered, he need never tell a direct untruth. Lies were not English, not even good form. Looking down his nose, he said slowly:

"Well, I let them know that I knew that woman's name."

Fleur frowned; Mr. Blythe reached out and took some salted almonds.

"What did I tell you, sir?" said Michael. "They always get back on you. The Press has a tremendous sense of dignity; and corns on both feet; eh, Mr. Blythe?"

Mr. Blythe said weightily: "It's a very human institution, young man. It prefers to criticise rather than to be criticised."

"I thought," said Fleur icily, "that I was to be left to my own cudgels."

The discussion broke back to Foggartism, but Soames sat brooding. He would never again interfere in what didn't concern himself. Then, like all who love, he perceived the bitterness of his fate. He had only meddled with what *did* concern himself—her name, her happiness; and she resented it. Basket in which were all his eggs, to the end of his days he must go on walking gingerly, balancing her so that she was not upset, spilling his only treasure.

She left them over the wine that only Mr. Blythe was drinking. Soames heard an odd word now and then, gathered that this great frog-chap was going to burst next week in *The Outpost*, gathered that Michael was to get on to his hind legs in the House at the first opportunity. It was all a muzz of words to him. When they rose, he said to Michael:

"I'll take myself off."

"We're going down to the House, sir: won't you stay with Fleur?"

"No," said Soames; "I must be getting back."

Michael looked at him closely.

"I'll just tell her you're going."

Soames had wrapped himself into his coat, and was opening the door when he smelled violet soap. A bare arm had come round his neck. He felt soft pressure against his back. "Sorry, Dad, for being such a pig."

Soames shook his head.

"No," said her voice; "you're not going like that."

She slipped between him and the door. Her clear eye looked into his; her teeth gleamed, very white. "Say you forgive me!"

"There's no end to it," said Soames.

She thrust her lips against his nose. "There! Good-night, ducky! I know I'm spoiled!"

Soames gave her body a convulsive little squeeze, opened the door and went out without a word.

Under Big Ben boys were calling—political news, he supposed. Those Labour chaps were going to fall—some editor had got them into trouble. He would! Well—one down, t'other come on! It was all remote to him. She alone—she alone mattered.

## Chapter XII

### MICHAEL MUSES

MICHAEL and Mr. Blythe sought the Mother of Parliaments and found her in commotion. Liberalism had refused, and Labour was falling from its back. A considerable number of people were in Parliament Square contemplating Big Ben and hoping for sensation.

"I'm not going in," said Michael. "There won't be a division to-night. General Election's a foregone conclusion, now. I want to think."

"One will go up for a bit," said Mr. Blythe; and they parted, Michael returning to the streets. The night was clear, and he had a longing to hear the voice of his country. But—where? For his countrymen would be discussing this pro and that con, would be mentioning each his personal 'grief'—here the Income Tax, there the dole, the names of leaders, the word Communism. Nowhere would he catch the echo of the uneasiness in the hearts of all. The Tories—as Fleur had predicted—would come in now. The country would catch at the anodyne of 'strong stable government'. But could strong stable government remove the inherent canker, the lack of balance in the top-heavy realm? Could it still the gnawing ache which everybody felt, and nobody would express?

'Spoiled,' thought Michael, 'by our past prosperity. We shall never admit it,' he thought, 'never! And yet in our bones we feel it!'

England with the silver spoon in her mouth and no longer the teeth to hold it there, or the will to part with it! And her very qualities—the latent 'grit', the power to take things smiling, the lack of nerves and imagination! Almost vices, now, perpetuating the rash belief that England could still 'muddle through' without special effort, although with every year there was less chance of recovering from shock, less time in which to exercise the British 'virtues'. 'Slow in the uptak',' thought Michael, 'it's a ghastly fault in 1924.'

Thus musing, he turned East. Mid-theatre-hour, and the 'Great Parasite'—as Sir James Foggart called it—was lying inert and bright. He walked the length of wakeful Fleet Street into the City so delirious by day, so dead by night. Here England's wealth was snoozing off the day's debauch. Here were all the frame and filaments of English credit. And based on—what? On food and raw material from which England, undefended in the air, might be cut off by a fresh war; on Labour, too big for European boots. And yet that credit stood high still, soothing all with its 'panache' —save, perhaps, receivers of the dole. With her promise to pay, England could still purchase anything, except a quiet heart.

And Michael walked on—through Whitechapel, busy still and coloured—into Mile End. The houses had become low, as if to give the dwellers a better view of stars they couldn't reach. He had crossed a frontier. Here was a different race almost; another England, but as happy-go-lucky and as hand-to-mouth as the England of Fleet Street and the City. Aye, and more! For the England in Mile End knew that whatever she felt could have n(

effect on policy. Mile on mile, without an end, the low grey streets stretched towards the ultimate deserted grass. Michael did not follow them, but coming to a cinema, turned in.

The show was far advanced. Bound and seated in front of the bad cowboy on a bronco, the heroine was crossing what Michael shrewdly suspected to be the film company's pet paddock. Every ten seconds she gave way to John T. Bronson, manager of the Tucsonville Copper Mine, devouring the road in his 60-h.p. Packard, to cut her off before she reached the Pima river. Michael contemplated his fellow gazers. Lapping it up! Strong stable government —not much! This was their anodyne and they could not have enough of it. He saw the bronco fall, dropped by a shot from John T. Bronson, and the screen disclose the words: "Hairy Pete grows desperate. . . . 'You shall not have her, Bronson.'" Quite! He was throwing her into the river instead, to the words: "John T. Bronson dives." There he goes! He has her by her flowing hair! But Hairy Pete is kneeling on the bank. The bullets chip the water. Through the heroine's fair perforated shoulder the landscape is almost visible. What is that sound? Yes! John T. Bronson is setting his teeth! He lands, he drags her out. From his cap he takes his automatic. Still dry—thank God!

"Look to yourself, Hairy Pete!" A puff of smoke. Pete squirms and bites the sand—he seems almost to absorb the desert. "Hairy Pete gets it for keeps!" Slow music, slower! John T. Bronson raises the reviving form. Upon the bank of the Pima river they stand embraced, and the sun sets. "At last, my dinky love!"

'Pom, pom! that's the stuff!' thought Michael, returning to the light of night: 'Back to the Land! "Plough the fields and scatter" —when they can get this? Not much!' And he turned West again, taking a seat on the top of a bus beside a man with grease-stains on his clothes. They travelled in silence till Michael said:

"What do you make of the political situation, sir?"

The possible plumber replied, without turning his head:

"I should say they've over-reached theirselves."

"Ought to have fought on Russia—oughtn't they?"

"Russia—that cock won't fight either. No—ought to 'ave 'eld on to the Spring, an' fought on a good stiff Budget."

"Real class issue?"

"Yus!"

"But do you think class politics can wipe out unemployment?"

The man's mouth moved under his moustache as if mumbling a new idea.

"Ah! I'm fed up with politics; in work to-day and out to-morrow —what's the good of politics that can't give you a permanent job?"

"That's it."

"Reparations," said his neighbour; "*we're* not goin' to benefit by reparations. The workin' classes ought to stand together in every country." And he looked at Michael to see how he liked *that*.

"A good many people thought so before the war; and see what happened."

"Ah!" said the man, "and what good's it done us?"

"Have you thought of emigrating to the Dominions?"

The man shook his head.

"Don't like what I see of the Austrylians and Canydians."

"Confirmed Englishman—like myself."

"That's right," said the man. "So long, Mister," and he got off.

Michael travelled till the bus put him down under Big Ben, and it was nearly twelve. Another election! Could he stand a second time without showing his true colours? Not the faintest hope of making Foggartism clear to a rural constituency in three weeks! If he spoke from now till the day of the election, they would merely think he held rather extreme views on Imperial Preference. which, by the way, he did. He could never tell the electorate that he thought England was on the wrong tack—one might just as well not stand. He could never buttonhole the ordinary voter, and say to him: "Look here, you know, there's no earthly hope of any real improvement for another ten years; in the meantime we must face the music, and pay more for everything, so that twenty years hence we may be safe from possible starvation, and self-supporting within the Empire." It wasn't done. Nor could he say to his Committee: "My friends, I represent a policy that no one else does, so far."

No! If he meant to stand again, he must just get the old wheezes off his chest. But did he mean to stand again? Few people had less conceit than Michael—he knew himself for a lightweight. But he had got this bee into his bonnet; the longer he lived the more it buzzed, the more its buzz seemed the voice of one crying in the wilderness, and that wilderness his country. To stop up that buzzing in his ears; to turn his back on old Blythe; to stifle his convictions, and yet remain in Parliament—he could not! It was like the war over again. Once in, you couldn't get out. And he was 'in'—committeed to something deeper far than the top dressings of Party politics. Foggartism had a definite solution of England's troubles to work towards—an independent, balanced

Empire; an England safe in the air, and free from unemployment
—with Town and Country once more in some sort of due proportion! Was it such a hopeless dream? Apparently!

'Well,' thought Michael, putting his latch-key in his door, 'they
may call me what kind of a bee fool they like—I shan't budge.'
He went up to his dressing-room and, opening the window, leaned
out.

The rumourous town still hummed; the sky was faintly coloured
by reflection from its million lights. A spire was visible, some
stars; the tree foliage in the Square hung flat, unstirred by wind.
Peaceful and almost warm—the night. Michael remembered a
certain evening—the last London air-raid of the war. From his
convalescent hospital he had watched it for three hours.

'What fools we all are not to drop fighting in the air,' he thought.
'Well, if we don't, I shall go all out for a great air force—all hangs,
for us, on safety from air attack. Even the wise can understand
that.'

Two men had stopped beneath his window, talking. One was
his next-door neighbour.

"Mark my words," said his neighbour, "the election'll see a big
turnover."

"Yes; and what are you going to do with it?" said the other.

"Let things alone; they'll right themselves. I'm sick of all this
depressing twaddle. A shilling off the Income Tax, and you'll see."

"How are you going to deal with the Land?"

"Oh! damn the Land! Leave it to itself, that's all the farmers
really want. The more you touch it, the worse it gets."

"Let the grass grow under your feet?"

The neighbour laughed. "That's about it. Well, what else *can*
you do—the Country won't have it. Good night!"

Sounds of a door, of footsteps. A car drove by; a moth flew in
Michael's face. "The Country won't have it!" Policies! What but
mental yawns, long shrugs of the shoulders, trustings to Luck!
What else could they be? *The Country wouldn't have it!* And
Big Ben struck twelve.


## Chapter XIII

### INCEPTION OF THE CASE

THERE are people in every human hive born to focus talk; perhaps
their magnetism draws the human tongue, or their lives are lived

at an acute angle. Of such was Marjorie Ferrar—one of the most talked-of young women in London. Whatever happened to her was rumoured at once in that collection of the busy and the idle called Society. That she had been ejected from a drawing-room was swiftly known. Fleur's letters about her became current gossip. The reasons for ejectment varied from truth to a legend that she had lifted Michael from the arms of his wife.

The origins of lawsuits are seldom simple. And when Soames called it all 'a storm in a tea-cup', he might have been right if Lord Charles Ferrar had not been so heavily in debt that he had withdrawn his daughter's allowance; if, too, a Member for a Scottish borough, Sir Alexander MacGown, had not for some time past been pursuing her with the idea of marriage. Wealth made out of jute, a rising Parliamentary repute, powerful physique, and a determined character, had not advanced Sir Alexander's claims in twelve months so much as the withdrawal of her allowance advanced them in a single night. Marjorie Ferrar was, indeed, of those who can always get money at a pinch, but even to such come moments when they have seriously to consider what kind of pinch. In proportion to her age and sex, she was 'dipped' as badly as her father, and the withdrawal of her allowance was in the nature of a last straw. In a moment of discouragement she consented to an engagement, not yet to be made public. When the incident at Fleur's came to Sir Alexander's ears, he went to his betrothed flaming. What could he do?

"Nothing, of course; don't be silly, Alec! Who cares?"

"The thing's monstrous. Let me go and exact an apology from this old blackguard."

"Father's been, and he wouldn't give it. He's got a chin you could hang a kettle on."

"Now, look here, Marjorie, you've got to make our engagement public, and let me get to work on him. I won't have this story going about."

Marjorie Ferrar shook her head.

"Oh! no, my dear. You're still on probation. I don't care a tuppenny ice about the story."

"Well, I do; and I'm going to that fellow to-morrow."

Marjorie Ferrar studied his face—its brown, burning eyes, its black, stiff hair, its jaw—shivered slightly, and had a brain-wave.

"You will do nothing of the kind, Alec, or you'll spill your ink. My father wants me to bring an action. He says I shall get swinging damages."

305

The Scotsman in MacGown applauded, the lover quailed.

"That may be very unpleasant for you," he muttered, "unless the brute settles out of Court."

"Of course he'll settle. I've got all his evidence in my vanity-bag."

MacGown gripped her by the shoulders and gave her a fierce kiss.

"If he doesn't, I'll break every bone in his body."

"My dear! He's nearly seventy, I should think."

"H'm! Isn't there a young man in the same boat with him?"

"Michael? Oh! Michael's a dear. I couldn't have his bones broken."

"Indeed!" said MacGown. "Wait till he launches this precious .Foggartism they talk of—dreary rot! I'll eat him!"

"Poor little Michael!"

"I heard something about an American boy, too."

"Oh!" said Marjorie Ferrar, releasing herself from his grip. "A bird of passage—don't bother about him."

"Have you got a lawyer?"

"Not yet."

"I'll send you mine. He'll make them sit up!"

She remained pensive after he had left her, distrusting her own brain-wave. If only she weren't so hard up! She had learned during this month of secret engagement that "Nothing for nothing and only fair value for sixpence" ruled North of the Tweed as well as South. He had taken a good many kisses and given her one trinket which she dared not take to 'her Uncle's'. It began to look as if she would have to marry him. The prospect was in some ways not repulsive—he was emphatically a man; her father would take care that she only married him on terms as liberal as his politics; and perhaps her motto 'Live dangerously' could be even better carried out with him than without. Resting inert in a long chair, she thought of Francis Wilmot. Hopeless as husband, he might be charming as lover, naïve, fresh, unknown in London, absurdly devoted, oddly attractive, with his lithe form, dark eyes, engaging smile. Too old-fashioned for words, he had made it clear already that he wanted to marry her. He was a baby. But until she was beyond his reach, she had begun to feel that he was beyond hers. After? Well, who knew? She lived in advance, dangerously, with Francis Wilmot. In the meantime this action for slander was a bore! And shaking the idea out of her head, she ordered her horse, changed her clothes, and repaired to the Row. After that she again

306

changed her clothes, went to the Cosmopolis Hotel, and danced with her mask-faced partner and Francis Wilmot. After that she changed her clothes once more, went to a first night, partook of supper afterwards with the principal actor and his party, and was in bed by two o'clock.

Like most reputations, that of Marjorie Ferrar received more than its deserts. If you avow a creed of indulgence, you will be indulged by the credulous. In truth she had only had two love-affairs passing the limits of decorum; had smoked opium once, and been sick over it; and had sniffed cocaine just to see what it was like. She gambled only with discretion, and chiefly on race-horses; drank with strict moderation and a good head; smoked of course, but the purest cigarettes she could get, and through a holder. If she had learned suggestive forms of dancing, she danced them but once in a blue moon. She rarely rode at a five-barred gate, and that only on horses whose powers she knew. To be in the know she read, of course, anything 'extreme', but would not go out of her way to do so. She had flown, but just to Paris. She drove a car well, and of course fast, but never to the danger of herself, and seldom to the real danger of the public. She had splendid health, and took care of it in private. She could always sleep at ten minutes' notice, and when she sat up half the night, slept half the day. She was 'in' with the advanced theatre, but took it as it came. Her book of poems, which had received praise be-cause they emanated from one of a class supposed to be unpoetic, was remarkable not so much for irregularity of thought as for irregularity of metre. She was, in sum, credited with a too strict observance of her expressed creed: 'Take life in both hands, and eat it.'

This was why Sir Alexander MacGown's lawyer sat on the edge of his chair in her studio the following morning, and gazed at her intently. He knew her renown better than Sir Alexander. Messrs. Settlewhite and Stark liked to be on the right side of a matter before they took it up. How far would this young lady, with her very attractive appearance and her fast reputation, stand fire? For costs—they had Sir Alexander's guarantee and the word 'traitress' was a good enough beginning; but in cases of word against word, it was ill predicting.

Her physiognomy impressed Mr. Settlewhite favourably. She would not 'get rattled' in Court, if he was any judge; nor had she the Aubrey Beardsley cast of feature he had been afraid of, that might alienate a jury. No! an upstanding young woman with a good blue eye and popular hair. She would do, if her story were all right.

Marjorie Ferrar, in turn, scrutinised one who looked as if he might take things out of her hands. Long-faced, with grey deep eyes under long dark lashes, all his hair, and good clothes, he was as well preserved a man of sixty as she had ever seen.

"What do you want me to tell you, Mr. Settlewhite?"

"The truth."

"Oh! but naturally. Well, I was just saying to Mr. Quinsey that Mrs. Mont was very eager to form a 'salon', and had none of the right qualities, and the old person who overheard me thought I was insulting her——"

"That all?"

"Well, I may have said she was fond of lions; and so she is."

"Yes; but why did he call you a traitress?"

"Because she was his daughter and my hostess, I suppose."

"Will this Mr. Quinsey confirm you?"

"Philip Quinsey?—oh! rather! He's in my pocket."

"Did anybody else overhear you running her down?"

She hesitated a second. "No."

'First lie!' thought Mr. Settlewhite, with his peculiar sweet-sarcastic smile. "What about an American?"

Marjorie Ferrar laughed. "He won't say so, anyway."

"An admirer?"

"No. He's going back to America."

'Second lie!' thought Mr. Settlewhite. 'But she tells them well.'

"You want an apology you can show to those who overheard the insult; and what we can get, I suppose?"

"Yes. The more the better."

'Speaking the truth there,' thought Mr. Settlewhite. "Are you hard up?"

"Couldn't well be harder."

Mr. Settlewhite put one hand on each knee, and reared his slim body.

"You don't want it to come into Court?"

"No; though I suppose it might be rather fun."

Mr. Settlewhite smiled again.

"That entirely depends on how many skeletons you have in your cupboard."

Marjorie Ferrar also smiled.

"I shall put everything in your hands," she said.

"Not the skeletons, my dear young lady. Well, we'll serve him and see how the cat jumps; but he's a man of means and a lawyer."

"I think he'll hate having anything about his daughter brought out in Court."

"Yes," said Mr. Settlewhite, drily. "So should I."

"And she *is* a little snob, you know."

"Ah! Did you happen to use that word?"

"N-no; I'm pretty sure I didn't."

'Third lie!' thought Mr. Settlewhite: 'not so well told.'

"It makes a difference. Quite sure?"

"Not quite."

"He says you did?"

"Well, I told him he was a liar."

"Oh! did you? And they heard you?"

"Rather!"

"That may be important."

"I don't believe he'll say I called her a snob, in Court, anyway."

"That's very shrewd, Miss Ferrar," said Mr. Settlewhite. "I think we shall do."

And with a final look at her from under his long lashes, he stalked, thin and contained, to the door.

Three days later Soames received a legal letter. It demanded a formal apology, and concluded with the words "failing it, action will be taken." Twice in his life he had brought actions himself; once for breach of contract, once for divorce; and now to be sued for slander! In every case he had been the injured party, in his own opinion. He was certainly not going to apologise. Under the direct threat he felt much calmer. He had nothing to be ashamed of. He would call that 'baggage' a traitress to her face again to-morrow, and pay for the luxury, if need be. His mind roved back to when, in the early 'eighties, as a very young lawyer, he had handled his Uncle Swithin's defence against a fellow member of the Walpole Club. Swithin had called him in public "a little touting whipper-snapper of a parson." He remembered how he had whittled the charge down to the word 'whipper-snapper', by proving the plaintiff's height to be five feet four, his profession the church, his habit the collection of money for the purpose of small-clothing the Fiji islanders. The jury had assessed 'whipper-snapper' at ten pounds—Soames always believed the small clothes had done it. His Counsel had made great game of them—Bobstay, Q.C. There *were* Counsel in those days; the Q.C.'s had been better than the K.C.'s were. Bobstay would have gone clean through this 'baggage' and come out on the other side. Uncle Swithin had asked him to dinner afterwards and given him York ham with Madeira sauce, and his special Heidsieck. He had never given anybody anything else. Well! There must still be cross-examiners who could tear a reputation to tatters, especially if there wasn't one to tear. And one could always settle at the last moment if one wished. There was no possibility anyway of Fleur being dragged in as witness or anything of that sort.

He was thunder-struck, a week later, when Michael rang him up at Mapledurham to say that Fleur had been served with a writ for libel in letters containing among others the expression 'a snake of the first water' and 'she hasn't a moral about her.'

Soames went cold all over. "I told you not to let her go about abusing that woman."

"I know; but she doesn't consult me every time she writes a letter to a friend."

"Pretty friend!" said Soames into the mouthpiece. "This is a nice pair of shoes!"

"Yes, sir; I'm very worried. She's absolutely spoiling for a fight —won't hear of an apology."

Soames grunted so deeply that Michael's ear tingled forty miles away.

"In the meantime, what shall we do?"

"Leave it to me," said Soames. "I'll come up to-night. Has she any evidence to support those words?"

"Well, she says——"

"No," said Soames, abruptly, "don't tell me over the phone." And he rang off. He went out on to the lawn. Women! Petted and spoiled—thought they could say what they liked! And so they could till they came up against another woman. He stopped by the boat-house and gazed at the river. The water was nice and clean, and there it was—flowing down to London to get all dirty! That feverish, quarrelsome business up there! Now he would have to set to and rake up all he could against this Ferrar woman, and frighten her off. It was distasteful. But nothing else for it, if Fleur was to be kept out of Court! Terribly petty. Society lawsuits— who ever got anything out of them, save heart-burning and degradation? Like the war, you might win and regret it ever afterwards, or lose and regret it more. All temper! Jealousy and temper!

In the quiet autumn light, with the savour of smoke in his nostrils from his gardener's first leaf bonfire, Soames felt moral. Here was his son-in-law, wanting to do some useful work in Parlia-

310

THE SILVER SPOON

ment, and make a name for the baby, and Fleur beginning to settle
down and take a position; and now this had come along, and all
the chatterers and busy mockers in Society would be gnashing on
them with their teeth—if they had any! He looked at his shadow
on the bank, grotesquely slanting towards the water as if wanting
to drink. Everything was grotesque, if it came to that! In Society,
England, Europe—shadows scrimmaging and sprawling, scuffling
and posturing; the world just marking time before another Flood!
H'm! He moved towards the river. There went his shadow, plung-
ing in before him! They would all plunge into that mess of cold
water if they didn't stop their squabblings. And, turning abruptly,
he entered his kitchen-garden. Nothing unreal there, and most
things running to seed—stalks, and so on! How to set about raking
up the past of this young woman? Where was it? These young
sparks and fly-by-nights! They all had pasts, no doubt; but the
definite, the concrete bit of immorality alone was of use, and when
it came to the point, was unobtainable, he shouldn't wonder.
People didn't like giving chapter and verse! It was risky, and not
the thing! Tales out of school!

And, among his artichokes, approving of those who did not tell
tales, disapproving of anyone who wanted them told, Soames
resolved grimly that told they must be. The leaf-fire smouldered,
and the artichokes smelled rank, the sun went down behind the
high brick wall mellowed by fifty years of weather; all was peaceful and chilly, except in his heart. Often now, morning or evening,
he would walk among his vegetables—they were real and restful,
and you could eat them. They had better flavour than the green-
grocer's and saved his bill—middlemen's profiteering and all that.
Perhaps they represented atavistic instincts in this great-grandson
of 'Superior Dosset's' father, last of a long line of Forsyte 'agri-
culturists'. He set more and more store by vegetables the older he
grew. When Fleur was a little bit of a thing, he would find her
when he came back from the City, seated among the sunflowers
or blackcurrants, nursing her doll. He had once taken a bee out
of her hair, and the little brute had stung him. Best years he ever
had, before she grew up and took to this gadabout Society business,
associating with women who went behind her back. Apology! So
she wouldn't hear of one? She was in the right. But to be in the
right and have to go into Court because of it, was one of the most
paniful experiences that could be undergone. The Courts existed
to penalise people who were in the right—in divorce, breach of
promise, libel and the rest of it. Those who were in the wrong

311

went to the South of France, or if they did appear, defaulted afterwards and left you to pay your costs. Had he not himself had to
pay them in his action against Bosinney? And in his divorce suit
had not Young Jolyon and Irene been in Italy when he brought it?
And yet, he couldn't bear to think of Fleur eating humble-pie to
that red-haired cat. Among the gathering shadows, his resolve
hardened. Secure evidence that would frighten the baggage into
dropping the whole thing like a hot potato—it was the only way!

## Chapter XIV

### FURTHER CONSIDERATION

THE Government had 'taken their toss' over the Editor—no one
could say precisely why—and Michael sat down to compose his
address. How say enough without saying anything? And having
impetuously written: "Electors of mid-Bucks," he remained for
many moments still as a man who has had too good a dinner. "If"
he traced words slowly—"if you again return me as your representative, I shall do my best for the country according to my lights.
I consider the limitations of armaments, and, failing that, the
security of Britain through the enlargement of our air defences;
the development of home agriculture; the elimination of unemployment through increased emigration to the Dominions; and the
improvement of the national health particularly through the abate-
ment of slums and smoke, to be the most pressing and immediate
concerns of British policy. If I am returned, I shall endeavour to
foster these ends with determination and coherence; and try not to
abuse those whose opinions differ from my own. At my meetings
I shall seek to give you some concrete idea of what is in my mind,
and submit myself to your questioning."

Dared he leave it at that? Could one issue an address containing
no disparagement of the other side, no panegyric of his own?
Would his Committee allow it? Would the electors swallow it?
Well, if his Committee didn't like it—they could turn it down, and
himself with it; only—they wouldn't have time to get another
candidate!

The Committee, indeed, did not like it, but they lumped it; and
the address went out with an effigy on it of Michael, looking, as he
said, like a hairdresser. Thereon he plunged into a fray, which,
like every other, began in the general and ended in the particular.

During the first Sunday lull at Lippinghall, he developed his poultry scheme—by marking out sites, and deciding how water could be laid on. The bailiff was sulky. In his view it was throwing away money. "Fellers like that!" Who was going to teach them the job? He had no time, himself. It would run into hundreds, and might just as well be poured down the gutter. "The townsman's no mortal use on the land, Master Michael."

"So everybody says. But, look here, Tutfield, here are three 'down and outs', two of them ex-Service, and you've got to help me put this through. You say yourself this land's all right for poultry—well, it's doing no good now. Bowman knows every last thing about chickens, set him on to it until these chaps get the hang. Be a good fellow and put your heart into it; you wouldn't like being 'down and out' yourself."

The bailiff had a weakness for Michael, whom he had known from his bottle up. He knew the result, but if Master Michael liked to throw his father's money away, it was no business of his. He even went so far as to mention that he knew "a feller" who had a hut for sale not ten miles away; and that there was "plenty of wood in the copse for the cuttin'."

On the Tuesday after the Government had fallen Michael went up to town and summoned a meeting of his 'down and outs'. They came at three the following day, and he placed them in chairs round the dining-table. Standing under the Goya, like a general about to detail a plan of attack which others would have to execute, he developed his proposal. The three faces expressed little, and that without conviction. Only Bergfeld had known anything of it, before, and his face was the most doubting.

"I don't know in the least," went on Michael, "what you think of it; but you all want jobs—two of you out of doors, and you, Boddick, don't mind what it is, I think."

"That's right, sir," said Boddick, "I'm on."

Michael instantly put him down as the best man of the three.

The other two were silent till Bergfeld said:

"If I had my savings——"

Michael interrupted quickly:

"I'm putting in the capital; you three put in the brains and labour. It's probably not more than a bare living, but I hope it'll be a healthy one. What do *you* say, Mr. Swain?"

The hairdresser, more shadow-stricken than ever, in the glow of Fleur's Spanish room, smiled.

"I'm sure it's very kind of you. I don't mind havin' a try—only, who's goin' to boss the show?"

313

"Co-operation, Mr. Swain."

"Ah!" said the hairdresser; "thought so. But I've seen a lot of tries at that, and it always ends in one bloke swallerin' the rest."

"Very well," said Michael, suddenly, "I'll boss it. But if any of you crane at the job, say so at once, and have done with it. Otherwise I'll get that hut delivered and set up, and we'll start this day month."

Boddick got up, and said: "Right, sir. What about my children?"

"How old, Boddick?"

"Two little girls, four and five."

"Oh! yes!" Michael had forgotten this item. "We must see about that."

Boddick touched his forelock, shook Michael's hand, went out. The other two remained standing.

"Good-bye, Mr. Bergfeld; good-bye, Mr. Swain!"

"If I might——"

"Could I speak to you for a minute?"

"Anything you have to say," said Michael, astutely, "had better be said in each other's presence."

"I've always been used to hair."

'Pity,' thought Michael, 'that Life didn't drop that "h" for him— poor beggar!' "Well, we'll get you a breed of birds that can be shingled," he said. The hairdresser smiled down one side of his face. "Beggars can't be choosers," he remarked.

"I wished to ask you," said Bergfeld, "what system we shall adopt?"

"That's got to be worked out. Here are two books on poultry-keeping; you'd better read one each, and swop."

He noted that Bergfeld took both without remonstrance on the part of Swain.

Seeing them out into the Square, he thought: 'Rum team! It won't work, but they've got their chance.'

A young man who had been standing on the pavement came forward.

"Mr. Michael Mont, M.P.?"

"Yes."

"Mrs. Michael Mont at home?"

"I think so. What do you want?"

"I must see her personally, please."

"Who are you from?"

"Messrs. Settlewhite and Stark—a suit."

"Dressmakers?"

The young man smiled.

"Come in," said Michael. "I'll see if she's at home."

Fleur was in the 'parlour'.

"A young man from some dressmaker's for you, dear."

"Mrs. Michael Mont? In the suit of Ferrar against Mont—libel. Good-day, madam."

Between those hours of four and eight, when Soames arrived from Mapledurham, Michael suffered more than Fleur. To sit and see a legal operation performed on her with all the scientific skill of the British Bar, it was an appalling prospect; and there would be no satisfaction in Marjorie Ferrar's also being on the table, with her inside exposed to the gaze of all! He was only disconcerted, therefore, when Fleur said:

"All right; if she wants to be opened up, she shall be. I know she flew to Paris with Walter Nazing last November; and I've always been told she was Bertie Curfew's mistress for a year."

A Society case—cream for all the cats in Society, muck for all the blowflies in the streets—and Fleur the hub of it! He waited for Soames with impatience. Though 'Old Forsyte's' indignation had started this, Michael turned to him now, as to an anchor let go off a lee shore. The 'old man' had experience, judgment, and a chin; he would know what, except bearing it with a grin, could be done. Gazing at a square foot of study wall which had escaped a framed caricature, he reflected on the underlying savagery of life. He would be eating a lobster to-night that had been slowly boiled alive! This study had been cleaned out by a charwoman whose mother was dying of cancer, whose son had lost a leg in the war, and who looked so jolly tired that he felt quite bad whenever he thought of her. The Bergfelds, Swains and Boddicks of the world —the Camden Towns, and Mile Ends—the devastated regions of France, the rock villages of Italy! Over it all what a thin crust of gentility! Members of Parliament and ladies of fashion, like himself and Fleur, simpering and sucking silver spoons, and now and then dropping spoons and simper, and going for each other like Kilkenny cats!

"What evidence has she got to support those words?" Michael racked his memory. This was going to be a game of bluff. That Walter Nazing and Marjorie Ferrar had flown to Paris together appeared to him of next to no importance. People could still fly in couples with impunity; and as to what had happened afterwards in the great rabbit-warren Outre Manche—Pff! The Bertie Curfew affair was different. Smoke of a year's duration probably had fire

315

behind it. He knew Bertie Curfew, the enterprising director of the 'Ne Plus Ultra Play Society', whose device was a stork swallowing a frog—a long young man, with long young hair that shone and was brushed back, and a long young record; a strange mixture of enthusiasm and contempt, from one to the other of which he passed with extreme suddenness. His sister, of whom he always spoke as 'Poor Norah,' in Michael's opinion was worth ten of him. She ran a Children's House in Bethnal Green, and had eyes from which meanness and evil shrank away.

Big Ben thumped out eight strokes; the Dandie barked, and Michael knew that Soames had come.

Very silent during dinner, Soames opened the discussion over a bottle of Lippinghall Madeira by asking to see the writ.

When Fleur had brought it, he seemed to go into a trance.

'The old boy,' thought Michael, 'is thinking of his past. Wish he'd come to!'

"Well, Father?" said Fleur at last.

As if from long scrutiny of a ghostly Court of Justice, Soames turned his eyes on his daughter's face.

"You won't eat your words, I suppose?"

Fleur tossed her now de-shingled head. "Do you want me to?"

"Can you substantiate them? You mustn't rely on what was told you—that isn't evidence."

"I know that Amabel Nazing came here and said that she didn't mind Walter flying to Paris with Marjorie Ferrar, but that she did object to not having been told beforehand, so that she herself could have flown to Paris with somebody else."

"We could subpœna that young woman," said Soames.

Fleur shook her head. "She'd never give Walter away in Court."

"H'm! What else about this Miss Ferrar?"

"Everybody knows of her relationship with Bertie Curfew."

"Yes," Michael put in, "and between 'everybody knows' and 'somebody tells' is a great gap fixed."

Soames nodded.

"She just wants money out of us," cried Fleur; "she's always hard up. As if she cared whether people thought her moral or not! She despises morality—all her set do."

"Ah! Her view of morality!" said Soames, deeply; he was suddenly seeing a British jury confronted by a barrister describing the modern view of morals: "No need, perhaps, to go into personal details."

Michael started up.

316

"By Jove, sir, you've hit it! If you can get her to admit that she's read certain books, seen or acted in certain plays, danced certain dances, worn certain clothes——" He fell back again into his chair; what if the other side started asking Fleur the same questions? Was it not the fashion to keep abreast of certain things, however moral one might really be? Who could stand up and profess to be shocked, to-day?

"Well?" said Soames.

"Only that one's own point of view isn't quite a British jury's, sir. Even yours and ours, I expect, don't precisely tally."

Soames looked at his daughter. He understood. Loose talk—afraid of being out of the fashion—evil communication corrupting all profession of good manners! Still, no jury could look at her face without—who could resist the sudden raising of those white lids? Besides, she was a mother, and the older woman wasn't; or if she was—she shouldn't be! No, he held to his idea. A clever fellow at the Bar could turn the whole thing into an indictment of the fast set and modern morality, and save all the invidiousness of exposing a woman's private life.

"You give me the names of her set and those books and plays and dancing clubs and things," he said. "I'll have the best man at the Bar."

Michael rose from the little conference somewhat eased in mind. If the matter could be shifted from the particular to the general; if, instead of attacking Marjorie Ferrar's practice, the defence could attack her theory, it would not be so dreadful. Soames took him apart in the hall.

"I shall want all the information I can get about that young man and her."

Michael's face fell.

"You can't get it from me, sir, I haven't got it."

"She must be frightened," said Soames. "If I can frighten her, I can probably settle it out of Court without an apology."

"I see; use the information out of Court, but not in."

Soames nodded. "I shall tell them that we shall justify. Give me the young man's address."

"Macbeth Chambers, Bloomsbury. It's close to the British Museum. But do remember, sir, that to air Miss Ferrar's linen in Court will be as bad for us as for her."

Again Soames nodded.

When Fleur and her father had gone up, Michael lit a cigarette, and passed back into the 'parlour'. He sat down at the clavichord.

The instrument made very little noise—so he could strum on it without fear of waking the eleventh baronet. From a Spanish tune picked up three years ago on his honeymoon, whose savagery always soothed him, his fingers wandered on: "I got a crown, you got a crown—all God's childern got a crown! Eb'ryone dat talk 'bout 'Eaben ain't goin' dere. All God's childern got a crown."

Glass lustres on the wall gleamed out at him. As a child he had loved the colours of his aunt Pamela's glass chandeliers in the panelled rooms at Brook Street; but when he knew what was what, he and everyone had laughed at them. And now lustres had come in again; and Aunt Pamela had gone out! "She had a crown—he had a crown——" Confound that tune! *"Auprès de ma blonde— il fait bon—fait bon—fait bon; Auprès de ma blonde, il fait bon dormir."*

His 'blonde'—not so very blonde, either—would be in bed by now. Time to go up! But still he strummed on, and his mind wandered in and out—of poultry and politics, Old Forsyte, Fleur, Foggartism, and the Ferrar girl—like a man in a mælstrom whirling round with his head just above water. Who was it said the landing-place for modernity was a change of heart; the re-birth of a belief that life was worth while, and better life attainable? 'Better life?' Prerogative of priests? Not now. Humanity had got to save itself! To save itself—what was that, after all, but expression of 'the will to live'? But did humanity will to live as much as it used? That was the point. Michael stopped strumming and listened to the silence. Not even a clock ticking—time was inhospitable in 'parlours'; and England asleep outside. Was the English 'will to live' as strong as ever; or had they all become so spoiled, so sensitive to life, that they had weakened on it? Had they sucked their silver spoon so long that, threatened with a spoon of bone, they preferred to get down from table? 'I don't believe it,' thought Michael, 'I won't believe it. Only where are we going? Where am I going? Where are all God's children going?' To bed, it seemed!

And Big Ben struck: One.

# PART II

## Chapter I

## MICHAEL MAKES HIS SPEECH

WHEN in the new Parliament Michael rose to deliver his maiden effort towards the close of the debate on the King's Speech, he had some notes in his hand and not an idea in his head. His heart was beating and his knees felt weak. The policy he was charged to express, if not precisely new in concept, was in reach and method so much beyond current opinion that he awaited nothing but laughter. His would be a stray wind carrying the seed of a new herb into a garden, so serried and so full that no corner would welcome its growth. There was a plant called Chinese weed which having got hold never let go, and spread till it covered everything. Michael desired for Foggartism the career of Chinese weed; but all he expected was the like of what he had seen at Monterey on his tour round the world after the war. Chance had once brought to that Californian shore the seeds of the Japanese yew. In thick formation the little dark trees had fought their way inland to a distance of some miles. That battalion would never get farther now that native vegetation had been consciously roused against it; but its thicket stood—a curious and strong invader.

His first period had been so rehearsed that neither vacant mind nor dry mouth could quite prevent delivery. Straightening his waistcoat and jerking his head back, he regretted that the speech from the throne foreshadowed no coherent and substantial policy such as might hope to free the country from its present plague of under-employment and over-population. Economically speaking, any foreseeing interpretation of the course of affairs must now place Britain definitely in the orbit of the overseas world. . . . ("Oh! oh!") Ironical laughter so soon and sudden cleared Michael's mind and relaxed his lips; and, with the grin that gave his face a certain charm, he resumed:

Speakers on all sides of the House, dwelling on the grave nature of the Unemployment problem, had pinned their faith to the full recapture of European trade, some in one way, some in another. August as they were, he wished very humbly to remark that they could not eat cake and have it. (*Laughter*.) Did they contend that wages in Britain must come down and working hours be lengthened; or did they assert that European wages must go up, and European working hours be shortened? No, they had not had the temerity. Britain, which was to rid itself of unemployment in the ways suggested, was the only important country in the world which had to buy about seven-tenths of its food, and of whose population well-nigh six-sevenths lived in towns. It employed those six-sevenths in producing articles in some cases too dearly for European countries to buy, and yet it had to sell a sufficient surplus above the normal exchanges of trade to pay for seven-tenths of the wherewithal to keep its producers alive. (*A laugh*.) If this was a joke, it was a grim one. (*A voice: "You have forgotten the carrying trade."*) He accepted the honourable Member's correction, and hoped that he felt happy about the future of that trade. It was, he feared, a somewhat shrinking asset.

At this moment in his speech Michael himself became a somewhat shrinking asset, overwhelmed by a sudden desire to drop Foggartism and sit down. The cool attention, the faint smiles, the expression on the face of a past Prime Minister, seemed conspiring towards his subsidence. 'How young—oh! how young you are!' they seemed to say. 'We sat here before you were breeched.' And he agreed with them completely. Still there was nothing for it but to go on—with Fleur in the Ladies' Gallery, old Blythe in the Distinguished Strangers'; yes, and something stubborn in his heart! Clenching the notes in his hand, therefore, he proceeded:

In spite of the war, and because of the war, the population of their island had increased by 2,000,000. Emigration had fallen from over 200,000 to 100,000. And this state of things was to be remedied by the mere process of recapturing to the full European trade which, quite obviously, had no intention of being so recaptured. What alternative, then, was there? Some honourable Members, he was afraid not many, would be familiar with the treatise of Sir James Foggart, entitled *The Parlous State of England*. (*"Hear, hear:" from a back Labour bench*.) He remembered to have read in a certain organ, or perhaps he should say harmonium, of the Press, for it was not a very deep-voiced instrument—(*laughter*) —that no such crack-brained policy had ever been devised for British consumption. (*"Hear, hear!"*) Certainly Foggartism was mad enough to look ahead, to be fundamental, and to ask the

320

country to face its own position and the music into the bargain. . . .

About to go over 'the top'—with public confession of his faith trembling behind his lips—Michael was choked by the sudden thought: 'Is it all right—is it what I think it, or am I an ignorant fool?' He swallowed vigorously, and staring straight before him, went on:

"Foggartism deprecates surface measures for a people in our position; it asks the country to fix its mind on a date—say twenty years hence—a minute in a nation's life—and to work steadily and coherently up to that date. It demands recognition of the need to make the British Empire, with its immense resources mostly latent, a self-sufficing unit. Imperialists will ask: What is there new in that? The novelty lies in degree and in method. Foggartism urges that the British people should be familiarised with the Empire by organised tours and propaganda on a great scale. It urges a vast increase—based on this familiarisation—of controlled and equipped emigration from these shores. But it has been found impossible, as honourable members well know, to send out suitable grown folk in any adequate quantity, because confirmed town-dwellers with their town tastes and habits, and their physique already impaired by town life, are of little use in the Dominions, while the few still on the English land cannot be spared. Foggartism, therefore, would send out boys and girls, between the ages of fifteen, or perhaps sixteen, and eighteen, in great numbers. The House is aware that experiments in this direction have already been made, with conspicuous success, but such experiments are but a drop in the bucket. This is a matter which can only be tackled in the way that things were tackled during the war. Development of child emigration is wanted, in fact, on the same scale and with the same energy as was manifested in Munitions after a certain most honourable Member had put his shoulder to that wheel—multiplication a hundredfold. Although the idea must naturally prove abortive without the utmost good-will and co-operating energy on the part of the Dominions, I submit that this co-operation is not beyond the bounds of hope. The present hostility of people in the Dominions towards British immigrants is due to their very reasonable distrust of the usefulness of adult immigrants from this country. Once they have malleable youth to deal with, that drawback vanishes. In fact, the opening up of these vast new countries is like the progress of a rolling snowball, each little bit of 'all right'—I beg the House's pardon—picks up another little bit; and there is no limit to the cumulative possibilities if a start is made at the right end

321

and the scheme pushed and controlled by the right people." Some-one behind him said: "Talking through his hat." Michael paused, disconcerted; then, snatching at his bitt, went on: "A job of this sort half done is better left alone, but in the war, when something was found necessary, it *was* done, and men were always available for the doing of it. I put it to the House that the condition of our country now demands efforts almost as great as then."

He could see that some members were actually listening to him with attention, and, taking a deep breath, he went on:

"Leaving out Ireland——" (*A voice: "Why?"*) "I prefer not to touch on anything that does not like to be touched——" (*laughter*) "the present ratio of white population between Britain and the rest of the Empire is roughly in the nature of five to two. Child Emigra-tion on a great scale will go far to equalise this ratio within twenty years; the British character of the British Empire will be established for ever, and supply and demand between the Mother Country and the Dominions will be levelled up." (*A voice: "The Dominions will then supply themselves."*) "The honourable Member will forgive me if I doubt that, for some time to come. We have the start in the machinery of manufacture. It may, of course, be five, seven, ten years before unemployment here comes down even to the pre-war rate, but can you point to any other plan which will really decrease it? I am all for good wages and moderate working hours. I believe the standard in Britain and the new countries, though so much higher than the European, is only a decent minimum, and in some cases does not reach it; I want better wages, even more moderate working hours; and the want is common among working men wherever the British flag flies." (*"Hear, hear!"*) "They are not going back on that want; and it is no good supposing that they are!" (*"Hear, hear!" "Oh! oh!"*) "The equalisation of demand and supply *within the Empire* is the only way of preserving and improving the standards of life, which are now recognised as necessary on British soil. The world has so changed that the old maxim 'buy in the cheapest, sell in the dearest market' is standing on its head so far as England is concerned. Free Trade was never a principle——" (*"Oh! oh!" "Hear, hear!" and laughter.*) "Oh! well, it was born twins with expediency, and the twins have got mixed, and are both looking uncommonly peeky." (*Laughter.*) "But I won't go into that. . . ." (*A voice: "Better not!"*) Michael could see the mouth it came from below a clipped moustache in a red, black-haired face turned round at him from a Liberal bench. He could not put a name to it, but he did not like the unpolitical expression it wore. Where was he? Oh! yes. . . . "There is another point in the Foggart programme: England as she now is, insufficiently protected in the air, and lamentably devoid of food-producing power, is an abiding temptation to the aggressive feelings of other nations. And here I must beg the House's pardon for a brief reference to Cinderella—in other words, the Land. The speech from the throne gave no lead in reference to that vexed question, beyond implying that a conference of all interested will be called. Well, without a definite intention in the minds of all the political Parties to join in some fixed and long-lasting policy for rehabilitation, such a conference is bound to fail. Here again Foggartism——" ("Ho! ho!") "Here again Foggartism steps in. Foggartism says: Lay down your Land policy *and don't change it.* Let it be as sacred as the Prohibition Law in America." (*A voice:* "*And as damned!*" *Laughter.*) "The sacred and damned—it sounds like a novel by Dostoievski." (*Laughter.*) "Well, we shall get nowhere without this damned sanctity. On our Land policy depends, not only the prosperity of farmers, landlords, and labourers, desirable and important though that is, but the very existence of England, if unhappily there should come another war under the new conditions. Yes, and in a fixed land policy lies the only hope of preventing the permanent deterioration of the British type. Foggartism requires that we lay down our land policy, so that within ten years we may be growing up to seventy per cent of our food. Estimates made during the war showed that as much as eighty-two per cent could be grown at a pinch; and the measures then adopted went a long way to prove that this estimate was no more than truth. Why were those measures allowed to drop? Why was all that great improvement allowed to run to seed and grass? What is wanted is complete confidence in every branch of home agriculture; and nothing but a policy guaranteed over a long period can ever produce that confidence." Michael paused. Close by, a member yawned; he heard a shuffle of feet; another old Prime Minister came in; several members were going out. There was nothing new about 'the Land'. Dared he tackle the air—that third plank in the Foggart programme? There was nothing new about the air either! Besides, he would have to preface it by a plea for the abolition of air fighting, or at least for the reduction of armaments. It would take too long! Better leave well alone! He hurried on:

"Emigration! The Land! Foggartism demands for both the same sweeping attention as was given to vital measures during the war. I feel honoured in having been permitted to draw the attention of all Parties to this—I will brave an honourable Member's disposition to say 'Ho, ho!'—great treatise of Sir James Foggart. And I beg the House's pardon for having been so long in fulfilling my task."

He sat down, after speaking for thirteen minutes. Off his chest! An honourable Member rose.

"I must congratulate the Member for mid-Bucks on what, despite its acquaintanceship with the clouds, and its Lewis Carrollian appeal for less bread, more taxes, we must all admit to be a lively and well-delivered first effort. The Member for Tyne and Tees, earlier in the Debate, made an allusion to the Party to which I have the honour to belong, which—er——"

'Exactly!' thought Michael, and after waiting for the next speech, which contained no allusion whatever to his own, he left the House.

## Chapter II

## RESULTS

HE walked home, lighter in head and heart. That was the trouble—a light weight! No serious attention would be paid to him. He recollected the maiden speech of the Member for Cornmarket. At least he had stopped, to-day, as soon as the House began to fidget. He felt hot, and hungry. Opera-singers grew fat through their voices, Members of Parliament thin. He would have a bath.

He was half clothed again when Fleur came in.

"You did splendidly, Michael. That beast!"

"Which?"

"His name's MacGown."

"Sir Alexander MacGown? What about him?"

"You'll see to-morrow. He insinuated that you were interested in the sale of the Foggart book, as one of its publishers."

"That's rather the limit."

"And all the rest of his speech was a cut-up; horrid tone about the whole thing. Do you know him?"

"MacGown? No. He's Member for some Scottish borough."

"Well, he's an enemy. Blythe is awfully pleased with you, and wild about MacGown; and so is Bart. I've never seen him so angry. You'll have to write to *The Times* and explain that you've had no interest in Danby & Winter's since before you were elected. Bart

324

and your mother are coming to dinner. Did you know she was with me?"

"Mother? She abhors politics."

"All she said was: 'I wish dear Michael would brush his hair back before speaking. I like to see his forehead.' And when Mac-Gown sat down, she said: 'My dear, the back of that man's head is perfectly straight. D'you think he's a Prussian? And he's got thick lobes to his ears. I shouldn't like to be married to him!' She had her opera-glasses."

Sir Lawrence and Lady Mont were already in the 'parlour' when they went down, standing opposite each other like two storks, if not precisely on one leg, still very distinguished. Pushing Michael's hair up, Lady Mont pecked his forehead, and her dove-like eyes gazed at the top of his head from under their arched brows. She was altogether a little Norman in her curves; she even arched her words. She was considered 'a deah; but not too frightfully all there'.

"How did you manage to stick it, Mother?"

"My dear boy, I was thrilled; except for that person in jute. I thought the shape of his head insufferable. Where did you get all that knowledge? It was so sensible."

Michael grinned. "How did it strike you, sir?"

Sir Lawrence grimaced.

"You played the *enfant terrible*, my dear. Half the party won't like it because they've never thought of it; and the other half won't like it because they *have*."

"What! Foggartists at heart?"

"Of course; but in Office. You mustn't support your real convictions in Office—it's not done."

"This nice room," murmured Lady Mont. "When I was last here it was Chinese. And where's the monkey?"

"In Michael's study, Mother. We got tired of him. Would you like to see Kit before dinner?"

Left alone, Michael and his father stared at the same object, a Louis Quinze snuff-box picked up by Soames.

"Would you take any notice of MacGown's insinuation, Dad?"

"Is that his name—the hairy haberdasher! I should."

"How?"

"Give him the lie."

"In private, in the Press, or in the House?"

"All three. In private I should merely call him a liar. In the Press you should use the words: 'Reckless disregard for truth.'

And in Parliament—that you regret he 'should have been so mis-informed.' To complete the crescendo you might add that men's noses have been pulled for less."

"But you don't suppose," said Michael, "that people would believe a thing like that?"

"They will believe anything, my dear, that suggests corruption in public life. It's one of the strongest traits in human nature. Anxiety about the integrity of public men would be admirable, if it wasn't so usually felt by those who have so little integrity themselves that they can't give others credit for it." Sir Lawrence grimaced, thinking of the P.P.R.S. "And talking of that—why wasn't Old Forsyte in the House to-day?"

"I offered him a seat, but he said: He hadn't been in the House since Gladstone moved the Home Rule Bill, and then only because he was afraid his father would have a fit."

Sir Lawrence screwed his eye-glass in.

"That's not clear to me," he said.

"His father had a pass, and didn't like to waste it."

"I see. That was noble of Old Forsyte."

"He said that Gladstone had been very windy."

"Ah! They were even longer in those days. You covered your ground very quickly, Michael. I should say with practice you would do. I've a bit of news for Old Forsyte. Shropshire doesn't speak to Charlie Ferrar because the third time the old man paid his debts to prevent his being posted, he made that a condition, for fear of being asked again. It's not so lurid as I'd hoped. How's the action?"

"The last I heard was something about administering what they call interrogatories."

"Ah! I know. They answer you in a way nobody can make head or tail of, and that without prejudice. Then they administer them to you, and you answer in the same way; it all helps the lawyers. What is there for dinner?"

"Fleur said we'd kill the fatted calf when I'd got my speech off."

Sir Lawrence sighed.

"I'm glad. Your mother has Vitamins again rather badly; we eat little but carrots, generally raw. French blood in a family is an excellent thing—prevents faddiness about food. Ah! here they come! . . ."

It has often been remarked that the breakfast-tables of people who avow themselves indifferent to what the Press may say of them are garnished by all the newspapers on the morning when

326

there is anything to say. In Michael's case this was a waste of almost a shilling. The only allusions to his speech were contained in four out of thirteen dailies. *The Times* reported it (including the laughter) with condensed and considered accuracy. The *Morning Post* picked out three imperial bits, prefaced by the words: 'In a promising speech.' The *Daily Telegraph* remarked: "Among the other speakers were Mr. Michael Mont." And the *Manchester Guardian* observed: "The Member for Mid-Bucks in a maiden speech advocated the introduction of children into the Dominions."

Sir Alexander MacGown's speech received the added attention demanded by his extra years of Parliamentary service, but there was no allusion to the insinuation. Michael turned to Hansard. His own speech seemed more coherent than he had hoped. When Fleur came down he was still reading MacGown's.

"Give me some coffee, old thing."

Fleur gave him the coffee and leaned over his shoulder.

"This MacGown is after Marjorie Ferrar," she said; "I remember now."

Michael stirred his cup. "Dash it all! The House is free from that sort of pettiness."

"No. I remember Alison telling me—I didn't connect him up yesterday. Isn't it a disgusting speech?"

"Might be worse," said Michael, with a grin.

"'As a member of the firm who published this singular production, he is doubtless interested in pressing it on the public, so that we may safely discount the enthusiasm displayed.' Doesn't that make your blood boil?"

Michael shrugged his shoulders.

"Don't you ever feel angry, Michael?"

"My dear, I was through the war. Now for *The Times*. What shall I say?

"'SIR,

"'May I trespass upon your valuable space' (that's quite safe), 'in the interests of public life——' (that keeps it impersonal) 'to—' er— Well?"

"To say that Sir Alexander MacGown in his speech yesterday told a lie when he suggested that I was interested in the sale of Sir James Foggart's book."

"Straight," said Michael, "but they wouldn't put it in. How's this?

"'To draw attention to a misstatement in Sir Alexander Mac-

Gown's speech of yesterday afternoon. As a matter of fact' (always useful) 'I ceased to have any interest whatever in the firm which published Sir James Foggart's book, *The Parlous State of England*, even before I became a member of the late Parliament; and am therefore in no way interested, as Sir Alexander MacGown suggested, in pressing it on the public. I hesitate to assume that he meant to impugn my honour' (must get in 'honour') 'but his words might bear that construction. My interest in the book is simply my interest in what is truly the 'parlous state of England'.

'Faithfully, etc.'

That do?"

"Much too mild. Besides, I shouldn't say that you really believe the state of England is parlous. It's all nonsense, you know. I mean it's exaggerated."

"Very well," said Michael, "I'll put the state of the country instead. In the House I suppose I rise to a point of order. And in the Lobby to a point of disorder, probably. I wonder what the *Evening Sun* will say?"

The *Evening Sun*, which Michael bought on his way to the House, gave him a leader, headed: "Foggartism again," beginning as follows: "Young Hopeful, in the person of the Member for Mid-Bucks, roused the laughter of the House yesterday by his championship of the insane policy called Foggartism, to which we have already alluded in these columns;" and so on for twenty lines of vivid disparagement. Michael gave it to the door-keeper.

In the House, after noting that MacGown was present, he rose at the first possible moment.

"Mr. Speaker, I rise to correct a statement in yesterday's debate reflecting on my personal honour. The honourable member for Greengow, in his speech said——" He then read the paragraph from Hansard. "It is true that I was a member of the firm which published Sir James Foggart's book in August, 1923, but I retired from all connection with that firm in October, 1923, before ever I entered this House. I have therefore no pecuniary or other interest whatever in pressing the claims of the book, beyond my great desire to see its principles adopted."

He sat down to some applause; and Sir Alexander MacGown rose. Michael recognised the face with the unpolitical expression he had noticed during his speech.

"I believe," he said, "that the honourable Member for Mid-Bucks was not sufficiently interested in his own speech to be present when I made my reply to it yesterday. I cannot admit that my words bear the construction which he has put on them. I said, and I still say, that one of the publishers of a book must necessarily be interested in having the judgment which induced him to publish it vindicated by the public. The honourable Member has placed on his head a cap which I did not intend for it." His face came round towards Michael, grim, red, provocative.

Michael rose again.

"I am glad the honourable Member has removed a construction which others besides myself had put on his words."

A few minutes later, with a certain unanimity, both left the House.

The papers not infrequently contain accounts of how Mr. Swash, the honourable Member for Topcliffe, called Mr. Buckler, the honourable Member for Tooting, something unparliamentary. ("*Order!*") And of how Mr. Buckler retorted that Mr. Swash was something worse. ("*Hear, hear!*" *and* "*Order!*") And of how Mr. Swash waved his fists (*uproar*), and Mr. Buckler threw himself upon the Chair, or threw some papers ("*Order! order! order!*") And of how there was great confusion, and Mr. Swash, or Mr. Buckler, was suspended, and led vociferous out of the Mother of Parliaments by the Serjeant-at-Arms, with other edifying details. The little affair between Michael and Sir Alexander went off in other wise. With an instinct of common decency, they both made for the lavatory; nor till they reached those marble halls did either take the slightest notice of the other. In front of a roller towel Michael said:

"Now, sir, perhaps you'll tell me why you behaved like a dirty dog. You knew perfectly well the construction that would be placed on your words."

Sir Alexander turned from a hair-brush.

"Take that!" he said, and gave Michael a swinging box on the ear. Staggering, Michael came up wildly with his right, and caught Sir Alexander on the nose. Their movements then became intensive. Michael was limber, Sir Alexander stocky; neither was over proficient with his fists. The affair was cut short by the honourable Member for Wasbaston, who had been in retirement. Coming hastily out of a door, he received simultaneously a black eye, and a blow on the diaphragm, which caused him to collapse. The speaker, now, was the Member for Wasbaston, in language stronger than those who knew the honourable gentleman would have supposed possible.

329

"I'm frightfully sorry, sir," said Michael. "It's always the innocent party who comes off worst."

"I'll dam' well have you both suspended," gasped the Member for Wasbaston.

Michael grinned, and Sir Alexander said: "To hell!"

"You're a couple of brawling cads!" said the Member for Wasbaston. "How the devil am I to speak this afternoon?"

"If you went in bandaged," said Michael, dabbing the damaged eye with cold water, "and apologised for a motor accident, you would get special hearing, and a good Press. Shall I take the silver lining out of my tie for a bandage?"

"Leave my eye alone," bellowed the Member for Wasbaston, "and get out, before I lose my temper!"

Michael buttoned the top of his waistcoat loosened by Sir Alexander's grip, observed in the glass that his ear was very red, his cuff bloodstained, and his opponent still bleeding from the nose, and went out.

'Some scrap!' he thought, entering the fresher air of Westminster. 'Jolly lucky we were tucked away in there! I don't think I'll mention it!' His ear was singing and he felt rather sick, physically and mentally. The salvational splendour of Foggartism already reduced to a brawl in a lavatory! It made one doubt one's vocation. Not even the Member for Wasbaston, however, had come off with dignity, so that the affair was not likely to get into the papers.

Crossing the road towards home, he sighted Francis Wilmot walking west.

"Hallo!"

Francis Wilmot looked up, and seemed to hesitate. His face was thinner, his eyes deeper set; he had lost his smile.

"How is Mrs. Mont?"

"Very well, thanks. And you?"

"Fine," said Francis Wilmot. "Will you tell her I've had a letter from her cousin Jon. They're in great shape. He was mighty glad to hear I'd seen her, and sent his love."

"Thanks," said Michael, drily. "Come and have tea with us."

The young man shook his head.

"Have you cut your hand?"

Michael laughed. "No, somebody's nose."

Francis Wilmot smiled wanly. "I'm wanting to do that all the time. Whose was it?"

"A man called MacGown's."

330

# THE SILVER SPOON

Francis Wilmot seized Michael's hand. "It's the very nose!" Then, apparently disconcerted by his frankness, he turned on his heel and made off, leaving Michael putting one and one together.

Next morning's papers contained no allusion to the blood-letting of the day before, except a paragraph to the effect that the Member for Wasbaston was confined to his house by a bad cold. The Tory journals preserved a discreet silence about Foggartism; but in two organs—one Liberal and one Labour—were little leaders, which Michael read with some attention.

The Liberal screed ran thus: "The debate on the King's speech produced one effort which at least merits passing notice. The policy alluded to by the Member for mid-Bucks under the label of Foggartism, because it emanates from that veteran Sir James Foggart, has a certain speciousness in these unsettled times, when everyone is looking for quack specifics. Nothing which departs só fundamentally from all that Liberalism stands for will command for a moment the support of any truly Liberal vote. The risk lies in its appeal to backwoodism in the Tory ranks. Loose thought and talk of a pessimistic nature always attracts a certain type of mind. The state of England is not really parlous. It in no way justifies any unsound or hysterical departure from our traditional policy. But there is no disguising the fact that certain so-called thinkers have been playing for some time past with the idea of reviving a 'splendid isolation', based (whether they admit it or not) on the destruction of Free Trade. The young Member for mid-Bucks in his speech handled for a moment that corner-stone of Liberalism, and then let it drop; perhaps he thought it too weighty for him. But reduced to its elements, Foggartism is a plea for the abandonment of Free Trade, and a blow in the face of the League of Nations."

Michael sighed and turned to the Labour article, which was signed, and struck a more human note:

"And so we are to have our children carted off to the Antipodes as soon as they can read and write, in order that the capitalist class may be relieved of the menace lurking in Unemployment. I know nothing of Sir James Foggart, but if he was correctly quoted in Parliament yesterday by a member for an agricultural constituency, I smelled Prussianism about that old gentleman. I wonder what the working man is saying over his breakfast-table? I fear the words: 'To hell!' are not altogether absent from his discourse. No, Sir James Foggart, English Labour intends to call its own hand; and with all the old country's drawbacks, still prefers it for itself and its children. We are not taking any, Sir James Foggart."

331

'There it is naked,' thought Michael. 'The policy ought never to have been entrusted to me. Blythe ought to have found a Labour townsman.'

Foggartism, whittled to a ghost by jealousy and class-hatred, by shibboleth, section and Party—he had a vision of it slinking through the purlieus of the House and the corridors of the Press, never admitted to the Presence, nor accepted as flesh and blood!

"Never mind," he muttered; "I'll stick it. If one's a fool, one may as well be a blazing fool. Eh, Dan?"

The Dandie, raising his head from his paws, gave him a lustrous glance.

## Chapter III

### MARJORIE FERRAR AT HOME

FRANCIS WILMOT went on his way to Chelsea. He had a rendezvous with Life. Over head and ears in love, and old-fashioned to the point of marriage, he spent his days at the tail of a petticoat as often absent as not. His simple fervour had wrung from Marjorie Ferrar confession of her engagement. She had put it bluntly: She was in debt, she wanted shekels and she could not live in the back-woods.

He had promptly offered her all his shekels. She had refused them with the words:

"My poor dear, I'm not so far gone as that."

Often on the point of saying 'Wait until I'm married,' the look on his face had always deterred her. He was primitive; would never understand her ideal: Perfection, as wife, mistress, and mother, all at once. She kept him only by dangling the hope that she would throw MacGown over; taking care to have him present when MacGown was absent, and absent when MacGown was present. She had failed to keep them apart on two occasions, painful and productive of more lying than she was at all accustomed to. For she was really taken with this young man; he was a new flavour. She 'loved' his dark 'slinky' eyes, his grace, the way his 'back-chat' grew, dark and fine, on his slim comely neck. She 'loved' his voice and his old-fashioned way of talking. And, rather oddly, she 'loved' his loyalty. Twice she had urged him to find out whether Fleur wasn't going to 'climb down' and 'pay up'. Twice he had refused. saying: "They were mighty nice to me; and I'd never tell you what they said, even if I did go and find out."

She was painting his portrait, so that a prepared canvas with a little paint on it chaperoned their almost daily interviews, which took place between three and four when the light had already failed. It was an hour devoted by MacGown to duty in the House. A low and open collar suited Francis Wilmot's looks. She liked him to sit lissom on a divan with his eyes following her; she liked to come close to him, and see the tremor of his fingers touching her skirt or sleeve, the glow in his eyes, the change in his face when she moved away. His faith in her was inconvenient. P's and Q's were letters she despised. And yet, to have to mind them before him gave her a sort of pleasure, made her feel good. One did not shock children!

That day, since she expected MacGown at five, she had become uneasy, before the young man came in saying:

"I met Michael Mont; his cuff was bloody. Guess whose blood!"

"Not Alec's?"

Francis Wilmot dropped her hands.

"Don't call that man 'Alec' to me."

"My dear child, you're too sensitive. I thought they'd have a row—I read their speeches. Hadn't Michael a black eye? No? Tt—tt! Al—er—'that man' will be awfully upset. Was the blood fresh?"

"Yes," said Francis Wilmot, grimly.

"Then he won't come. Sit down, and let's do some serious work for once."

But throwing himself on his knees, he clasped his hands behind her waist.

"Marjorie, Marjorie!"

Disciple of Joy, in the forefront of modern mockery, she was yet conscious of pity, for him and for herself. It was hard not to be able to tell him to run out, get licence and ring, or whatever he set store by, and have done with it! Not even that she was ready to have done with it without ring or licence! For one must keep one's head. She had watched one lover growing tired, kept her head, and dismissed him before he knew it; grown tired of another, kept her head, and gone on till he was tired too. She had watched favourites she had backed go down, kept her head and backed one that didn't; had seen cards turn against her, and left off playing before her pile was gone. Time and again she had earned the good mark of Modernity.

So she kissed the top of his head, unclasped his hands, and told him to be good; and, in murmuring it, felt that she had passed her prime.

"Amuse me while I paint," she said. "I feel rotten."

And Francis Wilmot, like a dark ghost, amused her.

Some believe that a nose from which blood has been drawn by a blow swells less in the first hour than it does later. This was why Sir Alexander MacGown arrived at half-past four to say that he could not come at five. He had driven straight from the House with a little bag of ice held to it. Having been led to understand that the young American was 'now in Paris,' he stood stock still, staring at one whose tie was off and whose collar was unbuttoned. Francis Wilmot rose from the divan, no less silent. Marjorie Ferrar put a touch on the canvas.

"Come and look, Alec; it's only just begun."

"No, thanks," said MacGown.

Crumpling his tie into his pocket, Francis Wilmot bowed and moved towards the door.

"Won't you stay for tea, Mr. Wilmot?"

"I believe not, thank you."

When he was gone Marjorie Ferrar fixed her eyes on the nose of her betrothed. Strong and hard, it was, as yet, little differentiated from the normal.

"Now," said MacGown, "why did you lie about that young blighter? You said he was in Paris. Are you playing fast and loose with me, Marjorie?"

"Of course! Why not?"

MacGown advanced to within reach of her.

"Put down that brush."

Marjorie Ferrar raised it; and suddenly it hit the wall opposite.

"You'll stop that picture, and you'll not see that fellow again; he's in love with you."

He had taken her wrists.

Her face, quite as angry as his own, was reined back.

"Let go! I don't know if you call yourself a gentleman?"

"No, a plain man."

"Strong and silent—out of a dull novel. Sit down, and don't be unpleasant."

The duel of their eyes, brown and burning, blue and icy, endured for quite a minute. Then he did let go.

"Pick up that brush and give it to me."

"I'm damned if I will!"

"Then our engagement is off. If you're old-fashioned, I'm not.

You want a young woman who'll give you a whip for a wedding-present."

MacGown put his hands up to his head.

"I want you too badly to be sane."

"Then pick up the brush."

MacGown picked it up.

"What have you done to your nose?"

MacGown put his hand to it.

"Ran it against a door."

Marjorie Ferrar laughed. "Poor door!"

MacGown gazed at her in genuine astonishment.

"You're the hardest woman I ever came across; and why I love you, I don't know."

"It hasn't improved your looks or your temper, my dear. You were rash to come here to-day."

MacGown uttered a sort of groan. "I can't keep away, and you know it."

Marjorie Ferrar turned the canvas face to the wall, and leaned there beside it.

"I don't know what you think of the prospects of our happiness, Alec; but I think they're pretty poor. Will you have a whisky and soda? It's in that cupboard. Tea, then? Nothing? We'd better understand each other. If I marry you which is very doubtful, I'm not going into purdah. I shall have what friends I choose. And until I marry you, I shall even see them. If you don't like it, you can leave it."

She watched his clenched hands, and her wrists tingled. To be perfect wife to him would 'take a bit of doing'! If only she knew of a real 'good thing' instead, and had a 'shirt to put on it'! If only Francis Wilmot had money and did not live where the cotton came from and darkies crooned in the fields; where rivers ran red, Florida moss festooned the swamps and the sun shone; where grapefruit grew—or didn't?—and mocking-birds sang sweeter than the nightingale. South Carolina, described to her with such enthusiasm by Francis Wilmot! A world that was not her world stared straight into the eyes of Marjorie Ferrar. South Carolina! Impossible! It was like being asked to be ancient!

MacGown came up to her. "I'm sorry," he said. "Forgive me, Marjorie."

On her shrugging shoulders he put his hands, kissed her lips, and went away.

And she sat down in her favourite chair, listless, swinging her

foot. The sand had run out of her dolly—life was a bore! It was
like driving tandem, when the leader would keep turning round;
or the croquet party in 'Alice in Wonderland', read in the butter-
cup-fields at High Marshes not twenty years ago that felt like
twenty centuries!

What did she want? Just a rest from men and bills? or that
fluffy something called 'real love'? Whatever it was, she hadn't
got it! And so! Dress, and go out, and dance; and later dress again,
and go out and dine; and the dresses not paid for!

Well, nothing like an egg-nog for 'the hump'!

Ringing for the ingredients, she made one with plenty of brandy,
capped it with nutmeg, and drank it down.

## Chapter IV

### FONS ET ORIGO

TWO mornings later Michael received two letters. The first, which
bore an Australian post-mark, ran thus:

"DEAR SIR,

"I hope you are well and the lady. I thought perhaps you'd like
to know how we are. Well, Sir, we're not much to speak of out
here after a year and a half. I consider there's too much gilt on
the ginger-bread as regards Australia. The climate's all right when
it isn't too dry or too wet—it suits my wife fine, but Sir when
they talk about making your fortune all I can say is tell it to the
marines. The people here are a funny lot they don't seem to have
any use for us and I don't seem to have any use for them. They
call us Pommies and treat us as if we'd took a liberty in coming to
their blooming country. You'd say they wanted a few more out
here, but they don't seem to think so. I often wish I was back in
the old Country. My wife says we're better off here, but I don't
know. Anyway they tell a lot of lies as regards emigration.

"Well, Sir, I've not forgotten your kindness. My wife says please
to remember her to you and the lady.

"Yours faithfully,
"ANTHONY BICKET."

With that letter in his hand, Michael, like some psychometric
medium, could see again the writer, his thin face, prominent eyes,
large ears, a shadowy figure of the London streets behind his

336

coloured balloons. Poor little snipe—square peg in round hole
wherever he might be; and all those other pegs—thousands upon
thousands, that would never fit in. Pommies! Well! He wasn't
recommending emigration for them; he was recommending it for
those who could be shaped before their wood had set. Surely they
wouldn't put that stigma on to children! He opened the other letter.

"Roll Manor,
"Nr. Huntingdon.

"MY DEAR SIR,

"The disappointment I have felt since the appearance of my book
was somewhat mitigated by your kind allusions to it in Parliament,
and your championship of its thesis. I am an old man, and do not
come to London now, but it would give me pleasure to meet you.
If you are ever in this neighbourhood, I should be happy if you
would lunch with me, or stay the night, as suits you best.

"With kind regards,

"Faithfully yours,
"JAS: FOGGART."

He showed it to Fleur.

"If you go, my dear, you'll be bored to tears."

"I must go," said Michael; *"Fons et Origo!"*

He wrote that he would come to lunch the following day.

He was met at the station by a horse drawing a vehicle of a
shape he had never before beheld. The green-liveried man to whose
side he climbed introduced it with the words: "Sir James thought,
sir, you'd like to see about you; so 'e sent the T cart."

It was one of those grey late autumn days, very still, when the
few leaves that are left hang listless, waiting to be windswept. The
puddled road smelled of rain; rooks rose from the stubbles as if in
surprise at the sound of horses' hoofs; and the turned earth of
ploughed fields had the sheen that betokened clay. To the flat
landscape poplars gave a certain spirituality; and the russet-tiled
farmhouse roofs a certain homeliness.

"That's the manor, sir," said the driver, pointing with his whip.
Between an orchard and a group of elms, where was obviously a
rookery, Michael saw a long low house of deeply weathered brick
covered by Virginia creeper whose leaves had fallen. At a little
distance were barns, out-houses, and the wall of a kitchen-garden.
The T cart turned into an avenue of limes and came suddenly on

the house unprotected by a gate. Michael pulled an old iron bell. Its lingering clang produced a lingering man, who, puckering his face, said: "Mr. Mont? Sir James is expecting you. This way, sir."

Through an old low hall smelling pleasantly of wood-smoke, Michael reached a door which the puckered man closed in his face.

Sir James Foggart! Some gaitered old countryman with little grey whiskers, neat, weathered and firm-featured; or one of those short-necked John Bulls, still extant, square and weighty, with a flat top to his head, and a flat white topper on it?

The puckered man reopened the door, and said:

"Sir James will see you, sir."

Before the fire in a large room with a large hearth and many books was a huge old man, grey-bearded and grey-locked, like a superannuated British lion, in an old velvet coat with whitened seams.

He appeared to be trying to rise.

"Please don't, sir," said Michael.

"If you'll excuse me, I won't. Pleasant journey?"

"Very."

"Sit down. Much touched by your speech. First speech, I think?"

Michael bowed.

"Not the last, I hope."

The voice was deep and booming; the eyes looked up keenly, as if out of thickets, so bushy were the eyebrows, and the beard grew so high on the cheeks. The thick grey hair waved across the forehead and fell on to the coat collar. A primeval old man in a high state of cultivation. Michael was deeply impressed.

"I've looked forward to this honour, sir," he said, "ever since we published your book."

"I'm a recluse—never get out now. Tell you the truth, don't want to—see too many things I dislike. I write, and smoke my pipe  Ring the bell, and we'll have lunch. Who's this Sir Alexander MacGown? His head wants punching!"

"No longer, sir," said Michael.

Sir James Foggart leaned back and laughed. His laugh was long, deep, slightly hollow, like a laugh in a trombone.

"Capital! And how did those fellows take your speech? Used to know a lot of 'em at one time—fathers of these fellows, grand-fathers, perhaps."

"How do you know so well what England wants, sir," said Michael, suavely, "now that you never leave home?"

To all whom this writeth a will bring a sight
Quot homines
tot sententiae.

Christopher Wordman
Reading... de
Prorogation
so many men,
so many
minds

Guanatem neometuit tuba: m t
omes meosus aut tinerme narma

# THE SILVER SPOON

Sir James Foggart pointed with a large thin hand covered with hair to a table piled with books and magazines.

"Read," he said; "read everything—eyes as good as ever—seen a good deal in my day." And he was silent, as if seeing it again.

"Are you following your book up?"

"M'm Something for 'em to read when I'm gone. Eighty-four, you know."

"I wonder," said Michael, "that you haven't had the Press down."

"Have—had 'em yesterday; three by different trains; very polite young men; but I could see they couldn't make head or tail of the old creature—too far gone, eh?"

At this moment the door was opened, and the puckered man came in, followed by a maid and three cats. They put a tray on Sir James's knees and another on a small table before Michael. On each tray was a partridge with chipped potatoes, spinach and bread sauce. The puckered man filled Sir James's glass with barley-water, Michael's with claret, and retired. The three cats, all tortoise-shells, began rubbing themselves against Sir James's trousers, purring loudly.

"Don't mind cats, I hope? No fish to-day, pussies!"

Michael was hungry and finished his bird. Sir James gave most of his to the cats. They were then served with fruit salad, cheese, coffee and cigars, and everything removed except the cats, who lay replete before the fire curled up in a triangle.

Michael gazed through the smoke of two cigars at the fount and origin, eager, but in doubt whether it would stand pumping—it seemed so very old! Well! anyway, he must have a shot!

"You know Blythe, sir, of *The Outpost?* He's your great supporter; I'm only a mouthpiece."

"Know his paper—best of the weeklies; but too clever by half."

"Now that I've got the chance," said Michael, "would you mind if I asked you one or two questions?"

Sir James Foggart looked at the lighted end of his cigar. "Fire ahead."

"Well, sir, can England really stand apart from Europe?"

"Can she stand with Europe? Alliances based on promise of assistance that won't be forthcoming—worse than useless."

"But suppose Belgium were invaded again, or Holland?"

"The one case, perhaps. Let that be understood. Knowledge in Europe, young man, of what England will or will not do in given cases is most important. And they've never had it. *Perfide Albion!* Heh! We always wait till the last moment to declare our policy.

Great mistake. Gives the impression that we serve Time—which, with our democratic system, by the way, we generally do."

"I like that, sir," said Michael, who did not. "About wheat? How would you stabilise the price so as to encourage our growth of it?"

"Ha! My pet lamb. We want a wheat loan, Mr. Mont, and Government control. Every year the Government should buy in advance all the surplus we need and store it; then fix a price for the home farmers that gives them a good profit; and sell to the public at the average between the two prices. You'd soon see plenty of wheat grown here, and a general revival of agriculture. '

"But wouldn't it raise the price of bread, sir?"

"Not it."

"And need an army of officials?"

"No. Use the present machinery properly organised."

"State trading, sir?" said Michael, with diffidence.

Sir James Foggart's voice boomed out. "Exceptional case—basic case—why not?"

"I quite agree," said Michael, hastily. "I never thought of it, but why not? . . . Now as to the opposition to child emigration in this country. Do you think it comes from the affection of parents for their children?"

"More from dislike of losing the children's wages."

"Still, you know," murmured Michael, "one might well kick against losing one's children for good at fifteen!"

"One might; human nature's selfish, young man. Hang on to 'em and see 'em rot before one's eyes, or grow up to worse chances than one's own—as you say, that's human nature."

Michael who had not said it, felt somewhat stunned.

"The child emigration scheme will want an awful lot of money, and organisation."

Sir James stirred the cats with his slippered foot.

"Money! There's still a mint of money—misapplied. Another hundred million loan—four and a half millions a year in the Budget; and a hundred thousand children at least sent out every year. In five years we should save the lot in unemployment dole." He waved his cigar, and its ash spattered on his velvet coat.

"Thought it would," said Michael to himself, knocking his own off into a coffee-cup. "But can children sent out wholesale like that be properly looked after, and given a real chance, sir?"

"Start gradually; where there's a will there's a way."

"And won't they just swell the big towns out there?"

THE SILVER SPOON

"Teach 'em to want land, and give it 'em."

"I don't know if it's enough," said Michael, boldly; "the lure of the towns is terrific."

Sir James nodded. "A town's no bad thing till it's overdone, as they are here. Those that go to the towns will increase the demand for our supplies."

'Well,' thought Michael, 'I'm getting on. What shall I ask him next?' And he contemplated the cats, who were stirring uneasily. A peculiar rumbling noise had taken possession of the silence. Michael looked up. Sir James Foggart was asleep! In repose he was more tremendous than ever—perhaps rather too tremendous; for his snoring seemed to shake the room. The cats tucked their heads farther in. There was a slight smell of burning. Michael picked a fallen cigar from the carpet. What should he do now? Wait for a revival, or clear out? Poor old boy! Foggartism had never seemed to Michael a more forlorn hope than in this sanctum of its fount and origin. Covering his ears, he sat quite still. One by one the cats got up. Michael looked at his watch. 'I shall lose my train,' he thought, and tiptoed to the door, behind a procession of deserting cats. It was as though Foggartism was snoring the little of its life away! "Good-bye, sir!" he said softly, and went out. He walked to the station very thoughtful. Foggartism! That vast if simple programme seemed based on the supposition that human beings could see two inches before their noses. But was that supposition justified; if so would England be so town-ridden and over-populated? For one man capable of taking a far and comprehensive view and going to sleep on it, there were nine—if not nine-and-ninety—who could take near and partial views and remain wide awake. Practical politics! The answer to all wisdom however you might boom it out. "Oh! Ah! Young Mont—not a practical politician!" It was public death to be so labelled. And Michael, in his railway carriage, with his eyes on the English grass, felt like a man on whom everyone was heaping earth. Had pelicans crying in the wilderness a sense of humour? If not, their time was poor. Grass, grass, grass! Grass and the towns! And, nestling his chin into his heavy coat, he was soon faster asleep than Sir James Foggart.

341

## Chapter V

## PROGRESS OF THE CASE

WHEN Soames said "Leave it to me," he meant it, of course; but it was really very trying that whenever anything went wrong, he, and not somebody else, had to set it right!

To look more closely into the matter he was staying with his sister Winifred Dartie in Green Street. Finding his nephew Val at dinner there the first night, he took the opportunity of asking him whether he knew anything of Lord Charles Ferrar.

"What do you want to know, Uncle Soames?"

"Anything unsatisfactory. I'm told his father doesn't speak to him."

"Well," said Val, "it's generally thought he'll win the Lincolnshire with a horse that didn't win the Cambridgeshire."

"I don't see the connection."

Val Dartie looked at him through his lashes. He was not going to enter for the slander stakes. "Well, he's got to bring off a *coup* soon, or go under."

"Is that all?"

"Except that he's one of those chaps who are pleasant to you when you can be of use, and unpleasant when you can't."

"So I gathered from his looks," said Soames. "Have you had any business dealings with him?"

"Yes; I sold him a yearling by Torpedo out of Banshee."

"Did he pay you?"

"Yes," said Val, with a grin; "and she turned out no good."

"H'm! I suppose he was unpleasant afterwards? That all you know?"

Val nodded. He knew more, if gossip can be called 'more'; but what was puffed so freely with the smoke of racing-men's cigars was hardly suited to the ears of lawyers.

For so old a man of the world Soames was singularly unaware how in that desirable sphere, called Society, everyone is slandered daily, and no bones broken; slanderers and slandered dining and playing cards together with the utmost good feeling and the intentions of re-slandering each other the moment they are round the corner. Such genial and hair-raising reports reach no outside ears, and Soames really did not know where to begin investigation.

"Can you ask this Mr. Curfew to tea?" he said to Fleur.

"What for, Father?"

"So that I can pump him."

"I thought there were detectives for all that sort of thing."

Soames went a special colour. Since his employment of Mr. Polteed, who had caught him visiting his own wife's bedroom in Paris, at the beginning of the century, the word detective produced a pain in his diaphragm. He dropped the subject. And yet, without detectives, what was he to do?

One night, Winifred having gone to the theatre, he sat down with a cigar, to think. He had been provided by Michael with a list of 'advanced' books and plays which 'modern' people were reading, attending and discussing. He had even been supplied with one of the books: *Canthar*, by Perceval Calvin. He fetched it from his bedrom, and, turning up a lamp, opened the volume. After reading the first few pages, in which he could see nothing, he turned to the end and read backwards. In this way he could skip better, and each erotic passage, to which he very soon came, led him insensibly on to the one before it. He had reached the middle of the novel, before he had resort in wonder to the title-pages. How was it that the publisher and author were at large? Ah! The imprint was of a foreign nature. Soames breathed more freely. Though sixty-nine, and neither judge, juryman nor other-wise professionally compelled to be shocked, he was shaken. If women were reading this sort of thing, then there really was no distinction between men and women nowadays. He took up the book again, and read steadily on to the beginning. The erotic passages alone interested him. The rest seemed rambling, discon-nected stuff. He rested again. What was this novel written for? To make money, of course. But was there another purpose? Was the author one of these 'artist' fellows who thought that to give you 'life'—wasn't that the phrase? they must put down every visit to a bedroom, and some besides? 'Art for Art's sake', 'realism'— what did they call it? In Soames's comparatively bleak experience 'life' did not consist wholly of visiting bedrooms, so that he was unable to admit that this book was life, the whole of life, and nothing but life. "Calvin's a crank, sir," Michael had said, when he handed him the novel. "He thinks people can't become con-tinent except through being excessively incontinent; so he shows his hero and heroine arriving gradually at continence." 'A Bedlam,' thought Soames. They would see what a British jury had to say to that, anyway. But how elicit a confession that this woman and her set had read it with gusto? And then an idea

343

occurred to him, so brilliant that he had to ponder deeply before
he could feel any confidence in it. These 'advanced' young people
had any amount of conceit; everyone who didn't share their views
was a 'dud', or a 'grundy'. Suppose the book were attacked in the
Press, wouldn't it draw their fire? And if their fire could be drawn
in print, could it not be used afterwards as evidence of their views
on morality? H'm! This would want very nice handling. And first
of all, how was he to prove that Marjorie Ferrar had read this
book? Thus casting about him, Soames was rewarded by another
brilliant thought: Young Butterfield—who had helped him to
prove the guilt of Elderson in that matter of the P.P.R.S. and owed
his place at Danby & Winter's, the publishers, to Soames's recom-
mendation! Why not make use of him? Michael always said the
young man was grateful. And obscuring the title of the book
against his flank, in case he should meet a servant, Soames sought
his own bedroom.

His last thought that night was almost diagnostic.

'In my young days we read that sort of book if we could get
hold of it, and didn't say so; now, it seems, they make a splash of
reading it, and pretend it does them good!'

Next morning from the Connoisseurs' he telephoned to Danby
& Winter's, and asked to speak to Mr. Butterfield.

"Yes?"

"Mr. Forsyte speaking. Do you remember me?"

"Yes, indeed, sir."

"Can you step round to the Connoisseurs' Club this morning
some time?"

"Certainly, sir. Will twelve-thirty suit you?"

Secretive and fastidious in matters connected with sex, Soames
very much disliked having to speak to a young man about an
'immoral' book. He saw no other way of it, however, and, on his
visitor's arrival, shook hands and began at once.

"This is confidential, Mr. Butterfield."

Butterfield, whose dog-like eyes had glowed over the handshake,
answered:

"Yes, sir. I've not forgotten what you did for me, sir."

Soames held out the book.

"Do you know that novel?"

Butterfield smiled slightly.

"Yes, sir. It's printed in Brussels. They're paying five pounds a
copy for it."

"Have you read it?"

344

The young man shook his head. "It's not come my way, sir."

Soames was relieved. "Well, don't! But just attend a moment. Can you buy ten copies of it, at my expense, and post them to ten people whose names I'll give you? They're all more or less connected with literature. You can put in slips to say the copies are complimentary, or whatever you call it. But mention no names."

The young man Butterfield said deprecatingly:

"The price is rising all the time, sir. It'll cost you well on sixty pounds."

"Never mind that."

"You wish the book boomed, sir?"

"Good Gad—no! I have my reasons, but we needn't go into them."

"I see, sir. And you want the copies to come—as if—as if from heaven?"

"That's it," said Soames. "I take it that publishers often send doubtful books to people they think will support them. There's just one other thing. Can you call a week later on one of the people to whom you've sent the books, and offer to sell another copy as if you were an agent for it? I want to make quite sure it's already reached that person, and been read. You won't give your name, of course. Will you do this for me?"

The eyes of the young man Butterfield again glowed.

"Yes, sir. I owe you a great deal, sir."

Soames averted his eyes; he disliked all expression of gratitude.

"Here's the list of names, then, with their addresses. I've underlined the one you call on. I'll write you a cheque to go on with; and you can let me know later if there's anything more to pay."

He sat down, while the young man Butterfield scrutinised the list.

"I see it's a lady, sir, that I'm to call on."

"Yes; does that make any difference to you?"

"Not at all, sir. Advanced literature is written for ladies nowadays."

"H'm!" said Soames. "I hope you're doing well?"

"Splendidly, sir. I was very sorry that Mr. Mont left us; we've been doing better ever since."

Soames lifted an eyebrow. The statement confirmed many an old suspicion. When the young man had gone, he took *Canthar*. Was he capable of writing an attack on it in the Press, over the signature 'Paterfamilias'? He was not. The job required someone used to that sort of thing. Besides, a real signature would be needed

345

to draw fire. It would not do to ask Michael to suggest one; but Old Mont might know some fogey at the 'Parthenæum' who carried metal. Sending for a bit of brown paper, he disguised the cover with it, put the volume in his overcoat pocket, and set out for 'Snooks'.

He found Sir Lawrence about to lunch, and they sat down together. Making sure that the waiter was not looking over his shoulder, Soames, who had brought the book in with him, pushed it over, and said:

"Have you read that?"

Sir Lawrence whinnied.

"My dear Forsyte, why this morbid curiosity? Everybody's reading it. They say the thing's unspeakable."

"Then you haven't?" said Soames, keeping him to the point.

"Not yet, but if you'll lend it me, I will. I'm tired of people who've enjoyed it asking me if I've read 'that most disgusting book'. It's not fair, Forsyte. Did you enjoy it?"

"I skimmed it," said Soames, looking round his nose. "I had a reason. When you've read it, I'll tell you."

Sir Lawrence brought it back to him at the Connoisseurs' two days later.

"Here you are, my dear Forsyte," he said. "I never was more glad to get rid of a book! I've been in a continual stew for fear of being overseen with it! Perceval Calvin—*quel sale Monsieur!*"

"Exactly!" said Soames. "Now, I want to get that book attacked."

"You! Is Saul also among the prophets? Why this sudden zest?"

"It's rather roundabout," said Soames, sitting on the book. He detailed the reason, and ended with:

"Don't say anything to Michael, or Fleur."

Sir Lawrence listened with his twisting smile.

"I see," he said, "I see. Very cunning, Forsyte. You want me to get someone whose name will act like a red rag. It mustn't be a novelist, or they'll say he's jealous—which he probably is: the book's selling like hot cakes—I believe that's the expression. Ah! I think—I rather think, Forsyte, that I have the woman."

"Woman!" said Soames. "They won't pay any attention to that."

Sir Lawrence cocked his loose eyebow. "I believe you're right—the only women they pay attention to nowadays are those who go one better than themselves. Shall I do it myself, and sign 'Outraged Parent'?"

"I believe it wants a real name."

"Again right, Forsyte; it does. I'll drop into the 'Parthenæum', and see if anyone's alive."

Two days later Soames received a note.

"The Parthenæum.
"Friday.

"MY DEAR FORSYTE,

"I've got the man—the editor of the *Protagonist;* and he'll do it under his own name. What's more, I've put him on to the right line. We had a spirited argument. He wanted to treat it *de haut en bas* as the work of a dirty child. I said: 'No. This thing is symptomatic. Treat it seriously; show that it represents a school of thought, a deliberate literary attitude; and make it a plea for censorship.' Without the word censorship, Forsyte, they will never rise. So he's leaving his wife and taking it into the country for the week-end. I admire your conduct of the defence, my dear Forsyte; it's very subtle. But if you'll forgive me for saying so, it's more important to prevent the case coming into Court than to get a verdict if it does.

"Sincerely yours,
"LAWRENCE MONT."

With which sentiment Soames so entirely agreed, that he went down to Mapledurham, and spent the next two afternoons going round and round with a man he didn't like, hitting a ball, to quiet his mind.

Chapter VI

MICHAEL VISITS BETHNAL GREEN

THE feeling of depression with which Michael had come back from the fount and origin was somewhat mitigated by letters he was receiving from people of varying classes, nearly all young. They were so nice and earnest. They made him wonder whether after all practical politicians were not too light-hearted, like the managers of music-halls who protected the public carefully from their more tasteful selves. They made him feel that there might be a spirit in the country that was not really represented in the House, or even in the Press. Among these letters was one which ran:

# A MODERN COMEDY

"Sunshine House,
"Bethnal Green.

"Dear Mr. Mont,

"I was so awfully glad to read your speech in *The Times*. I instantly got Sir James Foggart's book. I think the whole policy is simply splendid. You've no idea how heart-breaking it is for us who try to do things for children, to know that whatever we do is bound to be snowed under by the life they go to when school age ends. We have a good opportunity here of seeing the realities of child life in London. It's wonderful to see the fondness of the mothers for the little ones, in spite of their own hard lives—though not all, of course, by any means; but we often notice, and I think it's common experience, that when the children get beyond ten or twelve, the fondness for them begins to assume another form. I suppose it's really the commercial possibilities of the child making themselves felt. When money comes in at the door, disinterested love seems to move towards the window. I suppose it's natural, but it's awfully sad, because the commercial possibilities are generally so miserable; and the children's after-life is often half ruined for the sake of the few shillings they earn. I do fervently hope something will come of your appeal; only—things move so slowly, don't they? I wish you would come down and see our House here. The children are adorable, and we try to give them sunshine.

"Sincerely yours,
"Norah Curfew."

Bertie Curfew's sister! But surely that case would not really come to anything! Grateful for encouragement, and seeking light on Foggartism, he decided to go. Perhaps Norah Curfew would take the little Boddicks! He suggested to Fleur that she should accompany him, but she was afraid of picking up something unsuitable to the eleventh baronet, so he went alone.

The house, facing the wintry space called Bethnal Green, consisted of three small houses converted into one, with their three small back yards, trellised round and gravelled, for a playground. Over the door were the words: 'SUNSHINE HOUSE' in gold capitals. The walls were cream-coloured, the woodwork dark, and the curtains of gay chintz. Michael was received in the entrance-lobby by Norah Curfew herself. Tall, slim and straight, with dark hair brushed back from a pale face, she had brown eyes, clear, straight and glowing.

# THE SILVER SPOON

'Gosh!' thought Michael, as she wrung his hand. 'She *is* swept and garnished. No basement in her soul!'

"It *was* good of you to come, Mr. Mont. Let me take you over the house. This is the play-room."

Michael entered a room of spotless character, which had evidently been formed from several knocked into one. Six small children dressed in blue linen were seated on the floor, playing games. They embraced the knees of Norah Curfew when she came within reach. With the exception of one little girl Michael thought them rather ugly.

"These are our residents. The others only come out of school hours. We have to limit them to fifty, and that's a pretty good squeeze. We want funds to take the next two houses."

"How many of you are working here?"

"Six. Two of us do the cooking; one the accounts; and the rest washing, mending, games, singing, dancing and general chores. Two of us live in."

"I don't see your harps and crowns."

Norah Curfew smiled.

"Pawned," she said.

"What do you do about religion?" asked Michael, thinking of the eleventh baronet's future.

"Well, on the whole we don't. You see, they're none of them more than twelve; and the religious age, when it begins at all, begins with sex about fourteen. We just try to teach kindness and cheerfulness. I had my brother down the other day. He's always laughed at me; but he's going to do a matinée for us, and give us the proceeds."

"What play?"

"I think it's called 'The Plain Dealer'. He says he's always wanted to do it for a good object."

Michael stared. "Do you know 'The Plain Dealer'?"

"No; it's by one of the Restoration people, isn't it?"

"Wycherley."

"Oh! yes!" Her eyes remaining clearer than the dawn, Michael thought: 'Poor dear! It's not my business to queer the pitch of her money-getting; but Master Bertie likes his little joke!'

"I must bring my wife down here," he said; "she'd love your walls and curtains. And I wanted to ask you. You haven't room, have you, for two more little girls, if we pay for them? Their father's down and out, and I'm starting him in the country—no mother."

Norah Curfew wrinkled her straight brows, and on her face came the look Michael always connected with haloes, an anxious longing to stretch good-will beyond power and pocket.

"Oh! we must!" she said. "I'll manage somehow. What are their names?"

"Boddick—Christian, I don't know. I call them by their ages— Four and Five."

"Give me the address. I'll go and see them myself; if they haven't got anything catching, they shall come."

"You really are an angel," said Michael simply.

Norah Curfew coloured, and opened a door. "That's silly," she said, still more simply. "This is our mess-room."

It was not large. and contained a girl working a typewriter, who stopped with her hands on the keys and looked round; another girl beating up eggs in a bowl, who stopped reading a book of poetry; and a third, who seemed practising a physical exercise, and stopped with her arms extended.

"This is Mr. Mont," said Norah Curfew, "who made that splendid speech in the House. Miss Betts, Miss La Fontaine, Miss Beeston."

The girls bowed, and the one who continued to beat the eggs, said: "It was bully."

Michael also bowed. "Beating the air, I'm afraid."

"Oh! but, Mr. Mont, it must have an effect. It said what so many people are really thinking."

"Ah!" said Michael, "but their thoughts are so deep, you know."

"Do sit down."

Michael sat on the end of a peacock-blue divan.

"I was born in South Africa," said the egg-beater, "and I know what's waiting."

"My father was in the House," said the girl, whose arms had come down to her splendid sides. "He was very much struck. Anyway, we're jolly grateful."

Michael looked from one to the other.

"I suppose if you didn't all believe in things, you wouldn't be doing this? *You* don't think the shutters are up in England, anyway?"

"Good Lord, no!" said the girl at the typewriter; "you've only to live among the poor to know that."

"The poor haven't got every virtue, and the rich haven't got every vice—that's nonsense!" broke in the physical exerciser.

Michael murmured soothingly.

"I wasn't thinking of that. I was wondering whether something doesn't hang over our heads too much?"

"D'you mean poison-gas?"

"Partly; and town blight, and a feeling that Progress had been found out."

"Well, I don't know," replied the egg-beater, who was dark and pretty. "I used to think so in the war. But Europe isn't the world. Europe isn't even very important, really. The sun hardly shines there, anyway."

Michael nodded. "After all, if the Millennium comes and we do blot each other out in Europe, it'll only mean another desert about the size of the Sahara, and the loss of a lot of people obviously too ill-conditioned to be fit to live. It'd be a jolly good lesson to the rest of the world, wouldn't it? Luckily the other continents are far off each other."

"Cheerful!" exclaimed Norah Curfew.

Michael grinned.

"Well, one can't help catching the atmosphere of this place. I admire you all frightfully, you know, giving up everything, to come and do this."

"That's tosh," said the girl at the typewriter. "What is there to give up—bunny-hugging? One got used to doing things in the war."

"If it comes to that," said the egg-beater, "we admire you much more for not giving up Parliament."

Again Michael grinned.

"Miss La Fontaine—wanted in the kitchen!"

The egg-beater went towards the door.

"Can you beat eggs? D'you mind—shan't be a minute." Handing Michael the bowl and fork, she vanished.

"What a shame!" said Norah Curfew. "Let me!"

"No," said Michael; "I can beat eggs with anybody. What do you all feel about cutting children adrift at fifteen?"

"Well, of course, it'll be bitterly opposed," said the girl at the typewriter. "They'll call it inhuman, and all that. It's much more inhuman really to keep them here."

"The real trouble," said Norah Curfew, "apart from the shillings earned, is the class-interference idea. Besides, Imperialism isn't popular."

"I should jolly well think it isn't," muttered the physical exerciser.

"Ah!" said the typist, "but this isn't Imperialism, is it, Mr.

351

# A MODERN COMEDY

Mont? It's all on the lines of making the Dominions the equal of the Mother Country."

Michael nodded. "Commonwealth."

"That won't prevent their camouflaging their objection to losing the children's wages," said the physical exerciser.

A close discussion ensued between the three young women as to the exact effect of children's wages on the working-class budget. Michael beat his eggs and listened. It was, he knew, a point of the utmost importance. The general conclusion seemed to be that children earned on the whole rather more than their keep, but that it was 'very shortsighted in the long run', because it fostered surplus population and unemployment, and a 'great shame' to spoil the children's chances for the sake of the parents.

The re-entrance of the egg-beater put a stop to it.

"They're beginning to come in, Norah."

The physical exerciser slipped out, and Norah Curfew said:

"Now, Mr. Mont, would you like to see them?"

Michael followed her. He was thinking: 'I wish Fleur had come!' These girls seemed really to believe in things.

Downstairs the children were trickling in from school. He stood and watched them. They seemed a queer blend of anæmia and vitality, of effervescence and obedience. Unselfconscious as puppies, but old beyond their years; and yet looking as if they never thought ahead. Each movement, each action was as if it were their last. They were very quick. Most of them carried something to eat in a paper bag or a bit of grease-paper. They chattered, and didn't laugh. Their accent struck Michael as deplorable. Six or seven at most were nice to look at; but nearly all looked good-tempered, and none seemed to be selfish. Their movements were jerky. They mobbed Norah Curfew and the physical exerciser; obeyed without question, ate without appetite, and grabbed at the house cat. Michael was fascinated.

With them came four or five mothers, who had questions to ask, or bottles to fill. They too were on perfect terms with the young women. Class did not exist in this house; only personality was present. He noticed that the children responded to his grin, that the women didn't, though they smiled at Norah Curfew and the physical exerciser; he wondered if they would give him a bit of their minds if they knew of his speech.

Norah Curfew accompanied him to the door.

"Aren't they ducks?"

"I'm afraid if I saw much of them, I should give up Foggartism."

352

"Oh! but why?"

"Well, you see, it designs to make them men and women of property."

"You mean that would spoil them?"

Michael grinned. "There's something dangerous about silver spoons. Here's my initiation fee." He handed her all his money.

"Oh! Mr. Mont, we didn't——!"

"Well, give me back sixpence, otherwise I shall have to walk home."

"It's frightfully kind of you. Do come again; and please don't give up Foggartism."

He walked to the train thinking of her eyes; and, on reaching home, said to Fleur:

"You absolutely must come and see that place. It's quite clean, and the spirit's topping. It's bucked me up like anything. Norah Curfew's perfectly splendid."

Fleur looked at him between her lashes.

"Oh!" she said. "I will."

## Chapter VII

## CONTRASTS

THE land beyond the coppice at Lippinghall was a ten-acre bit of poor grass, chalk and gravel, fenced round, to show that it was property. Except for one experiment with goats, abandoned because nobody would drink their milk in a country that did not demean itself by growing food, nothing had been done with it. By December this poor relation of Sir Lawrence Mont's estate was being actively exploited. Close to the coppice the hut had been erected, and at least an acre converted into a sea of mud. The coppice itself presented an incised and draggled appearance, owing to the ravages of Henry Boddick and another man, who had cut and stacked a quantity of timber, which a contractor was gradually rejecting for the fowl-house and granary. The incubator-house was at present in the nature of a prophecy. Progress, in fact, was somewhat slow, but it was hoped that fowls might be asked to begin their operations soon after the New Year. In the meantime Michael had decided that the colony had better get the worst over and go into residence. Scraping the Manor House for furniture, and sending in a store of groceries, oil-lamps, and soap, he installed Boddick on the left, earmarked the centre for the Bergfelds, and the right hand for Swain. He was present when the Manor car brought them from the station. The murky day was turning cold, the trees dripped, the car-wheels splashed up the surface water. From the doorway of the hut Michael watched them get out, and thought he had never seen three more untimely creatures. Bergfeld came first; having only one suit, he had put it on, and looked what he was—an actor out of a job. Mrs. Bergfeld came second, and having no outdoor coat, looked what she was—nearly frozen. Swain came last. On his shadowy face was nothing quite so spirited as a sneer; but he gazed about him, and seemed to say: "My hat!"

Boddick, with a sort of prescience, was absent in the coppice. 'He,' thought Michael, 'is my only joy!'

Taking them into the kitchen mess-room of the hut, he deployed a thermos of hot coffee, a cake, and a bottle of rum.

"Awfully sorry things look so dishevelled; but I think the hut's dry, and there are plenty of blankets. These oil-lamps smell rather. You were in the war, Mr. Swain; you'll feel at home in no time. Mrs. Bergfeld, you look so cold, do put some rum into your coffee; we always do when we go over the top."

They all put rum into their coffee, which had a marked effect. Mrs. Bergfeld's cheeks grew pink, and her eyes darkened. Swain remarked that the hut was a "bit of all right"; Bergfeld began making a speech. Michael checked him. "Boddick knows all the ropes. I'm afraid I've got to catch a train; I've only just time to show you round."

While whirling back to town afterwards he felt that he had, indeed, abandoned his platoon just as it was going over the top. That night he would be dining in Society; there would be light and warmth, jewels and pictures, wine and talk; the dinner would cost the board of his 'down and outs' for a quarter at least; and nobody would give them and their like a thought. If he ventured to draw Fleur's attention to the contrast, she would say:

"My dear boy, that's like a book by Gurdon Minho; you're getting sentimental." And he would feel a fool. Or would he? Would he not, perhaps, look at her small distinguished head and think: 'Too easy a way out, my dear; those who take it have little heads!' And, then, his eyes, straying farther down to that white throat and all the dainty loveliness below, would convey a warmth to his blood and a warning to his brain not to give way to blasphemy, lest it end by disturbing bliss. For what with Foggartism, poultry, and the rest of it, Michael had serious thoughts sometimes that Fleur had none; and with wisdom born of love, he knew that if she hadn't, she never would have, and he must get used to it. She was what she was, and could be converted only in popular fiction. Excellent business for the self-centred heroine to turn from interest in her own belongings to interest in people who had no belongings; but in life it wasn't done. Fleur at least camouflaged her self-concentration gracefully; and with Kit——! Ah! but Kit was herself!

So he did not mention his 'down and outs' on their way to dinner in Eaton Square. He took instead a lesson in the royal Personage named on their invitation card, and marvelled at Fleur's knowledge. "She's interested in social matters. And do remember, Michael, not to sit down till she asks you to, and not to go away before her, and to say 'ma'am'."

Michael grinned. "I suppose they'll all be nobs, or sn—er—why the deuce did they ask us?"

But Fleur was silent, thinking of her curtsey.

Royalty was affable, the dinner short but superb, served and eaten off gold plate, at a rate which suited the impression that there really wasn't a moment to spare. Fleur took a mental note of this new necessity. She knew personally five of the twenty-four diners, and the rest as in an illustrated paper, darkly. She had seen them all there at one time or another, stepping hideously in paddocks, photographed with their offspring or their dogs, about to reply for the Colonies, or 'taking a lunar' at a flying grouse. Her quick instinct apprehended almost at once the reason why she and Michael had been invited. His speech! Like some new specimen at the Zoo, he was an object of curiosity, a stunt. She saw people nodding in the direction of him, seated opposite her between two ladies covered with flesh and pearls. Excited and very pretty, she flirted with the Admiral on her right, and defended Michael with spirit from the Under-Secretary on her left. The Admiral grew warm, the Under-Secretary, too young for emotion, cold.

"A little knowledge, Mrs. Mont," he said at the end of his short second innings, "is a dangerous thing."

"Now where have I heard that?" said Fleur. "Is it in the Bible?"

The Under-Secretary tilted his chin.

"We who have to work departments know too much, perhaps; but your husband certainly doesn't know enough. Foggartism is an amusing idea, but there it stops."

"We shall see!" said Fleur. "What do you say, Admiral?"

"Foggartism! What's that—new kind of death ray? I saw a fellow yesterday, Mrs. Mont—give you my word!—who's got a

355

ray that goes through three bullocks, a nine-inch brick wall, and gives a shock to a donkey on the other side; and only at quarter strength."

Fleur flashed a look round towards the Under-Secretary, who had turned his shoulder, and, leaning towards the Admiral, murmured:

"I wish you'd give a shock to the donkey on *my* other side; he wants it, and I'm not nine inches thick."

But before the Admiral could shoot his death ray, Royalty had risen.

In the apartment to which Fleur was withdrawn, she had been saying little for some minutes, and noticing much, when her hostess came up and said·:

"My dear, Her Royal Highness——"

Fleur followed, retaining every wit.

A frank and simple hand patted the sofa beside her. Fleur sat down. A frank and simple voice said:

"What an interesting speech your husband made! It was so refreshing, I thought."

"Yes, ma'am," said Fleur; "but there it will stop, I am told."

A faint smile curled lips guiltless of colouring matter.

"Well, perhaps. Has he been long in Parliament?"

"Only a year."

"Ah! I liked his taking up the cudgels for the children."

"Some people think he's proposing a new kind of child slavery."

"Oh! really! Have you any children?"

"One," said Fleur, and added honestly: "And I must say I wouldn't part with him at fourteen."

"Ah! And have you been long married?"

"Four years."

At this moment the royal lady saw someone else she wished to speak to, and was compelled to break off the conversation, which she did very graciously, leaving Fleur with the feeling that she had been disappointed with the rate of production.

In the cab trailing its way home through the foggy night, she felt warm and excited, and as if Michael wasn't.

"What's the matter, Michael?"

His hand came down on her knee at once.

"Sorry, old thing! Only, really—when you think of it—eh?"

"Of what? You were quite a li—object of interest."

"The whole thing's a game. Anything for novelty!"

"The Princess was very nice about you."

"Ah! Poor thing! But I suppose you get used to anything!"
Fleur laughed. Michael went on:

"Any new idea gets seized and talked out of existence. It never gets farther than the brain, and the brain gets bored; and there it is, already a back number!"

"That can't be true, Michael. What about Free Trade, or Woman Suffrage?"

Michael squeezed her knee. "All the women say to me: 'But how interesting, Mr. Mont; I think it's most thrilling!' And the men say: 'Good stunt, Mont! But not practical politics, of course.' And I've only one answer: 'Things as big got done in the war.' By George, it's foggy!"

They were going, indeed, at a snail's pace, and through the windows could see nothing but the faint glow of the street lamps emerging slowly, high up, one by one. Michael let down a window and leaned out.

"Where are we?"

"Gawd knows, sir."

Michael coughed, put up the window again, and resumed his clutch of Fleur.

"By the way, Wastwater asked me if I'd read *Canthar*. He says there's a snorting cut-up of it in *The Protagonist*. It'll have the usual effect—sends sales up."

"They say it's very clever."

"Horribly out of drawing—not fit for children, and tells adults nothing they don't know. I don't see how it can be justified."

"Genius, my dear. If it's attacked, it'll be defended."

"Sib Swan won't have it—he says it's muck."

"Oh! yes; but Sib's getting a back number."

"That's very true," said Michael, thoughtfully. "By Jove! how fast things move, except in politics, and fog."

Their cab had come to a standstill. Michael let down the window again.

"I'm fair lost, sir," said the driver's hoarse voice. "Ought to be near the Embankment, but for the life of me I can't find the turning." Michael buttoned his coat, put up the window again, and got out on the near side.

The night was smothered, alive only with the continual hootings of creeping cars. The black vapour, acrid and cold, surged into Michael's lungs.

"I'll walk beside you; we're against the kerb; creep on till we strike the river, or a bobby."

The cab crept on, and Michael walked beside it, feeling with his foot for the kerb.

The refined voice of an invisible man said: "This is sanguinary!"

"It is," said Michael. "Where are we?"

"In the twentieth century, and the heart of civilisation."

Michael laughed, and regretted it; the fog tasted of filth.

"Think of the police!" said the voice, "having to be out in this all night!"

"Splendid force, the police!" replied Michael. "Where are you, sir?"

"Here, sir. Where are you?"

It was the exact position. The blurred moon of a lamp glowed suddenly above Michael's head. The cab ceased to move.

"If I could only smell the 'Ouses of Parliament," said the cabman. "They'll be 'avin' supper there be now."

"Listen!" said Michael—Big Ben was striking. "That was to our left."

"At our back," said the cabman.

"Can't be, or we should be in the river; unless you've turned right round!"

"Gawd knows where I've turned," said the cabman, sneezing. "Never saw such a night!"

"There's only one thing for it—drive on until we hit something. Gently does it."

The cabman started the cab, and Michael, with his hand on it, continued to feel for the kerb with his foot.

"Steady!" he said, suddenly. "Car in front." There was a slight bump.

"Nah then!" said a voice. "Where yer comin'? Cawn't yer see?"

Michael moved up alongside of what seeemed to be another taxi.

"Comin' along at that pice!" said its driver; "and full moon, too!"

"Awfully sorry," said Michael. "No harm done. You got any sense of direction left?"

"The pubs are all closed—worse luck! There's a bloomin' car in front o' me that I've hit three times. Can't make any impression on it. The driver's dead, I think. Would yer go and look, Guv'nor?"

Michael moved towards the loom in front. But at that moment it gave way to the more universal blackness. He ran four steps to hail the driver, stumbled off the kerb, fell, picked himself up and spun round. He moved along the kerb to his right, felt he was going wrong, stopped and called: "Hallo!" A faint "Hallo!" replied from—where? He moved what he thought was back, and called again. No answer! Fleur would be frightened. He shouted. Half a dozen faint hallos replied to him; and someone at his elbow said: "Don't cher know where y'are?"

"No; do you?"

"What do you think? Lost anything?"

"Yes; my cab."

"Left anything in it?"

"My wife."

"Lawd! You won't get 'er back to-night." A hoarse laugh, ghostly and obscene, floated by. A bit of darkness loomed for a moment, and faded out. Michael stood still. 'Keep your head!' he thought. 'Here's the kerb—either they're in front, or they're behind; or else I've turned a corner.' He stepped forward along the kerb. Nothing! He stepped back. Nothing! "What the blazes have I done?" he muttered: "or have they moved on!" Sweat poured down him in spite of the cold. Fleur would be really scared! And the words of his election address sprang from his lips: "Chiefly by the elimination of smoke!"

"Ah!" said a voice, "got a cigarette, Guv'nor?"

"I'll give you all I've got and half a crown, if you'll find a cab close by with a lady in it. What street's this?"

"Don't arst me! The streets 'ave gone mad, I think."

"Listen!" said Michael sharply.

"That's right, 'Someone callin' so sweet.' "

"Hallo!" cried Michael. "Fleur!"

"Here! Here!"

It sounded to his right, to his left, behind him, in front. Then came the steady blowing of a cab's horn.

"Now we've got 'em," said the bit of darkness. "This way, Guv'nor, step slow, and mind my corns!"

Michael yielded to a tugging at his coat.

"It's like no-man's-land in a smoke barrage!" said his guide.

"You're right. Hallo! Coming!"

The horn sounded a yard off. A voice said: "Oh! Michael!"

His face touched Fleur's in the window of the cab.

"Just a second, darling. There you are, my friend, and thanks awfully! Hope you'll get home!"

"I've 'ad worse nights out than this. Thank you, Captain! Wish you and the lady luck." There was a sound of shuffling on, and the fog sighed out: "So long!"

"All right, sir," said the hoarse voice of Michael's cabman. "I know where I am now. First on the left, second on the right. I'll bump the kerb till I get there. Thought you was swallered up, sir!"

Michael got into the cab, and clasped Fleur close. She uttered a long sigh, and sat quite still.

"Nothing more scaring than a fog!" he said.

"I thought you'd been run over!"

Michael was profoundly touched.

"Awfully sorry, darling. And you've got all that beastly fog down your throat. We'll drown it out when we get in. That poor chap was an ex-service man. Wonderful the way the English keep their humour and don't lose their heads."

"I lost mine!"

"Well, you've got it back," said Michael, pressing it against his own to hide the emotion he was feeling. "Fog's our sheet-anchor, after all. So long as we have fog, England will survive." He felt Fleur's lips against his.

He belonged to her, and she couldn't afford to have him straying about in fogs or Foggartism! Was that the——? And then, he yielded to the thrill.

The cabman was standing by the opened door. "Now, sir, I'm in your Square. P'r'aps you know your own 'ouse."

Wrenched from the kiss, Michael stammered: "Righto!" The fog was thinner here; he could consult the shape of trees. "On and to your right, third house."

There it was—desirable—with its bay trees in its tubs and its fanlight shining. He put his latch-key in the door.

"A drink?" he said.

The cabman coughed: "I won't say no, sir."

Michael brought the drink.

"Far to go?"

"Near Putney Bridge. Your 'ealth, sir!"

Michael watched his pinched face drinking.

"Sorry you've got to plough into that again!"

The cabman handed back the glass.

"Thank'ee, sir; I shall be all right now; keep along the river, and down the Fulham Road. Thought they couldn't lose me in London. Where I went wrong was trying for a short cut instead of takin' the straight road round. 'Ope the young lady's none the worse, sir. She was properly scared while you was out there in the dark. These fogs ain't fit for 'uman bein's. They ought to do somethin' about 'em in Parliament."

"They ought!" said Michael, handing him a pound note. "Good-night, and good luck!"

"It's an ill wind!" said the cabman, starting his cab. "Good-night, sir, and thank you kindly."

"Thank *you*!" said Michael.

The cab ground slowly away, and was lost to sight.

Michael went into the Spanish room. Fleur, beneath the Goya, was boiling a silver kettle, and burning pastilles. What a contrast to the world outside—its black malodorous cold reek, its risk and fear! In this pretty glowing room, with this pretty glowing woman, why think of its tangle, lost shapes, and straying cries?

Lighting his cigarette, he took his drink from her by its silver handle, and put it to his lips.

"I really think we ought to have a car, Michael!"

## Chapter VIII

### COLLECTING EVIDENCE

THE editor of *The Protagonist* had so evidently enjoyed himself that he caused a number of other people to do the same.

"There's no more popular sight in the East, Forsyte," said Sir Lawrence, "than a boy being spanked; and the only difference between East and West is that in the East the boy at once offers himself again at so much a spank. I don't see Mr. Perceval Calvin doing that."

"If he defends himself," said Soames, gloomily, "other people won't."

They waited, reading daily denunciations signed: 'A Mother of Three'; 'Roger: Northampton'; 'Victorian'; 'Alys St. Maurice'; 'Plus Fours'; 'Arthur Whiffkin'; 'Sportsman if not Gentleman'; and 'Pro Patria'; which practically all contained the words: 'I cannot say that I have read the book through, but I have read enough to——'

It was five days before the defence fired a shot. But first came a letter above the signature: 'Swishing Block', which, after commenting on the fact that a whole school of so-called literature had been indicted by the editor of *The Protagonist* in his able letter of the 14th inst., noted with satisfaction that the said school had grace enough to take its swishing without a murmur. Not even an anonymous squeak had been heard from the whole apostolic body.

"Forsyte," said Sir Lawrence, handing it to Soames, "that's my very own mite, and if it doesn't draw them—nothing will!"

But it did. The next issue of the interested journal in which the correspondence was appearing contained a letter from the greater

novelist L. S. D. which restored everyone to his place. This book
might or might not be Art, he hadn't read it; but the editor of *The
Protagonist* wrote like a pedagogue, and there was an end of him.
As to the claim that literature must always wear a flannel petticoat,
it was 'piffle', and that was that. From under the skirts of this letter
the defence, to what of exultation Soames ever permitted himself,
moved out in force. Among the defenders were as many as four
of the selected ten associates to whom young Butterfield had pur-
veyed copies. They wrote over their own names that *Canthar*
was distinctly LITERATURE; they were sorry for people who
thought in these days that LITERATURE had any business with
morals. The work must be approached æsthetically or not at all.
ART was ART, and morality was morality, and never the twain
could, would, or should meet. It was monstrous that a work of this
sort should have to appear with a foreign imprint. When would
England recognise genius when she saw it?

Soames cut the letters out one after the other, and pasted them
in a book. He had got what he wanted, and the rest of the discussion interested him no more. He had received, too, a communication from young Butterfield.

"SIR,

"I called on the lady last Monday, and was fortunately able to
see her in person. She seemed rather annoyed when I offered her
the book. 'That book,' she said: 'I read it weeks ago.' 'It's exciting
a great deal of interest, Madam,' I said. 'I know,' she said. 'Then
you won't take a copy; the price is rising steadily, it'll be very
valuable in time?' 'I've got one,' she said. That's what you told
me to find out, sir; so I didn't pursue the matter. I hope I have done
what you wanted. But if there is anything more, I shall be most
happy. I consider that I owe my present position entirely to
you."

Soames didn't know about that, but as to his future position—
he might have to put the young man into the box. The question of
a play remained. He consulted Michael.

"Does that young woman still act in the advanced theatre place
you gave me the name of?"

Michael winced. "I don't know, sir; but I could find out."

Inquiry revealed that she was cast for the part of Olivia in Bertie
Curfew's matinée of 'The Plain Dealer'.

" 'The Plain Dealer'?" said Soames. "Is that an advanced play?"

"Yes, sir, two hundred and fifty years old."

"Ah!" said Soames; "they were a coarse lot in those days How is it she goes on there if she and the young man have split?"

"Oh! well, they're very cool hands. I do hope you're going to keep things out of Court, sir?"

"I can't tell. When's this performance?"

"January the seventh."

Soames went to his club library and took down "Wycherley". He was disappointed with the early portions of 'The Plain Dealer', but it improved as it went on, and he spent some time making a list of what George Forsyte would have called the 'nubbly bits'. He understood that at that theatre they did not bowdlerise. Excellent! There were passages that would raise hair on any British jury. Between *Canthar* and this play, he felt as if he had a complete answer to any claim by the young woman and her set to having 'morals about them'. Old professional instincts were rising within him. He had retained Sir James Foskisson, K.C., not because he admired him personally, but because if he didn't, the other side might. As junior he was employing very young Nicholas Forsyte; he had no great opinion of him, but it was as well to keep the matter in the family, especially if it wasn't to come into Court.

A conversation with Fleur that evening contributed to his intention that it should not.

"What's happened to that young American?" he said.

Fleur smiled acidly. "Francis Wilmot? Oh! he's 'fallen for' Marjorie Ferrar."

" 'Fallen for her'?" said Soames. "What an expression!"

"Yes, dear; it's American."

" 'For' her? It means nothing, so far as I can see."

"Let's hope not, for his sake! She's going to marry Sir Alexander MacGown, I'm told."

"Oh!"

"Did Michael tell you that he hit him on the nose?"

"Which—who?" said Soames testily. "Whose nose?"

"MacGown's dear; and it bled like anything."

"Why on earth did he do that?"

"Didn't you read his speech about Michael?"

"Oh!" said Soames. "Parliamentary fuss — that's nothing. They're always behaving like schoolboys, there. And so she's going to marry him. Has he been putting her up to all this?"

"No; *she's* been putting him."

Soames discounted the information with a sniff; he scented the

363

hostility of woman for woman. Still, chicken and egg—political feeling and social feeling, who could say which first promoted which? In any case, this made a difference. Going to be married—was she? He debated the matter for some time, and then decided that he would go and see Settlewhite and Stark. If they had been a firm of poor repute or the kind always employed in 'causes célèbres', he wouldn't have dreamed of it; but, as a fact, they stood high, were solid family people, with an aristocratic connection and all that.

He did not write, but took his hat and went over from the Connoisseurs' to their offices in King Street, St. James's. The journey recalled old days—to how many such negotiatory meetings had he not gone or caused his adversaries to come! He had never cared to take things into Court if they could be settled out of it. And always he had approached negotiation with the im-personality of one passionless about to meet another of the same kidney—two calculating machines, making their livings out of human nature. He did not feel like that to-day; and, aware of this handicap, stopped to stare into the print and picture shop next door. Ah! There were those first proofs of the Roussel engrav-ings of the Prince Consort Exhibition of '51, that Old Mont had spoken of—he had an eye for an engraving, Old Mont. Ah! and there was a Fred Walker, quite a good one! Mason, and Walker—they weren't done for yet by any means. And the sensation that a man feels hearing a blackbird sing on a tree just coming into blossom, stirred beneath Soames's ribs. Long—long since he had bought a picture! Let him but get this confounded case out of the way, and he could enjoy himself again. Riving his glance from the window, he took a long breath, and walked into Settlewhite and Stark's.

The chief partner's room was on the first floor, and the chief partner standing where chief partners stand.

"How do you do, Mr. Forsyte? I've not met you since 'Bobbin against the L. & S. W.' That must have been 1900!"

"1899," said Soames. "You were for the Company."

Mr. Settlewhite pointed to a chair.

Soames sat down and glanced up at the figure before the fire. H'm! a long-lipped, long-eyelashed, long-chinned face; a man of his own calibre, education, and probity! He need not beat about the bush.

"This action," he said, "is a very petty business. What can we do about it?"

Mr. Settlewhite frowned.

"That depends, Mr. Forsyte, on what you have to propose? My client has been very grossly libelled."

Soames smiled sourly.

"She began it. And what is she relying on—private letters to personal friends of my daughter's, written in very natural anger! I'm surprised that a firm of your standing——"

Mr. Settlewhite smiled.

"Don't trouble to compliment my firm? I'm surprised myself that you are acting for your daughter. You can hardly see all round the matter. Have you come to offer an apology?"

"That!" said Soames. "I should have thought it was for your client to apologise."

"If such is your view, I'm afraid it's no use continuing this discussion."

Soames regarded him fixedly.

"How do you think you're going to prove damage? She belongs to the fast set."

Mr. Settlewhite continued to smile.

"I understand she's going to marry Sir Alexander MacGown," said Soames.

Mr. Settlewhite's lips tightened.

"Really, Mr. Forsyte, if you have come to offer an apology and a substantial sum in settlement, we can talk. Otherwise——"

"As a sensible man," said Soames, "you know that these Society scandals are always dead sea fruit—nothing but costs and vexations, and a feast for all the gossips about town. I'm prepared to offer you a thousand pounds to settle the whole thing, but an apology I can't look at. A mutual expression of regret—perhaps; but an apology's out of the question."

"Fifteen hundred I might accept—the insults have had wide currency. But an apology is essential."

Soames sat silent, chewing the injustice of it all. Fifteen hundred! Monstrous! Still he would pay even that to keep Fleur out of Court. But humble-pie! She wouldn't eat it, and he couldn't make her, and he didn't know that he wanted to. He got up.

"Look here, Mr. Settlewhite, if you take this into Court, you will find yourself up against more than you think. But the whole thing is so offensive to me, that I'm prepared to meet you over the money, though I tell you frankly I don't believe a jury would award a penny piece. As to an apology, a 'formula' could be found perhaps"—why the deuce was the fellow smiling?—"Something like this: 'We regat that we have said hasty things about each other,' to be signed by both parties."

Mr. Settlewhite caressed his chin.

"Well, I'll put your proposition before my client. I join with you in wishing to see the matter settled, not because I'm afraid of the result"—'Oh, no!' thought Soames—"but because these cases, as you say, are not edifying." He held out his hand.

Soames gave it a cold touch.

"You understand that this is entirely 'without prejudice'," he said, and went out. 'She'll take it!' he thought. Fifteen hundred pounds of his money thrown away on that baggage, just because for once she had been labelled what she was; and all his trouble to get evidence wasted! For a moment he resented his devotion to Fleur. Really it was fatuous to be so fond as that! Then his heart rebounded. Thank God! He had settled it.

Christmas was at hand. It did not alarm him, therefore, that he received no answering communication. Fleur and Michael were at Lippinghall with the ninth and eleventh baronets. He and Annette had Winifred and the Cardigans down at 'The Shelter'. Not till the 6th of January did he receive a letter from Messrs. Settlewhite and Stark.

"DEAR SIR,

"In reference to your call of the 17th ultimo, your proposition was duly placed before our client, and we are instructed to say that she will accept the sum of £1,500—fifteen hundred pounds—and an apology, duly signed by your client, copy of which we enclose.

"We are, dear Sir,
"Faithfully yours,
"SETTLEWHITE AND STARK."

Soames turned to the enclosure. It ran thus:

"I, Mrs. Michael Mont, withdraw the words concerning Miss Marjorie Ferrar contained in my letters to Mrs. Ralph Ppynrryn and Mrs. Edward Maltese of October 4th last, and hereby tender a full and free apology for having written them.

"(Signed)"

Pushing back the breakfast-table, so violently that it groaned, Soames got up.

"What is it, Soames?" said Annette. "Have you broken your plate again? You should not bite so hard."

"Read that!"

Annette read.

"You would give that woman fifteen hundred pounds? I think you are mad, Soames. I would not give her fifteen hundred pence! Pay this woman, and she tells her friends. That is fifteen hundred apologies in all their minds. Really, Soames— I am surprised. A man of business, a clever man! Do you not know the world better than that? With every pound you pay, Fleur eats her words!"

Soames flushed. It was so French, and yet somehow it was so true. He walked to the window. The French—they had no sense of compromise, and every sense of money!

"Well," he said, "that ends it anyway. She won't sign. And I shall withdraw my offer."

"I should hope so. Fleur has a good head. She will look very pretty in Court. I think that woman will be sorry she ever lived! Why don't you have her what you call shadowed? It is no good to be delicate with women like that."

In a weak moment he had told Annette about the book and the play; for, unable to speak of them to Fleur and Michael, he had really had to tell someone; indeed, he had shown her *Canthar*, with the words: "I don't advise you to read it, it's very French."

Annette had returned it to him two days later, saying: "It is not French at all; it is disgusting. You English are so coarse. It has no wit. It is only nasty. A serious nasty book—that is the limit. You are so old-fashioned, Soames. Why do you say this book is French?"

Soames, who really didn't know why, had muttered:

"Well, they can't get it printed in England." And with the words: "Bruxelles, Bruxelles, you call Bruxelles——" buzzing about his ears, had left the room. He had never known any people so touchy as the French!

Her remark about 'shadowing', however, was not easily forgotten. Why be squeamish, when all depended on frightening this woman? And on arriving in London he visited an office that was not Mr. Polteed's, and gave instructions for the shadowing of Marjorie Ferrar's past, present, and future.

His answer to Settlewhite and Stark, too, was brief, determined, and written on the paper of his own firm.

# A MODERN COMEDY

"Jan. 6th, 1925.

"DEAR SIRS,

"I have your letter of yesterday's date, and note that your client has rejected my proposition, which, as you know, was made entirely without prejudice, and is now withdrawn *in toto*.

"Yours faithfully,

"SOAMES FORSYTE."

If he did not mistake, they would be sorry. And he gazed at the words '*in toto*'; somehow they looked funny. *In toto*! And now for ' The Plain Dealer '!

The theatre of the 'Ne Plus Ultra' Play-Producing Society had a dingy exterior, a death-mask of Congreve in the hall, a peculiar smell, and an apron stage. There was no music. They hit something three times before the curtain went up. There were no footlights. The scenery was peculiar—Soames could not take his eyes off it till, in the first Entr'acte, its principle was revealed to him by the conversation of two people sitting just behind.

"The point of the scenery here is that no one need look at it, you see. They go farther than anything yet done."

"They've gone farther in Moscow."

"I believe not. Curfew went over there. He came back raving about the way they speak their lines."

"Does he know Russian?"

"No. You don't need to. It's the timbre. I think he's doing pretty well here with that. You couldn't give a play like this if you took the words in."

Soames, who had been trying to take the words in—it was, indeed, what he had come for—squinted round at the speakers. They were pale and young and went on with a strange unconcern

"Curfew's doing great work. He's shaking them up."

"I see they've got Marjorie Ferrar as Olivia."

"Don't know why he keeps on an amateur like that."

"Box office, dear boy; she brings the smart people. She's painful, I think."

"She did one good thing—the dumb girl in that Russian play. But she can't speak for nuts; you're following the sense of her words all the time. She doesn't rhythmatise you a little bit."

"She's got looks."

"M'yes."

At this moment the curtain went up again. Since Marjorie Ferrar had not yet appeared, Soames was obliged to keep awake:

368

indeed, whether because she couldn't 'speak for nuts', or merely from duty, he was always awake while she was on the stage, and whenever she had anything outrageous to say he noted it carefully; otherwise he passed an excellent afternoon, and went away much rested. In his cab he mentally rehearsed Sir James Foskisson in the part of cross-examiner:

"I think, madam, you played Olivia in a production of 'The Plain Dealer' by the 'Ne Plus Ultra' Play-Producing Society?. . . Would it be correct to say that the part was that of a modest woman? . . . Precisely. And did it contain the following lines (Quotation of nubbly bits.) . . . Did that convey anything to your mind, madam? . . . I suppose that you would not say it was an immoral passage? . . . No? Nor calculated to offend the ears and debase the morals of a decent-minded audience? . . . No. In fact, you don't take the same view of morality that I, or, I venture to think, the jury do? . . . No. The dark scene—you did not remonstrate with the producer for not omitting that scene? . . . Quite. Mr. Curfew, I think, was the producer? Yes. Are you on such terms with that gentleman as would have made a remonstrance easy? . . . Ah! Now, madam, I put it to you that throughout 1923 you were seeing this gentleman nearly every day. . . . Well, say three or four times a week. And yet you say that you were not on such terms as would have made it possible for you to represent to him that no modest young woman should be asked to play a scene like that. . . . Indeed! The jury will form their own opinion of your answer. You are not a professional actress, dependent for your living on doing what you are told to do? . . . No. And yet you have the face to come here and ask for substantial damages because of the allegation in a private letter that you haven't a moral about you? . . . Have you? . . ." And so on, and so on. Oh! no. Damages! She wouldn't get a farthing.

## Chapter IX

### VOLTE FACE

KEEPING Sir Alexander MacGown and Francis Wilmot in the air, fulfilling her week-end and other engagements, playing much bridge in the hope of making her daily expenses, getting a day's hunting when she could, and rehearsing the part of Olivia, Marjorie Ferrar had almost forgotten the action, when the offer of fifteen hundred pounds and the formula were put before her by Messrs. Settlewhite and Stark. She almost jumped at it. The money would wipe out her more pressing debts; she would be able to breathe, and reconsider her future.

She received their letter on the Friday before Christmas, just as she was about to go down to her father's, near Newmarket, and wrote hastily to say she would call at their office on her way home on Monday. The following evening she consulted her father. Lord Charles was of opinion that if this attorney fellow would go as far as fifteen hundred, he must be dead keen on settling, and she had only to press for the apology to get it. Anyway, she should let them stew in their juice for a bit. On Monday he wanted to show her his yearlings. She did not, therefore, return to Town till the 23rd, and found the office closed for Christmas. It had never occurred to her that solicitors had holidays. On Christmas Eve she herself went away for ten days; so that it was January the 4th before she was again able to call. Mr. Settlewhite was still in the South of France, but Mr. Stark would see her. Mr. Stark knew little about the matter, but thought Lord Charles's advice probably sound; he proposed to write accepting the fifteen hundred pounds if a formal apology were tendered; they could fall back on the formula if necessary, but it was always wise to get as much as you could. With some misgiving Marjorie Ferrar agreed.

Returning from the matinée on January 7th, tired and elated by applause, by Bertie Curfew's words: "You did quite well, darling," and almost the old look on his face, she got into a hot bath, and was just out when her maid announced Mr. Wilmot.

"Keep him, Fanny; say I'll be with him in twenty minutes."

Feverish and soft, as if approaching a crisis, she dressed hastily, put essence of orange-blossom on her neck and hands, and went to the studio. She entered without noise. The young man, back to the door, in the centre of the room, evidently did not hear her. Approaching within a few feet, she waited for the effect on him of orange-blossom. He was standing like some Eastern donkey, that with drooped ears patiently awaits the fresh burdening of a sore back. And suddenly he spoke: "I'm all in."

"Francis!"

The young man turned.

"Oh! Marjorie!" he said, "I never heard." And taking her hands, he buried his face in them.

She was hampered at that moment. To convert his mouth from despairing kissing of her hands to triumphal flame upon her lips would have been so easy if he had been modern, if his old-fashioned

370

love had not complimented her so subtly; if, too, she were not feeling for him something more—or was it less?—than passion. Was she to know at last the sensations of the simple—a young girl's idyll—something she had missed? She led him to the divan, sat down by his side, and looked into his eyes. Fabled sweetness, as of a spring morning—Francis and she, children in the wood, with the world well lost! She surrendered to the innocence of it; deliberately grasped something delicious, new. Poor boy! How delightful to feel him happy at last—to promise marriage and mean to perform it! When? Oh! when he liked—— Soon, quite soon; the sooner the better! Almost unconscious that she was 'playing' a young girl, she was carried away by his amazement and his joy. He was on fire, on air; yet he remained delicate—he was wonderful! For an hour they sat—a fragrant hour for memory to sniff—before she remembered that she was dining out at half-past eight. She put her lips to his, and closed her eyes. And thought ran riot. Should she spoil it, and make sure of him in modern fashion? What was his image of her but a phlizz, but a fraud? She saw his eyes grow troubled, felt his hands grow fevered. Something seemed drowning before her eyes. She stood up.

"Now, my darling, you must fly!"

When he had flown, she threw off her dress and brushed out her hair that in the mirror seemed to have more gold than red. . . . Some letters on her dressing-table caught her eye. The first was a bill, the second a bill; the third ran thus:

"DEAR MADAM,

"We regret to say that Cuthcott Kingson & Forsyte have refused to give the apology we asked for, and withdrawn their verbal offer *in toto*. We presume, therefore, that the action must go forward. We have every hope, however, that they may reconsider the matter before it comes into Court.

"Your obedient servants,
"SETTLEWHITE & STARK."

She dropped it and sat very still, staring at a little hard line on the right side of her mouth and a little hard line on the left. . . .

Francis Wilmot, flying, thought of steamship-lines and state-rooms, of registrars and rings. An hour ago he had despaired; now it seemed he had always known she was 'too fine not to give up this fellow whom she didn't love'. He would make her the queen of South Carolina—he surely would! But if she didn't like it out there, he would sell the 'old home', and they would go and live where she wished—in Venice; he had heard her say Venice was wonderful; or New York, or Sicily; with her he wouldn't care! And London in the cold dry wind seemed beautiful, no longer a grey maze of unreality and shadows, but a city where you could buy rings and steamship passages. The wind cut him like a knife and he did not feel it. That poor devil MacGown! He hated the sight, the thought of him, and yet felt sorry, thinking of him with the cup dashed from his lips. And all the days, weeks, months himself had spent circling round the flame, his wings scorched and drooping, seemed now but the natural progress of the soul towards Paradise. Twenty-four—his age and hers; an eternity of bliss before them! He pictured her on the porch at home. Horses! A better car than the old Ford! The darkies would adore her—kind of grand, and so white! To walk with her among the azaleas in the spring, that he could smell already; no—it was his hands where he had touched her! He shivered, and resumed his flight under the bare trees, well-nigh alone in the east wind; the stars of a bitter night shining.

A card was handed to him as he entered his hotel.

"Mr. Wilmot, a gentleman to see you."

Sir Alexander was seated in a corner of the lounge, with a crush hat in his hand. He rose and came towards Francis Wilmot, grim and square.

"I've been meaning to call on you for some time, Mr. Wilmot."

"Yes, sir. May I offer you a cocktail, or a glass of sherry?"

"No, thank you. You are aware of my engagement to Miss Ferrar?"

"I was, sir."

This red aggressive face, with its stiff moustache and burning eyes, revived his hatred; so that he no longer felt sorry.

"You know that I very much object to your constant visits to that young lady. In this country it is not the part of a gentleman to pursue an engaged young woman."

"That," said Francis Wilmot coolly, "is for Miss Ferrar herself to say."

MacGown's face grew even redder.

"If you hadn't been an American, I should have warned you to keep clear a long time ago."

Francis Wilmot bowed.

"Well! Are you going to?"

"Permit me to decline an answer."

MacGown thrust forward his face.

"I've told you," he said. "If you trespass any more, look out for yourself."

"Thank you; I will," said Francis Wilmot softly.

MacGown stood for a moment swaying slightly. Was he going to hit out? Francis Wilmot put his hands into his trouser pockets.

"You've had your warning," said MacGown, and turned on his heel.

"Good-night!" said Francis Wilmot to that square receding back. He had been gentle, he had been polite, but he hated the fellow, yes, indeed! Save for the triumphal glow within him, there might have been a fuss!

## Chapter X

### PHOTOGRAPHY

SUMMONED to the annual Christmas covert-shooting at Lipping-hall, Michael found there two practical politicians and one member of the Government.

In the mullion-windowed smoking-room, where men retired, and women too sometimes, into chairs old, soft, leathery, the ball of talk was lightly tossed, and naught so devastating as Foggartism mentioned. But in odd minutes and half-hours Michael gained insight into political realities, and respect for practical politicians. Even on this holiday they sat up late, got up early, wrote letters, examined petitions, dipped into Blue Books. They were robust, ate heartily, took their liquor like men, never seemed fatigued. They shaved clean, looked healthy, and shot badly with enjoyment. The member of the Government played golf instead, and Fleur went round with him. Michael learned the lesson: Have so much on your mind that you have practically nothing in it; no time to pet your schemes, fancies, feelings. Carry on, and be careful that you don't know to what end.

As for Foggartism, they didn't—à la Evening Sun—pooh-pooh it; they merely asked, as Michael had often asked himself: "Yes, but how are you going to work it? Your scheme might be very good, if it didn't hit people's pockets. Any addition to the price of living is out of the question—the country's taxed up to the hilt. Your Foggartism's going to need money in every direction. You may swear till you're blue in the face that ten or twenty years hence it'll bring fivefold return; nobody will listen. You may say: 'Without it we're all going to the devil'; but we're accustomed to that—some people think we're there already, and they resent its being said. Others, especially manufacturers, believe what they want to. They can't bear anyone who cries 'stinking fish', whatever his object. Talk about reviving trade, and less taxation, or offer more wages and talk of a capital levy, and, according to Party, we shall believe you've done the trick—until we find you haven't. But you're talking of less trade and more taxation in the present with a view to a better future. Great Scott! In politics you can shuffle the cards, but you mustn't add or subtract. People only react to immediate benefit, or, as in the war, to imminent danger. You must cut out sensationalism."

In short, they were intelligent, and completely fatalistic.

After these quiet talks, Michael understood, much better than before, the profession of politics. He was greatly attracted by the member of the Government; his personality was modest, his manner pleasant, he had Departmental ideas, and was doing his best with his own job according to those ideas; if he had others he kept them to himself. He seemed to admire Fleur, and he listened better than the other two. He said, too, some things they hadn't. "Of course, what we're able to do may be found so inadequate that there'll be a great journalistic outcry, and under cover of it we may bring in some sweeping measures that people will swallow before they know what they're in for."

"The Press," said Michael; "I don't see them helping."

"Well! It's the only voice there is. If you could get fast hold of the vociferous papers, you might even put your Foggartism over. What you're really up against is the slow town growth of the last hundred and fifty years, an ingrained state of mind which can only see England in terms of industrialism and the carrying trade. And in the town-mind, of course, hope springs eternal. They don't like calamity talk. Some genuinely think we can go on indefinitely on the old lines, and get more and more prosperous into the bargain. Personally, I don't. It's possible that much of what old Foggart advocates may be adopted bit by bit, even child emigration, from sheer practical necessity; but it won't be called Foggartism. Inventor's luck! *He'll* get no credit for being the first to see it. And," added the Minister gloomily, "by the time it's adopted, it'll probably be too late."

Receiving the same day a request for an interview from a Press syndicate whose representative would come down to suit his convenience, Michael made the appointment, and prepared an elaborate exposition of his faith. The representative, however, turned out to be a camera, and a photograph entitled: 'The Member for mid-Bucks expounding Foggartism to our Representative,' became the only record of it. The camera was active. It took a family group in front of the porch: 'Right to left, Mr. Michael Mont, M.P., Lady Mont, Mrs. Michael Mont, Sir Lawrence Mont, Bt.' It took Fleur: 'Mrs. Michael Mont, with Kit and Dandie.' It took the Jacobean wing. It took the Minister, with his pipe, 'enjoying a Christmas rest'. It took a corner of the walled garden: 'In the grounds.' It then had lunch. After lunch it took the whole house-party: 'At Sir Lawrence Mont's, Lippinghall Manor, Bucks'; with the Minister on Lady Mont's right and the Minister's wife on Sir Lawrence's left. This photograph would have turned out better if the Dandie, inadvertently left out, had not made a sudden onslaught on the camera legs. It took a photograph of Fleur alone: 'Mrs. Michael Mont—a charming young Society hostess.' It understood that Michael was making an interesting practical experiment—could it take Foggartism in action? Michael grinned and said: "Yes, if it would take a walk, too."

They departed for the coppice. The colony was in its normal state—Boddick, with two of the contractor's men cheering him on, was working at the construction of the incubator-house; Swain, smoking a cigarette, was reading the *Daily Mail*; Bergfeld was sitting with his head in his hands, and Mrs. Bergfeld was washing up.

The camera took three photographs. Michael, who had noted that Bergfeld had begun shaking, suggested to the camera that it would miss its train. It at once took a final photograph of Michael in front of the hut, two cups of tea at the Manor, and its departure.

As Michael was going upstairs that night, the butler came to him.

"The man Boddick's in the pantry, Mr. Michael; I'm afraid something's happened, sir."

"Oh!" said Michael blankly.

Where Michael had spent many happy hours, when he was young, was Boddick, his pale face running with sweat, and his dark eyes very alive.

"The German's gone, sir."

"Gone?"

"Hanged hisself. The woman's in an awful state. I cut him down and sent Swain to the village."

"Good God! Hanged! But why?"

375

"He's been very funny these last three days; and that camera upset him properly. Will you come, sir?"

They set out with a lantern, Boddick telling his tale.

"As soon as ever you was gone this afternoon he started to shake
and carry on about having been made game of. I told 'im not to be
a fool, and went out to get on with it. But when I came in to tea,
he was still shakin', and talkin' about his honour and his savin's;
Swain had got fed-up and was jeerin' at him, and Mrs. Bergfeld
was as white as a ghost in the corner. I told Swain to shut his head;
and Fritz simmered down after a bit, and sat humped up as he does
for hours together. Mrs. Bergfeld got our tea. I had some chores to
finish, so I went out after. When I come in at seven, they was at it
again hammer and tongs, and Mrs. Bergfeld cryin' fit to bust her
heart. 'Can't you see,' I said, 'how you're upsettin' your wife?'
'Henry Boddick,' he said, 'I've nothing against *you*, you've always
been decent to me. But this Swain,' he said, ''is name is Swine!'
and he took up the bread-knife. I got it away from him, and spoke
him calm. 'Ah!' he said, 'but *you've* no pride.' Swain was lookin'
at him with that sort o' droop in his mouth he's got. 'Pride,' he
says, 'you silly blighter, what call 'ave *you* to 'ave any pride?'
Well, I see that while we was there he wasn't goin' to get any
better, so I took Swain off for a glass at the pub. When we came
back at ten o'clock, Swain went straight to bed, and I went into
the mess-room, where I found his wife alone. 'Has he gone to
bed?' I said. 'No,' she said, 'he's gone out to cool his head. Oh!
Henry Boddick,' she said, 'I don't know what to do with him!' We
sat there a bit, she tellin' me about 'im brooding, and all that—
nice woman she is, too; till suddenly she said: 'Henry Boddick,'
she said, 'I'm frightened. Why don't he come?' We went out to
look for him, and where d'you think he was, sir? You know that
big tree we're just goin' to have down? There's a ladder against it,
and the guidin' rope all fixed. He'd climbed up that ladder in the
moonlight, put the rope round his neck, and jumped off; and there
he was, six feet from the ground, dead as a duck. I roused up
Swain, and we got him in, and—— Well, we 'ad a proper time!
Poor woman, I'm sorry for her, sir—though really I think it's just
as well he's gone—he couldn't get upsides with it, anyhow. That
camera chap would have given something for a shot at what we
saw there in the moonlight."

'Foggartism in action!' thought Michael bitterly. 'So endeth the
First Lesson!'

The hut looked lonely in the threading moonlight and the bitter

wind. Inside, Mrs. Bergfeld was kneeling beside the body placed on the deal table, with a handkerchief over its face. Michael put a hand on her shoulder. She gave him a wild look, bowed her head again, and her lips began moving. 'Prayer!' thought Michael. 'Catholic—of course!' He took Boddick aside. "Don't let her see Swain. I'll talk to him."

When the police and the doctor came in, he button-holed the hairdresser, whose shadowy face looked ghastly in the moonlight. He seemed much upset.

"You'd better come down to the house for the night, Swain."

"All right, sir. I never meant to hurt the poor beggar. But he did carry on so, and I've got my own trouble. I couldn't stand 'im monopolisin' misfortune the way he does. When the inquest's over, I'm off. If I can't get some sun soon, I'll be as dead as 'im."

Michael was relieved. Boddick would be left alone.

When at last he got back to the house with Swain, Fleur was asleep. He did not wake her to tell her the news, but lay a long time trying to get warm, and thinking of that great obstacle to all salvation—the human element. And, mingled with his visions of the woman beside that still, cold body, were longings for the warmth of the young body close to him.

The photographs were providential. For three days no paper could be taken up which did not contain some allusion, illustrated, to 'The Tragedy on a Buckinghamshire estate' 'German actor hangs himself'; 'The drama at Lippinghall'; 'Tragic end of an experiment'; 'Right to Left: Mr. Michael Mont, Member for mid-Bucks; Bergfeld, the German actor who hanged himself; Mrs. Bergfeld.'

The *Evening Sun* wrote more in sorrow than in anger:

'The suicide of a German actor on Sir Lawrence Mont's estate at Lippinghall has in it a touch of the grotesquely moral. The unfortunate man seems to have been one of three "out-of-works" selected by the young Member for mid-Bucks, recently conspicuous for his speech on "Foggartism", for a practical experiment in that peculiar movement. Why he should have chosen a German to assist the English people to return to the Land is not perhaps very clear; but, largely speaking, the incident illustrates the utter unsuitability of all amateur attempts to solve this problem, and the futility of pretending to deal with the unemployment crisis while we still tolerate among us numbers of aliens who take the bread out of the mouths of our own people.' The same issue contained a short leader entitled: 'The Alien in Our Midst.' The inquest was well attended. It was common knowledge that three men and one

377

woman lived in the hut, and sensational developments were expected. A good deal of disappointment was felt that the evidence disclosed nothing at all of a sexual character.

Fleur, with the eleventh baronet, returned to town after it was over. Michael remained for the funeral—in a Catholic cemetery some miles away. He walked with Henry Boddick behind Mrs. Bergfeld. A little sleet was drifting out of a sky the colour of the gravestones, and against that whitish sky the yew trees looked very stark. He had ordered a big wreath laid on the grave, and when he saw it thus offered up, he thought: 'First human beings, then rams, now flowers! Progress? I wonder!'

Having arranged that Norah Curfew should take Mrs. Bergfeld as cook in Bethnal Green, he drove her up to London in the Manor car. During that long drive he experienced again feelings that he had not had since the war. Human hearts, dressed-up to the nines in circumstance, interests, manners, accents, race, and class, when stripped by grief, by love, by hate, by laughter were one and the same heart. But how seldom were they stripped! Life was a clothed affair! A good thing too, perhaps—the strain of naked-ness was too considerable! He was, in fact, infinitely relieved to see the face of Norah Curfew, and hear her cheerful words to Mrs. Bergfeld:

"Come in, my dear, and have some tea!" She was the sort who stripped to the heart without strain or shame.

Fleur was in the drawing-room when he got home, furred up to her cheeks, which were bright as if she had just come in from the cold.

"Been out, my child?"

"Yes. I——" She stopped, looked at him rather queerly, and said: "Well, have you finished with that business?"

"Yes; thank God. I've dropped the poor creature on Norah Curfew."

Fleur smiled. "Ah! Yes, Norah Curfew! *She* lives for every-body but herself, doesn't she?"

"She does," said Michael, rather sharply.

"The new woman. One's getting clean out of fashion."

Michael took her cheeks between his hands.

"What's the matter, Fleur?"

"Nothing."

"There is."

"Well, one gets a bit fed up with being left out, as if one were fit for nothing but Kit, and looking appetising."

378

Michael dropped his hands, hurt and puzzled. Certainly he had not consulted her about his 'down and outs'; had felt sure it would only bore or make her laugh—— No future in it! And had there been?

"Any time you like to go shares in any mortal thing, Fleur, you've only to say so."

"Oh! I don't want to poke into your affairs. I've got my own. Have you had tea?"

"Do tell me what's the matter?"

"My dear boy, you've already asked me that, and I've already told you—nothing."

"Won't you kiss me?"

"Of course. And there's Kit's bath—would you like to go up?"

Each short stab went in a little farther. This was a spiritual crisis, and he did not know in the least how to handle it. Didn't she want him to admire her, to desire her? What did she want? Recognition that she was as interested as he in—in the state of the country? Of course! Only—was she?

"Well," she said, "I want tea, anyway. Is the new woman dramatic?"

Jealousy? The notion was absurd. He said quietly:

"I don't quite follow you."

Fleur looked up at him with very clear eyes.

"Good God!" said Michael, and left the room.

He went upstairs and sat down before 'The White Monkey'. In that strategic position he better perceived the core of his domestic moment. Fleur had to be first—had to take precedence. No object in her collection must live a life of its own! He was appalled by the bitterness of that thought. No, no! It was only that she had a complex—a silver spoon, and it had become natural in her mouth. She resented his having interests in which she was not first; or rather, perhaps, resented the fact that they were not her interests too. And that was to her credit, when you came to think of it. She was vexed with herself for being egocentric. Poor child! 'I've got to mind my eye,' thought Michael, 'or I shall make some modern-novel mess of this in three parts.' And his mind strayed naturally to the science of dishing up symptoms as if they were roots—ha! He remembered his nursery governess locking him in; he had dreaded being penned up ever since. The psycho-analysts would say that was due to the action of his governess. It wasn't—many small boys wouldn't have cared a hang; it was due to a nature that existed before that action. He took up the photograph of Fleur that stood on his desk. He loved the face, he would always love it. If she had limitations—well! So had he—lots! This was comedy. one mustn't make it into tragedy! Surely she had a sense of humour, too! Had she? Had she not? And Michael searched the face he held in his hands. . . .

But, as is usual with husbands, he had diagnosed without knowledge of all the facts.

Fleur had been bored at Lippinghall, even collection of the Minister had tried her. She had concealed her boredom from Michael. But self-sacrifice takes its revenge. She reached home in a mood of definite antagonism to public affairs. Hoping to feel better if she bought a hat or two, she set out for Bond Street. At the corner of Burlington Street, a young man bared his head.

"Fleur!"

Wilfrid Desert! Very lean and very brown!

"You!"

"Yes. I'm just back. How's Michael?"

"Very well. Only he's in Parliament."

"Great Scott! And how are you?"

"As you see. Did you have a good time?"

"Yes. I'm only perching. The East has got me!"

"Are you coming to see us?"

"I think not. The burnt child, you know."

"Yes; you *are* brown!"

"Well, good-bye, Fleur! You look just the same, only more so. I'll see Michael somewhere."

"Good-bye!" She walked on without looking back, and then regretted not having found out whether Wilfrid had done the same.

She had given Wilfrid up for—well, for Michael, who—who had forgotten it! Really she was too self-sacrificing!

And then at three o'clock a note was brought her:

"By hand, ma'am; answer waiting."

She opened an envelope, stamped 'Cosmopolis Hotel.'

"MADAM,

"We apologise for troubling you, but are in some perplexity. Mr. Francis Wilmot, a young American gentleman, who has been staying in this hotel since early October, has, we are sorry to say, contracted pneumonia. The doctor reports unfavourably on his condition. In these circumstances we thought it right to examine his effects, in order that we might communicate with his friends;

380

but the only indication we can find is a card of yours. I venture to ask you if you can help us in the matter.

        "Believe me to be, Madam,

               "Your faithful servant,

                       "(for the Management)."

Fleur stared at an illegible signature, and her thoughts were bitter. Jon had dumped Francis on her as a herald of his happiness; her enemy had lifted him! Well, then, why didn't that Cat look after him herself? Oh! well, poor boy! Ill in a great hotel—without a soul!

"Call me a taxi, Coaker."

On her way to the hotel she felt slight excitement of the 'ministering angel' order.

Giving her name at the bureau, she was taken up to Room 209. A chambermaid was there. The doctor, she said, had ordered a nurse, who had not yet come.

Francis Wilmot, very flushed, was lying back, propped up; his eyes were closed.

"How long has he been ill like this?"

"I've noticed him looking queer, ma'am; but we didn't know how bad he was until to-day. I think he's just neglected it. The doctor says he's got to be packed. Poor gentleman, it's very sad. You see, he's hardly there!"

Francis Wilmot's lips were moving; he was evidently on the verge of delirium.

"Go and make some lemon tea in a jug as weak and hot as you can; quick!"

When the maid had gone, she went up and put her cool hand to his forehead.

"It's all right, Francis. Much pain?"

Francis Wilmot's lips ceased to move; he looked up at her and his eyes seemed to burn.

"If you cure me," he said, "I'll hate you. I just want to get out, quick!"

She changed her hand on his forehead, whose heat seemed to scorch the skin of her palm. His lips resumed their almost soundless movement. The meaningless, meaningful whispering frightened her, but she stood her ground, constantly changing her hand, till the maid came back with the tea.

"The nurse has come, miss; she'll be up in a minute."

"Pour out the tea. Now, Francis, drink!"

His lips sucked, chattered, sucked. Fleur handed back the cup, and stood away. His eyes had closed again.

"Oh! ma'am," whispered the maid, "he *is* bad! Such a nice young gentleman, too."

"What was his temperature; do you know?"

"I did hear the doctor say nearly 105. Here is the nurse, ma'am."

Fleur went to her in the doorway.

"It's not just ordinary, nurse—he *wants* to go. I think a love-affair's gone wrong. Shall I stop and help you pack him?"

When the pneumonia jacket had been put on, she lingered, looking down at him. His eyelashes lay close and dark against his cheeks, long and innocent, like a little boy's.

Outside the door, the maid touched her arm.

"I found this letter, ma'am; ought I to show it to the doctor?"

Fleur read:

"MY POOR DEAR BOY,

"We were crazy yesterday. It isn't any good, you know. Well, I haven't got a breakable heart; nor have you really, though you may think so when you get this. Just go back to your sunshine and your darkies, and put me out of your thoughts. I couldn't stay the course. I couldn't possibly stand being poor. I must just go through it with my Scotsman and travel the appointed road. What is the good of thinking we can play at children in the wood, when one of them is

"Your miserable (at the moment)

"MARJORIE."

"I mean this—I mean it. Don't come and see me any more, and make it worse for yourself. M."

"Exactly!" said Fleur. "I've told the nurse. Keep it and give it him back if he gets well. If he doesn't, burn it. I shall come to-morrow." And, looking at the maid with a faint smile, she added: "*I* am not that lady!"

"Oh! no, ma'am—miss—no, I'm sure! Poor young gentleman! Isn't there nothing to be done?"

"I don't know. I should think not. . . ."

She had kept all these facts from Michael with a sudden retaliatory feeling. He couldn't have private—or was it public—life all to himself!

After he had gone out with his 'Good God!' she went to the

window. Queer to have seen Wilfrid again! Her heart had not fluttered, but it tantalised her not to know whether she could attract him back. Out in the Square it was as dark as when last she had seen him before he fled to the East—a face pressed to this window that she was touching with her fingers. 'The burnt child!' No! She did not want to reduce him to that state again; to copy Marjorie Ferrar, who had copied her. If, instead of going East, Wilfrid had chosen to have pneumonia like poor Francis! What would she have done? Let him die for want of her? And what ought she to do about Francis, having seen that letter? Tell Michael? No, he thought her frivolous and irresponsible. Well! She would show him! And that sister—who had married Jon? Ought she to be cabled to? But this would have a rapid crisis, the nurse had said, and to get over from America in time would be impossible! Fleur went back to the fire. What kind of girl was this wife of Jon's? Another in the new fashion—like Norah Curfew; or just one of those Americans out for her own way and the best of everything? But they would have the new fashion in America, too —even though it didn't come from Paris. Anne Forsyte!—Fleur gave a little shiver in front of the hot fire.

She went upstairs, took off her hat, and scrutinised her image. Her face was coloured and rounded, her eyes were clear, her brow unlined, her hair rather flattened. She fluffed it out, and went across into the nursery.

The eleventh baronet, asleep, was living his private life with a very determined expression on his face; at the foot of his cot lay the Dandie, with his chin pressed to the floor, and at the table the nurse was sewing. In front of her lay an illustrated paper with the photograph inscribed: 'Mrs. Michael Mont, with Kit and Dandie.'

"What do you think of it, nurse?"

"I think it's horrible, ma'am; it makes Kit look as if he hadn't any sense—giving him a stare like that!"

Fleur took up the paper; her quick eyes had seen that it concealed another. There on the table was a second effigy of herself: 'Mrs. Michael Mont, the pretty young London hostess, who, rumour says, will shortly be defendant in a Society lawsuit.' And, above, yet another effigy, inscribed: 'Miss Marjorie Ferrar, the brilliant granddaughter of the Marquis of Shropshire, whose engagement to Sir Alexander MacGown, M.P., is announced.'

Fleur dropped paper back on paper.

## Chapter XI

## SHADOWS

THE dinner, which Marjorie Ferrar had so suddenly recollected, was MacGown's, and when she reached the appointed restaurant, he was waiting in the hall.

"Where are the others, Alec?"

"There are no others," said MacGown.

Marjorie Ferrar reined back. "I can't dine with you alone in a place like this!"

"I had the Ppynrryns, but they fell through."

"Then I shall go to my club."

"For God's sake, no, Marjorie. We'll have a private room. Go and wait in there, while I arrange it."

With a shrug she passed into a little 'lounge'. A young woman whose face seemed familiar idled in, looked at her, and idled out again, the ormolu clock ticked, the walls of striped pale grey stared blankly in the brilliant light, and Marjorie Ferrar stared blankly back—she was still seeing Francis Wilmot's ecstatic face.

"Now!" said MacGown. "Up those stairs, and third on the right. I'll follow in a minute."

She had acted in a play, she had passed an emotional hour, and she was hungry. At least she could dine before making the necessary scene. And while she drank the best champagne Mac-Gown could buy, she talked and watched the burning eyes of her adorer. That red-brown visage, square, stiff-haired head, and powerful frame—what a contrast to the pale, slim face and form of Francis! This was a man, and when he liked, agreeable. With him she would have everything she wanted except—what Francis could give her. And it was one or the other—not both, as she had thought it might be. She had once crossed the 'striding edge' on Helvellyn, with a precipice on one side and a precipice on the other, and herself, doubting down which to fall, in the middle. She hadn't fallen, and—she supposed—she wouldn't now! One didn't, if one kept one's head!

Coffee was brought; and she sat, smoking, on the sofa. Her knowledge of private rooms taught her that she was now as alone with her betrothed as money could make them. How would he behave?

He threw his cigar away, and sat down by her side. This was

384

THE SILVER SPOON

the moment to rise and tell him that he was no longer her
betrothed. His arm went round her, his lips sought her face.
"Mind my dress; it's the only decent one I've got."

And, suddenly, not because she heard a noise, but because her
senses were not absorbed like his, she perceived a figure in the open
doorway. A woman's voice said: "Oh! I beg your pardon; I
thought——" Gone!

Marjorie Ferrar started up.

"Did you see that young woman?"

"Yes. Damn her!"

"She's shadowing me."

"What?"

"I don't know her, and yet I know her perfectly. She had a good
look at me downstairs, when I was waiting."

MacGown dashed to the door and flung it open. Nobody was
there! He shut it, and came back.

"By heaven! Those people, I'll——! Well, that ends it!
Marjorie, I shall send our engagement to the papers to-morrow."

Marjorie Ferrar, leaning her elbows on the mantelpiece, stared
at her own face in the glass above it. 'Not a moral about her!'
What did it matter? If only she could decide to marry Francis out
of hand, slide away from them all—debts, lawyers, Alec! And
then the 'You be damned' spirit in her blood revolted. The
impudence of it! Shadowing her! No! She was not going to leave
Miss Fleur triumphant—the little snob; and that old party with
the chin!

MacGown raised her hand to his lips; and somehow the caress
touched her.

"Oh! well," she said, "I suppose you'd better."

"Thank God!"

"Do you really think that to get me is a cause for gratitude?"

"I would go through Hell to get you."

"And after? Well, as we're public property, let's go down and
dance."

For an hour she danced. She would not let him take her home,
and in her cab she cried. She wrote to Francis when she got in.
She went out again to post it. The bitter stars, the bitter wind, the
bitter night! At the little slurred thump of her letter dropping, she
laughed. To have played at children! It was too funny! So that
was done with! 'On with the dance!'

Extraordinary, the effect of a little paragraph in the papers!
Credit, like new-struck oil, spurted sky-high. Her post contained,

385

not bills for dresses, but solicitations to feed, frizz, fur, flower, feather, furbelow, and photograph her. London offered itself. To escape that cynical avalanche she borrowed a hundred pounds and flew to Paris. There, every night, she went to the theatre. She had her hair done in a new style, she ordered dresses, ate at places known to the few—living up to Michael's nickname for her; and her heart was heavy.

She returned after a week, and burned the avalanche—fortunately all letters of congratulation contained the phrase 'of course you won't think of answering this.' She didn't. The weather was mild; she rode in the Row; she prepared to hunt. On the eve of departure, she received an anonymous communication.

"Francis Wilmot is very ill with pneumonia at the Cosmopolis Hotel. He is not expected to live."

Her heart flurried round within her breast and flumped; her knees felt weak; her hand holding the note shook; only her head stayed steady. The handwriting was 'that little snob's'. Had Francis caused this message to be sent? Was it his appeal? Poor boy! And must she go and see him if he were going to die? She so hated death. Did this mean that it was up to her to save him? What did it mean? But indecision was not her strong point. In ten minutes she was in a cab, in twenty at the hotel. Handing her card, she said:

"You have a Mr. Wilmot here—a relative of mine. I've just heard of his serious illness. Can I go up and see the nurse?"

The management looked at the card, inquisitively at her face, touched a bell, and said:

"Certainly, madam. . . . Here, you—take this lady up to room —er—209."

Led by what poor Francis called a 'bell-boy' into the lift, she walked behind his buttons along a pale-grey river of corridor carpet, between pale-grey walls, past cream-coloured after cream-coloured door in the bright electric light, with her head a little down.

The 'bell-boy' knocked ruthlessly on a door.

It was opened and in the lobby of the suite stood Fleur. . . .

386

## Chapter XII

## DEEPENING

HOWEVER untypically American according to Soames, Francis Wilmot seemed to have the national passion for short cuts.

In two days from Fleur's first visit he had reached the crisis, hurrying towards it like a man to his bride. Yet, compared with the instinct to live, the human will is limited, so that he failed to die. Fleur, summoned by telephone, went home cheered by the doctor's words: "He'll do now, if we can coax a little strength into him." That, however, was the trouble. For three afternoons she watched his exhausted indifference seeming to increase. And she was haunted by cruel anxiety. On the fourth day she had been sitting for more than an hour when his eyes opened.

"Yes, Francis?"

"I'm going to quit all right, after all."

"Don't talk like that—it's not American. Of course you're not going to quit."

He smiled, and shut his eyes. She made up her mind then.

Next day he was about the same, more dead than alive. But her mind was at rest; her messenger had brought back word that Miss Ferrar would be in at four o'clock. She would have had the note by now; but would she come? How little one knew of other people, even when they were enemies!

He was drowsing, white and strengthless, when she heard the 'bell-boy's' knock. Passing into the lobby, she closed the door softly behind her, and opened the outer door. So she *had* come!

If this meeting of two declared enemies had in it something dramatic, neither perceived it at the moment. It was just intensely unpleasant to them both. They stood for a moment looking at each other's chins. Then Fleur said:

"He's extremely weak. Will you sit down while I tell him you're here?"

Having seen her settled where Francis Wilmot put his clothes out to be valeted in days when he had worn them, Fleur passed back into the bedroom, and again closed the door.

"Francis," she said, "someone is waiting to see you."

Francis Wilmot did not stir, but his eyes opened and cleared strangely. To Fleur they seemed suddenly the eyes she had known; as if all these days they had been 'out', and someone had again put a match to them.

"You understand what I mean?"

The words came clear and feeble: "Yes; but if I wasn't good enough for her before, I surely am not now. Tell her I'm through with that fool business."

A lump rose in Fleur's throat.

"Thank her for coming!" said Francis Wilmot, and closed his eyes again.

Fleur went back into the lobby. Marjorie Ferrar was standing against the wall with an unlighted cigarette between her lips.

"He thanks you for coming; but he doesn't want to see you. I'm sorry I brought you down."

Marjorie Ferrar took out the cigarette. Fleur could see her lips quivering. "Will he get well?"

"I don't know. I think so—now. He says he's 'through with that fool business'."

Marjorie Ferrar's lips tightened. She opened the outer door, turned suddenly, and said:

"Will you make it up?"

"No," said Fleur.

There was a moment of complete stillness: then Marjorie Ferrar gave a little laugh, and slipped out.

Fleur went back. He was asleep. Next day he was stronger. Three days later Fleur ceased her visits; he was on the road to recovery. She had become conscious, moreover, that she had a little lamb which, wherever Mary went, was sure to go. She was being shadowed! How amusing! And what a bore that she couldn't tell Michael; because she had not yet begun again to tell him anything.

On the day that she ceased her visits he came in while she was dressing for dinner, with a 'weekly' in his hand.

"Listen to this," he said:

### FONDOUK

'When to God's fondouk the donkeys are taken—
  Donkeys of Africa, Sicily, Spain—
If peradventure the Deity waken,
  He shall not easily slumber again.

Where in the sweet of God's straw they have laid them
  Broken and dead of their burdens and sores,
He, for a change, shall remember He made them—
  One of the best of His numerous chores—

388

Order from someone a sigh of repentance—
Donkeys of Araby, Syria, Greece—
Over the fondouk distemper the sentence:
"God's own forsaken—the stable of peace." '

"Who's that by? It sounds like Wilfrid."

"It is by Wilfrid," said Michael, and did not look at her. "I met him at the Hotch-Potch."

"And how is he?"

"Very fit."

"Have you asked him here?"

"No. He's going East again soon."

Was he fishing? Did he know that she had seen him? And she said:

"I'm going down to father's, Michael. He's written twice."

Michael put her hand to his lips.

"All right, darling."

Fleur reddened; her strangled confidence seemed knotted in her throat. She went next day with Kit and Dandie. The 'little lamb' would hardly follow to 'The Shelter'.

Annette had gone with her mother to Cannes for a month; and Soames was alone with the English winter. He was paying little attention to it, for the 'case' was in the List, and might be reached in a few weeks' time. Deprived of French influence, he was again wavering towards compromise. The announcement of Marjorie Ferrar's engagement to MacGown had materially changed the complexion of affairs. In the eyes of a British jury, the character of a fast young lady, and the character of the same young lady publicly engaged to a Member of Parliament, with wealth and a handle to his name, would not be at all the same thing. They were now virtually dealing with Lady MacGown, and nothing, Soames knew, was so fierce as a man about to be married. To libel his betrothed was like approaching a mad dog.

He looked very grave when Fleur told him of her 'little lamb'. It was precisely the retaliation he had feared; nor could he tell her that he had 'told her so', because he hadn't. He had certainly urged her to come down to him, but delicacy had forbidden him to give her the reason. So far as he could tell through catechism, there had been nothing 'suspect' in her movements since Lippinghall, except those visits to the Cosmopolis Hotel. But they were bad enough. Who was going to believe that she went to this sick young man out of pure kindness? Such a motive was not current in a

Court of Law. He was staggered when she told him that Michael didn't know of them. Why not?

"I didn't feel like telling him."

"Feel? Don't you see what a position you've put yourself in? Here you are, running to a young man's bedside, without your husband's knowledge."

"Yes, darling; but he was terribly ill."

"I dare say," said Soames; "so are lots of people."

"Besides, he was over head and ears in love with *her*."

"D'you think he's going to admit that, even if we could call him?"

Fleur was silent, thinking of Francis Wilmot's face.

"Oh! I don't know," she said at last. "How horrid it all is!"

"Of course it's horrid," said Soames. "Have you had a quarrel with Michael?"

"No; not a quarrel. Only he doesn't tell *me* things."

"What things?"

"How should I know, dear?"

Soames grunted. "Would he have minded your going?"

"Of course not. He'd have minded if I hadn't. He likes that boy."

"Well, then," said Soames, "either you or he, or both, will have to tell a lie, and say that he did know. I shall go up and talk to him. Thank goodness we can prove the illness. If I catch anybody coming down here after you——!"

He went up the following afternoon. Parliament being in recess, he sought the Hotch-Potch Club. He did not like a place always connected in his mind with his dead cousin, that fellow young Jolyon, and said to Michael at once: "Can we go somewhere else?"

"Yes, sir; where would you like?"

"To your place, if you can put me up for the night. I want to have a talk with you."

Michael looked at him askance.

"Now," said Soames, after dinner, "what's this about Fleur—she says you don't tell her things?"

Michael gazed into his glass of port.

"Well, sir," he said slowly, "I'd be only too glad to, of course, but I don't think they really interest her. She doesn't feel that public things matter."

"Public! I meant private."

"There aren't any private things. D'you mean that she thinks there are?"

Soames dropped his scrutiny.

"I don't know—she said 'things'."

"Well, you can put that out of your head, and hers."

"H'm! Anyway, the result's been that she's been visiting that young American with pneumonia at the Cosmopolis Hotel, without letting you know. It's a mercy she hasn't picked it up."

"Francis Wilmot?"

"Yes. He's out of the wood, now. That's not the point. She's been shadowed."

"Good God!" said Michael.

"Exactly! This is what comes of not talking to your wife. Wives are funny—they don't like it."

Michael grinned.

"Put yourself in my place, sir. It's my profession, now, to fuss about the state of the country, and all that; and you know how it is—one gets keen. But to Fleur, it's all a stunt. I quite understand that; but, you see, the keener I get, the more I'm afraid of boring her, and the less I feel I can talk to her about it. In a sort of way she's jealous."

Soames rubbed his chin. The state of the country was a curious sort of co-respondent. He himself was often worried by the state of the country, but as a source of division between husband and wife it seemed to him cold-blooded; he had known other sources in his time!

"Well, you mustn't let it go on," he said. "It's trivial."

Michael got up.

"Trivial! Well, sir, I don't know, but it seems to me very much the sort of thing that happened when the war came. Men had to leave their wives then."

"Wives put up with that," said Soames, "the country was in danger."

"Isn't it in danger now?"

With his inveterate distrust of words, it seemed to Soames almost indecent for a young man to talk like that. Michael was a politician, of course; but politicians were there to keep the country quiet, not to go raising scares and talking through their hats.

"When you've lived a little longer," he said, "you'll know that there's always something to fuss about if you like to fuss. There's nothing in it really; the pound's going up. Besides, it doesn't matter what you tell Fleur, so long as you tell her something."

"She's intelligent, sir," said Michael.

391

Soames was taken aback. He could not deny the fact, and answered:

"Well, national affairs are too remote; you can't expect a woman to be interested in them."

"Quite a lot of women are."

"Blue-stockings."

"No, sir; they nearly all wear 'nude'."

"H'm! Those! As to interest in national affairs—put a tax on stockings, and see what happens!"

Michael grinned.

"I'll suggest it, sir."

"If you expect," said Soames, "that people—women or not—are going to put themselves out of the way for any scheme like this—this Foggartism of yours, you'll be very much disappointed."

"So everybody tells me. It's just because I don't like cold water at home as well as abroad, that I've given up worrying Fleur."

"Well, if you take my advice, you'll take up something practical —the state of the traffic, or penny postage. Drop pessimism; people who talk at large like that, never get trusted in this country. In any case you'll have to say you knew about her visits to that young man."

"Certainly, sir, wife and husband are one. But you don't really mean to let them make a circus of it in Court?"

Soames was silent. He did not *mean* them to; but what if they did?

"I can't tell," he said, at last. "The fellow's a Scotchman. What did you go hitting him on the nose for?"

"He gave me a thick ear first. I know it was an excellent opportunity for turning the other cheek, but I didn't think of it in time."

"You must have called him something."

"Only a dirty dog. As you know, he suggested a low motive for my speech."

Soames stared. In his opinion this young man was taking himself much too seriously.

"Your speech! You've got to get it out of your mind," he said, "that anything you can say or do will make any difference."

"Then what's the good of my being in Parliament?"

"Well, you're in the same boat with everybody else. The country's like a tree; you can keep it in order, but you can't go taking it up by the roots to look at them."

Michael looked at him, impressed.

"In public matters," said Soames, "the thing is to keep a level head, and do no more than you're obliged."

"And what's to govern one's view of necessity?"

"Common sense. One can't have everything."

And rising, he began scrutinising the Goya.

"Are you going to buy another Goya, sir?"

"No; if I buy any more pictures, I shall go back to the English School."

"Patriotism?"

Soames gave him a sharp look.

"There's no patriotism," he said, "in fussing. And another thing you've got to remember is that foreigners like to hear that we've got troubles. It doesn't do to discuss our affairs out loud."

Michael took these sayings to bed with him. He remembered, when he came out of the war, thinking: 'If there's another war, nothing will induce me to go.' But now, if one were to come, he knew he *would* be going again. So Old Forsyte thought he was just 'fussing'! Was he? Was Foggartism a phlizz? Ought he to come to heel, and take up the state of the traffic? Was everything unreal? Surely not his love for Fleur? Anyway he felt hungry for her lying there. And Wilfrid back, too! To risk his happiness with her for the sake of—what? *Punch* had taken a snap at him this week, grinning and groping at a surrounding fog. Old England, like Old Forsyte, had no use for theories. Self-conscious national efforts were just pomposity. Pompous! He? The thought was terribly disturbing. He got out of bed and went to the window. Foggy! In fog all were shadows; and he the merest shadow of them all, an unpractical politician, taking things to heart! One! Two! Big Ben! How many hearts had he turned to water! How many dreams spoiled, with his measured resonance! Line up with the top-dressers, and leave the country to suck its silver spoon!

393

# PART III

## Chapter I

### 'CIRCUSES'

IN his early boyhood Soames had been given to the circus. He had outgrown it; 'Circuses' were now to him little short of an abomination. Jubilees and Pageants, that recurrent decimal, the Lord Mayor's Show, Earl's Court, Olympia, Wembley—all he disliked. He could not stand a lot of people with their mouths open. Dressing up was to him a symptom of weak-mindedness, and the collective excitement of a crowd an extravagance that offended his reticent individualism. Though not deeply versed in history, he had an idea, too, that nations who went in for 'circuses' were decadent. Queen Victoria's funeral, indeed, had impressed him—there had been a feeling in the air that day; but, ever since, things had gone from bad to worse. They made everything into a 'circus' now! A man couldn't commit a murder without the whole paper-reading population—himself included—looking over each other's shoulders; and as to these football-matches, and rodeos—they interfered with the traffic and the normal course of conversation; people were so crazy about them!

Of course, 'circuses' had their use. They kept the people quiet. Violence by proxy, for instance, was obviously a political principle of some value. It was difficult to gape at the shedding of blood and shed it at the same time; the more people stood in rows to see others being hurt, the less trouble would they take to hurt others, and the sounder Soames could sleep by night. Still sensation-hunting had become a disease, in his opinion, and no one was being inoculated for it, so far as he could see!

As the weeks went on and the cases before it in the List went off, the 'circus' they were proposing to make of his daughter appeared to him more and more monstrous. He had an instinctive distrust of Scotchmen—they called themselves Scotsmen nowadays, as if it helped their character!—they never let go, and he could not approve in other people a quality native to himself. Besides, 'Scotchmen' were so—so exuberant—always either dour or else

394

hearty—extravagant chaps! Towards the middle of March, with the case in the List for the following week, he took an extreme step and entered the Lobby of the House of Commons. He had spoken to no one of his determination to make this last effort, for it seemed to him that all—Annette, Michael, Fleur herself—had done their best to spoil the chance of settlement.

Having sent in his card, he waited a long while in that lofty purlieu. 'Lobbying', he knew the phrase, but had never realised the waste of time involved in it. The statues consoled him somewhat. Sir Stafford Northcote—a steady chap; at old Forsyte dinner-parties in the 'eighties his character had been as much a standby as the saddle of mutton. He found even 'that fellow Gladstone' bearable in stucco, or whatever it was up there. You might dislike, but you couldn't sneeze at him, as at some of these modern chaps. He was sunk in coma before Lord Granville when at last he heard the words:

"Sir Alexander MacGown," and saw a square man with a ruddy face, stiff black hair, and clipped moustache, coming between the railings, with a card in his hand.

"Mr. Forsyte?"

"Yes. Can we go anywhere that's not quite so public?"

The 'Scotchman' nodded, and led him down a corridor to a small room.

"Well?"

Soames smoothed his hat. "This affair," he said, "can't be any more agreeable to you than it is to me."

"Are you the individual who was good enough to apply the word 'traitress' to the lady I'm engaged to?"

"That is so."

"Then I don't see how you have the impudence to come and speak to me."

Soames bit his lips.

"I spoke under the provocation of hearing your fiancée call my daughter a snob, in her own house. Do you want this petty affair made public?"

"If you think that you and your daughter can get away with calling the lady I'm going to marry 'a snake', 'a traitress', 'an immoral person', you're more mistaken than you ever were in your life. An unqualified apology that her Counsel can announce in Court is your only way out."

"That you won't get; mutual regret is another thing. As to the question of damages——"

395

"Damn the damages!" said MacGown violently. And there was that in Soames which applauded.

"Well," he said, "I'm sorry for you and her."

"What the devil do you mean, sir?"

"You will know by the end of next week, unless you revise your views in between. If it comes into Court, we shall justify."

The 'Scotchman' went so red that for a moment Soames was really afraid he would have an apoplectic fit.

"You'd better look out what you say in Court."

"We pay no attention to bullies in Court."

MacGown clenched his fists.

"Yes," said Soames, "it's a pity I'm not your age. Good-evening!"

He passed the fellow and went out. He had noted his way in this 'rabbit warren', and·was soon back among the passionless statues. Well! He had turned the last stone and could do no more, except make that overbearing fellow and his young woman sorry they'd ever been born. He came out into the chilly mist of West-minster. Pride and temper! Sooner than admit themselves in the wrong, people would turn themselves into an expensive 'circus' for the gaping and the sneers, the japing and the jeers of half the town! To vindicate her 'honour', that 'Scotchman' would have his young woman's past dragged out! And fairly faced by the question whether to drag it out or not, Soames stood still. If he didn't, she might get a verdict; if he did, and didn't convince the jury, the damages would be shockingly increased. They might run into thousands. He felt the need of definite decision. One had been drifting in the belief that the thing wouldn't come into Court! Four o'clock! Not too late, perhaps, to see Sir James Foskisson. He would telephone to very young Nicholas to arrange a con-ference at once, and if Michael was at South Square, he would take him down to it. . . .

In his study, Michael had been staring with lugubrious relish at Aubrey Greene's cartoon of himself in a Society paper. On one leg, like Guy—or was it Slingsby?—in the Edward Lear 'Nonsense' book, he was depicted crying in a wilderness where a sardonic smile was rising on the horizon. Out of his mouth the word 'Foggartism' wreathed like the smoke of a cigar. Above a hole in the middle distance, a meercat's body supported the upturned face and applauding forepaws of Mr. Blythe. The thing was devastating in treatment and design—not unkind, merely killing. Michael's face had been endowed with a sort of after-dinner rapture, as if he were enjoying the sound of his own voice. Ridicule! Not even a personal friend, an artist, could see that the wilderness was at least as deserving of ridicule as the pelican! The cartoon seemed to write the word 'futility' large across his page. It recalled to him Fleur's words at the outset: "And by the time the Tories go out you'll have your licence." She was a born realist! From the first she had foreseen for him the position of an eccentric, picturesquely beating a little private drum! A dashed good cartoon! And no one could appreciate it so deeply as its victim. But why did every-one smile at Foggartism? Why? Because among a people who naturally walked, it leaped like a grasshopper; to a nation that felt its way in fog, it seemed a will-o'-the-wisp. Yes, he was a fool for his pains! And—just then, Soames arrived.

"I've been to see that Scotchman," he said. "He means to take it into Court."

"Oh! Not really, sir! I always thought you'd keep it out."

"Only an unqualified apology will do that. Fleur can't give it; she's in the right. Can you come down with me now and see Sir James Foskisson?"

They set out in a taxi for the Temple.

The chambers of very young Nicholas Forsyte were in Paper Buildings. Chinny, mild and nearly forty, he succeeded within ten minutes in presenting to them every possible doubt.

"He seems to enjoy the prospect of getting tonked," murmured Michael while they were going over to Sir James.

"A poor thing," Soames responded; "but careful. Foskisson must attend to the case himself."

After those necessary minutes during which the celebrated K.C. was regathering from very young Nicholas what it was all about, they were ushered into the presence of one with a large head garnished by small grey whiskers, and really obvious brains. Since selecting him, Soames had been keeping an eye on the great advocate; had watched him veiling his appeals to a jury with an air of scrupulous equity; very few—he was convinced—and those not on juries, could see Sir James Foskisson coming round a corner. Soames had specially remarked his success in cases concerned with morals or nationality—no one so apt at getting a co-respondent, a German, a Russian, or anybody at all bad, non-suited! At close quarters his whiskers seemed to give him an intensive respecta-bility—difficult to imagine him dancing, dicing, or in bed. In spite of his practice, too, he enjoyed the reputation of being thorough; he might be relied on to know more than half the facts of any case by the time he went into Court, and to pick up the rest as he went along—or at least not to show that he hadn't. Very young Nicholas, knowing all the facts, had seemed quite unable to see what line could possibly be taken. Sir James, on the other hand, appeared to know only just enough. Sliding his light eyes from Soames to Michael, he retailed them, and said: "Eminently a case for an amicable settlement."

"Indeed!" said Soames.

Something in his voice seemed to bring Sir James to attention.

"Have you attempted that?"

"I have gone to the limit."

"Excuse me, Mr. Forsyte, but what do you regard as the limit?"

"Fifteen hundred pounds, and a mutual expression of regret. They'd accept the money, but they ask for an unqualified apology."

The great lawyer rested his chin. "Have you tried the unqualified apology without the money?"

"No."

"I would almost be inclined. MacGown is a very rich man. The shadow and the substance, eh? The expressions in the letters are strong. What do you say, Mr. Mont?"

"Not so strong as those she used of my wife."

Sir James Foskisson looked at very young Nicholas.

"Let me see," he said, "those were——?"

"Lion-huntress and snob," said Michael curtly.

Sir James wagged his head precisely as if it were a pair of scales.

"Immoral, snake, traitress, without charm—you think those weaker?"

"They don't make you snigger, sir, the others do. In Society it's the snigger that counts."

Sir James smiled.

"The jury won't be in Society, Mr. Mont."

"My wife doesn't feel like making an apology, anyway, unless there's an expression of regret on the other side; and I don't see why she should."

Sir James Foskisson seemed to breathe more freely.

"In that case," he said, "we have to consider whether to use the detective's evidence or not. If we do, we shall need to subpœna the hall porter and the servants at Mr.—er—Curfew's flat."

"Exactly," said Soames; "that's what we're here to decide." It was as if he had said: 'The conference is now opened.'

Sir James perused the detective's evidence for five silent minutes.

"If this is confirmed, even partially," he said at last, "we win."

Michael had gone to the window. The trees in the garden had

tiny buds; some pigeons were strutting on the grass below. He heard Soames say:

"I ought to tell you that they've been shadowing my daughter. There's nothing, of course, except some visits to a young American dangerously ill of pneumonia at his hotel."

"Of which I knew and approved," said Michael, without turning round.

"Could we call him?"

"I believe he's still at Bournemouth. But he was in love with Miss Ferrar."

Sir James turned to Soames.

"If there's no question of a settlement, we'd better go for the gloves. Merely to cross-examine as to books and play and clubs is very inconclusive."

"Have you read the dark scene in 'The Plain Dealer'?" asked Soames; "and that novel, *Canthar*?"

"All very well, Mr. Forsyte, but impossible to say what a jury would make of impersonal evidence like that."

Michael had come back to his seat.

"I've a horror," he said, "of dragging in Miss Ferrar's private life."

"No doubt. But do you want me to win the case?"

"Not that way. Can't we go into Court, say nothing, and pay up?"

Sir James Foskisson smiled and looked at Soames. 'Really,' he seemed to say, 'why did you bring me this young man?'

Soames, however, had been pursuing his own thoughts.

"There's too much risk about that flat; if we failed there, it might be a matter of twenty thousand pounds. Besides, they would certainly call my daughter. I want to prevent that at all costs. I thought you could turn the whole thing into an indictment of modern morality."

Sir James Foskisson moved in his chair, and the pupils of his light-blue eyes became as pin-points. He nodded almost imperceptibly three times, precisely as if he had seen the Holy Ghost.

"When shall we be reached?" he said to very young Nicholas.

"Probably next Thursday—Mr. Justice Brane."

"Very well. I'll see you again on Monday. Good evening." And he sank back into an immobility, which neither Soames nor Michael felt equal to disturbing.

They went away silent—very young Nicholas tarrying in conversation with Sir James's devil.

399

Turning at the Temple station, Michael murmured:

"It was just as if he'd said: 'Some stunt!' wasn't it? I'm look-ing in at *The Outpost*, sir. If you're going back to Fleur, will you tell her?"

Soames nodded. There it was! He had to do everything that was painful.


## Chapter II

### "NOT GOING TO HAVE IT"

IN the office of *The Outpost* Mr. Blythe had just been in conversa-tion with one of those great business men who make such deep impression on all to whom they voice their views in strict con-fidence. If Sir Thomas Lockit did not precisely monopolise the control of manufacture in Great Britain, he, like others, caused almost anyone to think so—his knowledge was so positive and his emphasis so cold. In his view the country must resume the posi-tion held before the Great War. It all hinged on coal—a question of this seven hours a day; and they were 'not going to have it'. A shilling, perhaps two shillings, off the cost of coal. They were 'not going to have' Europe doing without British produce. Very few people knew Sir Thomas Lockit's mind; but nearly all who did were extraordinarily gratified.

Mr. Blythe, however, was biting his finger, and spitting out the result.

"Who was that fellow with the grey moustache?" asked Michael.

"Lockit. He's 'not going to have it'."

"Oh!" said Michael, in some surprise.

"One sees more and more, Mont, that the really dangerous people are not the politicians, who want things with public passion —that is, mildly, slowly; but the big business men, who want things with private passion, strenuously, quickly. They know their own minds; and if we don't look out they'll wreck the country."

"What are they up to now?" said Michael.

"Nothing for the moment; but it's brewing. One sees in Lockit the futility of will-power. He's not going to have what it's entirely out of his power to prevent. He'd like to break Labour and make it work like a nigger from sheer necessity. Before that we shall be having civil war. Some of the Labour people, of course, are just as bad—they want to break everybody. It's a bee nuisance. If

400

we're all to be plunged into industrial struggles again, how are we to get on with Foggartism?"

"I've been thinking about the country," said Michael. "Aren't we beating the air, Blythe? Is it any good telling a man who's lost a lung that what he wants is a new one?"

Mr. Blythe puffed out one cheek.

"Yes," he said, "the country had a hundred very settled years—Waterloo to the War—to get into its present state; it's got its line of life so fixed and its habits so settled that nobody—neither editors, politicians nor business men—can think except in terms of its bloated town industrialism. The country's got beyond the point of balance in that hundred settled years, and it'll want fifty settled years to get back to that point again. The real trouble is that we're not going to get fifty settled years. Some bee thing or other—war with Turkey or Russia, trouble in India, civil ructions, to say nothing of another general flare-up—may knock the bottom out of any settled plans at any time. We've struck a disturbed patch of history, and we know it in our bones, and live from hand to mouth, according."

"Well, then!" said Michael glumly, thinking of what the Minister had said to him at Lippinghall.

Mr. Blythe puffed out the other cheek.

"No backsliding, young man! In Foggartism we have the best goods we can see before us, and we must bee well deliver them, as best we can. We've outgrown all the old hats."

"Have you seen Aubrey Greene's cartoon?"

"I have."

"Good—isn't it? But what I really came in to tell you is that this beastly libel case of ours will be on next week."

Mr. Blythe's ears moved.

"I'm sorry for that. Win or lose—nothing's worse for public life than private ructions. You're not going to have it, are you?"

"We can't help it. But our defence is to be confined to an attack on the new morality."

"One can't attack what isn't," said Mr. Blythe.

"D'you mean to say," said Michael, grinning, "that you haven't noticed the new morality?"

"Certainly not. Formulate it if you can."

" 'Don't be stupid, don't be dull.' "

Mr. Blythe grunted. "The old morality used to be: 'Behave like a gentleman.' "

"Yes! But in modern thought there ain't no sich an animal."

401

"There are fragments lying about; they reconstructed Neander-thal man from half a skull."

"A word that's laughed at can't be used, Blythe."

"Ah!" said Mr. Blythe. "The chief failings of your generation, young Mont, are sensitiveness to ridicule and terror of being behind the times. It's bee weak-minded."

Michael grinned.

"I know it. Come down to the House. Parsham's Electrification Bill is due. We may get some lights on Unemployment."

Having parted from Mr. Blythe in the Lobby, Michael came on his father walking down a corridor with a short bright old man in a trim grey beard.

"Ah! Michael, we've been seeking you. Marquess, my hopeful son! The Marquess wants to interest you in electricity."

Michael removed his hat.

"Will you come to the reading-room, my lord?"

This, as he knew, was Marjorie Ferrar's grandfather, and might be useful. In a remote corner of a room lighted so that nobody could see anyone else reading, they sat down in triangular formation.

"You know about electricity, Mr. Mont?" said the Marquess.

"No, sir, except that more of it would be desirable in this room."

"Everywhere, Mr. Mont. I've read about your Foggartism; if you'll allow me to say so, it's quite possibly the policy of the future; but nothing will be done with it till you've electrified the country. I should like you to start by supporting this Bill of Parsham's."

And, with an engaging distinction of syllable, the old peer proceeded to darken Michael's mind.

"I see, sir," said Michael at last. "This Bill ought to add considerably to Unemployment."

"Temporarily."

"I wonder if I ought to take on any more temporary trouble. I'm finding it difficult enough to interest people in the future as it is—they seem to think the present so important."

Sir Lawrence whinnied.

"You must give him time and pamphlets, Marquess. But, my dear fellow, while your Foggartism is confined to the stable, you'll want a second horse."

"I've been advised already to take up the state of the traffic or penny postage. And, by the way, sir, that case of ours *is* coming into Court next week."

THE SILVER SPOON

Sir Lawrence's loose eyebrow shot up:

"Oh!" he said. "Do you remember, Marquess—your grand-daughter and my daughter-in-law? I came to you about it."

"Something to do with lions? A libel, was it?" said the old peer. "My aunt——"

While Michael was trying to decide whether this was an ejaculation or the beginning of a reminiscence, his father broke in:

"Ah! yes, an interesting case that, Marquess—it's all in Betty Montecourt's Memoirs."

"Libels," resumed the Marquess, "had flavour in those days. The words complained of were: 'Her crinoline covers her considerable obliquity.' "

"If anything's to be done to save scandal," muttered Michael, "it must be done now. We're at a deadlock."

"Could you put in a word, sir?" said Sir Lawrence.

The Marquess's beard quivered.

"I see from the papers that my granddaughter is marrying a man called MacGown, a Member of this House. Is he about?"

"Probably," said Michael. "But I had a row with him. I think, sir, there would be more chance with her."

The Marquess rose. "I'll ask her to breakfast. I dislike publicity. Well, I hope you'll vote for this Bill, Mr. Mont, and think over the question of electrifying the country. We want young men interested. I'm going to the Peers' Gallery now. Good-bye!"

When briskly he had gone, Michael said to his father: "If he's not going to have it, I wish he'd ask Fleur to breakfast, too. There are two parties to this quarrel."

Chapter III

SOAMES DRIVES HOME

SOAMES in the meantime was seated with one of those parties in her 'parlour'. She had listened in silence, but with a stubborn and resentful face. What did he know of the loneliness and frustration she had been feeling? Could he tell that the thrown stone had starred her mirrored image of herself; that the words 'snob' and 'lion-huntress' had entered her very soul? He could not understand the spiritual injury she had received, the sudden deprivation of that self-importance, and hope of rising, necessary to all. Concerned by the expression on her face, preoccupied with the practical aspects of the 'circus' before them, and desperately in-

403

# A MODERN COMEDY

volved in thoughts of how to keep her out of it as much as possible, Soames was reduced to the closeness of a fish.

"You'll be sitting in front, next to me," he said. "I shouldn't wear anything too bright. Would you like your mother there, too?"

Fleur shrugged her shoulders.

"Just so," said Soames. "But if she wants to come, she'd better, perhaps. Brane is not a joking judge, thank goodness. Have you ever been in a Court?"

"No."

"The great thing is to keep still and pay no attention to anything. They'll all be behind you, except the jury—and there's nothing in them really. If you look at them, don't smile!"

"Why? Aren't they safe, Dad?"

Soames put the levity aside.

"I should wear a small hat. Michael must sit on your left. Have you got over that—er—not telling each other things?"

"Yes."

"I shouldn't begin it again. He's very fond of you."

Fleur nodded.

"Is there anything you want to tell *me*? You know I—I worry about you."

Fleur got up and sat on the arm of his chair; he had at once a feeling of assuagement.

"I really don't care now. The harm's done. I only hope *she'll* have a bad time."

Soames, who had the same hope, was somewhat shocked by its expression.

He took leave of her soon after and got into his car for the dark drive back to Mapledurham. The spring evening was cold and he had the window up. At first he thought of very little; and then of still less. He had passed a tiring afternoon, and was glad of the slight smell of stephanotis provided by Annette. The road was too familiar to rouse his thoughts, beyond wonder at the lot of people there always seemed to be in the world between six and seven. He dozed his way into the new cut, woke, and dozed again. What was this—Slough? Before going to Marlborough he had been at school there with young Nicholas and St. John Heyman, and after his time, some other young Forsytes. Nearly sixty years ago! He remembered his first day—a brand-new little boy in a brand-new little top-hat, with a playbox stored by his mother with things to eat, and blessed with the words: "There, Summy dear, that'll make

404

you popular." He had reckoned on having command of that corruption for some weeks; but no sooner had he produced a bit of it than they had taken the box, and suggested to him that it would be a good thing to eat the lot. In twenty-two minutes twenty-two boys had materially increased their weight, and he himself, in handing out the contents, had been obliged to eat less than a twenty-third. They had left him one packet of biscuits, and those had caraway seeds, for which he had constitutionally no passion whatever. Afterwards, three other new boys had complained that he was a fool for having it all eaten up like that, instead of saving it for them, and he had been obliged to sit on their heads one by one. His popularity had lasted twenty-two minutes, and, so far as he knew, had never come back. He had been against Communism ever since.

Bounding a little on the cushioned seat, he remembered poignantly his own cousin St. John Heyman pushing him into a gorse-bush and holding him there for an appreciable minute. Horrid little brutes, boys! For a moment he felt quite grateful to Michael for trying to get them out of England. And yet——! He had some pleasant memories even of boys. There was his collection of butter-flies—he had sold two Red Admirals in poor condition to a boy for one-and-threepence. To be a boy again—h'm—and shoot peas at passengers in a train that couldn't stop, and drink cherry brandy going home, and win a prize by reciting two hundred lines of 'The Lady of the Lake' better than 'Cherry-Tart' Burroughes—Um? What had become of 'Cherry-Tart' Burroughes, who had so much money at school that his father went bankrupt! 'Cherry-Tart' Burroughes!

The loom of Slough faded. One was in rank country now, and he ground the handle of the window to get a little fresh air. A smell of trees and grass came in. Get boys out of England! They had funny accents in those great places overseas. Well, they had funny accents here, too. The accent had been all right at Slough— for if it wasn't a boy got lammed. He remembered the first time his father and mother—James and Emily—came down; very genteel (before the word was fly-blown), all whiskers and crinoline; the beastly boys had made personal remarks which had hurt him! Get 'em out of England! But in those days there had been nowhere for boys to go. He took a long breath of the wayside air. They said England was changed, spoiled, some even said 'done for' Bosh! It still smelt the same! His great-uncle, one of 'Superior Dosset's' brothers, had gone as a boy to Bermuda at the beginning of the last century, and had he been heard of since? Not he. Young Jon Forsyte and his mother—his own first, unfaithful, still not quite forgotten wife—had gone to the States—would they be heard of again? He hoped not. England! Some day, when he had time and the car was free, he would go and poke round on the border of Dorset and Devon where the Forsytes came from. There was nothing there—he understood, and he wouldn't care to let anybody know of his going; but the earth must be some sort of colour, and there would be a graveyard, and—ha! Maidenhead! These sprawling villas and hotels and gramophones spoiled the river. Funny that Fleur had never been very fond of the river; too slow and wet, perhaps—everything was quick and dry now, like America. But had they such a river as the Thames anywhere out of England? Not they! Nothing that ran green and clear and weedy, where you could sit in a punt and watch the cows, and those big elms, and the poplars. Nothing that was safe and quiet, where you called your soul your own and thought of Constable and Mason and Walker.

His car bumped something slightly, and came to a stand. That fellow Riggs was always bumping something! He looked out. The chauffeur had got down and was examining his mudguard.

"What was that?" said Soames.

"I think it was a pig, sir."

"Where?"

"Shall I drive on, or see?"

Soames looked round. There seemed no inhabitants in sight.

"Better see."

The chauffeur disappeared behind the car. Soames remained seated. He had never had any pigs. They said the pig was a clean animal. People didn't treat pigs properly. It was very quiet! No cars on the road; in the silence the wind was talking a little in the hedgerow. He noticed some stars.

"It *is* a pig, sir; he's breathing."

"Oh!" said Soames. If a cat had nine, how many lives had a pig? He remembered his father James's only riddle: 'If a herring and a half cost three-ha'pence, what's the price of a gridiron?' When still very small, he had perceived that it was unanswerable.

"Where is he?" he said.

"In the ditch, sir."

A pig was property, but if in the ditch, nobody would notice it till after he was home. "Drive on," he said. "No! Wait!" And, opening the near door, he got out. After all, the pig was in distress.

"Show me," he said, and moved in the tail-light of his car to where the chauffeur stood pointing. There, in the shallow ditch, was a dark object emitting cavernous low sounds, as of a man asleep in a club chair.

"It must belong to one of them cottages we passed a bit back," said the chauffeur.

Soames looked at the pig.

"Anything broken?"

"No, sir; the mudguard's all right. I fancy it copped him pretty fair."

"In the pig, I meant."

The chauffeur touched the pig with his boot. It squealed, and Soames quivered. Someone would hear! Just like that fellow, drawing attention to it—no gumption whatever! But how, without touching, did you find out whether anything was broken in a pig? He moved a step and saw the pig's eyes; and a sort of fellow-feeling stirred in him. What if it had a broken leg! Again the chauffeur touched it with his foot. The pig uttered a lamentable noise, and, upheaving its bulk, squealing and grunting, trotted off. Soames hastily resumed his seat. "Drive on!" he said. Pigs! They never thought of anything but themselves; and cottagers were just as bad—very unpleasant about cars. And he wasn't sure they weren't right—tearing great things! The pig's eye seemed looking at him again from where his feet were resting. Should he keep some, now that he had those meadows on the other side of the river? Eat one's own bacon, cure one's own hams! After all, there was something in it—clean pigs, properly fed! That book of old Foggart said one must grow more food in England, and be independent if there were another war. He sniffed. Smell of baking—— Reading town already! They still grew biscuits in England! Foreign countries growing his food—something unpleasant about living on sufferance like that! After all, English meat and English wheat—as for a potato, you couldn't get one fit to eat in Italy, or France. And now they wanted to trade with Russia again! Those Bolshevists hated England. Eat their wheat and eggs, use their tallow and skins? *Infra dig*, he called it! The car swerved and he was jerked against the side cushions. The village church!—that fellow Riggs was always shying at something. Pretty little old affair, too, with its squat spire and its lichen—couldn't see that out of England—graves, old names, yew trees. And that reminded him: One would have to be buried, some day. Here, perhaps. Nothing flowery! Just his name, 'Soames Forsyte', standing out on rough stone, like that grave he had sat on at Highgate; no need to put 'Here lies'—of course he'd lie! As to a cross, he didn't know. Probably they'd put one, whatever he wished. He'd like to be in a corner, though, away from people—with an apple tree or something, over him. The less they remembered him, the better. Except Fleur—and she would have other things to think of!

The car turned down the last low hill to the level of the river. He caught a glimpse of it flowing dark between the poplars, like the soul of England, running hidden. The car rolled into the drive, and stopped before the door. He shouldn't tell Annette yet about this case coming into Court—she wouldn't feel as he did—she had no nerves!

## Chapter IV

### CATECHISM

MARJORIE FERRAR'S marriage was fixed for the day of the Easter Recess; her honeymoon to Lugano; her trousseau with Clothilde; her residence in Eaton Square; her pin-money at two thousand a year; and her affections on nobody. When she received a telephone message: Would she come to breakfast at Shropshire House? she was surprised. What could be the matter with the old boy?

At five minutes past nine, however, on the following day she entered the ancestral precincts, having left almost all powder and pigment on her dressing-table. Was he going to disapprove of her marriage? Or to give her some of her grandmother's lace, which was only fit to be in a museum?

The marquess was reading the paper in front of an electric fire. He bent on her his bright, shrewd glance.

"Well, Marjorie? Shall we sit down, or do you like to breakfast standing? There's porridge, scrambled eggs, fish—ah! and grapefruit—very considerate of them! Pour out the coffee, will you?"

"What'll you have, Grandfather?"

"Thank.you, I'll roam about and peck a bit. So you're going to be married. Is that fortunate?"

"People say so."

"He's in Parliament, I see. Do you think you could interest him in this Electricity Bill of Parsham's?"

"Oh! yes. He's dead keen on electricity."

"Sensible man. He's got Works, I suppose. Are they electrified?"

"I expect so."

The marquess gave her another glance.

"You know nothing about it," he said. "But you're looking very charming. What's this I hear of a libel?"

She might have known! Grandfather was too frightfully spry! He missed nothing!

"It wouldn't interest you, dear."

"I disagree. My father and *old* Sir Lawrence Mont were great friends. Why do you want to wash linen in Court?"

"I don't."

"Are you the plaintiff?"

"Yes."

"What do you complain of?"

"They've said things about me."

"Who?"

"Fleur Mont and her father."

"Ah! the relation of the tea-man. What have they said?"

"That I haven't a moral about me."

"Well, have you?"

"As much as most people."

"Anything else?"

"That I'm a snake of the first water."

"I don't like that. What made them say so?"

"Only that I was heard calling her a snob; and so she is."

The marquess, who had resigned a finished grapefruit, placed his foot on a chair, his elbow on his knee, his chin on his hand, and said:

"No divinity hedges our Order in these days, Marjorie; but we still stand for something. It's a mistake to forget that."

She sat very still. Everybody respected grandfather; even her father, to whom he did not speak. But to be told that she stood for something was really too dull for anything! All very well for grandfather at his age, and with his lack of temptations! Besides, *she* had no handle to her name, owing to the vaunted nature of British institutions. Even if she felt that—by Lord Charles out of Lady Ursula—she ought not to be dictated to, she had never put on frills—had always liked to be thought a mere Bohemian. And, after all, she did stand—for not being stuffy, and not being dull.

"Well, Grandfather, I tried to make it up, but she wouldn't. Coffee?"

"Yes, coffee. But tell me, are you happy about yourself?"

Marjorie Ferrar handed him the cup.

"No. Who is?"

"A hit," said the marquess. "You're going to be very well off, I hear. That means power. It's worth using well, Marjorie. He's a Scotsman, isn't he? Do you like him?" Again the shrewd bright glance.

"At times."

"I see. With your hair, you must be careful. Red hair is extraordinarily valuable on occasion. In the Eton and Harrow Match, or for speaking after dinner; but don't let it run away with you after you're married. Where are you going to live?"

"In Eaton Square. There's a Scotch place, too."

"Have your kitchens electrified. I've had it done here. It saves the cook's temper. I get very equable food. But about this libel. Can't you all say you're sorry—why put money into the lawyers' pockets?"

"She won't, unless I do, and I won't, unless she does."

The marquess drank off his coffee.

"Then what is there in the way? I dislike publicity, Marjorie. Look at that suit the other day. Anything of this nature in Society, nowadays, is a nail in our coffins."

"I'll speak to Alec, if you like."

"Do! Has he red hair?"

"No; black."

"Ah! What would you like for a wedding-present—lace?"

"Oh! no, please, dear. Nobody's wearing lace."

With his head on one side, the marquess looked at her. "I can't get that lace off." he seemed to say.

"Perhaps you'd like a colliery. Electrified, it would pay in no time."

Marjorie Ferrar laughed. "I know you're hard up, Grandfather; but I'd rather not have a colliery, thanks. They're so expensive. Just give me your blessing."

"I wonder," said the marquess, "if I could sell blessings? Your uncle Dangerfield has gone in for farming; he's ruining me. If only he'd grow wheat by electricity; it's the only way to make it pay at the present price. Well, if you've finished breakfast, good-bye. I must go to work."

Marjorie Ferrar, who had indeed begun breakfast, stood up and pressed his hand. He was a dear old boy, if somewhat rapid! . . .

That same evening, in a box at the St. Anthony, she had her opportunity, when MacGown was telling her of Soames's visit.

"Oh, dear! Why on earth didn't you settle it, Alec? The whole thing's a bore. I've had my grandfather at me about it."

"If they'll apologise," said MacGown, "I'll settle it to-morrow. But an apology they must make."

"And what about me? I don't want to stand up to be shot at."

"There are some things one can't sit down under, Marjorie. Their whole conduct has been infamous."

Visited by a reckless impulse, she said:

"What d'you suppose I'm really like, Alec?"

MacGown put his hand on her bare arm.

"I don't suppose I know."

"Well?"

"Defiant."

Curious summary! Strangely good in a way—only——!

"You mean that I like to irritate people till they think I'm—what I'm not. But suppose"—her eyes confronted his—"I really am."

MacGown's grasp tightened.

"You're not; and I won't have it said."

"You think this case will whitewash my—defiance?"

"I know what gossip is; and I know it buzzes about you. People who say things are going to be taught, once for all, that they can't."

Marjorie Ferrar turned her gaze towards the still life on the dropped curtain, laughed and said:

"My dear man, you're dangerously provincial."

"I know a straight line when I see one."

"Yes; but there aren't any in London. You'd better hedge, Alec, or you'll be taking a toss over me."

MacGown said, simply: "I believe in you more than you believe in yourself."

She was glad that the curtain rose just then, for she felt confused and rather touched.

Instead of confirming her desire to drop the case, that little talk gave her a feeling that by the case her marriage stood or fell. Alec would know where he was when it was over, and so would she! There would be precious little secret about her and she would either not be married to him, or at least not married under false pretences. Let it rip! It was, however, a terrible bore; especially the preparatory legal catechism she had now to undergo. What effect, for instance, had been produced among her friends and acquaintances by those letters? From the point of view of winning, the point was obviously not without importance. But how was she to tell? Two hostesses had cancelled week-end invitations: a rather prim countess, and a Canadian millionairess married to a decaying

411

baronet. It had not occurred to her before that this was the reason, but it might have been. Apart from them she would have to say she didn't know, people didn't tell you to your face what they heard or thought of you. They were going to try and make her out a piece of injured innocence! Good Lord! What if she declared her real faith in Court, and left them all in the soup! Her real faith —what was it? Not to let a friend down; not to give a man away; not to funk; to do things differently from other people; to be always on the go; not to be 'stuffy'; not to be dull! The whole thing was topsy-turvy! Well, she must keep her head!

## Chapter V

## THE DAY

ON the day of the case Soames rose, in Green Street, with a sort of sick impatience. Why wasn't it the day after?

Renewed interviews with very young Nicholas and Sir James Foskisson had confirmed the idea of defence by attack on modern morality. Foskisson was evidently going to put his heart into attacking that from which he had perhaps suffered; and if he were at all like old Bobstay, who, aged eighty-two, had just published his reminiscences, that cat would lose her hair and give herself away. Yesterday afternoon Soames had taken an hour's look at Mr. Justice Brane, and been very favourably impressed; the learned judge, though younger than himself—he had often briefed him in other times—looked old-fashioned enough now for anything.

Having cleaned his teeth, put in his plate, and brushed his hair, Soames went into the adjoining room and told Annette she would be late. She always looked terribly young and well in bed, and this, though a satisfaction to him, he could never quite forgive. When he was gone, fifteen years hence, perhaps, she would still be under sixty, and might live another twenty years.

Having roused her sufficiently to say: "You will have plenty of time to be fussy in that Court, Soames," he went back and looked out of his window. The air smelled of spring—aggravating! He bathed and shaved with care—didn't want to go into the Box with a cut on his chin!—then went back to see that Annette was not putting on anything bright. He found her in pink underclothes.

"I should wear black," he said.

Annette regarded him above her hand-mirror.

"Whom do you want me to fascinate, Soames?"

412

"These people will bring their friends, I shouldn't wonder; anything conspicuous——"

"Don't be afraid; I shall not try to be younger than my daughter."

Soames went out again. The French! Well, she had good taste in dress.

After breakfast he went off to Fleur's. Winifred and Imogen would look after Annette—they too were going to the Court, as if there were anything to enjoy about this business!

Spruce in his silk hat, he walked across the Green Park, conning over his evidence. No buds on the trees—a late year; and the Royal Family out of town! Passing the Palace, he thought: 'They're very popular!' He supposed they liked this great Empire group in front of them, all muscle and flesh and large animals! The Albert Memorial, and this—everybody ran them down; but, after all, peace and plenty—nothing modern about them! Emerging into Westminster, he cut his way through a smell of fried fish into the Parliamentary backwater of North Street, and, between its pleasant little houses, gazed steadily at the Wren Church. Never going inside any church except St. Paul's, he derived a sort of strength from their outsides—churches were solid and stood back, and didn't seem to care what people thought of them! He felt a little better, rounding into South Square. The Dandie met him in the hall. Though he was not over-fond of dogs, the breadth and solidity of this one always affected Soames pleasurably—better than that little Chinese abortion they used to have! This dog was a character—masterful and tenacious—you would get very little out of *him* in a witness-box! Looking up from the dog, he saw Michael and Fleur coming down the stairs. After hurriedly inspecting Michael's brown suit and speckled tie, his eyes came to anchor on his daughter's face. Pale but creamy, nothing modern—thank goodness! no rouge, salve, powder, or eye-blacking; perfectly made-up for her part! In a blue dress, too, very good taste, which must have taken some finding! The desire that she should not feel nervous stilled Soames's private qualms.

"Quite a smell of spring!" he said: "Shall we start?"

While a cab was being summoned, he tried to put her at ease.

"I had a look at Brane yesterday; he's changed a good deal from when I used to know him. I was one of the first to give him briefs."

"That's bad, isn't it, sir?" said Michael.

"How?"

"He'll be afraid of being thought grateful."

Flippant, as usual!

413

"Our judges," he said, "are a good lot, take them all round."

"I'm sure they are. Do you know if he ever reads, sir?"

"How d'you mean—reads?"

"Fiction. We don't, in Parliament."

"Nobody reads novels, except women," said Soames. And he felt Fleur's dress. "You'll want a fur; that's flimsy."

While she was getting the fur, he said to Michael: "How did she sleep?"

"Better than I did, sir."

"That's a comfort, anyway. Here's the cab. Keep away from that Scotchman."

"I see him every day in the House, you know."

"Ah!" said Soames; "I forgot. You make nothing of that sort of thing there, I believe." And taking his daughter's arm, he led her forth.

"I wonder if old Blythe will turn up," he heard Michael say, when they passed the office of *The Outpost*. It was the first remark made in the cab, and, calling for no response, it was the last.

The Law Courts had their customary air, and people, in black and blue, were hurrying into them. "Beetle-trap!" muttered Michael. Soames rejected the simile with his elbow—for him they were just familiar echoing space, concealed staircases, stuffy corridors, and the square enclosures of one voice at a time.

Too early, they went slowly up the stairs. Really, it was weak-minded! Here they had come—they and the other side—to get—what? He was amazed at himself for not having insisted on Fleur's apologising. Time and again in the case of others, all this had appeared quite natural—in the case of his own daughter, it now seemed almost incredibly idiotic. He hurried her on, however, past lingering lawyers' clerks, witnesses, what not. A few low words to an usher, and they were inside, and sitting down. Very young Nicholas was already in his place, and Soames so adjusted himself that there would only be the thickness of Sir James, when he materialised, between them. Turning to confer, he lived for a cosy moment in the past again, as might some retired old cricketer taking block once more. Beyond young Nicholas he quartered the assemblage with his glance. Yes, people had got wind of it! He knew they would—with that cat always in the public eye—quite a lot of furbelows up there at the back, and more coming. He reversed himself abruptly; the jury were filing in—special, but a common-looking lot! Why were juries always common-looking? He had never been on one himself. He glanced at Fleur. There she sat, and what she was feeling he couldn't tell. As for young Michael, his ears looked very pointed. And just then he caught sight of Annette. She'd better not come and sit down here, after all—the more there were of them in front, the more conspicuous it would be! So he shook his head at her, and waved towards the back. Ah! She was going! She and Winifred and Imogen would take up room—all rather broad in the beam; but there were still gaps up there. And suddenly he saw the plaintiff and her lawyer and MacGown; very spry they looked, and that insolent cat was smiling! Careful not to glance in their direction, Soames saw them sit down, some six feet off. Ah! and here came Counsel—Foskisson and Bullfry together, thick as thieves. They'd soon be calling each other 'my friend' now, and cutting each other's throats! He wondered if he wouldn't have done better after all to let the other side have Foskisson, and briefed Bullfry—an ugly-looking customer, broad, competent and leathery. He and Michael with Fleur between them, and behind—Foskisson and his junior; Settlewhite and the Scotchman with 'that cat' between them, and behind—Bullfry and his junior! Only the Judge wanted now to complete the pattern! And here he came! Soames gripped Fleur's arm and raised her with himself. Bob! Down again! One side of Brane's face seemed a little fuller than the other; Soames wondered if he had toothache, and how it would affect the proceedings.

And now came the usual 'shivaree' about such and such a case, and what would be taken next week, and so on. Well! that was over, and the Judge was turning his head this way and that, as if to see where the field was placed. Now Bullfry was up:

"If it please Your Lordship——"

He was making the usual opening, with the usual flowery description of the plaintiff—granddaughter of a marquess, engaged to a future Prime Minister . . . or so you'd think! . . . prominent in the most brilliant circles, high-spirited, perhaps a thought too high-spirited. . . . Baggage! . . . the usual smooth and subacid description of the defendant! . . . Rich and ambitious young married lady. . . . Impudent beggar! . . . Jury would bear in mind that they were dealing in both cases with members of advanced Society, but they would bear in mind, too, that primary words had primary meanings and consequences, whatever the Society in which they were uttered. H'm! Very sketchy reference to the incident in Fleur's drawing-room—minimised, of course—ha! an allusion to himself—man of property and standing—thank you for nothing! Reading the libellous letter now! Effect of them

415

. . . very made-up, all that! . . . Plaintiff obliged to take action. . . . Bunkum! "I shall now call Mrs. Ralph Ppynrryn."

"How do you spell that name, Mr. Bullfry?"

"With two p's two y's, two n's and two r's, my lord."

"I see."

Soames looked at the owner of the name. Good-looking woman of the flibberty-gibbet type! He listened to her evidence with close attention. Her account of the incident in Fleur's drawing-room seemed substantially correct. She had received the libellous letter two days later; had thought it her duty, as a friend, to inform Miss Ferrar. Should say, as a woman in Society, that this incident and these letters had done Miss Ferrar harm. Had talked it over with a good many people. A public incident. Much feeling excited. Had shown her letter to Mrs. Maltese, and been shown one that she had received. Whole matter had become current gossip. H'm!

Bullfry down, and Foskisson up!

Soames adjusted himself. Now to see how the fellow shaped— the manner of a cross-examiner was so important! Well, he had seen worse—the eye, like frozen light, fixed on unoccupied space while the question was being asked, and coming round on to the witness for the answer; the mouth a little open, as if to swallow it; the tongue visible at times on the lower lip, the unoccupied hand clasping something under the gown behind.

"Now, Mrs.—er—Ppynrryn. This incident, as my friend has called it, happened at the house of Mrs. Mont, did it not? And how did you come there? As a friend. Quite so! And you have nothing against Mrs. Mont? No. And you thought it advisable and kind, madam, to show this letter to the plaintiff and to other people—in fact, to foment this little incident to the best of your ability?" Eyes round!

"If a friend of mine received such a letter about me, I should expect her to tell me that the writer was going about abusing me."

"Even if your friend knew of the provocation and was also a friend of the letter-writer?"

"Yes."

"Now, madam, wasn't it simply that the sensation of this little quarrel was too precious to be burked? It would have been so easy, wouldn't it, to have torn the letter up and said nothing about it? You don't mean to suggest that it made *you* think any the worse of Miss Ferrar—you knew her too well, didn't you?"

"Ye-es."

"Exactly. As a friend of both parties you knew that the expressions were just spleen and not to be taken seriously?"

"I can't say that."

"Oh! You regard them as serious? Am I to take it that you thought they touched the hambone? In other words, that they were true?"

"Certainly not."

"Could they do Miss Ferrar any harm if they were palpably untrue?"

"I think they could."

"Not with you—you were a friend?"

"Not with me."

"But with other people, who would never have heard of them but for you. In fact, madam, you enjoyed the whole thing. Did you?"

"Enjoyed? No."

"You regarded it as your duty to spread this letter? Don't you enjoy doing your duty?"

The dry cackle within Soames stopped at his lips.

Foskisson down, and Bullfry up!

"It is, in fact, your experience, Mrs. Ppynrryn, as well as that of most of us not so well constituted, perhaps, as my learned friend, that duty is sometimes painful."

"Yes."

"Thank you. Mrs. Edward Maltese."

During the examination of this other young woman, who seemed to be dark and solid, Soames tried to estimate the comparative effect produced by Fleur and 'that cat' on the four jurymen whose eyes seemed to stray towards beauty. He had come to no definite conclusion, when Sir James Foskisson rose to cross-examine.

"Tell me, Mrs. Maltese, which do you consider the most serious allegation among those complained of?"

"The word 'treacherous' in my letter, and the expression 'a snake of the first water' in the letter to Mrs. Ppynrryn."

"More serious than the others?"

"Yes."

"That is where you can help me, madam. The circle you move in is not exactly the plaintiff's, perhaps?"

"Not exactly."

"Intersecting, um?"

"Yes."

"Now, in which section, yours or the plaintiff's, would you say

417

the expression 'she hasn't a moral about her' would be the more, or shall we say the less, damning?"

"I can't say."

"I only want your opinion. Do you think your section of Society as advanced as Miss Ferrar's?"

"Perhaps not."

"It's well known, isn't it, that her circle is very free and easy?"

"I suppose so."

"Still, *your* section is pretty advanced—I mean, you're not 'stuffy'?"

"Not what, Sir James?"

"Stuffy, my lord; it's an expression a good deal used in modern Society."

"What does it mean?"

"Strait-laced, my lord."

"I see. Well, he's asking you if you're stuffy?"

"No, my lord. I hope not."

"You hope not. Go on, Sir James."

"Not being stuffy, you wouldn't be exactly worried if somebody said to you: 'My dear, you haven't a moral about you'?"

"Not if it was said as charmingly as that."

"Now come, Mrs. Maltese, does such an expression, said charmingly or the reverse, convey any blame to you or to your friends?"

"If the reverse, yes."

"Am I to take it that the conception of morality in your circle is the same as in—my lord's?"

"How is the witness to answer that, Sir James?"

"Well, in your circle are you shocked when your friends are divorced, or when they go off together for a week in Paris, say, or wherever they find convenient?"

"Shocked? Well, I suppose one needn't be shocked by what one wouldn't do oneself."

"In fact, you're not shocked?"

"I don't know that I'm shocked by anything."

"That would be being stuffy, wouldn't it?"

"Perhaps."

"Well, will you tell me then—if that's the state of mind in your circle; and you said, you know, that your circle is less free and easy than the plaintiff's—how it is possible that such words as 'she hasn't a moral about her' can have done the plaintiff any harm?"

"The whole world isn't in our circles."

418

"No. I suggest that only a very small portion of the world is in your circles. But do you tell me that you or the plaintiff pay any——?"

"How can she tell, Sir James, what the plaintiff pays?"

"That *you*, then, pay any attention to what people outside your circle think?"

Soames moved his head twice. The fellow was doing it well. And his eye caught Fleur's face turned towards the witness; a little smile was curling her lip.

"I don't personally pay much attention even to what anybody *in* my circle thinks."

"Have you more independence of character than the plaintiff, should you say?"

"I dare say I've got as much."

"Is she notoriously independent?"

"Yes."

"Thank you, Mrs. Maltese."

Foskisson down, Bullfry up!

"I call the plaintiff, my lord."

Soames uncrossed his legs.


## Chapter VI

### IN THE BOX

MARJORIE FERRAR stepped into the Box, not exactly nervous, and only just 'made-up'. The papers would record a black costume with chinchilla fur and a black hat. She kissed the air in front of the book, took a deep breath, and turned to Mr. Bullfry.

For the last five days she had resented more and more the way this case had taken charge of her. She had initiated it, and it had completely deprived her of initiative. She had, in fact, made the old discovery, that when the machinery of quarrel is once put in motion, much more than pressure of the starting button is required to stop its revolutions. She was feeling that it would serve Alec and the lawyers right if all went wrong.

The voice of Mr. Bullfry, carefully adjusted, soothed her. His questions were familiar, and with each answer her confidence increased, her voice sounded clear and pleasant in her ears. And she stood at ease, making her figure as boyish as she could. Her performance, she felt, was interesting to the Judge, the jury, and all those people up there, whom she could dimly see. If only 'that

419

little snob' had not been seated, expressionless, between her and her Counsel! When at length Mr. Bullfry sat down and Sir James Foskisson got up, she almost succumbed to the longing to powder her nose. Clasping the Box, she resisted it, and while he turned his papers, and hitched his gown, the first tremor of the morning passed down her spine. At least he might look at her when he spoke!

"Have you ever been party to an action before, Miss Ferrar?"

"No."

"You quite understand, don't you, that you are on your oath?"

"Quite."

"You have told my friend that you had no animus against Mrs. Mont. Look at this marked paragraph in *The Evening Sun* of October 3rd. Did you write that?"

Marjorie Ferrar felt exactly as if she had stepped out of a conservatory into an east wind. Did they know everything, then?

"Yes; I wrote it."

"It ends thus: 'The enterprising little lady is losing no chance of building up her 'salon' on the curiosity which ever surrounds any buccaneering in politics.' Is the reference to Mrs. Mont?"

"Yes."

"Not very nice, is it—of a friend?"

"I don't see any harm in it."

"The sort of thing, in fact, you'd like written about yourself?"

"The sort of thing I should expect if I were doing the same thing."

"That's not quite an answer, but let me put it like this: The sort of thing your father would like to read about you, is it?"

"My father would never read that column."

"Then it surprises you to hear that Mrs. Mont's father did? Do you write many of these cheery little paragraphs about your friends?"

"Not many."

"Every now and then, eh? And do they remain your friends?"

"It's not easy in Society to tell who's a friend and who isn't."

"I quite agree, Miss Ferrar. You have admitted making one or two critical—that was your word, I think—remarks concerning Mrs. Mont, in her own house. Do you go to many houses and talk disparagingly of your hostess?"

"No; and in any case I don't expect to be eavesdropped."

"I see; so long as you're not found out, it's all right, eh? Now, on this first Wednesday in October last, at Mrs. Mont's, in speaking to this gentleman, Mr. Philip—er—Quinsey, did you use the word 'snob' of your hostess?"

"I don't think so."

"Be careful. You heard the evidence of Mrs. Ppynrryn and Mrs. Maltese. Mrs. Maltese said, you remember, that Mr. Forsyte—that is Mrs. Mont's father—said to you on that occasion: 'You called my daughter a snob in her own house, madam—be so kind as to withdraw; you are a traitress.' Is that a correct version?"

"Probably."

"Do you suggest that he invented the word 'snob'?"

"I suggest he was mistaken."

"Not a nice word, is it—'snob'? Was there any other reason why he should call you a traitress?"

"My remarks weren't meant for his ears. I don't remember exactly what I said."

"Well, we shall have Mr. Forsyte in the Box to refresh your memory as to exactly what you said. But I put it to you that you called her a snob, not once but twice, during that little conversation?"

"I've told you I don't remember; he shouldn't have listened."

"Very well! So you feel quite happy about having written that paragraph and said nasty things of Mrs. Mont behind her back in her own drawing-room?"

Marjorie Ferrar grasped the Box till the blood tingled in her palms. His voice was maddening.

"Yet it seems, Miss Ferrar, that you object to others saying nasty things about you in return. Who advised you to bring this action?"

"My father first; and then my fiancé."

"Sir Alexander MacGown. Does he move in the same circles as you?"

"No; he moves in Parliamentary circles."

"Exactly; and he wouldn't know, would he, the canons of conduct that rule in your circle?"

"There are no circles so definite as that."

"Always willing to learn, Miss Ferrar. But tell me, do you know what Sir Alexander's Parliamentary friends think about conduct and morality?"

"I can guess. I don't suppose there's much difference."

"Are you suggesting, Miss Ferrar, that responsible public men take the same light-hearted view of conduct and morals as you?"

"Aren't you rather assuming, Sir James, that her view *is* light-hearted?"

421

"As to conduct, my lord, I submit that her answers have shown the very light-hearted view she takes of the obligations incurred by the acceptance of hospitality, for instance. I'm coming to morals now."

"I think you'd better, before drawing your conclusions. What have public men to do with it?"

"I'm suggesting, my lord, that this lady is making a great to-do about words which a public man, or any ordinary citizen, would have a perfect right to resent, but which she, with her views, has no right whatever to resent."

"You must prove her views then. Go on!"

Marjorie Ferrar, relaxed for a moment, gathered herself again. Her views!

"Tell me, Miss Ferrar—we all know now the meaning of the word 'stuffy'—are public men 'stuffier' than you?"

"They may say they are."

"You think them hypocrites?"

"I don't think anything at all about them."

"Though you're going to marry one? You are complaining of the words: 'She hasn't a moral about her.' Have you read this novel *Canthar*? He was holding up a book.

"I think so."

"Don't you know?"

"I've skimmed it."

"Taken off the cream, eh? Read it sufficiently to form an opinion?"

"Yes."

"Would you agree with the view of it expressed in this letter to a journal? 'The book breaks through the British "stuffiness". which condemns any frank work of art—and a good thing, too!' Is it a good thing?"

"Yes. I hate Grundyism."

" 'It is undoubtedly Literature.' The word is written with a large L. Should you say it was?"

"Literature—yes. Not great literature, perhaps."

"But it ought to be published?"

"I don't see why not."

"You know that it is not published in England?"

"Yes."

"But it ought to be?"

"It isn't everybody's sort of book, of course."

"Don't evade the question, please. In your opinion ought this

422

novel *Canthar* to be published in England? . . . Take your time, Miss Ferrar."

The brute lost nothing! Just because she had hesitated a moment trying to see where he was leading her.

"Yes. I think literature should be free."

"You wouldn't sympathise with its suppression if it were published?"

"No."

"You wouldn't approve of the suppression of any book on the ground of mere morals?"

"I can't tell you unless I see the book. People aren't bound to read books, you know."

"And you think your opinion generally on this subject is that of public men and ordinary citizens?"

"No; I suppose it isn't."

"But your view would be shared by most of your own associates?"

"I should hope so."

"A contrary opinion would be 'stuffy', wouldn't it?"

"If you like to call it so. It's not my word."

"What is your word, Miss Ferrar?"

"I think I generally say 'ga-ga'."

"Do you know, I'm afraid the Court will require a little elaboration of that."

"Not for me, Sir James; I'm perfectly familiar with the word; it means 'in your dotage'."

"The Bench is omniscient, my lord. Then anyone, Miss Ferrar, who didn't share the opinion of yourself and your associates in the matter of this book would be 'ga-ga', that is to say, in his or her dotage?"

"Æsthetically."

"Ah! I thought we should arrive at that word. You, I suppose, don't connect art with life?"

"No."

"Don't think it has any effect on life?"

"It oughtn't to."

"When a man's theme in a book is extreme incontinence, depicted with all due emphasis, that wouldn't have any practical effect on his readers, however young?"

"I can't say about other people, it wouldn't have any effect on me."

"You are emancipated, in fact."

423

"I don't know what you mean by that."

"Isn't what you are saying about the divorce of art from life the merest clap-trap; and don't you know it."

"I certainly don't."

"Let me put it another way: Is it possible for those who believe in current morality to hold your view that art has no effect on life?"

"Quite possible; if they are cultured."

"Cultured! Do you believe in current morality yourself?"

"I don't know what you call current morality."

"I will tell you, Miss Ferrar. I should say, for instance, it was current morality that women should not have *liaisons* before they're married, and should not have them after."

"What about men?"

"Thank you; I was coming to men. And that men should at least not have them after."

"I shouldn't say that was *current* morality at all."

In yielding to that satiric impulse she knew at once she had made a mistake—the judge had turned his face towards her. He was speaking.

"Do I understand you to imply that in your view it is moral for women to have *liaisons* before marriage, and for men and women to have them after?"

"I think it's current morality, my lord."

"I'm not asking you about current morality; I'm asking whether in *your* view it is moral?"

"I think many people think it's all right who don't say it, yet."

She was conscious of movement throughout the jury; and of a little flump in the well of the Court. Sir Alexander had dropped his hat. The sound of a nose being loudly blown broke the stillness, the face of Bullfry, K.C., was lost to her view. She felt the blood mounting in her cheeks.

"Answer my question, please. Do *you* say it's all right?"

"I—I think it depends."

"On what?"

"On—on circumstances, environment, temperament; all sorts of things."

"Would it be all right for *you*?"

Marjorie Ferrar became very still. "I can't answer that question, my lord."

"You mean—you don't want to!"

"I mean I don't know."

And, with a feeling as if she had withdrawn her foot from a bit of breaking ice, she saw Bullfry's face re-emerge from his handkerchief.

"Very well. Go on, Sir James!"

"Anyway, we may take it, Miss Ferrar, that those of us who say we don't believe in these irregularities are hypocrites in your view?"

"Why can't you be fair?"

He was looking at her now; and she didn't like him any the better for it.

"I shall prove myself fair before I've done, Miss Ferrar."

"You've got your work cut out, haven't you?"

"Believe me, madam, it will be better for you not to indulge in witticism. According to you, there is no harm in a book like *Canthar*?"

"There ought to be none."

"You mean if we were all as æsthetically cultured—as you."— Sneering beast!—"But are we?"

"No."

"Then there is harm. But you wouldn't mind that harm being done. I don't propose, my lord, to read from this very unpleasant novel. Owing apparently to its unsavoury reputation, a copy of it now costs nearly seven pounds. And I venture to think that is in itself an answer to the plaintiff's contention that 'art' so called has no effect on life. We have gone to the considerable expense of buying copies, and I shall ask that during the luncheon interval the jury may read some dozen marked passages."

"Have you a copy for me, Sir James?"

"Yes, my lord."

"And one for Mr. Bullfry? . . . If there is any laughter, I shall have the Court cleared. Go on."

"You know the 'Ne Plus Ultra' Play-Producing Society, Miss Ferrar? It exists to produce advanced plays, I believe."

"Plays—I don't know about 'advanced'."

"Russian plays, and the Restoration dramatists?"

"Yes."

"And you have played in them?"

"Sometimes."

"Do you remember a play called 'The Plain Dealer', by Wycherley, given at a matinée on January 7th last—did you play in that the part of Olivia?"

"Yes."

"A nice part?"

"A very good part."

"I said 'nice'."

"I don't like the word."

"Too suggestive of 'prunes and prisms', Miss Ferrar? Is it the part of a modest woman?"

"No."

"Is it, towards the end, extremely immodest? I allude to the dark scene."

"I don't know about extremely."

"Anyway, you felt no hesitation about undertaking and playing the part—a little thing like that doesn't worry you?"

"I don't know why it should. If it did, I shouldn't act."

"You don't act for money?"

"No; for pleasure."

"Then, of course, you can refuse any part you like?"

"If I did, I shouldn't have any offered me."

"Don't quibble, please. You took the part of Olivia not for money but for pleasure. You enjoyed playing it?"

"Pretty well."

"I'm afraid I shall have to ask the jury, my lord, to run their eyes over the dark scene in 'The Plain Dealer'."

"Are you saying, Sir James, that a woman who plays an immoral part is not moral—that would asperse a great many excellent reputations."

"No, my lord; I'm saying that here is a young lady so jealous of her good name in the eyes of the world, that she brings a libel action because someone has said in a private letter that she 'hasn't a moral about her'. And at the same time she is reading and approving books like this Canthar, playing parts like that of Olivia in 'The Plain Dealer', and, as I submit, living in a section of Society that really doesn't know the meaning of the word morals, that looks upon morals, in fact, rather as we look upon measles. It's my contention, my lord, that the saying in my client's letter: 'She hasn't a moral about her', is rather a compliment to the plaintiff than otherwise."

"Do you mean that it was intended as a compliment?"

"No, no, my lord."

"Well, you want the jury to read that scene. You will have a busy luncheon interval, gentlemen. Go on, Sir James."

"Now, Miss Ferrar—my friend made a point of the fact that you are engaged to a wealthy and highly respected Member of Parliament. How long have you been engaged to him?"

"Six months."

"You have no secrets from him, I suppose?"

"Why should I answer that?"

"Why should she, Sir James?"

"I am quite content to leave it at her reluctance, my lord."

Sneering brute! As if everybody hadn't secrets from everybody!

"Your engagement was not made public till January, was it?"

"No."

"May I take it that you were not sure of your own mind till then?"

"If you like."

"Now, Miss Ferrar, did you bring this action because of your good name? Wasn't it because you were hard up?"

She was conscious again of blood in her cheeks.

"No."

"*Were* you hard up when you brought it?"

"Yes."

"Very?"

"Not worse than I have been before."

"I put it to you that you owed a great deal of money, and were hard pressed."

"If you like."

"I'm glad you've admitted that, Miss Ferrar; otherwise I should have had to prove it. And you didn't bring this action with a view to paying some of your debts?"

"No."

"Did you in early January become aware that you were not likely to get any sum in settlement of this suit?"

"I believe I was told that an offer was withdrawn."

"And do you know why?"

"Yes, because Mrs. Mont wouldn't give the apology I asked for."

"Exactly! And was it a coincidence that you thereupon made up your mind to marry Sir Alexander MacGown?"

"A coincidence?"

"I mean the announcement of your engagement, you know?"

Brute!

"It had nothing to do with this case."

"Indeed! Now when you brought this action, did you really care one straw whether people thought you moral or not?"

427

"I brought it chiefly because I was called 'a snake'."

"Please answer my question."

"It isn't so much what *I* cared, as what my friends cared."

"But their view of morality is much what yours is—thoroughly accommodating?"

"Not my *fiancé's.*"

"Ah! no. He doesn't move in your circle, you said. But the rest of your friends. You're not ashamed of your own accommodating philosophy, are you?"

"No."

"Then why be ashamed of it for them?"

"How can I tell what *their* philosophy is?"

"How can she, Sir James?"

"As your lordship pleases. Now, Miss Ferrar! You like to stand up for your views, I hope. Let me put your philosophy to you in a nutshell: You believe, don't you, in the full expression of your personality; it would be your duty, wouldn't it, to break through any convention—I don't say law—but any so-called moral convention that cramped you?"

"I never said I had a philosophy."

"Don't run away from it, please."

"I'm not in the habit of running away."

"I'm so glad of that. You believe in being the sole judge of your own conduct?"

"Yes."

"You're not alone in that view, are you?"

"I shouldn't think so."

"It's the view, in fact, of what may be called the forward wing of modern Society, isn't it—the wing you belong to, and are proud of belonging to? And in that section of Society—so long as you don't break the actual law—you think and do as you like, eh?"

"One doesn't always act up to one's principles."

"Quite so. But among your associates, even if you and they don't always act up to it, it *is* a principle, isn't it, to judge for yourselves and go your own ways without regard to convention?"

"More or less."

"And, living in that circle, with that belief, you have the effrontery to think the words: 'She hasn't a moral about her', entitles you to damages?"

Her voice rang out angrily: "I have morals. They may not be yours, but they may be just as good, perhaps better. I'm not a hypocrite, anyway."

Again she saw him look at her, there was a gleam in his eyes; and she knew she had made another mistake.

"We'll leave my morals out of the question, Miss Ferrar. But we'll go a little farther into what you say are yours. In your own words, it should depend on temperament, circumstances, environment, whether you conform to morality or not?"

She stood silent, biting her lip.

"Answer, please."

She inclined her head. "Yes."

"Very good!" He had paused, turning over his papers, and she drew back in the Box. She had lost her temper—had made him lose his; at all costs she must keep her head now! In this moment of search for her head she took in everything—expressions, gestures, even the atmosphere—the curious dramatic emanation from a hundred and more still faces; she noted the one lady juryman, the judge breaking the nib of a quill, with his eyes turned away from it as if looking at something that had run across the well of the Court. Yes, and down there, the lengthening lip of Mr. Settlewhite, Michael's face turned up at her with a rueful frown, Fleur Mont's mask with red spots in the cheeks, Alec's clenched hands, and his eyes fixed on her. A sort of comic intensity about it all! If only she were the size of Alice in 'Wonderland', and could take them all in her hands and shake them like a pack of cards—so motionless, there, at her expense! That sarcastic brute had finished fiddling with his papers, and she moved forward again to attention in the box.

"Now, Miss Ferrar, his lordship put a general question to you which you did not feel able to answer. I am going to put it in a way that will be easier for you. Whether or no it was right for you to have one"—she saw Michael's hand go up to his face—"have you *in fact* had a—*liaison*?" And from some tone in his voice, from the look on his face, she could tell for certain that her persecutor knew she had.

With her back to the wall, she had not even a wall to her back. Ten, twenty, thirty seconds—judge, jury, that old fox with his hand under the tail of his gown, and his eyes averted! Why did she not spit out the indignant: No! which she had so often rehearsed? Suppose he proved it—as he had said he would prove her debts?

"Take your time, Miss Ferrar. You know what a *liaison* is, of course."

Brute! On the verge of denial, she saw Michael lean across, and

429

heard his whisper: 'Stop this!' And then 'that little snob' looked up at her—the scrutiny was knowing and contemptuous: 'Now hear her lie!' it seemed to say. And she answered quickly: "I consider your question insulting."

"Oh! come, Miss Ferrar, after your own words! After what——"

"Well! I shan't answer it."

A rustle, a whispering in the Court.

"You won't answer it?"

"No."

"Thank you, Miss Ferrar." Could a voice be more sarcastic?

The brute was sitting down.

Marjorie Ferrar stood defiant, with no ground under her feet. What next? Her counsel was beckoning. She descended from the Box and, passing her adversaries, resumed her seat next her betrothed. How red and still he was! She heard the judge say:

"I shall break for lunch now, Mr. Bullfry," saw him rise and go out, and the jury getting up. The whispering and rustling in the Court swelled to a buzz. She stood up. Mr. Settlewhite was speaking to her.

## Chapter VII

### 'FED UP'

GUIDED by him into a room designed to shelter witnesses, Marjorie Ferrar looked at her lawyer.

"Well?"

"An unfortunate refusal, Miss Ferrar—very. I'm afraid the effect on the jury may be fatal. If we can settle it now, I should certainly say we'd better."

"It's all the same to me."

"In that case you may take it I shall settle. I'll go and see Sir Alexander and Mr. Bullfry at once."

"How do I get out quietly?"

"Down those stairs. You'll find cabs in Lincoln's Inn Fields. Excuse me." He made her a grave little bow and stalked away.

Marjorie Ferrar did not take a cab; she walked. If her last answer had been fatal, on the whole she was content. She had told no lies to speak of, had stood up to 'that sarcastic beast', and given him sometimes as good as she had got. Alec! Well, she couldn't help it! He had insisted on her going into Court; she hoped he liked it now she'd been! Buying a newspaper, she went into a restaurant and read a description of herself, accompanied by a photograph. She ate a good lunch, and then continued her walk along Piccadilly. Passing into the Park, she sat down under a tree coming into bud, and drew the smoke of a cigarette quietly into her lungs. The Row was almost deserted. A few persons of little or no consequence occupied a few chairs. A riding mistress was teaching a small boy to trot. Some sparrows and a pigeon alone seemed to take a distant interest in her. The air smelled of spring. She sat some time with the pleasant feeling that nobody in the world knew where she was. Odd, when you thought of it—millions of people every day, leaving their houses, offices, shops, on their way to the next place, were as lost to the world as stones in a pond! Would it be nice to disappear permanently, and taste life incognita? Bertie Curfew was going to Moscow again. Would he take her as secretary, and *bonne amie*? Bertie Curfew—she had only pretended to be tired of him! The thought brought her face to face with the future. Alec! Explanations! It was hardly the word! He had a list of her debts, and had said he would pay them as a wedding-present. But—if there wasn't to be a wedding? Thank God, she had some ready money. The carefully 'laid-up' four-year-old in her father's stable had won yesterday. She had dribbled 'a pony' on at a nice price. She rose and sauntered along, distending her bust—in defiance of the boy-like fashion, which, after all, was on the wane—to take in the full of a sweet wind.

Leaving the Park, she came to South Kensington station and bought another paper. It had a full account under the headlines: 'Modern Morality Attacked.' 'Miss Marjorie Ferrar in the Box.' It seemed funny to stand there reading those words among people who were reading the same without knowing her from Eve, except, perhaps, by her clothes. Continuing her progress towards Wren Street, she turned her latch-key in the door, and saw a hat. Waiting for her already! She took her time; and, pale from powder, as though she had gone through much, entered the studio.

MacGown was sitting with his head in his hands. She felt real pity for him—too strong, too square, too vital for that attitude! He raised his face.

"Well, Alec!"

"Tell me the truth, Marjorie. I'm in torment."

She almost envied him the depth of his feeling, however unreasonable after her warnings. But she said ironically:

"Who was it knew me better than I knew myself?"

431

In the same dull voice he repeated:

"The truth, Marjorie, the truth!"

But why should she go into the confessional? Was he entitled to her past? His rights stopped at her future. It was the old business—men expecting more from women than they could give them. Inequality of the sexes. Something in that, perhaps, in the old days when women bore children, and men didn't; but now that women knew all about sex and only bore children when they wanted to, and not always even then, why should men be freer?

And she said slowly: "In exchange for your adventures I'll tell you mine."

"For God's sake don't mock me; I've had hell these last hours."

His face showed it, and she said with feeling:

"I said you'd be taking a toss over me, Alec. Why on earth did you insist on my bringing this case? You've had your way, and now you don't like it."

"It's true, then?"

"Yes. Why not?"

He uttered a groan, recoiling till his back was against the wall, as if afraid of being loose in the room.

"Who was he?"

"Oh! no! That I can't possibly tell you. And how many affairs have you had?"

He paid no attention. He wouldn't! He knew she didn't love him; and such things only mattered if you loved! Ah! well! His agony was a tribute to her, after all!

"You're well out of me," she said sullenly; and, sitting down, she lighted a cigarette. A scene! How hateful! Why didn't he go? She'd rather he'd be violent than deaf and dumb and blind like this.

"Not that American fellow?"

She could not help a laugh.

"Oh! no, poor boy!"

"How long did it last?"

"Nearly a year."

"My God!"

He had rushed to the door. If only he would open it and go! That he could feel so violently! That figure by the door was just not mad! His stuffy passions!

And then he did pull the door open and was gone.

She threw herself at full length on the divan; not from lassitude, exactly, nor despair—from a feeling rather as if nothing mattered.

How stupid and pre-war! Why couldn't he, like her, be free, be supple, take life as it came? Passions, prejudices, principles, pity— old-fashioned as the stuffy clothes worn when she was a tot. Well! Good riddance! Fancy living in the same house, sharing the same bed, with a man so full of the primitive that he could 'go off his chump' with jealousy about her! Fancy living with a man who took life so seriously, that he couldn't even see himself doing it! Life was a cigarette to be inhaled and thrown away, a dance to be danced out. On with that dance! . . . Yes, but she couldn't let him pay her debts, now, even if he wanted to. Married, she would have repaid him with her body; as it was—no! Oh! why didn't someone die and leave her something? What a bore it all was! And she lay still, listening to the tea-time sounds of a quiet street— taxis rounding the corner from the river; the dog next door bark- ing at the postman; that one-legged man—ex-Service—who came most afternoons and played on a poor fiddle. He expected her shilling—unhappy fellow! she'd have to get up and give it him. She went to the little side window that looked on to the street, and suddenly recoiled. Francis Wilmot in the doorway with his hand up to the bell! Another scene! No, really! This was too much! There went the bell! No time to say 'Not at home!' Well, let them all come—round her past, like bees round a honey- pot!

"Mr. Francis Wilmot."

He stood there, large as the life he had nearly resigned—a little thinner, that was all.

"Well, Francis," she said, "I thought you were 'through with that fool business'?"

Francis Wilmot came gravely up and took her hand. "I sail to- morrow."

Sail! Well, she could put up with that. He seemed to her just a thin, pale young man with dark hair and eyes and no juices in his system.

"I read the evening papers. I wondered if, perhaps, you'd wish to see me."

Was he mocking her? But he wore no smile; there was no bitter- ness in his voice; and, though he was looking at her intently, she could not tell from his face whether he still had any feeling. She said:

"You think I owe you something? I know I treated you very badly."

He looked rather as if she'd hit him.

"For heaven's sake, Francis, don't say you've come out of chivalry. That'd be too funny."

"I don't follow you; I just thought, perhaps, you didn't like to answer that question about a love affair—because of me."

Marjorie Ferrar broke into hysterical laughter.

"Senor Don Punctilio! Because of you! No, no, my dear!"

Francis Wilmot drew back, and made her a little bow.

"I shouldn't have come," he said.

She had a sudden return of feeling for that slim unusual presence, with its grace and its dark eyes.

"I'm a free-lance again now, Francis, anyway."

A long moment went by, and then he made her another little bow. It was a clear withdrawal.

"Then for God's sake," she said, "go away! I'm fed up!" And she turned her back on him.

When she looked round, he *had* gone, and that surprised her. He was a new variety, or a dead one, dug up! He didn't know the rudiments of life—old-fashioned, *à faire rire!* And, back at full length on the divan, she brooded. Well, her courage was 'not out'! To-morrow was Bella Magussie's 'At Home' to meet—some idiot. Everybody would be there, and so would she!

## Chapter VIII

### FANTOCHES

WHEN Michael, screwed towards Sir James Foskisson's averted face, heard the words: "Well, I shan't answer", he spun round. It was just as if she had said: 'Yes, I have.' The judge was looking at her, everyone looking at her. Wasn't Bullfry going to help her? No! He was beckoning her out of the Box. Michael half rose, as she passed him. By George! He was sorry for MacGown! There he sat, poor devil! with everyone getting up all round him, still, and red as a turkey-cock.

Fleur! Michael looked at her face, slightly flushed, her gloved hands clasped in her lap, her eyes fixed on the ground. Had his whisper: 'Stop this!' his little abortive bow, offended her? How could one have helped sympathising with the 'Pet of the Panjoys' in so tight a place! Fleur must see that! The Court was empty-ing—fine birds, many—he could see her mother and her aunt and cousin, and Old Forsyte, talking with Foskisson. Ah! he had finished; was speaking: "We can go now."

They followed him along the corridor, down the stairs, into the air.

"We've time for a snack," Soames was saying. "Come in here!"

In one of several kennels without roofs in a celebrated room with a boarded floor, they sat down.

"Three chump chops, sharp," said Soames, and staring at the cruet-stand, added: "She's cooked her goose. They'll drop it like a hot potato. I've told Foskisson he can settle, with both sides paying their own costs. It's more than they deserve."

"He ought never to have asked that question, sir."

Fleur looked up sharply.

"Really, Michael!"

"Well, darling, we agreed he shouldn't. Why didn't Bullfry help her out, sir?"

"Only too glad to get her out of the Box; the judge would have asked her himself in another minute. It's a complete fiasco, thank God!"

"Then we've won?" said Fleur.

"Unless I'm a Dutchman," answered Soames.

"I'm not so sure," muttered Michael.

"I tell you it's all over; Bullfry'll never go on with it."

"I didn't mean that, sir."

Fleur said acidly: "Then what do you mean, Michael?"

"I don't think we shall be forgiven, that's all."

"What for?"

"Well, I dare say I'm all wrong. Sauce, sir?"

"Worcester—yes. This is the only place in London where you can rely on a floury potato. Waiter—three glasses of port, quick!"

After fifteen minutes of concentrated mastication, they returned to the Court.

"Wait here," said Soames, in the hall; "I'll go and find out."

In that echoing space, where a man's height was so inconsiderable, Fleur and Michael stood, not speaking, for some time.

"She couldn't know that Foskisson had been told not to follow it up, of course," he said at last. "Still, she must have expected the question. She should have told a good one and have done with it. I couldn't help feeling sorry for her."

"You'd feel sorry for a flea that bit you, Michael. What do you mean by our not being forgiven?"

"Well! The drama was all on her side, and it's drama that counts. Besides, there's her engagement!"

"That'll be broken off."

435

"Exactly! And if it is, she'll have sympathy; while if it isn't, he'll have it. Anyway, we shan't. Besides, you know, she stood up for what we all really believe nowadays."

"Speak for yourself."

"Well, don't we talk of everyone being free?"

"Yes, but is there any connection between what we say and what we do?"

"No," said Michael.

And just then Soames returned.

"Well, sir?"

"As I told you, Bullfry caught at it. They've settled. It's a moral victory."

"Oh! not moral, I hope, sir."

"It's cost a pretty penny, anyway," said Soames, looking at Fleur. "Your mother's quite annoyed—she's no sense of propor-tion. Very clever the way Foskisson made that woman lose her temper."

"He lost his, at the end. That's his excuse, I suppose."

"Well," said Soames, "it's all over! Your mother's got the car; we'll take a taxi."

On the drive back to South Square, taking precisely the same route, there was precisely the same silence.

When a little later Michael went over to the House, he was edified by posters.

'Society Libel Action.'

'Marquess's Granddaughter and K.C.'

'Dramatic evidence.'

'Modern Morality!'

All over—was it? With publicity—in Michael's opinion—it had but just begun! Morality! What was it—who had it, and what did they do with it? How would he have answered those questions himself? Who could answer them, nowadays, by rote or rule? Not he, nor Fleur! They had been identified with the Inquisition, and what was their position now? False, if not odious! He passed into the House. But, try as he would, he could not fix his attention on the Purity of Food, and passed out again. With a curious long-ing for his father, he walked rapidly down Whitehall. Drawing blank at 'Snooks'' and the 'Aeroplane', he tried the 'Parthenæum' as a last resort. Sir Lawrence was in a corner of a forbidden room, reading a life of Lord Palmerston. He looked up at his son.

"Ah! Michael! They don't do justice to old Pam. A man with-out frills, who worked like a nigger. But we mustn't talk here!"

And he pointed to a member who seemed awake. "Shall we take a turn before the old gentleman over there has a fit? The books here are camouflage; it's really a dormitory."

He led the way, with Michael retailing the events of the morning.

"Foskisson?" said Sir Lawrence, entering the Green Park. "He was a nice little chap when I left Winchester. To be professionally in the right is bad for a man's character—counsel, parsons, police-men, they all suffer from it. Judges, High Priests, Arch-Inspectors, aren't so bad—they've suffered from it so long that they've lost consciousness."

"It was a full house," said Michael glumly, "and the papers have got hold of it."

"They would." And Sir Lawrence pointed to the ornamental water. "These birds," he said, "remind me of China. By the way, I met your friend Desert yesterday at the 'Aeroplane'—he's more interesting now that he's dropped Poetry for the East. Everybody ought to drop something. I'm too old now, but if I'd dropped baronetcy in time, I could have made quite a good contortionist."

"What would you recommend for Members of Parliament?" asked Michael, with a grin.

"Postmanship, my dear—carrying on, you know; a certain importance, large bags, dogs to bark at you, no initiative, and con-versation on every door-step. By the way, do you see Desert?"

"I have seen him."

Sir Lawrence screwed up his eyes.

"The providential," he said, "doesn't happen twice."

Michael coloured; he had not suspected his father of such shrewd observation. Sir Lawrence swung his cane.

"Your man Boddick," he said, "has persuaded some of his hens to lay; he's giving us quite good eggs."

Michael admired his reticence. But somehow that unexpected slanting allusion to a past domestic crisis roused the feeling that for so long now had been curled like a sleepy snake in his chest, that another crisis was brewing and must soon be faced.

"Coming along for tea, sir? Kit had tummy-ache this morn-ing. How's your last book doing? Does old Danby advertise it properly?"

"No," said Sir Lawrence, "no; he's keeping his head wonderfully; the book is almost dead."

"I'm glad I dropped *him*, anyway," said Michael, with emphasis. "I suppose, sir, you haven't a tip to give us, now this case is over?"

Sir Lawrence gazed at a bird with a long red bill.

"When victorious," he said at last, "lie doggo. The triumphs of morality are apt to recoil on those who achieve them."

"That's what I feel, sir. Heaven knows *I* didn't want to achieve one. My father-in-law says my hitting MacGown on the boko really brought it into Court."

Sir Lawrence whinnied.

"The tax on luxuries. It gets you everywhere. I don't think I will come along, Michael—Old Forsyte's probably there. Your mother has an excellent recipe for child's tummy-ache; you almost lived on it at one time. I'll telephone it from Mount Street. Good-bye!"

Michael looked after that thin and sprightly figure moving North. Had he troubles of his own? If so, he disguised them wonderfully. Good old Bart! And he turned towards South Square.

Soames was just leaving.

"She's excited," he said, on the door-step. "It's the reaction. Give her a Seidlitz powder to-night. Be careful, too; I shouldn't talk about politics."

Michael went in. Fleur was at the open window of the drawing-room.

"Oh! here you are!" she said. "Kit's all right again. Take me to the Café Royal to-night, Michael, and if there's anything funny anywhere, for goodness' sake, let's see it. I'm sick of feeling solemn. Oh! And, by the way, Francis Wilmot's coming in to say good-bye. I've had a note. He says he's all right again."

At the window by her side, Michael sniffed the unaccountable scent of grass. There was a south-west wind, and slanting from over the house-tops, sunlight was sprinkling the soil, the buds, the branches. A blackbird sang; a piano-organ round a corner was playing 'Rigoletto'. Against his own, her shoulder was soft, and to his lips her cheek was warm and creamy. . . .

When Francis Wilmot left them that evening after dinner at the Café Royal, Fleur said to Michael:

"Poor Francis! Did you ever see anyone so changed? He might be thirty. I'm glad he's going home to his river and his darkies. What are live oaks? Well! Are we going anywhere?"

Michael cloaked her shoulders.

" 'Great Itch', I think; there's no other scream so certain."

After their scream they came out into a mild night. High up in red and green the bright signs fled along the air: 'Tomber's Tires for Speed and Safety', 'Milkoh Makes Mothers Merry'.

Through Trafalgar Square they went and down Whitehall, all moonlight and Portland stone.

"The night's unreal," said Fleur. " *'Fantoches'!*"

Michael caught her waist.

"Don't! Suppose some Member saw you!"

"He'd only sympathise. How nice and solid you feel!"

"No. *Fantoches* have no substance."

"Then give me shadow."

"The substance is in Bethnal Green."

Michael dropped his arm.

"That's a strange thought."

"I have intuitions, Michael."

"Because I can admire a good woman, can I not love you?"

"*I* shall never be 'good'; it isn't in me."

"Whatever you are's enough for me."

"Prettily said. The Square looks jolly to-night! Open the doll's house."

The hall was dark, with just a glimmer coming through the fan-light. Michael took off her cloak and knelt down. He felt her fingers stir his hair; real fingers, and real all this within his arms; only the soul elusive. Soul?

"*Fantoches!*" came her voice, soft and mocking. "And so to bed!"

## Chapter IX

### ROUT AT MRS. MAGUSSIE'S

THERE are routs social, political, propagandic; and routs like Mrs. Magussie's. In one of Anglo-American birth, inexhaustible wealth, unimpeachable widowhood, and catholic taste, the word hostess had found its highest expression. People might die, marry, and be born with impunity so long as they met, preferably in her house, one of the largest in Mayfair. If she called in a doctor, it was to meet another doctor; if she went to church, it was to get Canon Forant to meet Dean Kimble at lunch afterwards. Her cards of invitation had the words: 'To meet' printed on them; and she never put 'me'. She was selfless. Once in a way she had a real rout, because once in a way a personality was available, whose name everybody, from poets to prelates, must know. In her intimate belief people loved to meet anybody sufficiently distinguished; and this was where she succeeded, because almost without exception they did.

439

Her two husbands had 'passed on', having met in their time nearly everybody. They had both been distinguished, and had first met in her house; and she would never have a third for Society was losing its landmarks, and she was too occupied. People were inclined to smile at mention of Bella Magussie, and yet, how do without one who performed the function of cement? Without her, bishops could not place their cheeks by the jowls of ballet girls, or Home Secretaries be fertilised by disorderly dramatists. Except in her house, the diggers-up of old civilisation in Beluchistan never encountered the levellers of modern civilisation in London. Nor was there any chance for lights of the Palace to meet those lights of the Halls—Madame Nemesia and Top Nobby. Nowhere else could a Russian dancer go to supper with Sir Walter Peddel, M.D., F.R.S.T.R., P.M.V.S., 'R.I.P.' as Michael would add. Even a bowler with the finest collection of ducks' eggs in first-class cricket was not without a chance of wringing the hand of the great Indian economist Sir Banerjee Bath Babore. Mrs. Magussie's, in fine, was a house of chief consequence; and her long face, as of the guardian of some first principle, moving about the waters of celebrity, was wrinkled in a great cause. To meet or not to meet? She had answered the question for good and all.

The 'met' or 'meetee' for her opening rout in 1925 was the great Italian violinist Luigi Sporza, who had just completed his remarkable tour of the world, having in half the time played more often than any two previous musicians. The prodigious feat had been noted in the Press of all countries with every circumstance—the five violins he had tired out, the invitation he had received to preside over a South American Republic, the special steamer he had chartered to keep an engagement in North America, and his fainting fit in Moscow after the Beethoven and Brahms concertos, the Bach chaconne, and seventeen encores. During the lingering year of his great effort, his fame had been established. As an artist he had been known to a few, as an athlete he was now known to all.

Michael and Fleur, passing up the centre stairway, saw a man 'not 'arf like a bull'—Michael muttered—whose hand people were seizing, one after the other, to move away afterwards with a look of pain.

"Only Italy can produce men like that," said Michael in Fleur's ear. "Give him the go-by. He'll hurt you."

But Fleur moved forward.

"Made of sterner stuff," murmured Michael. It was not the part of his beloved to miss the hand of celebrity, however horny! No portion of her charming face quivered as the great athlete's grip closed on hers, and his eyes, like those of a tired minotaur, traversed her supple body with a gleam of interest.

'Hulking brute!' thought Michael, disentangling his own grasp, and drifting with her over shining space. Since yesterday's ordeal and its subsequent spring-running, he had kept his unacceptable misgivings to himself; he did not even know whether, at this rout, she was deliberately putting their position to the test, or merely, without forethought, indulging her liking to be in the swim. And what a swim! In that great pillared 'salon', Members of Parliament, poets, musicians, very dry in the smile, as who should say: 'I could have done it better,' or 'Imagine doing that!' peers, physicians, dancers, painters, Labour Leaders, cricketers, lawyers, critics, ladies of fashion, and ladies who 'couldn't bear it'—every mortal person that Michael knew or didn't know seemed present. He watched Fleur's eyes quartering them, busy as bees beneath the white lids he had kissed last night. He envied her that social curiosity; to live in London without it was like being at the sea without bathing. She was quietly—he could tell—making up her mind whom she wanted to speak to among those she knew, and whom, among those she didn't yet know, she wanted to speak to her. 'I hope to God she's not in for a snubbing,' he thought, and when she was engaged in talk, he slipped towards a pillar. A small voice behind him said: "Well, young Mont!" Mr. Blythe, looking like a Dover sole above Kew Bridge, was squeezed against the same pillar, his eyes goggling timorously above his beard.

"Stick to me!" he said. "These bees are too bee busy."

"Were you in Court yesterday?" asked Michael.

"No; one read about it. You did well."

"She did better."

"H'm!" said Mr. Blythe. "By the way, *The Evening Sun* was at us again this afternoon. They compared us to kittens playing with their tails. It's time for your second barrel, Mont."

"I thought—on the agricultural estimates."

"Good! Governmental purchase and control of wheat. Stress use of the present machinery. No more officials than are absolutely necessary."

"Blythe," said Michael suddenly, "where were you born?"

"Lincolnshire."

"You're English, then?"

"Pure," said Mr. Blythe.

"So am I; so's old Foggart—I looked him up in the stud-book. It's lucky, because we shall certainly be assailed for lack of patriotism."

"We *are*," said Mr. Blythe. " 'People who can see no good in their own country. . . . Birds who foul their own nest. . . . Gentry never happy unless running England down in the eyes of the world. . . . Calamity-mongers. . . . Pessimists. . . .' You don't mind that sort of gup, I hope?"

"Unfortunately," said Michael, "I do; it hurts me inside. It's so damned unjust. I simply can't bear the idea of England being in a fix."

Mr. Blythe's eyes rolled.

"She's bee well not going to be, if we can help it."

"If only I amounted to something," murmured Michael; "but I always feel as if I could creep into one of my back teeth."

"Have it crowned. What you want is brass, Mont. And talking of brass: there's your late adversary! *She's* got it all right. Look at her!"

Michael saw Marjorie Ferrar moving away from the great Italian, in not too much of a sea-green gown, with her red-gold head held high. She came to a stand a small room's length from Fleur, and swept her eyes this way and that. Evidently she had taken up that position in deliberate challenge.

"I must go to Fleur."

"So must I," said Mr. Blythe, and Michael gave him a grateful look.

And now it would have been so interesting to one less interested than Michael. The long, the tapering nose of Society could be seen to twitch, to move delicately upwards, and like the trunk of some wild elephant scenting man, writhe and snout this way and that, catching the whiff of sensation. Lips were smiling and moving closer to ears; eyes turning from that standing figure to the other; little reflective frowns appeared on foreheads, as if, beneath cropped and scented scalps, brains were trying to make choice. And Marjorie Ferrar stood smiling and composed; and Fleur talked and twisted the flower in her hand; and both went on looking their best. So began a battle without sign of war declared, without even seeming recognition of each other's presence. Mr. Blythe, indeed, stood pat between the two of them. Bulky and tall, he was an effective screen. But Michael, on the other side of her, could see and grimly follow. The Nose was taking time to apprehend the full of the aroma; the Brain to make its choice. Tide seemed at balance, not moving in or out. And then, with the slow implac-ability of tides, the water moved away from Fleur and lapped round her rival. Michael chattered, Mr. Blythe goggled, using the impersonal pronoun with a sort of passion; Fleur smiled, talked, twisted the flower. And, over there, Marjorie Ferrar seemed to hold a little court. Did people admire, commiserate, approve of, or sympathise with her? Or did they disapprove of himself and Fleur? Or was it just that the 'Pet of the Panjoys' was always the more sensational figure? Michael watched Fleur growing paler, her smile more nervous, the twitching of the flower spasmodic. And he dared not suggest going; for she would see in it an admission of defeat. But on the faces, turned their way, the expression became more and more informative. Sir James Foskisson had done his job too well; he had slavered his clients with his own self-righteousness. Better the confessed libertine than those who brought her to judgment! And Michael thought: 'Dashed natural, after all! Why didn't the fellow take my tip, and let us pay and look pleasant.'

And just then close to the great Italian he caught sight of a tall young man with his hair brushed back, who was looking at his fingers. By George! It was Bertie Curfew! And there behind him, waiting for his turn 'to meet', who but MacGown himself! The humour of the gods had run amok! Head in air, soothing his mangled fingers, Bertie Curfew passed them, and strayed into the group around his former flame. Her greeting of him was elaborately casual. But up went the tapering Nose, for here came MacGown! How the fellow had changed—grim, greyish, bitter! The great Italian had met his match for once. And he too, stepped into that throng.

A queer silence was followed by a burst of speech, and then by dissolution. In twos and threes they trickled off, and there were MacGown and his betrothed standing alone. Michael turned to Fleur.

"Let's go."

Silence reigned in their homing cab. He had chattered himself out on the field of battle, and must wait for fresh supplies of camouflage. But he slipped his hand along till it found hers, which did not return his pressure. The card he used to play at times of stress—the eleventh baronet—had failed for the last three months; Fleur seemed of late to resent his introduction as a remedy. He followed her into the dining-room, sore at heart, bewildered in mind. He had never seen her look so pretty as in that oyster-coloured frock, very straight and simply made, with a swing out above the ankles. She sat down at the narrow dining-table, and he seated himself opposite, with the costive feeling of one who cannot find words that will ring true. For social discomfiture he himself didn't care a tinker's curse; but she——!

And, suddenly, she said:

"And you don't mind?"

"For myself—not a bit."

"Yes, you've still got your Foggartism and your Bethnal Green."

"If *you* care, Fleur, I care a lot."

"*If* I care!"

"How—exactly?"

"I'd rather not increase your feeling that I'm a snob."

"I never had any such feeling."

"Michael!"

"Hadn't you better say what you mean by the word?"

"You know perfectly well."

"I know that you appreciate having people about you, and like them to think well of you. That isn't being a snob."

"Yes; you're very kind, but you don't admire it."

"I admire *you*."

"You mean, desire me. You admire Norah Curfew."

"Norah Curfew! For all I care, she might snuff out to-morrow."

And from her face he had the feeling that she believed him.

"If it isn't her, it's what she stands for—all that I'm not."

"I admire a lot in you," said Michael, fervently; "your intelligence, your flair; I admire you with Kit and your father; your pluck; and the way you put up with me."

"No, I admire you much more than you admire me. Only, you see, I'm not capable of devotion."

"What about Kit?"

"I'm devoted to myself—that's all."

He reached across the table and touched her hand.

"Morbid, darling."

"No. I see too clearly to be morbid."

She was leaning back, and her throat, very white and round, gleamed in the alabaster-shaded light; little choky movements were occuring there.

"Michael, I want you to take me round the world."

"And leave Kit?"

"He's too young to mind. Besides, my mother would look after him."

If she had got as far as that, this was a deliberate desire!

"But your father——"

"He's not really old yet, and he'd have Kit."

"When we rise in August, perhaps——"

"No, now."

"It's only five months to wait. We'd have time in the vacation to do a lot of travelling."

Fleur looked straight at him.

"I knew you cared more for Foggartism now than for me."

"Be reasonable, Fleur."

"For five months—with the feeling I've got here!" she put her hand to her breast. "I've had six months of it already. You don't realise, I suppose, that I'm down and out?"

"But, Fleur, it's all so——"

"Yes, it's always petty to mind being a dead failure, isn't it?"

"But, my child——"

"Oh! If you can't feel it——!"

"I can—I felt wild this evening. But all you've got to do is to let them see that you don't care; and they'll come buzzing round again like flies. It would be running away, Fleur."

"No," said Fleur, coldly, "it's not that—I don't try twice for the same prize. Very well, I'll stay and be laughed at."

Michael got up.

"I know you don't think there's anything to my job. But there is, Fleur, and I've put my hand to it. Oh! don't look like that. Dash it! This is dreadful!"

"I suppose I could go by myself. That would be more thrilling."

"Absurd! Of course you couldn't! You're seeing blue to-night, old thing. It'll all seem different to-morrow."

"To morrow and to-morrow! No, Michael, mortification has set in, my funeral can take place any day you like!"

Michael's hands went up. She meant what she was saying! To realise, he must remember how much store she had set on her powers as hostess; how she had worked for her collection and shone among it! Her house of cards all pulled about her ears! Cruel! But would going round the world help her? Yes! Her instinct was quite right. He had been round the world himself, nothing else would change her values in quite that way; nothing else would so guarantee oblivion in others and herself! Lippinghall, her father's, the sea for the five months till vacation came—they wouldn't meet her case! She needed what would give her back her importance. And yet, how could he go until vacation? Foggartism—that lean and lonely plant—unwatered and without its only gardener, would wither to its roots, if, indeed, it had any. There was some movement in it now, interest here and there—this Member and that were

445

pecking at it. Private efforts in the same direction were gathering
way. And time was going on—Big Ben had called no truce; unemployment swelling, trade dawdling, industrial trouble brewing—
brewing, hope losing patience! And what would old Blythe say to
his desertion now?

"Give me a week," he muttered. "It's not easy. I must think
it over."

## Chapter X

### THE NEW LEAF

WHEN MacGown came up to her, Marjorie Ferrar thought: 'Does
he know about Bertie?' Fresh from her triumph over 'that little
snob', fluttered by the sudden appearance of her past, and confronted with her present, she was not in complete possession of
her head. When they had moved away into an empty side room,
she faced him.

"Well, Alec, nothing's changed. I still have a past as lurid as
yesterday. I'm extremely sorry I ever kept it from you. But I did
practically tell you, several times; only you wouldn't take it."

"Because it was hell to me. Tell me everything, Marjorie!"

"You want to revel in it?"

"Tell me everything, and I'll marry you still."

She shook her head. "Marry! Oh! no! I don't go out of my
depth any more. It was absurd anyway. I never loved you, Alec."

"Then you loved that—you still——"

"My dear Alec, enough!"

He put his hands to his head, and swayed. And she was touched
by genuine compassion.

"I'm awfully sorry, I really am. You've got to cut me out;
that's all."

She had turned to leave him, but the misery in his face stopped
her. She had not quite realised. He was burnt up! He was——!
And she said quickly:

"Marry you I won't; but I'd like to pay up, if I could——"

He looked at her.

Quivering all over from that look, she shrugged her shoulders,
and walked away. Men of an old fashion! Her own fault for stepping outside the charmed circle that took nothing too seriously.
She walked over the shining floor, conscious of many eyes, slipped
past her hostess, and soon was in a cab.

446

# THE SILVER SPOON

She lay awake, thinking. Even without announcement the return of presents would set London by the ears and bring on her again an avalanche of bills. Five thousand pounds! She got up and rummaged out the list, duplicate of that which Alec had. He might still want to pay them! After all, it was he who had spilled the ink by making her go into Court! But then his eyes came haunting her. Out of the question! And, shivering a little, she got back into bed. Perhaps she would have a brain-wave in the morning. She had so many in the night, that she could not sleep. Moscow with Bertie Curfew? The stage? America and the 'movies'? All three? She slept at last, and woke languid and pale. With her letters was one from Shropshire House.

"DEAR MARJORIE,
   "If you've nothing better to do, I should like to see you this morning.

"Affectionately,
   "SHROPSHIRE."

What now? She looked at herself in the glass, and decided that she *must* make-up a little. At eleven o'clock she was at Shropshire House. The marquess was in his work-room at the top, among a small forest of contraptions. With coat off, he was peering through a magnifying-glass at what looked like nothing.

"Sit down, Marjorie," he said: "I'll have done in a minute."

Except the floor, there seemed nowhere to sit, so she remained standing.

"I thought so," said the marquess; "the Italians are wrong."

He put the spy-glass down, ran his hand through his silvery hair, and drew his ruffled beard into a peak. Then, taking an eyebrow between finger and thumb, he gave it an upward twist, and scratched himself behind one ear.

"They're wrong; there's no reaction whatever."

Turning towards his granddaughter, he screwed up his eyes till they were bright as pins. "You've never been up here before. Sit in the window."

She seated herself on a broad window-ledge covering some sort of battery, with her back to the light.

"So you brought that case, Marjorie?"

"I had to."

"Now why?" He was standing with his head a little to one side, his cheeks very pink, and his eyes very shrewd. And she thought: 'After all, I'm his granddaughter. I'll plunge.'

"Common honesty, if you want to know."

The marquess pouted, as if trying to understand the words.

"I read your evidence," he said, "if you mean that."

"No. I meant that I wanted to find out where I stood."

"And did you?"

"Very much so."

"Are you still going to be married?"

Really, he was a spry old boy!

"No."

"Whose doing? Yours or his?"

"He still says he'll marry me if I tell him everything. But I don't choose to."

The marquess moved two steps, placed his foot on a box, and assumed his favourite attitude. He had a red silk tie this morning which floated loose; his tweed trousers were of a blue-green, his shirt of a green-blue. He looked wonderfully bright.

"Is there much to tell?"

"A good deal."

"Well, Marjorie, you know what I said to you."

"Yes, Grandfather, but I don't quite see it. *I* don't want to stand for anything."

"Ah! you're an exception in our class—luckily! But it's the exceptions that do the harm."

"If people took one as any better than themselves, perhaps. But they don't nowadays."

"Not quite honest, that," interrupted the marquess; "what about the feeling in your bones?"

She smiled.

"It's good to mortify oneself, Grandfather."

"By having a better time than you ought, um? So your marriage is off?"

"Very much so."

"Are you in debt?"

"Yes."

"How much do you owe?"

Marjorie Ferrar hesitated. Should she compromise, or blurt it out?

"No heel-taps, Marjorie."

"Well, then, five thousand about."

The old peer screwed up his lips, and a melancholy little whistle escaped.

"A good deal of it, of course, is due to my engagement."

"Your father won a race the other day, I see."

The old boy knew everything!

"Yes; but I believe it's all gone."

"It would be," said the marquess. "What are you going to do now?"

She had a strong desire to answer: "What are *you?*" but restrained it, and said:

"I thought of going on the stage."

"Well, I suppose that might be suitable. Can you act?"

"I'm not a Duse."

"Duse?" The marquess shook his head. "One must go back to Ristori for really great acting. Duse! Very talented, of course, but always the same. So you don't choose to marry him now?" He looked at her intently. "That, I think, is right. Have you a list of your debts?"

Marjorie Ferrar rummaged in her vanity bag. "Here it is."

She could see his nose wrinkling above it, but whether at its scent, or its contents, she could not tell.

"Your grandmother," he said, "spent about a fifth of what you seem to on about five times the acreage of clothes. You wear nothing nowadays, and yet it costs all this."

"The less there is, Grandfather, the better it has to be cut, you know."

"Have you sent your presents back?"

"I've had them packed."

"They must all go," said the marquess. "Keep nothing he or anyone else gave you."

"Of course not."

"To frank you," he said, suddenly, "I should have to sell the Gainsborough."

"Oh, no!"

Gainsborough's picture of his own grandmother as a little girl— that beautiful thing! She stretched out her hand for the list. Still holding it, he put his foot to the ground, and stood peering at her with his bright, intent old eyes.

"The question is, Marjorie, how far it's possible to strike a bargain with you. Have you a 'word' to keep?"

She felt the blood mounting in her cheeks.

"I think so. It depends on what I've got to promise. But Grandfather, I don't *want* you to sell the Gainsborough."

"Unfortunately," said the marquess, "without doing your uncle Dangerfield in the eye, I've nothing else. It's been my fault, I suppose, for having had expensive children. Other people don't seem to have had them to the same degree."

She stifled a smile.

"Times are hard," went on the marquess. "Land costs money, collieries cost money, Shropshire House costs money; and where's the money? I've got an invention here that ought to make my fortune, but nobody will look at it."

The poor old boy—at his age! She said with a sigh:

"I really didn't mean to bother you with this, Grandfather. I'll manage somehow."

The old peer took several somewhat hampered steps, and she noticed that his red slippers were heel-less. He halted, a wonderfully bright spot among the contraptions.

"To come back to what we were saying, Marjorie. If your idea of life is simply to have a good time, how can you promise anything?"

"What do you want me to promise?"

He came and stood before her again, short and a little bent.

"You look as if you had stuff in you, too, with your hair. Do you really think you could earn your living?"

"I believe I can; I know a lot of people."

"If I clear you, will you give me your word to pay ready money in future? Now don't say 'Yes', and go out and order yourself a lot of fallals. I want the word of a lady, if you understand what that implies."

She stood up.

"I suppose you've every right to say that. But I don't want you to clear me if you have to sell the Gainsborough."

"You must leave that to me. I might manage, perhaps, to scrape it up without. About that promise?"

"Yes; I promise that."

"Meaning to keep it?"

"Meaning to keep it."

"Well, that's something."

"Anything else, Grandfather?"

"I should have liked to ask you not to cheapen our name any more, but I suppose that would be putting the clock back. The spirit of the age is against me."

Turning from his face, she stood looking out of the window. The spirit of the age! It was all very well, but he didn't understand what it was. Cheapen? Why! she had *raised* the price of the family name; hoicked it out of a dusty cupboard, and made of it a current

450

coin. People sat up when they read of her. Did they sit up when they read of grandfather? But he would never see that! And she murmured:

"All right, dear, I'll be careful. I think I shall go to America."

His eyes twinkled.

"And start a fashion of marrying American husbands? It's not yet been done, I believe. Get one who's interested in electricity, and bring him over. There are great things for an American to do here. Well, I'll keep this list and work it off somehow. Just one thing, Marjorie: I'm eighty, and you're—what are you—twenty-five? Don't get through life so fast—you'll be dreadfully bored by the time you're fifty, and there's no greater bore than a bored person. Good-bye!" He held out his hand.

She took a long breath. Free!

And seizing his hand, she put it to her lips. Oh! He was gazing at it—oh! Had her lips come off? And she hurried out. The old boy! He was a darling to have kept that list! A new leaf! She would go at once to Bertie Curfew and get him to turn it over for her! The expression in his eye last night!

## Chapter XI

## OVER THE WINDMILL

DURING his period of indecision Michael struck no attitudes, and used practically no words; the thing was too serious. Perhaps Kit would change Fleur's mood, or she would see other disadvantages, such as her father. The complete cessation, however, of any social behaviour on her part—no invitation issued, or received, no function attended, or even discussed, during that rather terrible week, proved that the iron had really seared her spirit. She was not sulky, but she was mum and listless. And she was always watching him, with a wistful expression on her face, and now and then a resentful look, as if she had made up her mind that he was going to refuse. He could consult no one, too, for to any who had not lived through this long episode, Fleur's attitude would seem incomprehensible, even ridiculous. He could not give her away; could not even go to old Blythe, until he had decided. Complicating his mental conflict was the habitual doubt whether he was really essential to Foggartism. If only his head would swell! He had not even the comfort of feeling that a sturdy negative would impress Fleur; she thought his job a stunt, useful to make him conspicuous, but of no real importance to the country. She had the political cynicism of the woman in the street; only that which threatened property or Kit would really ruffle her. He knew that his dilemma was comic. The future of England against the present of a young woman socially snubbed! But, after all, only Sir James Foggart and old Blythe so far seriously connected Foggartism with the future of England; and if, now, he went off round the world, even they would lose their faith.

On the last morning of that week, Michael, still in doubt, crossed Westminster Bridge and sought the heart of the Surrey side. It was unfamiliar, and he walked with interest. Here, he remembered, the Bickets had lived; the Bickets who had failed, and apparently were failing in Australia, too. Street after mean street! Breeding-ground of Bickets! Catch them early, catch them often, catch them before they were Bickets, spoiled for the land; make them men and women of property, give them air and give them sun—the most decent folk in the world, give them a chance! Ugly houses, ugly shops, ugly pubs! No, that wouldn't do! Keep Beauty cut of it; Beauty never went down in 'the House'! No sentiment went down! At least, only such as was understood—'British stock', 'Patriotism', 'Empire', 'Moral Fibre'. Thews and productive power—stick to the clichés! He stood listening outside a school to the dull hum of education. The English breed with its pluck and its sense of humour and its patience, all mewed-up in mean streets!

He had a sudden longing for the country. His motor-cycle! Since taking his seat in Parliament he had not been on a machine so inclined to bump his dignity. But he would have it out now, and go for a run—it might shake him into a decision!

Fleur was not in, and no lunch ordered. So he ate some ham, and by two o'clock had started.

With spit and bluster he ran out along the road past Chiswick, Slough and Maidenhead; crossed the river and sputtered towards Reading. At Caversham he crossed again, and ran on to Pang-bourne. By the towing path he tipped his machine into some bushes and sat down to smoke a pipe. Quite windless! The river between the bare poplars had a grey, untroubled look; the catkins were forming on the willows. He plucked a twig, and stirred it round the bowl of his pipe before pressing in tobacco. The shaking had done him good; his mind was working freely. The war! One had no hesitations then; but then—one had no Fleur. Besides, that was a clear, a simple issue. But now, beyond this 'to stay or not to stay', Michael seemed seeing the future of his married life.

The decision that he made would affect what might last another fifty years. To put your hand to the plough, and at the first request to take it off again! You might be ploughing crooked, and by twilight; but better plough by dim light than no light; a crooked furrow than none at all! Foggartism was the best course he could see, and he must stick to it! The future of England! A blackbird, close by, chuckled. Quite so! But, as old Blythe said, one must stand up to laughter! Oh! Surely Fleur would see in the long run that he couldn't play fast and loose; see that if she wanted him to remain in Parliament—and she did—he must hang on to the line he had taken, however it amused the blackbirds. She wouldn't like him to sink to the nonentity of a turntail. For after all she was his wife, and with his self-respect her own was bound up.

He watched the smoke from his pipe, and the low grey clouds, the white-faced Herefords grazing beyond the river, and a man fishing with a worm. He took up the twig and twirled it, admiring the yellowish-grey velvet of its budding catkins. He felt quiet in the heart, at last, but very sorry. How make up to Fleur? Beside this river not two miles away, he had wooed—queer word—if not won her! And now they had come to this snag. Well, it was up to her now, whether or no they should come to grief on it. And it seemed to him, suddenly, that he would like to tell Old Forsyte. . . .

When he heard the splutter of Michael's motor-cycle, Soames was engaged in hanging the Fred Walker he had bought at the emporium next to Messrs. Settlewhite and Stark, memorialising his freedom from the worry of that case, and soothing his itch for the British School. Fred Walker! The fellow was old-fashioned; he and Mason had been succeeded by a dozen movements. But—like old fiddles, with the same agreeable glow—there they were, very good curiosities such as would always command a price.

Having detached a Courbet, early and about ripe, he was standing in his shirt-sleeves, with a coil of wire in his hand, when Michael entered.

"Where have you sprung from?" he said, surprised.

"I happened to be passing, sir, on my old bike. I see you've kept your word about the English School."

Soames attached the wire.

"I shan't be happy," he said, "till I've got an old Crome—best of the English landscapists."

"Awfully rare, isn't he, old Crome?"

"Yes, that's why I want him."

The smile on Michael's face, as if he were thinking: 'You mean that's why you consider him the best,' was lost on Soames giving the wire a final twist.

"I haven't seen your pictures for a long time, sir. Can I look round?"

Observing him sidelong, Soames remembered his appearance there one summer Sunday, after he had first seen Fleur in that Gallery off Cork Street. Only four years? It seemed an age! The young fellow had worn better than one had hoped; looked a good deal older, too, less flighty; an amiable chap, considering his up-bringing, and that war! And suddenly he perceived that Michael was engaged in observing him. Wanted something, no doubt—wouldn't have come down for nothing! He tried to remember when anybody had come to see him without wanting something; but could not. It was natural!

"Are you looking for a picture to go with that Fragonard?" he said. "There's a Chardin in the corner."

"No, no, sir; you've been much too generous to us already."

Generous! How could one be generous to one's only daughter?

"How is Fleur?"

"I wanted to tell you about her. She's feeling awfully restless."

Soames looked out of the window. The spring was late!

"She oughtn't to be, with that case out of the way."

"That's just it, sir."

Soames gimleted the young man's face. "I don't follow you."

"We're being cold-shouldered."

"How? You won."

"Yes, but you see, people resent moral superiority."

"What's that? Who——?" Moral superiority—he resented it himself!

"Foskisson, you know; we're tarred with his brush. I told you I was afraid of it. It's the being laughed at Fleur feels so bitterly."

"Laughed at? Who has the impudence——?"

"To attack modern morality was a good stunt, sir, with the judge and the jury, and anyone professionally pompous; but it makes one ridiculous nowadays in Society, you know, when everybody prides himself on lack of prejudice."

"Society!"

"Yes, sir; but it's what we live in. I don't mind, got used to it over Foggartism; but Fleur's miserable. It's natural, if you think of it—Society's her game."

"She ought to have more strength of mind," said Soames. But

he was gravely perturbed. First she'd been looked on as a snob, and now there was this!

"What with that German actor hanging himself at Lipping-hall," Michael went on, "and my Foggartism, and this Ferrar rumpus, our pitch is badly queered. We've had a wretched week of it since the case. Fleur feels so out of her plate, that she wants me to take her round the world."

A bomb bursting on the dove-cote down there could not have been more startling. Round the world! He heard Michael murmuring on:

"She's quite right, too. It might be the very best thing for her; but I simply can't leave my job until the long vacation. I've taken up this thing, and I must stick to it while Parliament's sitting."

Sitting! As if it were a hen, addling its precious eggs! Round the world!

But Michael ran on:

"It's only to-day I've quite decided. I should feel like a deserter, and that wouldn't be good for either of us in the long run. But she doesn't know yet."

For Soames the dove-cote was solidifying again, now that he knew Michael was not going to take her away for goodness knew how long!

"Round the world!" he said. "Why not—er—Pontresina?"

"I think," answered Micahel slowly, like a doctor diagnosing, "that she wants something dramatic. Round the world at twenty-three! She feels somehow that she's lost caste."

"How can she think of leaving that little chap?"

"Yes, that shows it's pretty desperate with her. I wish to good-ness I could go."

Soames stared. The young fellow wasn't expecting him to do anything about it, was he? Round the world? A crazy notion!

"I must see her," he said. "Can you leave that thing of yours in the garage and come up with me in the car? I'll be ready in twenty minutes. You'll find tea going downstairs."

Left alone with the Fred Walker still unhung, Soames gazed at his pictures. He saw them with an added clarity, a more pene-trating glance, a sort of ache in his heart, as if—— Well! A good lot they were, better than he had thought, of late! *She* had gone in for collecting people! And now she'd lost her collection! Poor little thing! All nonsense, of course—as if there were any satisfac-tion in people! Suppose he took her up that Chardin? It was a good Chardin. Dumetrius had done him over the price, but not too much. And, before Chardin was finished with, he would do Dumetrius. Still—if it would give her any pleasure! He unhooked the picture and, carrying it under his arm, went downstairs.

Beyond certain allusions to the characteristics of the eleventh baronet, and the regrettable tendencies of the police to compel slow travelling over the new cut constructed to speed up traffic, little was said in the car. They arrived in South Square about six o'clock. Fleur had not been in since lunch; and they sat down uneasily to wait for her. The Dandie, having descended to look for strange legs, had almost immediately ascended again, and the house was very quiet. Michael was continually looking at his watch.

"Where do you think she's got to?" said Soames at last.

"Haven't an idea, sir; that's the worst of London, it swallows people up."

He had begun to fidget; Soames, who also wanted to fidget, was thinking of saying 'Don't!' when from the window Michael cried:

"Here she is!" and went quickly to the door.

Soames sat on, with the Chardin resting against his chair.

They were a long time out there! Minute after minute passed, and still they did not come.

At last Michael reappeared. He looked exceedingly grave.

"She's in her little room upstairs, sir. I'm afraid it's upset her awfully. Perhaps you wouldn't mind going up."

Soames grasped the Chardin.

"Let's see, that's the first door on the left, isn't it?" He mounted slowly, his mind blank, and without waiting for her to answer his mild knock, went in.

Fleur was sitting at the satinwood bureau, with her face buried on her arms. Her hair, again in its more natural 'bob', gleamed lustrously under the light. She seemed unconscious of his entry. This sight of private life affected Soames, unaccustomed to give or receive undefended glimpses of self, and he stood, uncertain. Had he the right to surprise her, with her ears muffled like that, and her feelings all upset? He would have gone out and come in again, but he was too concerned. And, moving to her side, he put his finger on her shoulder and said:

"Tired, my child?"

Her face came round—queer, creased, not like her face; and Soames spoke the phrase of her childhood:

"See what I've brought you!"

He raised the Chardin; she gave it just a glance and he felt hurt. After all, it was worth some hundreds of pounds! Very pale, she had crossed her arms on her chest as if shutting herself up. He recognised the symptom. A spiritual crisis! The sort of thing his whole life had been passed in regarding as extravagant; like a case of appendicitis that will not wait decently.

"Michael," he said, "tells me you want him to take you round the world."

"Well, he can't; so that ends it."

If she had said: 'Yes, and why can't he?' Soames would have joined the opposition automatically. But her words roused his natural perversity. Here she was, and here was her heart's desire—and she wasn't getting it! He put the Chardin down and took a walk over the soft carpet.

"Tell me," he said, coming to a halt, "where do you feel it exactly?"

Fleur laughed: "In my head, and my eyes, and my ears, and my heart."

"What business," muttered Soames, "have they to look down their confounded noses!" And he set off again across the room. All the modern jackanapes whom from time to time he had been unable to avoid in her house, seemed to have come sniggering round him with lifted eyebrows, like a set of ghosts. The longing to put them in their places—a shallow lot—possessed him at that moment to the exclusion of a greater sanity.

"I—I don't see how *I* can take you," he said, and stopped short.

What was that he was saying? Who had asked him to take her? Her eyes, widely open, were fixed on him.

"But of course not, Dad!"

Of course not! He didn't know about that!

"I shall get used to being laughed at, in time."

Soames growled.

"I don't see why you should," he said. "I suppose people do go round the world."

Fleur's pallor had gone, now.

"But not you, dear; why, it would bore you stiff! It's very sweet of you, even to think of it; but of course I couldn't let you—at your age!"

"At my age?" said Soames. "I'm not so very old."

"No, no, Dad; I'll just dree my weird."

Soames took another walk, without a sound. Dree her weird, indeed!

"I won't have it," he ejaculated; "if people can't behave to you, I—I'll show them!"

457

She had got up, and was breathing deeply, with her lips parted and her cheeks very flushed. So she had stood, before her first party, holding out her frock for him to see.

"We'll go," he said gruffly. "Don't make a fuss! That's settled."

Her arms were round his neck; his nose felt wet. What nonsense! as if——! . . .

He stood unbuttoning his braces that night in the most peculiar state of mind. Going round the world—was he? Preposterous! It had knocked that young fellow over, anyway—he was to join them in August wherever they were by that time! Good Lord! It might be China! The thing was fantastic; and Fleur behaving like a kitten! The words of a comic ditty, sung by a clergyman, in his boyhood, kept up a tattoo within him:

> "I see Jerusalem and Madagascar,
> And North and South Amerikee. . . ."

Yes! Indeed! His affairs were in apple-pie order, luckily! There was nothing to do, in Timothy's or Winifred's Trusts—the only two he had on his hands now; but how things would get on without him, he couldn't tell. As to Annette! She wouldn't be sorry, he supposed. There was no one else to care, except Winifred, a little. It was, rather, the intangible presence of England that troubled him, about to forsake her for months on end! Still, the cliffs of Dover would be standing, he supposed, and the river still running past his lawn, when he came back, if he ever came back! You picked up all sorts of things out there—microbes, insects, snakes—never knew what you'd run into! Pretty business, steering Fleur clear of all that. And the sightseeing he would have to do! For *she* wouldn't miss anything! Trust her! Going round among a lot of people with their mouths open—he couldn't stand that; but he would have to! H'm! A relief when that young fellow could join them. And yet—to have her to himself; he hadn't, for a long time now. But she would pick up with everybody, of course. He would have to make himself agreeable to Tom, Dick, and Harry. A look at Egypt, then to India, and across to China and Japan, and back through that great sprawling America— God's own country, didn't they call it! She had it all mapped out. Thank goodness, no question of Russia! She hadn't even proposed that—it was all to pieces now, they said! Communism! Who knew what would happen at home before they got back? It seemed to Soames as if England, too, must all go to pieces, if he

458

left it. Well, he'd said he would take her! And she had cried over it. Phew! He threw the window up, and in the Jaeger dressing-gown, kept there for stray occasions, leaned into the mild air. No Westminster Square did he seem to see out there, but his own river and its poplars, with the full moon behind them, a bright witness—the quiet beauty he had never put into words, the green tranquillity he had felt for thirty years, and only permitted to seep into the back of his being. He would miss it—the scents, the sighs of the river under the wind, the chuckle down at the weir, the stars. They had stars out there, of course, but not English stars. And the grass —those great places had no grass, he believed! The blossom, too, was late this year—no blossom before they left! Well, the milk was spilled! And that reminded him: The dairyman would be certain to let the cows go out of milk—he was a 'natural', that chap! He would have to warn Annette. Women never seemed to understand that a cow didn't go on giving milk for ever, without being attended to. If he only had a man to rely on in the country, like old Gradman in Town! H'm! Old Gradman's eyes would drop out when he heard this news! Bit of old England there; and wouldn't be left long, now! It would be queer to come back and find old Gradman gone. One—Two—Three—Eleven! That clock! It had kept him awake before now; still—it was a fine old clock! That young fellow was to go on sitting under it. And was there anything in the notions that kept him sitting there, or were they just talk? Well, he was right to stick to his guns, anyway. But five months away from his young wife—great risk in that! 'Youth's a stuff'—Old Shakespeare knew the world. Well! Risk or no risk, there it was! After all, Fleur had a good head; and young Michael had a good heart. Fleur had a good heart, too; he wouldn't have it said that she hadn't! She would feel leaving the baby when it came to the point. She didn't realise, yet. And Soames felt within him the stir of a curious conflict, between hope that, after all, she might give it up, and apprehension lest she should. Funny—that! His habits, his comfort, his posses-sions . . . and here he was, flinging them all over the windmill! Absurd! And yet——!

## Chapter XII

### ENVOI

AWAY from Fleur five months at least!

Soames's astounding conduct had indeed knocked Michael over. And yet, after all, they had come to a crisis in their life together, the more serious because concerned with workaday feelings. Perhaps out there she would become afflicted, like himself, with an enlarged prospect; lose her idea that the world consisted of some five thousand people of advanced tastes, of whom she knew at the outside five hundred. It was she who had pushed him into Parliament, and until he was hoofed therefrom as a failure, their path was surely conjoined along the crest of a large view. In the fortnight before her departure he suffered and kept smiling; wryly thankful that she was behaving 'like a kitten', as her father called it. Her nerves had been on edge ever since the autumn over that wretched case—what more natural than this reaction? At least she felt for him sufficiently to be prodigal of kisses—great consolation to Michael while it lasted. Once or twice he caught her hanging with wet eyes over the eleventh baronet; once found her with a wet face when he awoke in the morning. These indications were a priceless assurance to him that she meant to come back. For there were moments when possibilities balled into a nightmare. Absurd! She was going with her father, that embodiment of care and prudence! Who would have thought old Forsyte could uproot himself like this? He, too, was leaving a wife, though Michael saw no signs of it. One didn't know much about old Forsyte's feelings, except that they centred round his daughter, and that he was continually asking questions about labels and insects. He had bought himself, too, a life-saving waistcoat and one for Fleur. Michael held with him only one important conversation.

"I want you," Soames said, "to keep an eye on my wife, and see she doesn't go getting into a mess with the cows. She'll have her mother with her, but women are so funny. You'll find her first-rate with the baby. How will you be off for money?"

"Perfectly all right, sir."

"Well, if you want some for any good purpose, go to old Gradman in the City; you remember him, perhaps?"

"Yes, and I'm afraid he'll remember me."

"Never mind; he's a faithful old fellow." And Michael heard him

460

sigh. "I'd like you to look in at Green Street, too, now and then. Your aunt-in-law may feel my being away a little. I'll let you have news of Fleur from time to time—now they've got this wireless she'll want to know about the baby. I'm taking plenty of quinine. Fleur says she's a good sailor. There's nothing like champagne for that, I'm told. And, by the way, you know best, but I shouldn't press your notions too far in Parliament; they're easily bored there, I believe. We'll meet you at Vancouver, at the end of August. She'll be tired of travelling by then. She's looking forward to Egypt and Japan, but I don't know. Seems to me it'll be all travelling."

"Have you plenty of ducks, sir? You'll want them at this time of year in the Red Sea; and I should take a helmet."

"I've got one," said Soames; "they're heavy great things," and, looking suddenly at Michael, he added:

"I shall look after her, and you'll look after yourself, I hope."

Michael understood him.

"Yes, sir. And thank you very much. I think it's most frightfully sporting of you."

"It's to be hoped it'll do her good; and that the little chap won't miss her."

"Not if I can help it."

Soames, who was seated in front of 'The White Monkey', seemed to go into a trance. At last he stirred in his chair and said:

"The war's left everything very unsettled. I suppose people believe in something nowadays, but *I* don't know what it is."

Michael felt a fearful interest.

"Do you mind telling me, sir, what you believe in yourself?"

"What was good enough for my fathers is good enough for me. They expect too much now; there's no interest taken in being alive."

"Interest taken in being alive!" The words were singularly comprehensive. Were they the answer to all modern doubt?

The last night, the last kiss came; and the glum journey to the Docks in Soames's car. Michael alone went to see them off! The gloomy dockside, and the grey river; the bustle with baggage, and the crowded tender. An aching business! Even for her, he almost believed—an aching business. And the long desultory minutes on the ship; the initiation of Soames into its cramped, shining, strangely odoured mysteries. The ghastly smile one had to keep on the lips, the inane jokes one had to make. And then that moment, apart, when she pressed her breast to his and gave him a clinging kiss.

461

"Good-bye, Michael; it's not for very long."

"Good-bye, darling! Take care of yourself. You shall have all the news I can send you, and don't worry about Kit."

His teeth were clinched, and her eyes—he saw—were wet! And, then, once more:

"Good-bye!"

"Good-bye!"

Back on the tender, with the strip of grey water opening, spreading, between him and the ship's side, and that high line of faces above the bulwark—Fleur's face under the small fawn hat, her waving hand; and, away to the left, seen out of the tail of his eyes, old Forsyte's face alone—withdrawn so that they might have their parting to themselves—long, chinny, grey-moustached, very motionless; absorbed and lonely, as might be that of some long-distance bird arrived on an unknown shore, and looking back towards the land of its departure. Smaller and smaller they grew, merged in blur, vanished.

For the whole journey back to Westminster, Michael smoked cigarette on cigarette, and read the same sentence over and over in the same journal, and the sentence was:

'Robbery at Highgate, Cat Burglar gets clear away.'

He went straight into the House of Commons. And all the afternoon sat listening and taking in a few words now and then, of a debate on education. What chance—what earthly chance—had his skyscraping in this place, where they still talked with calm disagreement, as if England were the England of 1906, and the verdict on him was: 'Amiable but very foolish young man!' National unity—national movement! No jolly fear! The country wouldn't have it! One was battering at a door which everybody said must be opened, but through which nobody could pass. And a long strip of grey water kept spreading between him and the talkers; the face under the fawn hat confused itself with that of the Member for Wasbaston; the face of Old Forsyte above the bulwark rail appeared suddenly between two Labour Leaders; and the lines of faces faded to a blur on a grey river where gulls were flighting.

Going out, he passed a face that had more reality—MacGown's! Grim! It wasn't the word. No one had got any change out of that affair. *Multum ex parvo! Parvum ex multo!* That was the modern comedy!

Going home to have a look at Kit and send Fleur a wireless, he passed four musicians playing four instruments with a sort of fury. They had able bodies in shabby clothes. 'By Jove!' thought

Michael, 'I know that chap's face!—surely he was in my company in France!' He watched till the cheeks collapsed. Yes! A good man, too! But they had all been good men. By George, they had been wonders! And here they were! And he within an ace of abandoning them! Though everybody had his nostrum, and one perhaps was as good as another, still one could only follow what light one had! And if the Future was unreadable, and Fate grinned, well—let it grin!

How empty the house felt! To-morrow Kit and the dog were to go down to 'The Shelter' in the car, and it would be still emptier. From room after room he tried to retrieve some sight or scent of Fleur. Too painful! His dressing-room, his study were the only places possible—in them he would abide.

He went to the nursery and opened the door softly. Whiteness and dimity; the dog on his fat silver side, the Magicoal fire burning; the prints on the white walls so carefully selected for the moment when the eleventh baronet should begin to take notice— prints slightly comic, to avoid a moral; the high and shining fender-guard that even Magicoal might not be taken too seriously; the light coming in between bright chintz. A charming room! The nurse, in blue, was standing with her back to the door, and did not see him. And, in his little high chair, the eleventh baronet was at table; on his face, beneath its dark chestnut curls, was a slight frown; and in his tiny hand he held a silver spoon, with which over the bowl before him he was making spasmodic passes.

Michael heard the nurse saying:

"Now that mother's gone, you must be a little man, Kit, and learn to use your spoon."

Michael saw his offspring dip at the bowl and throw some of its contents into the air.

"That's not the way at all."

The eleventh baronet repeated the performance, and looked for applause, with a determined smile.

"Naughty!"

"A—a!" said the eleventh baronet, plopping the spoon. The contents spurted wastefully.

"Oh! you spoiled boy!"

' "England, my England!" ' thought Michael, 'as the poet said.'

# INTERLUDE

## PASSERS BY

# Chapter I

IN Washington, District of Columbia, the 'Fall' sun shone, and all that was not evergreen or stone in Rock Creek Cemetery was glowing. Before the Saint Gaudens statue Soames Forsyte sat on his overcoat, with the marble screen to his back, enjoying the seclusion and a streak of sunlight passaging between the cypresses.

With his daughter and her husband he had been up here already, the afternoon before, and had taken a fancy to the place. Apart from the general attraction of a cemetery, this statue awakened the connoisseur within him. Though not a thing you could acquire, it was undoubtedly a work of art, and produced a very marked effect. He did not remember a statue that made him feel so thoroughly at home. That great greenish bronze figure of seated woman within the hooding folds of her ample cloak seemed to carry him down to the bottom of his own soul. Yesterday, in the presence of Fleur, Michael, and other people, all gaping like himself, he had not so much noted the mood of the thing as its technical excellence, but now, alone, he could enjoy the luxury of his own sensations. Some called it 'Nirvana', some 'The Adams Memorial'. He didn't know, but in any case there it was, the best thing he had come across in America, the one that gave him the most pleasure, in spite of all the water he had seen at Niagara and those skyscrapers in New York. Three times he had changed his position on that crescent marble seat, varying his sensations every time. From his present position the woman had passed beyond grief. She sat in a frozen acceptance deeper than death itself, very remarkable! There was something about death! He remembered his own father, James, a quarter of an hour after death, as if—as if he had been told at last!

A red oak leaf fell on to his lapel, another on to his knee; Soames did not brush them off. Easy to sit still in front of that thing! They ought to make America sit there once a week!

He rose, crossed towards the statue, and gingerly touched a fold in the green bronze, as if questioning the possibility of everlasting nothingness.

"Got a sister living in Dallas—married a railroad man down there as a young girl. Why! Texas is a wonderful State. I know my sister laughs at the idea that the climate of Texas isn't about right."

Soames withdrew his hand from the bronze and returned to his seat. Two tall, thin, elderly figures were entering the sanctuary. They moved into the middle and stood silent. Presently one said "Well!" and they moved out again at the other end. A little stir of wind fluttered some fallen leaves at the base of the statue. Soames shifted along to the extreme end. From there the statue was once more woman—very noble! And he sat motionless in his attitude of a thinker, the lower part of his face buried in his hand.

Considerably browned and distinctly healthy-looking, he was accustomed to regard himself as worn out by his long travel, which, after encircling the world, would end, the day after to-morrow, by embarkation on the *Adelphic*. This three-day run to Washington was the last straw, and he was supporting it very well. The city was pleasing; it had some fine buildings and a great many trees with the tints on, there wasn't the rush of New York, and plenty of houses that people could live in, he should think. Of course the place was full of Americans, but that was unavoidable. He was happy about Fleur too; she had quite got over that unpleasant Ferrar business, seemed on excellent terms with young Michael, and was looking forward to her home and her baby again. There was, indeed, in Soames a sense of culmination and of peace—a feeling of virtue having been its own reward, and, beyond all, the thought that he would soon be smelling English grass and seeing again the river flowing past his cows. Annette, even, might be glad to see him—he had bought her a really nice emerald bracelet in New York. To such general satisfaction this statue of 'Nirvana' was putting the finishing touch.

"Here we are, Anne."

An English voice, and two young people at the far end—going to chatter, he supposed! He was preparing to rise when he heard the girl say in a voice American, indeed, but soft and curiously private:

"John, it's terribly great. It makes me sink here." From the gesture of the hand, Soames saw that it was where the thing had made *him* sink, too.

"Everlasting stillness. It makes me sad, John."

As the young man's arm slid under hers his face came into view. Quick as thought, half of Soames's face disappeared again into his hand. "John?" "Jon" was what she had meant to say. Young Jon Forsyte—not a doubt of it! And this girl, his wife, sister—as he had heard—of that young American, Francis Wilmot! What a mischance! He remembered the boy's face perfectly, though he had only seen it in that Gallery off Cork Street, and the pastrycook's after, and once on that grim afternoon when he had gone down to Robin Hill to beg his own divorced first wife to let *her* son marry *his* daughter! Never had he been more pleased to be refused. Never had the fitness of things been better confirmed; and yet, the pain of telling Fleur of that refusal remained in his memory like a still-live ember, red and prickly under the ashes of time. Behind his shadowing hat and screening hand Soames made sure.

The young man was standing bareheaded, as if in reverence to the statue. A Forsyte look about him, in spite of too much hair. A poet—he had heard! The face wasn't a bad one; it had what they called charm; the eyes were deep set, like his grandfather's, old Jolyon's, and the same colour, dark grey; the touch of brightness on his head came from his mother, no doubt; but the chin was a Forsyte's chin. Soames looked at the girl. A fair height, brownish pale, brown hair, dark eyes; pretty trick of the neck, nice way of standing too; very straight, an attractive figure! But how could the young man have taken to her áfter Fleur? Still, for an American she looked natural; a little bit like a nymph, with a kind of privacy about her.

Nothing in America had struck Soames so much as the lack of privacy. If you wanted to be private you had to disconnect your telephone and get into a bath—otherwise they rang you up just as you were going to sleep, to ask if you were Mr. and Mrs. Newberg. The houses, too, were not divided from each other, nor even from the roads. In the hotels the rooms all ran into each other, and as likely as not there'd be a drove of bankers in the hall. Dinner too—nothing private about that; even if you went out to dinner, it was always the same: lobster-cocktails, shad, turkey, asparagus, salad, and ice-cream; very good dishes, no doubt, and you put on weight, but nothing private about them.

Those two were talking; he remembered the young man's voice.

"It's the greatest man-made thing in America, Anne. We haven't

469

anything so good at home. It makes me hungry—we'll have to go to Egypt."

"Your mother would just love that, Jon; and so would I."

"Come and see it from the other side."

Soames rose abruptly and left the alcove. Though not recognised, he was flustered. A ridiculous, even a dangerous encounter. He had travelled for six months to restore Fleur's peace of mind, and now that she was tranquil, he would not for the world have her suddenly upset again by a sight of her first love. He remembered only too well how a sight of Irene used to upset himself. Yes—and as likely as not Irene was here too! Well, Washington was a big place. Not much danger! They were going to Mount Vernon in the afternoon, and to-morrow morning early were off again! At the top of the cemetery his taxicab was waiting. One of those other cars must belong to those two young people; and he glanced at them sidelong. Did there rise in him some fear, some hope, that in one of them he would see her whom, in another life, he had seen, day by day, night by night, waiting for what—it seemed—he could not give her. No! only the drivers and their voices, their 'Yeahs!' and their 'Yeps!' Americans no longer said 'Yes', it seemed. And getting into his taxi, he said:

"Hotel Pótomac."

"Hotel Potómac?"

"If you prefer it."

The driver grinned and shut Soames in. The Soldiers' Home! They said the veterans had pretty well died off. Still, they'd have plenty coming on from this last war. Besides, what was space and money to America? They had so much they didn't know what to do with it. Well, he didn't mind that, now that he was leaving. He didn't mind anything. Indeed, he had invited quite a number of Americans to come and see his pictures if they came to England. They had been very kind, very hospitable; he had seen a great many fine pictures too, including some Chinese; and a great many high buildings, and the air was very stimulating. It wouldn't suit him to live here, but it was all very much alive, and a good tonic, for a bit. 'I can't see *her* living here!' he thought suddenly. 'There never was anyone more private.' The cars streamed past him, or stood parked in rows. America was all cars and newspapers! And a sudden thought disturbed him. They put everything into the newspapers over here; what if his name was among the arrivals?

Reaching his hotel, he went at once towards the kiosk in the hall

470

where you could buy newspapers, tooth-paste, 'candy' to pull your teeth out—teeth to replace them, he shouldn't be surprised. List of arrivals? Here it was: 'Hotel Potomac: Mr. and Mrs. Cyrus K. McGunn; the Misses Errick; Mr. H. Yellam Root; Mr. Semmes Forsyth; Mr. and Mrs. Munt.' As large as life, but, fortunately, only half as natural! Forsyth! Munt! They never could get anything right in the papers. 'Semmes!' Unrecognisable, he should hope. And going over to the bureau, he turned the register towards him. Yes! he had written the names quite clearly. Lucky, too, or they'd have got 'em right, by mistake. And then, turning the leaf, he read: 'Mr. and Mrs. Jolyon Forsyte.' Here! At this hotel—those two! A day before them; yes, and at the very top, dated some days ago: 'Mrs. Irene Forsyte.' His mind travelled with incredible swiftness. He must deal with this at once. Where were Fleur and Michael? They had seen the Freer Gallery with him yesterday, and a beautiful little gallery it was, he had never seen anything better, and the Lincoln Memorial, and that great tower thing which he had refused to go up. This morning they had said they should go to the Corcoran Gallery, where there was a Centenary Exhibition. He had known what that meant. He had seen English centenaries in his time. All the fashionable painters of their day—and the result too melancholy for words! And to the clerk he said:

"Is there a restaurant here where I can get a good lunch?"

"Sure; they cook fine at Filler's."

"Good! If my daughter and her husband come in, kindly tell them to meet me at Filler's at one o'clock."

And, going back to the kiosk, he bought some tickets for the opera, so that they should be out in the evening, and in ten minutes was on his way to the Corcoran Gallery. From Filler's they would go straight off to Mount Vernon; they would dine at another hotel before the opera, and to-morrow be off by the first train—he would take no chances. If only he could catch them at the Corcoran!

Arriving, he mechanically bought a catalogue and walked upstairs. The rooms opened off the gallery and he began at the end room. Ah! there they were, in front of a picture of the setting sun! Sure of them now, but not sure of himself—Fleur was so sharp—Soames glanced at the pictures. Modern stuff, trailing behind those French extravagances Dumetrius had shown him six months ago in London. As he had thought, too, a wholesale lot; might all have been painted by the same hand. He saw Fleur touch Michael's arm and laugh. How pretty she looked! A thousand

471

pities to have her apple-cart upset again! He came up behind them. What? That setting sun was a man's face, was it? Well, you never knew nowadays.

And he said: "I thought I'd have a look in. We're lunching at Filler's; they tell me it's better than the hotel; and we can go straight on from there to Mount Vernon. I've got some seats for the opera to-night, too."

And conscious of Fleur's scrutiny, he stared at the picture. He did not feel too comfortable.

"Are the older pictures better?" he asked.

"Well, sir, Fleur was just saying—how can anyone go on painting in these days?"

"How do you mean?"

"If you walk through, you'll say the same. Here's a hundred years of it."

"The best pictures never get into these shows," said Soames; "they just take anything they can get. Ryder, Innes, Whistler, Sargent—the Americans have had some great painters."

"Of course," said Fleur. "But do you really want to go round, Dad? I'm frightfully hungry."

"No," said Soames; "after that Saint Gaudens thing I don't feel like it. Let's go and lunch."

## Chapter II

MOUNT VERNON! The situation was remarkable! With all that colour on the trees, the grassy cliff, and below it the broad blue Potomac, which, even Soames confessed, was more imposing than the Thames. And the low white house up here, dignified and private, indeed, except for the trippers, almost English, giving him a feeling he had not had since he left home. He could imagine that fellow George Washington being very fond of it. One could have taken to the place oneself. Lord John Russell's old house on the hill at Richmond was something like this, except, of course, for the breadth of river, and the feeling you always had in America and Canada, so far as he had seen, that they were trying to fill the country and not succeeding—such a terrific lot of space, and apparently no time. Fleur was in raptures, and young Michael had remarked that it was "absolutely topping". The sun fell warmly on his cheek while he took his last look from the wide porch, before entering the house itself. He should remember this—

472

America had not all been run up yesterday! He passed into the hall and proceeded, mousing through the lower rooms. Really! They had done it extraordinarily well. Nothing but the good old original stuff, from a century and a half ago, reminding Soames of half-hours spent in the antique shops of Taunton and Tunbridge Wells. Too much 'George Washington' of course! George Washington's mug, George Washington's foot-bath, and his letter to so-and-so, and the lace on his collar, and his sword and his gun and everything that was his! Still, that was unavoidable! Detached from the throng, detached even from his daughter, Soames moved —covered, as in a cloak, by his collector's habit of silent appraisement; he so disliked his judgments to be confused by uncritical imbecilities. He had reached the bedroom upstairs where George Washington had died, and was gazing through the grille, when he heard sounds which almost froze his blood; the very voices he had listened to that morning before the Saint Gaudens statue, and with those voices Michael's voice conjoined! Was Fleur there too? A backward glance relieved him. No! the three were standing at the head of the main stairs exchanging the remarks of strangers casually interested in the same thing. He heard Michael say: "Jolly good taste in those days." And Jon Forsyte answering: "All hand-made, you see."

Soames dived for the back stairs, jostled a stout lady, recoiled, stammering, and hurried on down. If Fleur was not with Michael it meant that she had got hold of the curator. Take her away, while those three were still upstairs! That was the thought in his mind. Two young Englishmen were not likely to exchange names or anything else, and, if they did, he must get hold of Michael quickly. But how to get Fleur away? Yes, there she was—talking to the curator in front of George Washington's flute laid down on George Washington's harpsichord in the music-room! And Soames suffered. Revolting to be unwell, still more revolting to pretend to be! And yet—what else? He could not go up to her and say: "I've had enough. Let's go to the car!" Swallowing violently, he put his hand to his head and went towards the harpsichord.

"Fleur!" he said, and without pausing to let her take him in, went on: "I'm not feeling the thing. I must go to the car."

The words no doubt were startling, coming from one so un-dramatic.

"Dad! What is it?"

"I don't know," said Soames; "giddy. Give me your arm."

Really dreadful to him—the whole thing! On the way to the car, parked at the entrance, her concern was so embarrassing that he very nearly abandoned his ruse. But he managed to murmur:

"I've been doing too much, I expect; or else it's that cookery. I'll just sit quiet in the car."

To his great relief she sat down with him, got out her smelling-bottle, and sent the chauffeur to tell Michael. Soames was touched, though incommoded by having to sniff the salts, which were very strong.

"Great fuss about nothing," he muttered.

"We'd better get home, dear, at once, so that you can lie down."

In a few minutes Michael came hurrying. He too expressed what seemed to Soames a genuine concern, and the car was started. Soames sat back with his hand in Fleur's, and eyes tight closed, feeling perhaps better than he'd ever felt in his life. Before they reached Alexandria he opened his lips to say that he had spoiled their trip for them; they must go home by way of Arlington, and he would stay in the car while they had a look at it. Fleur was for going straight on, but he insisted. Arrived, however, at this other white house, also desirably situated on the slope above the river, he almost had a fit while waiting for them in the car. What if the same idea had occurred to Jon Forsyte and he were suddenly to drive up? It was an intense relief when they came out again, saying that it was nice but not a patch on Mount Vernon: the porch columns were too thick. When the car was again traversing the bright woods Soames opened his eyes for good.

"I'm all right again now. It was liver, I expect."

"You ought to have some brandy, Dad. We can get some on a doctor's prescription."

"Doctor? Nonsense. We'll dine upstairs and I'll get over the waiter; they must have something in the house."

Dine upstairs! That was a happy thought!

In their sitting-room he lay down on the sofa, touched and gratified, for Fleur was propping up his cushions, shading the light, looking over the top of her book to see how he was. He did not remember when he had felt so definitely that she really did care about him. He even thought: 'I ought to be ill a little, every now and then!' And yet, if he ever complained of feeling ill at home, Annette at once complained of feeling worse!

Close by, in the little 'salon' opposite the stairs, a piano was being played.

"Does that music worry you, dear?"

Into Soames's mind flashed the thought: 'Irene!' If it were, and

Fleur were to go out to stop it, then, indeed, would fat be in the fire!

"No; I rather like it," he said, hastily.

"It's a very good touch."

Irene's touch! He remembered how June used to praise her touch; remembered how he had caught that fellow Bosinney listening to her, in the little drawing-room in Montpelier Square, with the wildcat look on his face, the fellow had; remembered how she used to stop playing when he himself came in—from consideration, or the feeling that it was wasted on him—which? He had never known. He had never known anything! Well—another life! He closed his eyes, and instantly saw Irene in her emerald-green dinner-gown, standing in the Park Lane hall, first feast after their honey-moon, waiting to be cloaked! Why did such pictures come back before closed eyes—pictures without rhyme or reason? Irene brushing her hair—grey now, of course! As he was seventy, she must be nearly sixty-two! How time went; Hair *feuille morte*—old Aunt Juley used to call it with a certain pride in having picked up the expression—and eyes so velvet dark! Ah! but handsome was as handsome did! Still—who could say! Perhaps, if he had known how to express his feelings! If he had understood music! If she hadn't so excited his senses! Perhaps—oh, perhaps your grand-mother! No riddling that out! And here—of all places. A tricksy business! Was one never to forget?

Fleur went to pack and dress. Dinner came up. Michael spoke of having met a refreshing young couple at Mount Vernon, "an Englishman; he said Mount Vernon made him awfully homesick."

"What was his name, Michael?"

"Name? I didn't ask. Why?"

"Oh! I don't know. I thought you might have."

Soames breathed again. He had seen her prick her ears. Give it a chance, and her feeling for that boy of Irene's would flare up again. It was in the blood!

"Bright Markland," said Michael, "has been gassing over the future of America—he's very happy about it because there are so many farmers still, and people on the land; but he's also been gas-sing over the future of England—he's very happy about it, and there's hardly anybody on the land."

"Who's Bright Markland?" muttered Soames.

"Editor of our *Scrutator*, sir. Never was a better example of optimism, or the science of having things both ways."

"I'd hoped," said Soames heavily, "that seeing these new

475

countries would have made you feel there's something in an old one, after all."

Michael laughed. "No need to persuade me of that, sir. But you see I belong to what is called the fortunate class, and so I believe, do you."

Soames stared. This young man was getting sarcastic!

"Well," he said, "I shall be glad to be home. Are you packed?"

They were; and presently he telephoned for a cab to take them to the opera. So that they might not hang about in the hall, he went down, himself, to see them into it. The incident passed without let or hindrance; and with a deep sigh of relief he resumed his place in the lift, and was restored to his room.

### Chapter III

HE stood there at the window, looking out at the tall houses, the cars moving below and the clear starry sky. He was really tired now; another day of this and he would not need to simulate indisposition. A narrow squeak, indeed—a series of them! He wished he were safe home. To be under the same roof with that woman— how very queer! He had not passed a night under the same roof with her since that dreadful day in November '87, when he walked round and round Montpelier Square in such mortal agony, and came to his front door to find young Jolyon there. One lover dead, and the other already on his threshold! That night she had stolen away from his house; never again till this night had the same roof covered them. That music again—soft and teasing! *Was* it she playing? To get away from it, he went into his bedroom and put his things together. He was not long about that, for he had only a suitcase with him. Should he go to bed? To bed, and lie awake? This thing had upset him. If it were she, sitting at that piano, a few yards away, what did she look like now? Seven times—no, eight— he had seen her since that long ago November night. Twice in her Chelsea flat; then by that fountain in the Bois de Boulogne; at Robin Hill when he delivered his ultimatum to her and young Jolyon; at Queen Victoria's funeral; at Lord's Cricket Ground; again at Robin Hill when he went to beg for Fleur; and in the Goupenor Gallery just before she came out here. Each meeting he could remember in every detail, down to the lifting of her gloved hand at the last—the faint smiling of her lips.

And Soames shivered. Too hot—these American rooms! He went

476

back into the sitting-room; they had cleared away and brought him the evening paper; no good in that! He could never find anything in the papers over here. At this distance from the past, all this space and all this time—what did he feel about her? Hate? The word was too strong. One didn't hate those who weren't near one. Besides, he had never hated her! Not even when he first knew she was unfaithful. Contempt? No. She had made him ache too much for that. He didn't know what he felt. And he began walking up and down, and once or twice stood at the door and listened, as might a prisoner in his cell. Undignified! And going to the sofa he stretched himself out on it. He would think about his travels. Had he enjoyed them? One long whirl of things, and—water. And yet, all had gone according to programme, except China, to which they had given as wide a berth as possible, owing to its state. The Sphinx and the Taj Mahal, Vancouver Harbour, and the Rocky Mountains, they played a sort of hide-and-seek within him; and now—that strumming; was it She? Strange! You had, it seemed, only just one season of real heat. Everything else that happened to you was in a way tepid, and perhaps it was as well, or the boiler would burst. His emotions in the years when he first knew her—would he go through them again? Not for the world. And yet! Soames got up. That music was going on and on; but when it stopped, the player—She or not She!—would be no longer visible. Why not walk past that little 'salon'—just walk past, and—and take a glimpse? If it were She, well, probably she'd lost her looks—the beauty that had played such havoc with him! He had noticed the position of the piano; yes—the player would be in profile to him. He opened the door; the music swelled, and he stole forth.

The breadth of Fleur's room, only, separated him from that little 'salon' opposite the stairs. No one was in the corridor, not even a bell-boy. Very likely some American woman after all, possibly that girl—Jon's wife! Yet no—there was something—something in the sound! And holding up the evening paper before him, he moved along. Three pillars, with spaces between them, divided the 'salon' from the corridor, avoiding what Soames so missed in America—the fourth wall. At the first of these pillars he came to a stand. A tall lamp with an orange shade stood by the keyboard, and the light from it fell on the music, on the keys, on the cheek and hair of the player. *She!* Though he had supposed her grey by now, the sight of that hair without a thread in it of the old gold affected him strangely. Curved, soft, shining, it covered her like a silver casque. She was in evening dress, and he could see that her shoulders, neck and arms were still rounded and beautiful. All her body from the waist was moving lightly to the rhythm of her playing. Her frock was of a greyish heliotrope. Soames stood behind his pillar gazing, his hand over his face, lest she should turn her head. He did not exactly feel—the film of remembrance was unrolled too quickly. From the first sight of her in a Bournemouth drawing-room to the last sight of her in the Goupenor Gallery—the long sequence passed him by in its heat and its frost and its bitterness; the long struggle of sense, the long failure of spirit; the long aching passion, and its long schooling into numbness and indifference. The last thing he wanted, standing there was to speak with her, and yet he could not take his eyes away. Suddenly she stopped playing; bending forward she closed the music and reached to turn out the lamp. Her face came round in the light, and, cowering back, Soames saw it, still beautiful, perhaps more beautiful, a little worn, so that the eyes looked even darker than of old, larger, softer under the still dark eyebrows. And once more he had that feeling: 'There sits a woman I have never known.' With a sort of anger he craned back till he could see no longer. Ah! she had had many faults, but the worst of her faults had always been, was still, her infernal mystery! And, stepping silently like a cat, he regained his room.

He felt tired to death now, and, going into his bedroom, undressed hurriedly and got into bed. He wished with all his heart that he were on board, under the British flag. 'I'm old,' he thought suddenly, 'old.' This America was too young for him, so full of energy, bustling about to ends he could not see. Those Eastern places had been different. And yet, after all, he was a mere seventy. His father had lived to be ninety—old Jolyon eighty-five, Timothy a hundred, and so with all the old Forsytes. At seventy *they* weren't playing golf; and yet they were younger, younger anyway than he felt to-night. The sight of that woman had—had——! Old!

'I'm not going back to be old,' he thought. 'If I feel like this again I shall consult someone.' They had some monkey things nowadays they could inject. He shouldn't try that. Monkeys indeed! Why not pigs or tigers? Hold on somehow another ten or fifteen years! By that time they would have found out where they were in England. That precious capital levy would have been exploded. He would know what he had to leave to Fleur; would see her baby grow into a boy and go to school—public school—even! Eton? No—young Jolyon had been there. Winchester, the Monts' school? Not there either, if he could help it. Harrow was handy; or his own school—Marlborough? Perhaps he would see him play at Lord's. Another fifteen years before Kit could play at Lord's! Well—something to look forward to, something to hold on for. If you hadn't that, you felt old and if you *felt* old, you *were* old, and the end soon came. How well that woman had worn! She——! There were his pictures too; take them up more seriously. That Freer Gallery! Leave them to the nation, and your name lived—much comfort in *that*! She! *She* would never die!

A crack of light on the wall close to the door.

"Asleep, Dad?"

So Fleur had remembered to come and have a look at him!

"How are you now, dear?"

"All right; tired. How was the opera?"

"Middling."

"I've told them to call us at seven. We'll breakfast on the train."

Her lips touched his forehead. If—if that woman—but never— never once—never of her own accord——!

"Good-night," he said. "Sleep well!"

The light on the wall narrowed and was gone! Well! He was drowsy now. But, in this house—Shapes—Shapes! Past—present— at the piano—at his bedside—passing—passing by—and there, be- hind them, the great bronze-hooded woman, with the closed eyes, deep sunk in ever-lasting—profound—pro——! And from Soames a gentle snore escaped.

*This book,*
*designed by William B. Taylor*
*is a production of*
*Heron Books, London*

*Printed in Great Britain by offset litho at Taylor*
*Garnett Evans & Co. Ltd, Watford, Herts, and*
*bound by Wm. Brendon & Son Ltd, Tiptree, Essex*